MARTYRS AL-SABRA

Dan M. Kalin

FERAL CAT PUBLISHERS
MELBOURNE, FL USA
2019

Feral Cat
PUBLISHERS

Published by Feral Cat Publishers, Melbourne, FL 32940 USA
www.feralcatpublishers.com

Version 1.0, January 2018

Cover Art by tatlin.net

Book layout by www.ebooklaunch.com

KDP Print ISBN: 978-1970-087055
IngramSpark Print ISBN: 978-1970-087062
ebook ISBN: 978-1970-087048

*For Jan Vincek,
and first belief*

Acknowledgements

My first sketches of plot and text for a Martyrs series began back in 2006, but the bulk of the writing took place during 2017. The current version went someplace completely different from where I first imagined, as the characters themselves decided where the story would go as it was written.

I had a lot of valuable help, especially with the editing. I handed my editor, Sarah Kalin of Dreamlined.com, a manuscript weighing in at 270,000 words in early 2018. Rather than send me away, she rolled up her sleeves, firmly grasped a chainsaw, and carved off 66,000 words quite early in the process. Much of that story will be told in the second installment of the Martyrs series. Even with the cuts, editing a 204,000 word manuscript is not a trivial task. Sarah did a great job of making the plot hold together and the end result is much better for her amazing work. Thank you!

I also want to thank my intrepid team of beta readers; John Kalin, Michele Kalin, Adam Ramsay, and Marie Tex. Their comments and suggestions were consistently useful; and they made a huge positive impact on the finished product. Thank you!

Any remaining nits, gnats, errors, mixed-fonts, unnecessary puns, or gerbils-in-the-attic are entirely my fault and should be attributed accordingly.

Contents

Acknowledgements i

Prologue 1

Election Night 3

Venture Capital 25

Hunt Camp 43

Madame President 77

First Shots 121

Feeding Frenzy 173

Maritime Maneuvers 203

Light In The Tunnel 207

Closing Doors 247

Last Call 283

Command Performances 303

Terminal Sacrifices 369

Friday The 16th 421

Rendezvous In Riyadh 435

Epilogue 529

PROLOGUE

Summer, 2006

The tramp freighter decisively pointed its bow northward towards home. Alone at the stern railing, a small figure gazed back to a home being left behind, perhaps forever. Gaza City still burned from the day's explosions, the rising smoke of which could be seen amidst the normal night lighting of the city.

The boy stood in man's fatigues, his body gangly from recent growth which he had yet to complete. An adult in height, a child in form. The grey-steel eyes were ancient, however, having seen too much to ever reclaim childhood. Deep anger burned within those eyes.

Looking back at the fires, oaths are taken, to remaining family and friends, but especially to his many enemies. Someday, he promises, the oaths will be kept.

ELECTION NIGHT

The man stood still in a dark hotel penthouse, overlooking the Potomac River and the city beyond, as his call was being put through.

"As-Salaam-Alaikum. This is Hammer. I need to speak with him." His voice was modified by a small device before being transmitted to the handset's bluetooth connection.

There was a flurry of activity on the other end of the planet as 'He' was located and the telephone delivered.

"Speak," a noncommittal voice said.

"Have you monitored the results of the American election? I think there is a rare opportunity here for us. I would like to discuss it with you in person."

"I will be in Riyadh for the next three weeks, contact the usual channels for an appointment. How big and how much?"

"Very cost effective with a huge ROI. Perhaps the biggest ever," The Hammer said.

"I'm intrigued. Don't disappoint me."

"Disappointing you could prove fatal."

"As long as you understand that. As-Salaam-Alaikum"

"Wa-Alaikum-Salaam," The Hammer said as the connection ceased.

Stripping the battery from the prepaid phone which would have to be disposed of after leaving the hotel, the terrorist known to western powers as "The Hammer of Allah" buttoned his dress shirt as he paced the bedroom suite. Now it was time to meet with his contact downstairs.

Leaving the room, he took an elevator with three other guests who were giddy with excitement and in the mood to celebrate. He smiled for their benefit, nodding when hearing disparaging comments about the incumbent president as if he fully agreed. The elevator doors opened, and the newly-bonded Brown supporters went their separate ways.

Picking up a glass of wine, he stood against a wall in plain sight, along with other celebrants. Soon, the most beautiful woman in the room came over to stand next to him.

"Were you able to make contact with our target?" The Hammer asked as though he was talking about the election.

"Yes, it was much easier than I thought it would be," Nayla said seriously.

"How is his protection detail?"

"As expected. Two on and others in the building. He also had a pair of babysitters from his wife's team."

"Nothing he can't slip if he wants to, it sounds like."

"That's right," Nayla said. "He seemed motivated, rubbing himself all over me in our slow dance."

"That dress does show your body's perfection quite well," The Hammer sniffed at the air, enjoying the amalgam of scents that was Nayla and her expensive perfume.

"I always feel unclean after we run one of these operations. This guy is a typical American pig, and it takes time to wash the smell of pig off of you," Nayla complained.

"Then I won't keep you from your bath. Continue and keep me informed, as usual."

"Yes, I will," Nayla said as she formally extended her hand for a professional parting. The Hammer shook her hand with a smile, and went back to the bar for a refill before leaving the ballroom.

•••

Earlier that Evening

Democratic Party presidential candidate Lucinda Brown sat watching the election returns in a private suite atop the Gaylord National Resort, with her campaign manager, Sidney Rosenbloom, and running mate Michael Rodriquez. The mood in the room was tense, but upbeat: the electoral college appeared to be swinging their way.

It had been a brutal campaign for the record books, as the Republican incumbent president was a billionaire reality show star whose demagoguery had been honed over twenty years of live television.

In the prior 2016 election, he had upset a Democratic candidate everyone, including the candidate herself, was confident would win. The loss devastated party leadership and the next four years saw widespread denial, protests, and active resistance; all to no avail. Republicans closed ranks around a man they could barely stand to acknowledge. The President seemed to go out of his way to offend those opposed to his efforts, taunting them daily on social media, and changing positions on a dime.

While his first two years in office were anarchic, the economy improved and intransigent foreign relation issues had some break-throughs, in spite of the backdrop of take-no-prisoners partisan warfare. Poll after poll suggested constant street agitation was working against Democrats; and Republicans were making unearned gains because of it.

Finally, a core strategic group coalesced within the party, who offered a less confrontational style for their many objections. Senator Lucinda Brown of Missouri was chosen as the reasonable face of Democrat opposition, and America responded.

The final two years didn't go as well for the incumbent President. Midterm elections had resulted in a House of Representatives majority for the Democrats. The Senate was still held by Republicans, but their majority was diminished significantly.

The President responded after the midterm election rebuke with a flurry of almost daily invective and provocative statements transmitted through social media. The difference now, was a lack of animus in the Democrat response. Americans, generally, are a polite people who eschew bullying, so gains were made by projecting a dignified demeanor without emotional outbursts during formal Democratic Party response statements. Nonetheless, the election had always promised to be difficult running against a sitting president.

• • •

"Lucy, it looks like things are going our way." Sidney Rosenbloom said as the television analysis showed more state poll results showing blue. You never knew exactly how the votes would come in, and there had been some notable pre-vote polling failures in recent years, which meant, even while polls were predicting a Brown win, no one was going to celebrate just yet.

Michael Rodriguez, her running mate, was very excited by all of the state results coming through. The pundits were already talking about what the Brown Presidency could accomplish during its first 100 days, but fully recognizing the Republicans would continue to hold the Senate. Lucy's coat-tails appeared to have improved their dominant position in the House, and eroded the Senate majority for Republicans, confirming the country's rejection of the serving President's policies.

"Lucy, or should I say Madame President? Do you mind if I check in on my wife for a few minutes?" Michael asked. "It looks like we still have some time before the Big Man formally concedes."

"*Lucy* is fine for a few more minutes, and always in private." She smiled at Michael. "Certainly, go check on Celia, she'll be tired at this point I expect. Stay close to your phone, though, Sid will call when we have the word."

Michael's wife Celia was pregnant with their third child, and busy keeping the other two in line. Michael and Celia had taken a room in the hotel so the children could see their father's victory speech, but knew it would be very late before it finally happened. Michael nodded at Lucy and Sidney then walked out of the room briskly.

"Did we ever have that much energy?" Lucy asked Sidney.

Sidney snorts, "He needs it with the work and his kids. I took them for an hour earlier to give Celia a break and they about wore this grandfather out touring the resort. What about you, Lucy? Did you ever want to have children?"

"I did. But every time I was ready to, something always came up which took precedence. But can you imagine children growing up with Jonny Ray as their daddy and principle caregiver?" she smiled tightly. "We'd have to keep a close watch on young nannies and the like, given his proclivities."

Sidney chuckled appreciatively.

Lucy had a very pragmatic view of Jonny Ray's strengths and weaknesses, and was always frank with Sid. It was one of the things that made them such a powerful team. Early on, Sid had said that the more he knew, the more he could be useful. It took a while for Lucy to fully trust anyone with her thinking, but, once she had, life became that much easier.

Sid made sure that Jonny Ray's continued propensity to stray did not impact Lucy. Sid handled things. Sid's staff also ensured that Jonny Ray arrived sober, presentable and on-message for his many political engagements. Sidney had the harried look of any political Chief-of-Staff: the prematurely grey hair, substantial belly, multiple phones, and badly-worn very expensive suits. Only two inches taller than Lucy, they appeared to be the same height whenever she was in heels.

The phone rang. Sid quickly determined it was the phone they were wanting to ring and signaled Lucy. She muted the TV.

"Sidney Rosenbloom," he said.

Sid listened to the voice on the other end of the call for a few seconds. "Thank you, sir. Those are very kind words. Yes, I'll put her on now."

Handing the phone to Lucy, he signed a thumbs-up.

"Hello, this is Lucinda Brown." She listened for a few seconds in silence. "Thank you! Yes, I agree it was a difficult campaign. I want to also thank you for calling the race early, a lot of children can get to bed now. I like to think I would have done the same in your position."

They exchanged a few more pleasantries before terminating the call.

"Sid, he is about to do his concession speech. Please go round up Jonny Ray, Michael, Celia and his kids. I want them all up on the stage with me for the victory speech. Did Meryl come? If so, I'd like her to join us as well," Lucy directed.

"Yes, Madame President-Elect."

"God, that sounds awful. Maybe it should stay Lucy or Senator until I'm sworn in," Lucy said.

"That, Madame President, is a topic for tomorrow," Sidney said with a wicked grin.

Lucy waved him out and went to a large mirror to prepare for her speech. A quick knock at the door, heralded the arrival of the hair and cosmetics team. She smiled mockingly at her reflection. Sid always seemed to know her needs before she did.

• • •

In the ballroom of the Gaylord National Resort, Farid Amir Monsour Royce al Haj stood talking with his sister, Lindsey Royce Hamilton, and Nayla Kaldah. Lindsey and Nayla had been classmates at Harvard Law School, now both worked beltway politics in their own ways. Lindsey had set Nayla up with Farid on a blind date once, and the two remained more than good friends in spite of it.

Farid leaned in close to Lindsey, "Lindsey, have you met the Browns yet?" Farid Royce was recognized wherever he went as television's smooth-speaking expert on all matters Muslim. He spoke American English without an accent, moved with the world's elite, and had high-level personal contacts in the US, Europe and the Middle-East.

Lindsey was a DC socialite and heiress to most of the Royce fortune, as well as Farid's younger sister. Heavily involved in beltway progressive politics, she knew everyone who mattered in the Democratic Party and was happily married to a banking executive. She smiled back up at him.

"Of course I have, both of them! She is so nice, and he is such a character. Would you like to meet them? I see Jonny Ray over there next to the blonde at the bar. Since our lovely Nayla is here," she said with a smirk, "I should have little trouble getting him to come over."

"Why would we need Nayla to lure him over? You're still packing heat, Sis," Farid teased. Nayla was used to the nonstop banter and made a show of rolling her eyes.

"Oh, no!" Lindsey exclaimed. "Jonny Ray doesn't trouble himself with old married women with young children and stretch marks. No, Nayla is our bait! Look mysterious and exotic, Nayla."

Nayla struck a pose, which made Lindsey laugh and Farid smile.

Lindsey headed over to where Jonny Ray was holding court.

Nayla was indeed a very attractive Palestinian-American woman. Appearing Italian or Castilian Spanish in features, she spoke four languages fluently and worked as a lawyer for a prominent lobbyist firm on K-Street in Washington, DC. Like Lindsey, she worked the progressive DC social world like a maestro, in spite of the barely concealed bias against Muslims. Lindsey was able to call upon old family connections, whereas Nayla's access was down to her hard work and beauty.

"Nayla, would you like a refill on your wine?" Farid asked.

"Yes, please. I may need some reinforcement before talking to Jonny Ray," Nayla said.

"I hear he can be quite charming. But I doubt his handlers will allow him to get too far off message tonight," Farid said while indicating two of Sidney Rosenbloom's assistants following Jonny Ray.

"That man - you have no idea! I've heard stories of him ditching his minders and working his magic in the nearest broom closet. His paramours definitely need to bring their own cab fare."

Farid smiled and headed for the cash bar. In the meantime, Lindsey had worked her way to the head of the pack surrounding Jonny Ray and was talking with him. Jonny Ray looked over to where Nayla was standing, and nodded to Lindsey after pointing at his watch.

Farid came back with two wine glasses and handed one to Nayla along with a fresh napkin.

"Thanks. It's amazing how fast you get served!" Nayla said.

"It had everything to do with what I tipped on the first round," Farid said, with a self-deprecating smirk.

Lindsey came back, claiming Farid's wine glass as her own, "Is that for me? Thank you! Jonny Ray will be over in a few minutes, he is working his way through a few donors."

"Of course, it is yours. A brother's work is never done," Farid sighed in mock martyrdom as he headed back for another glass of Cabernet.

"Nayla, look at you! If I didn't know better, I would think you were hunting big game tonight in that smashing outfit. Believe me, no one here is worth your time!" Lindsey said.

"Maybe I am just taking another run at Farid," Nayla smiled into her glass.

"I wish somebody would! I would die for some nieces and nephews for the kids to grow up with. Seriously, I always thought you two were perfect for each other. And good God! The kids you two would have: beautiful and brilliant! It would almost be unfair. You're already like a sister, having it formalized would be wonderful."

A look of pain quickly passed through Nayla's eyes before she looked down, "Please don't badger him about it. We're fine as things stand, really."

Farid came back to rejoin the group, "So what are we talking about?" he asked.

"Oh, Jonny Ray will be over in a few minutes," Lindsey said, ignoring the question. "Can you believe Lucy Brown's comeback? I thought the President had her down and out. I'm glad that he seems to be losing. He was a real throwback to the 1980's, without the personal character. Lucy will have her work cut out for her with a split Congress, though, but she has never been about making enemies - so it might work."

Just then, the solar system of planets surrounding Jonny Ray's sun started to move in their direction. Jonny Ray seemed to be annoyed with Sid's team and obviously told them to stay where they were.

"I swear to sweet Jesus, Lindsey, those hound dogs stick to me like glue!" Jonny Ray said as he joined the group.

"Thanks for coming over, Jonny Ray. I wanted to introduce you to a couple of people. First, my brother Farid Royce al Haj. Farid, Jonny Ray Brown," Lindsey said.

Jonny Ray shook Farid's hand, "My God, I know you! You're the television news expert on Muslim affairs! Must say, I am a big fan of yours. I didn't make the connection with your name, but should have known. Plus, I do recall you being on our list of generous donors! Thank you, we couldn't have made it without you!"

"I'm flattered that you would remember," Farid said. "Normally, those of us in the media donate equivalent amounts to both candidates to ensure access to the winner, but this time it was different. Besides the Reality King, as Lindsey so aptly put it, didn't need my contribution."

"No, but I imagine tonight he is feeling a big sucking sound where his cash used to be. Couldn't happen to a nicer fella! By the way, I really appreciate the way you explain issues on the Middle East in your broadcasts. It almost feels like I have a shot at understanding both sides of the issues," Jonny Ray's easy-going personal charm was on full display.

"My pleasure, sir. Since Lindsey has forgotten to do so, please allow me to formally introduce our dear friend, Nayla Kaldah. Nayla works K Street as a lawyer and is a supporter as well," Farid said.

"Nayla Kaldah, yes I remember your name from the donor list, too. Talk about combining work with pleasure! I'm very pleased to meet such a beautiful and accomplished supporter of our future president," Jonny Ray shook her hand by enveloping it with both of his. "I hope you will be sticking around for the announcement and after party. I hear there might be some dancing and, if there is, you need to save one for me."

"It's a pleasure to meet you, as well. I'll definitely save a dance. I'm planning to stay unless the bar closes early."

"Well, Darlin', that's going to be open all night if I have anything to say about it, and I do," Jonny Ray said with a wink. "Say, Farid. You're drinking wine? Don't Muslims normally have an issue over that?"

"Yes, a lot of us do, but many do not. Think Christian branches like Catholic versus Southern Baptists; Catholics are able to drink, whereas Southern Baptists still long for prohibition," Farid explained.

"I'll say they do! See, you explain things so well that I just learned something new. That, sir, is a gift," Jonny Ray said as he glanced back towards his entourage.

"Well, it looks like I have to check in with Frick and Frack, they just got off the phone and are motioning me over. It was a pleasure to meet you both, I look forward to speaking more with you more later on tonight." Jonny Ray waved and headed back to the Brown campaign team.

"See, he mostly behaved himself," Farid said. "It looks like we might be getting to an announcement soon. Wait, look! The Reality King is on the tube."

The room erupted with cheers and applause as it became clear the Republican President had conceded. Farid raised his glass to both Nayla and Lindsey. "Four years! Congratulations, Linds!"

They reveled in the moment, as Lucy Brown took the stage. Lucy surrounded herself with her team and their families. Jonny Ray stood directly behind her, Sid and Meryl Rosenbloom on her left, Michael and Celia Rodriguez on her right. The President-elect made a passionate speech about unifying the country and thanked all of the supporters who enabled their come-from-behind victory. Then she handed off to Michael so that he could say a few words as well. All told, it was short, but very, very, sweet for Lucy's supporters.

• • •

After the initial quick walking tour of the ballroom Sid got Lucy's attention, "Madame President-Elect, we have a few more celebrations to pop in on. Shall we go?"

Jonny Ray hugged Lucy, "I knew you would do it, Lu! Congratulations, I'm very proud of you!"

"Thanks, Jonny. Are you coming along for the victory tour?" Lucy asked.

"No, I'm pretty sure the best venue is this one. Plus, this way I just have to make it upstairs when things wind down," Jonny said.

"Alright, you behave yourself, there are about a thousand phone cameras here tonight. We don't want a social media thing to talk down tomorrow."

"Naw, I'll be good. Most of the big money donors are here, so I can start twisting arms for the Congressional races in two years." He chuckled in anticipation.

Lucy and Sid headed for the security cavalcade which was waiting to take them on the tour.

"Is he going to be alright staying here?" Sid asked, referring to Jonny Ray as they climbed in the armored SUV.

"I'm inclined to let him have some fun, and it is a bit of a relief to not have him to worry about. His Secret Service detail will be all over him so he's unlikely to get into any trouble tonight," Lucy said.

Sid kept his thoughts to himself. He knew how much trouble Jonny Ray could get into and how quickly it could develop, since it was his team that cleaned up the messes. *Perhaps it would be a good idea to have a junior cabinet position whose sole role was keeping Jonny Ray out of trouble,* Sid mused to himself. *Another problem to consider tomorrow.*

• • •

Back inside the resort, the party was just getting started. Farid nursed his glass of wine as Nayla and Lindsey headed off to refresh their war paint. Jonny Ray came up beside Farid and raised his highball in a silent toast.

"Now the madness will truly begin," Jonny said. "We worked very hard to get here, but now that it's real the consequences are starting to sink in. No more privacy at all! I was known when Lucy became a Senator, but occasionally people would still serve me a drink without knowing exactly who I was. Now, I'm the *first-fella.*"

"Cheer up, I think the drinks will all be free now!" Farid said with a smile.

"Well, there is that. You have this issue also, don't you?"

"Not as much as you might think. People often say I look familiar, but most don't recognize me on the street. Of course, I don't have a bevy of Secret Service agents clearing my way either."

"You're God-damned right! Shit, those guys are going to be a major pain in my ass," Jonny Ray lamented.

"I expect you'll do what others have done in your position. There are ways to lose your detail when needed, but it is a lot harder these days. I always heard stories of Presidents slipping away for a few hours to do various things, but again it isn't widely advertised. Call it the Secret History of the White House," Farid laughed.

Jonny Ray nodded and pulled at his drink. "Say, how well do you know Nayla? Are you two an item?"

"No, we're just good friends. Nayla and my sister were roommates at Harvard, so we're all very close. We're both from the same part of the world. I was born in Lebanon and adopted by the Royces when I was five. Nayla grew up in Gaza City, believe it or not, went to college in France, then did her law degree at Harvard."

"Wow! That is a story I would like to hear sometime. Both of them," Jonny Ray said.

"I hope we have the opportunity someday. Nayla has some bad memories from her time there, though, her brother was killed during an incident between Fatah and Hamas," Farid confided.

"I can never keep those two separate in my mind," Jonny Ray said while shaking his head.

"Well, think of them as the Palestinian Republicans versus Democrats, but everyone is armed. The metaphor holds," Farid said. "Looks like the band is starting to tune up for the dancing. I expect you will have a lot of commitments."

"A bunch of fat donor's wives or widow donors that are 105 years old. I'd better dance with Lindsey and Nayla first while I am reasonably unfatigued. Ah, here they come. Ladies, you look marvelous!"

Lindsey and Nayla joined Farid and Jonny Ray. Hovering nearby, two Secret Service agents kept a close eye on things, periodically talking into their radios.

"Ladies, can I refresh your drinks?" Farid asked. "Jonny Ray wants to dance with you two before he gets overwhelmed by the room's demands."

"Thanks, Farid. Please do," Lindsey said and Nayla nodded in assent. "I have to wrap things up here in a bit anyway and that will be a nice end to the evening. You are saving a dance for your sister?"

"Of course, Nayla too. I'll be right back."

"Lindsey, shall we show them how it is done?" Jonny Ray asked holding out his hand.

"Certainly, let's go!" Lindsey and Jonny Ray headed out onto the dance floor. The Secret Service talked into their radios again and moved to a better vantage point to watch over Jonny Ray.

Farid came back with the drinks, handing one to Nayla with a slight bow. She smiled and raised the glass in salute prior to taking a sip.

"Jonny Ray asked about you earlier. I told him a little bit about your background, I hope that was appropriate?" Farid asked.

"Thanks for letting me know. It's alright, he could know every-thing about all of us by this time tomorrow if he asked his Secret Service detail," Nayla said with an elegant shrug. "He might want to reconsider our dance."

"It's true: the Secret Service will be all over this by tomorrow. I hope your papers are in order?" Farid teased in a fake German accent. "But I think he was looking forward to your dance even more."

"I've heard he is an equal opportunity hound: not just the young ones anymore. Will you be jealous watching us dance?" Nayla asked.

"No, because I will be dancing with you first," Farid said smoothly as he set his drink down. He took her hand and headed for the dance floor.

• • •

At the next break, Farid said his goodbyes to Lindsey and Nayla after finishing off his glass. Jonny Ray, as promised, whisked Nayla away for what turned out to be a slow number.

"So, Nayla. How is it that someone as sexy as you came alone to what turned into the biggest party of the year?" Jonny Ray said.

"Who says I came alone? Perhaps you were misinformed," Nayla said with a shake of her head. Nayla was beautiful with her face in a neutral state, but when she smiled, or moved, it took her into beauty pageant territory.

Some men would be intimidated by the combination of beauty and intelligence, but Jonny Ray was not some men.

"Alright, I'll play. Why are you alone now?"

"I'm not alone, I'm dancing with you. By the way, you seem much taller in person, and are quite a good dancer. But soon our dance will be finished and then, perhaps, I'll be alone. Maybe some of the old widows' boy toys will want a dance and I'll be able to console myself."

"Ah, Honey. You are killing me! I've got to go work them after, as well," Jonny Ray said.

"Yes, our jobs are somewhat similar. I provide non-specific support to progressive causes nationwide, while you have more of a focus on the President-Elect. It isn't any wonder we end up talking to the same people. I am hoping winning this election will make it easier to raise funding," Nayla said.

"I'm thinking it won't. Some of these folks can't be convinced to part with a nickel unless there is an emergency or crisis," Jonny Ray drily commented. "Even with a split congress, they'll see tonight as a triumph with all threats banished."

"Well, then people like you and I will have to convince them otherwise," Nayla said.

"I wouldn't mind working closer with you, both personally and professionally," Jonny Ray said as he held the small of Nayla's trim back snugly with one large hand, dancing a little closer than was strictly proper at his wife's party.

After a few seconds of increased sexual tension, Nayla moved back a little as she eyed the room. "I do look forward to our professional collaboration. Anything else would seem to be impossible given all of your entourage," Nayla said with an ironic smile as she indicated the Secret Service detail and Sidney's two assistants who were still on the job watching him.

Jonny Ray took in his virtual jailers with an annoyed glance, "Yes, these guys are going to be a real pain to deal with after tonight. I know it is doable, though, I just have to see how things shake out. How can I reach you?"

The music ended and they broke off again into their own separate spaces. "I'll give you my card, you can call or text my mobile. Of course, you could have obtained this from any of your team, but discretion is probably better. Text is best, simply because I don't answer calls unless I recognize the ID," Nayla said as she reached into her purse for a card. "Oh my, I don't have any that are pristine. I'm sorry. Will you take one with an old grocery list on it?"

"Whatever it takes, my dear. Now, I need to gird my considerable loins and see to the needs of our biggest donors. Wish me luck!" Jonny Ray said as he took her card and placed it in his wallet. Nayla nodded as he headed off to work through his list of patrons.

Lindsey came over. "You're playing with fire there - that was a pretty steamy dance you had going," Lindsey said.

"Sometimes the best dancing is with those who are not real possibilities. The drama is so much greater, don't you agree?" Nayla said.

"Girl, if you get a knock at your door and find a tall, naked, and disgraced former politician holding his prick and looking hopeful, don't say I didn't warn you!"

"I don't think it will come to that, but if it does I'll just call his Secret Service detail and tell them where he is," Nayla laughed. "Speaking of pricks, supposedly his has a kink in it? Did you hear that one?"

"I heard it and Jonny Ray isn't shy about telling it. I think the story goes that he told the woman in question it naturally kinks to the left due to his politics," Lindsey tittered.

"Allah save him from one that kinks to the right! He'd have to change his party affiliations. He did mention his considerable loins," Nayla joked as they both laughed.

"I think I am done for the evening, are you alright here by yourself?" Lindsey asked.

"Absolutely, I was planning a few more work-related dances, then I will leave as well. Where is Gerald tonight?"

"He's watching Benny and Claire, and all too glad to skip these festivities. I'm sure they were watching the broadcast before heading off to bed. Maybe they got to see Mommy on television!"

"Give them their Aunt Nayla's love, and say I will see them soon," Nayla said.

"I will. Don't stay too late. Let's do something this weekend at the house, okay?"

"I won't stay much later. I think this weekend is open, but I'll call later to confirm," Nayla kissed Lindsey's cheek in farewell.

· · ·

Deep in the warren of an electronic listening post, the lead technician alerted the Interagency Terrorism Task Force team about some interesting voice traffic. "Sir, you'll want to listen to this one. It was a call from the DC area to ZBag5 in Riyadh tonight after the election announcement. We're narrowing down an exact origin location but it will take a few more minutes."

Justin Simons, lead FBI Special Agent on the task force headed for the secure listening room, picking up the Code Name binder as he went. His counterparts from NSA and CIA came along as well. All of them sat down around a small conference room table after closing the door. The walls were covered with computer monitors, and there was one control station at the end of the table where the technician readied the digital file for playback.

"Sirs, we picked this up about an hour ago. I'll play it back for you now." As it played back the Arabic language audio a print translation transcript came up on the main video monitor.

"As-Salaam-Alaikum. This is Hammer. I need to speak with him." (effects modified voice - DC)

"Speak." (Riyadh)

"Have you monitored the results of the American election? I think there is a rare opportunity here for us. I would like to discuss it with you in person." (DC)

"I will be in Riyadh for the next three weeks, contact the usual channels for an appointment. How big and how much?" (Riyadh)

"Very cost effective with a huge ROI. Perhaps the biggest ever." (DC)

"I'm intrigued. Don't disappoint me." (Riyadh)

"Disappointing you could prove fatal." (DC)

"As long as you understand that. As-Salaam-Alaikum" (Riyadh)

"Wa-Alaikum-Salaam." (DC)

The team was fully awake now. Justin flipped open the Code Name binder and looked up "ZBag5" on the list of names.

"Shit, we're talking Zufar Azzizi al-Saud. He is a Saudi prince suspected of bankrolling a number of extreme terrorist actions," Justin said. "Has he done anything here in the past or has it been mostly in other jurisdictions?"

"We haven't had any objective proof of his involvement in any action. NSA identified a number of terrorist groups which have contacted him, but we've never been able to link him to anything other than a conversation. He is so well-connected in Saudi Arabia our friends there are very cautious dealing with him. He is also relatively famous in Western financial markets as a large investor. You'll even occasionally see televised interviews with him on cable financial networks," Tom Franklin of the CIA said.

"He is flagged for coverage at all times, but rarely do we have a caller masking his own voice. It always gets our attention," Thang Duy of the NSA added seriously.

"Who is 'The Hammer'?" Justin asked.

"He's considered a myth, from all I have heard. Some of the things he is reported to have done seem impossible for one man. The Hammer may not even be an actual person, but rather a group. I think the stories reflect a Muslim tendency to exaggerate. He's reputed to be Palestinian, or Jordanian, or Lebanese, or Egyptian depending on who is telling the story. You get the picture," Tom said.

"What kind of things has The Hammer done?" Justin asked.

"Political assassination of rivals, attacks against Israeli tour groups in far-flung places, assassinations of Western tourists, and cybercrime," Tom said, ticking them off on his fingers.

"I can see why people would think this is more than one person. Why haven't I heard of him?" Justin asked.

"He avoids notoriety and, of course, the associated cruise missiles which come with it," Tom said.

"Where did this call come from, do we know yet?" Justin asked.

A map overlay of the Washington, DC metro area came up on one of the screens. There was a pie-shaped graphic corresponding to the mobile phone tower and sector used during the call.

Justin looked at the map and had an instant feeling of panic, "Where was the President-Elect's announcement hotel? Gaylord National, right? It's inside this coverage map. Whoever made that call might have been within a few feet of our next president. SHIT! Get Secret Service on the line immediately and notify them to be on alert. This incident has to be upgraded across the board. Is there any way to isolate and repair the voice print?"

"We've been trying. We're having trouble, though. It wasn't a simple digital filter overlay, the signal went through several analog-digital conversions before final transmission. Without knowing the hardware involved, it will be very difficult, if not impossible, to get to a voice fingerprint. It also looks as though some pronunciation games were played as well, so we can't even hang our hat on repeating speech patterns," Thang finished with a groan.

"Why would the election results prove to be an opportunity for a terrorist? He's talking ROI, Return on Investment, are we sure this wasn't just a call about an investment opportunity?" Justin asked.

"It could be. Normally, those types of calls are longer and include more details about the opportunity, but now even investment deals are kept highly secret. Companies assume there are industrial spies listening at all times. So it could be that or it could be a terrorist cloaking his request in financial terms to throw us off the trail. We won't know until we follow the lead all the way," Thang said.

"OK, first order of business is to find where the phone was used. I suppose it is unlikely the GPS coordinates were transmitted by the handset. Get the RF crew out there right away. Do we have the back-office logs with signal strengths from multiple towers? We can possibly triangulate from those," Justin said. "Did we have anything else of similar value to work?"

"No, it was pretty quiet tonight. This was the hottest one."

"Alright, we're going mobile. Let's get over there and start seeing what we can find out," Justin instructed. "You're with me," he said to Thang.

The drive over was going to take an hour and a half due to traffic on the beltway. Justin wished, once again, he had a helicopter to get over the herd animals which always clogged DC traffic. He knew whatever The Hammer had planned for tonight, it would be over long before they got there. The Secret Service had been notified and were taking additional precautions.

Somehow, the task force was going to have to get visibility into the movements of Zufar for the next three weeks on the off-chance it would lead them to The Hammer.

He was also going to have to put together a detailed workup on The Hammer, with a full accounting of all the rumors and legends, to yield a better picture of what the task force needed to look for. Right now, there were too many unknowns. The only concrete lead was the upcoming meeting arranged with Zufar. Writing down notes in his ever-present Moleskine, he made a reminder to check into whoever made appointments for Zufar. They might prove an easier target.

As the team pulled into the resort entry area, there was an unusual amount of activity for as late as it was on a weeknight.

"How much do you want to bet this is where the after-parties were held, or at least one of them?" Justin said. The passersby seemed to be in good spirits and a number were openly intoxicated. "Let's chat with the hotel security manager."

Justin walked into the lobby followed by the team, he looked around until he identified a hotel security staff member. He was standing next to what had to be a Secret Service agent looking directly at Justin and his investigative team. Justin turned back to his pack of followers, "Folks, stay here for a few seconds while I speak to these guys."

He walked over and held out his credentials for inspection, "Simons, FBI Joint Terrorism Task Force. I need to speak with the detail leads, can you point me to them?"

"Adam Rungate, facility security services," the guard introduced himself. "Dinesh here can help you, I expect."

"Dinesh Patel," the Secret Service Agent said, shaking Justin's hand. "Yes, I can take you to our lead agent. He's working close to the Ballroom Party. Adam, thanks for helping. I'll come back with any information which would impact your interests as soon as possible," Adam nodded curtly. "Follow me, Agent Simons," Dinesh said.

Justin motioned for the team to settle in the lobby area and followed Agent Patel through the labyrinth of resort hallways.

"Are you the one who called in the alert earlier?" Dinesh asked.

"Yes. We were on an international surveillance detail and we heard someone, presumably in the hotel area, make a call to one of our monitored overseas baddies. We couldn't get out here in time to check it out, and knew you were on the scene," Justin explained.

"I'm sure Agent Jones appreciated it, I know I do. A lot better than being kept in the dark until it is too late, even if it does raise our blood pressures for a bit. One sec," Agent Patel keyed his communicator informing Agent Jones that he was en route with FBI.

The sound of a live band still in service began to filter into the hallways as they headed for the command center which had been prepared for the Secret Service. Passing by the agent stationed at the door, Justin's eyes adjusted to the dark room lit by live computer screens tracking video and agent telemetry. Agent Jones grunted and rose to his feet, stretching to his full 6'4" height. Agent Patel waved and headed back towards the lobby.

"Are you Agent Simons? Hello, I'm Alex Jones, detail lead. We're tasked with the President Elect's husband's safety. The President Elect, and her team, left prior to your alert. What are we supposed to be watching for exactly?"

"We don't know, I'm afraid. We intercepted a call made from this area to a monitored overseas person of interest. Putting two and two together, we realized that this was also where the President Elect was waiting for the poll results. We might have erred on the side of caution alerting you, but the caller referred to the name of an internationally-known terrorist operative. I can't brief you in on full details tonight - we don't have much to go on when it comes to the operative. No one knows what he looks like, or even if it is really a group of people. We do know they are of Middle East extraction," Justin explained.

"Well, that narrows it down, but not by much. I don't like the idea the President Elect was so close to a terror suspect. I don't like it at all," Agent Jones tugged at his neck in thought before abruptly deciding. "We're going to make alternate arrangements for both of them tonight. She is making a victory tour of the poll-watching parties, and should just about be done with it by now. Jonny Ray is still here, dancing with the faithful in the ballroom. We have eyes on him. We were expecting he would stay here tonight, but plans change."

"If you decide to take him offsite, could you do it in a stealthy way? I mean, we could set up surveillance on where he is supposed to be staying and see if anyone shows up. It's a long shot, but that's all we have at the moment," Justin said.

"Yes, we can easily do that and set your team up. What else can I do for you? I need to get onto alternate arrangements for Jonny Ray," Agent Jones said in clipped tones, eager to set plans in motion.

"You knew there would be something else," Justin said with a smile. "Yes, we're going to need a full list of names for the party, guests, workers, etc. We'll do the same with the hotel itself. Then start the sifting of data."

"I do not envy your job on this one. There are close to 2,000 rooms in this hotel, mostly full tonight. There's over 500K square feet of conference space and about 10 restaurants. You're going to want logs for the docks on the river, too. There are a lot of ways to leave this place, and most of them aren't monitored. Shoot, you could kayak across the Potomac to Jones Point and you're in Virginia. One thing to keep in mind: politics. A good portion of the worthies that were here tonight are far above our pay grades, a word to the wise."

"Thanks for those kind words of encouragement," Justin said.

"I do what I can," Agent Jones smiled in shared suffering.

Justin could feel this turning into an all-night affair, so he got out his phone and texted his wife, Janice, that he was into extra innings. She and the kids were probably already in bed, but the message would be there if she got worried.

His team straggled into the command center and started to set up equipment.

Who is The Hammer and what was he doing around the next President? Justin thought to himself as he started working through the immediate tasks before them.

VENTURE CAPITAL

".. American Muslims are cautiously optimistic with the vote count selecting Senator Lucinda Brown as President-Elect, especially those who travel internationally. One comment which keeps coming up is they welcome a return to predictability in treatment.."

Farid Monsour al Haj for World News Corporation.

Farid picked up his electronic book reader and sipped at his cocktail. He was sitting in a Lufthansa First-Class recliner on his way to Riyadh, Saudi Arabia; it was a 13-hour nonstop flight from Washington- Dulles Airport. The broadcast network had called Farid, two days after the election, on a newly-urgent assignment. Farid was tasked to poll his connections in the Muslim world on their thoughts concerning the first woman President. Specifically, what could be expected in terms of relationships that had been forged with the prior administration. The West expected little to no change, but things are rarely so simple in the Middle East. So Farid was dispatched, along with his faithful cameraman Marc Crosse, to points east. Their first round of interviews would be in Riyadh, and from there they would work their way around the Gulf States. There was no point in polling Iran, as they maintained their intransigent position on "The Great Satan", the United States.

Setting his ebook down, Farid went back towards the Business Class cabin to check on Marc. As he walked, he could see Marc had button-holed a hapless, sweating, German businessman and was talking nonstop. Marc was a short, unkempt man whose hair was a dyed black not normally seen in nature. His age was indeterminate: it could be argued either late 30's or mid-40's, but Farid suspected 40's.

There was plenty of evidence that Marc had enjoyed the open bar on all of these flights a bit too much, but that was one of the fringe benefits of following Farid on his trips. Marc didn't speak any foreign languages, which limited what he could do on these assignments, and Farid preferred the privacy Marc's ignorance afforded.

"Marc, how are you doing? I see you are already boring the ears off of your seatmates," Farid asked.

Marc looked up interrupting his soliloquy, "Hey Farid, we're doing alright back here in the cheap seats. Only ten more hours to go before I have to live without alcohol. Did the network upgrade you?"

"No, I got a mileage upgrade," Farid had, in fact, paid for the upgrade, but didn't like to parade his wealth unnecessarily.

"Damn, I tried to get one, but didn't."

"Guess they just upgraded me on my good looks. That's what happens when you make me famous," Farid joked. "It could be worse, you know. You could have been even further back and paying for your own drinks."

"God save me from such a fate!" Marc said.

"Seriously, though, try to get some sleep if you can. We will have a very short rest on the ground before we meet with our first Ministry contact," Farid advised.

"What do you think I am doing? I'll be dropping off after the dinner service. These seats are alright, much better than the last trip to Indonesia," Marc said.

Farid nodded. "Lufthansa is always reliable in their customer treatment. Plus you get to hear such lovely German. Excuse me for a second."

Turning to the businessman, Farid spoke to him in flawless Berliner German, "Stick with it, he will be falling asleep after the dinner so there is not much more to endure."

The businessman brightened with a relieved chuckle, and nodded his thanks to Farid.

"What did you say to him? That is the first smile I've seen so far!" Marc asked.

"I told him that you were traveling to Riyadh due to your preference for being with desert goats, and your affinity for small animals of all types. I called it Animal Husbandry in German. He was very amused." Farid said with a smile that was mirrored by the German businessman.

"You evil bastard! No way of checking that out, I suppose. Guess it's time for me to catch up on my subscriptions," Marc said after his face had cycled from indignation to rueful humor.

"My work here is done. I'll check in with you later on," Farid patted Marc's shoulder and went back to the First Class cabin.

Sitting back down, he ran through the interview questions for the next day. They were essentially multiple ways of asking the same question: *Will you work with the new American President?* Farid expected he already knew the answers, but having video footage of the players fed the Internet's insatiable need for new content. The delivery mechanism for the news had never been more complicated. The Internet wanted new content nonstop, it wasn't as simple as a network television 2-minute segment at 6 p.m. anymore. Now the story would be dribbled out in a series of 15-30 second snippets that would be released as best-suited the generation of advertising clicks. There was no non-subscription news source where a complete story would be told anymore. Complete news was now the province of the wealthy, who could afford to purchase it.

Farid thought about his upcoming meetings with the Saudi elite. They tended to look down upon him, since he was Palestinian in background. From his American employer's perspective, the Saudis loved him, hence all of the network assignments. But the truth was much more complex. The former clan of the desert, made into royalty by the British Empire, never lost an opportunity to sneer at a mere Palestinian. Of course, in the distant past, the Palestinians had sneered at the desert-dwellers. The desert clans remembered old slights and continued to demand payment. Oil wealth had reset the scales, and the Saudis continued to dominate politics in the Middle East. Farid sighed. Once the one-upmanship rituals were completed, he knew useful business could still be done with his fellow Muslims.

The first meeting on Farid's agenda was with Zufar Azzizi al-Saud, one of several hundred Saudi princes. Zufar was different from most of his fellow princes in that he had been educated in London, and routinely managed his international investments in conjunction with

Western firms. Never one to duck a television interview, Zufar was photogenic and articulate in several languages. Farid had interviewed him on-camera several years before, and it had been relatively easy to set up another appointment.

The balance of the officials Farid hoped to interview were less certain as to timing, which was to be expected in Saudi Arabia. Generally, officials would schedule meetings during the periods between prayers, but not with any finer resolution than that. Farid knew he could, and would be, kept waiting for as much as six hours, depending on what else the person was doing that day. Workplace stress was not something that government workers in Saudi Arabia worried much about. No, that was the sole province of the foreigners brought in from around the world to do the jobs no Saudi wanted to do.

Marc's assessment of the recreational possibilities in Saudi Arabia was fairly bleak: no movies, no legal booze, and no fraternization with women. Farid knew that it wouldn't be as bad as all that. They would be there for several days; they'd eat some splendid meals; then they'd be off for the next stop. Marc would have to be careful but, as an obvious foreigner, the religious police would likely warn him of transgressions before taking any action. In Farid's case, as a fellow Muslim, the rules would be much more strictly enforced.

Farid's status as a Muslim who had participated in the Hajj pilgrimage after his college graduation was announced every time his formal name was presented. It was, of course, much easier for a resident of Saudi Arabia to participate in the Hajj, but there was a level of respect accorded to all of those who had made the effort. Farid even enjoyed a small celebrity locally because his reporting segments were occasionally picked up for local re-broadcasts.

Relegating the worries of his trip until tomorrow, Farid ate a light meal, read one of his books, and slept for the balance of the flight. They were being met by a hotel driver once they had cleared customs services.

Exiting the airport into the cool winter weather, Farid and Marc's bags were carried by the driver while Marc carried all of his video equipment himself. Marc's load had gotten a lot smaller over the years due to the huge advances in the video arts. There was still some bulk which came from an assortment of lenses, but it was a small fraction of what a team used to carry. Of course, the old crews had several people on the team instead of the one-man show who was Marc.

"Marc, we'll head over to check into the hotel, get cleaned up and see if we can't get in to see Zufar Azzizi this afternoon. I think we will be able to squeeze the time there," Farid said.

"Sounds good to me, I'd appreciate having an early evening. I got some sleep, but you know I'm better after sleeping in a real bed. Getting a quick shower now should get me through what we have to do today," Marc said.

They checked in to their rooms, and agreed to meet back in the lobby in an hour. Farid arranged for a car to take them to meet with Zufar. Feeling refreshed they relaxed in the back of the large hotel Mercedes sedan as their driver navigated the wild driving streets of Riyadh. Pulling up to a building that had the look of a post-modern palace, they were let out in front of the lobby.

Two very large doormen, wearing uniforms, stood impassively at attention until Farid approached the door, when one of them opened the glass and gold door with a gloved hand. Farid nodded at the doorman and headed for the lobby desk which had a very attractive young man managing visitors.

"Hello, my name is Farid Amir Mansour Royce al-Haj. I am here to conduct an interview with Prince Zufar Azzizi. I believe we are expected," Farid said in Arabic as he passed over their press credentials and identification.

"Thank you. Yes, you are expected. Did you have a good flight coming to Riyadh?" the receptionist asked as he perused the documentation.

"Yes, it is always a gift from Allah to enter the Kingdom. This is the best time of the year to visit as well," Farid said politely.

Marc stood patiently holding his equipment without fidgeting around. Over the years he had learned it made their interviewees nervous or distracted if he appeared bored or looked around too much during the process. Marc on-the-job focused solely on what needed to be done for Farid, which was one of the reasons why he was such a well-regarded addition to any traveling delegation.

"Please follow Mussa back through the security checkpoint into the waiting lounge," the receptionist said as he dismissed them.

"Come, Marc. Time for security," Farid indicated that they should follow Mussa, a very large man, to the checkpoint.

The security checkpoint was not as overtly sophisticated as the ones manned by TSA in American airports, but that was only from the surface. The metal detector could be seen, but the backscatter X-Ray array was hidden behind a 2 meter hallway choke point which opened into an area to retrieve handheld items.

"Stand here," Mussa rumbled to Farid in Arabic. Farid held his arms out and Mussa ran a hand-held scanner over his entire body. Once complete, he supplemented the scan with a physical pat-down. Afterwards he motioned for Farid to continue and gestured for Marc to approach.

"Marc, come here and be inspected," Farid said in English. Marc had paid close attention and assumed the position without comment or drama.

Once Marc was also cleared, Mussa led them to a very plush waiting lounge. "Please wait here until the Prince sends for you," Mussa said as though he begrudged each word spoken. The lounge was very well appointed, and as they picked a table a steward came over to ask if they would like some refreshment. Farid indicated that a coffee service would be appreciated and the steward bustled off.

"Do you know where we will do the interview?" Marc asked. "Any notion on the light environment we're dealing with?"

"I'm not certain, it has been several years since the last time I was here. But generally you can count on a low light setting, you might also want to go hard-wire for the mics as the Bluetooth environment might be too crowded for good sound," Farid advised.

The coffee arrived along with a selection of local pastries. Farid took out his ebook and started reading. Marc did the same while sampling the delicious array. After about 45 minutes, Mussa reappeared and told Farid that the Prince would see them now.

Mussa led the way to another imposing door, which looked very solid and might have been armored as the hinges were quite robust.

Farid, with Marc one step behind, made his way to Prince Zufar. The Prince was wearing an expertly tailored Western business suit, which appeared to be English in origin. He had well-oiled dark black hair cut short, strong cologne, medium height, flashing eyes, long straight nose of the Saud family, small mustache, and a body which had not completely given itself over to fat.

After the initial exchanges of greetings in Arabic, introduction of Marc, the ritual offering of refreshments, and inquiries after relatives or friends which were a prerequisite to any business being done in most Muslim cultures, the Prince came to their business.

"Welcome, my old friend. What is the reason for our discussion today?" Prince Zufar asked, in English for Marc's benefit.

Zufar, of course, had been fully briefed on the television interview topic and potential broadcast market audience before agreeing to meet with Farid in the first place. But making a supplicant ask once again was something also common in Saudi Arabian business dealings.

"Your Royal Highness, as you are aware, the people of the United States have elected Lucinda Brown for the office of President of the United States. We want to understand your view of the implications for doing business with Saudi Arabia as well as any political ones," Farid said formally.

"Very well, shall we move to my studio setting? My publicist and make-up team are waiting. The make-up team can do yours as well, everyone should look their best for media segments," Prince Zufar said brightly. "I think you will find the lighting and sound to be quite acceptable, Mr. Crosse."

The Prince stood up and they followed him down a hallway into a small studio which was set up for a coffee table interview format. The tableau was indeed well lit. One of the chairs, the Prince's clearly, was quite ornate while a second chair was tastefully expensive but much lower key. At the side of the room was a make-up station which the Prince immediately made use of.

"May I set up microphones?" Marc asked the Prince's Australian publicist, gesturing at the set.

"No need to set mics, mate, you can patch direct into our mixing panel. You'll find our equipment to be state-of-the-art," the publicist said while motioning Marc over to the panel. "Farid, did you bring copies of the questions as we discussed?"

"Yes, here is your copy. I think you will find it to be exactly as we discussed," Farid said.

"Farid, come over and get a touch up. I can see a little fatigue in your eyes, doubtless a result of your trip but not something the camera will miss," Prince Zufar called. "Flying commercial will do that to you."

"Thank you, Your Royal Highness," Farid said as he sat down for a touch-up.

"Farid, we're fully set up and can start whenever His Royal Highness is ready," Marc had been briefed on the correct form of address, and who was really setting the pace in this interview.

"Thank you Marc. Your Royal Highness?" Farid asked.

Prince Zufar nodded assent and gestured Farid towards his seat. The publicist came over and attached a small microphone onto Farid's suit, hiding the thin antenna wire behind his lapel. He then went to the Prince and carefully attached another one.

"Testing, testing, testing," Farid and the Prince said until Marc finished adjusting the microphone gain for each. Marc signaled ready with a thumbs-up gesture.

"Your Royal Highness, are we ready to begin?" Farid asked.

"Yes, I believe so. Proceed." Prince Zufar ordered.

"We are here with His Royal Highness, Prince Zufar Azzizi al-Saud, a highly-regarded member of the Royal Family and well-known international business leader. Thank you for granting us this interview today, Your Royal Highness," Farid said.

"It is my pleasure, Farid. And 'Prince Zufar' is sufficient in this context," Prince Zufar said with a genial smile.

"Thank you, Prince Zufar. As you know, the people of the United States have elected Senator Lucinda Brown for the office of President of the United States. What are your views on the implications for doing business with Saudi Arabia?" Farid asked.

Prince Zufar nodded. "Senator Brown is well-known to us. We have found her to always be receptive to hearing our views, and expressing her own. There already exists a mutual respect. I am optimistic on the potential for improved business, especially if we can agree to find a way to stabilize world oil supplies," The Prince said.

"President-elect Brown will have an uphill battle with a split congress, do you see that as something which may be an impediment in US-KSA business relations?" Farid asked.

"I think that will be less of an issue when it comes to KSA than it will be for other countries. As an example, I understand both Democrats and Republicans are concerned about American jobs leaving the country for lower-cost international workers. Wouldn't the Congress be more or less united when it comes to sanctioning companies who move their operations off-shore?" Prince Zufar asked.

"Yes, you would certainly think so," Farid laughed. "Oil has traditionally been the largest single trade good associated with the Kingdom, do you see that continuing under the new administration?"

"Oil will continue to be the single largest element in our exports to the United States, but we have begun to diversify. We now bring a good deal of investment capital to American firms. President Elect Brown could encourage more investment and we would be willing to do so. Several points on that topic. I would point out that countries with extensive economic ties, such as investments, very seldom have serious conflicting interests. It is when they have little in common that problems arise. If the new administration is serious about increasing USA exports, then they must focus on creating smoother regulatory approvals on their side. In the end, business is business. We can find a buyer for our products and we can find the products we want to buy, regardless of whether the United States is a key partner. We prefer that they would be, however," Prince Zufar finished with a winning smile.

"Thank you, Prince Zufar. Let's change gears to the political considerations. During the years following the second Gulf War, the United States and the Kingdom have worked together to maintain order and peace within the Gulf region. Do you see that continuing under the new administration?" Farid asked.

"The relationship between the Kingdom and the United States has been a stabilizing factor, but there are still areas of conflict in the region, and without being more interventionist there is little reason to think that will change. I would caution however that there are perpetual issues which create an environment for conflict and terrorism, where the Kingdom and the United States respectfully differ.

An example would be the issue of Israel's building new settlements in occupied territories. That situation enables fringe Muslims, who are dissatisfied with their status quo, an easy unifying reason to engage in destabilization. As long as the United States is committed to veto any proposed United Nations sanctions of Israel for violating their international agreements, people in the region will not fully trust the United States. Another factor, is the USA tendency to withdraw early from destabilizing engagements, such as Iraq and Afghanistan. Removing American forces before reestablishing a national political power has enabled groups like ISIS to fill that void. Now, America is having to fight some of the same battles again. When intervening, there needs to be a sustainable long-term plan, rather than an early exit for political expedience at home. If the new administration could be more focused on long term strategic issues it would be an improvement."

"President Elect Brown is, of course, a woman. Do you consider that it will cause any issues in relations with the Kingdom?" Farid asked.

"The United States is coming late to the party when it comes to having a female head of state. We have worked successfully in the past with many woman leaders. Germany has had one for more than ten years. We find that as long as there is mutual respect on both sides of the table, we can be fully productive. Would we be more comfortable with a man? Of course! But as long as there is mutual respect, it is not the most critical factor," Prince Zufar said.

"On the topic of world oil supply, the worldwide economic slowdown as well as increased crude oil production has put downward pressure on the price of oil. What is the most critical thing the new administration should consider on this topic, from the perspective of the Kingdom?" Farid asked.

"I would express the observation that many third world oil-based economies are a fairly recent phenomenon, and that low oil prices impacts their development more adversely than one would expect. Smaller economies in developing countries are bank-financed, secured by future cash flows from oil production. If those countries cannot pay their loans, there is a wider risk of economic destabilization and political upheaval. Also, consider countries with third world economies and first world militaries. Bringing such nations to the brink of bankruptcy is counterproductive to stability. It might be better to chart a middle course which sets oil pricing higher in order to prevent those outcomes. The Kingdom is better situated than most to survive long periods of low oil prices, but even we will suffer eventually if a more balanced policy isn't achieved," Prince Zufar said while illustrating his final points with hand gestures.

"Prince Zufar, thank you very much for granting us your time to consider these important issues, which will face the new American administration!" Farid said.

"It was my pleasure, Farid. I look forward to the inauguration of President Elect Brown, along with the American people," Prince Zufar concluded by flashing his extremely white teeth once more.

Farid signaled Marc to turn off the camera.

"Your Royal Highness, I think the segment will play very well with American audiences. If it is not an imposition, perhaps we could do a follow-up interview after the President-Elect's first 100 days?" Farid asked.

"Certainly. In fact, my publicist would have set one up if you hadn't suggested it first," Prince Zufar laughed. Switching to Arabic, "I like how your camera man behaves. He is respectful and appears to know his work; perhaps I should offer him a position on my staff."

"It would be an honor for him, I am sure. But I wish you would not, it took quite some time to train him properly. He would probably have difficulty making the adjustment in his personal life, too, he likes women and alcohol," Farid said.

"Ah, I was only half-serious. Riyadh is indeed difficult for Americans to enjoy over the long-term. You have other interviews tomorrow, I hear?"

"Yes, that is true. We will take dinner and use tonight to adjust to the new time zone."

The usual parting rituals, which take more than twenty minutes if done politely, were observed. After which, Marc and Farid were ushered back through the front lobby to where their driver waited. Both climbed into the car and sat back against the cushions.

"I think that went well," Marc said, "or at least it looked good from my side of the camera."

"Yes, Prince Zufar is always talkative, but this time he brought up things that aren't usually on the agenda when talking about the Kingdom-USA relationship. He, or the people above him, must really think there is an opportunity. He was impressed with you by the way. He mentioned making you an offer to work on his staff," Farid said.

"The equipment was top-flight and it looked like they had a production facility as well. I don't know, this is one of those places where they cut off your cock if they catch you with the local talent, isn't it?"

"At the very least, unfortunately," Farid laughed.

"Not for me then," Marc said tiredly.

Farid chuckled. "I am planning on turning in early tonight, do you mind getting dinner on your own?" He asked.

"Sure, I brought plenty to do, although I will probably go to bed early myself," Marc said.

"Let's reconvene for breakfast tomorrow at 8 a.m. We have a few things to go over before our next interview," Farid said as they entered the lobby of their hotel and headed for their separate rooms.

• • •

Prince Zufar had a very different type of meeting scheduled for the evening. This man came alone, with a small laptop computer, and was let in by Mussa through a door behind the compound, away from the street cameras. The man's movements were graceful, fluid, and economic. To those with the experience to know, his bearing was that of someone extremely dangerous. Mussa took it all in stride, escorting the man to a table where he was relieved of a small machine pistol, a very sharp knife, and a saw-garrote, all of which were offered up silently by the man. Mussa gestured, and the man extended his arms for Mussa's pat-down. Nothing additional was found, and Mussa brought him into Prince Zufar's sitting room. Indicating that the man should sit down, Mussa left the room.

Looking around, the man noticed the decor had been arranged to mimic the inside of a tent in the desert. The man allowed himself a moment of internal amusement at the irony; most Saudi princes wouldn't be caught dead traveling the desert in a real tent. Somehow it wasn't the same thing with air conditioning and without the omnipresent smell of camel shit. Ironic, too, that persons maintaining such a pretence of history and simplicity in their surroundings, now wanted Microsoft PowerPoint slide presentations for proposals such as the one the man carried.

Mussa came in bearing coffee and refreshments on a large tray. Silently, he placed them on a low table for the man and left the room again. The man took a coffee and touched it to his lips without drinking deeply. He sat motionless, with only his breathing to show that he was not a statue. He was about 1.8 m in height, slim yet powerful, in the prime of life, with jet-black hair and a well-trimmed mustache. His fingernails were well-manicured, and his hands hard as bricks in spite of their masculine beauty.

"I was hoping to make my favorite Palestinian freedom fighter nervous by making him wait longer than usual, but I cannot see any reaction from you so the fun has gone out of it," Prince Zufar said as he entered the room.

"Your Royal Highness, supplicants should get used to waiting, and who has been waiting longer than the Palestinians?" The Hammer said without irony.

"Most Palestinians look for someone else to take back their land for them," Zufar countered. "People such as that would have been nervous. But you have never been one of them, have you?" He asked.

"No. I fight enemies on my own terms. It is the only rational way to fight. Fighting losing battles is a mistake I do not make."

"No, you do not. Speaking of fighting, is Amin still your second? He's probably here as well, isn't he? He should be very careful, several of the King's Intelligence officers would love to have him as a permanent guest in one of their facilities," Prince Zufar said.

"He would be very careful if he were here. Yes, he is still my loyal second."

"So let's hear about this opportunity you mentioned before. I am eager to see it, and I have something for you as well," Prince Zufar said with barely contained excitement. "Here is a video dock, and I will lower the presentation screen," Zufar indicated a small drawer. The Hammer opened it and started to connect his laptop into the system. Zufar dimmed the lights and nodded to The Hammer. The cover page came up with a well-known logo.

"I call this operation *The Martyrs al-Sabra*. We will use the *Martyrs* incident as justification for the actions which are taken. There are two main efforts which will occur in a seemingly-unrelated manner. The combination will bring the United States to its knees in fear. One action creates widespread fear in the people and the second creates political destabilization. No matter what happens, the United States will be weakened," The Hammer said.

The presentation went on for about thirty minutes until the funding slide.

"The cost for executing this strategy is $2.8M USD. This covers the entire cost and the ongoing maintenance expenses of the network we create for 24 months. Keep in mind nothing here is expendable, and everything can be reused, as needed, for future actions," The Hammer said.

"The cost is minimal and the strategy seems to be sound. If all goes as planned, wouldn't the United States simply declare martial law in order to deal with it? Or increase the persecution of their Muslim citizens?" Prince Zufar said.

"No doubt the conservatives in the Congress will want to do so, but Democrats will simply label them racists and nothing will be done. This president simply cannot do that; Democrats are too proud of their protection of peaceful Muslims. That is the beauty of this opportunity. Congress might successfully implement sanctions on American Muslims, but it would mobilize the entire Muslim population to protest. If international news broadcasts show American police beating Muslims in the streets, it would mobilize world Muslim support and condemnation of the United States. In this action, we goad and goad until the bull charges the sword to its death. No matter what happens, it is a win for us," The Hammer said.

"I like it. But, I have one addition to make, in conjunction with the political destabilization effort," Prince Zufar said with a commanding tone. "Our Russian friends mislaid one, or two, of their suitcase nukes. I acquired one through intermediaries in Kazakhstan and have been looking for the perfect opportunity to use it. For a long time I thought that Israel was the right target, but it is too difficult to get one into that country. Not to mention they would be well-able to reconstruct how it came in."

"Those particular weapons are easily detectable," The Hammer protested. "Their neutron shielding is almost non-existent, if I remember correctly. The Americans have very sophisticated scanning for neutron emitters, they would lock onto it almost at once. How would you prevent that from happening?" The Hammer asked.

"I? I'm not going to prevent anything; it is your job. I'll agree to fund the Martyrs operation, but my price is that you incorporate the use of this device against an American city," Prince Zufar smugly stated. "At this point, you don't really have a choice. We're either moving forward or you're not leaving this building alive, since you now know of my prized toy."

For several long seconds the two locked gazes, until The Hammer broke the impasse by looking down at his coffee.

"Where would we have to take possession of it?" The Hammer asked quietly.

"I can arrange a high seas transfer or the Mediterranean port of your choice. How would you bring it in?"

"High seas is probably best, the Med is too closely watched by Americans and Israelis. I'm not sure yet on the how. I'll want the physical details of the device, model numbers and manuals. Are those things available?" The Hammer asked.

"Yes, I have several copies of the manuals which have those details. They're written in Russian, of course."

"As you said, it is my worry. However, we cannot do the revised operation for the budget I presented earlier, I think this change would require about double the resources discussed. Especially if we have to bribe shippers to get our people aboard as crew on a container ship. We can't just put the device into a container and ship it; it would be detected easily," The Hammer said.

"Shall we call it an even $5M USD? I like round numbers. One condition just suggested itself, you mentioned tying the threads together using the *Martyrs* incident. The weapon has to be tied in as well."

"Is that the final condition placed on our operational plans?" The Hammer asked softly.

"Yes."

"Then transfer the funding to this offshore account and we will begin. Do you have the technical data we discussed here tonight?" The Hammer said.

"Yes, I had it prepared in the event your plan was suitable. Mussa will get it. I'll be happy to have it out of my home, truth be told. Funding will be in place before you leave the Kingdom. Now, a more important concern: where do we invest to reap the most benefit from this operation?" Prince Zufar asked.

"I would expect all of the automatic video surveillance analysis firms will do well. The makers of wide-area neutron scanners will rise also. You could make a case for oil futures, either direction. Or a currency play; European and Asian currencies should strengthen against the dollar. Equities will take a real dive after the device explodes: there is opportunity there as well. I think the equity play might be safest, as it would look as though we were simply being supportive," The Hammer said.

"I largely concur with your analysis. We might make a billionaire of you yet! People who make things happen should be rewarded commensurately."

"My biggest reward is to humble the infidel and turn their triumphs into dust. They already work so hard at their destruction, I only want to help it along. In the meantime, we have to be careful and perfect, so we live long enough to see that day," The Hammer said.

The Hammer disconnected the laptop and placed it within his bag. Prince Zufar signaled for Mussa to rejoin them.

"Mussa, you have the documentation package for The Hammer? Good. Please be so good as to show him out the same way he arrived," Prince Zufar said and turned to The Hammer. "I'll watch events very closely. I should warn you once more our bargain needs to stand or you will earn my lasting enmity. I don't think you would survive that."

The Hammer nodded his head in assent, thinking the Prince lacked sophistication if he needed to make such obvious threats but saying only, "I will keep it in the forefront of my thoughts, as always."

Turning to Mussa, he took the package of documentation and placed it within his computer bag.

Retracing their steps, Mussa repatriated The Hammer's small weapons arsenal and escorted him to the back door once more. Reviewing a television monitor which showed the alley from a number of angles, he opened the door and nodded at The Hammer in farewell as he vanished into the darkness outside.

Mussa went back into the Prince's presence and said, "He is gone. I did not see anyone waiting for him. I'm surprised he accepted responsibility for the package, I expected he would refuse at first."

"What choice did he have? The Palestinians have ever been the tools of their betters, eating whatever shit is placed in front of them, because they have no choice. A race of beggars. I could have denied him extra funding and he still would have had to accept it. I do not want The Hammer to fail, though, so the extra funding is not significant especially considering what I will make the day the device goes off. Easily one hundred times what I have advanced to him! I just need to be liquid in order to take full advantage; that will be my task for the next 60 days," Prince Zufar said.

· · ·

The Hammer was met silently by Amin, who scanned his leader's face for clues as to how the meeting had progressed. As usual, The Hammer's face was imperturbable. At the curb was a hotel limousine driven by Amin, which they quickly entered.

The Hammer reached over the front seat and laid the documentation on the front seat for Amin. "The Prince has added a special condition to our operation. How is your Russian?"

"My Russian is well used. Are we talking intelligence or technical manuals?" Amin asked.

"Technical manuals, old school suitcase."

"Shit! Those things are portable but not at all stealthy. Where is it to be used?"

"I thought as much. Please read the documentation and we'll decide how best to use it. It is our choice where, but the demand is one of the cities."

"I will. Do you think the prince is planning something against our interests?" Amin asked.

"I do, but he has reached the point of liability even if he is not. We may have to bring forward the retirement plan we discussed. As for the operation, funding should land tomorrow. Once confirmed, launch the training phase. Operation should go live in mid-April, is that doable?"

"Noted. Mid-April is doable but tight. We'll make it. I'll look into the hunting clubs. Do you need me to stay here for a few days in case things fall apart?" Amin asked.

"No, you have a lot to accomplish in a very short time. The first thing we need to figure out is the device handover. Can you get me an ops plan for that before you go? I'll coordinate with the prince before I leave."

"I can. No later than tomorrow midnight. I will contact you the usual way," Amin said.

"Don't worry overly about the device addition, as I consider, the more I think it can be turned to our benefit. Allah has sent a priceless opportunity to us, we just have to grasp it without burning our hands."

"From your lips to the ears of Allah!"

Hunt Camp

"..Muslim leaders in the Gulf expect a productive relationship with President Brown's administration, citing a need for flexible new approaches on Middle East issues. Several pointed out they had worked closely with Germany's Chancellor Merkel for many years, as an indication President Brown's sex will not be an impediment for them.."

Farid Monsour al Haj for World News Corporation.

Amin Zafir al Tikriti sat in a dark hotel room on the outskirts of Columbus, Ohio lit only by the laptop computer open before him. He sat waiting for his VPN connection to a Ventrilo server located in Russia to indicate his online meeting had started. Vent was one way to avoid the notice of the major intelligence services who monitored worldwide voice telecommunications for terrorist traffic. It wasn't completely secure, but very little was. The key was to communicate quickly, with decent encryption, and move on before the conversations could be decrypted. Amin had checked into a hotel with a false ID and credit card but didn't plan on staying the night. Excellent Internet service was the key requirement. Vent worked much like a walkie-talkie, used very little bandwidth, and was very hard to spot when encapsulated within a VPN.

The laptop flashed and a tone signifying the arrival of a new member to the conference sounded. Amin sat down in front of the laptop and pushed the transmit key.

"Amin, standing by for instruction," in Iraqi-accented English.

"We have a go for the operation. Acquire the Wisconsin site for two weeks. Sponsor has asked if we can support 30 hunters. Over." A digitally modified voice intoned.

"Acknowledged Wisconsin. 30 doable with full mirror. Timing? Over," Amin said through his own voice modification device.

"Wisconsin session within six weeks. Doable? Over."

"Doable. Over," Amin acknowledged.

"Engraving status? Over."

"Complete 300. 10 each. Acceptable? Over." Amin asked.

"Excellent. Next meeting status 01021015. Over."

"Next meet 01021015. Over and out."

Amin changed Vent rooms and rang for the woman he knew would be waiting. After she answered, he spoke with her in Arabic for an hour. His cover story would be he had hoped to meet with his lover, but she was unable to leave her home, so he had to be satisfied with the sound of her voice. Vent carried much less risk of a private detective being able to wiretap their conversation, which is an important consideration when your lover is the wife of a powerful man. Who suspects a man with a hard-on for another man's wife as a terrorist? Classic intelligence service training. Misdirection and a mundane reason for otherwise suspicious behavior.

Amin had served years as an Iraqi intelligence operative, assigned to support the hidden world of terrorism shortly before the events of 9/11/2001. In the aftermath, he was one of the operatives who had been dispersed nameless into the world, landing in Lebanon where he trained and led terrorist candidates. A solid, forgettable man, he looked somewhat dull, which was anything but true. In the years following the 9/11 mission, he concentrated his efforts on smaller factions. During that time, he met The Hammer of Islam. Amin trained him extensively in the tradecraft of intelligence work. The Hammer mastered everything taught in a remarkably short time. Soon, it became clear The Hammer was the leader Amin had been waiting for, and he volunteered to become The Hammer's second for operations.

Of all the secrets that Amin held, The Hammer's identity was the greatest. In order for their strategic efforts to succeed, no one could know who he was. Amin was one of only four people who knew that detail. Amin had no illusions of what The Hammer would do to him, or the others, if betrayed; after all, Amin himself had taught that lesson early on.

Amin packed up his laptop, surveyed the room for anything else he might have touched, and exited to his car in an unhurried manner. Placing his bag in the passenger seat, he pulled out of the hotel and headed back to his small 3-bedroom house in Columbus, Ohio.

Taking another mobile phone out of the computer bag, he made a call to the rental manager of the Oversight Hunting Lodge in Wisconsin. Set on a small lake in a thousand acres of private forest, it was perfect for the next phase of the operation.

"Hello, this Andro Simonetti of the Sons of Italy Hunt Club. We spoke last week about the possibility of a two week rental of the entire property," Amin said.

"Mr. Simonetti! Yes, I remember it well. We still have that early February availability, is that what you wanted?" Property manager Frances Singleton gushed, anticipating a healthy commission.

"Yes, would that run from February 1 through the 14th? If so, that would be perfect for us," Amin said.

"Yes, a two-week reservation would be split that way, or from the 15th through 28th. How many hunters are coming?"

"The total party will be about 60-70 people, but only 20-30 of those will actually be hunting. We'll bring our own staff for the game rendering, so we won't need that. How many beds are available?"

"We can handle those kinds of numbers easily; we have over 120 beds in fifty rooms. The main lodge dining room seats 100. All deer shot on the property are private, so you won't need permits or tags. If you go onto the neighboring public parkland, though, you will."

"I think we will confine ourselves to the property itself. Just to confirm, is there a full target range on the site?"

"Yes, there is a ten-shooter range, with demarcations at 50, 100, and 200 yards. We also have a small snow-cat to remove snow if you get a storm. Our caretakers can come out anytime, they live within 20 miles of the property."

"And, finally, it is ridiculous I have to ask this question, but you know how it is: how is the Internet service for the property?" Amin asked.

Frances laughed, "These days, everyone wants that. They don't care about the telephones in the rooms, but they want to be able to upload pictures of their kill to Facebook immediately. To answer your question, we have a dedicated 12 Mbps connection, and excellent WiFi coverage throughout the buildings. You won't be able to stream movies for everyone, but I think you will be pleased with the performance."

"That's all I had for questions other than needing a price, and payment terms," Amin said. "Rather than having everyone pay via credit card, is there a discount for a group wire transfer instead?"

"Yes, we pay a 2.2% fee normally for credit card acceptance and we'll discount by that much for a group wire transfer. The price for the two weeks is based on no onsite support services; you're on your own with no kitchen staff, maid service, or grounds crew. If something breaks or isn't understood the local caretakers can be called in at no charge, but if they get into providing services additional charges would apply."

"Yes, that is exactly what we want," Amin said.

"Then we are talking $208,000 for the two weeks, discounted down to $203,424, payable in advance. Please note, we will want a damages deposit of $50,000 in advance as well, which would be returned less repair costs once the rental is complete."

"On the damages deposit, we're talking about other than reasonable and customary damage, correct?" Amin asked.

"Let me put it this way, unless your party acts like an English rock band and intentionally start destroying things, the deposit is usually fully refunded."

"That makes perfect sense. Let me give you my email for the contracts. I'll also need wiring instructions for the payments," Amin said.

Frances promised to send the paperwork shortly and thanked Mr. Simonetti effusively for the club's business.

One thing out of the way, Amin thought to himself. He would have to check his list of candidates to select the thirty best suited for the mission.

Upon arrival home, Amin pulled into the garage, shutting the door once inside. It never paid to advertise your presence by always parking in the driveway. Amin couldn't understand the American habit of buying a home with a large garage and never parking in it.

He had seen some home garages in his neighborhood full to the brim with storage boxes, and cars worth more than $50K sitting in the driveways, exposed to the fierce winter weather.

Amin was known in the neighborhood as an Italian to those who weren't Italian, and Bosnian to those who were. His standard explanation was everyone knows where Italy is, but Bosnia? It helped Americans understand which part of the world he was from.

Opening the door to his home, Amin reset the codes of his custom alarm system and accessed the security terminal. He checked the continually captured video footage for identified anomalies; no one had approached the exterior doors while he was gone. The new software eliminated the need to watch hours of video footage, and it amused Amin mightily that Israelis were the original inventors. The system took continuous feeds from twelve video cameras, passed it to a hidden system storage array in the attic and held a rolling 48 hours of video footage. The system automatically reviewed all video files and flagged potential issues for later human review. During their upcoming Wisconsin hunting trip, Amin would have to check in remotely to monitor things here. There wouldn't be a lot of evidence if his home was raided, but such a superb security system in a residential neighborhood would raise eyebrows.

Sitting down with a laptop, he reviewed potential candidates: one from each of the thirty largest metropolitan areas of the United States. In most cases, there were multiple candidates in the area, but Amin was looking for a very specific profile. This operation wasn't going to include disaffected young men or women intent on martyrdom. No, for this mission he wanted steady, upstanding, family men who were motivated to survive. Furthermore, they should be solidly from within the ranks of the middle class. No one with financial difficulties would even be considered. Amin was looking for guys with dad-bellies, kids, and a loving wife.

Looking over the list of cities, Amin knew he had several trips ahead of him over the next two weeks. Some of the metro areas like Chicago, Kansas City, Pittsburgh, and St. Louis were within driving range of Ohio. The coastal cities would probably be best dealt with a combination of flying and rental cars. Leaving the cities needing be accessed solely by air travel for the very last would save on airfares and be far less noticeable. Tomorrow he would head for Cincinnati and work through the central states.

Pulling the telephone number of his mosque contact in Cincinnati, he dialed the number using one of his prepaid telephones.

"Hello, this is Sabir al-Qasim from Columbus, Ohio. I am heading your way tomorrow on a business trip."

"Yes, it is wonderful to hear from you again," an unctuous voice eagerly said.

"Would it be possible for me to have coffee with the potential investor we spoke of recently? I can be there in the early morning. As we discussed, if the investor participates, you will be given a percentage as a reflection of our gratitude," Amin said.

"Would that be the first, second, or third party we discussed?"

"The second. Do you think he will have any problems being able to meet tomorrow? Also, was he fully motivated to be a part of our venture? Does he need convincing?"

"No, he is fully committed and waiting only to understand what must be done to join the group."

"Excellent, please contact me as soon as you have a time and location for our discussion. I'll be up late tonight, so please do not hesitate," Amin said.

Amin hung up the phone and placed a checkmark next to Cincinnati.

Amin made telephone calls to the cities of St. Louis, Kansas City, Denver, and Minneapolis then sat back to wait for confirmations to start coming in. The intermediaries would be monitored throughout the operation to ensure they were not playing both sides of the game for profit. This had the potential to be the largest operation since the hugely successful 9/11 mission. Unlike 2001, the infidel enemy was fully alert and always canvassing the potential battlefield for indication of a pending attack. Millions of eyes and untold millions of lines of computer code searched for people like Amin day and night. Intermediaries were always the weakest link. The security risk of leaving them alive had to be balanced against the cost in time to develop new contacts. It had taken Amin more than five years of painstaking work to build his current network, and he was the only person who knew the entire asset list.

By the time he had to reestablish contact with The Hammer, in nine days, he should have a significant number of the operatives lined up and some trips to make to round up the rest. Amin sat down in a recliner with the telephone on the arm and dozed waiting for the phone to ring.

The next day, Amin drove the hundred miles to Cincinnati for the first stop on his tour. He was scheduled to meet with a Mufid Aziz, whose family owned and operated two Circle K convenience stores in the Cincinnati area, at 10 a.m. in a coffee shop. Amin had picked a location which was far enough from Mufid's normal business so it would be unlikely anyone would know him.

Amin sat drinking the heaviest coffee he could order and watched the door for Mufid. Mufid came in several minutes late, a medium to smallish man with a middle age paunch around his waist and a thinning head of black hair. He was wearing worn black store slacks and a white long sleeve shirt with the cuffs rolled up. Amin was pleased to see a Circle K logo was nowhere to be found on his person. Waving his arm to get Mufid's attention, he signaled the waitress to attend Mufid's order.

"Good morning, Mufid Aziz. I am Sabir al-Qasim. Thank you for meeting with me today. Will you have some coffee as we discuss our business?" Amin said.

"Thank you, yes I will," Mufid placed his order with the bored waitress. Warily he looked back at Sabir and switching to Arabic, "My brother from mosque said I should meet with you today, so I am here. What business do we have?"

Amin changed his manner to be more confidential and less friendly, "I'm told you are interested in being a part of our struggle to liberate Palestine from the infidel. More than simply donating money as you do now, but by being a resource we can count on in Cincinnati."

"Yes, that is my desire. I want to be a part of future actions."

"Our future actions will not be martyrdom actions. These will cause much greater pain to the infidel, and strike a bigger blow than even the blessed event of 2001. If our plan works, it will be as though a powerful bull is maddened by the sting of a thousand bees," Sabir said.

"What will I have to do?" Mufid asked nervously.

"I have several questions for you first. Are you happy with your family and your business, is everything going well there?"

"Yes, it is very good. My children are doing well in school, my wife loves me, my business will make us rich some day. There are long hours to work, but it is good," Mufid said.

"Excellent. We do not want someone who simply wants to die or to escape their life into paradise. We want people who have a lot to live for in their life. This effort is something which will take a long time. My next question is more critical, would you be able to kill or injure infidels without concern?"

"Yes, I could. I'm not in the best of physical condition as you can see, but I would be willing, even eager, to do so."

"May I understand why you feel that way, living here in the belly of America? Surely you have infidel friends whom you would not harm," Sabir probed.

"I used to have such friends, until I heard what they say of me when they thought I could not hear. They despise our prophet's teachings and secretly hate us, even as they smile politely to our face. Me, they do not fear as I am only the little man working in the convenience store. They have contempt for me and my children. I would give much to change that," Mufid said bitterly.

"Understand that the actions we are engaging will be anonymous. You personally would not be suspected or identified, if things go as planned. The credit would go to the larger cause. We do not want any soldier to be expendable in this battle. You will see the fear show on all their faces, though, I promise you that much."

"I am yours," Mufid said simply, with conviction.

"Very well. We will need your time, away from family and work, during the first two weeks of February. You will drive alone to a hunting lodge in Wisconsin, where you will learn to hunt deer and elk. You have joined a Muslim hunting club, if asked. You will even bring home coolers full of hallal meat which is taken in our hunts, so your wife should be very happy. I will provide additional details concerning location when it is closer to the date."

"I do not know how to shoot rifles, even though I have a shotgun at the store," Mufid admitted.

"Do not fear, you will be taught everything you need to know. I must caution you now, this is very important. You must not talk about our conversations or plans with anyone, including your family and the person who sent you here today. In these actions, a story will be created and it must be followed exactly. The consequences are terrible for being considered a traitor, both in this life and the one to come," Sabir said seriously. "All of us are being watched for signs of such and we must be very careful."

"I understand," Mufid acknowledged.

"Good. It is very important to understand that we are not playing children's games. There are severe consequences for failure. Between now and our trips to Wisconsin, you will use this mobile phone to contact me. My number is the only one entered. Don't use the phone for anything else. You don't have to carry the phone with you all the time, but you do need to check and see if I have tried to contact you every few hours," Sabir said. "Now, are there any questions you wish to ask me while I am here?"

"No. I am pleased to be part of the upcoming action. Thank you, my brother."

"It will be my pleasure to teach you how to hunt, as well as introduce you to some of the many brothers who are a part of our effort."

They said the low key goodbyes of Muslims in public American spaces and went their separate ways. Amin-Sabir was satisfied with the selection of Mufid. *One down, twenty-nine more to go*, he thought to himself as he started the car.

• • •

Amin was able to report that he had made contact with 13 candidates thus far, with no fall out due to lack of commitment, when he spoke to The Hammer again. He anticipated the winter weather would start to impact progress, which is why he had started with the central northern parts of the United States and saved the South and West for last. The Hammer set a time for mid-January to discuss status updates, and of course Amin was to contact him if there were adverse developments in the interim.

Several of the remaining candidates either refused the opportunity outright, or were judged unsuitable by Amin, so they had to be replaced within those cities. Each of the candidates who fell out were soberly advised of the extreme need for secrecy, and the horrific consequences for those who did not stay loyal. Then Amin assigned mirrors to each of them. A mirror is an oversight asset whose job it was to watch the operational staff for any sign of disloyalty. In cases where disloyalty was proven, the mirrors would kill the offending party. The operatives did not personally know the mirrors and, if the mirrors were good, the operatives didn't even realize they were there. All of the mirrors reported directly to Amin, just as the operatives did. The candidates who fell out would be watched even more closely, their home, emails, and telephone calls would be monitored closely especially once the operation unfolded. Talking to their wife or family about Amin's offer would prove fatal.

By mid-January, Amin finished his recruitment efforts. The contracts with the lodge had been signed and payment funding transferred directly by wire from several bank holding companies in the Caribbean. Amin planned to drive to the hunt camp in an unmarked commercial van, acquired specifically for the occasion. This was the truly risky part of the operation. Inside the van, were forty Winchester Model 70 rifles with scopes, chambered for .30-06 Springfield rounds. There were also 6,000 rounds of ammunition. In support of their cover story, there were also hunting vests, coveralls, eye protectors, and a case of industrial-strength insect repellent.

Amin had ready documentation for the Hunt Club rental of the lodge in the event that he was pulled over and searched. Non-perishable food items filled the rest of the van's empty space, so the cover story would seem complete and consistent. On a good day, he would not be pulled over at all, and he definitely didn't plan on driving significantly over any posted speed limits.

If traffic were in line with plan, it would take a little over ten hours of driving to arrive at the camp. Amin would only drive from dawn until early evening, the times where there would be the most vehicles on the highway. The last thing he wanted was to be the only car on a road, driving past a bored state trooper, with out-of-state license plates.

In addition, Amin had a very special package which was hidden amongst the many ammunition cases. Three hundred rounds of rifle ammunition with Arabic text engraved on the shell casings.

• • •

At the end of January, Amin made the drive to Wisconsin in very good time, considering a winter storm had dropped several feet of snow along the route a few days prior. Anyone who has lived in places with snow can attest to the almost paradoxical ease of traveling several days after a storm. Perhaps the traffic wasn't as bad due to the fact fewer people were on the roads, but regardless, the traffic moved and there were no delays. The only close brush with law enforcement came when an Illinois State Trooper was sizing up the van, riding behind it for several miles. It was made moot by a carload of young people in a Dodge Charger blowing by in the fast lane at high speed. The Trooper lost interest in the van and headed out in the hot pursuit of youth.

Amin checked into a small well-lit motel where he could park directly next to his room. The van had a custom alarm system and Amin was carrying a small arsenal should anyone be foolish enough to set it off. No one sought to test his resolve overnight and he got a good night's rest.

The next morning, Amin got a breakfast of coffee and scrambled eggs with sausage at the cafe next to the motel. One action which convinced infidels a person wasn't Muslim was to partake in eating pork sausage. While most observant Muslims would eschew pork, those who worked as spies did whatever was necessary to fit into the local culture. Amin had to wait until the property management office opened for the day to take possession of the lodge rental. He also needed to coordinate with the rest of his incoming staff who were also driving vans filled with equipment. His technology lead, Reem Moussa, had networking equipment and 75 high-end laptop computers. The thirty trainees would each receive an identical computer for the operation; the thirty mirrors would be given specially-configured computers to aid with the monitoring their charges; and there were fifteen spares because shit happens. A large quantity of special burner mobile phones which were to only be used in emergency situations.

Reem texted that he was about thirty miles out and would soon join Amin in the cafe. Reem was a former IT consultant for one of the largest defense contractor firms serving the DC beltway. His clearances had been very high when he had worked on projects for the NSA and FBI. The clearances themselves had lapsed long ago, since he no longer accepted the lucrative service contracts, but the knowledge of how the clients systems and procedures operated were still fresh in his mind. The NSA and FBI managed the physical flow of information very closely indeed, however they did not always perceive the threat of a talented individual with an excellent memory. Reem could recite lines of code from memory; if he thought it could prove useful later, he memorized it. Physically unimposing, he had the classic look of a Pakistani technical lead: unkempt appearance, large glasses optimized for the reading of computer and mobile device screens, and a manic coffee-fueled energy when working on a problem.

Amin's tradecraft lead, Qazi Wahdan, was also driving a van, but this one was primarily dedicated to the balance of the provisions to get them through the first few meals prior to finding local sources for fresh food. He also carried an array of winter coats and gloves, as it was likely some candidates would be less than fully prepared. He too was less than an hour from the cafe.

Amin ordered another round of coffee and had them take the breakfast plate. That gave him some room to start writing notes on next steps, last details to see complete prior to the arrival of the candidates. Reem was first to arrive, parking his van next to Amin's. Amin waved him over to his table.

"Hello, Nico, over here!" Amin called.

"Andro! Traffic wasn't bad after all," Nico-Reem said quietly as he slid into the booth. "From your greeting I assume we are using Italian covers."

"Si. Grazie mille," Andro said. "Not too much of that obviously but enough to sell the Sons of Italy charter. Antonio should be right behind you."

"Antonio was probably tailing me for practice, I'd be insulted but it's always good to have a backup," Nico said with a smirk.

Just then, Antonio entered the cafe, glanced around the room, nodded at Amin and headed for their booth.

"Ah, Antonio! Come sit and have some of this fine coffee," Andro-Amin said jovially indicating the empty place.

"Brothers, we have a few things to sort out when the hunters arrive. First, I want to run a no-real-names protocol between the hunters. I'm using the Sabir cover, you should use your Level 2 ones as well. We'll greet each hunter and assign them a nametag number with screen-names, which will be their name for the duration. The hunters must not be allowed to compare notes with their counterparts, no names, no cities, and no backgrounds. When we assign roommates for the sleeping arrangements, it will be a mirror for each case. Antonio, how are the mirrors coming along?" Andro asked.

"Very well. We started remote training about a month ago; they are all familiar with the toolset. We can use them to police the hunters during the training process as live practice. They start arriving later today through tomorrow. They will all be on-site by tomorrow evening," Antonio-Qazi said.

"The hunters will start arriving tomorrow, but many of them will need an extra day to get here. It is a bit of a risk to have them all drive here, but it seemed to be safest given what they have to carry back with them. Once they are safely back home with their tools it will be very difficult for to find them. Nico, how much time will you need to get the network set up at the lodge?" Andro asked.

"Probably it can be done within four hours. I will need a few more to sweep the facilities for listening devices. Does the Lodge have security cameras or systems?" Nico asked.

"Not sure, we can ask when we head over in a few minutes. Are there any other questions we need cleared up prior to seeing the property managers?"

"We should understand whether the property is gated. That would solve a lot of day-to-day security issues once everyone is there," Antonio said as he looked up from the menu.

"Agreed! Let's head over to meet with the property manager, you two can stay with your vans and follow us out to the Lodge."

"What? No breakfast for us? Antonio needs a good breakfast!" Antonio said with a grin.

"Sure, you know where the property is, you can join us later. How about you Nico?" Andro-Amin asked.

"I'll come along with you, I was able to grab something when I got gas earlier." Nico said.

"Antonio has no problem eating alone. It breaks his heart, but it is one of the things he must endure with friends such as yourselves," Antonio said while perusing the menu. "Ah, pork sausage! Bene!"

"Don't overdo it!" Andro said with a smile.

Andro and Nico headed for their respective vans and drove to the property manager's office. Andro went in with his folder of paperwork and came out five minutes later followed by Frances Singleton who climbed into a sporty Mercedes coupe. Andro and Nico followed her car on the winding roads to the Lodge property. She had to open the gate for the small cavalcade, then they drove up a long wooded gravel road to the main buildings.

Frances handed over a large set of keys and walked the two around the property to see where everything was kept. The Lodge had been leased many times to hunting parties similar to the Sons of Italy, so they even had a large three ring binder with information on how things worked. The tour included the generator building, kitchen, dining hall, and guest lodging. She didn't think there would be any snow for the next few weeks, but if it changed, there was a tractor with a snow plow so access to the road could be maintained. Nico was very pleased to see a very large television screen in the main dining/lobby area, as he would need to set one up if it had not been there. He also confirmed there was a security camera setup; if needed, all that was required was to turn it on.

"The property boundaries are well marked? I want to make sure we don't inadvertently wander off of it when hunting and run afoul of the game warden," Andro said.

"Yes, there are posts with wire strung across the entire boundary. If you go under one of those, you might have an issue," Frances said.

"How likely is it that we would see someone else on the property when we're hunting?" Andro asked.

"The locals all know this is private land, and do not trespass. This time of year, you won't see the casual hunters because it's too cold. So it would be unlikely. The security system is mostly keyed to watch the boundary, the wire is tied to sensors, which capture video footage. We use it primarily to keep track of the private deer herd. Most of the time they stay here because of the food, but occasionally they wander a bit."

"Thanks, those are all the questions I have. Nico?" Andro asked.

"No, I've seen what I need to. Just got to unload and start setting up."

Ms. Singleton tendered her thanks for the rental, made sure Andro had contact information for any conceivable issue, and made her departure. An hour later Antonio, presumably well-fed, pulled his van up to the lodge as well.

"Let's get to work. Antonio should have all the energy necessary," Andro said with a smirk. "From now on, we'll use level 2 alias unless we see Ms. Singleton or other camp workers."

Both men nodded their heads in agreement.

Together, they started on unloading the trucks. Slowly but surely the main room of the lodge began to be filled with equipment. One particularly nice feature of the lodge, was an empty lockable equipment room which had many gun racks and shelves for ammunition. Amin-Sabir quickly had the guns, ammo, targets organized within the room, with the inventory sheets left for signing out the guns.

"Hassan-Qazi, we have ample space in the equipment room for the cold weather gear, let's get all of that in here. Karim-Reem, we might have space for the laptops as well. Perhaps this is where the candidates sign in and get their badges. It would be a good way to keep control of things." Sabir said.

It turned out there was plenty of room for their entire store of equipment, which simplified the plan considerably. Foodstuffs went into the kitchen pantries and large walk-in freezers.

Later that afternoon the mirrors started to trickle in. Upon arrival, they were assigned nametags which had numbers instead of names and their custom laptops which had the same number on the case. They were put to work immediately, getting the guest rooms ready for the candidates, filling up the kitchen with supplies of coffee and snacks. Each mirror operative would share a guest room with a candidate, but not the person they were assigned to mirror, as it would not do for the candidate to later recognize them so easily. The mirror would monitor their roommate and report any behavior slips within the mirror group sessions. The protocol was to correct the candidate's error immediately, but also report the transgression back to the mirror group.

Sabir called a meeting with the mirrors that evening.

"A quick word, many of you have noticed the unusual program installed on your laptops. I am speaking of Fantasy Conquests. By show of hands, how many of you are familiar with the game?" Sabir asked, and close to half raised their hands uncertainly.

"Good! Have any played the game before?" The response was close to a third of the assembled men.

"Excellent! Those of you who have played before will be resources for those who have not. Each laptop has an installed paid-up account, the login details are in a file called FC_Login. The account comes with a character that was created specifically for each person. Each character belongs to a very special guild within the game, which comprises all of your brothers for the operation. We will be using the game for several things. First, to solidify our group into a real team by doing something together which can be fun. Second, and most important, we will be using the game to communicate orders during our operation. Done correctly, the infidel will not be able to decipher our communication medium even when they are tearing out their hair looking for a solution. More on that later. But for now, I want you to set up in the dining hall and become familiar with your main characters. Again, those of you who already know how this works need to help those new to the game. And no jokes about noobs, we are all brothers here and need to help bring the new ones up to the necessary standard," Sabir said.

"Question, how can we communicate safely with this? I know there is chat, but I think those are logged and monitored," Number 33 asked.

"That is a very good question. I will explain it in complete detail for the entire group later, but in summary this method uses the concept of virtual presence and coded gestures," Sabir explained.

"Ah, very interesting and quite ingenious I think," Number 33 said in frank admiration.

"Yes, this is just the beginning of using this channel, if it works. Now you know why the mirrors are critical to our success. The only way this message medium will be broken is if one of our own number explains it to an outsider. It is the one thing which must not happen. There are other measures in place to confuse the trail even further, but again those will be discussed later. In the meantime, go get some coffee and snacks, and sit down for some gaming," Sabir commanded.

The mirrors all took their laptops into the dining hall, and sat down intermixing the experienced players with the new ones. Soon the hall was filled with the sounds of game combat and music. When the sound became distracting, they all started using the earphones provided in their kit. Sabir watched satisfied, as another purpose was to have some activity to burn time between other tasks, so the candidates wouldn't be tempted to compare personal data in boredom. No, each one needed to be unaware of who or where their brothers actually were, to promote safety for everyone.

Sabir checked in with Karim-Reem, who reported the networks were completely in place for the training and no external monitoring devices had been detected.

"Karim, I think we should keep the video camera security net operational so we can spot any unwanted parties entering the property. Just make sure any archival files are fully eliminated prior to our departure," Sabir ordered.

"Will do. I'll turn those on now, and start assigning mirror monitors in four shifts per day,"

As the rest of the mirrors came in and got established with new laptops, the candidates began to straggle in as well.

• • •

Munir Hammayil was feeling aggrieved as he drove from his home in Roseville, California to Wisconsin. Munir had acquired a used Honda Accord sedan for the operation, as his contact Sabir insisted, but Munir hated every minute of driving it. Not because the car was unreliable or difficult to handle, but rather it was beneath Munir Hammayil, DDS! Were it not for the cause, he wouldn't be caught dead driving something so undistinguished. To think he would have to drive over 4,500 miles in one gave him a headache. Better to think about his attractive new dental assistant sitting in the passenger seat gazing at him worshipfully. Better to think of the BMW 7, safely parked in his garage at home.

People on Highway 80 East didn't respect a person driving an Accord either. Munir was used to zooming through traffic which moved over to accommodate a man who clearly was more important. No one ever moved over for an Accord, unless it was being driven erratically. Sabir had expressly forbidden Munir calling attention to himself or his cover. At first it was exciting, having a cover, but it wasn't a lifestyle natural to him. He didn't build a successful dental practice to be lumped together with middle class Americans, but it was a sacrifice he was making for the liberation of Palestine. As instructed, he even purchased an inexpensive watch to wear for the trip rather than his $40,000 Rolex Oyster. *How was anyone to understand his importance without some indication of status?* Munir wondered.

Munir planned to make the trip in three days, leaving Saturday, January 30th and arriving at the camp the evening of February 1st. The first night would be spent in Salt Lake City, Utah and the second in Lincoln, Nebraska. Day 2 would be the longest spent driving. The drive itself was hugely boring when it came to scenery, and the Honda's radio channels soon failed to provide interesting content.

Somehow, Munir made it to Wisconsin without major incident. There were many small slights, he imagined suffering, from other drivers and wait-staff which fueled even more suppressed rage at the infidel oppressors. He also couldn't help but notice the population became more Caucasian the closer he came to Wisconsin, which made him question the wisdom of his contacts. Munir couldn't stand out with his car or his jewelry, but a clearly ethnic team of color was being assembled somewhere lily-white. No way would it be ignored by the locals.

He drove until he reached the access road to the camp, and joined many other Honda Accords in the ample parking area. After a quick check-in, he received a name tag with the number 27 and the nonsensical name Sullnpsych.

Munir recognized Sabir, who was clearly in charge, and walked over to pay his respects. Sabir's demeanor was polite, however he immediately interrupted Munir's attempt to reintroduce himself by insisting Munir only use the name or number on his tag going forward. Munir acquiesced, but felt as though he had been punched in the stomach. Keeping to himself, he took his new equipment to his room and took a nap to recover from the long days of driving.

The next day, everyone had arrived and Munir was summoned with the rest to be addressed by their new commander. Munir joined the rest of the team in the large dining room which held a large flat television screen. Looking around the room, he saw an assortment of clearly different Muslim nationalities, but resisted the impulse to introduce himself to learn more about them.

Sabir turned to Karim and asked, "Are the gates locked and the security system activated?"

"Yes, everything is active, and everyone is here but for the security team."

"Thank you, Karim. Brothers, we are gathered to hear our leader's words," Sabir said and indicated the television screen.

A common Muslim symbol that most of the audience recognized came on the screen, the Martyrs al-Sabra logo. After a few seconds, the logo dissolved into a shot of a man's face covered by a black balaclava.

"Assalaamu 'Alaikum!" the man said with a voice deeper than humanly possible.

"Wa'alaykumu s-salām!" Amin and Reem said together respectfully. The room also responded once they realized the video was a conference.

"Sabir, are we ready to begin?" the masked man asked.

"Yes, everyone is here to hear your words," Amin said.

Munir could see flashing dark eyes and flawless white teeth as the masked man spoke to them.

"I greet all of you in the sight of Allah, the most glorious. You are the new swords of Islam. I am The Hammer." A murmur swept through the room, and Munir's jaw dropped, with the hearing of the name. "We are beginning a new fight against the infidel. One they have never seen before, one that will cause terror far in excess of the glorious events of 9/11. The infidel will drive themselves crazy trying to find you, and they will not, if we execute our operation as designed. We will not announce our efforts, but we will leave a small token behind each of our actions for the perfection of their dismay."

"In the past, our bothers have engaged in martyrdom operations, many which were successful. They worked for a very short time, because the infidel understands very well that martyrs can hurt them no more, as they are dead. So the faithful were losing our youth in a lost cause, a bomb set off by a martyr who will set off no more bombs. After the infidels bury their dead, a week later none of them remember the martyr with fear. It changes now! We will not be martyrs by design. If we die in an unplanned fight with the infidel, InShaAllah! But it will not happen because we planned on seeking martyrdom. No, our bothers will live to strike the infidel over and over again! It will bring more terror to the infidel than a thousand martyrdom operations. That is the reason why we wanted only seasoned mature fighters for this mission, we do not want the impulsiveness of youth."

"How will we strike the infidel? We adapt the plan that another man with a Muslim name executed poorly, but to great effect. It was not reported whether he was a brother, but his method was inspired to terrify the infidel, and it did. I am speaking of John Allen Muhammad, the DC sniper of 2002. If you remember, he and a young man killed 17 people during a 23-day period. The entire DC area was paralyzed with fear; hundreds of aircraft and police were involved in the search to little avail, and the normal operation of the city was severely impacted. This was done by one man, on his own, with no means to plan a proper terror campaign."

"Our plan is different. We have expertise and financial backing to protect our shooters. We have a plan to paralyze an entire country. If we are successful, the United States might have to resort to martial law, which would be a huge victory for the faithful. Even so, they will not find us. Every American will worry they could be a target, this will be in the forefront of their mind, fear like a cancer."

"There are more than sixty brothers here in our effort. Each is from a different major city in the United States. Each will be taught how to be a sniper in the service of our jihad. We will make all of you proficient in the use of the rifle you will take home."

"At this point you might ask yourself how you would avoid being caught when shooting. The answer is that you will not be blindly firing your weapon. You will only do so at the command of myself. In addition, you will take only one shot and make your escape. You see, it doesn't matter if the shot fails to immediately kill or even hit the infidel. What matters is the terror produced by taking the shot in the first place. Snipers are caught when they take more than one shot. Unless someone is looking directly at the sniper, they cannot tell where the shot came from until there are more shots. The first shot wakes them up to the presence of danger, but not where it is coming from. In our scheme, you will take one shot, eject the shell casing, and then escape to be ready on another day. Who you shoot is not important, the only rule is that it can be no one who is guarded or personally known to you."

"Remember the logo on our screen when we started? The Martyrs al-Sabra? The same martyrs commemorated by the charity to help orphans in war zones. We have inscribed the name on each shell casing. It must be left behind so the infidel knows each shot is connected to our effort, since the gun ballistics will obviously be different from city to city."

"Why did we pick the Martyrs to commemorate? Because Zionist killing of innocents created the Martyrs. We now will target the innocent as well, so that the infidel will feel our pain. Killing their young children and mothers will inflame them as nothing else has."

"What is our greatest fear as human beings? Is it something that is fierce, ferocious, and known? Or is it something undefined that cannot be predicted? I would argue it is the one which takes away their control. The Americans whine about post traumatic stress now with a small number of people, what will happen when all Americans suffer from it? That is our goal. And when we have accomplished it, we will vanish like the morning mist of the fields, until Americans have again forgotten their fear and need a new reminder. Once the Americans fear us completely, the Zionists will lose American support and fall to the sword when we take back our lands."

"In the next few days, you will be taught how to shoot and care for your rifle. You will learn how to choose a target and devise the best escape strategies. You will be given a communications channel that is very difficult to intercept. I say difficult, but not impossible. If all of us stay safe and true to our cause, it is closer to impossible than to difficult. Which brings me to the last topic: operational security."

"Do not mistake my wanting no martyrs to mean that I will not punish traitors. There will be no mercy for traitors. This is the only warning you will have. If you remain true, I will protect you and yours as though you were my own family. If you are a traitor to this operation, I will personally ensure that none of your seed remains on this earth. You know my reputation, I think, let it be your guide. A traitor will tell friends or family he is involved in our efforts, or he knows someone who is. Talk to no one about our mission. It will bring the infidel to your door very quickly. None of you are permitted to talk about the city you are from, or your real names, while here. It is for the safety of all of you. If one of you is accidently caught, it limits the damage."

"Once your training is complete you will go back to your homes and act as if there is nothing changed, until you are activated by our command. Some of you have already played the game installed on your laptops, it is very important to our scheme, so take it seriously. You are permitted, even encouraged, to enjoy it," The Hammer smiled his bright smile. "If you're spoken to online by others not in our guild, tell them you're a teenager, but don't engage further. Our guild name is *Crusaders for Truth*, which is even more diversion, for any watchers there may be."

"One other aspect of this training time is the hunting of deer, and perhaps elk, after your instruction in shooting on the range. This will help you pull the trigger when the time comes for the mission, as well as provide an acceptable cover for this training trip. If you are stopped or detained on the ride home and they find your gun, they will also find your frozen deer meat. Everything works together in our story and our plan. Fresh deer or elk meat is a wonderful treat - you'll see. The instructors will teach you to kill the deer hallal. This, too, you should enjoy. May Allah protect you all!" The video feed winked out, and Sabir brought the house lights back up.

"You've heard from our leader, you know the main action that we execute. Are there any questions that I can address now?" Sabir asked.

"Sir, we are to take one shot and escape. How do we choose our targets?" A man to Munir's right asked.

"A very good question. The answer is that the choice is completely up to you. We will teach you to identify the best places to shoot from, ones that offer security and a quick escape. After a site is found, you will choose a target from the opportunities Allah then presents. You will learn the middle-of-body method of aiming, where you do not have to be the world's best marksman to hit your target. Even if your aim is not accurate, your chances of hitting the target are much better. The alternate method of choosing a victim in advance, means that you might have to compromise on your safety to successfully stalk them. We do not want you to ever do that. Any target, except a Muslim, will do for our purpose," Sabir said.

"Sir, how will the communications orders be passed?" A man behind Munir asked.

"Another good question. In the game, we will gather as a group in a virtual circle at a regularly scheduled time. The commander will point at the next shooter. Then the commander will communicate the schedule by gestures. You will all learn the gestures and the codes by memory, but it will not be complicated. Note that if you were not selected as the next shooter, there is nothing else for you to do other than watch. The next shooter has to pay attention to the schedule and make the right responses back to the commander. There will be no text instructions, no telephone calls, no emails; in short very little for our enemies to track."

"How will our hunting be hallal?" Munir's roommate asked from the seat beside him.

"If you shoot a rifle when hunting deer or elk, and you say the name of Allah when pulling the trigger, then it will be hallal, even if you find it already dead from the wounds, because the Prophet (peace and blessings of Allah be upon him) said: "Whatever causes the blood to flow and the name of Allah has been mentioned over it, then eat." But if it is still alive and able to move then you must slaughter it properly and mention the name of Allah over it when slaughtering it," Sabir said. "Are there any further questions?" The men remained silent. "Let's break and those not involved in making dinner can play the game."

The meeting broke up, and soon more than forty heads were bent over their laptops engaged in virtual mayhem. Munir logged into his account, clicking on the pointy-eared character called Sullnpsych. A swell of music sounded in his headphones as he leaned forward to begin playing the character. He found the game fun, much to his surprise, and had eagerly taken to it by spending every free moment building up his character online.

• • •

The next day training started in earnest. Munir joined a group of ten shooters, working their way through the training regimen. The first phase consisted of learning how to maintain the rifle, first by cleaning it, and checking all of its functions prior to using it. Munir found his rifle to be unnaturally heavy, at first, but soon grew used to the solid weight. In some sense, his work in dentistry helped his understanding of what needed to be done and why. He was soon very comfortable with the rifle and its component parts. Later in the training session, he found himself helping several of the others who weren't doing as well, but had to be reminded to not use real names in idle chitchat.

From there, Munir's group was shown to the shooting range to fire their weapons. Munir had never before fired a gun and had to break himself of some involuntary flinching when he pulled the trigger.

Hassan made it easy to learn, though, as video was taken of each shooter so they could easily understand what they were doing wrong. Each person would position themselves for a shot, prone, and then take the shot. Munir was able to hit the body-sized target consistently within a few tries, but not very close to the bulls-eye mark.

"Sullnpsych, try exhaling as you sight on target and pull the trigger at the end of your breath-cycle. Your chest will be still then, and your whole body should also be still. It will help your accuracy," Hassan demonstrated with exaggerated motions.

Munir slowly breathed out, his eye looking through the scope at the target. Hassan was right, the rifle moved less and less as the breath left. Just before he began to inhale, Munir squeezed the trigger. The shot hit the edge of the six-inch bulls-eye mark, his best shot so far.

"Very good, Sullnpsych! Now do it again so it becomes natural to you."

Munir took another shot, then another. He was beginning to enjoy the shooting training, the feeling of power which the gun represented. He wasn't going to win any marksmanship awards, but he could definitely hit the target!

After the day's allocation of ammunition was spent, Munir then spent time on learning how to break down the weapon for escape, after all it wouldn't do to be seen leaving the scene of a shooting with something which looked like a rifle. Exercises were timed, and scored so that each shooter could see the improvement as they progressed.

Each phase of the training was carefully documented by Sabir, Hassan, and three of the mirrors. After each session, the groups would gather for results, with Sabir and Hassan announcing what each shooter had accomplished currently against their prior efforts. A lot of good-natured competitiveness was displayed, but it could not be denied the entire group was progressing. Sabir closed with a list of things to be covered the next day and the group dismissed. The next group took their place and started through the same process.

Munir found himself checking his rifle during his off-time, practicing both maintenance and fast disassembly, when he wasn't playing Fantasy Conquests.

The next day, when Munir's team reported to the shooting range, they found the targets were now twice as far away. The instructors demonstrated how to adjust the rifle scopes for the new range and the shooters took the field. Munir found it more difficult, but realized he would have to cultivate an even greater stillness in order to consistently hit his target. Before long, he had made the adjustment.

The instructors had one more surprise for the group.

"Hold firing! We're going to move the targets to various places for each shooter. While the instructors do it, I'll explain. Suppose you set your scope for a specific distance, but a better opportunity presents itself closer in? You don't have time to adjust the scope," Sabir said.

Number 17 spoke up, "You adjust the aim lower to correct for distance?"

"Very good! It is very difficult to be exact doing it but essentially you aim at a point lower on the body than the target zone. The key to success is to place the shot in the same place left-right, but aimed lower," Sabir instructed. "Notice each of you has a different distance, take your places. We're sighted in at 100 yards today, the rounds we're using will drop 3-4 inches shooting at 200 yards, so what happens at 60 yards?"

"It will be 1-2 inches higher?" Munir said.

"Yes it will be higher, but not as much as that. The reason is the bullet travels slower the further from the gun it gets, so extending range has a bigger effect on placement than reducing it," Sabir instructed. "Take your shots everyone and see for yourself."

Munir took his place and worked through his regimen before taking the shot. He did overcompensate, but was still in the body outline. After a few shots the instructors called another halt, for changing the targets, but this time further out. Munir began to understand the relationship to distance and soon was able to place shots close to where he wanted. The day resounded with the crack of rifle fire almost non-stop.

By the third day, everyone in Munir's group could hit a body-shaped target out to 300 yards more than 90% of the time. Some of them had potential as marksmen, while others were merely good enough for the exercise. Munir's metrics were solidly mid-group, which made him very proud of himself, having just learned to do it.

Sabir dismissed the final group for the day, then turned to Hassan who was gathering up the statistics for later review.

"Tomorrow, we should start the groups on hunting," Sabir said.

"These city men are not very quiet, the deer will hear them a mile away," Hassan said.

"Exactly, I want them to understand how noisy they are, this will demonstrate it."

"Yes, it will. It will play nicely into the tradecraft training which begins tomorrow as well," Hassan agreed.

• • •

Munir heard their next test would be hunting. He had never killed anything larger than an insect before. The instructors, of course, expected the shooters to be inexperienced. The training objective for hunting deer was twofold, first to get the hunter used to have something living in the crosshairs of the rifle scope when pulling the trigger, and the second was working on their stealth walking through the woods.

The next day, Sabir gathered Munir's group together with their rifles and ammunition.

"We'll be going out in groups of five for our hunts. The hunt will last until a deer is taken or the day is over. We'll be taking shots in turn, if your shot kills the deer, we'll bring the deer back to the lodge and you will be done for the day. The thing to remember is to say *bismillah* before taking the shot. If the deer is only wounded, you would say it again before killing it. That way, the food is fully hallal. If Allah wills, we may take 30-40 deer for our use," Sabir instructed. "I will take one group, Hassan will take another. We'll be on different sides of the property, even so you will follow our instructions before shooting at a deer."

Sabir and Hassan stressed that in order to have a successful hunt, the hunter needed to be as quiet as was possible. The same would be true for snipers. Initially, the hunters all made little noises that they were completely unaware of, coming as they did from city life. After a few days in the hunt camp, things that were unheard before now had the impact of a crashing cymbal. The snap of a broken twig, the slight rasp sound of the gun rubbing onto the fabric of their coverall as they walked, the automatic clearing of their nose, a deep sigh, deep breathing due to not being in the best physical shape. Sabir used this burgeoning awareness on the part of his students to make the point that people in and from cities are noisy, but a person who is quiet in a city is well on their way to invisibility.

With that they were off, two groups of six men wearing hunter camouflage coveralls. They looked exactly what they were supposed to look like, urban middle-aged men out to enjoy a hunt in early spring. Most of the men had never killed anything, it was important to blood them so that taking the step to killing a human being would not be as large of a leap for each of them personally. Sabir knew that some of the group would attempt to fudge the results by intentionally missing, that was another reason why the marksmanship scores were being kept. When and how a shooter would be disciplined was something only The Hammer would determine, but history suggested Sabir had better anticipate the problem in advance.

Initially, the men predictably made too much noise. Sabir would gesture at the offending party's issue and slowly but surely the group tightened up to where they were much more quiet. Munir changed his method of movement until he was as quiet as he could be. Sabir knew of a likely place to find deer next to a natural watering spot. Gauging the wind direction, he led Munir's group on a circuitous track until the right level of group stealth was achieved. Then he led the now-silent team on a downwind approach to the watering spot. There was a slight overlook where they set up, Sabir gestured the entire group should sight-in on the watering spot in preparation. He gestured that the group should relax, but quietly, as they waited for a likely deer to show up.

Sabir had a ringer in his pocket as the first shooter, No. 43 was a mirror and an excellent shot, plus he had enthusiastically taken to the idea of hunting the entire time. *Nothing breeds success like success,* Sabir thought. *The finishing touch will be when they have enjoyed fresh meat put on the table by their own efforts. Nothing tastes as good.*

After a half hour of waiting, a small buck approached the watering spot. Sabir gestured at No. 43, who happily set up to take the shot. He released his breath slowly, whispered *bismallah*, and squeezed the trigger. The sharp crack rang through the silent woods. The buck jumped up, but not in time, the middle-of-body shot hit solidly above and behind its front legs. The deer collapsed within ten feet of the ambush.

No. 43 was very excited about his success. Sabir looked the deer over and made several complimentary remarks on what No. 43 had done well. Sabir had several of the other party members move the body away from the water hole, so that it wouldn't scare off other deer from the water hole. He then took out a very sharp knife and cut a sapling down so that the deer could be easily carried by two men. It was a small buck, only about 120 pounds, but would difficult for one man to carry without field rendering. Sabir had the two men hand their rifles to other party members, then the two men picked up the sapling supporting the deer and they all headed back to the lodge.

Once back, Sabir showed the interested men how to dress the deer and dispose of the offal. Setting aside some particularly choice cuts of meat for the evening meal, he wrapped the rest in 1 to 2 pound packages, and wrote a notation on the paper of the meat cut, with the No. 38 clearly marked. He placed all of those packages inside the quick freezer on one of the empty shelves. No. 38 was in paradise, bragging about his shot to the avidly listening group. Taking a break to get cleaned up, Sabir got ready to take out another group. He was able to get three more groups out and back that day. Dinner was prepared using the meat from the hunt, and the delicious smell filled the dining room as it was being prepared. After the meal, the consensus was that the meat was uncommonly delicious and all of their wives would be very grateful to receive it. The ones who had not taken their deer were now quite enthused to get their turn.

Each day, the remaining men got an opportunity to get their first shots in while hunting. The freezer slowly filled up with the results. Sabir and Hassan made sure that the unsuccessful ones received additional instruction as they strove to get their own deer. The ones who already had theirs spent their days in the shooting range, being further instructed in tradecraft, and the finer points of Fantasy Conquests play. Between those activities and the normal prayer breaks throughout the day, the men were kept very busy. But the uncontested high point of each day was dinner and the latest dish prepared from the hunts.

Three days prior to the end of their time at the camp, shooters living on the coasts prepared for their long drives home. Sabir called a meeting to go over final details.

"Some of our brothers are preparing to depart for their homes. There are a few more things that must be transferred before commending them to the highways. Each person will take home some additional items from their time here. First, each will have their own rifle with a supply of standard hunting rounds which will be placed out of sight in the automobile. In addition, each will receive a small ammo pouch with ten *Martyrs al-Sabah* inscribed rifle rounds. These are the ones we will use on our mission. When you have taken an assigned shot at an infidel, you will eject the spent shell casing for the police to find at the scene where the shot was taken. It is very important to never touch these with your bare hands after you have polished them. I will pass several samples now so that you can see what the shells look like and understand how we will play with the minds of the police. They are beautiful, are they not?" Sabir asked.

The men passed the samples to each other after feeling the cold purpose embedded in the design. The bullets were a work of art, and indeed quite beautiful. Munir shivered as he felt the sample, he would both strike the infidel and live his wonderful life as a dentist. It was almost too much to contemplate.

"When you get your ten rounds, I recommend taking them out of the casing, asking Allah to bless their use, and polishing them while wearing surgical gloves in order to remove any trace of yourself," Sabir said. "On your long trip back, you must not be suspicious and attract the notice of the highway police. That means driving close to the speed limit, being respectful of other drivers, and being friendly if stopped. As we have discussed, if an officer stops you, be friendly and polite.

If they ask where you're going, tell them you are going home from a wonderful fishing trip in Wisconsin. Under no circumstances agree to letting the officer search your car. Refuse politely. Each of you have been issued a new phone, one of the features of the phone is an app to record conversations. When you are pulled over, turn on the recorder app and leave it running on the seat next to you. We will later use this recording to get you out of trouble, if you are arrested. The recording is sent to the cloud, so unless there is no network coverage, we will have a record even if the police confiscate your phone. You will have done nothing wrong enough to be arrested hopefully, and the only way for the police to find the rifle will be an illegal search."

"If you are arrested or detained, answer no questions, engage in no conversation with the police. Instead immediately ask to speak with a lawyer. If they ask why you need a lawyer, tell them you think they hate Muslims and you are being discriminated against. That is why you need a lawyer. They will either let you go then, or they will let you speak with a lawyer. Your lawyer's card shall be carried in your wallet. The lawyer works for us, and will extract you from the problem."

"If you are in an automobile accident, do exactly what you would do if you were at home. Exchange insurance details with the other party and go on your way, if possible. If the car is unable to continue, contact me, rent a car, and continue your trip. We will arrange for someone to deal with the car. It is most important that you get back to your home and life with minimal delay."

Sabir didn't point out that if the shooter lost their special bullets to the police, or vanished for any length of unexplained time, it would be the equivalent of a death sentence for them and their families. Unraveling the operation could be done to protect the human assets, but the loss of one person balanced against the objective was not a hard decision to make.

"Remember to never miss our twice weekly raid night in-game. We will communicate instructions and new contact telephone number then, plus confirm that you are still safely in place. In emergency situations, use the phone to contact the current phone number. In that call, tell me what you need using the code terms previously learned in training. We will deal with the situation and move on. Of course, in those situations the contact phone will be deactivated and a new one set up in the next raid meeting. I will be in-game every day for the same several hours, so send a mail saying that we need to speak and I will reach out," Sabir said.

"You have all your equipment, and your ice chests are full of frozen deer meat. All that is left is for us who remain to ask Allah's protection for you during your journey home."

The only people who didn't have a number for a name were Sabir, Karim, and Hassan. Regardless, the men felt friendships were formed even in the absence of real names. They knew the online personas and already had friendly banter experiences between their favorites within the game itself. Sabir knew the online game would reinforce the feeling of teamwork and camaraderie, even though they were still strangers when it came to real names and where they lived. The formation of online gaming communities all worked that way, and proved an opportunity to build networks unremarked. Fifteen men including Munir left that evening, more would go the next morning. Sabir would be uneasy until all of the shooters were accounted for and safely home. He was less worried about the mirrors, as they had been trained much more extensively before they had even arrived at the camp. They knew how to blend in, pass unnoticed, and get themselves out of trouble. It was the shooters who were the amateurs, but beyond suspicion as established elder members of their communities.

Munir found his drive back was much more enjoyable, as he anticipated being a part of the biggest operation in terrorism history.

• • •

Two days later, all of the shooters and mirrors had departed the camp. The equipment closet was empty, but for a few spare rifles, ammunition, phones, and laptops. Karim had already decommissioned his network upgrades and the van was loaded for departure. The man-shaped shooting range targets had all been burned and the security video storage wiped clean.

"Let's fire off some of these rounds before we leave, shall we?" Sabir said. "Hassan's reputation as a master marksman is overstated, don't you think, Karim?"

"Hah, we shall see!" Hassan said. "Shall we wager something on the contest?"

"Not me, I do alright but I am not in the same league as you two," Karim said.

"OK, whoever loses has to transport and dispose of the rifles. And not on eBay, Hassan!" Sabir said.

"I hadn't even thought of doing that, but now the contest has a different objective. Perhaps you'll win Sabir!" Hassan joked.

They headed for the range with the last several hundred rounds and fired them all off. Sabir won, barely, to good natured ribbing from all sides. Word trickled in that evening as shooters started arriving home and were checked off in Sabir's roster. Mirrors were checked off in Hassan's roster.

The next day, they policed the grounds, security systems, countertops for anything that could be linked back to their shooters. Some things required cleaning, and they all pitched in with a will. Hassan loaded up the balance of the guns in good grace, and they all were ready to depart. The camp had achieved its purpose, it was time for the next phase of the operation.

Madame President

"..Inauguration day is fast approaching and the entire nation awaits the new White House Administration. Rumors abound on what initiatives we can expect from President Brown's first 100 days. My sources indicate a comprehensive review of immigration policy may be in the works. Obviously, it would be of huge interest to her Muslim constituents. Stay tuned.."

Farid Monsour al Haj for World News Corporation

Justin Simons reviewed the sparse file that had been started concerning The Hammer and Prince Zufar Azzizi with something like disgust. In spite of an enhanced listening regime on the prince, no other indications or traffic concerning The Hammer had appeared. The assistant angle had turned into a dry hole, as there appeared to be no public-facing assistant that worked for the prince. The closest anyone came was the receptionist to the prince's palace. CIA had tried to get someone in to speak with the prince under cover as a financial journalist, but they'd been routed to the prince's Australian publicist. For a time, a team of operatives placed the building under visual surveillance, but decided to pull back due to repeated stops by Kingdom police. Clearly, the men had been made by the prince's security forces and they were probably calling the police to check the operative's credentials. So the team was pulled out and everything went back to satellite or network surveillance. So far that had turned up precisely zero new information.

The file entries for The Hammer were also frustrating. Conflicting reports said that he was Palestinian, or Jordanian, or Lebanese; that he was tall, short, middle-aged or old. Either there wasn't much more than gossip and rumor, or The Hammer had engaged in a deliberate effort to muddy the water. He had never taken credit for any operations, but was rumored to have done several in Lebanon, Greece, and Italy. One factor which argued for the existence of The Hammer was a strange execution of the leader of another group. Evidently, the leader had taken credit in the press for an operation that was rumored to have really been done by The Hammer. The leader was killed within a week and his forehead branded with the word "Liar" in Arabic. Justin thought to himself that he could probably get a better understanding of The Hammer's activities by simply collating operations for which no one took credit. The Hammer never took credit, which made him much harder to track.

In the background, a television monitor was on and tuned to a cable news channel. Justin was barely paying attention until he heard an upcoming segment announcement mentioning his friend, Farid Royce. Grabbing a fresh cup of coffee, he hurried back to see what Farid was up to. Evidently, Farid was traveling the Middle East doing a Muslim opinion survey concerning the U.S.A. presidential election results.

When Prince Zufar's name popped up, Justin was shocked. He called the rest of his team in to watch the interview. "Get in here, we have Prince Zufar Azzizi giving an interview. Is there any way we can get a full copy of this?"

Steve Roberts, the team's technical support, pressed several buttons to begin immediate capture, then went deeper into the FBI network to see if the interview had been cached in their system. "Sir, we started recording just now and don't have a cache for the previous few minutes. Do you want me to contact the network and ask for a full copy of the segment?"

"No, not just yet. This channel repeats everything several times in a day. See if you can't get the whole thing when they replay it," Justin said. "I want impressions and observations on this guy's behavior, people. Remember, we're listening to everything coming out of his complex and that one intercept pegs this guy as a sponsor. Steve, have we gotten anywhere on tracking his money?"

"No sir, we have a lot of data to wade through. Prince Zufar is close to being a multi-billionaire, if not one. So money is moving in and out of his empire all of the time. He owns hundreds of millions of dollars in shares of major American firms directly, and that doesn't account for his holdings through nominees. We'll get there, but it won't be anything like a real-time summary," Steve said.

"I know the journalist who is interviewing him, I'll talk to him about Zufar when he gets back."

An authoritative voice cut in, "You know Farid Monsour al Haj? Could he be the interface we're looking for to The Hammer?" The voice belonged to Quinton Jameson II, Justin's boss and primary pain in his ass. He was a well-connected Ivy League WASP prick who lived for the political infighting necessary to rise to command rank in the FBI. He was a tall man starting to show his age in posture and an expansive stomach, but still maintaining a perfect haircut. Part of his job description seemed to be the oppression of every working asset under his command, especially ones with talent, like Justin.

"I know him very well. He went to elementary school in Alexandria with me. For Chrissake, he was best man at my wedding," Justin said.

"No need to get worked up, it was just a question," Jameson said. "Isn't this how breakthroughs come about: we watch a player and then investigate who they talk to?"

"Yes, sir. Could I speak to you privately for a moment?" Justin asked.

"Certainly, come to my office," Quinton said.

They walked silently through the halls together until they came to Jameson's soundproof office which was regularly swept for listening devices. Such offices were on the interior of the building, to prevent windows being used to watch the executives. One joke said high-level executives at the FBI, CIA, and NSA could be identified by the unnatural pallor of their skin.

Quinton entered and Justin followed, closing the door.

Motioning to a chair in front of his desk, Quinton said, "OK, tell me what this is all about."

"Yes, sir. I didn't want to say this in the open environment, but Farid is actually one of our better confidential informants in the Muslim community. He's helped us on a number of occasions. In fact, I am planning to get in front of him when he's back in-country to talk about Zufar," Justin said. "I've been his handler since he indicated a willingness to participate. We have a natural cover story being childhood friends."

"Why didn't I know about it?" Quinton asked.

"As you know, normally the identities are held very close until there is a need to be told, in order to better protect the informants. That's why I told you now. You have seen his input before, in briefings on Muslim threat profiles. He was the one who tipped us off on the radical mullah who was recruiting in the Fairfax Mosque," Justin said.

"Oh, the mullah who suddenly had visa issues and was forcibly repatriated to his eagerly waiting homeland?" Quinton smiled with a feral grin.

"The very one. We've had to be very circumspect with how we use the information Farid brings, since he is a trusted person within the greater Muslim community. He's on the board of a number of Muslim charities and is well-placed to hear things. So far, the biggest contribution he makes is to identify people we should take a hard look at. Most of what he knows is in the realm of hearsay, and not usable for building a case," Justin said.

"Have we ever done a deep dive on Farid, to make sure we're not missing something important?"

"No sir, we've done the standard vetting process and followed his money, but not a full-depth source investigation. As far as I know, he's not aware that we've even looked at his financials. But, if we do a full-depth, he will find out about it and it may compromise our relationship. Another thing to consider is that he is extremely well-connected inside the beltway. If we struck out on a fishing expedition and he took exception to it, there might be some adverse political impacts," Justin said.

Quinton frowned. "Sounds like you might have a problem being objective with this informant."

"Sir, he's wealthy, brilliant, and politically connected at the highest levels. Even if I didn't know him, I would be concerned about making a potentially career-limiting move here, which could happen if anything went wrong. I've still got a mortgage, I need this job," Justin said.

"You let me worry about the politics, but if you are unable to treat this informant like any other, we might want to change things up."

"Sir, most informants are criminals and we have significant leverage over them because of it. Farid is a volunteer - we don't have leverage over him. He can simply refuse to play along," Justin cautioned.

"What if we threatened him with the inadvertent release of the information he is a FBI informant?" Quinton mused.

"Sir, I know you don't mean that. Not only is it completely unethical, it would poison all of our other informant relationships. Who would work with us if it came out that the FBI wasn't diligent in protecting informants?" Justin said.

"Justin, I didn't say we would release the data, I said that we should threaten to do so. Sometimes you are too conservative on these things. You're a good special agent, smart, but you don't even see some strategies which might help. I don't like anyone having leverage over the FBI, we leverage others. Why is he a volunteer?"

"Because he loves his adopted country and hates what extremists do within his religion? He is a passive, not an active, sensor for us: by that I mean he doesn't go out shaking the bushes to find this data, he reports it when it lands in his lap."

"Well, we might need him to do some bush-shaking on this Hammer-Azizzi thing. Would he wear a wire?" Quinton asked.

"I doubt it. With all due respect, he wouldn't be talking to Prince Zufar inside the territorial boundaries of the United States, which means it would be out of our jurisdiction. Do we really want to hand this over to CIA?"

Quinton grimaced and leaned forward. "No, you're right. I'm mostly just thinking out loud here. I am a little concerned we haven't made any headway on this. If there is a legitimate threat, we should have something to show for it. If there isn't a threat, we can wind this effort down and move onto to other, more productive, tasks."

"I plan to meet with Farid when he gets back to the USA. I'll find out what he knows about the prince, and if there are any avenues of inquiry which might pay off," Justin said.

"Do that, and keep me informed as things develop. I may want to sit down with Farid myself, just to get a sense of who he is for myself.

If this all turns to shit, I'll need to know whether he should be protected or pulled in as a possible accessory. I know, you don't believe that of him, but I need to feel the same way if we're going to continue the unleveraged relationship with him," Quinton said.

"I will. Thank you, sir," Justin said.

"One more thing, Justin. In order for me to have a better shot at the next job on the ladder, I need to have a viable replacement. I think that person is you, but I want to ensure we're on the same page. People like Farid can either help one move up or take one all the way to the bottom. We just have to make sure it isn't the latter."

"I agree wholeheartedly. I'll be sure to report in with the results of my conversation with Farid. I will also bring up the fact that you want to meet with him."

"Good! I'll let you get back to fighting the good fight," Quinton nodded his head in dismissal.

Justin's head was swirling with the prospect of the promotion, for which he had diligently spent the long hours, but having it come up so baldly in conversation with Quinton was a surprise. Either Quinton was bringing him into his circle of trust, or he was playing him somehow. Regardless, he would need to get in contact with Farid.

Taking out his mobile phone, he texted Farid, "*Farid, I just saw one of your interviews. When are you back in town?*"

He replaced his phone in the front pocket of his slacks and headed back towards the task force room. Several steps down the hall, he heard an incoming message chime and he pulled out the phone once more with a laugh. He wasn't expecting a reply for a while, but it was just like Farid to be fast on the draw.

"*I'll be back next Thursday, why don't we get together Saturday sometime? I should be back on VA time by then.*" Farid's text said.

"*That was a fast response!*" Justin replied.

"*It's dinner time here. You should be flattered, I'm ignoring a belly dancer to text you. Need anything in particular?*"

"*Nothing that can't wait, I just want to run something work-related by you.*"

"*Alright. Meet in Georgetown?*"

"*Come out to Sterling. Jan and the kids would love seeing you.*"

"Those two hellions? I'll wear something durable. Will confirm. Got to run."

"Thanks! See you then", Justin closed.

Nothing more to do on that topic until next week, Justin thought. Turning around he went back to Quinton's closed door and rapped quietly.

"Come in," Quinton said.

"Just a quick update: I contacted Farid and he will be back in the United States next Thursday. We're getting together at my house on Saturday. I'll keep you apprised," Justin said from the doorway.

"Thank you," Quinton said as Justin closed the door.

Once Justin was gone, Quinton picked up his phone and keyed in a number.

"I want a team to monitor a potential suspect 24/7 starting next Thursday. The subject's name is Farid Monsour Royce al Haj. He should be returning to Dulles International that day from an overseas trip. I want to know everything he does, with daily reports," Quinton said.

He listened to a voice asking several questions, then said "No, we don't need to get a wiretap at this time or network surveillance other than our global take on international calls. I do want him flagged for that. Let's see what we can get with it. I don't expect the effort to require more than 10 days. One note, the surveillance is my eyes only and highly sensitive. Especially if he is clean. Start the reports on 12 hours: morning and evening to start."

The voice acknowledged the instructions and rang off.

Now we should see some action, Quinton thought to himself.

• • •

In an anonymous apartment in Georgetown, the sounds of sweaty afternoon lovemaking trended towards inevitable conclusion.

"Damn, that's it for me Darlin'. Got to catch my breath," Jonny Ray gasped as he lay back on his pillow.

Nayla stretched like a cat, then rolled over onto her side facing him. "You never told me how you managed to shake your Secret Service detail for today." Each time they had managed to meet, Jonny

Ray would brag about the various and sundry ways he had escaped his Secret Service handlers. Hearing him tell it, made it sound as though he were James Bond, but without the property destruction.

"I can't keep doing it the same way, those boys are too smart and catch on pretty quick. Today it was a meet and greet with an old friend at a hotel conference and I just ducked out a window," Jonny Ray chortled. "They keep thinking of me as an old man, but I still have a few moves in me."

"You certainly do," Nayla purred as she lightly caressed his chest with the finger tips of one hand. It had not been hard to encourage an advance from Jonny Ray, she just had to be friendly and wear clothing which flattered her excellent figure. Following the election, they had attended several of the same fundraising events, to the point where they were each arranging to be at the same ones. Initially, she had played the *willing-but-with-reservations* card, until his entreaties were allowed to overcome her resistance. She had insisted on security, for both of their sakes, so she arranged for a small one bedroom apartment in Georgetown. The building had underground parking and multiple street exits.

A hidden video camera was set up to capture HD video of Jonny Ray's bedroom exploits in real time. Nayla knew exactly where the camera was placed and artfully obscured her face for as much of the time as was possible, in order to yield the most useable footage after editing. This was Jonny Ray's third visit and The Hammer had indicated that several more were most likely required, until another operation had fully begun. Nayla had achieved her objective quicker than was originally anticipated, so she would have to endure its continuance a bit more.

Jonny Ray regarded his mistress with an admiring gaze. She was absolutely perfect. Lying on her side both breasts showed the effects of gravity but were still firm. Her light brown skin and dark brown nipples excited him far more than he cared to admit. Jonny Ray was not all that discriminating when it came to bedding willing women; willing, wet, and not hideous were his primary requirements. So when Jonny Ray had the opportunity to be with someone like Nayla, it was something he wanted to fully experience. She was beautiful, fearsomely intelligent, and wanted him. Jonny Ray had few illusions as to why she had wanted him, at least initially, but now Jonny Ray was thinking this should be a long-term relationship. It was going to be a lot harder after next week's inauguration ceremony, when Lucy and Jonny Ray moved into the White House, but he continued to give the idea additional thought.

"I've always meant to ask, but your beauty is such a distraction that I always forget. Those two medallions that you wear on your necklace chain, what are they?" Jonny Ray asked.

Nayla hesitated for a moment, "The silver one was my mother's and the stainless steel coin reminds me of my brother. My mother died with I was 17, and my brother was lost a year later. The coin was something we both had."

Jonny Ray wasn't the world's most empathetic person but he did know how to pretend, "I'm so sorry, I didn't mean to make you sad or offend."

Nayla waved it off, "Thank you, it was a long time ago. I actually appreciate you asking, even though it is sad, because then I honor their memory by thinking of it. That doesn't happen often these days in spite of having the reminder right in front of me. But enough of that, you look as though you have recovered your … breath."

"Ah, Lover, you are going to be the death of me," Jonny Ray said as he reached for her waist.

• • •

Jonny Ray thought he had given the Secret Service the slip, but the fact was that he had not. They had followed him discretely after his first visit and since then had fully investigated the apartment block. They knew of his exploits and had been instructed to allow Jonny Ray some slack, as long as his safety wasn't endangered. It looked like he was setting up a long-term mistress, which would be a big help to the Secret Service as it would allow for some predictability. That way, if Jonny Ray really slipped his leash they would know where to look first.

They had also started a file on Nayla Rakhshan Kaldah, but there wasn't anything in it that was considered worthy of concern. In past administrations, being a first generation immigrant of Palestinian extraction would have been enough to deny access to any White House official. The former and incoming Democrat administrations hewed to a more inclusive, diverse standard. It was not unusual to now see Palestinians as staff members at the highest levels. In this case, she was a heavy-hitting fundraiser for lobbying groups politically aligned with the Democratic Party. One agent joked that at least Jonny Ray wasn't diving dumpsters or the local trailer parks for his strange anymore.

Jonny Ray drifted off to sleep after a second leisurely bout of lovemaking, blissfully unaware of all that was centered on his person. Nayla stood and took the opportunity to draw down the apartment's meager hot water supply for a long shower. Nayla didn't consider Jonny Ray to be a particularly bad person, just a weak one when it came to his idée fixe of chasing extramarital sex.

Nayla had no idea what The Hammer had planned, but she had waited for a long time to strike a solid blow for the cause. Palestine for Palestinians! Nayla had never considered moving back to the lands currently governed by the Palestinian Authority, conditions there remained too primitive to appeal to someone of her background. But she supported the cause nonetheless, due to the family she had lost in the struggles, and the bad memories of her late teenage years in Gaza City. It was not the first time she had been called upon to climb into bed with someone she would not have chosen. Hopefully, this operation would be the last. Maybe this time, the world would change. The Hammer had said it would.

• • •

In an office space not too far away from the apartment, Lucy Brown's transition team was putting the final touches on her inaugural address, as well as poring through short lists of candidates for cabinet appointments.

Sidney Rosenbloom was engaged in a never-ending whirl of activity as functionaries would engage, impart their message, receive guidance, and leave to accomplish whatever new task had been assigned. Very seldom did Sid knock upon the large double door behind which Lucy was practicing her upcoming address and reading policy briefings. Sid acted as an effective filter and dealt with most issues himself, but occasionally something rose to the level that needed input from Lucy.

The head of the President Elect's Secret Service detail signaled from the door that he needed a word.

Sid nodded his head towards a small conference room that served him as a space for private consultations.

"Special Agent. To what do I owe this visit?" Sid asked.

"I'm sorry, Mr. Rosenbloom. This regards Jackalope," Jackalope was the code name assigned to Jonny Ray Brown. The detail thought it perfect, a rabbit with prongs.

Sid rolled his eyes and shook his head. "What has he done now?"

"I just wanted to report on further developments. You remember we allowed him to appear to escape surveillance at your instruction? He has what appears to be a longer term liaison with this Nayla Kaldah, she has taken an apartment in Georgetown used solely for their assignations. We've got the place secured when he is there, but I wanted you to know he is settling into a routine. I also wanted to understand something as well. Is the President-Elect aware of this situation?"

"The President-Elect is aware of the overall situation and tolerates it, but leaves the details to me," Sid said, "Why are you asking?"

"Because it could change the way we deal with this going forward, in a good way, from a security perspective. What if the security detail worked directly with Jonny Ray and told him that he doesn't need to shake off pursuit every time he wants to visit his lover? That way it would much easier to protect him, as it would remove the chance of him actually shaking us off."

"I, personally, would have no objection to that approach as long as complete confidentiality is maintained. We can't have this coming up in the newspapers, especially not in the early days of her presidency," Sid said.

"I'd also like a chance to hear from the President-Elect directly that we're handling this in the correct way."

"I understand the concern, you want to confirm that this is more than just my idea?" Sid asked.

"Essentially, yes. Our charter is to protect the President Elect and her family, and while we do accept direction from her staff it does need to be confirmed on occasion. This situation has the potential to blow up and I will not have the Secret Service being blamed for getting into it."

"Part of what we are doing here is building a working relationship between all of the departments of the upcoming administration, including the Secret Service. You'll learn how we work, but that won't be immediately apparent. Very well, let's go speak to her now. I will voice the question in a way calculated not to offend, if that works for you?" Sid asked.

Together they went to the double door, and Sid spoke to the detail agent at the door. She went inside and spoke to the President Elect, then came out and waved them in. Lucy was sitting on a sofa with reading material in her lap and spread around her.

"Yes, Sid?"

"Madame President Elect, the Secret Service want to confirm my directions concerning Jonny Ray's extracurricular activities," Sid said.

Something like pain flashed across Lucy's face for a split second. Turning to the Special Agent she said, "Jonny Ray and I have led separate lives for quite some time. Now I have a country to lead, and Jonny Ray doesn't have an operational role yet. As long as his safety is assured, I tolerate his need to find something else to do. Sid, my chief of staff, has my authority to make decisions on the details surrounding that topic. Is that sufficient?"

"Yes, Madame President Elect, thank you," the agent said.

Sid nodded his head to Lucy who went back to her papers, and motioned they should take their leave.

"Thank you, sir, for confirming our instruction. I apologize for the need to have asked," the agent said to Sid once they were clear of the office doors.

"No need for an apology. We're not about running a monolithic administration here, it is better to ask the question than have your actions constrained by unvoiced doubt. Please do not hesitate to bring your concerns to my attention in the future," Sid said.

"I won't, sir."

Sid looked upon these types of situations as team-building exercises, if the troops see that the leader supports the second tier, managing gets a lot easier. Now if there were only a simple solution to Jonny Ray.

• • •

Nayla was meeting The Hammer at a safe house in Alexandria tonight. She decided to prepare a traditional meal for the two of them similar to the ones she'd made for her lost brother Adeeb, so very long ago. It had been a long time since Nayla had the luxury of spending time with family, and The Hammer was as close to it as anyone. Her American friends could not understand the pain she felt every time she thought about Gaza City and the things she had lost. Every Muslim convenience store was a reminder, with its Martyrs al-Sabra collection jar, half-filled with change. Not many knew of her connection to those events or what she had lost that day.

As a successful lawyer she was able to afford the best ingredients, but never quite recaptured the tastes of those first meals prepared as a young orphan girl under the tutelage of a widow who lived in the same building. Nayla hadn't thought of the Widow Faruqi in quite a long time. She'd lost touch with her after starting university. Nayla wondered if she was still alive, and if she had ever married Kamal. Someday Nayla would visit Gaza again and see if either could be found. Burying her past in the deep well it was usually confined in, Nayla set about preparing a Palestinian feast. She knew The Hammer would not arrive until it was full dark, so she had several hours.

Her phone signaled the arrival of a text, from Farid Royce, "*Hi Nayla, I'm back from my Gulf tour, are you doing anything tonight?*"

She smiled and typed, "*Gulf tour? You were gone? I forgot.*"

"*Sharp as a serpent's tooth, a woman's tongue. {wilted emoji} But seriously, do you want to do something tonight? {hopeful emoji}*"

"*Sorry, have a previous commitment. Next time!*"

"*I'll ask earlier next time. Seeing Justin, Jan and monsters Saturday night.*"

"*Pass along my love to the scamps!*" Nayla sent, and received a final thumbs-up from Farid.

Nayla hummed to herself as she cut the vegetables into the bite sized bits common to Palestinian cuisine, the hours passed quickly as she worked.

The Hammer walked in a little after 8 p.m., wearing dark clothes and a bushy fake mustache. "Ah, Nayla you shouldn't have. It smells wonderful though."

Nayla looked at him and stifled a giggle, surprising even herself. "You look like an Iraqi with that mustache, except in much better shape than the Husseins."

"That wouldn't be too hard, since they are all dead. This is what happens when using one of Sabir's pre-packaged disguise kits. How do you like the gold chain?" The Hammer smiled.

"I take it back, even the Husseins wouldn't wear that! That looks more Los Angeles Persian or Greek. Americans are too clueless to understand that Muslim males do not wear gold necklace jewelry, so the subtlety is probably wasted."

"One thing that should not be wasted is this food. Let's sit. I'll get a bottle of wine, if you will join me?"

"Of course. I'll set the table."

As Nayla positioned all of the dishes within reach, she sat down and watched as The Hammer's strong hands had their way with a particularly stubborn cork. He poured them each a glass and sat down.

"Bismillahi wa 'ala baraka-tillah," The Hammer said in blessing of the food, echoed by Nayla.

"So tell me, Nayla, how are things going with your objective?" The Hammer asked as he filled his plate.

"Jonny Ray is well entertained for the time being. The video has been capturing everything, as far as I know. How much longer do we need to continue?" Nayla said.

"Yes, Sabir has been collating and editing the footage for the operation. You have done very well with hiding your face, it will be very important later. As for how much longer you must continue to entertain the infidel, the inauguration happens in a week's time. The next phase of the operation will begin in March. You'll be able to stop sometime in mid-April. How are you holding up?" The Hammer asked.

"As you know, I have no desire for other men, so it is hard to pretend and it will be a relief to stop. My personal discomfort has not affected the operation, I assure you. One thing, Jonny Ray is a pig in many ways but not as bad as many in this country. He doesn't look down on Muslims."

"Yes, that is true. Unfortunately, that, combined with his penchant for women, is the key to this part of the operation. It would have been impossible to use this gambit with the Republicans in power. They are just as susceptible to sex as anyone, but they want very little to do with Muslims or any minority. You wouldn't have been able to get within a mile of a Republican protected by the Secret Service." The Hammer said.

"Do you think he will be able to keep escaping his detail to come to the apartment after next week?" Nayla asked.

The Hammer smiled, "Funny thing, that. Sabir said that the Secret Service is in place when he visits you. Evidently they know all about the trysts and follow him to provide hidden protection. I'm betting that the protection will become more overt after the inauguration, and will not stop. The Secret Service has already investigated you and your cover is holding up. The rumor that his marriage has an arrangement is probably true. I do not doubt the President Elect knows of his dalliances."

"Isn't that dangerous? What if she decides I should be killed?" Nayla asked.

"Again, the Democrats are capable of many things, but killing a top fundraiser for their causes is not one of them. Democrats launch cruise missiles rather than get their hands dirty by killing someone face-to-face. They're not above bribing you to cease and desist, though. I wouldn't worry; very soon they will have bigger issues than what you represent."

"Can't you share the overall plan? I can't see how this would impact anything in a major way," Nayla said.

"Nayla, I won't give you the operational details, you should know better than to ask. But I will say that you will be the straw that breaks the infidel camel's back. This meal was wonderful, thank you for preparing it."

"Alham do lillah hilla-thee At Amana wa saquana waja 'alana minal Muslimeen," The Hammer said at the close of the meal.

Nayla stood up and placed her hands on The Hammer's broad shoulders. She bent down until her mouth was next to his ear, her hands moving to hug his chest, "Will you stay a while longer?"

The Hammer gently placed his palms on her circling arms, "How could I refuse such an offer? And I'll confess to thinking of little else while I was working."

"Ah, and now that you are here?"

"Nayla, you always have my heart in your keeping, you have from the day we first met," The Hammer said softly.

"Then, there will there be a time when we can stop and live a life? It is almost too much to hope for," Nayla said wistfully.

"I have my hopes, and I think this operation must be our last. After, we will see what comes, maybe something more normal."

"Do you hate me when I have to do my part of the operation?"

"No. I hate that it has to be done for our cause. I hate that any other man touches your skin. Perhaps I'll have you wear the chador once we marry, and never share you again. Then only your voice would be left to entice the strangers."

"So you would still have me as your wife, in spite of everything?"

He turned and looked seriously into her lovely eyes, "I will marry no one, if not you." Taking one of her hands, he stood and led her to the single bedroom.

• • •

Saturday afternoon, Farid turned his Tesla Model S onto Kentwell Place in Potomac Falls Virginia and parked in front of Justin and Jan's colonial tract home. Gathering together a gift bag, he closed his car door and headed for the front of their house. As he walked up the brick steps, a small boy's face looked out one of the two side windows at the front doors. Seeing Farid approach, he turned and shouted back towards the kitchen before flinging the door open and hugging him fiercely.

"Uncle Farid! Come in, Mom and Dad are in the kitchen," Michael grabbed Farid's hand and pulled him bodily into the house.

As Michael closed the front door, his sister Rebecca (Becky to most) came running down the staircase for her own hug. Adding to the general clamor was a Golden Retriever named Beth who followed Becky down the stairs.

"Hold on, you two. I need to check in with your parents first," Farid said laughing.

Beth led the procession into the kitchen which was of open design. The entire back half of the home was dedicated to a kitchen, small breakfast nook and family room, all overlooking the Algonkibahn, as Algonkian Parkway was called by the locals. The house was set on a hill about fifty feet above the road, with windows overlooking the road and parkland trail heads of Sugarland Run. The neighborhood was replete with government employees of one type or another. State Department, CIA, FBI, World Bank, and others made up the mix of families. Reasonably close to the District of Columbia, it offered excellent schools, and miles of wooded parkland along the Potomac River.

"Farid, it's been too long!" Janice said as she kissed his cheek. Jan had been one of Farid's very first school friends when he was adopted by the Royces.

"It is good to see you too, Jan. Here, I've brought you some of that Swiss chocolate liqueur you like so much. But first," reaching into the bag, he pulled out two small boxes, "these go to soothe the two wild beasts, who share their mother's undying love for chocolate."

Mike and Becky stood in front of Farid, at war with the manners that had been drilled into them by their mother, waiting to be given their prizes.

"The only thing I'll say about these is that you should eat them slowly, otherwise they will be gone too soon," Farid said as he formally handed a finely wrapped package to each of them.

"Thank you, Uncle Farid!" they chorused and Becky held onto his arm until he bent down to receive her kiss. Then the two children ran into the family room and sat down to open their boxes.

"Don't eat all of those before dinner, you two! Really, Farid, those are probably too good for them."

"Never too early to develop refined taste in chocolate. They're never going to do that with M&Ms," Farid said as he watched the children take their first piece of the rich chocolate, smiling as their eyes widened with the taste.

"Thank you for the liqueur, after dinner we'll have it with some coffee. Justin is outside on the deck cursing over the grill, as usual. Beth got into the grease pan last week and made quite the mess," Jan said. Beth, hearing her name, slowly wagged her tail as she leaned against Farid.

Reaching into the huge five door refrigerator, she extracted two local craft brew beer bottles and handed them to Farid. "Here, take one of these out for Justin, I think he has probably worked up a thirst with all the colorful language he has been using."

Farid dutifully took the bottles from Jan and headed out onto the large wood deck.

"Just-In-Time! Here, Jan thought you could use this," Farid opened a bottle and handed it to his friend.

"Hi Farid! Thanks for coming out. I tell you, that dog is getting senile in her old age. When she was young she could steal the grill drip pan without spilling a drop. These days, she gets it all over the place. Damn thing will catch fire if I start her up without getting all of it cleaned up." Justin said.

"What? This sweet dog here?" Farid asked archly. Beth had followed him out onto the deck and sat leaning into his leg whenever he stopped moving.

"Oh, before I forget about it, Jan tried to get Lindsey and Nayla out as well. Lindsey was out of town and Nayla said she was otherwise engaged. So it's just us. That works better for me anyway, because I wanted to talk to you about something we're working on at the office. But hey, that can wait until after dinner. You think Nayla has a date?" Justin asked.

"She might, I haven't talked to her, other than a quick text, since I got back."

"You probably ought to move on that soon, you're not getting any younger," Justin joked.

"You, Jan, and Lindsey ganging up on me?" Farid laughed. "No, she is a wonderful person but the timing has just never been quite right."

"It's just that we know what a wonderful father you would be, and we all want to see you happy," Justin said.

"What, and give up all of my married mistresses?" Farid said waggling his eyebrows until Justin threw a crumpled up paper towel ball at him. There was some truth to that, as married women seemed to fall into Farid's lap with some frequency. A television reporter was slightly more respectable than a reality show cast member, so he tended to get a lot of attention when he was out and about. Farid was that handsome Muslim fellow from the news channel; if Farid wanted female companionship all he had to do was respond to one of many unsolicited offers.

"Well, I can report to Jan later that I had the conversation with you. Extra points for me: the grist of a good marriage. Looks like I can fire this grill up now without burning down the deck," Justin lit the gas burner and relaxed when he heard the corresponding *whump* sound.

The brisk January air was the perfect temperature to be cooking outdoors. Most of the trees were still without their leaves, so the day had a greyish feel to it that wasn't warranted by how good the air felt. Farid enjoyed the slight winter bite in the air, preferring it over the dry weather of the Arabian Gulf.

Justin slapped a few Costco steaks on the hot grill and poked his head into the house. "Steaks are on in about 20 minutes, was there anything else for the grill?"

Jan said, "No, everything else is ready, just keeping warm."

Returning to the deck, Justin said, "I saw your interview with Prince Zufar Azzizi on television. It was very interesting, for a number of reasons. How did the rest of your interviews go? Were they all resigned to working with a woman?"

"You know how it is, there is a spectrum of opinion. Some people have no issues working with whoever is in power in the United States, others are more reactionary. I'd say on balance, it was more positive than negative. The region doesn't really trust the current president. So their view is that a change at the top might be good for them," Farid said. "Prince Zufar is a bit of a character though. Hard to tell what his real opinion is since he is so sophisticated in his approach to press relations. Do you know, I interviewed him in his palace television studio, which had better equipment than we have at the network?"

"Prince Zufar is part of what I wanted to talk to you about. He is one of the Saudis suspected of funneling money to worldwide terrorism efforts, so we keep pretty close tabs on who calls him from the USA and elsewhere," Justin said.

"Really? I've never even gotten a whiff of something like that. He is a definite capitalist and usually that kind of thing would impact his profits. Is there evidence or is it just a rumor? Kingdom security tends to deal pretty harshly with people caught doing that," Farid observed.

"Rumor mostly, which is why we've kept this to ourselves. My boss, Quinton Jameson, may want to meet with you at some point. Actually, I had to fend him off as he wanted to come today to talk over what we've got. He is, of course, aware that you've helped us in the past and is concerned enough about our current situation to want to hear your thoughts first hand," Justin said.

"Quinton Jameson? Hmm, I think I met this guy once at a Congressional Republican fundraiser. Kind of a classic Ivy League prick, if I recall correctly," Farid mused.

"That would be him." Justin laughed.

"So what is this situation that you referred to earlier?"

"Short version: the night of the election, we listened to a telephone call between Prince Zufar and a suspected terrorist known as The Hammer of Islam. The Hammer asked for a short meeting, which Zufar agreed to. The worst part is that we tracked The Hammer's mobile phone to the Gaylord Resort in Maryland. So, yes, people have their knickers in a bunch right now," Justin explained.

"Allah forfend! Lindsey, Nayla, and I were there at the ballroom through the election result announcements. The President Elect and her husband were there as well! I left just after the dancing started, but Nayla and Lindsey were there for a while longer," Farid said.

"I knew that you three were on the list of people in attendance. I was meaning to speak with you earlier about what you might have seen, but you left on your trip before I got the chance. Then we saw your interview with Zufar, so it became even more critical to chat," Justin said.

"It would be a problem for me to be seen going into the FBI offices without a good reason. I don't mean dangerous so much as that people might not trust me as much if that got out."

"I know, that is why I pressed for today rather than something more formal. Besides, it looks as though Beth will be going home with you, which is plenty of cover story," Justin pointed at the Golden Retriever camped next to Farid's leg.

"Ah, Beth knows I am just slumming. Islam prevents me from constant exposure to dog saliva, which is considered unclean. I'm sorry, Beth, but you know it does," Farid said as he rubbed Beth's massive chest. Beth wasn't impressed with his logic.

"The steaks are done, let's talk more about this after dinner," Justin said as he loaded up a platter with the juicy cuts.

Farid extricated himself from the adoration of Beth and picked up the empty beer bottles before heading back inside for dinner.

Dinner was seated in the breakfast nook, which is where most of the Simons' meals were held. Occasionally they dusted off the formal dining room in the front of the house, but the views weren't as nice and it had less convenient access to the kitchen. Farid was an old hand at this, sitting at Jan's end of the table next to Becky. Farid had told Mike long ago that western gunfighters always sat with their back to the sunlight, so he always insisted on sitting with his back to the windows. That meant that Becky and Farid got the great views of parkland and the occasional squirrel running across their deck.

Jan and Justin never talked down to their children when conversing. As a result, Mike and Becky lost the baby voice early in life, so regular adult conversations could be had at the table. The adults self-censored topics, but those that were discussed weren't dumbed-down for children. Mike and Becky wanted to hear about Farid's latest trip, as they had seen him on television as well. Farid kept them entertained with stories of exotic meals eaten from communal dishes using only his hand. Jan wasn't so enamored with it, but was mollified by the added story of hand cleaning basins and towels. They all weren't too sure about eating a goat's eyeball, but Farid insisted that it was a very great honor and quite delicious. This was a regular feature of their dinners together: trying to test the stomachs around the table. Farid, Jan, and

Justin had known each other since they were children themselves. Becky and Mike sometimes brought those times back to the adults, and the kids were always delighted when their parents confessed to having been children themselves in the far-distant past.

As the meal wound down, Jan served up coffee for the adults doctored with the liqueur that Farid had brought. Farid gave a small sip to Becky, with a conspiratorial wink. Mike was insisting that Farid see his new computer game before heading to Justin's office. Farid looked at Justin, shrugged his shoulders and followed Mike down to the entertainment center in the basement. Justin and Jan tidied up the kitchen, explaining to Becky that she couldn't have her own cup of doctored coffee. After about twenty minutes, Justin headed down to rescue Farid.

"Dad, Farid is really good at video games. We are killing the online players all over the place, he's increasing my rating," Mike said.

Justin said, "Probably shouldn't do too much of that, otherwise you'll be fighting people that are a lot harder."

"He'll just have to play up," Farid said. "Here, Mike, take over. I'm going to go talk with your Dad."

They went into Justin's office retreat and closed the door. Justin had large cubicle furniture set up there with a conference room sized white board. Farid sat down in front of the desk and Justin plopped his large frame into his oversized office chair.

"That meal really hit the spot," Justin said with his hands over his flat belly.

"Good protein always leaves me feeling that way," Farid said in agreement. "So tell me what you can about this situation."

"Sure, of course everything we discuss is off-the-record," Farid nodded in agreement and Justin continued. "As I mentioned earlier, we have been watching Prince Zufar for a long while. Rumor is that he bankrolls Muslim terror operations worldwide. So far we haven't actually caught him doing anything we can take action on. But the list of people who call him includes some pretty shady characters. We don't know too much about The Hammer, but he got our attention by being so physically close to the next president. Have you ever heard of The Hammer?"

Farid was silent for a few seconds as if considering what to say, "Yes, I have heard of him. Not too many details, though. Supposedly he doesn't take overt credit for operations, but kills others who take credit for his work."

Justin interjected, "Yes, we've heard that as well. Does anyone know what his goals are, or anything else about him?"

"Not really, but there is a fair amount of contradictory information. Most of the things he is credited with were small efforts like political assassinations and kidnappings. No one really knows his nationality either with certainty, you'll hear that he is all kinds of things. I suspect that is exactly how he wants it. You know, the war on terrorism has primarily killed off the dumb ones. I wouldn't be surprised if we start seeing more from people too smart to make a target of themselves," Farid said.

"What do you mean?" Justin asked.

"Think about it, every time a terrorist makes themselves known, the USA works very hard to capture or kill them. If you don't want to wake up to a bomb that kills you and everyone around you, it might make more sense to tone down the ego and keep a low profile."

"Unfortunately, that makes a lot of sense. What is your take on Prince Zufar? What kind of person is he?" Justin asked.

"I think there are a lot of layers to Zufar. One layer is the urbane, sophisticated, world investor, welcome at all western ports of call. Another is the arrogant Saudi royal family member, who thinks that everyone else in the world is beneath them. I don't think he is particularly fundamentalist when it comes to religion, as his lifestyle seems to indicate otherwise. He isn't really in the chain of succession for King; well he is, but there are about 100 people in front of him. One thing that gives him more influence in the Kingdom, is his diversification. When the price of oil goes down, he is one of the people in Saudi Arabia that are hurt the least. I wouldn't say that I personally know him all that well, I am a Palestinian American and we don't rate all that well with the Saudis. He likes talking to me because I know how to treat him during an interview and I am a Muslim. A WASP interviewer wouldn't show the proper deference to his position. Zufar, as all Saudi princes, really likes being deferred to. Not much help I am afraid," Farid said.

"Actually that gives me a little to work with, or at least begin to investigate. How much footage did you get that wasn't used for broadcast? Any chance that we could see the original take? Our profilers would have a better sense of the man," Justin said.

"We videoed about 30 minutes of interview, and probably used something like 3 minutes. I assume you don't want to formally request a copy from the network? I could probably get a copy, but it would prove a problem if anyone found out about it."

"Maybe we tell the analysts it was picked it up illicitly, stole it as it were," Justin suggested.

"That would probably be the best option. I can get the memory card from my cameraman, then it can be stolen or misplaced. Marc has a backup, so it should prove no more than an inconvenience. Coffee on Monday?"

"Good deal! That brings us to the election night soiree, what were you all doing there?" Justin asked.

"Besides drinking some of the booze we paid for with our donations? Lindsey and Nayla were there due to their fundraising prowess. Lindsey got me in, as a prominent donor connected to the media. There was a decent band and open bar. We didn't get to see much of the President-Elect, but Jonny Ray spent some time with us, doubtless due to the beauty of the two ladies. In fact, the Secret Service could probably validate that if needed. I left after the first couple of dances, which happened after the victory speech. I think Nayla and Lindsey stayed a while longer," Farid said.

"Did you see any other Muslims there?" Justin asked.

"Nayla and I, plus a few of the regular donors who should already be on your list. I didn't know everyone, though. Do you think The Hammer was actually in the ballroom?"

"We don't know. He was very likely in the resort somewhere, but it is a big place."

"What did his voice sound like?" Farid asked.

"Indeterminate. He was using voice modification technology, so it is hard to tell. That's pretty much all I had, oh wait. Remember I mentioned Quinton Jameson? Are you up for a meeting?" Justin said.

"That's fine, bring him along for coffee. That should give him enough tire-kicking to feel comfortable," Farid suggested.

"I'll suggest it. From what he said, he prefers informants who are criminals due to the leverage. So a private citizen helping out the FBI doesn't ring true to him," Justin said.

"Justin, I'm not helping the FBI out, I'm helping you. I wouldn't be doing it at all with someone I didn't fully trust. While I am very grateful to my adopted country, I don't trust political careerists to do the right thing. Ivy-League WASPs are not my favorites either. Don't worry, I'll play nice unless he doesn't want it that way."

"I hope it doesn't come to that, but you're right. The higher up you get in government service, the less trustworthy they are. Since I work for them, I will deny I ever said that," Justin said with a rueful smile. "That's all I had, but if you have any ideas on topic I'd appreciate hearing about them. Thanks for helping me out on this. Shall we rejoin the others?"

"My pleasure, 'Time. Yes, let's rejoin the lovely ladies," Farid said.

They went up and visited a bit more before Farid cited jet-lag, despite protests from Beth, Becky and Jan. He promised to come again soon and left for home.

Heading east on Route 7, Farid noticed what looked like a government-issue car with two men hanging back behind him. Turning on his mobile phone, he called Justin.

"Say, Justin. Do you think WASP's concerns rise to the level of putting me under surveillance? I've got a couple of federal-looking types on my six."

"Not that I am aware of, I'll look into it. Are you worried and want to come back in?" Justin asked.

"No, it might just be a coincidence. My place is pretty secure, due to all my crazed fans," Farid laughed, "I usually keep tabs on people who make the same turns I do, just in case. One more thing to talk about on Monday."

"Keep your eyes open, and if you have concerns drive to a police station."

"Will do. I'll ping you when I have what we discussed. Pass my thanks to Jan once more for the lovely dinner. Cheers," Farid hung up the phone. In his rear view he could still see the car following. Looking at the license plate during a red traffic light, it wasn't a government-issue plate, so it could easily be the FBI. The postures indicated military or police, which was oddly reassuring. Farid considered that having it be FBI was probably better than another alternative, such as private detectives or hitmen.

Farid hadn't been completely kidding when he mentioned married mistresses to Justin. His latest conquest was a 42 year old married woman, with children in High School, who fancied herself a journalist like Farid. Her husband was a corporate finance director for a local telecommunications firm on the Dulles Corridor, and reliably spent most of his time at work.

She had recently announced they could no longer continue the relationship. From Farid's perspective, that closed out the chapter, but he understood full well that husbands could take exception long after the offense was actually committed. Looking at it in that fashion opened the door to a lot of potentially aggrieved husbands. Yes, Farid hoped it was the FBI following him.

As he pulled into his neighborhood, the trailing car was still there. It was highly unlikely to be a coincidence after driving 30 miles to the same place. Pulling up to the gate of his apartment building, he pressed the access code which allowed him into the basement parking garage. The other car stayed on the street and they appeared to be looking for a place to park. As the gate closed behind Farid, he felt relief and parked the car in his reserved spot complete with its charging station. Farid entered his access card into the elevator and rode silently up to his penthouse apartment overlooking the river. The security system had not been tampered with and no one had tried to contact him.

Taking out his mobile phone, he dialed a contact. "Marc, sorry to disturb you on a Saturday! I wanted to know if you still have a copy of the full Prince Zufar interview? I need to look it over as we may want to do a follow-up."

"No problem, I was just watching the game. Yes, I still have it with me actually. Do you want me to load the files onto our cloud drop box?"

"How big are the files? If it takes too long to upload, I can wait until Monday morning," Farid said.

"Not too bad, about 1.5 GB. It won't take me very long to upload. I'll do it now. Give it about an hour and it should be there."

"Thanks, I'll let you get back to your game. See you Monday," Farid rang off.

• • •

The phone rang in the posh McLean, Virginia home of Quinton Jameson, late Saturday evening.

"This had better be important," Quinton said.

"Sir, the team monitoring Farid Royce was made by the subject."

"How did they find out?"

"They didn't. We got a call from Justin Simons asking whether we had any details following Mr. Royce. Evidently, he noticed the team and called Agent Simons to ask about it. This happened after he had dinner with Agent Simons and his family."

"Fucking incompetents. Let me guess, a dead end residential street and two guys sitting in a government car sticking out like sore thumbs?" Quinton said.

"That sounds about right. We didn't tell Agent Simons there was a detail, but thought you should know it was spotted. Should we continue on with the surveillance?"

"No, damn it! I was hoping to get more visibility into this guy before bringing him in, but we have what we have. Stand down, and indicate my displeasure to the team in no uncertain terms. Get a final report on my desk first thing Monday morning," Quinton shook his head in disgust. Now he would have to meet Farid without much information. Quinton liked to shock his subjects with how much he already knew, but that worked best on someone who didn't expect it.

Quinton pulled Farid Royce's last five years of tax returns and had looked through them over the weekend. So far, there were no irregularities. The man didn't even arrange to avoid being taxed in the District of Columbia for his news network earnings. The returns were about what you would expect for a seriously wealthy individual, without the usual shelters CPAs could arrange. The salary from his job, while significant, paled in comparison to his other earnings. *I'll have to ask him why his taxes aren't optimized, it is almost like he is trying not to be noticed by paying more than he has to.* Quinton thought. *Of course, a lot of people did that to avoid running afoul of the IRS.*

I'll instruct Justin to set up a meeting for next week, it's time to fire a shot across the bow.

Quinton made a note to himself to pull Justin's financial records as well, in order to see if his employee had been compromised by this Royce character.

• • •

Late Monday morning, Farid was sitting in an upscale coffee bistro nursing the strongest coffee on offer. Justin was running late, but he had a longer subway ride. Farid checked in with Lindsey via text, chuckling when she described the latest exploits of his niece and nephew.

"Farid!" Justin called as he entered the store, waving as he got into line. With him was an older man with fading blond hair wearing an upscale rack suit. Farid waved and went back to the texts. Within a few minutes Justin arrived, "Farid, this is Quinton Jameson, the head of our department. I mentioned him over the weekend."

Farid stood up and firmly shook Quinton's outstretched hand, "Hello, Quinton, I am glad to make your acquaintance. Justin mentioned that you might be joining us. Please sit."

"Hello Farid, I am likewise pleased to meet you. Your work has been very informative, especially for those of us tasked with understanding Muslim issues and concerns," Quinton said.

"That is very kind of you to say," Farid said. "Of course, some of what needs to be relayed can only happen in back-channels like the one between myself and Justin."

"Which brings us to today's subject. Justin, here is a memory card with the raw file footage of the complete interview we discussed. It even has the off-camera and positioning footage. I thought that it would be better to give you the entire sitting, so you can simply pick and choose what you're interested in. No need to return the card, it is disposable. Please make sure that it doesn't get back to the network: that may raise some eyebrows and get back to the prince," Farid said, sliding a memory card across the table.

"Thank you, Farid," Quinton said as Justin nodded. "What is your impression of the prince? What kind of man is he?"

"He is of a type with other western-educated Saudi princes: intelligent, entitled, and arrogant. Those are his good qualities," Farid said lightly with a small smile. "That was my poor attempt at a joke. He differs from his peers in that he is more independent of the oil industry, having diversified across many market segments. He views himself as superior to his Kingdom peers, and perhaps even his betters. Is that the kind of observation you were looking for?"

"Yes. Why do you think a guy with those advantages would entertain or consort with terrorists?" Quinton asked.

"I'll take it as a given that he has done that, for the sake of this discussion, but I've not seen any evidence of it myself. Perhaps he feels that strife, upset, and uncertainty benefits him in some way. As an investor, a person could get very wealthy if they knew when those type of events were to occur in advance. Consider for a moment, if you knew of the 9/11 attack in advance, you could sell the equities and currency markets short and make a killing."

"I'm not sure how that addresses the issue. Wouldn't it cost him money to fund terrorist operations as well as be dangerous to him personally?" Quinton asked.

"It is a matter of the cost of doing business. Terrorism doesn't cost much money to execute. Something like 9/11 was probably done with less than $5 million investment. That cost is miniscule when compared to the potential of making hundreds of millions in investment gains within six months. The personal danger is a deterrent certainly, but billionaires can afford to spend money on security. Having just visited his palace, I can vouch for his security being state of the art," Farid said and sipped at his drink.

"You're a fairly wealthy man, Mr. Royce, you certainly do not have to work for someone else as you do. If you don't mind my asking, why do you put up with the inconvenience?" Quinton asked.

"Farid, please! And I work for the fun of being able to ask questions of important people who I would never have access to otherwise. I'm small potatoes when it comes to wealth and power: something like a moderately successful actor. That doesn't get you invited into the billionaires' clubs. In my work, however, that is who I get to talk to the most."

"Farid, I have to ask. Have you ever considered working for the Bureau more actively?"

"Not really, no. What I do now is just about the optimum blend of risk and reward. If I learn something that could impact our country adversely, I pick up the phone and chat with Justin. Then my part is done, and I am on to other things."

"But what about your patriotic duty to our country? You have an unusual skill set which would be very useful to us," Quinton probed, leaning forward in his seat.

Farid paused, considering how best to answer. "As an immigrant, I do feel that obligation deeply. The best thing about America today is being able to choose how one contributes. In my case, I pay an enormous amount of taxes and occasionally help flag national threats. Working for a government agency would put ridiculous restraints on my lifestyle. I'm patriotic, but I'm also a libertarian politically, which means it wouldn't be a good fit."

He continued, "One more thing you should understand about the prince. People like him are not really subject to the same rules or constraints we live by here in the United States. An example, if during my visit I somehow insulted him, he could absolutely get away with killing me then and there. There would be little to no consequences for him. At worst he would get a public reprimand from the King, in order to quell American complaints, but nothing more. As long as we need the Saudis, there is little we can do to change those facts. The FBI's jurisdiction is law enforcement within the USA, and I suspect things get rather more complicated when you try to play internationally."

"That's a political issue, and these days the various agencies are working together much better. Changing gears a little, what do you know about this Hammer character? What is his objective and reputation?" Quinton asked.

"I don't know much about that, as I told Justin over the weekend. He is tied up with the Palestinian struggle or is just anti-Zionist, could be either. The rumor is if you meet him, you die. I think the origin of that was when some other faction leaders took credit for his work and died promptly thereafter. No one really knows his nationality, what he looks like, or even where he is based," Farid said.

"Yes, that is pretty much what we heard too. Thank you, Farid. It was good meeting you today. Look, if anything develops on these topics, I want you to call Justin or me immediately. In fact, here is my card with contact information where I can be reached 24/7. I know you understand how seriously we are taking the situation. If there is something planned that affects the President Elect, we need to nip it in the bud," Quinton said.

Farid took the card, stood and shook Quinton's hand, "Thanks, I will. Justin, I'll be in touch if I hear anything new," Farid left the two behind to finish their coffees.

"I think he knows more than he is saying," Quinton said.

"How so?" Justin asked with a displeased twist to his mouth.

"Just an impression I have. I hope our profilers will be able to get a read on the prince from the footage. How much do you know about Farid's movements?"

"Not much more than a friend would know. Most of the time, I hear when he is leaving town, but day-to-day I wouldn't know. He has a sister in town, Lindsey Royce, who often knows. In the past I have called her when I was looking for him, but she doesn't always know either," Justin said.

"Who was the other woman at the election night party?"

"Nayla Kaldah? She is a former college roommate of Lindsey's and good friend of Farid's. She has been over to our home many times. Works as a lobbyist and fundraiser for progressive interests, similar to Lindsey," Justin said.

"I think we should open this up a bit. Where is Nayla from and what is her citizen status?" Quinton asked.

"Gaza City, went to university in France and did her JD in the USA. Nayla is fully naturalized, I believe, as I attended the party celebrating her receipt of American citizenship."

"Gaza City, Palestinian. Maybe she knows something about this Hammer, and she was at the same party," Quinton mused.

"Farid is also Palestinian but came here by way of Beiruit when he was five or six years old. Nayla was in her mid-teens when she left for France. I'll set up an appointment to see Nayla and Lindsey to ask the same set of questions this week," Justin said.

"No, I'll do that. Given the fact that you know those subjects, I think you should work the ones you don't know. I don't want any perceived conflict of interest. There are still several hundred people to be contacted, correct?" Quinton said.

"Yes, there are a lot more people to interview, and I'll get on that. I'll also get you Lindsey and Nayla's contact information later today. Shall we head back to the office?"

"Yes, let's go. Hopefully The Hammer isn't planning anything for next week's inauguration," Quinton said. Justin nodded in full agreement.

• • •

Nayla saw the special chalk marking on her building that The Hammer used when he wanted to meet. While worried about what he had to tell her, she looked forward to seeing him and smiled as she remembered their last evening together. He wouldn't arrive at the apartment until after full dark, but she would be waiting.

A little after 9 p.m., she heard a key inserted into the door lock. Quickly, The Hammer entered the apartment.

"Hello, can I get you something before we sit down?" Nayla asked.

"Sparkling water, if you have it," The Hammer said.

Nayla set down a glass filled with the popping liquid and set the bottle close by.

"Thank you. I came tonight to warn you. You'll be contacted in the next day or two by the FBI to talk about the night of the election party. They have a recording of my call to our benefactor in Saudi, and traced it back to the hotel's location. So they are looking for me. Use the story we agreed upon. If they focus on you being Palestinian, point out that the President Elect has many Muslim supporters and that some of the more prominent ones were at the event."

"That should prove to be no problem, especially since it is true. Should I admit to having heard of The Hammer?" Nayla asked.

"I would say that you've heard of him, but think he is just a myth. You don't mix in the circles that would know more about that kind of thing."

"Anything else?"

"Yes, I have been thinking about your operation, and it needs to continue for sixty days after the inauguration. The primary effort will begin forty-five days after the inauguration. That time overlap should prove most effective. Keep in mind that Jonny Ray will be very busy in the first week or two and likely will not call upon you."

"Sixty days? How do you want the close out to go? Do I just break it off with him?"

"No need. At the end he will either break things off himself or just disappear. I doubt he has much stomach for breaking bad news, so I expect it will be the latter," The Hammer said. "Let me know immediately if he gives any sign of breaking off before then."

"Understood."

The Hammer touched Nayla's cheeks with the fingertips of his right hand, "It will be over soon, and this blow will be struck. Persevere, my Love," he breathed as he kissed her lips softly. Extricating himself from her arms, "I have to go see several more of our friends. Be careful as you leave tonight."

The Hammer used the security peephole to scan the hallway, then quietly left the apartment. Nayla sat quietly for a few minutes listening for any sound that would show The Hammer had run into difficulties. When nothing out of the ordinary occurred, she cleaned up the apartment, and readied it for the next rendezvous with Jonny Ray. Only then did she gather her things and go home.

•••

Quinton sat in his office considering how the conversation earlier had gone with Farid Royce. He didn't trust the man. Royce was many of the things Quinton despised; rich, handsome, intelligent, and an immigrant Muslim with good political connections. Quinton thought many of America's security problems would vanish overnight if all Muslims were deported and the religion banned within its borders. He couldn't say that aloud in the politically correct world he lived in every day, but that was how he felt.

He had read the file on Nayla upon his return to the office. His first question about how an orphan from Gaza City could have gotten a green card and be fast-tracked to citizenship was answered. Benton Royce's old connections at the State Department had accrued to his orphaned daughter Lindsey after he and his wife Claire died in a tragic 2004 automobile accident on Georgetown Pike. Later when Lindsey became close to Nayla, she has used her connections at the State Department to assist the process. Going over the file further, he noticed some handwritten markings in several places with notes.

He reached over and pressed the intercom button on his desk phone, "Margery, get whoever dropped off the last set of files in here as soon as possible. Thanks!"

Jameson didn't have long to wait before there was a soft knock on the door, "Come in."

The department's latest file-runner, Ismael, opened the door slowly, "Sir, you asked to see me?"

"Yes, Ismael, isn't it? Did you bring in the last bunch of files, this one on Nayla Kaldah?" Jameson asked.

"I believe so, if I may see the file? Yes, I did," Ismael responded.

"Here, let me show you something. Do you see these handwritten notes? Do we have any way of finding out who made the notations? I think there should be more information in the file, as these seem to reference things that are not in it. What do you think?"

"Sir, this is the one I had to retrieve from the Secret Service last week. Special Agent Simons had asked for them all, and this one had been checked out to Alex Jones over at Secret Service," Ismael said.

"Thank you, Ismael. That will be all." Jameson watched Ismael leave, "Margery, please get me the mobile phone number for Alex Jones of Secret Service."

For a few moments Jameson considered bringing Justin into the conversation, but concluded that he was too close to Nayla for objectivity.

Jameson rang Alex Jones' number, "Alex, this is Section Chief Quinton Jameson at FBI. Do you have a few minutes to speak with me now?"

"Certainly, what is this about?" Jones said.

"I wanted to talk with you about Nayla Kaldah, I was reviewing her file and saw that your team had recently made some notations within it, which didn't have backup source material in the file."

"Yes, I run the detail for the President Elect's husband Jonny Ray Brown. In fact, I was working closely with Justin Simons on the Election Night investigation, providing our data on the guests on site that evening," Jones said.

"We're talking about the same investigation then. Did you have more detail on Nayla than what is in her file that we sent over? It might save us some steps."

Jones heaved a deep sigh and said, "Yes. There is more, but I am not comfortable speaking about it over the telephone. Are you downtown now? Meet me at this coffee shop, I'm sending you text with the link. In an hour if that works?"

"That will work, I look forward to meeting you there," Jameson said as he rang off.

The location was in a neighborhood dominated by residential buildings. The coffee shop was on the first floor of one, a half-block away from a Metro stop. Jameson got himself a cup of coffee and settled in for the wait. Agent Jones was fairly easy to spot, as was Jameson, so they quickly got down to the business at hand.

"Do you see that apartment building across the street there?" Agent Jones asked. "Nayla Kaldah took a six month lease on an apartment there that she doesn't live in, two weeks after Election Night."

"Alright. What am I missing?" Jameson asked.

Looking around before answering, Jones covered his mouth with his hand and said, "She is using it when she meets with our charge several times a week. He finds a way to sneak out of wherever he is, and comes there for a few hours of afternoon delight. We secure the perimeter and he does his thing."

"Holy crap! I can appreciate why you didn't want that on the wire. I really appreciate you telling me about it, because it saves me from stepping in some major shit. We are in the process of interviewing everyone, and she would be on the list shortly. I know you guys did an in-depth on her. What was the takeaway on it?" Jameson said.

"The takeaway was that she was clean and well-connected. Her teenage years would have been problematic in some circles, but she wasn't directly involved in those issues. Have you ever heard of The Martyrs al-Sabra? Her brother was one of the people who precipitated that fiasco, and no one can agree whether he is living or dead. She was in Paris at the time, getting set to start University. She lost her parents and her brother all within the space of a year," Jones said.

"I remember it had something to do with a massacre of school children? I'll look into it more later. You say she had a brother, who was he?" Jameson asked.

"Adeeb Kaldah, her younger brother. Of course, Palestinian families are run by the men, so he was in charge of their little family unit once their parents were killed, in spite of being 15 years or so old. The parents were killed by a stray Israeli bomb; how many times have we heard that story? When things blew up with the Martyrs, they never found Adeeb's body. But you know the Palestinian Authority, they aren't the best and brightest when it comes to documentation. Most of what we know about it comes from our Israeli colleagues," Jones said. "The Israeli assessment was that she wasn't involved directly and the Martyrs Incident was likely a Hamas/Fatah dispute which turned ugly."

"You know we are trying to figure out who The Hammer is? What if he is Adeeb Kaldah? That could explain why no one has been able to figure out who he is. I wonder what the Israelis know about the Hammer?" Jameson said.

"I'd ask them. Nayla Kaldah we have a pretty good handle on. The Hammer we'll leave to you, unless he threatens any of the principals."

"I would love to know what they talk about during their trysts. Jonny Ray probably isn't briefed in on much, but if we're wrong and Nayla is part of some operation we could be in a real mess," Jameson said.

"I'm with you on that, however, I would hate to be the one explaining why I wired the love nest for video. No, we'll stick to physical protection on this one," Jones said. "Your folks could put her under surveillance otherwise, wearing your counterterrorism hat, but even that could prove problematic if there is nothing there and they are caught at it."

"Yes. You've given me a lot to think about, thank you for briefing me in on this. If we hear anything new I'll get back in touch with you," Jameson said.

"What about Justin?"

"Keep working with him as he wades through the rest of this. I had to take Justin off of a few subjects that he knew personally. We want to do this right and avoid any appearance of impropriety. He knows Nayla and a few others on the list personally, " Jameson explained.

"Ah, makes sense. OK, we'll stay in touch," Agent Jones took his cup and headed for the Metro station.

Jameson added the name *Adeeb Kaldah* to his list as something he should investigate further. He didn't personally have an Israeli contact, so he would have to share his concerns with the CIA or escalate within the FBI. Either way came with disadvantages for him personally. Whoever he took it to at FBI would get credit if the investigation proved fruitful. A similar thing would happen at CIA, only then it would be the FBI losing out and not just himself. No, this required more thought. Quinton knew Nayla was the key to something, he just wasn't sure what it was. He would sit down with her before the inauguration, because he wanted to see the look on her face when he asked about her brother. He had a bit of homework to do there, but he could see a path forward and it was all his.

• • •

On Wednesday morning, two days prior to the inauguration ceremony, Jameson called Nayla from his office. "Ms. Kaldah, this is Section Chief Jameson of the FBI. I would like to speak with you for about an hour concerning your recollections of the Election night festivities you attended."

"The election night last November?" Nayla asked.

"Yes, that's right. We had a national security incident occur and we are talking to everyone who attended the event at the Gaylord Resort. In fact, we've already spoken to your friends Lindsey Hamilton and Farid Royce. It has taken a while to work through everyone, as there were a lot of supporters in attendance," Jameson said.

"An hour? Are you located downtown? I can block an hour for you today, if you're willing to meet at my office. If I need to come to you, then tomorrow would be better," Nayla offered.

"I can come to you. K-Street, right?"

"Yes, how about 4 p.m.?" Nayla said.

"Thank you, I will see you then," Jameson rang off.

Nayla sat at her desk for a few minutes, seemingly lost in thought. Then she stood up and closed the blinds completely on her south-facing window. Across the street, the webcam focused on that window transmitted a signal to a waiting party.

The phone rang on the front desk of Nayla's firm.

"Hello, this is Sandwich Specialties. May I please speak with Nayla Kaldah?"

"Is she expecting your call?" the receptionist inquired.

"No, it's a little embarrassing. She left an order, but there was a spill on the ticket and her direct number was destroyed along with her order. I'm calling to get her order straightened out."

"I'll forward you now," the receptionist said and rang the call through.

"Nayla Kaldah."

"Hello. This is Sandwich Specialties, we lost your order under a spill and wanted to make sure we got it right."

"No problem, I ordered a turkey club with rye bread. Delivered as close to noon as possible. One question, how long is that sandwich good for? I tend to eat half and let it sit for a while. Would it last as late as 4 p.m.?" Nayla asked.

"Got it, we'll include a free order of the cookies you like, our treat. The sandwich will last about six hours, after that it should be disposed of," The Hammer said.

"Good, I'll be eating it before 4 p.m. in my conference room then. Thank you for calling, and for the cookies!"

Nayla was calmer now that she knew The Hammer was informed. He had told her to expect the call, but it still made her uncomfortable. Standing up, she returned the blind to its normal position. At 12 p.m., a delivery man dropped off Nayla's sandwich basket, complete with the soft chocolate chip cookies that she loved. Nothing to do now but wait until 4 p.m.

Quinton Jameson took a perverse pride in handing his card to the receptionist, saying he was there for his 4 p.m. appointment with Ms. Kaldah. That will work its way through the grapevine, he thought to himself. The firm's lobby was resplendent in the understated classic look of old money: real leather seats and wooden furniture. At exactly 4 p.m., he was shown into a small, four-chair conference room where Nayla rose to greet him.

"Section Chief Jameson? I'm Nayla Kaldah, please be seated. Before we start, would you like any coffee or water?"

"No thank you. I'll get right to the point, as I know you are quite busy. On Election Night, we intercepted a telephone call between a known terrorist and a Saudi prince. We were able to trace the terrorist's phone location back to the area surrounding the Gaylord Resort. This terrorist is known as The Hammer of Allah. Have you ever heard of him?"

Nayla recoiled, "The Hammer? I honestly thought he was just a fantasy used to scare children. You know, like telling children not to lie or The Hammer would kill them."

"Much more than a fantasy I'm afraid. Did you happen to see any memorable Muslims you didn't know previously at the event?"

"No, most of the people there were well-known donors to the Democratic Party and their affiliated influence groups. In fact, now that I think of it, I was acquainted with all the people I knew were Muslim. That doesn't mean that someone couldn't have been there without appearing to be Muslim. I didn't know everyone at the party," Nayla said slowly as she thought it through. "I was only in the President-Elect's party, the resort is pretty big and there were a number of other election night events."

"We're following up on all of them. You came to the United States on a student visa when?" Jameson asked.

"In 2009, to attend Harvard Law School."

"That's where you met Lindsey Royce?" Jameson asked.

"Yes. I answered an ad she placed for a roommate."

"She is wealthy, why did she need to get a roommate?"

"Probably for the same reason I did; to know someone there. It helps to have someone local who has your back without having to hire an assistant. I'm not as wealthy as Lindsey, but I had plenty of money of my own from my parents' estate," Nayla explained.

"Were you the sole heir of your parents' estate?"

"No, I had a brother who died in Gaza after I had left for Paris and university. I'm all that is left," Nayla said as a sad expression flitted across her face and was quickly brought under control.

"Your bother was Adeeb Kaldah? One of the persons responsible for the Martyrs al-Sabra incident? Are you sure he is dead?"

Surprised by the turn in the questions, but trained in the cut and thrust of legal deposition, Nayla took a deep breath and said, "Yes, Adeeb was my brother. I've also heard that he was one of the persons blamed for that incident. No, I'm not sure he's dead, but it has been so many years without contact I have given up hope that he survived. A body was never found. Many of those bodies were not found. There was a huge fire which destroyed an entire city block."

"Do you think there is any chance that he is alive, and in fact might be The Hammer?" Jameson asked.

"I don't think it works with the timing involved. Adeeb was a small 16 year-old boy when the Martyrs incident occurred, and he had no training or influence. I don't know when The Hammer was first heard from, but I think it was probably earlier than that. Your sources are better than mine on that topic," Nayla was beginning to become angry with Section Chief Jameson, it appeared he had some theories of his own.

"I'll have to check into that, I hadn't heard about him myself until this year. We have to go down all the lines of inquiry until we find what we're looking for, or the situation resolves itself. I apologize if I have given offense, but that is why we are having informal discussions rather than a more formal deposition," Jameson said in an officious way.

"With all due respect, Section Chief, the people in that room would not prove easy to depose. We all have teeth. From what I have heard, all you have is a telephone call that as many as five thousand people could have made. I hope you took the time to track them all down and talk with them as well, otherwise you might be accused of racial profiling. I'm sure that's not your intent, especially since that is the quickest path in today's FBI to a posting in the rural Midwest. I think we're done here today, if there are further questions I'll address them in the presence of my counsel," Nayla stood and held the door open for Jameson.

"Why would you need counsel, if you have nothing to hide?" Jameson said.

"Who do you think you're talking to, some stupid drug dealer? I have a limited tolerance for bureaucrats, especially those who go off-topic on their own racist political agendas. Having counsel present would enable me to protect myself from a witch hunt, as well as give me cause for future action against the persons and agencies responsible. That's what smart people with teeth do. Goodbye, Section Chief Jameson!" Nayla showed him the door.

Well, that didn't go as well as I hoped. I'll have to look into the time line a little more. Quinton thought to himself. *She didn't seem all that surprised that I asked about her brother, or indeed surprised at all. I wonder if someone told her to expect the call. Of course, she may have heard from her friends Lindsey or Farid. I'll have to see if Lindsey has already been talked to, if not it will have been Farid. I can't push her much more, but keeping a close eye on her wouldn't be a bad idea. Maybe we can wiretap her mobile phone and track her using the GPS sensors. Could blow up in my face, but that is probably the best way to get to the truth of her.*

Quinton was so absorbed in his planning that he didn't notice The Hammer follow him towards the Metro station. As was usual that time of day, most of the commute traffic had died down, and the streets belonged to the transients again. Coming up behind Quinton as he passed an alley access, The Hammer swung a sap expertly against Quinton's temple, dropping him instantly. The Hammer dragged his limp form behind a dumpster, quickly stole his wallet, mobile phone, badge, and service pistol. The Hammer straightened up and walked normally out the back side of the alley; the entire episode took less than 20 seconds.

Quinton awoke some time later and dragged himself to the sidewalk attempting to attract some help. He grasped the shoe of a passing lawyer, "Please, call the police, I am with the FBI and was just attacked," he said as he passed out again.

The next thing he remembered were flashes of consciousness during the ambulance ride, an emergency physician shining a bright light into his eyes, and finally waking up in a hospital bed. Two DC police officers were there to speak to him. He gave his name and a contact at the FBI to notify.

"Mr. Jameson, it appears you were the victim of a mugging. You had no wallet, badge, or mobile phone on you. Did you have them before?" an officer asked.

"Yes, I had those as well as my service weapon. What about that?" Jameson asked.

"Sorry, sir, there was no sign of one."

"What about video surveillance? Is there any footage that can be reviewed?"

"No, sir, there was a camera in the alley but it had been vandalized."

Quinton laid his pounding head against his pillow. While he wasn't ruling out a simple mugging, it seemed more professional than the usual smash and grab. For one thing, the assailant had only hit him a single time with expert force. Second, most muggers would see his FBI credentials and have second thoughts. He couldn't believe he had been so distracted by the Palestinian bitch that he hadn't seen it coming. Maybe she had something to do with it. No point wasting time thinking about it now, with Nayla's hackles up it would not be easy to get anything more from her. No, if there was a break in the investigation, it would have to come from somewhere else.

Justin Simons came in with the FBI internal investigation lead. Quinton waved feebly from his hospital bed. "Justin, there is something I need you to look into. Nayla Kaldah had a brother who disappeared, presumed dead, about ten years ago. Please look into the earliest reports we have of The Hammer, e.g. when those were. I want to know whether it is possible he is our man."

"I will. How are you, boss? You got hit pretty hard," Justin's open face was twisted with concern.

"The physician thinks I may have a concussion, so they are holding me for a while. Honestly, my head spins when I try to stand up, so he may be right. But we're running out of time on the Hammer investigation. I spoke with Nayla this afternoon. In fact, it is where I was before running into the brick wall. I antagonized her by asking about her brother, so she will be lawyering up for future discussions. There's more to her story, but we'll have to come back to it," Quinton said. "Go back and get started on the Kaldah brother deep-dive. Hopefully, I'll be able to join you before it is finished."

• • •

In the Georgetown apartment, Nayla waited for The Hammer. Upon full darkness, he entered the apartment.

"How did your meeting with the FBI go?"

"As expected, but it took a negative turn," Nayla recapped the entire meeting with Section Chief Jameson.

"Nayla, you handled it perfectly! So they think Adeeb might be The Hammer. Interesting," The Hammer said.

"I don't think they do, I suspect it is a pet notion of Jameson's. Normally, FBI investigators operate in pairs and this one came alone. I think we have an ambitious functionary who smells a chance to garner significant credit for capturing and neutralizing The Hammer. His coming alone is simply a testament to his greed. Did you ever learn anything about Adeeb's fate? I only got the one message saying the person named Adeeb had to die so his replacement could live," Nayla said.

"While not completely sure, I believe Adeeb lives, but has changed his name. It was a very wise decision, given the events of the Martyrs incident. There was also a rumor that he left Gaza on a Greek freighter under false papers. Who got him the papers, arranged for the boat, and what name was on those papers is unclear. The trail is lost at that point," The Hammer said. "There is still a reward for his capture, offered by the Obeidat family, but no one has collected so far. Actually, I am surprised the Obeidats haven't tried to come after you."

"I know why. It is because I am not in Gaza City. The Obeidats have been under siege themselves, as a good number have been assassinated in recent years. Clearly they had problems with more than one family. I can't say I pity them - they deserve all of it."

"Don't worry about your FBI agent, he had a little setback which will inconvenience him for a few days. Are you attending the inauguration?"

"Yes, my firm got me a seat close in and I'm looking forward to it," Nayla said.

"Good, continue with the operation. Don't worry, we'll be looking out for you," The Hammer said. "If anything else comes up, set the regular signals and I'll be in contact."

"You be careful as well. Do I want to know what happened to that asshole?" Nayla asked.

"I would say, no. I'll be careful." As before The Hammer previewed the hallway before opening the door and silently leaving the apartment.

• • •

"Please repeat after me. I, Lucinda Mary Brown, do solemnly swear that I will faithfully execute the Office of President of the United States, and will to the best of my ability, preserve, protect, and defend the Constitution of the United States," The Chief Justice of the United States Supreme Court said.

Lucinda with her right hand raised and her left hand resting on the Bible held by her husband, repeated the words in a strong and clear voice. The historic Presidency of Lucinda Brown had begun.

First Shots

"..Beltway pundits are calling it the 'War of Orders', before leaving office the President issued hundreds of executive orders on a number of contentious topics, given the election results. Much of President Brown's time has been spent unraveling or negating his lame-duck efforts. The former president continues to publicly campaign against President Brown's initiatives, in spite of the transgression of decorum it represents. Past time for him to play some golf and show some dignity.."

Farid Monsour al Haj for World News Corporation

The Massively Multiplayer Online Role-Playing Game (MMORPG) Fantasy Conquests where the Crusaders for Truth guild members played was one of the largest in the world. More than ten million accounts were active at any given moment. The Crusaders for Truth met three times a week: Monday, Wednesday, and Friday. On those occasions, there would be a short meeting in one of the capital cities contained in the virtual world. There, the entire group of 45-50 players would form a loose circle in an open area. In the center of the circle were the Guildmaster and his two Officers. The group would discuss which raids they would tackle after the meeting, and select members needing upgrades in equipment would speak up in guild-chat to schedule equipment dungeon runs. The first week of March, the meetings were short before the members headed off on whatever activities had been agreed upon.

The drives home from the hunt camp had been completely uneventful. Only two of the thirty shooters encountered police officers. One had a tire blowout, and the police officer blocked the car from traffic, using his lights to provide a safer environment to change the tire. The officer also recommended a reasonably priced garage nearby, and got the hunter back on the road quickly.

The second hunter was stopped for traveling 5 mph over the speed limit on a surface street in a small town while stopping for gasoline and a short rest. The hunter reviewed his training and affected an unconcerned demeanor as he waited. The police officer, almost apologetically, handed over a speeding ticket with an admonition to "Have a safe trip home!" The trainers had briefed all of the hunters on how small town police departments were funded by out-of-state drivers. The hunter was pleased things went according to plan, and continued onward to his home.

The shooters were all safely home in their major cities. As they had been instructed at camp, they set aside regular times daily to play the online game so it would become one of their normal home behaviors. They also spent several hours twice a week scouting for potential shot sites. That too, became part of their normal routine. All of the shooters had rented a small self-service storage unit where their gun was kept. The special ammunition was kept in a more secure location: a small safety deposit box at their local bank.

Each shooter had a mirror, whose sole job was to monitor the everyday life of their assigned shooter. The laptops provided to the shooters had spy software which the mirrors used to infiltrate the networks of each shooter. The mirror knew what was said in the home, what financial transactions were taking place, and if the family was becoming suspicious of the shooter's new behaviors. All mirrors were linked to Amin-Sabir using encrypted channels forwarded through foreign proxy servers.

Everything was in full readiness for the operation to begin.

Forty-five days after the inauguration of President Lucinda Brown, the first action was readied for execution. In the Monday guild meeting, on March 8th, a special selection was about to be communicated. Earlier that day, The Hammer had used a random number generator to select the first target city: Sacramento metropolitan area, the nation's 27th most populous region. The Sacramento shooter's in-game persona was named Sullnpsych, played by Munir Hammayil the dentist from Roseville. The Hammer's in-game persona was named Redonkulus, Amin's was Snaptime, and Reem's was Snacksnick.

The Crusaders of Truth guild gathered in the human race capital in the city cemetery. The thirty shooters gathered in a circle, as always. Redonkulus, Snaptime, and Snacksnick stood in the center of the circle. First, Redonkulus started to dance, then Snaptime, and then Snacksnick. After 30 seconds or so, the three in the center ran around inside the circle jumping around until Redonkulus pointed at Sullnpsych then started dancing again. Snaptime and Snacksnick pointed at different players. Sullnpsych indicated, after his initial shock, he had seen his selection and acknowledged by starting to dance himself. The selections of Amin and Reem also started dancing. Redonkulus stopped and jumped two times. Sullnpsych stopped and jumped two times. Amin and Reem did similar things with a different number of jumps. The message had been passed: Sacramento's hunter was to shoot, as trained, in two days. Amin and Reem were nothing but a distraction for other eyes, and all other city shooters knew that they were not operational during this episode. The entire group joked around on chat, commenting on the dance moves, and what they were going to do in-game. No indication of the true message was reflected in the chat channels.

Sullnpsych, Munir Hammayil, lived in Roseville, just outside of Sacramento. He had come to the movement due to the slights, real and imagined, he suffered as a Muslim. In order for his business to be successful, he had to serve a wide mostly Christian customer base. Most of them were simple folk who had never traveled the world, and simply had strange or ignorant ideas about Muslims. While he would have liked to shoot some of his clients, he knew there had to be no connection to him at all, which meant he could not know the target victim. Munir's children were in college and his wife had long ago given herself over to the comforts of food and home. As long as Munir brought home his income and didn't press her for sex, she did not worry aloud about Munir's activities. Over the years, Munir had arranged for a mistress or two, but not frequently enough to be caught doing so.

Munir was excited to be the operation's first shooter, there was notoriety in it, suitable for his position in life. It meant, of course, he would have to drive the Honda Accord but it wasn't the trial it had been before the hunt club trip.

Several weeks ago, Munir had picked the spot for his shooting position. Off of Fairway Drive in Roseville, there was a Home Helper with a large parking lot. To the west, an open field with trees along the edges culminating in a FoodCo Foods supermarket and parking lot. He hadn't decided whether the target should be at FoodCo or at the Home Helper, but he would travel there tonight to decide, once it was fully dark. He suspected the best opportunity would be the supermarket, as the Home Helper's parking lot was connected to many other establishments which would make it easy to disappear quickly.

Munir parked his car in the Home Helper lot, with the trunk facing the field. Getting out of the car, he looked around for security cameras and didn't see any covering that edge of the parking lot. Munir walked in between the trees bordering the field and out towards the supermarket. There was a fair amount of knee-high scrub grass, but it wasn't hard going. The field itself had no lighting and the parking lots shone like islands of light in the surrounding darkness. Munir's instructor had talked about how light-adapted eyes aren't able to see well into relatively darker areas. That would help shield Munir's retreat across the field, that and the dark clothing he would wear. Working his way along the tree line to the FoodCo parking lot, he found several sheltered areas which would work for shooting from a recumbent position. Getting back up, he hurried back towards his car in the Home Helper parking lot. As Munir approached the tree line, he slowed in order to assess whether anyone noticed his appearance next to the car. When he had parked a few minutes prior, there had been no cars or trucks parked next to him in the far reaches of the parking lot. Now there were two. Munir looked for any persons heading or looking towards his direction. Seeing none, Munir stepped up to his car door and got in. Driving around the parking lot, Munir tried to gauge how quickly he could get to a major street and established the best exit for his purposes. Afterwards he headed for home.

His mirror had been driving the pick-up truck parked next to Munir's car. He watched Munir go through his paces and stayed out of his sight. It was going to be a long three days for the mirror, as he had to not miss anything Munir was doing.

Munir arrived at his home, greeted his wife who was watching television, and sat down to play some more of their MMORPG game. All was ready for the first shot.

• • •

In Washington, Lucy Brown was discovering that her predecessor had left a much greater mess than anyone could have imagined. Hundreds of executive orders had been issued between the time of her election and inauguration. Sorting through all of the special interest giveaways and deciding how to best unwind the most egregious had taken up most of her time in her first forty-five days as President. None of those provisions had been part of the transition team's debriefs during that period.

Not only that, but he was not willing to accept the reduced role all previous presidents had: that of being an emeritus leader. In a normal succession, a past president would take a long vacation and not do anything to take attention away from their successor for some period of time.

Lucy's predecessor was so narcissistic that he was on television a week later, second-guessing her decisions in a public forum.

"Sid, what are we going to do about this guy? He's already got people wondering who is really in charge. If I do something other than what he says, it is because I am just being contrary. If I do what he says, others say he is still pulling the strings. We need to have this stop, immediately. Any ideas?" Lucy asked.

"I've been thinking about it, and I have an idea which is close to being evil but can be spun to appear righteous," Sid said.

"Tell me more," Lucy said.

"Well, you know how he has been giving speeches for something like $250K per engagement all over the world? In every case, he has had his Secret Service protection at taxpayer expense. In fact, the American people have kicked in more than $3M just to protect him as he travels the world. His current wealth is estimated at more than $3 billion. So here is a rich man getting richer and taking shameless advantage of the American taxpayer. Surely he can afford to pay for his own security when engaged on private commercial ventures, the same as that of all of his peers in the speaking community."

"So how would we go about doing something about that?" Lucy said.

"This is one of the parts that I think will get his attention. All of the past presidents who are still alive are multimillionaires, none of them until now, have used the Secret Service when pursuing commercial activities. So what if you, in conjunction with Congress, ask for a bill that includes a means test for provision of Secret Service protection as well as a strict prohibition of protection support for commercial activities? If a past president doesn't have enough money to fund it themselves, protection would be provided as before, except for instances where they are engaged in commercial activities. If they are wealthy enough, then no Secret Service protection at all, except in the case where a credible threat exists. It is sold as a savings for the American people, and elimination of an entitlement as well. What do you think?" Sid said.

"Spending other people's money is definitely something he enjoys, he will hate having to pay out of pocket for security. Is that all of it?" Lucy asked.

"No, Madame President, there is more. You know how past presidents maintain security clearances and are afforded security briefings as a courtesy by the sitting president? I propose that you stop the practice immediately, cancelling past president security clearances and eliminating briefings, by issuing an executive order. One justification is that by removing up-to-date security data from past presidents, it reduces the chance that they would be considered an active intelligence target, thus requiring even less Secret Service protection. The best part is that them being out of the loop allows you to observe that the past president isn't in possession of all the facts surrounding whatever issue he is spouting on," Sid said.

"What about push-back from allies in Congress and his party?" Lucy asked.

"This can play out a couple of ways. One way is to stage the entire package and call him in for a discussion. The second option is to work with his enemies in Congress, who coincidentally control one house and would love to stick a spoke in his wheels, in order to get the bill passed. The executive order on security clearances you could issue at any time," Sid explained.

"I really like it. Ideally, I would like to work with this guy and not burn a bridge, but we need to get his attention somehow without making the approach public. Call him in for a discussion," Lucy directed.

"Yes, Madame President. Have you given any more thought to how we're going to task Jonny Ray?" Sid asked.

Lucy's face tightened subtly at the change in topic, "I have. I think we should have him helping progressive election campaigns in key battleground regions. He can fundraise, fly the flag for us, and build up a group of key people who owe us for their position. We have to start thinking about the run-up to a second term."

"Great idea - it definitely plays to Jonny Ray's strengths. Do you want to ask him about it yourself or shall I?" Sid asked.

"I'll do it," Lucy said flatly. "How is Michael settling in as VP?"

"Very well. He's been willing and eager on everything we've asked him to do. I think a large part of what drives it is you requiring him to be involved in all of the day-to-day decisions. He is truly getting the experience without having the responsibility, which will serve him well in years to come. Most VPs don't get anywhere near this close to a decision," Sid said.

"Ah, well. He will still have to do some lousy jobs on my behalf, so the least we can do is make the overall experience bearable. Plus, if something were to happen to me, I don't want him fumbling around trying to figure out how things work," Lucy said. "What else do you have for me?"

• • •

The Hammer waited in the coffee shop across the street from Nayla's apartment rental, watching as the Secret Service closed down the entrances to the building after Jonny Ray arrived, letting only residents enter or depart. This tryst was expected to be short, as Jonny Ray was meeting with Sid Rosenbloom later that afternoon. As expected, within two hours the Secret Service reversed their previous exercise as they rolled up their detail coverage and departed. About thirty minutes later, Nayla emerged, dressed for the light sprinkles that accompanies springtime in Washington, DC and headed for the Metro station. The Hammer watched to see if anyone was following her, and was relieved to see there was not. It was important to know how much FBI attention was being paid to Nayla's movements, for future planning.

Walking down the stairs, he entered the Metro station heading to a different rendezvous with Amin, in a seedier section of the city. Amin had contracted a safe house in an older, mostly low-income black, city ward. The Hammer tapped the door twice, then used his key. Entering slowly, he acknowledged Amin who had been standing with a drawn handgun at the ready beside the door.

"Report," The Hammer said as he removed his dark overcoat.

"Sacramento is proceeding according to plan. The mirror reports no suspicious behavior from the shooter. The target site appears to be a supermarket next to a Home Helper," Amin said.

"Excellent. Of course, the Feds won't get involved on the first or possibly even the second shots, it will take them some time to identify this as terrorism," The Hammer said.

"Do you think you should reconsider taking credit in some way to speed that up? I know that is not your usual policy, but perhaps this once?"

"Perhaps. If they prove to be obtuse, perhaps we could leak a taste of it to a press outlet and let them do the rest," The Hammer said.

"Any candidates in mind?"

"Not immediately, but this town is full of reporters who will do anything for a breaking story. It won't be hard to set up if we decide to go there. How about our seagoing venture?"

"The container ship will meet our transport off the coast of Oman, where the special container will be transferred aboard. We have specified the container be carried below the waterline to help mitigate neutron detection. The container itself is mostly shielding of various kinds to limit scanning. In fairness, though, this will never make it through a normal port security scan," Amin cautioned.

"It won't have to - I have something different in mind for this. Our patron will have to be satisfied with our alternate plan. I'm still unhappy he placed it upon us unasked, and will find some way to express my displeasure at some point. Here, let me explain what I am thinking."

The Hammer spoke quietly for several minutes and afterwards Amin shook his head in admiration. "This will make the security of America almost impossible to maintain and, by itself, will eclipse the twin towers."

"Yes, it might even kill an industry in one blow. How many security personnel are we deploying to the container ship?"

"Ten, with a full complement of weapons. The cover story is pirate security when passing Somalia. They will stay aboard and return with the ship. If pirates do show up, they will provide some target practice," Amin laughed.

"Did you engage these gentlemen through cut-outs? It may be that this detail becomes doomed at some point. Especially if they are unwise enough to open the container. The triggering system should be connected to the ship WiFi for remote activation, or at a minimum for GPS. How is it secured against the security team?" The Hammer asked.

"No cut-outs other than the Sabir identity, which can be retired if necessary afterwards. The container is welded shut, but there is also a signaling relay built in to notify the controller when an attempt to open it is being made via satellite link. The controller would then call the ship's captain via satphone and ask to speak to the offending party. They shouldn't be so stupid as to ignore the message, especially since the anti-tamper provisions would kick in and detonate. I also promised them a completion bonus equal to the entire fee, so hopefully greed will triumph over curiosity," Amin said.

"That sounds like an excellent plan. When does the cargo transfer to the freighter take place?"

"End of next week. From the pickup off of the coast of Oman, it will take another 14 days for the freighter to get to the Atlantic. The cargo should be off the USA coast about 10 days after the freighter clears Gibraltar. So, about four weeks from today we'll have it in hand," Amin said.

"Perfect, the Americans will be crazed from our other two actions when this hits. It might well push the country into martial law, which would be a huge win for our cause. Then they, too, can see what living under military rule is like. I'll check in with you in a couple of days. We'll choose the second city tomorrow. Do you have enough support to monitor all of this?"

"Not really, but we don't have time to properly recruit new people that can be trusted. We can get it done, the project is laid out and we just have to follow up with the players," Amin said.

They turned off the lights and checked the street prior to exiting the house. As they walked together towards the Metro station, two young black men fell in behind them. The Hammer and Amin eyed each other and kept walking at a calm pace, until they came upon a service alley between two buildings. Quickly, both ran into the alley. Amin peeled off behind a dumpster and stopped. The Hammer kept running down the alley noisily. The two thugs ran right past Amin after The Hammer, who tripped on a piece of debris and fell to the ground.

"Yo, boy! Hand over your wallet or we'll fuck you up!"

The Hammer stood, "Boy, you say? Why should I give you anything?"

"Because if you don't, I'll cut you," The young, tattooed street thug said as he produced a switchblade, waving it slowly back and forth.

"But, I have a knife as well. If you leave now, I'll give you your life and your mother won't have to cry over your body tomorrow," The Hammer produced a small short knife with a wide blade.

"Tyrese, shoot this fucker and let's jam."

Tyrese drew a small handgun and as he pointed it at The Hammer, Amin shot him through the back of the head. The second thug turned to face Amin's gun, and The Hammer deftly cut his throat from behind. The thug stared at the blood spurting uncontrollably out, trying to stop the flow, until his brain finally fell silent. The Hammer wiped his blade on the back of the thug's boxer underwear. Amin had secured the pistol already.

"This safe house is blown. Add the gun to our arsenal. Let's go," The Hammer said.

They left the bodies where they lay.

The Hammer felt invigorated by the night's news as well as the closing act. He hadn't had a chance to personally kill anyone in some time, and even relentless practice was never quite the same thing. His blood zinged through his body in anticipation of tomorrow night, when more blood would be shed and the Martyrs al-Sabra would be heard once more.

• • •

The President of the United States entered the family quarters of the White House. She had her own suite, as did her husband. Lucy Brown hadn't slept in the same bed as her husband ever since his disgrace as Governor, almost twenty years earlier. Their relationship was one of mutual respect and friendship, but never romantic love. Sometimes Lucy missed that part of her marriage, but never to the extent that she considered finding someone else or reaching out to Jonny Ray. She knew that Jonny Ray continued to philander, but didn't really expect him to do otherwise since she would not open that part of her life to him. She was still deeply fond of him, though, and cared for his happiness.

She approached the Secret Service agent stationed outside of Jonny Ray's suite, "Hello, is Jonny Ray available?"

"Of course, Madame President. I will announce you," He entered the suite and a few seconds later opened the door.

Lucy went into a suite that was a bit smaller than her own, but very spacious regardless. Jonny Ray was sitting in golf clothes on a couch watching a college basketball game. As she came in, he turned it off and waited.

"Jonny Ray, how are you settling in?" Lucy asked.

"Well, Darlin', this is a long ways from Missouri but it does grow on you. The food in this house is excellent, and all the drinks are top-shelf.

What's not to like?" Jonny Ray said, and paused. "Come on, Girl, what's on your mind?"

"Jonny Ray, we agreed you wouldn't perform all of the traditional presidential spouse engagements. I wanted to ask if you are interested in a role doing some other things instead?" Lucy asked.

"I guess it depends on what it is. My life is pretty sweet right now. What are you thinking?"

"Well, as you know, we need to maintain a national view of things. There are a number of races in progress that could use someone like you to raise funds, help candidates lacking in charisma, and represent my administration," Lucy said.

"After all, who is closer to the president than her husband, right?" Jonny Ray said with a touch of bitterness. His large blue eyes stared into hers, letting her see his longing.

Lucy straightened. "Jonny, this ground has been well-covered for years. We, together, made the decision that our partnership was more than just a marriage long ago. We both had something to offer the other that would be hard to replace."

"Yes, but still it would be nice to know you cared about more than that," Jonny Ray said.

Lucy was silent for a moment, "I care, Jonny Ray, I always have. But things being what they are, what would be the benefit of dwelling upon that?"

"I don't know what's worse: being completely out of a relationship or still in it without any of the feelings that normally accompany one. I still struggle with that, every day, Luce. Make no mistake, I am very comfortable where I am, but sometimes it feels like it isn't enough."

"What there is, is all there is. I'm sorry, truly. Are you willing to consider helping some of our less fortunate cousins to succeed?" Lucy asked.

"Sure, as long as I am spending most of my time here. If that is the case, then I am fine with it, and will enjoy helping the charisma-challenged into office," Jonny said.

"That would be great! I'll ask Sid to put a plan together with you tomorrow. Thank you, Jonny Ray, I really appreciate your contribution. I'll let you get back to your game."

"My pleasure, Madame President," Jonny Ray said as he switched the game back on, refusing to watch her walk away again.

• • •

Quinton Jameson's injuries had faded to mere memory, but his pride continued to feel the sting of having lost his service weapon and badge to what still appeared to be a random street thug. The entire incident would reflect badly upon him when it came time for a promotion, especially the fact that he was alone while interviewing a subject. Unless an agent was undercover, FBI agents never did anything alone, specifically to avoid outcomes similar to what he had experienced. His thin excuse, manpower was tight and the threat level justified his action, was barely sufficient.

The Bureau hadn't made much more progress on The Hammer task force, but in a few minutes he had a meeting with Justin Simons to discuss findings on the Martyrs al-Sabra incident and Adeeb Kaldah's role within it. Quinton still thought there was a connection here somewhere, Nayla had something to hide, even though her actions were simply those of any seasoned lawyer. Getting up from behind his desk, Quinton grabbed his notebook and headed for the small conference room to meet with Justin and the team.

Justin was setting up his laptop to present slides to the gathering group. After everyone settled in, he dimmed the lights and displayed the cover slide entitled "Martyrs al-Sabra".

"Good morning. Last week, Section Chief Jameson determined that The Hammer and The Martyrs al-Sabra incident might be linked in some fashion. Since then, we have learned a few things about the latter, mostly from our colleagues in Israel. The incident was the result of a conflict between two wealthy families in Gaza City: the Kaldahs and the Obeidats. If you recognize the name Kaldah, remember Nayla Kaldah is one of our Hammer interview subjects. In fact, cutting to the chase, the entire conflict was started due to one Mustafa Obeidat's lust for young Nayla Kaldah," Justin said.

"Are you saying Nayla was the reason for the incident?" Quinton broke in excitedly.

"No, sir. If anyone was responsible it was Mustafa Obeidat. I'll start at the beginning. One day in 2006, while Dr. Kaldah and his wife oversaw their daily business, an Israeli aircraft dropped a bomb on their home and offices completely destroying the building. Young Nayla and her brother Adeeb were at the market when it happened. Nayla was 17 and Adeeb almost 16 years old. The elder Kaldahs were close to the Fatah leadership, so Fatah stepped in to help the orphans. They gave Adeeb a job within the Brigades, think soldier/police/tax-collector, and Nayla managed their household on Adeeb's small income. The Kaldahs were moderately wealthy, but most of their wealth was offshore. Fatah helped Nayla and Adeeb with identity papers and to recover the stranded cash from the various jurisdictions involved. The problem started when Mustafa saw Nayla at the market. Mustafa Obeidat was a youngest son in a large Palestinian trading family which had relocated from Jordan. Evidently, he wasn't the sharpest tool in their box, so the family set him up within the Hamas brigades. Mustafa followed her home and started to harass the family, who he perceived as being poor and without influence. Mustafa formally asked Adeeb, as head of the family, to marry Nayla. Adeeb refused, respectfully by all accounts. Nayla refused marriage as her plan was to attend university once their funds were available," Justin said.

"It could have ended there, but Mustafa and his mother then started a rumor that Nayla had used her body sexually to trick him into a marriage, which he rightly refused after first enjoying her charms. In Gaza, it was tantamount to ruining her life. She couldn't go out in public without being shamed and bullied. In the meantime, Fatah had come through with access to the Kaldah millions, so the family now was powerful again. Nayla went to France and university, while Adeeb apparently plotted his revenge on Mustafa. Adeeb hired a group of Brigade comrades to assist his takedown of Mustafa. Somehow, it all went wrong. The problem, which Adeeb and his team evidently did not know, was that Hamas had been using the building for an armory as well as an elementary school. The school was on the upper floors. The firefight that ensued between the factions spilled over into the building, and an RPG set off the munitions stores. All 23 of the school children perished in the resulting inferno, they are "The Martyrs al-Sabra". Fifteen to twenty additional fighters perished as well. Mustafa died and his body was found. Adeeb was presumed to have died, but his body was not found," Justin explained.

"Do we have any data that suggests he might have survived?" Jameson asked.

"Yes, the Israelis provided some information. Evidently, elements within Fatah made arrangements for forged identity papers and smuggled him onto a passing Greek flag freighter at sea. They then declared Adeeb Kaldah dead. Much of the source material for it is unreliable however, due to the civil war between Hamas and Fatah which broke out later that year. Fatah wound up on the losing side in Gaza and much of their records were destroyed," Justin said.

"Did we have any luck with tracking the freighter?" Jameson asked.

"Yes, we were able to get copies of cargo and crew manifests from the ship, but there were no Palestinians aboard. Everyone had Greek papers. In order for it to work, Adeeb would have to pass as Greek. Given how beautiful Nayla is, Adeeb was probably quite handsome. There was also a reference to Adeeb speaking Greek as part of his language studies in school. If he escaped, he is now a Greek national," Justin said.

"Once in Greece though, he could recast his identity in a number of ways, couldn't he?" Jameson asked.

"Absolutely. In effect, he could go anywhere within the European Union. Given his physical appearance, he could pass as any of the darker complexion nationalities. There is one thing more, which is strictly top secret and for this room only. My Israeli contact provided one piece of incendiary information, if it is true. The Kaldah elders were Israeli informants for more than twenty years," Justin said.

"That seems unlikely, given that the Israelis bombed their home," Jameson said.

"Yes, sir. I mentioned that to my contact. He said, first, the bomber missed their actual target, and second, the Israeli military isn't always aware of the deep-cover Mossad operatives for obvious security reasons. He said when the bombing took place, the Mossad threw an internal tantrum worthy of note as it eliminated one of their best first-hand views into Fatah operations," Justin said.

"What the fuck! Is Nayla an Israeli operative?" Jameson asked.

"My contact denied it, which means very little. He did say that Mossad had plans to bring both Nayla and Adeeb into the fold, but all of this happened before they got the chance. But I also wonder why they are telling us now," Justin said.

"Everyone but Justin, clear the room. Thank you for your hard work looking into this. We'll reschedule as there is more to share," Jameson ordered. The larger group filed out and went back to their work stations.

"Justin, I have another piece of data to share that doesn't go beyond this room. Nayla is currently having an affair with Jonny Ray Brown, they meet at an apartment over in Georgetown. I learned it from Jonny Ray's Secret Service detail," Jameson said.

Justin sat down in shock. "I've known Nayla for years, somehow I never saw her doing something like that, are you sure?"

"Absolutely. Jonny Ray used to ditch his detail in order to meet her, but evidently that has now changed to where the detail works with him and maintains their security. But the possibility that she might be an Israeli agent turns this into something considerably more serious. In fact, I think we should place her under surveillance around the clock," Jameson said.

"Are we going to coordinate with Secret Service? They'll want to close it down as a potential security risk," Justin said.

"And rightly so, if she is in fact a security risk. The Secret Service head of detail told me that Jonny Ray doesn't have much of a security clearance at all and isn't briefed on national security matters. His view was that the affair didn't involve much risk in terms of national security. The danger here is political," Jameson said.

"Are we in danger here of going down a bit of a dirt road? I mean, The Hammer was known in 2005, so what we're finding here with Nayla may not be related to him at all, right?" Justin mused.

"I have a feeling that they are related somehow, but I am missing a few key pieces of information needed to prove it. Nayla will not be amenable to a casual interview again, and, as far as we know, she hasn't broken any laws so we have little leverage. If she is lawyered up, we have zero chance of getting her to inadvertently give us the information we are looking for. No one will thank us for outing Jonny Ray's affair either. I'm going to order surveillance of her phones, Internet, and bug her apartment. I'm not going to include the love nest, I'm not bugging the President's husband," Jameson said.

"This is quite a tightrope we're walking. How are we going to handle it operationally?" Justin asked.

"For now, the only people who know the whole story will be you and me. I'll order the surveillance on Nayla, which the greater team will monitor. The apartment will be excluded from the orders. How are we coming on the remaining interview subjects from November?" Jameson said.

"They are complete, as of last week. There were 27 persons of Muslim faith, and about the same number of those from Middle East but not Muslim. None of them fit the profile for The Hammer."

"I still say your friend Farid would fit the profile, if he hadn't grown up in the United States," Jameson said.

"He's a television network reporter, much too conspicuous for the reclusive Hammer. Plus, he continues to help us whenever we ask. He, like anyone else, cannot prove a negative. On the topic of The Hammer, I was speaking to a tech guy from Telecom Row on Dulles, he told me that mobile tower GPS headers can be forged if someone knows what they are doing. His point was that the call may not have originated at the Gaylord Resort at all. If I were a terrorist, having the FBI get all spun up investigating the wrong site, which happens to be a national security location, would definitely be amusing ," Justin said.

"Is there any way we can check the theory?"

"I already ran it by the NSA technician who provided the original site marker information, and he agreed that it was indeed possible to be spoofed. The telecom back office SS7 systems weren't originally designed for IP security, and once the call record circuit markers are recorded there is no way to retroactively validate that they are correct. He said that the skill set was fairly rare, however in the DC area alone there are about a hundred telecom engineers who could do it easily," Justin said.

"OK. Let's just hope something breaks on the Nayla front. Keep me up to speed, Justin."

"I will." Justin headed back to his desk, shaking his head at the thought that his friend Farid might be seriously hurt by Nayla's dalliance. Justin had always thought the two would eventually marry, but that notion was turned on its head by the Secret Service information. There was no legal way to let Farid know about it, though, and Justin knew he would just have to be supportive if the situation went public on its own. He couldn't even tell Jan. He didn't really think Nayla was an Israeli agent, as there would be no reason for his Israeli contact to have mentioned it. The fact he did suggested that the involvement of the Kaldah family was at an end, the past facts being diminished to merely an interesting anecdote. He sighed to himself, "Onward and upward."

• • •

In a small room at a local bank branch in Roseville, Munir opened his safety deposit box and, removed one of the special rounds, placing it in the bottom of the file portfolio he had brought with him. He placed some business papers on top of the remaining rounds and reclosed the box. Carrying it from the room, he found the bank clerk and signaled he was ready to put it back.

"That was quick, sir! Was everything in order?" The clerk asked.

"Yes, thank you. I get paranoid if I don't refresh my data backups every now and then," Munir said with a quick smile.

"I know what you mean. Having backups at home or work doesn't help if someone steals everything. I have to do mine, too, but I keep forgetting. Here we go," the clerk said, sliding the box back into its slot. "Is there anything else I can do for you today?"

"No, all good. Thanks and have a great day!" Munir repeated the meaningless words which were printed on the California entry card when people moved to the Golden State. Soon, different people would be smiling, after tomorrow night.

• • •

The Crusaders for Truth met again that evening in the capital city of the Elves. Again the circle formed and the three officers danced for the guild. Redonkulus pointed at Chunkmate, who acknowledged with his own dance. Redonkulus hopped twice, then Chunkmate did the same. The message was passed, and after some additional virtual merriment, the gathering broke up.

Chunkmate was the virtual identity of Khaled Hussein, a home and commercial painter from Sandy Springs, Georgia. Khaled was a self-employed contract laborer who worked with local construction companies in the Atlanta metro area. He lived alone, in bitterness, as his wife of many years had divorced him, taking half of the assets they had accumulated together. She had become American, so much so that she could completely disregard the man who had fed her and their children by the sweat of his hard labor. The children wanted nothing to do with him. His parents were long dead, they had arranged for his last marriage in Libya, and he had no idea how to go about finding a new companion. So he spent his surplus money on black prostitutes and hated America even as he smiled his way through each working day. The Martyrs operation was a gift for Khaled, it gave him purpose and an outlet for his hate.

Atlanta should prove easy for this type of operation. The city was wide-ranging with dense foliage all around. Similar to Munir's process, Khaled had scouted several locations but the one he kept coming back to was the Mt. Zion Christian School on Old Stone Mountain Road in Stone Mountain. The site was surrounded by woods which backed into a fire access road, which led to a GroceryCo Supercenter parking lot. He could set up in the woods next to the baseball diamond, on a school day, and shoot a teacher or student. It didn't matter which. Khaled felt it was an appropriate choice, given that the real Martyrs al-Sabra were Muslim school children. Shooting a child would prove a harder shot than a teacher, but Khaled had proven to be an excellent shot, taking two deer at the hunt camp. There were no innocents at the school, after all they proudly proclaimed their infidel status with the name of the institution. A daytime shoot would be more dangerous, but the school wasn't scheduled to have any evening events during the next two days. No, the infidel would recognize their danger with Khaled's shot. No one was safe. He still had a full day left for planning, but didn't expect to need it.

• • •

Munir, in Roseville, was getting ready for his action later that evening. As he spent the day performing routine dental exams and repairing fillings, he dreamed of the engraved 30-06 cartridge waiting in his car, ready for use. The honor of striking the first blow was overwhelming to him. His patients that day noticed the doctor seemed more distracted or less friendly than normal, but very careful in their mouth, which is all any dental patient really cares about. Already Munir was focused on the minutia of the tasks before him and determined to make no mistakes. He wasn't the best shot of the group, but he was consistent and dependable. Those traits had served him well when it became clear that he wasn't academically suited to practice medicine and made the transition to a focus on dentistry instead.

He closed the office just after 5 p.m. as usual and headed home for dinner. His wife had gone to visit a family friend and left his dinner in the refrigerator, ready for reheating in the microwave. Her absence worked well with his plans. As darkness fell, he donned his dark clothes: dull black jeans and dark grey long-sleeved shirt. His hiking shoes had also been blacked out with a Sharpie pen, so that the reflective surfaces were no longer apparent. Munir had splurged on a pair of night vision goggles, but had not had a chance to test them so they were not going tonight. He turned off the light in his bedroom and in the dark looked at himself in the mirror for any shiny surfaces he might have missed. He smiled, and could see the white flash as his eyes adjusted to the dark. *Have to be sure I don't smile tonight*, he thought to himself, *because a dentist has to have blazing white teeth but a sniper not so much.* On his wrist was a dull black sports watch he would use to time the operation.

Going out into the garage, he checked his car license plate cover was in place. It was one of those which presumably was designed to protect the license plate, but actually obscured visibility from most automated imaging cameras and casual police interest. In California, it paid to use these, especially as more and more traffic lights were set to issue traffic citations automatically. The Home Helper parking lot had video cameras, but not nearly enough to get a clear picture of every parking spot. Looking outside, it was full dark and time to begin.

Opening the trunk, he double checked the hunting rifle was safely enveloped in its black nylon case. He placed the single cartridge in his left pants pocket. Everything checked out - it was time to begin.

Munir closed the trunk and got into the driver's seat, triggering the garage door opener. Backing out of his driveway, he reclosed it and drove sedately out of his neighborhood.

Pulling into the Home Helper driveway, he looked around for the activity level in the parking lot. As usual, the number of after-work customers had fallen off a bit as everyone headed home for dinner. Pulling over to the same section of the parking lot, Munir backed into the parking space with the trunk facing the trees, just as he had before. Opening his window, he turned off the car lights and engine. Sitting there as though he was waiting for someone else, he watched people coming in and out of the store, waiting for an opportunity when no one was looking his way. A moment presented itself, Munir popped the trunk and got out of the car in one smooth move. Taking the rifle case, he closed the trunk softly so it wouldn't latch and stepped into the trees.

Once there, he stood still looking around for any indication he'd been noticed at the Home Helper and to let his eyes further adjust to the dark. He had picked the perfect moment. Munir took the rifle out of the bag and slung it onto his shoulder. Stowing the bag behind a tree near his car, he began slowly picking his way through the scrub of the field towards the lights of the nearby FoodCo Foods store. As he approached the tree line of the parking lot, he slowed his pace further to take in his new surroundings. Munir planned to shoot a target close to the store entrance, and he wanted to be sure there was no one close to his position when he took the shot.

No one was parked nearby, or out for a smoke. Munir headed for the spot he had picked before, nestled between three small trees, and laid down in a prone shooting position. He could smell the damp earth and pine tar under the bed of pine needles. Putting on a pair of huntsman gloves, he took out the cartridge and polished it to eliminate any of his latent fingerprints. Drawing back the bolt-action lever, he slid the single cartridge into the firing chamber, and slid the lever home. Uncapping the scope lens covers, he began to look for a potential victim. Since this was a supermarket, there were many mothers and small children. But Munir had it in his mind that the first target should be a large, slow-moving man, so his marksmanship would be sufficient to the task. It could be an obese woman too, he supposed, the key was having enough time to aim and fire. Some of the people seemed like they were in a hurry and walked quickly toward the store doors; he disregarded them.

Finally, Munir saw an obese woman getting out of her car parked in a handicapped slot. Barely able to walk, she looked like every grotesque caricature of trailer park trash. Her pendulous buttocks stretched a pair of pink sweat pants to their limit, she was emblematic of everything Munir hated about Americans. She was even snacking on her way into the store. Munir centered her on the scope then adjusted to the leading edge of her body in the direction she was moving. As he had been taught, he took a deep breath and exhaled slowly until the end of the breath when his body was absolutely still. Then, squeezing the trigger, he took the shot and the target went down.

Without waiting to see the result through the scope, Munir operated the bolt action to eject the cartridge, which flew out of the chamber with a puff of gunpowder gas, making sure not to touch it as it hit the ground. Fighting the urge to run, Munir activated his stopwatch and backed up further into the field. Then, rising from the ground, he headed back the way he had come to the Home Helper parking lot. Not running took all his willpower, but he concentrated on maintaining a fast walking speed, making as little noise as possible. Behind him, he could hear shouts of alarm in the now-distant parking lot, but no sounds of pursuit.

• • •

"Help, somebody! This woman has been shot. Call 911!" Jim Simpson had heard a shot from somewhere and thought *deer rifle* before seeing the woman crumple up and fall to the ground. He ran to her side and looked over the damage. She was lying on her side with her hands covering a spot on her lower stomach. Jim reached across to see if he could turn her over on her back, when his hand encountered a large wet spot on her back. Thinking better of turning her, he took off his t-shirt, bundled it up and held it against the wet place on her back. *Entrance wound*, he thought. He told her over and over help was on its way and to hold on. Her family would want her to hold on. He knew that if she died, it was better if she knew someone was there and trying to help.

A crowd had assembled, but so far no one could say whether an ambulance had actually been summoned. Jim had seen enough combat wounds during his tours in the Middle East that he wasn't shocked into immobility. Taking his smartphone into his left hand, he called 911 himself. One of the onlookers handed over their own t-shirt for the exit wound. After the 911 operator assured him that help was on the way, he went back to talking softly to her, words of encouragement, hope, and motivation - the words running together like an endless tape loop.

Finally, sirens sounded in the distance. A police officer tapped his shoulder, saying he would take it from here and not to go anywhere as they would need to speak with him. Jim nodded and sat down a few paces away, shirtless, with drying blood covering both of his hands. The crowd murmured and asked endless questions of each other. Jim knew he wouldn't be home for some time, so he called his ex-wife to tell her he would not be picking up his son this evening. She wasn't sympathetic, but Jim knew the news tomorrow would make her feel terrible so he didn't rise to the bait. He settled in and waited to be debriefed.

• • •

Munir drove slowly through the parking lot until he was able to turn right on Fairway Drive. He stopped his watch then and checked the time. It had taken a little more than three minutes from the shot to exiting onto a main street. Next time he would try to improve.

Munir turned on a local radio station to listen for news, but it was slow in coming. He was able to travel all the way home without any mention of the shooting. He parked his car in the garage, took off the grey shirt and replaced it with a short sleeve polo before going into his home. The gun, gloves, and dark shirt remained in the car trunk.

His wife still wasn't there, so he took a long, hot shower and put on a change of clothes. Munir was in a manic frame of mind, elated but keeping a lid on his glee as practice for the next few days. Earlier, he had worried that the taking of a life might be traumatic for him, but his experience was anything but that. He felt powerful, for the first time, in this country of infidels. As he had been trained, he worked through the list of things to do in order to cover his tracks. Leaving the television tuned to a local channel, he finally heard some news about the shooting.

"Police in Roseville report a shooting in a local supermarket parking lot. A woman was shot and remains in critical condition. Police have no comment on the details of the incident, but sources confirm a rifle was involved. We'll provide more detail as the story develops."

So, the woman wasn't immediately killed, Munir thought to himself. *I'll log into the game and see if there is any information to be had.* Munir logged into his character Sullnpsych, and an immediate notice popped up informing him of waiting mail. Sullnpsych went to a nearby mailbox and opened the mail interface. Waiting was an email from Redonkulus, the guildmaster. Sullnpsych opened the message, *Congratulations! An excellent beginning!* Attached to the email was 50,000 units of game currency. Munir was more elated than before! The Hammer approved of his work, and he could buy that new armor set he'd had his eye on. As guild members began to come online, they would pop messages congratulating Sullnpsych without any details of why. Munir continued playing the game until late in the night when at last his nervous energy ran out and then he slept like a tired child.

The next morning, the news confirmed the woman had died following emergency surgery. She was the mother of three teenage children, living in a local apartment. The Roseville Police put out a plea for anyone seeing anything unusual that evening to call into their tip line.

Munir was surprised how easy it was to get back into his genial dentist character for his customers. He found he enjoyed his work much more having a secret which would paralyze his patients with fear, if only they knew.

• • •

Sergeant Smith of the Roseville Police Department had a quandary. Roseville PD didn't get many homicide cases, on average it was less than two a year. And most of those were easily-solved: husbands or wives shooting each other. Roseville PD staffing was aimed at lower intensity crimes, unlike the neighboring state capital of Sacramento. On the one hand, all police departments like to keep their jurisdictional integrity when at all possible, but on the other hand they simply didn't have the staff and resources to support a murder investigation which wasn't clear cut.

This one was a puzzle. The victim, Lorie Lampson, didn't have any immediately obvious reason why someone would want to kill her. Her husband was long gone, and there were no simmering disputes. Furthermore, the shooting had been done with a 30-06 deer rifle round. Most crimes of passion involved handguns since the perpetrator usually wants the victim to know who is trying to kill them. In this case, the victim wouldn't have had a clue until the bullet entered their body. The Good Samaritan, Jim Simpson, hadn't been able to point to where the shot originated, he had just heard it and saw Lorie fall to the pavement. He did say it was a deer rifle, though. That information, along with the angle of her fall, indicated the shooter had hidden in the wooded area next to the parking lot.

Only one shell casing had been recovered on the ground just inside the tree line, early in the first light of morning. The casing had no latent fingerprints, but there was a strange engraving that looked like an Arabic script. The shooter had lain there on the ground to take the shot, but the entire area had been watered by an automatic sprinkler system overnight, leaving it a forensic mess. Sergeant Smith was still pissed off at the crime scene officers for not thinking to deactivate all automated sprinkler systems immediately after establishing control of the scene.

Sergeant Smith, like all California police officers, was also very sensitive about labeling something a hate crime or immediately deciding there was an Islamic connection. All major crimes involving any minorities of color were now legal minefields. The situation, if applicable, would have to be handled very delicately. Like many California communities, a small but vocal Islamic presence had been growing steadily in Roseville over recent years. Luckily, the police chief himself would be hands-on for that part of the investigation and doubtless would handle the politically-charged press relations.

Sergeant Smith had dispatched one of his detectives, armed with a picture of the shell casing, to a local mosque in order to get a translation of the engraving. This was going to be a very long day.

"Sergeant? I just spoke to the Imam at the mosque. You're not going to believe this, but the engraving says *Martyrs al-Sabra*. He was very shocked to see it on a rifle shell casing, and said the name itself corresponds to a famous worldwide Islamic charity to benefit orphans. In fact, he said the charity collects change from those collection boxes at convenience stores owned by Muslims all over the world."

"Thanks, I have a feeling that this is about to get a whole lot worse. Please check the evidence chain of custody on the shell casing and make double sure that it remains secure. There will probably be a number of people substantially above our pay grade who are going to want to see it," Sergeant Smith said in resignation.

As Roseville's finest continued the frustrating search for evidence on their biggest crime of the decade, events were in progress which would soon render Sergeant Smith's concerns moot.

One of the wonderful things that grew out of the events of 9/11, was police department reports were increasingly electronic and available to national law enforcement agencies almost as soon as they were filed. In truth, there was a several day delay before they were available, to allow the Big Data warehousing systems to index the newly-entered records into a searchable format. Other agencies, such as the FBI, could create scripts that would monitor key words and phrases for nationwide visibility into areas of interest. Thanks to the efforts of Section Chief Jameson and his Hammer team, one of the key phrases being searched was *Martyrs al-Sabra* in many iterations. But it would not be flagged immediately, and, by then, other events would be added to the fire.

• • •

Khaled watched the children stream from the school as the bell rang. He'd been observing the routines of the Christian school all day from the cover of nearby woods. Every 90 minutes or so, a large group of students would flood the playground. Each time, they stuck close to the basketball court or jungle gym, and had only fifteen minutes of recreation. It would be a longer shot, but it might be his best chance. Khaled knew his shot would very likely be the one to drive awareness of the operation to the national level, so he was determined to make a large impact. He kept coming back to the idea of targeting a young girl. It would be a much more difficult target, in terms of size, but Americans have a huge regard for the safety of their daughters and would feel the loss even more keenly. The lesson was that there would be no safety for the infidel.

Just as he was preparing to leave, Khaled saw an adult carrying a kit bag headed for the baseball diamond. The man appeared to be preparing for the afternoon school baseball team practice. He was a large man, which wasn't Khaled's preference, but could prove to be an alternate choice. Practicing his extrication, Khaled backed out of his makeshift blind and walked back to the GroceryCo parking lot. Khaled then got in his car and headed for the bank, where he had a cartridge to retrieve.

Khaled's mirror had observed Khaled's preparations with approval, and sent a text to Sabir that things appeared to be go for the next day. It would be a long 24 hours for the mirror, as he would only get to sleep when reasonably certain that Khaled was asleep as well.

• • •

In Washington, DC the first notice of *Martyrs al-Sabra* reference in the Roseville shooting made its way into a FBI analyst's review queue. So far, the Hammer task force analysts hadn't come up with much on the search terms provided by Justin and the team but wading through gross tons of information was what they did well. There were many references to The Martyrs al-Sabra international charity effort. Since Farid Royce was on their Board of Directors, the combination had produced thousands of references. Weeding out the false positives would take time and effort. The best analysts, however, kept a reasonable work-life balance. It enabled them to be fully alert and not miss a needle in the haystack when it presented itself. In this case, it also meant that the Roseville reference wouldn't be spotted until the next day, as the assigned analyst was headed to his son's soccer practice directly after his shift.

The FBI slept one more night in blissful ignorance of the unfolding terrorist operation. Justin Simons had plans as well, hoping he would be able to get to Becky's soccer game. Usually, he couldn't get to Algonkian Regional Park before the games started, but tonight he had high hopes to catch most of it. Becky's game was second on the lineup, so there was a good chance. Justin wasn't the only parent to show up in work clothes, and soccer was a big deal in Potomac Falls. Jan would have a cooler full of juice boxes, plus a few adult beverages to be parceled out cautiously. Striding up to the sidelines of the soccer pitch, he saw Becky playing mid-field. She waved with a big smile when she saw Justin, and he waved as well, then gestured that she should get back in the game.

Sitting down in the camp chair that Jan had deployed, "Hi Honey, how's she doing?"

"Pretty good, there is a bigger girl on the other team picking on her, but she is working around it. How was traffic?" Jan said as she handed Justin a beer wrapped in a concealing cozy.

"Well it got me here pretty quick so not too bad. That girl ought to be careful, I'm pretty sure Becky will be growing quite a bit in the next few years, and I doubt she will be forgetting any injustices on the soccer field," Justin laughed.

Just then, Justin's phone rang. It was Jameson. "Jan, I need to get this, the boss," Justin said as he walked a few feet away and answered the phone, "Justin Simons."

"Justin, Jameson here. Have we gotten anywhere on the surveillance on Nayla or with the analysts?"

"Nothing significant since we spoke two days ago, but on the surveillance the data is beginning to trickle in and people are being assigned to investigate new branches on our investigation tree. The analysts are getting a lot of hits on the charity, which clouds the issue significantly. Farid's involvement with them appears innocent, he was a major founding donor, and shows up at many of their fundraising functions," Justin said.

"Do we have any visibility into the charity and where the money goes? It struck me that a charity would be an excellent way to hide terrorist funding, especially an international charity," Jameson said.

"We're looking into it. We can see what is happening in the USA, but a lot of this charity's work is done overseas and we'd don't have a good view of that. We do see a line item of the money spent overseas in their form 990s, but no detail breakdowns. We could ask, but that would tip our hand," Justin said.

"If nothing breaks soon, I am thinking we up the pressure on some of our key subjects. Those include Farid and Nayla, but Nayla in particular," Jameson said.

"Didn't Nayla decide to lawyer-up for any new rounds of discussion?" Justin asked.

"Yes, she did. However, we can still ask some very intrusive questions, which she won't answer but she'll get an idea of what we suspect, which could increase the pressure on her. If she has anything to hide, she might break cover afterwards and surveillance could then catch it."

"Dangerous, but it might work. So do we start looking at that tomorrow?" Justin asked.

"Yes, let's reconvene tomorrow morning and see where we are. I'll see you then," Jameson hung up.

Justin returned the phone to his pocket and sat back down in his chair. "Where was I?, Oh yes, I was about to polish off this beverage," Justin picked up his beer and drained it. The small amount of alcohol nonetheless provided a pleasant buzz in his empty stomach, which felt good given the stress this investigation had stirred up.

"Trouble at work?" Jan asked with her eyes on Becky's play.

"Nothing more than the usual. Chasing bad guys who don't want us to find them. Why can't they make more mistakes? It would make my job so much easier," Justin said with a smile. He reached over and took possession of Jan's hand. The trees were just beginning to bud with new leaves and the air was still crisp: Northern Virginia at its finest. Together they sat contentedly watching their daughter dominate the soccer midfield.

· · ·

The next morning, Khaled put together a small backpack with water and snackbars, for his vigil in the woods. He didn't have to worry about insects very much, as the weather was just now starting to turn warmer. His biggest concern was the potential for rain which was in the forecast. He realized, belatedly, that he hadn't considered that factor when choosing a site for the attack. Specifically, he didn't have a fall-back location in the event of rain. Khaled knew that he didn't have time to waste now waiting for better weather, so he decided to remain on station in the woods until an opportunity presented itself.

Much like his colleague in California, Khaled took his time walking along the fire trail towards the Christian School. Passing motorists on Route 78 could have seen a glimpse of him, were they to look. There was one home whose backyard came dangerously close to the fire road, but Khaled took that section slow, working his way across. This was the most dangerous spot on his getaway route, and Khalid needed to take special care that he didn't panic and bolt through the area. Overnight, Khalid had realized that he could probably infiltrate another 100 yards and be able to shoot either the playground or baseball fields. Putting that plan into action, he worked his way slowly into the scrub at the corner of the playground and baseball field. He found a thick stand of brush and worked his way into the middle of it, positioning the rifle barrel towards the playground slide. He passed the time by adjusting his rifle scope, centered on the top of a complicated slide set for children. The children would be there on a platform waiting for their turn to go down one of several slides. That would be the optimal shot, if aimed correctly more than one child might be hit.

A distant bell sounded into the overcast morning, and children piled out of the school building heading for the playground. They were accompanied by a couple of adults who mostly watched the younger children. Khaled's heart rate increased as his moment of truth approached. Could he really shoot a child? Setting doubts aside, he whispered prayers to Allah as a means to sanctify his actions and calm his mind. The answer came to him quickly: these were not innocent children, they were infidels. Only Muslims could be reckoned as innocent in the gaze of the most high.

Looking through the scope, he watched as the young children grouped themselves on the slide platform, exactly as he'd expected. One little girl in particular drew his attention: long blonde hair, wearing a spring frock, and talking to her friends nonstop. This was the right target. Khaled settled in and aimed his shot. There was a boy with brown hair standing behind her in line, who was clearly smitten as he couldn't take his eyes off of his classmate. Khaled lined it up so the boy was in the same shot angle. A deep breath, slow exhale, squeezed trigger - the crack of a rifle shot in the crisp spring air.

Khaled cycled the spent cartridge shell onto the ground and began his escape.

• • •

Krysti Corbett watched in horror as she heard the rifle shot, which seemed to come from the woods, and then saw a spray of blood on the slide platform. Children started screaming, crying, and jumping off of the platform onto the sand pit underneath.

"Stacy, get the children back to the building, now!" Krysti screamed, as she struggled to gain access to the platform. *Please, Jesus, let the children be safe! Please, Jesus!* She prayed repetitively as she worked her way up to an area that was never meant for adults to enter. She saw a small body in a dress lying very still in a pool of blood, next to a hurt boy who was trying desperately to rouse the girl.

"Ms. Corbett, Jenni was shot. She won't wake up, I'm trying," Bennie Jacobs said in a panic.

"Bennie, you've been shot, too. Lie down now," Krysti said making sure he did. Taking out her mobile phone, Krysti called 911 and told them there was a shooting on the school playground. Jenni Cooper was in third grade and Bennie was in fourth. Krysti had some basic CPR training, as did all of the staff at the school, and quickly determined that Jenni didn't have a pulse. Taking a couple of seconds, she looked at Bennie's wound which was located about three inches above his right nipple. There was a fairly large entry wound which was leaking blood.

"Bennie, can you hold your hand over your chest here? Press here while you lay on your back. I'm going to try to wake up Jenni. Be brave, little man, help is on the way," Krysti said. She started in on CPR, fruitlessly repeating the chest compressions and mouth-to-mouth cycles. In the distance, numerous sirens were converging on the site. Krysti continued on until a male voice yelled from below.

"This is Officer Jeffreys of Stone Mountain Police force. What do you have there?"

"Thank, God! I have two children who were shot. I'm giving CPR to a girl but she isn't responding. The boy is conscious, and doing a good job holding his wound. Aren't you, Bennie? I'm Krysti Corbett, I work here at the school."

"Sit tight, ma'am, the paramedics are here, and will be up to help in a minute," Officer Jeffreys responded. Looking around the slide structure, Officer Jeffreys directed the paramedic team to an entrance ladder that was easiest for them to climb.

When the paramedics got to the top, one worked on Bennie and the other relieved Krysti. "Ma'am, can you operate the AMBU bag for me while I compress?" The paramedic cut Jenni's dress away, sucking in his breath as he saw the extent of the damage. He spoke into his radio using a series of code words, emphasizing the need for immediate transport. A small crowd of rescue responders were now gathered in the sand pit.

"Let's get the boy on a stretcher and out," The paramedic, with the help of a fireman, secured Bennie to a collapsible stretcher and lowered it down to the waiting hands of the others. Two firemen, ran to the ambulance carrying the stretcher between them.

Above, time was running out for Jenni. The second paramedic had placed bandages on both Jenni's entry and exit wounds, wrapping her torso in tape. A second stretcher was provided. Coordinating their movements, the paramedics stopped CPR for an instant, moving Jenni to the stretcher. One paramedic started CPR again, while the second secured her body to the stretcher.

"We have to get this one down fast, be ready," the lead paramedic said. "Now!" They paused the resuscitation efforts for the ten seconds it took to lower Jenni's stretcher to the ground. Again, two firefighters ran with the stretcher to the waiting ambulance. The paramedic grabbed one of the firemen to help continue resuscitation as the other paramedic drove. Sirens wailing, they sped out of the parking lot.

Krysti wanted to collapse, but there was still more to do. Parents had to be called, and she could tell that Officer Jeffreys wanted to speak with her. She realized that her hands and clothing were covered in blood, and she started looking for something to use as a hand cleaner.

Officer Jeffreys came over and handed her a package of wet-wipes. "Working with kids, you'd think I would always have these in my pocket, but no," Krysti said in a shaky voice.

"Krysti, I have to talk to you right now. The kids are being taken care of the best we can. Now we have to go after the person responsible. Please tell me what you saw happen," Officer Jeffreys said.

"I didn't see anything, but I heard a rifle shot, it sounded kind of like my Dad's deer rifle. I didn't see the children get hit either. I was watching kids come down the slides. The shot and the children's screams got my attention. I got up there as quickly as I could. I think she was dead when I got there, but I tried to bring her back."

"Krysti, you did great. Really, I mean that. Even if a doctor was right there, it would be hard with wounds like that. How many shots were there?" Officer Jeffreys asked.

"Just the one. I was afraid there would be more, but there weren't."

"Did you get an idea where the shot came from?"

"It sounded like it came from the woods behind the playground. It would have to be, Jenni was lying between Bennie and the woods. Bennie caught the same bullet after it went through Jenni, didn't he?" Krysti asked.

"Just a second, Krysti. Guys, we need to canvass the woods behind the playground, so tape it off. Get the forensics team here as soon as possible. Also, call dispatch and see if we can get Atlanta's FLIR helicopter unit out here ASAP, might be able to pick up the suspect's heat image in the woods. Krysti, when did the shot take place?"

"We came out at 10:30 a.m., it probably took a couple minutes to get over here from the school building. No more than five minutes after that," Krysti said.

"OK, it's 11:15 a.m. now, so the shooter has had a lot of time to get out of here. Krysti, did you hear the sound of any car engines leaving the area?"

"No, no more than the usual noise from Highway 78."

"Did you hear any dogs barking?" Officer Jeffreys asked.

"No, sir. There are houses between here and the GroceryCo, but the woods run all the way along the highway. There is a fire road there as well."

"Another moment, Krysti. Guys, we need to get someone over to the GroceryCo right away and request that the video footage of their parking lots be saved for our review. Tell them what happened, and that we'll get a warrant if necessary. Also, have a unit walk the fire road from the GroceryCo parking lot to here. Look for any signs that someone went through there in the last hour. Krysti, thanks for your help. One last question, who could we talk to at the school about possible parental grievances, disputes?" Officer Jeffreys asked.

"We haven't had any recent notifications, but the person who would know is Principal Perkins. He's right over there, and probably wants to talk to me, too," she said.

"Krysti, we still want you here until the forensics team can get samples, they are on their way. I'll speak to the Principal right now and tell him so. I'll also tell him what a heroic thing you did today. Try to sit down and catch your breath a bit."

The news had already started to spread throughout the town, doubtless from social media. The first television crew had already arrived and officers were enforcing a perimeter in the back half of the parking lot.

Officer Jeffreys walked over to the principal who was wringing his hands nervously. "Principal Perkins? My name is Officer Jeffreys, I need to speak with you for a few minutes."

"Certainly, Officer. How can I help?" This situation was something every school principal dreaded. Principal Perkins was a retired school teacher and administrator who had accepted the commission of his church to serve the school. Short, with thinning hair and comfortably middle-aged, Perkins looked as though he might need some emergency medical care himself before the day was over.

"Where are all the other school children right now?"

"We're keeping them in their classrooms at the moment, until their parents come to pick them up," Perkins said.

"Hold off on that. We need to identify the children who were potential witnesses and speak with them about the incident."

"What about the parents coming for their children?"

"We'd welcome the parents being in the room as we speak to each child. We're not going to interview all of them right now, but we do want to make a list of those who might have heard or seen something for later. We'll talk to the ones whose parents are here first, and clear them out as quickly as possible. Do you have a room we could use to speak with each of them?" Officer Jeffreys asked.

"Yes, we do. I can go get that set up now if you like," Principal Perkins said.

"Please. By the way, from what I can see, your Ms. Corbett handled herself very well. If either of those two children survive, it will be because of her quick thinking. I hope you and your staff are supportive, because she will be doubting herself and depressed - no escaping that."

"Thank you, I'll make sure of it. I expect we will have to be watchful for the children as well, it was a horrible thing to have experienced. We'll have to give it to Jesus, and pray for his strength."

Officer Jeffreys nodded and turned back to the crime scene. Thankfully, he saw Police Chief Edwards getting out of a cruiser with flashing lights and he headed over to brief the boss.

• • •

Khaled returned his rifle into its bag, zipped it up and slung the strap over his shoulder. He started walking briskly towards the highway and fire road. Behind him, Khaled could hear the screams and cries of the children. *Must have hit something then*, he thought to himself. Fear and elation fought for equal time in his mind. Gaining the fire road, he turned left towards the GroceryCo, staying on the right side of the path and decided that he should jog for a while. No one else was on the road with him, so he jogged a couple hundred yards and then slowed to a fast walk. The burst of effort had the effect of burning through his nervous energy and he was calm once more. Along the highway, trees and brush were fairly thick, and he planned to enter it for the approach to the parking lot, or if someone came along the road.

Khaled came upon the slight left turn that the fire road made as it approached GroceryCo. That was his cue to continue in a straight line, moving into the brush on the south side of GroceryCo's parking lot. He also slowed down and concentrated on being silent as he pushed through the brush. He could see the parking lot through the trees, and looked for his car. It wasn't anywhere in sight!

Starting to panic, Khaled realized there was now an 18 wheeler truck parked across the back row, which could be blocking the view of his car. Working his way past the truck facing him, while still in the woods, he did see his car behind the truck just as he had left it. Sirens could now be heard in the far distance, and time was of the essence. Khaled walked up to the edge of the woods, looking over at the back of the truck for any sign of the driver. Seeing no one on the truck or in the parking lot looking his way, Khaled stepped out from behind the tree, opened his trunk and stowed the rifle, gloves, and windbreaker. Without any sign of being in a hurry, he lit a cigarette then got into his car for departure. Rolling down his window, he smoked as he cruised the parking lot past the Hobby Lobby and made a right onto Rockbridge Road. The next right on Park Place Blvd allowed him to immediately enter Highway 78 West. As his passed the site where the school would be, he looked in vain for a sight of the scene, but the woods were too thick to even see the fire road, which Khaled took as a good sign.

He stayed on Highway 78 until exiting north on Highway 285 which took him all the way to Sandy Springs and home. Khaled found that he was very hungry and sat down to a large lunch while turning on the television to hear the news coverage begin.

At the GroceryCo, Khaled's mirror had watched from across the parking lot as Khaled made his getaway. Listening to a police scanner, he could tell that law enforcement would not be fast enough to catch Khaled. The mirror mentally applauded Khaled's plan and its execution. Taking out his mobile phone, he texted Amin the code words for success and received an acknowledgement. The mirror eased out of the parking lot as well, but headed south instead of north, on a roundabout track back to Khaled's home.

•••

"Sniper attacks Stone Mountain school children, one dead, one in critical condition. Police to make an informational announcement within the next thirty minutes."

Local Atlanta radio report which was picked up for national rebroadcast.

Justin had started his work-day going through the interview data once more to see if he had missed anything. A data analyst assigned to the task force came up and knocked on the wall of his cubicle.

"Sir, I think we have a legit hit on the Martyrs search terms. There was a sniper attack in the Sacramento, California area where a single round was fired at a woman in a supermarket parking lot, the 30-06 shell casing was left at the scene and had the words '*Martyrs al-Sabra*' in Arabic engraved on it."

Paying full attention now, Justin turned to the analyst "Good job! This might be really important. What else do we know about the case?"

"No suspect as of right now. Roseville PD is reviewing parking lot video coverage from a Home Helper which is separated from the supermarket by a wooded lot. The shooter was prone in the woods when he took his shot. No indication that the woman killed was engaged in any ongoing disputes or had enemies. I don't think they see a lot of murders in Roseville, but it is getting a lot of police attention and the investigation doesn't seem to be going anywhere."

"Thanks, is that your file? Let me take that, I need to meet with Jameson right away. I'll loop back with you afterwards," Justin said.

Justin walked quickly through the hallways leading to Jameson's office. It felt good to actually have something tangible to discuss on the case. Stopping just outside Jameson's office, he heard the television, but no ongoing conversation. Justin rapped gently on the door, and opened when he heard Jameson say "Enter."

"Sir, one of the data analysts has found something that might tie in to the Martyrs element of our case," Justin said.

"Just a second, listen to this," Jameson said. "Some sniper just shot a couple of school kids in the Atlanta area." They stopped to listen to the news announcement coming out of Atlanta. Justin heard the broadcast and something clicked in his mind.

"Sir, did they just say that only one shot was taken?" Justin said.

"Yes, one shot killed the little girl and wounded a boy. Why?"

"This might be connected to the terror operation we were expecting. Look at this incident which happened in the Sacramento area a couple of days ago. One shot was taken, a shell casing was left at the scene, and it was engraved with the words *Martyrs al-Sabra* in Arabic script," Justin said.

"That is a bit of a reach there, Justin. How do we know they are connected?" Jameson said.

"Just a hunch at this point, sir. The thing that triggered me is that there was only one shot fired in both cases. Most snipers fire lots of shots, but both of these were only one."

"Yes, that is unusual. Go ahead and get our Atlanta office involved immediately, see if they find a similar shell casing at the scene. You know, Justin, if the terrorists start acting like urban guerilla fighters things could get real ugly, real fast. Normally, they just keep trying to shoot until you kill them. This might be the start of something very unpleasant and new. If Atlanta finds that link, I'll want you to head down there as soon as possible. Reach out to our local guys in San Francisco and have them liaise with the Sacramento PD leads," Jameson ordered.

"Yes sir. What about the thing we discussed yesterday concerning Nayla?"

"Put it on hold. We can come back to it once we get a handle on the Sacramento/Atlanta situations. I really don't like what I am beginning to suspect here. If there is another related incident, we will be chasing our own tail," Jameson said.

"Maybe that is the idea," Justin said. "We probably ought to go through all sniper type incidents since the election to see if there are any more of these which were not previously connected."

"Good idea, I trust you'll start the ball rolling," Jameson said in dismissal.

• • •

Khaled went online to be with his colleagues in the game, and received a hero's welcome. Not only did he receive the game currency email from Redonkulus, but everyone said his efforts had taken things to a whole new level. His peers were so overcome with admiration the mirror monitors had to caution several on being too direct in their praise. Khaled enjoyed the notoriety and played the game for the hours remaining until the next meeting.

This time the entire group was energized, the shooters now fully understood what they were a part of and wholeheartedly approved. They formed their familiar circle of thirty, while the three officers danced again within it.

• • •

Farid went to his office to catch up on paperwork, when he noticed a thick, heavy envelope sitting on his desk. He opened it by cutting the end off, looked at the contents, and quickly set it back down. Taking out his mobile phone, he speed-dialed.

"Time? Hey, I just got a package that you need to see," Farid said.

"Hi, Farid. This is a pretty bad time. I don't know if you saw the news, but Atlanta has us all hands on deck," Justin said.

"I know. I think this has something to do with that, and might be a communication from that person you asked me about," Farid said elliptically.

"The prince?"

"No, the other one. And I think you are going to need your forensic evidence team. Once I realized what it was I set it back down, but my fingerprints are already on it. Can we meet at the same place in 30 minutes?"

"Yes, do you mind if Jameson comes along too?" Justin asked.

"Not at all. I just don't want to go to your main building. I'll see you then."

Justin ran down the hallways to Jameson's office. This time, he didn't pause after his two soft knocks, but opened the door.

Jameson looked up in annoyance, "Yes?"

"Sir, I just got a call from Farid and he thinks he just got a package from The Hammer. He wants to hand it over where we met last time. I am headed over there now."

"Really? Good! Let me get my coat."

"He mentioned that we might want to bring forensics along, want me to grab a guy?" Justin asked.

"No, we can get it back to forensics ourselves. I've come to agree with your previous points on protecting our source here, especially now that this is heating up."

Jameson and Simons headed out together to the same coffee shop where they had met with Farid several months earlier. They walked in together and saw Farid sitting at a back table.

"I'll get coffees for us and join you in a minute," Jameson said, motioning Justin towards the table.

Justin walked over to the table. Farid was acting strangely nervous, his hands wouldn't sit still and he played with his pen. "Farid, you're pretty nervous - I haven't seen you like this in years."

"See for yourself, tell me if you wouldn't be nervous receiving something like this," Farid gingerly handed over the strangely heavy envelope.

Justin sat down, pulled on a pair of sheer evidence gloves, wordlessly borrowed Farid's pen and looked into the end of the envelope. There were several sheets of paper filled with Arabic script, a wallet, a gun, and a badge. "Un-fucking believable," Justin swore. "Did you get a gist for what is on the papers?"

"Yes, whoever sent this wanted me to do a network story on the Martyrs al-Sabra operation which has just begun. They knew where I had been, where I would be, and don't seem inclined to take no for an answer. When I saw a reference to The Hammer, I knew you had to see it as soon as possible. I get stuff from cranks all the time, sometimes even death threats from local white supremacists, but these guys I worry about."

Jameson came up at that moment, set a coffee in front of Justin and sat down. He nodded to Farid in greeting and turned to Justin, "What have we got?"

"I think we have a shitstorm, sir. You should look at this. Need gloves?"

"No, I have a pair here somewhere," Jameson said as he checked his pockets. Pulling out a pair, he pulled them on and accepted the envelope. Looking down into the container, his face turned pale. "Is that what I think it is?"

Jameson reached into the envelope and pulled out the wallet. He opened it up, confirmed his suspicions and placed it back within the envelope. "It is. Farid, I was mugged a while back after meeting a contact. They got my wallet, badge, and service weapon. I think these are all mine."

Justin briefed Jameson on what the writing itself said, as related by Farid.

"Farid, what is it that they want you to report?"

"Something called the Martyrs al-Sabra Operation. It says that two blows have been struck so far, one in Sacramento and one in Atlanta, with many more to come. It goes on to say that all infidels shall fear the Hammer of Allah. That's when I picked up the phone to Justin," Farid said.

Jameson noticed that Farid was not his normal, confident self. He was full of nervous energy, and his eyes kept scanning the coffee shop and street, as if for early warning of an attack.

"Farid, you did exactly the right thing bringing this to us. I wouldn't worry overmuch, I think these guys need your help to publicize their terror campaign. The question we have to answer is whether you should or not. Like it or not, if you didn't pick it up, they can find five other people who will without too much effort. I would much prefer it to be you, as we have this working relationship in place," Jameson said.

"I think I know about the one in Atlanta - it hit the main newsfeeds hard. What happened in Sacramento? Also, the reports on Atlanta say nothing about a terrorist attack. I have some other concerns, too. I am on the Board of Directors for the Martyrs al-Sabra Charity, what if they are using it somehow for their effort? As far as I know, it has only helped orphans and their families. I have to worry, as this seems very personal to me," Farid said tersely.

"There was a one-shot sniper in Sacramento who left behind a rifle shell casing engraved with the Arabic words '*Martyrs al-Sabra*'. We don't know offhand if it is similar in Atlanta, but the one-shot and these papers say they are connected. OK, let's talk next steps because we have to get this package into forensics. I'll get you a copy of the papers later today, can you write a story about it? It will keep the source engaged and coming to you. Justin is getting on a plane for Atlanta tonight or first thing tomorrow. If you get any more packages, don't open them, we'll do it together to keep the evidence pristine."

"Yes, I can do that. Obviously, my network would kill to be first in line on this story. How much should I tell them?"

"I would show them the papers, and not mention the gun, badge, and wallet. That was a message to me, although I'm not sure what they want there," Jameson said.

"I'm pretty sure it was both a threat and a taunt. There was text that said you could not stop the effort, much like you could not stop losing your gear. That part isn't really newsworthy, in my opinion, as it seems off the main point," Farid said, sounding a bit more like his old self.

"I agree and appreciate your discretion. Don't share the full text. Justin will brief you in on what corroborating details from our investigation can be released in the series of stories," Jameson said.

"Farid, were there any personal threats or taunts to you in the text?" Justin asked.

Farid took a deep calming breath. "No, there were not. Section Chief Jameson might be right that they only want the publicity. It still makes me pretty nervous to be in this loop, these guys are historically not the most rational and tend to hold grudges."

Jameson took a long sip on his coffee, "I know exactly how you feel: unsafe. They know where I live and they are taunting me. Normally, a criminal or terrorist never has visibility into who is running their investigation. When they do, it changes things dramatically."

"How would they know anything if there wasn't someone inside feeding them information?" Farid asked.

"It could be anyone of thousands; it is a lot easier to find the task force leaders than it is task force participants," Jameson said officiously. "Thank you, Farid. This is very helpful. We'll head back now, Justin will contact you before the end of our work day with any details. Do you need to pitch your guys as well?"

"I will, yes. They may want to put another face in the lead role, given my national origin, but we'll see," Farid said as he, too, prepared to head back to his office.

• • •

"I like the new site," The Hammer nodded approvingly to Amin. A small house in an old section of Fairfax County, Virginia the new site was convenient to the district. Amin had rented it from a listing posted in a local mosque. The family was taking an extended six-month visit to relatives in Pakistan, and were only too happy to rent it to a brother Muslim with cash.

"Our man in Atlanta did an excellent job. I took your advice and dropped a fairly modest screed into the hands of a network reporter, along with a certain FBI Section Chief's personal belongings. It will be interesting to see if they report any of that story," The Hammer laughed.

"I would expect not," Amin smiled. "Khaled the painter definitely painted Stone Mountain blood red. Nothing gets the attention of infidels quite like the death of a young, white girl. Khaled even cheated a little by wounding another child with the same bullet. I haven't heard yet of a law enforcement tie between the two attacks in the news."

"My information packet made the connection for them. I think the FBI is already on the ground at both sites. We'll know soon enough, I expect. We'll give them four days to mill about, mobilize, and theorize before San Francisco. Then we will up the tempo next week. The mirrors will have to be extra vigilant because any of these could fall flat, through sheer bad luck. All of the hunt club trail is erased?"

"Yes, and we made sure that none of the shooters knew the names or cities of their peers. They will know the game personas now that the operation has commenced, but that was unavoidable. The prepaid accounts are all blind, and we'll have advance warning if someone tries to track proxies back to the shooters. I think we are in good shape there."

"How about the Nayla Kaldah portion of the operation?" The Hammer asked.

"We're ready for the next phase, we have a lot of video footage of the eminent Jonny Ray, in an astounding variety of flavors," Amin said.

"Any bondage or kinky footage?"

"Not really, he comes at it from wide number of directions, but nothing too outré."

"Hmm, we might want to change that. I'll think about it. How much time do you need to pull the equipment out before execution?"

"Ideally, 24 hours, just to be sure we aren't seen doing it," Amin said.

"Noted. We'll project the Nayla portion to take place after next week's feeding frenzy, probably in the following week. Then the prince's gambit two weeks afterwards. I have an idea on that. Do we have anyone besides yourself who knows how to captain a seagoing vessel?"

"Yes, we have one guy in the crew we placed on the container ship," Amin said.

"I've come up with a variation of the earlier plan, mainly because our timing is too tight for optimal effect. Here's what I think we should do," The Hammer spoke for a few more minutes.

• • •

The next meeting was held in Nayla's rented apartment. Once more, The Hammer entered cautiously, relaxing only when he was behind the closed door.

"Nayla, the time you've been waiting for has almost arrived. Given how things are going, we can wrap this up the week following next," The Hammer announced after kissing both of Nayla's cheeks.

"That is very good news, my love. One question, did you still want me to break things off at that point or just fade without explanation?"

"After a lot of thought, I don't think he should get any warning, after all we don't want him scrambling to clean things up, do we?"

"I suppose not. That makes it easier for me as well."

"I do have a request however. It occurred to me that it might be useful to get him on camera with some less common sexual behaviors. In particular, erotic asphyxiation. Has he shown any interest in choking you? That is a fairly common pornography motif these days," The Hammer asked smiling.

"I hate that, but now you mention it he has put his hands on my throat occasionally while in the act. It is something he might respond to. I'm the one being asphyxiated, right?"

"Yes, I wouldn't want anything to happen to him with the Secret Service standing just outside the door. Let's get some footage over the next visit or two and we will probably have everything we need," The Hammer said. "I'll have Sabir drop off some paraphernalia in the next couple of days. You'll have to reference online as to how it is used. I don't think the stuff comes with an instruction manual."

Nayla grabbed a small pillow off of the sofa and whacked The Hammer. "I think this is just your sneaky way of getting what you want, after all of this is done."

"Nayla, if that weren't true my feelings would be hurt," he smirked, and ducked under the follow-up swat to gather her in a hug. Placing his head next to hers, he smelled her hair and enjoyed the warmth of her bare neck. "Seriously, don't damage this beautiful neck as I have other plans for it," he whispered in her ear as he softly kissed a trail down to her shoulder to emphasize the point.

"Damn you, I am meeting my friend Lindsey in an hour and have to leave very soon," she whispered.

"Ah, disappointing. But ours is a passion that will keep. What is a couple more weeks when measured against a lifetime together?"

Nayla ran around the apartment getting herself ready to depart while The Hammer watched from the couch, enjoying the sight of a beautiful woman about to be late for a social engagement. Finally, she had everything together; she turned at the door and blew a kiss in his direction as she left.

The Hammer sighed to himself, then began the process of sweeping the apartment for anything other than what they had placed there. The cameras and microphones were intact, without any indication of tampering. There were no business cards or personalized touches, for all intents and purposes the apartment could be a hotel suite. Completing his task, he once more dimmed the lights and left the apartment to vanish into the night.

• • •

Justin's day had been a whirlwind of telephone calls with regional FBI offices in Atlanta and Roseville, as well as local Police Departments. The Atlanta shooting did indeed have a connection to the Martyrs al-Sabra, which was confirmed when the tell-tale spent cartridge was recovered. FBI officers had asserted leadership on the investigations, to secret sighs of relief by local law enforcement, and were bringing the best forensic minds onto the task force.

So far, the best evidence had been gathered by the Atlanta team, as the shooting happened during the day and law enforcement was fairly quickly on the scene. The Roseville investigation was hampered by a wet crime scene and law enforcement was slower to access local video camera footage.

The reconstruction of the Roseville shooting had the shooter in the woods next to the parking lot, making his escape through the wooded lot into the Home Helper parking lot. The FBI had notified both the supermarket and Home Helper that their parking lot security footage was required. Both management teams were helpful, but unwilling to release the footage without warrants due to corporate privacy policy concerns. The field office had the warrants in hand and would be getting the footage later that evening.

Atlanta moved a lot faster, likely due to the heinous nature of the crime; the warrants had been handed over the same day. The field office would have that footage later in the evening as well.

Justin had an interagency conference call scheduled for 9 p.m. ET, and would be traveling to both Atlanta and Sacramento to meet with the local offices. Jameson was in the process of forming a national task force with the bureau in DC, and had delegated Justin to kick things off that evening.

Doing some research, Justin had come up with some chilling thoughts. He recalled that in 2002, the entire DC metropolitan area had been paralyzed by the D.C. Sniper for three weeks until the pair of shooters were captured almost by accident. Law enforcement had been turned inside out during the period trying to chase every lead before the next shooting would occur. Neighboring communities had loaned additional police manpower to help sweep the streets. Planes and helicopters had flown the area using state-of-the-art imaging technologies to track movements, without success. Millions of dollars were spent fruitlessly, because law enforcement had to follow up on anything that might yield a result. Early profiles and tips proved to be next to useless, when reviewed in retrospect. The worst thing in Justin's opinion, was that the DC Snipers took additional shots at targets, which eventually led to their capture. So far, this terrorist had only taken one shot and run. It was as if The Hammer had studied past campaigns and designed a new one which would cause the most damage with the least effort. Justin had a feeling they were dealing with a new breed of terrorist; one less crazy by Western standards, one who dispassionately planned an operation and planned to survive for another day.

There were three days between the two attacks, enough time to have driven the distance, and easily enough time to have flown. It was possible this was a single shooter. The comparative ballistics report should be available that evening.

Justin stepped out for a quick dinner, then went back to the office for the conference call. He opened up the bridge and callers started announcing themselves. On the conference call were the local FBI agents assigned to the Roseville and Atlanta offices, as well as representatives of both Roseville and Stone Mountain Police Departments.

"Welcome, everyone. Thank you for attending this late call. We felt the information which was developed today needed to be shared with the entire team. As I go through this overview, please do not hesitate to interrupt me with any questions as they come up. I am Justin Simons, Special Agent and Task Force Lead in DC working for Quinton Jameson. My task force was formed in November of 2020 to run down intelligence about a potential terrorist cell in the US," Justin said.

"The terrorist in question goes by the alias *The Hammer of Allah* or *Allah's Hammer*. Our investigation has not been able to determine the identity of this Hammer, but in the course of our investigation the Martyrs al-Sabra incident came up. The short version of that story is that two factions of Palestinians, Fatah and Hamas, got into an urban firefight which ended up killing 23 children attending school classes upstairs from a Hamas armory. The 23 children are the martyrs referenced. There is an international charity formed in honor of them, to help orphans and their families. You've seen their change collection jars in many Muslim-run convenience stores. Are there any questions so far?" Justin asked.

"Yes, this is Roseville PD. Why would terrorists focus on something like this? Sounds like it was caused by their own groups."

"That is an excellent question. One answer is that the Muslim street blames the Israelis, and the US by proxy, for any mishap that occurs within Gaza and West Bank. The logic is that if it were not for the Israeli occupation of Palestine, there would be no need to fight their Muslim brothers over strategy and political power with weapons of war. In this case, one of the key players lost his parents to an Israeli bomb six months earlier and if that had not happened, it is very likely that the incident itself would not have happened. There is a lot more on Wikipedia and it is mostly accurate, for those who want additional information," Justin suggested.

Justin continued, "We were looking at that key player as a possible lead to the Hammer's identity; some even felt he might be the Hammer. The evidence wasn't conclusive, but it explains why we on the task force were focused on The Martyrs al-Sabra. Then these two separate shootings took place. We had search strings being run against the national crimes big data repository, and the Roseville sniper attack data with the Martyrs inscription raised the red flag for us. About the same time, the Stone Mountain attack took place. We confirmed the presence of another inscribed casing at that attack as well. That brings us up to date from this side. Any questions before we take status updates?"

"Yes, sir. Stone Mountain PD, can you share how the task force got the information about the Hammer?"

"I can't share the operational methods in play on this call, as they are classified. However, I can say that we could not use the received information in a US court of law. Evidence for a trial or indictment would have to be developed separately. Does that answer the question, albeit indirectly?" Justin said.

"Yes, it does. Thank you."

"One other thing, the only pieces of information we started with in November included the involvement of this Hammer, who was located within the US currently and planning an operation. What the operation was, where it would take place, when it would happen … all of those things were unknown. Sadly, it took the beginning of his campaign to start bringing the threads together."

"So let's open this up with status reports. Are the combined forensics results ready for discussion?"

"Yes. This is Michael Kang, FBI forensics lead. I would like to start by saying that Roseville and Stone Mountain PD's did a great job pulling together the evidence packages. As to our findings: both incidents were performed using a single shot with a Winchester Model 70 bolt action deer rifle. The round itself was a standard 30-06 Springfield 220 Grain, manufactured by Remington and available in every gun shop in the nation as well as online. The two shells appear to have come from the same lot. No fingerprints were found on either shell casing. The engraving on each casing was performed using the same equipment, and was machined rather than done free-hand. The recovered slugs and casings indicate different rifles, but the same type. That's all we have at the moment, but we will continue to track the shell lot and see if we can find where they were purchased."

"Any thoughts from anyone on whether we are dealing with one person traveling or different people?" Justin asked.

"Could be either, given what we have so far, right? In fact, different guns opens up the possibilities. Oh, sorry, this is Dan Adams of Roseville Branch Office."

"Yes, that is true. Timely question, have you been able to get the security video files from the retail establishments? Were there any other sources of video coverage available?" Justin asked.

"Yes, we just received them, and will be reviewing overnight. Roseville PD will be lending us extra eyeballs tonight - since this is familiar territory for them. In fact, they supplied the traffic camera captures as well. Hopefully, we will have a lot more to talk about tomorrow evening," Dan said.

"I've arranged for an online drop box for file notes and video files so that we can all stay up to date. Send me an email requesting access, to the email address used for this meeting invite, and I will get you set up. Roseville and Stone Mountain PD's, please nominate one point of contact for that access, and every communication will be routed to that person. We got a little off-track there, but it needed to be said," Justin said.

"Atlanta Field Office? Where are we?"

"Franklin Hsieh here. We have the security videos in for analysis, both traffic and store parking areas. We do know the route of the shooter. We found the place where he was laying down, and his footprints coming in and departing. We got a tracking dog out early, thanks to Atlanta PD, and tracked him to the south side of the GroceryCo parking lot. So we know where to look on the video reviews tonight. The forensics team hasn't had much luck with stray hairs or fabric threads yet, but the lay-down spot is covered now and secured. If there is something to find there, they will find it."

"Thank you, Franklin. To summarize where we are tonight, the shootings are connected, but we do not have any indication of how many different shooters are involved, or if they had to travel. We do not currently have any commonalities between the victims, other than the fact that both were female. The boy was hit only after the round went completely through the young girl. Let's see if we can narrow the field of investigation over the next few days. I'll be traveling to both Roseville and Atlanta to meet with the teams, and we'll hold tomorrow's call from Roseville most likely. I am going to recommend an alert go out to all branch offices, with enough details to identify new attacks, because I doubt this is all there will be. Is there anything else for tonight? If not, thanks again for supporting this call so late in the day," Justin closed.

• • •

Thirty shooters gathered in a circle on the plains to the southeast of the human capital. The dancing of guild officers commenced. Redonkulus pointed at the player named Bumbles. Bumbles started dancing. Redonkulus hopped once, twice, three times and is imitated by Bumbles. Once more the orders are confirmed: San Francisco in three days.

FEEDING FRENZY

"Following the story of the Stone Mountain sniper, who took the life of 3rd grader Jennifer Cooper and wounded 4th grader Benjamin Jacobs, confidential sources say that the incident is the action of a new band of radical Islamic terrorists. We have learned the first attack occurred in Roseville, California where a single mother of three, Lorie Lampson, was shot and killed outside a supermarket. The FBI has formed a task force and is coordinating a nationwide effort. The Section Chief in charge, Agent Quinton Jameson, has called a press briefing later this afternoon. More to follow.

- World News Corporation, Friday Night - 3/12/2021

Justin got home a little after 11 p.m., Jan was already in bed, and the only person still up was Beth who sat at the top of the stairs wagging her tail when she saw him. Taking a few minutes, he sat down with Beth at the top of the stairs, rubbing her fur as she leaned into him, and telling her how beautiful she was. Then, Justin stood and went quietly into the master bedroom. Tomorrow, he would have to pack an overnight bag and leave early as his flight for Atlanta left at 8:30 a.m. As stated in the teleconference, he planned to meet with the local team in the afternoon and head for the West Coast immediately after.

The primary purpose was to get a feel for the personalities of the team members in case he needed to pull them onto the national task force. Quinton had left this work up to him, as was often the case. Usually, Quinton was nowhere to be found when there was tedious investigative work to do. Justin didn't mind, he preferred to have a free hand when processing large amounts of data. Anything which was found would accrue to Quinton's credit, but it is the way the system worked. If Quinton was successful in his quest for promotion, it would open up an opportunity for Justin. Of course, if things went badly Justin would get most of the blame since he was in charge of the detail. *Still better than being a corporate lawyer,* Justin thought to himself, *although the hours were a lot more predictable and I could even coach one of the kids' teams.*

The next day, on the way to the airport, the radio news was dedicating a good portion of their broadcast to what they were calling the Martyrs sniper. They interviewed the Muslim chairman of the Martyrs al-Sabra charity, who categorically denied any involvement with terrorism. He went on to say it was possible that an Alt-Right or Skinhead group performed the killings and were trying stir up hatred against Muslims. Justin had sent a copy of the Hammer's communiqué back to Farid, along with a bulleted list of data to release to the news agencies. The Hammer's communication had not been released to the public, so the chairman's statements could not be refuted yet. The Hammer's missive didn't have any demands associated with it, other than the patently impossible return of the Palestinian homeland.

The word would get out soon, though, as leaks were bound to happen after releasing a case synopsis to fifty field offices. Justin's biggest fear was that this was just the beginning.

The hysteria was already starting to build. The randomness of the targets so far made it harder for people to rationalize their own safety. Also, with social media so prevalent, a shooting where there were mobile phones would be an instantly disseminated video before the police even had a chance to investigate and secure the crime scene. It might pay to retroactively look for social media coverage of both the Roseville and Atlanta killings. There might be something there.

Justin made a note to himself that he should have the team survey the online conspiracy publishers who would doubtless be very busy over the weekend. Sometimes it seemed like the only thing accomplished by the Internet was to make any type of crazy seem credible to its chosen audience.

• • •

The FBI's Atlanta field office was one of the most prominent in the South. The special agents assigned there were among the best in the nation, handling a wide array of crimes in the region. The Stone Mountain sniper case was no exception. Justin was pleasantly surprised upon his arrival to find that not only had the security videos been reviewed, but the team was engaged in tracking suspect vehicle owners. As each lead was being followed, an effort was made to track the vehicles through the use of traffic cameras. Most intersection signals now had traffic cameras in place in the Stone Mountain area. The GroceryCo parking lot the shooter had parked in was situated close to a freeway on-ramp, so it might prove difficult to follow all the vehicles to their homes. Another difficulty the team encountered was the resolution of the video was low and there were no close-up views of the extremity of the parking lots.

In the video footage, there were a number of vehicles parked along the wooded area south of the store. The dogs had tracked the shooter back to the area. There had also been a commercial trucker parked across a bunch of parking spots. For a moment, the FBI thought the trucker should be looked at as a potential suspect, but soon realized the driver would not have been able to drive a rig from Sacramento to Atlanta that quickly. They did intend to talk to the driver to ask if they'd seen anything unusual around the time of the shooting, though.

The real problem the team was encountering was the license numbers were not really visible in the videos. Some of the traffic cameras were designed to see license plates better, but tracking one suspect through the potential cameras was a case-by-case exercise. So far, the team had successfully identified a number of vehicles, and other agents were detailed to follow up on those leads in person. Justin suggested they look at people whose home address was further than 5 miles from the store; if the shooter didn't live in the area then, they shouldn't normally be shopping at that GroceryCo. Of course, if the shooter did live in Stone Mountain, the task force would be looking at the wrong end of the suspect list, but it was a quick way to prioritize leads.

Justin worked his way through the team, making sure those who needed access to the online drop box were properly set up, and mentally noting who should be drafted for the larger national team. After the first week of analysis by the local team, the task force roster would be reduced as new crimes would require their time. At that point, the national team would have to pick up the slack. Justin's plan was to have a least one local special agent on the national team in order to save time when additional local investigation was required.

Shortly after lunch, Justin packed up his gear and headed for the airport. In a little over five hours he would land in Sacramento, and immediately meet with the Roseville branch office. Justin parked himself in an airport bar while he waited for his flight. The television above him showed the first sign of a backlash against the Muslim population; clips of angry protesters interspersed with the reactions of American Muslim institutions. Rather than express sympathy for those who had lost their lives, the leaders of the Muslim community simply denied their own involvement without directly denouncing the perpetrators. Mothers filled out the ranks of protestors carrying signs calling Muslims murderers of children, and screaming at people entering or leaving mosques. *This could get out of hand very quickly*, Justin thought.

Taking out his phone, he placed a call to Jameson.

"Jameson."

"Justin Simons here. Do you have a few minutes to talk about Atlanta?" Justin asked.

"Yes, give me a second to get into my office. How did it go?"

"There is a good team in place; I identified two people we might want to bring onto the national task force. Atlanta did a much better job jumping onto the situation. It is probably partially due to the fact the Atlanta shooting occurred in the morning, rather than at night. They were able to get tracking dogs on the scene within an hour, which gave us pretty good data on what the shooter did. The video quality isn't as good as we hoped, but traffic cameras should help there. I did want to speak with you about the backlash we're already seeing in the news and social media. We haven't even released any information about The Hammer's claim of responsibility, but people are already manning the barricades outside of mosques. I guess what I am asking is whether we should release the data after all. Given where things are at, I think it would only confirm and expand the push against Muslims."

"I concur. I've already had to address high-level concern about the progress of the task force, supposedly due to the White House asking about it. They mentioned the President will be issuing a statement later this evening," Jameson said.

"Sir, I don't think The Hammer is done just yet. I authorized an information kit release to be distributed to all branch offices of the Bureau. It is marked classified, but you know how it is when there is a wide distribution of information: there will be leaks. I considered holding the information close, but decided the risk of an attack in another city was high, and I want the local teams to be aware of what to look for," Justin said.

"Good move. If there is another attack, having the information distributed shows we're working that possibility. If we can't get a handle on this situation soon, the folks upstairs will be lining up to bounce our asses off the team. And to be honest, the folks upstairs will be at risk as well due to Presidential displeasure."

"Depending on how late it is when I get to Sacramento, we might have to delay the status call tonight. I'll update the meeting invite when I land, if necessary," Justin said.

"That's fine. If I join tonight it will just be to sit in and listen - you're lead on this."

"I'll check my pay packet for the bump," Justin joked.

"Now, now. That is in progress as we discussed. But neither one of us will be seeing any increases or promotions if we can't close this case. Check in with me if there are any significant developments, no matter the time."

"Will do, sir," Justin said as he rang off.

• • •

"Sid, I want to make a statement on the Atlanta shooting. Did you get a briefing from the FBI on what progress has been made?" President Brown asked.

"Yes, Madame President. As it stands right now, they are fairly certain this is a terrorist action. There is a terrorist group that has taken responsibility for both the Roseville and Atlanta shootings. The public doesn't know yet about the terrorist claims, but are very close to violence against Muslims in some places. The Martyrs al-Sabra shell casing engravings link between the two shootings is known and has been reported. People are most upset by the targeting of mothers and children. They would be upset regardless, but this seems to have struck a raw nerve," Sid Rosenbloom said.

"Do we need to defuse the blowback against law-abiding Muslims? Maybe do a public statement bracketed by several Muslim leaders who also condemn the shootings?"

Sid's face looked grave. "That is part of the problem. It is very difficult to get Muslim leaders to condemn these attacks unequivocally. They will make general statements about how it is wrong to take a life, but they won't say that a specific act of life-taking was wrong. Most Americans interpret it as playing both sides. I'm not sure if it reflects a desire to play politics within their own constituencies or a cultural tendency to not take hard objective public positions. So having them on-camera without unequivocal condemnation of the killings could further enflame the protestors. If the Muslim leaders aren't on-camera, you could still reach out to them as part of what you say," Sid said.

"Yes, I have noticed that in the past," the President paused for a moment. "I don't want to make things worse, and I do think the American people want to hear their President is aware of the situation and concerned."

"I'll get a short statement put together, and notify the press pool of the time. Will you take questions?" Sid asked.

"Yes, let's do that for a few minutes afterwards. Do you think Michael might be a good face to put on the ongoing anti-terrorism effort?"

"Let me think about it. Offhand it sounds good, but we wanted him available to help explain your immigration reform proposal. We don't know how long this terrorist situation will take to resolve," Sid said. "If that's all for now, I'll go get the statement text ready for your review, Madame President."

•••

"I want to use this time to express my condolences to the families and communities touched by the cowardly and vicious attacks this last week. A mother and a young girl were killed by terrorist actions within our borders and our country as a whole has been wounded. The FBI has confirmed the shootings in Roseville, California and Stone Mountain, Georgia are linked and formed a national task force to apprehend the criminal perpetrators of these despicable acts," the President said.

"I also have reports of Americans harassing and threatening other Americans who are being unjustly blamed for these events: our strong community of law-abiding Muslims. We, as a country, are better than that. A real American understands the difference between criminals who happen to be Muslim and law-abiding citizens who happen to be Muslims. Do not let these heinous acts divide our nation or weaken our resolve. This administration will do its utmost to bring the criminal terrorists to justice and protect all law-abiding Americans, regardless of religious affiliation. That is who we are as a nation. Our prayers go out on behalf of the survivors, while we, as a nation, mourn. May God bless America, and keep you all safe."

The cameras panned out as the President departed the press room.

"I'll take a few questions now," Sid said.

"Miko Stans, Newstand. So far, the only information released was about an inscription on the shell casings at the sites of both shootings. How was it determined, the two incidents were linked?"

"Yes, the inscriptions matched exactly, and the shell casings came from the same manufacturing lot. There is some additional evidence which conclusively links the two attacks, but this will be held confidential during the course of the investigation. Next question."

"Phyllis Racner, Euronotes. Some have observed that these shootings illustrate again an urgent need for strict gun control in America. What are your thoughts?"

"Would stricter gun control laws have prevented these attacks? It is too early in the investigation to draw conclusions on that front. These shootings appear to have been carried out with single-shot rifles, commonly used in deer hunting, which are generally not the target of gun legislation. The FBI is investigating the weapon origins as part of their efforts. When the criminals are apprehended will be the best time to decide what legislative steps can help prevent future tragedy. The issue will not be overlooked - the President feels very strongly on the matter."

"Jeffrey Stinnis, Action News. The immigration reform legislation was scheduled to be unveiled in the next two weeks. Have these incidents changed the near-term focus of the administration?"

Sid nodded his head in acknowledgement, "Thank you for bringing it up. We plan to release the President's concept to Congressional Leadership in the next week, with proposed legislative language to follow. She considers the office of the Presidency requires maintaining a governing agenda in spite of the losses we as a nation have suffered this week. That being said, it also wouldn't be appropriate to detail our legislative agenda in this venue. Stay tuned, we will be talking more on the topic in weeks to come."

"Thank you, everyone, for coming on a Saturday evening," Sid turned and left the press room, trailing his aides.

When gathered safely back in the Oval Office, Lucy turned to Sid. "Do you think this set the right tone?"

"Definitely. I only went off the rails when it came to gun control, but those questions always cause problems. Otherwise it went well. I could kiss Stinnis' fat face for taking us over to immigration reform."

"You didn't pay him off?" Lucy asked with a smile.

"Not this time," Sid laughed. "But when I have something to leak, he has just earned himself a premium spot on my roster. In seriousness, though, if there are more shootings there is going to be a dramatic escalation of concern among common folk."

"This is a big deal. National Security tells me that key FBI resources are being reassigned to the Martyrs task force, which means they aren't available to do their normal tasks," the President paused in thought. "Sid, if we have another 5 or 6 of these shootings in separate cities, do we have the manpower to cover a situation like that? Also, what happens when the people are rioting against whatever enemy is tagged with the blame? We probably should have some contingency plans to deal with such situations."

"Yes, Madame President. I'll get a couple of our situation modelers on it," Sid said.

"Thanks, Sid. After you get it going, head home to Meryl and get some rest. I don't think we are going to get much of it next week."

"Thank you. Will that be all, Madame President?" Sid asked formally.

"Yes," Lucy sat down and wondered how to best navigate the swirling tempest she perceived all around them. She had successfully met with the former President, he had agreed to yield the stage and be more publicly supportive. The trouble with that accomplishment was the public would never know about it. A president is under pressure to accomplish something significant within their first hundred days in office. Fifty days were already gone, and the biggest issue of the day was something she couldn't actively manage: the Martyrs terrorist situation.

Pressing the intercom she rang her assistant, "Natalie, is the Vice President still in the building?"

"I'll find out. Do you want me to ask him to come over if he is?"

"Yes, please. Also, have the steward set up a small happy-hour assortment for us in the Oval Office if the VP is here."

"Yes, Madame President," Natalie rang off.

Michael would have to lead the charge on the immigration package. The two of them in tandem with Sid had spent hours on the key provisions over the last two months. It was time to kick things off.

After a few minutes, her assistant rang to say Michael was on his way. The steward came in and set about fixing up a small buffet of snacks and drinks for them. One of the best things about being President was the world-class staff at the White House who quickly learned what you liked and found new, interesting ways to present it. Lucy thanked the steward and got herself a small plate which she set down at one end of the coffee table. Heading to the wet bar, she made herself a rich gin-and-tonic before sitting down on the couch.

Michael was announced a few minutes later, and Lucy waved her hand at the buffet as she ate some hummus and pita squares.

After swallowing, she said "Michael, I'll only detain you for a few more minutes. Did you see the press statement earlier?"

"Yes, I did. We're in a tough place with this Martyrs business. Overall, though, I thought the statement went well for us," Vice President Michael Rodriquez said as he perused the buffet table.

"I do, too, but I suspect the Martyrs situation is going to get worse before it gets better. That's why I wanted to talk to you tonight. Are you completely on-board with the immigration reform proposals we've come up with?"

"Yes, I am. It is probably the most far-reaching immigration reform of the last 100 years. Of course, Congress will have to chivvied relentlessly to make sure they don't water it down," Michael said.

"I agree. Are you up to the task of leading the effort, from start to finish? I suspect I am going to be pulled into an unproductive cycle of responding to terrorist attacks; it would be impossible for me to do justice to both. The success of this immigration reform is more important than my personal leadership. Don't get me wrong: I will be there to back you up 100%, but you would be the face of the administration on that topic."

Michael's initial elation was almost immediately tempered, "Madame President, I apologize for my next question in advance. Is this notion a way to leverage my Hispanic heritage?"

"No apology necessary," Lucy said waving a hand holding a pita square. "Cynics will say it, regardless of my actual intent. I do have other reasons though. Immigration is bigger than just a Hispanic issue. This reform affects all of it. I'm asking because I trust that you will do the job we've worked towards, and will successfully do it while I am unavoidably preoccupied with other matters. This will be an accomplishment for you as well, when it comes time to pursue sitting in this office. Think about it overnight and let me know first thing in the morning."

"I will. I do appreciate the role you have allowed me to assume in the administration; not many presidents have done that."

"My view is that everything my team accomplishes benefits me as well. Why wouldn't I encourage that? I know, most feel the spotlight should always be on them, but this job is too big for one person to do everything. It doesn't cost me a thing to give credit over to the people who have done the work. Besides, vice presidents need to be ready to step in at a moment's notice. I will not be one of those presidents whose vice presidents aren't up to speed," Lucy set the empty plate down and sipped her drink. "Give my best to Celia," she said in dismissal.

"I will. She's finally able to get some rest! Rosa has decided to sleep through the night now, which helps a lot. I'll check in with you tomorrow. Good night, Madame President."

• • •

Justin's plane to Sacramento had been delayed. He arrived at 6:30 p.m. and quickly canceled the status teleconference for the day. Instead he arranged to have dinner at 7:30 p.m. with Special Agent Dan Adams, the Roseville branch office case lead. Justin was staying at a non-descript Hampton Inn, within walking distance of the branch office. They met at the BJ's Brewpub.

"Dan? It's a pleasure to meet you in person. Thanks for agreeing to meet with me tonight," Justin said.

"Well, my wife was getting tired of the regular hours. She keeps saying that is not why she married an FBI man," Dan said with a chuckle.

They made their way to a table near the back of the restaurant and placed orders for two steaks. While they waited, Justin briefed Dan on what he'd learned about the Atlanta investigation at a high level.

"So that's where we are as of five hours ago. I haven't received any text messages from Atlanta that something new has popped up, so it's probably close to up-to-date," Justin concluded as the waiter slid two sizzling platters onto the table.

"Well, on our side, we've made a bit of progress with the parking lot security footage. It has been slow going, though, as several of the timestamps were off and it took a while to synchronize everything. Not to mention watching it all!" Dan ran his hand through his hair in frustration. "We think we might have a video of the shooter. It's grainy and the resolution is poor, but we can see that he's driving a late-model Honda Accord sedan. The footage shows his car backed into the parking space; he comes out of the woods, puts something in the trunk, and then drives through the parking lot to exit. We're going through traffic camera videos to see which way he went, as well as try to get a license plate number."

"That is extremely good news! Is the team looking at it tonight?" Justin asked.

"Yes, they are. We may have something more tomorrow morning. In addition, however, we were able to isolate the sniper taking the shot from the woods next to the supermarket in one of the parking lot videos. Obviously, we don't have any facial detail, but it validates the theory on how it was done," Dan said.

"Great job! Atlanta is currently working towards that as well. The same problems apply there, I imagine. Is there anything special about the Accord?"

"No, it looks like a light grey or beige model, with no visible modifications. In short, it looks like every other Accord on the road," Dan said.

"The single most common car in the US, I know," Justin said. "Hopefully, getting a plate ID will help. How far were they able to track him?" Justin signaled the waiter for another round of beers.

"Well, we have him getting on Highway 80 South, but lost him after a few miles. There were several exits without traffic cameras, so the team is branching out into all the possible routes in the hope of picking up the trail again."

"The victim had three children at home, right? What is happening there?" Justin asked.

"Lorie Lampson was divorced and the children's father has stepped up for custody. Even the grandparents showed willing - so the kids will definitely have people to fall back on."

Justin took a pull on his house IPA, "Dan, if you were a terrorist, why would you shoot someone like Lorie Lampson?"

"I've thought a lot about that, and even more so about the choices in Atlanta. I can kind of understand Atlanta: shoot a blond Christian school girl and cause the biggest possible public reaction. But here, I don't know. The only thing that suggests itself to me is that Lorie was a large woman who could barely walk. Watching the tape where she is shot, she is barely moving as she walks to the store. What if the shooter isn't that good of a shot and simply picked someone who was slow?" Dan theorized.

"Interesting, that would suggest there were two shooters. The shooter in Atlanta was good enough to hit a small target, and line it up to try for more than one hit. That would also be supported by the fact that the rifles were different, albeit the same model. That would mean our checking all of the travelers between the cities will come up empty," Justin mused. "Are there only two snipers, is the next question I guess."

Dan shook his head ruefully. "God, I hope so. This is already shaping up to be a real problem. We've had to cannibalize staff on a number of other investigations to hit this hard, and so far do not have much to show for it. We need to get a break on this soon. The agency-critical tone in social media is already trending very negative, and will get more so if there are more shootings. We have a problem here in Roseville, but I cannot imagine what pressures our counterparts in Atlanta are under," Dan said.

"Yeah, sooner or later right wing pundits are going to shake themselves off and start making a mental connection between lax immigration controls and the current problem. Especially if we find the shooters are part of the un-vetted mass of people given refugee status. I don't think it is the case here, though; the shooters are too sophisticated. The refugee-type move is to attack people until they are killed while screaming '*InShAllah*'. These shooters want to live to fight again," Justin said.

"These guys are more dangerous, that's for sure. Say what you will about the other terror attacks, they don't last very long and usually end with a dead terrorist. That cycle of instant justice mitigates the psychological impact," Dan said.

"Damn, you have thought about this," Justin said.

"Past life hazard: I'm a recovering Psychology major."

The two finished their meals and made plans to hold a short work session at the office on Sunday morning. After parting, Justin headed for the hotel and a well-earned bed.

Sunday morning, Justin checked in with Quinton to bring him up-to-date on the identification of the Roseville shooter and promised to call prior to boarding his plane that afternoon. He wouldn't arrive at Dulles International until 11 p.m.; luckily home was only 8 miles from the airport. Monday would be upon him before he even fell asleep.

• • •

Michael Rodriquez accepted the commission to drive immigration reform legislation after due consideration. It was definitely true the effort would reflect favorably upon him, plus he believed in the package.

The proposed legislation had focused on the two largest problems posed by illegal immigration: the national security issue of unknown illegal immigrants and the economic costs imposed on the United States by providing government services to illegal immigrants. The proposal provided for several major changes to the process. In short, any foreign national could present themselves for admission to the United States, submit to fingerprinting, DNA registration, and pass a health screening. They would then be admitted and receive a provisional social security number and ID card. No immigrants with criminal records would be allowed entry - for prior offences considered crimes within the United States. Immigration identification must then be carried at all times and presented upon request. This would solve the problem of unknown illegal immigrants. Any immigrant found without their registration information would be summarily deported to their point of origin. Family units would be registered as a group, and the adults considered responsible for the whole.

The second issue of providing government services would be addressed by a probationary period, where a fixed-value wallet of services would be provided. After depletion the immigrant would be required to show employment or be deported. Immigrants would not be eligible for social support services until full citizenship was granted. Government services would no longer be provided to undocumented immigrants. This approach would also solve the issue of labor shortages, as the types of immigrant that were needed would find gainful employment.

Refugees would be treated no differently than other immigrants.

The issue of citizenship would be revised as well. In short, citizenship would be granted automatically at birth when one parent was an

American citizen regardless of where they were born. Children born in the United States would no longer automatically be granted citizenship. An immigrant could be granted citizenship with five years of qualified employment and a clean criminal record. If an immigrant was granted citizenship, their minor children in the USA would also be granted citizenship. Adult children would have to qualify on their own. In short the message was "be a productive member of society and become a citizen", which would be quite a change for the Democratic Party.

The largest existential threats to the United States in recent years had been security-related. As long as there was a large class of people without documentation, the security equation would never be addressable. *The Martyrs shootings illustrate the danger, and might even help get the immigration reform conversation started,* Michael thought to himself. *The Republicans will like the security and limited services portions, but will hate the increase to unskilled labor costs. The Democrats will like the clear path to citizenship, but may have issues with ID cards and limited services. The truth is that something different has to be done, and no one is going to get everything they want. Some provision will have to be made for those already in the country, but becoming legal residents will have benefits. No longer will they have to endure illegal rates of pay or be extorted by landlords to pay above-market rates. There is a good story here, I just need to figure out the best way to sell it.*

• • •

Justin dragged himself into the office Monday morning in time to see an email from the Atlanta team. They, too, had identified a Honda Accord suspect vehicle, and because the crime was committed in daylight were able to get decent video footage. The vehicle was a light grey, and the license plate number should be discernible with additional image processing. The car had been tracked south about five miles before being lost. The team was attempting to pick up the trail again, but it would take time. The process was similar to when a hound dog has lost a scent in a creek: they have to search along the bank until the trail becomes clear again.

As he waited for further developments on the Roseville and Atlanta investigations, Justin revisited the surveillance taken from the team monitoring Nayla. There wasn't anything of note: business discussions and the occasional meeting arrangement with Jonny Ray. Jonny Ray visited several times a week when he was in town, and seemed quite taken with her. As Justin riffled through the folder, his phone made the text message arrival tone. Taking a quick glance, he saw it was from Farid.

"Coffee?" the message read.

"Definitely. Meet you at the usual place in 30?" Maybe it would help put some spring back into his step.

When Justin arrived, he noticed Farid looking somewhat nervous, glancing all over the room as if watching for something or someone.

"Hi Farid, how is the famous broadcaster business?" Justin asked.

"You haven't seen any new ads featuring my suave visage, have you?" Farid said almost snappishly. "Being Muslim isn't exactly popular at the moment."

"I noticed the network went with another anchor to release the data we discussed."

"Yes, it was my idea. I didn't want The Hammer to consider me his puppet, but we still took the information and ran with it. That way it only helps me indirectly," Farid said. "How is the investigation going?"

"Jameson is the lead, and I'm the flunky doing the heavy lifting. Just got back from a tour of Atlanta and Sacramento, at midnight last night."

"Then you could really use the coffee. Thanks for coming out, 'Time, I heard something I thought should be shared with you. In mosque the other day, I was passing a group of men I don't know and heard the phrase 'Hammer'. So I dawdled a bit hoping to catch more, and heard something very disturbing. They were talking about a strike bigger than 9/11 and *Allah's Fire* was to be used," Farid said. "That is a metaphor sometimes used for nuclear weapons."

"Who were these people?" Justin interjected.

"I don't know. I did a little discrete digging, but they were said to be Florida tourists visiting the DC area. I could identify them if I see them again."

"Farid, this is a big deal. Jameson is going to want to bring you in, and he'll want to hit that mosque like a ton of bricks to see what he can find."

"I know - that is why I came to you. If he brings me in, my usefulness to the FBI will be over, and I will have trouble from the mosque as well. I thought I would try to stave that off. Check in with whoever is monitoring the mosque and see if there are photos from the last week."

"I don't know if we monitor that mosque. I'll ask Jameson, he would know."

"I would be very surprised if you do not. The question is whether there are photos that I can review and maybe get a lead on these visitors. I wonder if this 'Hammer' is watching me to see if I'm talking to the FBI. These guys are pretty serious, you think they are done with the two so far? Homeland Security has the entry port scanners for nukes, right?"

"Buddy, you know I can't speak to that," Justin said.

Farid made a disparaging noise. "That is one of the worst kept secrets in the world! The only unknown is what technology or technologies are being used. Smart money says neutron detection, though. So how would a group of terrorists smuggle something in, without setting off alarms from here to Baltimore?"

Justin sat there without responding.

"That's why I brought this to you. I think you need to get answers to those questions right quickly! Let me know if you have any pictures for me to look at. You might tell Jameson to not expect any cooperation from me, if he goes medieval on this tip. I'm keeping my lawyer on speed-dial."

"I don't think it will come to that, but we have to get to the bottom of any potential nuke. That trumps everything else. I'll tell Jameson he needs to go lightly," Justin said. "If he decides otherwise, I'll give you a heads-up."

"Thanks. For the very first time I understand the old saying about being nervous as a cat in a room full of rocking chairs."

"I wouldn't want to be noticed by a terrorist either. I expect Jameson has some angst on that score as well, considering the mugging. On the bomb issue, I'm not having Jan and the kids leave town, if that helps," Justin said.

"Thanks, I know you can't say much, but that is appreciated. Please give Jan and the kids my love."

"I will. I need to head back in and try not to fall asleep at my desk. I'll be in touch later today to give you an idea whether Hurricane Jameson is building."

"I'll keep my ears open as well, I hope what I heard was just some bullshit. Maybe I should do another round of foreign interviews. There is always a war somewhere, and it might be safer." Farid stood and walked out of the shop with Justin, parting when they passed the Metro stop.

Justin's body was running on coffee and adrenaline, as the demands of the job had allowed little to no downtime over the last few weeks. Farid's information threatened to overload his precarious grip on the demands of the task force. There wasn't enough time in a day to stay on top of all the details, and they were multiplying. One of the biggest problems faced in the modern Bureau was that specialization of the working level had created the need for big picture analysis, which the task force leads generally did themselves. The Martyrs task force already numbered more than a hundred agents nationwide doing their work. Someone needed to read it all, and make sense of it. He wanted about five more people like himself assigned as of yesterday. Now the nuclear weapon tip would create a fur ball of investigation as well. They would have to access whatever surveillance was in place on the mosque. It was fairly likely it was monitored, but the Bureau was sensitive about revealing it. Of course, the threat of a nuclear weapon would definitely get people's attention.

Justin got back to his desk, took off his coat, and then walked the maze of corridors to Jameson's office. He knocked lightly on the door and entered when beckoned.

"Sir, I just spoke to our contact, Farid, and he heard something very disturbing at mosque this week," Justin related the entire conversation to Jameson.

"So these guys were supposedly from Florida, just visiting DC?" Jameson asked.

"Yes, that's right. Farid said he could ID them if we had their photo."

"It is a good bet we do have a photo; the surveillance usually photographs people coming and going into the mosque. I'll contact the oversight team: see if they can provide a photo dump."

At that moment, Justin's phone signaled a text message, followed almost immediately by Jameson's as well. They both reached for their phones and read the message. It was from the San Francisco field office, a sniping incident had occurred at the Golden State Bridge Welcome Center, which had characteristics of the Martyrs terrorists. One jogger: male, wounded, and in intensive care. One shot, and a shell casing matching the earlier shootings.

"Goddamnit! Justin, go alert the team and let's get on the horn with San Francisco. This thing is going to eat us alive," Jameson said.

"Right away. Look, now isn't a good time, but we're going to need more high-level non-specialist eyeballs on this task force. At least five more people, hopefully with an integrationist mindset. Too many balls in the air."

"Are you saying you're not capable of handling it?"

"I don't think anyone is capable of handling it solely by themselves; there is not enough time in a day to read all the incoming data. We need a high-level strategic team splitting up the data, but working closely together," Justin said. "Right now it is just you and I who have all the facts, and The Hammer has us chasing our tails. Look, I'll go get San Francisco on the line now, I just brought it up because it bears some thought."

"OK. I'll come over to the task force in a few minutes."

• • •

"A third confirmed Martyrs sniping incident has been confirmed in San Francisco, California. The attack occurred this morning, injuring a man out for his morning run. So far, the FBI has only confirmed all three incidents are connected. No precautionary information, no suspects apprehended, and no information regarding the investigation's progress has been

offered. Meanwhile, online sentiment is rapidly turning against the Muslim community, as the number of hate-related postings has increased dramatically. There are reports across the country of mosques being vandalized and worshippers harassed. Meanwhile, the President has promised to protect law-abiding Muslims, which presumably means punishing those who vandalize mosques and harass Muslims. Perhaps the FBI will have more success against that sort of crime."

Online News Feed Editorial

"The Martyrs al-Sabra charity collects money in many Muslim-run convenience stores. Why isn't the government stopping them? If the government won't do it, maybe it is time to boycott businesses that support this charity. If you see a Martyrs change collecting jar like this (see below), just stop and leave the business without buying anything."

America for Americans - BLOG

"Boycott? When is someone going to do what needs to be done? Start shooting Muslims like they are shooting our children. Send them back to wherever they came from to rot..."

Comment to America for Americans - BLOG

"Rally to protect our Muslim citizens from the hate crimes of the far-right! We'll be organizing teams to protect Muslim businesses and mosques from reactionary forces."

Antifa

Nayla read the headlines, comments, and reactions on the Internet news sources. The Hammer's plan to stir up the American people was certainly working. She wasn't quite sure how she felt about using the Martyrs al-Sabra incident as a rallying cry, but understood The Hammer's point.

For years, Nayla had felt the crushing guilt of happily saying goodbye to her brother while he secretly planned to right the wrongs against her. The things he'd done were very hard and he must have known they could negate his future. Truly, Adeeb had been the head of the family for all of his youth. When The Hammer asked her to help the cause, years ago, she knew that she, too, had to give without concern for herself. She had money, she had status, but she didn't have family. If the Jonny Ray operation fell apart and became known to the world, who would want to be father to her children?

But Nayla had a secret; a secret no one, not even The Hammer, knew. A friend of hers from Greece, bore a striking resemblance to the brother she once had. She had to get word to him, in the event something happened to her, of the dangerous work she felt compelled to do. *A dead hand from beyond the grave*, she thought and wondered why she was being morbid. While not normally superstitious, she was feeling her mortality for no obvious reason.

The Ivy League lawyer quickly surfaced in her and determined what needed to be done. Her last will and testament was long prepared, but a lengthy letter needed to be written and sent separately. Nayla sat down with a fountain pen and fine paper, writing her missive in a flowing beautiful Arabic script. Occasionally, she had to stop as tears threatened to smear the ink script, but she eventually completed the letter and sealed the heavy envelope. She addressed it to a person and address in Greece, heaving a sigh as she considered what to do next. Picking up her phone, she dialed Lindsey.

"Hi Linds! I need to see you soon for something pretty important. How does your calendar look?" Nayla said.

"Oh Nayla, I'm so glad you called! I've been meaning to call you myself. How about tonight, is that too soon? I'm just doing mommy things with Benny and Claire."

"No, that would be just about perfect. What time?"

"How about after 6:30? The kids will have full stomachs and be less fractious. They'll be very excited to see their Aunt Nayla," Lindsey said.

"Perfect! I have a few errands to run, but I will be over afterwards. I'll see you then," Nayla rang off and started getting herself prepared to see two young children without crying.

At about 6:45 p.m., Nayla pulled up outside Lindsey's home in Alexandria, Virginia which had come to Lindsey when her parents were killed. Both Lindsey and Farid had grown up in the house. On the way, Nayla had stopped for some chocolates and a bottle of the wine she knew Lindsey preferred. Parking in the driveway, Nayla walked to the door, which opened as she approached and two small figures ran out to engulf her in the biggest hug they could manage.

"Gently, my small dears, I have something for you that I shouldn't drop," Nayla said as she maneuvered into the house without hurting her two leeches. Smiling, she handed the bottle and chocolates to Lindsey so that she could bend down and properly greet the children.

Bennie was four and Claire was two going on thirty. Turning to Lindsey, "Is Gerald home?"

"No, he'll be back a little later. He is having dinner at the club, with a couple of clients."

"It will be good to see him, too. So, Bennie and Claire, did you see the box I gave to your momma?"

"Yes, I did!" Bennie piped up. "Me too!" Claire said, not to be outdone.

"Inside are the most lovely chocolates I could find today. Did you two eat all of your dinner?"

"I did, but Claire didn't eat all of her corn. Mommy was mad," Bennie said helpfully.

"Can they have a piece?" Nayla asked Lindsey.

"Pleeeeease!" They chimed together.

"Sure, no more than two, though. The last thing I need are you bouncing around when you're supposed to be sleeping," Lindsey said in full mommy mode.

Nayla distributed the chocolates to her young fans and then handed the box to Lindsey.

"Thanks, was that a bottle of my favorite wine you handed me? And as I recall, you like it somewhat yourself. I'll pour us both a glass and you can spill whatever is on your mind," Lindsey said.

"That sounds good, I'll make sure Bennie and Claire don't drop any of their chocolate."

Lindsey popped the cork, and poured out two generous portions. Handing one glass to Nayla, she sat down on the couch next to her friend. The kids had gone back to their respective play, after having extracted their candy toll.

"So?"

"It's kind of hard to talk about, but I was putting together some of my contingency provisions and I realized I needed your help on something. I have a friend that I have known since childhood, which I would want to send a letter to right away if I died. I'm not really expecting to die soon, but I hadn't taken care of this detail. If it is alright with you, I would ask that you hold onto the letter confidentially and mail it immediately should something happen to me. My will and all of that is well in hand, but not as urgent as this would be," Nayla paused, staring into her wine glass. "I ask that you tell no one about the letter, Linds, not Gerald or Farid: no one. Will you do that for me?" Nayla asked.

"Of course, I will! Would I be breaking any laws?" She asked the question as if merely curious.

Nayla smiled at her friend's loyalty. "No, you wouldn't. Always so dramatic! No, this friend would be doing a few things before my will goes through probate, that's all. As a Greek national, he would have trouble doing what needs to be done if he wasn't given sufficient time. You know the Greeks: tomorrow is always a better day to do something. I've left some bequests for people who helped me in Gaza, and he would have to track them down," Nayla said.

"No worries. I should pull mine together, too, although I don't want to face that. You know my Mom and Dad died in an auto accident when I was 16: similar to you in timing. It is really hard to lose your parents so suddenly. I had Farid and other relatives, so I didn't have to fend for myself like you did. Yes, I'll do it. It will go in my personal safe and no one else will know."

"Thank you! Here it is, can you put it away now?" Nayla said.

"Certainly. Wait here, do you need a refresh on your wine?" Lindsey took the envelope into her office and placed it within her private wall safe, making sure the combination dial was spun afterwards.

"All done! We haven't spoken much since that election night party we were at, what's new in your life?"

"There has been something, well several somethings in fact. I can't tell you the details, but it could come out at some point to my general embarrassment," Nayla said.

"Ah, an illicit affair! Do tell me more!" Lindsey settled into the couch.

"I can't, but don't think less of me if it gets out in a big way. No, it's not Gerald. I don't know where it is going, or even how I got there, but it will be over soon I think."

"You're going to make me guess or speculate, aren't you? It isn't Farid; you wouldn't have to hedge if it were. In our work we meet too many powerful men, it will be hard to narrow down the candidates," Lindsey said mischievously.

"I'm not saying any more on that topic; it would just help you zero in. Different topic, the FBI has their hands full with this Martyrs al-Sabra terrorist plot. You know that this is the same thing they pulled us in to talk about earlier this year, right? The guy who interviewed me was a real dick, somebody named Jameson. Earlier I had spoken to Justin Simons, Farid's handsome friend, but then this Jameson guy took over. Did you talk to him or someone else?"

"Like you I started with Justin. Hey, tell me you're not sleeping with Justin!" Nayla shook her head no. "Anyhow, the interview with Justin was more just catching up. I met Jameson, he called me in for a follow-up. He's the guy who was asking about you, remember when I called? He had a lot of questions about Farid too. He wasn't all that bad in my conversation, just kept asking questions all over the map."

"In mine, I had to threaten to lawyer-up since he kept asking questions about my dead family. Clearly I was in his cross hairs for some reason. Once I did that, he went away. But the questions he asked indicated the current snipings are part of what they were investigating. Clearly they didn't get anywhere, as we now have three unsolved attacks. The one in Atlanta made me sick to my stomach. That poor little girl!" Nayla said.

"I know. My donors are starting to get itchy about the seeming lack of progress, they think the President should be doing more."

"Here it starts: a woman can't handle the crisis, right? We knew that was going to come out sooner or later, but too bad it happened in the first 100 days of her administration," Nayla bitterly observed.

"I've heard that Michael Rodriquez will be running with the administration's immigration reform push. He's a loyal guy, but I wonder if people will say she couldn't have gotten it done without him."

"I can see it happening. Too bad she doesn't have a female vice president. Did you hear what was in the reform package?" Nayla asked.

"I heard that it is only a whisper away from a national ID card that has to be carried by everyone. They will require immigrants to have something like it at all times or risk deportation. I don't know how they can realistically do that without everyone having to carry ID."

"These attacks might take us there anyway. If more happen and nothing develops I could see a declaration of martial law or something like it. I would hate to be wearing a hijab in this environment, the mob is only a step or two away from lashing out. If the sniping continues, there will be violence," Nayla said her face serious and grim.

"Yes, I think you're right. Nayla, you need to be really careful. DC is going to be full of people who are looking for targets." Lindsey reached over and squeezed Nayla's hand.

"I will. More than usual. I can pass for Italian, so it won't be as bad as it will be for those who are clearly Muslim. But then, the mob isn't that bright and may not make a distinction."

They chatted for a while longer, polishing off the bottle of wine and Nayla made her way home knowing that whatever happened would not go unmarked by loved ones.

• • •

Farid was spending the afternoon in the arms of his latest mistress, Marguerite ("call me Margo") Walsingham, the insatiable wife of Farid's boss. Although not naturally given to guilt, Farid knew Stuart Walsingham was spending his afternoon in the arms of his latest intern, so Farid felt even less than usual. Margo was in her mid-forties, and time had mostly been kind. Farid was just approaching forty himself, but he had found older women were the most fun from a recreational perspective. Especially, if she knew what a kegel was and when to use it.

Farid lay on Margo's bed, recovering his breath and looking around the otherwise immaculate room. He identified his clothes lying in a heap to one side, with a much smaller pile of hers topped by a hastily discarded black thong. *If there is anything more pathetic than a spent thong, I don't know what it is*, Farid thought to himself. It didn't matter how many times he indicated to her that he was most attracted to her everyday soccer mom garb; she still went the faux sex route made popular by strippers and mall lingerie shops when she wanted to feel sexy. Bad marketing on her part, or good marketing on the part of the strippers, it was hard to tell which.

Farid had seen the sniper news and decided that an afternoon with Margo was the best way he could spend his time while he waited to hear from Justin. He could imagine the FBI building as an angry hill of fire ants which had just been kicked. Woe to the hapless bystander who doesn't get the heck out of their way! Given the lack of announcement, it was pretty clear their investigation wasn't getting anywhere.

Margo came out of bathroom, looking as though she had never borne three grown children. Farid patted the bed next to himself and she climbed in.

"I saw your interview on the news yesterday, are you seeing any backlash over the sniper attacks?" Margo asked.

"You mean, because I am a known Muslim television personality? Not really. Most people who work with me are too embarrassed to ask the questions, and those in public mostly do not recognize me. You've seen both my made-up-for-television and the street versions, and the difference is pronounced. Besides, it isn't immediately obvious I am a Muslim."

"I just wondered if you should be concerned."

"I should probably be more concerned about my boss finding out I am in bed with his wife," Farid said as he ran his hand down to the small of her beautiful back, pulling her towards him once more.

"I won't tell," Margo gasped as the power of speech failed her once more.

• • •

President Brown took the bad news of another sniper attack with no outward reaction. As she had expected, another shooting had sent the online communities over the top with anger, fear, and blame. The press pool was getting restive as well.

"Sid, I'm thinking we make the Michael-Immigration announcement today and then talk about the sniping countermeasures we are considering. How does that play out in your mind?"

"Madame President, I think pairing the two is good politics, the same as you. That way, no one second guesses the division of labor or the reasons for it. That part is pretty straightforward, I think. What sniper countermeasures are you planning to talk about?" Sid Rosenbloom asked.

"I get the impression that the FBI doesn't know where these terrorists will strike next, so we cannot over deploy to any one place. If you remember the DC Sniper attacks, DC pulled in help from all the surrounding states as well as the FBI, and it still didn't flush them out. The problem here is a lot worse. We do not know how many snipers there are. What if there are ten, or even fifteen snipers? Which ten or fifteen cities do we send support to? As much as I hate to say it, we might have to institute night-time curfews nationwide. That won't stop any daytime attacks, but it will make night-time ones much more difficult. There is that citywide imagery platform we could deploy within a few cities, but it would be very expensive to keep those flying twenty-four hours a day. We might have to deploy National Guard at some point, which also gets expensive."

"I remember the DC Snipers. There was the feeling on the street that no one could stop them, and those guys were comparative amateurs. We've come a long way since in surveillance, but it is expensive to keep it up when nothing happens. I don't know that we can necessarily solve the problem, other than to deploy resources until it is dealt with. We're always going to be a step behind until there is a break in the case. So perhaps the message should be that you take the situation seriously and are focused upon it, examining all options as the situation develops," Sid said.

"This latest victim, how is he doing?"

"Jim Bledsloe, just a runner getting a jog in before going to work, African-American. He is expected to survive, but his condition is still guarded," Sid explained.

"So, are the victims random, do you think? I can't see a theme, other than the fact that they aren't Muslims."

"Thankfully, there are too few instances to truly call it random, but now we know it isn't just females being targeted. I don't think there is a target type, other than what you just said. How are they deciding which city is in play? If we knew that, we might be able to stop them. The FBI have identified three different guns, which means the San Francisco shooting wasn't necessarily the same shooter as Sacramento. Unfortunately, there are still too many possibilities in play. I think we will have to get lucky. Oh, you saw the report where all three shooters appeared to have been driving a Honda Accord? Keep in mind the DC Snipers were said to be driving a white panel truck, which turned out to be dead wrong. The Accord angle has yet to be released by the FBI, but as it is the single most popular car on the road it doesn't help all that much," Sid said.

"Did they get license plates on any of those cars?"

"Yes, and apparently they were all stolen plates from other Accords. The FBI is still trying to track them all down, but it might well be a dead end," Sid explained.

"The planning that went into this was substantial, and reflects a marked departure from the usual terrorist plot. How much credence do you place on this latest threat of a nuclear device?"

"Madame President, it would of course be catastrophic if true. So far, all the FBI has is an overheard conversation in a mosque. The FBI is all over it, but I wonder whether it is a terrorist tactic to overstress their resources? We've seen this terrorist group design their sniping operation to do exactly that. The armed forces assures me it would be extremely difficult to get a nuclear device inside the continental United States without it being noticed. The former Soviet weapons which were misplaced in the 1990's are all leaky older technology, and even easier to spot. Getting one inside the DC Beltway would be much more difficult. I'd say we take it seriously and investigate it, but try not to let it detract us from catching the snipers."

"I'll let the FBI do their job and stand ready to support them when needed. You know, Sid, we're going to remain vulnerable as a country to this kind of attack as long as we stubbornly remain the way we are. You know, in Israel this kind of attack would have been squelched almost immediately, because all citizens and visitors must carry identification at all times. They go through checkpoints and the security forces log movements. As long as 3% of our own population are unregistered aliens it provides a huge security hole terrorists can exploit. We can't address it, because we don't require that citizens carry IDs."

"Madame President, we don't know that illegal immigrants are behind the shootings," Sid cautioned.

"I know, but have you ever wondered why we don't, as a culture, carry IDs? Part of the reason, I believe, is it helps the employers of illegal aliens pay unlawfully low wages. There are powerful special interests, some donated to my campaign, who want that to continue happening. So it gets cast as a personal freedom issue for the masses, and the only ones who really benefit are criminals and special interests. I hate to say it, but this campaign might be just the catalyst to address illegal immigration."

"I wouldn't recommend saying it publicly, but there is a lot of truth in that observation. The question becomes what else do you want to accomplish this first term? Because if we go down this path towards a national ID card, it will be almost as big an effort as health care wound up being a few years ago. Religious folk will start talking about the Mark of the Beast accompanied by street protests. Their fears are behind popular opposition to ID schemes. They seem to also forget that Social Security Numbers do exactly the same thing, but aren't used for identification generally," Sid said.

"I don't need the religious core to get fractious, but we need to figure a way out of the Wild West which characterizes our approach to internal security. Let's table it for now. I'll make the announcement about Michael and promise all the support needed by the FBI. Have the terrorists made any demands? What is their objective?"

"The one letter received from the terrorists had the standard demands for return of Palestine to Palestinian rule, but no one really expects it to have been more than pro forma. I firmly believe The Hammer has simply taken terrorism to the next level and understands American culture far better than the previous groups who have attacked us. He is creating an ongoing atmosphere of nationwide fear and distrust, which he will encourage for as long as it is possible. The Hammer's product is continuous terror rather than the episodic variety. His ultimate objective might be destabilization of the country and its institutions. If this continues for long, the American people will turn on the government which isn't capable of protecting them and demand heads," Sid said.

"Continuing our stance of supporting the FBI might then be perceived as a weak response, and open my administration up to criticism. What would a stronger response look like?" Lucy asked.

"There isn't much in that playbook, but nationwide ID cards and martial law implemented with checkpoints. That would cause a completely different type of backlash, besides wrecking the economy. Our Hollywood campaign supporters would turn on us in an instant if they couldn't travel as freely as they want. You would see Internet conspiracy theories being propagated that have the government creating the whole crisis solely in order to seize power. Then domestic terror, known as freedom fighters to large segments of the country, would be seen much more frequently. That is before the backlash against Muslims even hits full stride. We are walking a really fine line here, and there are no power-related solutions which yield good results."

"Is there any good news?"

"Yes, Madame President. So far your popularity numbers are holding steady, Wall Street isn't panicking, and no one has been lynching Muslims even though harsh words are definitely in play."

"I'll make the Michael announcement, extend my concern over the shooters and ask the public to assist the FBI's investigation when requested. All the while, praying there aren't too many more shootings before there is a break in the investigation. Set it up, Sid."

"Yes, Madame President."

Maritime Maneuvers

"..With a third sniping attack committed by the Martyrs terrorists, questions are starting to be asked as to why the FBI is seemingly unable to find or apprehend the shooters. How many people are involved, where are they located? Having an entire nation looking over their shoulders in fear is not a sustainable solution in this reporter's opinion.."

Farid Monsour al Haj for World News Corporation

The Butler's Dosh, a small ocean-going motor yacht registered in the Dominican Republic, was a day en route to meet a container ship on the high seas. At the helm stood Amin, in his role as Sabir, while Reem formed the only crew. The ship had a range of 3,500 nautical miles with full fuel bunkers. They wouldn't need anything near the full capacity if everything went well. The container ship was destined for Houston; they planned to meet as it readied to pass the southern tip of Florida.

Sabir was at the helm and Reem manned the radio telephone to contact the ship. The security team was still aboard the container ship and ready to make the transfer. With the ship's bulk between Butler's Dosh and the distant coastline of the United States, the container ship powered down its engines and gradually slowed to a crawl. Sabir handed the helm over to Reem, slung the strap of a metal briefcase over his shoulder, and scrambled up the ladder which had descended from above. The security team lead and ship's captain met Sabir at the top.

"I can only do this speed for fifteen minutes before questions start coming in over the comsat transponder system," the captain informed Sabir.

"We won't be long; take me to the container and we'll be on our way," Sabir said.

Sabir followed his security lead down what seemed to be endless flights of metal stairs until they came to a large space filled with small-form containers. Their container was on the bottom of a large stack; the electronic security lock was still active and operative. Sabir turned to enter the codes necessary to safely open the container. The captain and security lead turned away after earning a dark look from Sabir. As the codes were entered, the device successfully cycled into an unlocked position.

"Here, give me a hand." Sabir opened the large doors wide to admit sufficient light into the container.

Working deftly, Sabir opened the coffin-like box which was secured to the middle of the container floor. There were additional electronic codes to be entered, which was done quickly as well. Sabir swung the hinged side of the box open. Inside, sat a large, canvas backpack looking like it carried something the size of a five-gallon water bottle. Wires snaked into a pocket within the backpack. Sabir opened the pocket flap and disconnected wires in the proper sequence to prevent accidental detonation. Then he grabbed several detonation devices from the walls of the box, placing them into pockets on the outside of the backpack.

He handed the briefcase over to his security lead, then turned to the captain, "Help me pick this up, please." With a heave the two men settled the bag upon his shoulders. "Damn, that's heavy! Is there an elevator to the deck?"

"Yes, over here. It's slow but better than bucking it up the stairs."

All three rode the elevator up to the main deck in silence and headed for the ladder. Sabir's security team was already gathered for their final instructions.

"Who are the three with maritime experience?" Sabir asked. Three men stepped forward, with their duffels already packed, and climbed down the ladder onto the Butler's Dosh. After they were safely aboard, Sabir turned to the captain motioning the security lead to open the briefcase. "This is for you, with another payment to be received when the balance of the team makes it back to the Gulf."

The captain eyed the open case, saw the bundled rows of hundred dollar bills, and nodded in satisfaction.

Sabir addressed the security lead, "Keep the men under tight control until they get back to the Gulf - they must not endanger our operation. The prince will not stand for it." Turning quickly, he backed down the ladder one step at a time to ensure his safe passage. Once he had arrived on the deck of the Butler's Dosh, he waved back up at the container ship and told Reem to warp them off away from the larger ship. The container ship engines began the rumbling that signified a return to cruising turns and slowly gained speed against the swells.

Turning to his crew of four, he said, "I hope you gentlemen are ready to spend some time in the Bahamas, you have a couple of weeks to wait. The beaches are nice; the food decent. I can think of worse places to spend some time. Let's get you checked out on how to operate the boat and familiar with your orders."

Leaving Reem at the helm, Sabir went below into the farthest cabin room where he deposited the 125 pounds of gear and securely locked the door before going back onto the deck.

The three were of Qatari origin, all with a background in maritime work. Mohammed, Khalid, and Nassir wasted no time becoming familiar with the Butler's Dosh. Mohammed had actually captained a small freighter in the Gulf, so he easily picked up what needed to be done to competently run the boat. It was actually a great deal more luxurious than the normal gulf freighter, or even the container ship, so the men planned to enjoy this adventure. Reem would return to the United States by way of British Virgin Islands after they docked in Nassau, in order to muddy the water a bit. Khalid and Nassir were tasked to report up to Mohammed on this voyage. The cover story, should anyone ask, was that they were the advance team for a Saudi royal family's Caribbean vacation and that they wanted a less noticeable presence than the usual massive yachts. This particular story was often used by royal family members with access to less funding, so it shouldn't raise any eyebrows.

The next day passed uneventfully as the crew got used to working together standing watches and conning the boat. Sabir made sure they were familiar with the operation of high-power magnetic hull connectors, most often used to attach booms to ships with oil leaks. He had quite another use in mind for these devices, though.

The Butler's Dosh stopped in Nassau long enough to drop Reem off.

"You have everything needed for the operation?" Reem asked Sabir.

"Yes, thank you. The devices are simple, yet sophisticated, I believe we will have no issues," Sabir said. "Be sure to monitor our channel closely in the event something unexpected is needed. Safe travels."

Reem nodded and strode off to catch a taxi at the front of the marina.

Sabir signaled Mohammed to pull off as he secured the lines aboard the boat. In short order, the Butler's Dosh was underway north and west. Several hours later they reached their temporary home, Andros Island.

Pulling into Andros Island harbor, Sabir made arrangements for docking the Butler's Dosh, and set a watch schedule which kept one person on the boat at all times. Otherwise, the crew was free to spend their time as they wished, but were cautioned against talking too much to the locals. The Qataris were unlikely to wander far as their English language skills were rudimentary.

Sabir-Amin made himself comfortable with the location, as he was to remain for the duration of this phase of the operation.

LIGHT IN THE TUNNEL

"..The FBI has so far produced no announced results on the Martyrs investigation. In the meantime, America is close to burning. Sources tell me hundreds if not thousands of law enforcement resources are currently tasked to the effort. Who is watching the rest of the store? Hate crimes against law abiding Muslim-Americans are on the rise, who will stop it? Who is left to be working on normal crimes like corruption, drugs, cartels, and so forth? .."

Farid Monsour al Haj for World News Corporation

Three shootings occurred in the week following the San Francisco sniper attack: in DC, Orlando, and Denver. The evidence for each showed a number of similarities, but Justin struggled to see how it could be used to predict the next target.

The snipers used different rifles of the same make in each city. Unfortunately, the model was one of the most popular sporting rifles ever made, the Winchester Model 70, and had been in general use for more than fifty years. Efforts to link the rifles themselves had proven fruitless, as large numbers had been in use prior to federal efforts to register firearms. The ammunition was definitely from the same production lot, maybe even from the same box. It had been shipped to an online seller who sold hundreds of thousands of rounds per month, and didn't track lots when shipping out the product. It had taken a significant amount of skill to inscribe the Arabic script on each shell casing, but there were no leads on that front.

The video captures from the shooting sites clearly established there was more than one shooter. In fact, so far not even one had been a repeat. None of the cameras had captured enough to make a firm identification, though. From what could be seen on camera, none of the shooters were poor drivers; they drove carefully and followed every traffic law. That worked against the possibility of a random traffic stop which provides a lucky break in the case. All the snipers appeared to be Middle Eastern, which wasn't widely communicated. The FBI and White House were trying to prevent an overreaction that would see Muslims persecuted.

Each of the shooters drove a late-model Honda Accord during their escape. The license plates were all stolen from similar Honda Accords.

Shoot, we don't even know which cities are involved! Justin thought. *How are we going to predict where they will strike next?* The task force was already stretched to the breaking point. Justin had expanded the scope of the investigation to include all field offices nationwide. Millions of budget dollars were being spent without much in the way of results. It would help a great deal to narrow the scope of the investigation down to a manageable number of potential sites. *We're trying to boil the ocean, and simply do not have the resources to do it.*

Justin sat up as a novel idea occurred to him. In his excitement, he dialed Quinton Jameson who by now had started to distance himself from Justin's failures on the task force.

"Boss, I just had a notion to help us narrow the field on which cities are in play," Justin said.

"Come over and tell me about it. I hope this one is better than what I've heard so far," Jameson sniped.

"Heading over," Justin said shaking his head. Jameson got to be even more of a prick as the pressure increased upstairs. Justin already knew he was nominated as the task force scapegoat if the investigation didn't break soon.

Knocking on the door frame, Justin entered Jameson's office and closed the door.

"So, what do you have?"

"Sir, you know how each of these shootings have the shooters using a late-model Honda Accord with stolen plates from another Accord? Well, I was wondering how we reduce the number of cities we have to cover with resources and it occurred to me. What if we go public, nationwide, and ask all owners of similar Honda Accords to check their cars and make sure that their correct license plate is installed? If it isn't, we have them contact the local FBI field office. We should be able to see the scope of the cities involved if there was a large enough publicity effort," Justin explained.

"By going public, aren't we tipping our hand to the terrorists?" Jameson asked.

"Yes, but then we would know what cities we have to watch. We need the help so we can concentrate the bureau's resources. It would also give us a pool of license numbers to watch for, if the shooters are operating in isolated cells, they may not be able to change their plans so easily."

"What if they are communicating in some fashion and recalibrate?" Jameson asked.

"In that case, we look at all sales transactions involving Honda Accords for the cities we identify. Putting the information out there would reduce the suspect list significantly. Frankly it gives us significantly more than we have right now, no matter how much it affects the terrorists' methods."

"Would you be looking for a high-level press conference to make the appeal?"

"Yes, I think we have a better shot getting to people if all the news outlets are participating," Justin said.

"OK, you've sold me. Let me take this upstairs, it might be something for the Director's office or even the President. She has been asking the Director if there is any way to be of assistance. I should have some initial feedback back to you in a couple of hours. In the meantime, please prepare a draft statement to use as a trial balloon for the discussions. The sooner I get it, the faster things will move along; especially if the President's speechwriters need to get involved."

"I'll go draft something short and sweet. You want me to forward the working file?" Justin asked.

"Yes, that way I can hand it off to whoever will be needing it. It's a good idea, Justin, and might help turn things around."

Justin headed back to his desk, already writing the press statement in his mind. An hour later, his smartphone lit up. Another shooting in Pittsburgh.

• • •

Nayla's smartphone rang with Jonny Ray's special ring-tone. She stood up from her desk and closed the office door.

"Hello, Darlin', you miss me?" Jonny Ray drawled.

"Hi JR! Of course, I did! When did you get back in town?"

"That's just it, I'm not quite there yet. But I thought I should call ahead and make some plans for us to get reacquainted. I'll be getting back Thursday night late, and was thinking we should spend Friday afternoon together. How does that sound?"

"That sounds wonderful! I'll block out the time from my schedule. How is the trip going? Making any progress with our less fortunate party members?" Nayla said.

"We were doing pretty good until all of these snipers got started. The Republicans are saying our lax security policies are the reason the attacks are possible. So: don't vote Democrat. As you know, the President put together an immigration program to work on those problems, but she didn't have time to get things going before this whole mess started. Mike is going to spearhead the effort, but the feeling in the field is: too little, too late. I don't think I've seen anything like what she's facing in her first 100 days. It's not fair, but then the world isn't. We're bringing in plenty of contributions, though."

"That is most likely due to your charismatic way of asking for them," Nayla said.

"My charisma is going to be focused on getting you out of your panties Friday afternoon. Wear something special, something that you wouldn't mind losing. I do miss seeing you. Being out of town for these couple of weeks has been hard."

"Please, Jonny Ray! A man like you has women in every campaign town," Nayla teased.

"That's been true my entire life, but right now there is only you. And Lucy, of course."

"Of course, and that, too, is as it should be. Hurry back, JR, Friday will be perfect."

"I will, Doll. My detail just poked his head in and said the Escalade is ready, so I have to go. I'll see you Friday, but will think of you a damn sight sooner," Jonny Ray hung up the call.

Nayla sat back at her desk. The Hammer had identified the end of this week as the last time she would need to see Jonny Ray. Strangely, she had come to like the man very much in spite of all the reasons she should hate him. Whatever The Hammer had planned, it was going to be very hard on Jonny Ray. Nayla forced herself to not think about it; there was nothing to be done at this point.

Nayla stood up and arranged her window blinds to signal she had information. Sitting back down, she turned her mind back to work-related matters.

After the day's work was completed, Nayla shut down her workstation and readied herself to spend the evening in her rented apartment. She stopped by a local grocery, picked up a bottle of wine, and some small snacks to set out for the upcoming meeting with The Hammer. Nayla recognized the emotional fatigue just under the surface of her consciousness and reflected the operation was ending at the right time for her peace of mind. Maybe a normal life waited sometime soon.

Letting herself into the apartment, she set about tidying up for her visitor, putting on some music in the background. Nayla found herself singing along to the American pop music fare as she worked. When she finished it seemed early enough to allow time for a quick shower and a change of clothing. She never felt completely clear of the workday until the thin coating of office dust had been washed from her body. As she stepped out of the small shower, she was surprised to see The Hammer standing in the doorway.

"My, you startled me!" Nayla said.

"Nayla, beautiful as always I see!" The Hammer observed. "What development did you have to report?"

"Let me get dressed, if you don't mind. Please open the bottle of wine sitting out in the kitchen, I'll be there in a few minutes."

Chuckling a little, The Hammer turned and went into the kitchen, opening drawers until he found a corkscrew. He deftly removed the foil and extracted the cork, pouring a glass for both Nayla and himself. Picking them up, he moved into the living room and sat upon the rich leather sofa. A few minutes later, as promised, Nayla joined him.

"I heard from Jonny Ray this afternoon. He is still out of town, but will return Thursday night. We scheduled to spend Friday afternoon and evening together."

"This is very good news. I'll make arrangements to remove our gear here tomorrow or Wednesday. You might want to get any personal items out as well. Plan on Friday being your last time with Jonny Ray," The Hammer said.

"You're not going to hurt him physically, are you? I know the attack is political and will fall upon him regardless, but he doesn't deserve to be killed doing it."

"I hadn't planned on doing so, besides it would be very difficult regardless, given all of the Secret Service protection which surrounds him most of the time. I think you can rest assured on that front."

"What are you planning to do to them?" Nayla asked casually.

The Hammer shook his head at her question. "Nayla, you know I will not share the operational details with you. It protects both of us. Aren't you happy you don't know the details on the Martyrs sniper operation?"

"I'm a woman. I can't help but feel regret when children are being killed. So, yes, I don't want to know more about it."

The Hammer's eyes flashed dangerously, "You know how many children have died in the Palestinian territories during the last fifty years? Their Palestinian mothers loved them just as much as these American mothers do, but no one cared what was being done by the Israeli armies. Israel would not exist today were it not for the American support. All Americans are therefore suitable targets for our operations, not just a select few. Americans need to feel the same hopelessness as that which prevails in Gaza and the West Bank. Maybe then they can gain some understanding and an appreciation of their sins."

"I'm not trying to make you angry. I am sorry if I have done so. You and I live a very nice life here that would not be possible anywhere else in the world. You have friends here, among the Americans, I know you do. I have American friends who have become like my own family," Nayla said softly.

"Of course I do. How can anyone exist in a place for a long time without making friends? You have to make friends in order to remain unnoticed. But I never forget why I am here, and I never let my friendships determine the course of my operations. Never."

"Never? And do you love anything or anyone? Love has been known to be exception-making."

"I love you, Nayla Kaldah. Most of those I love are dead."

"You've never said that before," Nayla said as her eyes filled. "I've always been the one telling you."

The Hammer set his glass down and turned to his love, "So now you've been told, what do you propose to do about it?"

She rushed into his arms, kissing his cheeks and lips before resting her head on his shoulder. "I'll be glad when this operation is over, and we can be seen together. Will you be making an American housewife of me?"

"You'll just have to wait and see. Unless you have already turned into an assertive American woman and plan on asking me instead? I've heard the Ivy League does that to a girl."

"That's Brown, not Harvard. Come with me and I'll show you some assertive!"

She stood and led The Hammer into the bedroom by his well-manicured hand.

• • •

Justin's desk phone rang; it was Jameson, "Justin, come down to my office."

"Yes sir, I'm on my way," Justin picked up his notebook and made the trek through the warren of cubicles that was the decaying J. Edgar Hoover building in DC. News of another Martyrs shooting had just come across his desk: Houston this time. It was the same modus operandi, but this time it happened in a suburban apartment complex in the early morning hours which left them with no video footage. The media coverage had become unhinged. Newsroom pundits even had their own profilers drawing up completely unauthorized profiles of the type of people who could be the snipers. Justin didn't have a lot of faith in the Bureau's own profilers, they seemed to always be fighting the last war, as the methods fit the past but not necessarily the future. The future was terrorism, not psychopaths. The shooters probably saw themselves as freedom fighters and were about as likely to be fingered by a profile as win a Lottery jackpot. The media was simply engaged in generating news content, even the President's announcement of a new immigration reform effort couldn't compete with stories of the Martyrs killers striking victims in various cities. Jameson had vanished yesterday afternoon after their discussion about a press release, and with this new incident Justin didn't know what kind of reception awaited him.

Justin rapped lightly on Jameson's door-jamb and entered his office. He was on the phone talking but motioned to one of the seats in front of the desk. Wrapping up the call, Jameson turned his attention to Justin.

"What a difference a day makes. I was struggling yesterday to get anyone to buy into your press release suggestion, but after this morning's shooting, minds have suddenly come into focus. Today makes seven shootings in seven different cities. Is it the same M.O. as all the others?"

"Yes, sir. The same model gun, and we're expecting the same ammunition source but tests come back on that later today. The Houston field office hit the ground running, given all of the data we've been sharing nationwide. One thing we weren't able to confirm is the Honda Accord angle on this one, as the traffic cams didn't come into play until some distance away from the site, and the timeframe was during the early morning work commute," Justin briefed.

Jameson nodded. "The Director wasn't in favor of any public release of information, even if it led to something which could possibly help the investigation. He believes strongly in keeping details secret during the process. That all changed this morning, when the Houston shooting occurred and the President called. You and I are heading over to speak with Sidney Rosenbloom at the White House in two hours."

"Does this mean the President will make the appeal?" Justin asked.

"It means the President is considering doing so. The public appeal is going to happen, the only issue now is who does it. The whole situation is fraught with political risk, especially if it leads to no benefits for the investigation. We'll make our case to Sid, and he'll decide whether it makes sense to have the President involved."

"Do we need to tweak the draft text before heading over?" Justin asked.

"No need, we'll bring a copy along for reference, but it will be rewritten by the President's speechwriting team if the White House decides to be involved. I'll meet you in the lobby in ninety minutes and we'll head over."

Justin went back to his desk and started pulling together data summarizing the current state of the investigation. He had already committed most of the details to memory, but having it in print made him feel more confident. The most recent data from Houston had yet to make it into the status update, so he added a couple of paragraphs to summarize. Justin had never been to the White House in a working capacity and didn't want to advertise his lack of experience. At the appointed time, he grabbed his suit coat and ran down a short list of things he needed to bring along before meeting Jameson in the Lobby. The weather was clear and crisp, as only a spring day in DC can be, so they decided to walk the five blocks to the White House.

As they were processing through White House security, both handed over their service weapons to be held at the guard station while they were inside. After donning their non-escort visitor's badges, Jameson led the way to the Chief of Staff's office. He checked in with Rosenbloom's administrative assistant, and then they sat down to wait.

Their appointment time had only passed by fifteen minutes, when the admin waved them into the Chief of Staff's office. Sidney was on the phone giving some rapid fire instructions to someone, and he waved the two over to a small sofa set in the middle of the room. A tired-looking woman sat in a chair next to the sofa, and she nodded to the two as they sat down.

Sid hung up the phone and joined the group. "Gentlemen, I invited Ashley Cohen to sit in as she will be the one tasked with a release rewrite, if we go that direction. Ashley, this is FBI Section Chief Quinton Jameson. Quinton?"

"Nice to meet you. This is Special Agent Justin Simons who works for me. We're tasked to the Martyrs terrorist case," Jameson said. Justin nodded his head to both Ashley and Sid.

"Alright, Quinton. Could you explain where we stand on the case and what you are proposing being done?" Sid asked.

"Certainly, Justin is the tactical lead of the task force, though, so he will do the briefing," Jameson said.

All eyes turned to Justin. *I guess this is my sink-or-swim moment,* he thought to himself. Justin was a little surprised Jameson allowed him to talk at all, but given the political situation it was probably the best play. If he did well, Jameson got credit for being a good manager, if things went sideways Jameson could deny responsibility. *Fortune doesn't favor the faint of heart, here goes.*

Justin started off by summarizing how the investigation got started in the first place, leaving out the top secret details of means and methods. Sid proved to be an attentive listener, occasionally stopping Justin with clarifying questions which were never off-topic. Ashley didn't say anything but was writing copious notes as they went.

As Justin went through the seven shootings, he pointed out similarities and differences so the extent of the Bureau's case was evident. As the briefing concluded, he outlined his proposal to ask the public for help in the area of the stolen license plates.

"Thank you for the summary, Justin. What outcome are you hoping for with the proposal?" Sid asked.

"Right now we have eight shootings in eight different cities by, what appears to be, eight different shooters. How many more cities are there? Given what we currently know, it has been very difficult to concentrate our resources to the right places. Right now, we have general alerts out to all of the FBI field offices, which means a lot of resources are potentially being wasted. If we know which cities have been targeted, we could pull resources from places that weren't to help with the investigation. So the benefit would hopefully be a list of targets," Justin explained.

"Interesting. I can think of a number of ways this might lead to a break in the case. If a public appeal is made, what would be the benefit of the President doing it?" Sid asked.

"Well, sir, initially I thought the Bureau would be the ones making the appeal so my draft release was written along those lines. But a key element here is driving citizen participation, which means mass exposure of the information. President Brown would bring an added level of exposure the Bureau press pool couldn't match. We have to reach as many of the right people as possible, and gain their full cooperation. I can't predict whether the President is absolutely needed for it, but she would add significantly to the media coverage," Justin said.

"Thank you, Justin. Ashley, do you have any questions?" Sid asked.

"Yes. Justin, how much of the overall story can be shared as part of the appeal?" Ashley asked.

"I can speak to that," Jameson said. "From a law enforcement perspective, we should share as little as possible in order to protect the investigation. Obviously, we have to share the detail about stolen license plates, but we don't have to mention the make or model of the cars. Sure, we'll get some extra data, but we can easily filter for Honda Accord later. If the terrorists shift car models after the appeal, we might get a lead there, too."

"I agree. I initially planned to release that information in my draft, but a general appeal is even better," Justin said.

"I think we have everything we need. Justin, please exchange your draft information with Ashley on the way out. Quinton, thank you for coming down here on short notice. I should be able to let you know how we want this to play out later this evening," Sid stood and shook both of the agents' hands in dismissal.

Justin stopped to hand Ashley the draft he carried and, taking her card, promised to send the file to her as soon as he got back to the FBI building. Justin and Quinton handed in their visitor badges at the security gate and retrieved their service weapons before heading back to the FBI building.

"Justin, you did a good job laying it all out for Sid. I'm pretty sure he was already in support, otherwise Ashley wouldn't have been in the room," Jameson said.

"Thank you, sir. I got the impression that you and Mr. Rosenbloom know each other."

"We do, old school ties and all of that. I have had occasion in the past to work with him as well. That information is known widely inside the beltway, which is another reason why you were tapped to lead the effort. The President and Sid are very sensitive to accusations of insider dealing when it comes to official work, so they prefer to hold those of us who are perceived to be close to them at arm's length. The Director couldn't do it, since he was one of the groomsmen at Sid's wedding. I'm sure Ashley was pulled into the meeting partially for that reason as well."

Great! Now I am a token participant, Justin thought. *It doesn't matter to me so long as we are able to catch the terrorists.*

"I'm going up to the Director's office to brief him on the meeting. I'll loop back with you later today," Jameson said.

Justin sat down at his desk and decided to call Farid. They hadn't spoken since the Orlando attack, which was only four days earlier, but it felt like much longer given the three shootings which had followed. "Farid, Justin here. Do you have a few minutes to chat?"

"Yes, let me get into a conference room for a little privacy. Here, that's better. What's up?" Farid asked.

"We haven't spoken since last Friday, and there have been three more shootings since then. I wanted to get a sense from you on how the local Muslim community is weathering the storm."

"Not very well. They're afraid people will blame them for all of the shootings. So far there hasn't been much along those lines: some vandalism, some name-calling, but no overt violence. Several of the businessmen said their business was down, and no one has the Martyrs al-Sabra charity collection jars out anymore. As you know, I sit on the board of that charity foundation, the loss of donations will be quite a blow to the work we've been doing overseas," Farid said.

"How about you?"

"More death threats than usual, mostly for having the effrontery to explain the Muslim point of view, not because I am a Muslim, oddly enough." Farid sounded exhausted.

"Did you report the death threats to the police?" Justin asked.

"No. Reporters get online death threats all the time. The good-looking women reporters get rape threats; it is all part of the job description. Most of us just have good security in place. You know I can take care of myself, karate-buddy! I take it a day at a time, In Sha Allah."

Justin laughed as he thought back upon the karate classes. Farid had taken up karate after being bullied in school. Justin had joined him in the classes after the two of them stood down the same bullies in a school hallway melee. Both students had attained a black belt before graduating high school. At first, Justin had an advantage being so large, but Farid was nimbly athletic and, after a growth spurt, was later able to spar with Justin on an equal basis. Some days, Farid's speed could not be countered by size and strength. No, as long as an attacker didn't shoot at him from a distance, Farid was fairly safe. "As long as they aren't snipers, I agree."

"This sniper thing is getting out of hand. I can't help but feel we are adding steam to a pressure cooker with every new shooting that is reported. You know at some point one or more of the rednecks are going to pop and who knows where that goes. How is Jan doing?"

"They have canceled all after-school activities for children in Potomac Falls, and she's not going to evening tennis any more. Jan knows the odds of being a target are very small but she is worried nonetheless. That is one lottery she does not want to win," Justin said. "Farid, has there been any other conversation in mosque about The Hammer?"

"Just one which seems to pop up every time there is a terrorist incident, namely that a Saudi prince had funded the effort."

"Why didn't you call me?" Justin said.

"I was going to mention it when we next spoke, but you have to understand. When anything happens in the Muslim world, a conspiracy of the powerful is always the first guess, and the favorite conspirator is usually a Saudi prince. Kind of similar to American rednecks and the Illuminati. If I hear something definite, like a Saudi prince's name, I'll call right away. Otherwise I would likely be wasting your time."

Justin reined in his annoyance. "One thing I have learned here at the Bureau, you don't know where the break in a case will come from, so we try to capture everything so we don't miss it when it happens.

Yes, it means we have a lot of extraneous data, but sorting through that data pays for my palatial manse in Loudoun County. You don't want me to have to resort to building a Disability Insurance Law practice, do you?" Justin said.

Farid fought back a laugh at the mental image of his friend, the former college linebacker, making bad television commercials in ill-fitting suits for local cable television audiences. "No, we definitely want to avoid that. Jan would have to leave you cold. Shoot, even Beth would be calling me for a new place to sleep."

"That's low, talking about taking a man's dog. Look, be careful, I have a feeling that things will heat up before they get better," Justin said.

"I agree. From the public point of view, it feels like the sniping attacks are just getting started. I hope I am wrong about that."

"You and me both, brother! Stay close to the office. I think some-thing along the lines of a press conference will happen later today or early tomorrow," Justin confided.

"Thanks, I will. Take no chances yourself, Justin. I'll call if I have something," Farid rang off.

No sooner had Justin hung up the phone, when it was ringing once more.

"Hi Justin, this is Ashley Cohen."

"Hi Ashley, did you have an issue with the file I sent over?" Justin asked.

"No, actually I didn't. I'm calling about another matter. Does the Bureau have a telephone tip line we want the public to use for this?"

"Why yes, we do. I'm sorry it wasn't in the draft. I'll find out which one we want to use and send it over. Thanks for asking, it would have been an embarrassment to make the appeal without a contact point."

"You're welcome. Don't worry, it gets a lot easier."

"I'm sorry, I don't follow."

"Today was your first White House visit, correct? That is what will get easier," Ashley said with a hint of humor.

"Now I'm embarrassed, it showed that much?"

"It showed to the discerning, but wasn't all that glaring. Everyone has to adjust to the rarified atmosphere when they first arrive. For what it is worth, Sid was impressed with your summary. He appreciates people who don't waste his time."

"I appreciate the feedback. I'll keep it in mind if I come back," Justin said.

"You were noticed, you'll be back."

"Thanks, I just sent that toll-free number over to you. We'll have the call center spun up to coincide with the appeal. So the President plans to present it?"

"Not determined yet. I am writing a draft however. I'll call if there are any further questions," Ashley rang off.

• • •

That evening, President Lucinda Brown addressed the nation, conveying her condolences to the victims of the Martyrs sniping attacks once more and asking everyone in the United States to check their car license plates - to make sure they were not stolen. An FBI toll-free contact number was provided. The President stated that, with the help of the entire nation, it would be possible to capture or eliminate the terrorists. Immediately after the President's speech, phones started ringing at the FBI.

• • •

Thirty minutes after the President's speech, a mobile phone rang in the Bahamas.

"Andro?"

"Yes," Amin said.

"Status?" The Hammer asked.

"Boat made it through the storm just fine. The new crew looks like they will work out also. We're still talking 47?"

"Yes, that sounds perfect. I have something else. The other crew needs to shift to second gear. The car's been found."

"Understood. Will get the word out immediately. The Internet is crap down here but Nico or Antonio will take care of it," Amin said.

"Good. The floater will be remote, right?"

"Yes, timer with about six hour start."

"Perfect. Will our kinsman be ready after that?"

"Yes, immediately after all the euphoria."

"Keep this phone charged, the next few days will be very important," the Hammer instructed.

"Understood," the connection ended.

• • •

The FBI response team had their work cut out for them, walking each caller through a standard set of questions, verifying the answers, and thanking them for their contribution. The Interactive Voice Response system was programmed to be very polite to the callers still in queue while the agents were busy, even going so far as to offer to telephone them back when an agent was available. Regardless the caller IDs were captured, so even the drops could be investigated.

As the agents entered the data into the system, back-end software filtered and extracted information from the current sniper cities. Justin was gratified to see twelve possible candidates quickly come up in Roseville, California. Those numbers were compared to the total list of newly-registered, late-model Honda Accords within the Sacramento area. Surreptitious filtering of those registrations with Arabic or Muslim surnames was run as well. That analysis yielded a list of six names with addresses.

Justin picked up the phone and dialed a number in the FBI Roseville Branch Office. "Dan Adams? Hello, this is Justin Simons. We might have something for you."

"Hi Justin. We saw the President's address, did it come out of that?" Dan Adams asked.

"Yes it did, very fast, too. I wanted to get to you first, because we don't know how much time the information will be useful. I'm sending you a list of six names, which popped out of the license plate analysis. We scanned for the numbers, recent registrations of similar vehicles, and possible Muslim ethnicity."

"I didn't hear that last piece, I assume?"

"That is correct. It should be in your email now. Please follow up on these and let me know if anything develops. If possible, we want to observe the suspects rather than bringing them in immediately so we can understand their process. Let me know if you need help obtaining wiretapping warrants, no one in DC is going to be amused by a judge getting a wild hair for civil liberties in the current environment," Justin said.

"Thank you. I can tell you no one is likely to cause an issue on this end. The metro area has been pretty much shut down with all the fear. We're not proud of being the first in line either. The Roseville and Sacramento PD will be anxious to help us out."

"Good. Good hunting, I have a few more folks to call. I'll be back in touch if more leads come in, it is going to be a long night, but it feels like progress is possible." Justin hung up and set up his next call to Atlanta.

• • •

That night in a partial meeting of the guild outside the virtual human capital city, the circle commenced with only one officer in the middle. Only twenty of the shooter characters had received word of the special meeting in time. It would be repeated at the regularly scheduled meeting Wednesday evening, but the instructions were too important to wait.

Reem's character SnackSnick stopped dancing and sat down without any additional movement. He held the position for three minutes without doing anything. Then he jumped up twice, and sat down again. He repeated cycle several times, until all members had acknowledged the instructions. Essentially, Reem had communicated the signal for phase two, which was to be invoked when there was a possible breach in operation security. Getaway vehicles would have to change for future shoots. Reem signed off, hoping that the message had gotten to the most vulnerable ones. One day wasn't much of a delay, but might make the critical difference.

One person who hadn't made the online session was Munir from Sacramento, whose wife had picked that evening to bring in a number of extended relatives for dinner. As head of the household, he had to maintain a presence and stay involved. Playing the online game had become something he enjoyed, but it was a solitary pursuit, certainly nothing you would share with relatives who revered you for being a successful dentist. The Honda Accord had remained in his garage ever since the shooting, and he planned to do the necessary license plate changes when his number came up again.

What he didn't count on was that his wife took the car out occasionally when he was at the office. It never occurred to him that she might have secrets of her own. Because the car was kept hidden in the garage, Munir's mirror hadn't seen the lapse in protocol. Munir's online activity still fell within acceptable parameters and he had a steady online presence in-game. No behavior red flags were obvious to any of the watchers.

Munir's name came up in the night's FBI screen for recent registrations of late model Honda Accords, and, unknown to Munir, traffic cameras had captured the stolen license plate during his getaway. Earlier, the owner of the stolen license plate had been investigated to a dead end. It was only the purest luck that the automated Big Data scan of the coordinated take of all the region's traffic cams didn't start until after the President's address. Any earlier and Munir's wife would have been flagged in one of her illicit outings. Munir suffered within the grip of his extended family, knowing he could not share the things he had done, and instead looked forward to his number coming up once more. In fact, he wanted to scout the next shooting site, so he sat distracted amidst the noise of less successful relatives eating the food his money had provided.

None of the other shooters had been so lax, each had immediately replaced the registered license plates on their cars after their shootings. Now that they received the phase two flag from the guild officer, they each placed ads to sell the Honda on Craigslist for a quite reasonable price. The next car could be any common one in their area which could be obtained inexpensively. Each of them had to concoct an excuse as to why they sold the Honda so soon after buying it, in the event law enforcement asked. Future shootings would involve different car models.

• • •

Early in the morning, Justin checked himself into an inexpensive hotel close by the FBI building to get a few hours of sleep. He had spoken to Jan shortly before she and the kids retired for the evening.

She was encouraged about the progress being made after the President's appeal, but less happy Justin wouldn't be home. But she agreed that an hour long drive home for three hours of sleep wasn't the best plan. Justin stripped off his sweaty work clothes and stood in the shower for a long twenty minutes. He always kept a spare set of clothes at the Bureau for occasions like this one, never quite knowing when it would be needed. After his shower, he collapsed on the hotel bed with the room AC set as cold as it would go and oblivion claimed him.

A few hours later the alarm woke him at 7 a.m. He got up slowly, started the substandard room coffee to brewing while he shaved and showered. Perusing the news on his mobile phone, Justin saw no further Martyrs shootings had been reported, which came as a bit of a relief. He called home to see how Jan was doing prior to checking out of the hotel. They were doing well, and the children were getting ready for their school day. Jan had taken to walking them to the corner where they caught the bus in the mornings. Normally, Justin would have accused her of being a helicopter parent, but in recent days one couldn't joke about it; especially if you were heading a task force in the stalled investigation. Justin passed on his love and promised to be home that evening come what may.

The office was much busier than normal due to the massive effort of reviewing the data off the telephone tip lines. Hundreds of files were being created and parceled out for teams to investigate. There were data summaries waiting for Justin on his desk, which he sat down to review. Almost immediately, he saw a fair amount of activity in the largest metro areas, which was to be expected. One of the challenges of the investigation was the lack of a historic baseline of incidences for license plate theft. It was one of those nuisance-type thefts which didn't rise to the same level of urgency as assault or murder. Justin shot off an email to the data team asking them to review DMV records to provide some basis of comparison.

The scan with the Muslim profiling filter yielded a manageable list of potential suspects in each major city. If any of those suspects had one of the stolen license plates, it would be like winning the lottery. Justin could see something very interesting, namely that the cities involved were among the largest in the United States and there appeared to be as many as 35 cities involved. Justin searched for a list of the biggest metro areas within the United States and was struck by the results. Just to be sure, he checked the list of stolen license plate cities against the large metro list. He picked up the phone and dialed Jameson's mobile number.

"Jameson," the boss sounded sleepy.

"Sir, Justin here. I apologize if I woke you, but, I just found something I think is significant. When I compare the list of stolen license plate reports for Honda Accords against the largest metro areas of the United States I am seeing a match. Every single one of the top twenty or so areas are represented, based on last night's take: an exact match. The further out you go there are gaps. What if the Hammer just picked the 30-40 largest metro areas and positioned shooters there? I think we may have our list."

"That is good news if it holds true. How likely is it that the data would appear that way even without our shooters?"

"Hard to tell, it is something we'll have to look at. No one really watches this kind of theft closely. It makes sense larger metro areas would see more of it, but usually the thief doesn't replace the missing license plate with another one."

"I'll be in within the next two hours. See what you can pull together in that time and let's jump on an action plan so that we don't lose the time advantage."

"Yes, sir," Justin said as Jameson hung up.

Justin spent the next few minutes putting together a small presentation deck comparing the incidences of stolen license plates to the existing shooter incident locations. While the correlation could simply be a function of city size driving more of this type of offence, it was hard to ignore the complete overlap between the two lists.

The new Big Data scanning engine, HORUS, wasn't something freely available or normally affordable to local law enforcement agencies. Justin wondered whether a public appeal would have been necessary had it been deployed from the first. Of course, in retrospect everything looks obvious. In all of the shootings where a license plate was identified, the local law enforcement agencies had flagged the plates so any officer spotting it would raise the alarm. However, that old school method depended on a human getting within range of the car. HORUS, which Brooster Technologies Corporation had been trying to sell to the FBI for almost five years, digested video feeds from thousands of traffic cameras at intersections and toll booths in near real-time. If any of these license plates were still in play, the software would point it out and track them.

Brooster Technologies had donated the use of the program installed in the cloud, with technical support, to the FBI and local law enforcement. The only constraint left was the size of the Internet connections necessary to securely stream the video from each of the jurisdictions involved. Justin wasn't really surprised that some of the local departments and FBI offices had extremely small connections in the interest of economy. In conjunction with national and local telecommunications companies, temporary "Big Pipes" were being deployed without consideration of cost, as fast as possible.

Initially, the installations had been limited to the eight cities where attacks had occurred. Justin added a slide advocating expanding that to include the top 40 metropolitan areas, and scanning for all of the stolen license plates. It would take some time to get approval to do so, as the expense was considerable even with the program and telecommunications being donated. But Justin had to try. The next shooting would be a terrible burden if it fell within the same modus operandi and the Bureau didn't do everything it could to prevent it.

• • •

Munir got ready to go to the office the morning after all of his relatives had departed. It had been a late night, and his patients would have suffered in the dental chair if not for the strong coffee his wife prepared for him.

In some ways, the office was a respite from the demands of family and Muslim friends. He was in control there. But never more so than the day after he had shot the fat woman in Roseville. That day he had felt as though his personal power could scarcely be contained. But again, the necessary restriction of secrecy diluted much of his pleasure. While being secretly powerful had its appeal, being publicly so was even more attractive. The respect he had in mosque for being a dentist and an educated man would have been seasoned with fear as well.

Munir, like many other intelligent men, was bullied as a child and considered, as some Americans would have called it, a nerd. Adults treat doctors and dentists with respect for their professional skills, but the respect that comes from fear is fairly rare. Munir watched the television coverage of the Martyrs campaign like a secret football fan in a home where sports were banned. It was all he could do to not crow aloud with the announcement of each shooting and say "I was the first!"

Munir decided to seduce his new dental assistant, Melanie Baker, over the next few weeks. She was an attractive blonde single-mother in her early thirties, fit but not fanatically so. She would definitely be receptive to someone with Munir's gifts. Melanie's work was good and would get better once she was comfortable with the office processes. Munir had been supportive of her schedule needs and respectful in front of others. Ever since the shooting, it felt as though he could easily influence her into a bedroom. For that reason, he decided to continue driving the BMW to work, as the Honda sedan didn't make the same impression.

"Munir, I'll drive you to work today, I need the car to run some errands," his wife Maryam said.

"No, I need it all week. The errands can wait until later in the evening," Munir said.

"Some of the stores are not open in the evening. I need to use the car during the day."

Munir was in no mood to hear it. "I said it can wait. It can wait. Have one of your friends take you if it is so important."

"It is my turn to take my friends this time."

"I have said all that I am going to say, woman! You have a good life with me, provided by my work, you need to remember that," Munir said.

When Munir got into this kind of mood, his wife knew better than to press the issue. Besides, she had another option sitting in the garage. "I'm sorry, you are right of course. I will wait. What meal would you like this evening after work?"

Slightly mollified, Munir said "I might be late tonight if the sales rep wants to buy dinner. So please do not plan anything special."

"Don't be too late," his wife called after him as he left the kitchen for the garage.

His thoughts were rushing ahead even as he closed the door. Tonight might be the right time to do some more area reconnaissance in the event that he was called upon to perform another shooting. If he wanted, he could copy his assistant's home address and combine the two tasks. It was too soon to show up at her door, but it would be good to see what her lifestyle looked like. Munir wordlessly hummed a tune as he drove off.

Behind Munir, his wife planned out her day as well. Perhaps an early lunch with friends and an afternoon spent shopping. The car keys were in the desk drawer. The day was all hers.

• • •

"We've got a hit on the license plate for the Roseville shooting. Roseville PD has been notified and they are following the car remotely. We're also seeing it come up in near real-time through the HORUS video feed. The driver appears to be a middle-aged woman, but we don't have an ID yet," Jameson said.

"That is fantastic news!" Justin watched as the driver pulled into the parking lot of a diner. She exited the car and stood at the entrance door, waiting. A few minutes later, a car load of women pulled into the parking lot. She waved at them, and they all went inside the diner together.

"Is there any way we can get a high resolution photo of the driver?" Justin asked the team that was linked together on a conference bridge.

"We have a plainclothes detective headed for the scene with a surveillance camera with a big lens. He'll set up across the street and get her as she leaves the diner," Dan Adams of the Roseville Branch Office replied. "We'll uplink immediately and see if we can get an ID."

"I wonder if the deer rifle is still in the trunk," Justin said. "That would almost be too much to ask. We know she isn't the shooter, we'll have to see whom she goes home to. Does anyone have an opinion on ethnicity?"

"She could be of Middle East, Greek, or Italian extraction from what little we saw," Dan said.

"I hope she is connected and not just someone the shooter used to replace license plates. Dan, your team has a Stinger available, right?" Justin asked.

The Stinger was a device that enabled the capture of a suspect's mobile phone traffic. Essentially, it would simulate a powerful cell site, drawing in phone connections in the surrounding area. Use of the device was occasionally controversial because the device captured all devices within range, rather than just the target device.

Suspects would make calls or send text messages not suspecting that it went through the surveillance gear first. The Stinger would be the first element of surveillance in place, once the suspect was identified, since it was the easiest to deploy. It would be followed by court orders to wiretap the home. Given the nature of the national security threat, Justin did not anticipate any delays putting things in place, but even abbreviated approvals took time.

"Yes, we have it standing by. The detective is on the scene now for the photo shoot."

The team sat watching the television monitors as the minutes ticked away.

"Maybe the detective or someone else, should go inside for a cup of coffee and see what can be learned?" Jameson said.

"His partner can go in. Hold on, I'll radio them," Dan said. "The partner will go in and try to take a pass by the group, if possible."

The team sat for another ten minutes with no new developments. The tension in the room was palpable. This woman's car was the first real lead in an otherwise completely opaque case.

"Dan, does the detective have any of the magnetic GPS tracker devices? Maybe one can be put onto the car, if she is still fully engaged with her friends," Justin asked.

"The partner is coming back out, let's hear what he has to say when he gets back to the car. I'll ask about the GPS tracker," Dan said.

A few more minutes passed. "The partner said the women don't look like they are going anywhere for a while longer. They just finished their meal and are ordering desserts. He also said they were speaking a foreign language amongst themselves. He thinks it is Arabic, but doesn't really know the language firsthand. The detective has a GPS tracker in his car, and will task his partner with placing it while watching the front door," Dan reported.

"Good idea, Justin. This way the follow vehicles can run a little further back. Don't want to spook our quarry at this point," Jameson said.

"She's come out, we've got some really good pictures. Those will be coming to the command center shortly. She's pulling out. We'll hang back and follow."

The next two hours were spent following the woman on her shopping expeditions to a local mall and various retail outlets. Finally, around 3 p.m., she appeared to be headed for home. Evidently, the HORUS software did an even better job tracking a car when it was already identified. There were only a few times the video coverage lapsed, and then only for a few seconds. In about twenty minutes, the coverage ceased as she pulled into an upper middle-class neighborhood with single family homes, pulling into her driveway and garage. The trailing officers reported the address over the bridge, and the task force had a name.

"The house belongs to Munir Hammayil and Maryam Said, husband and wife," Dan reported. "Munir is a dentist in Roseville; we have an office location. We're going to need another Stinger, Justin, if we want one each on the residence and office."

Justin picked up his mobile phone and dialed the Sacramento metro team to arrange for the extra unit.

"Dan, are we sending a plainclothes team to get eyes on the good dentist?" Jameson asked.

"Yes, sir, we'll have teams on both of them. Where should the first Stinger go? I'm thinking the office until we can get a second one in place?"

"I concur. We know the shooter wasn't her. Let's see if we can find some photos of Munir and compare against the shooter pictures. Hold on, we're getting immigration data. Munir was barely a teenager when his parents immigrated to the United States; he has been here for over forty years. Did all of his university and dental college work here," Jameson said. "Justin, let's get the wiretap warrant request over to the judge for approval, you have everything needed to complete it? I want an Internet tap on both the home and the office, in the next few hours."

"Yes, sir. The judge is standing by, I'll head over and call when it is in hand," Justin said.

"Good. Make sure the Internet provider knows it is coming, Dan. We can't have any delays on this," Jameson said.

On the way over to the judge's chambers, Justin sent a quick text message to Ashley Cohen "Suspect ID'd in Roseville, getting wire warrants." Ashley sent back a quick "Thanks, good luck!". Navigating the politics which were necessary to rise within the Bureau had not been a major consideration for Justin in the past. He was entering a brave new world, and recognized how easy it would be to stumble. Justin was always popular with his coworkers and generally so with superiors, but Jameson was one of those superiors who always had a quid pro quo in the back of his mind when doing something for his employees. Doing a great job was only table stakes with Jameson.

Justin was ushered into the judge's chambers quickly, as he was clearly expected. The judge asked a few questions about the need for the warrant and swiftly gave his approval. He, too, wished the Bureau well as the sniper threat had affected everyone who lived near a metro area. If the snipers were caught, maybe things could go back to the way it was before. Everyone hoped it would. Justin called into the team bridge and announced the warrants were in hand as he walked back to the office.

"We should be up with the cable Internet service provider very quickly. I've got a team headed that way now. The company was very cooperative, pending the receipt of the warrant paperwork. We also got lucky on this one. The central office location where we need to tap in is the same for both addresses. The Stinger will be in place in the next thirty minutes," Dan said.

"Good news. Now we wait for the data to start coming in. The East Coast team should grab some takeout dinner in shifts, I expect this will be a full staff event until lights-out on the West Coast," Jameson said.

The room emptied of about half the task force at the mention of dinner. There were a large number of take-out restaurants close by the building which seemed to have built their business on hungry special agents working late into the night. Justin made it back into the task force situation room, and started scanning the warrants for transmission to Roseville. One of the warrants kept getting jammed as he fed it through the combination scanner, copier and fax machine. The paper must have picked up some of the spring humidity on the way back, he thought. Finally, he had two electronic scans to forward to Roseville.

"Dan, look in the drop box under the Warrants folder, you should be good to go," Justin said.

"Thanks! Just-in time."

Justin shook his head, *everyone's a comedian.* Farid called him "'Time" as a nickname ever since Justin had waded into a school hall fight that Farid was losing. Somehow, it had stuck at the Bureau in spite of his attempts to let it die a natural death. *Funny how these things gain a life of their own.*

The task force changed shifts with the hungry remainder filing out to get some dinner. Justin offered to get Jameson an order as well, which Jameson accepted gratefully.

Justin could see that the next few hours were going to be unpleasant. The task force situation room was starting to reek with the hot smell of about twenty different kinds of fast food. The building air conditioning was usually up to the task of keeping things cool, but having twenty people wearing suits and ties in any smallish conference room was going to get warm. Since the previous year, the Bureau had implemented a "Green Building" program that turned up the thermostats after the normal work day, which meant any large task force was going to get ripe. So having an opportunity to enjoy the clean air of a spring evening, while getting dinner, was a welcome reprieve.

As Justin walked to a sandwich shop, he called Jan and delivered the bad news that he would be late coming home again. Jan wasn't happy about it, and made it clear he'd better make an appearance. Humbly, he allowed he would be. Justin had loved Jan since the day he met her in Junior High. His life was pretty good, both of his children were smart and attractive. Now all he had to manage was spending more time with them. Maybe the slippery career climb at the

Bureau wasn't worth what was lost in the process. Justin shelved the issue as something to explore after the country got through this Martyrs business.

By the time Justin had returned with food, the Stinger for the dental office was already deployed. There had not been any calls out from the suspect, but everything was captured just in case there were additional suspects identified. Word had come down the additional Stinger would be operational in Munir's neighborhood before 6 p.m. local time.

The task force sat down and listened to the feed whenever something came up. The dental office Stinger picked up no significant calls to or from a phone which could be attributed to Dr. Hammayil. The office closed at 5:30 p.m. local time and, from what the surveillance team could determine, only the dentist remained on-site. The BMW sitting in the parking lot had already been confirmed to be his, and a casual-seeming passerby had installed a GPS tracker on the frame as he stopped to tie his shoe. The team also confirmed the registration for the Honda Accord in Dr. Hammayil's name, and the correct license plate numbers. If those license plates could be found at the dentist's residence, the case for his involvement in the overall conspiracy could be made.

Finally, the dentist emerged into the evening. As before, the surveillance team hung back so their presence would not be perceived. The suspect didn't head directly for his home. He drove around shopping concourses as though he were looking for something. He drove slowly through parking lots, looking up at buildings and lighting poles.

"Dan, ask the surveillance team if the suspect is casing for a future action." Jameson said. "He seems to be engaged in meaningless activities. If there were hookers lining the streets, it would explain it, but not the case here."

"DC, they said it appears he is looking for something and not finding it. He might just have bad directions to somewhere, but the looking up is not usual," Dan reported.

"Justin, who else works in that dental office?" Jameson asked.

"We're checking the tax records right now, we should have contact details in the next hour or so. Are we going to interview them or put them under surveillance as well?"

"Just get the data queued for now, we have nothing objective to ask them just yet."

• • •

Munir continued his slow reconnaissance of new sites to stage a sniping. He wasn't really comfortable with the sites which so far suggested themselves because of his general lack of fitness. He saw a number of businesses where the roofs could be accessed, but it would be harder to get down safely in a getaway. But a roof shot really was the best option he was seeing.

Munir couldn't spend too much time tonight as he had to join the guild online later for the assignment dance. He hoped his number didn't come up yet, as he needed to spend some more time finding the perfect spot. Thus far, Munir had scouted close to the Roseville area, since he was most familiar with it. Perhaps it was time to widen the scope into some other part of the Sacramento Metro area.

One thing he wanted to do before heading home was to do a drive-by of his new assistant's home. Melanie Baker was a classic California woman in her early 30's: small and petite, long sun-bleached hair, her former-surfer physique still toned in spite of childbirth. Melanie's former husband, who she had supported through Law School with her dental assistant wages, had found her to be a social impediment after graduation and dropped her for an associate at the firm he joined. Melanie moved to Roseville to start over: close to her relatives who appreciated seeing young Emily more often. Munir had heard much of the story over the last few weeks and knew her schedule somewhat.

At this time of the evening, she and Emily should be inside their small apartment eating dinner. Munir checked the address and entered it into the GPS guidance system of the BMW. It shouldn't take more than a few minutes to drive by and get a feel for the place.

Munir knew Melanie was embarrassed by being in an apartment once more, and that she did enjoy the finer things in life. In all of her conversations, one got the impression she missed the prospect of having dual professional incomes more than she did her former husband. That was one avenue to explore: offer up higher-end entertainments as a distraction from her day-to-day life. It was certainly doable from his perspective. He had been fairly cautious with the money provided by the Hammer, and combining that with some of his office money would provide all the funding needed to pursue his target paramour.

As Munir entered the street where Melanie and Emily lived, he could see the apartment block parking lots filled with the cars of workers home for the day. He spotted the small Subaru which belonged to his assistant. He drove by the building slowly, taking in the details of the area leading to her front door. At the end of the street, he turned around and did one more pass before exiting the area for his home. *Yes, this will be easy*, he thought to himself as he drove.

"What did he just do?" Jameson asked as the GPS mapping video feed showed the turnaround.

"Yes, that was odd. This area only has residential apartment blocks. Maybe he is scouting here as well? Wait a minute, let me check that street name. Yes, this is the street his dental assistant, Melanie Baker, lives on. Do you think he is stalking her - or something else?" Justin said.

"Hard to tell at this point, but we know the connection here. The earlier drive we don't. Looks like he is finally headed for home. Are we in on his Internet yet?" Jameson said.

"Yes, sir. We're logging everything now both at home and in the office," Dan Adams said.

"Good deal, let's see where that leads us."

The team watched the GPS location indicator progress towards Dr. Hammayil's home. The Stinger and a surveillance team was fully deployed, ready to eavesdrop on any conversations the good dentist would have with his spouse with the latest remote recording technology. Technicians were already working to compromise any smart appliances in his home, and had already found a television which was quickly suborned. They would hit a goldmine if there were any security cameras, but so far the team had not found any.

Munir walked in and perfunctorily greeted his wife.

"I'm sorry there is no dinner prepared, I thought you would eat with the Sales Rep. tonight," Maryam said.

"Yes, he finished early and didn't offer this time. I can eat leftovers, and I need to join in online in a few minutes," Munir said.

"What do you see in that game? All you do is spend hours playing several times a week. It seems like something for a child," Maryam said.

"As opposed to the real brain damage I would suffer watching American television instead? At least this is fun and I enjoy it. I'll have to show you sometime how complicated it is, you might like it yourself. Many women play as well."

"You could do some work around the house. My friends were very surprised that you played games online for hours at a time," Maryam said.

"You told your friends I play online games? Why? That was not for you to tell anyone outside this home. Do I tell my friends that you snore and fart in your sleep? Or that your relatives remind me of hungry dogs eating at a carcass when they visit my home? No. Because I understand what can be said outside my home. The home I spent 10 hours today working to support. A long day smiling at infidels who openly hate us. Who are you to deny me anything?" Munir heatedly asked.

"I bore your children and maintain this home, which is falling apart. Nor is it suitable for one of your social standing. It was the best we could do starting out, but now we have money and stay in this old house. Don't bother threatening me with divorce! In this State I would be entitled to half and spousal support in addition. I could buy a car for myself instead of sneaking out in your Honda."

Munir turned his full attention on to Maryam. Softly he asked, "You took my Honda out? How many times?"

"Oh, I don't know. A few times in the last few weeks. Why?"

"When was the last time?"

"Today, if you must know. I told you I had to meet my friends."

Munir turned to Maryam and, for the first time in their marriage, slapped her with all of his strength. "You fool, you may have doomed us! You have no idea what you have done. I told you not to use the car and you chose to disobey me."

Maryam looked up at him, crying, "You cannot hit me here and get away with it. Divorce! I'll take your money and spousal support."

Munir became calm, "You will be very lucky to live through the next few days, given what you've done. I need to go online and see if this cannot be fixed."

"Go ahead and play your boy's game!" Maryam screamed from the floor.

• • •

"Do we send anyone in?" Dan asked as the task force heard Munir hit Maryam.

"No, we have no probable cause or an explanation of how we know he threatened and hit her. If he starts to kill her, then we move. Otherwise, we need to let this play out and keep recording." Jameson said.

"I concur," Justin said, although his mouth had become a hard line.

"What game is he talking about? It sounded like he needed to talk to someone."

"Didn't catch that, we'll know when he lights up the Internet," Dan said.

"It sounds like one of those MMORPG's doesn't it? Aren't you able to text and speak to other players in those games?" Justin asked.

One of the team members spoke up, "Yes, I play several. You can even talk to friends on the same platform while they are playing different games. Why?"

Justin turned to Jameson, "Sir, what if the Martyrs terrorists are communicating through one of these games? It would completely elude the normal NSA listening screens. Maybe that is why we haven't seen any traffic on this at all."

"Then finding out which game or platform is involved is of the highest priority. Let's see what we get."

A technician on the task force piped up, "The suspect is booting what appears to be a laptop, we're going to try and penetrate it once he gets going."

The room sat quietly for the time it took to boot the laptop. "Shit! He is using a VPN for all of his Internet access through a proxy server; it looks as though the server is located in Kansas. We're not going to see any of this in the clear tonight: it needs decrypting. We're capturing the entire stream, but it will take time to analyze. His wife is streaming movies in the next room and that device isn't going through the proxy. The laptop is definitely hardened for some reason."

"Justin, get a couple more warrants prepared. One for the data center where the server is located and one for the game server once we know which game is involved. Everyone else, you can stay if you want, but it doesn't look as though there will be any of the detail we need until tomorrow so the DC team should get some rest," Jameson said.

Justin went to his work station and prepared the necessary warrant request forms with blanks to be filled in as the data came back. A technician came in with IP addresses, the name of the data center owner with address and the scope of what they needed. Proxy servers were something security investigators dealt with on a regular basis. Essentially, it was a way to mask where you were physically located. Using a proxy server, all search engine queries and other Internet traffic would appear to originate from the location of the server, not the laptop. So Dr. Hammayil's laptop communications from Roseville appeared to be coming from somewhere in Kansas. Dr. Hammayil was up to something that was likely less than legal.

Justin drew up a small diagram of the client IP address, proxy server ports, and IP addresses to help him complete the warrant requests. The provider was not a large Internet services company, but one of the thousands of small companies who lease rack space from larger datacenters. Kansas City was a hub of the national Internet backbone and a natural location for a small firm to service the entire country. Justin knew enough about the technology to hope the company had sufficient logging tools and backups, otherwise this would be a very frustrating experience for the technical agents. NSA would have the encryption keys on tonight's take within a few hours so, one way or the other, the task force would have something to chew on.

Justin transmitted the warrant requests to the judge's chambers and waited for a response. He had briefed the judge on the overall investigation earlier so the background information would not have to be restated. Twenty minutes later, Justin's work station chirped with an email alert. As expected, the judge had signed off on all of the pending warrant requests. The game server request would have to wait until the team unraveled which game Dr. Hammayil was playing. Justin placed the files within their own folders in the cloud dropbox he had created for the larger task force, then headed back to the task force room.

The monitor screens were filled with the data being captured by the Internet take, so far it was all encrypted. The conference bridge was fairly silent, with the occasional noises of the extended team across the country.

"Kansas City Lead?" Justin asked.

"Here. Russell Lange."

"Thanks, Russell. I've just uploaded the signed warrants onto the drop box, in the warrants folder. You're good-to-go. The provider is a small firm named CryptProxy Networks, the contacts are also provided," Justin said.

"Sir, do we want to put surveillance on the owners of the company prior to serving up the warrants?" Justin asked Jameson.

"Absolutely! They probably don't have a connection with the terrorists, but you never know with these small firms."

"Did you hear that Russell?" Justin asked.

"Yes, sir. It won't take much time to organize, and we won't be able to serve the warrant tonight anyway, given the time. I doubt there are any company officers working onsite at the moment."

"I agree. Let's make sure we have everything in place to prevent leakage and hit these guys like a ton of bricks in the morning," Justin said.

Motioning to Jameson, Justin muted the call microphone. "I'm planning to head home for some sleep and fresh clothes, if that is alright."

"Yes, that is fine. The next couple of days will be eventful, so take the sleep when you can get it. I'm planning to only stay a couple more hours, just in the event the doctor decides to kill his wife, but I think it is unlikely."

Justin deactivated the muting switch, "I'm out until tomorrow morning, if anything breaks call my mobile or text me."

Justin's drive home was a race against the clock as it was closing in on midnight. Justin had always felt there is a huge difference between getting home tonight rather than the next day, even though it wasn't rational. But a successful marriage was about the small things, and the optics would be better if he could get through the door before midnight. Northern Virginia, for all of its proximity to Washington DC, still maintained a small town emptying of the streets after about 9 p.m., so traffic was no problem. Justin could get home in thirty minutes if he stayed long enough at work.

The President's address had given them a break in the case, simply by changing the rules of engagement. The dentist's car might have eventually been spotted by conventional means, but having the automated systems activated ensured it happened before the dentist's wife was forbidden to drive it. Justin suspected the dentist had simply neglected to change the license plate after the shooting, thinking incorrectly the car was safely hidden within the confines of his garage. Justin expected that tomorrow, the car would revert back to the plates issued with its registration, now that Dr. Hammayil was aware of his wife's perfidy.

Justin pressed the remote on his dashboard, opening his own garage door at 11:48 p.m. *Perfect!* he chortled to himself as he entered the home he hadn't seen in two days. Tonight he would sleep in his own bed. Jan was aware of his presence in a groggy, *I'm-not-getting-up*, way. Beth thumped her tail on the floor, signifying her approval as well. Justin bent over his wife's form and kissed her cheek. "We caught a break on the Martyrs case," he said softly.

"That's good, dear," Jan said half asleep.

Justin hopped into the shower, dried off quickly, and was sound asleep beside his wife in record time.

• • •

In Roseville, Munir's mirror drove slowly through the neighborhood doing a routine check. Almost immediately, he saw a technical van parked on a side street. Cautiously, he drove by the dentist's home, noting the government-issue sedan with line of sight to the house. Somehow Munir had drawn the attention of the authorities and word had to get back to The Hammer. He had nothing incriminating in the car, but he was driving through the dentist's cul-de-sac as though he was lost. The police or agents would doubtless want to know why. It was standard procedure during a surveillance to investigate all possible contacts of the target. Munir's mirror already had a cover story ready, there was a home for sale several streets over in which he would claim an interest.

The police or government watchers didn't break cover to pursue him, but he was sure his license plate had been noted. He drove over to the home with the real estate sign, and got out of his car looking over the outside of the home. The owners were in residence, so he satisfied himself by getting a brochure and getting back into the car. Turning on the dashboard reading light, he sat looking over the brochure. Within a minute, a car having the lines of government service drove slowly through the neighborhood. Munir's mirror maintained his perusal of the real estate sales brochure as the occupants of the unmarked cruiser looked him over. As before, the agents didn't break cover to engage him.

Breathing a sigh of relief, the mirror made a big show of folding up the brochure then turned off his reading light, started his car and drove out of the Munir's neighborhood. The mirror was especially careful to watch for anyone trailing him, stopping at a convenience store for an energy drink, all the while watching the cars on the road for too much similarity in destination. So far he could see no indication he was being followed, but he drove to his secure apartment cautiously all the same. The car was registered to a different address where the mirror's cover identity lived. If he wasn't immediately followed, he should be safe to send word to The Hammer.

Opening the door, he scanned the room for any changes during his absence. All of his markers were still in place, indicating no one had entered. Quickly, he sat down and activated his laptop. As it booted, he played the events of what had been seen over in his mind. The Hammer and his second were not men to accept haphazard reports, so it had to be crisp. The laptop automatically established its VPN connection to CryptProxy's server and sat ready for the mirror's input. He sat down and started up the game interface.

The initialization screens came and went, until his virtual character appeared where he had last left it outside the human capital city. Bringing up the guild membership listing, he looked for Redonkulus, Snaptime, or SnackSnick. As fortune would have it, both Redonkulus and SnackSnick were in game. Using the special texting interface of the game, he sent a text only to Redonkulus.

"Sullnpsych pwned as of one hour ago."

After a few seconds, Redonkulus replied, "He was just on and mentioned nothing."

"He may not know."

"Noted. See what can be done. Snaptime will contact you offline."

The mirror logged out of the game, and initialized a small program whose task was to cleanse the laptop of all records which would indicate how it had been used. The mirror satisfied himself the laptop was doing exactly that, then turned his mind to other matters.

In the game, Redonkulus disbanded the guild without making an announcement, and the few members still online immediately started logging off and running the cleansing program on each of their laptops. Redonkulus had ordered two additional sniping attacks in the regular guild meeting earlier in the evening. The timing would support the next phase of the operation and it wouldn't hurt to have the sniping network go dormant for that period. There could be no more communication using the game as the conduit, Crusaders for Truth no longer existed.

Using one of his burner phones, The Hammer texted the owner of a small business in Kansas City, "Guild finished, close the account effective immediately. Please acknowledge request."

After a few minutes, The Hammer's phone chimed the arrival of a response. "Acknowledged and have complied."

The Hammer took the phone and placed it in his "burn" bag. Once he finished with using a piece of equipment, he always made sure to immediately separate it from others that were still in use, pending the destruction of the bag contents. By this time tomorrow, the trail to the other snipers would be long gone. Only Sullnpsych-Munir remained at risk.

Picking up another mobile phone, he texted Amin in the Bahamas the code that signified the compromise of one or more of the sniper network. He would know what to do.

Munir's mirror also knew what to do. His bags were packed with everything which could be used to identify him. The laptop would be left inside the unlocked car on the wrong side of Sacramento. With luck, and normal criminal avarice, both the car and the laptop would be promptly stolen. The final task before he was free to leave Sacramento would be the most difficult of all.

Munir, in the meantime, had fixed himself a small snack and was headed back to his office to play some more of the game. After he logged on, he noticed that his guild status no longer appeared. Panicking, Munir searched the game for the Crusaders for Truth. *Guild not found*, was the message that was returned each time Munir typed in the request. Munir realized that he had no other listing for the specific members of the guild, and tried to remember what names he could. Either his system was down, or the Martyrs network had been compromised. After searching for the names of players he remembered, and finding none, Munir realized that it was the latter.

According to his training, he logged off of the game reluctantly and started the cleansing program. Munir hoped the breach had nothing to do with him, and resolved to acquire an account for the game himself once things became clear. Now what was he to do with his evening? He didn't really fear he was the party at risk, because things had gone well so far and he was special. The only lapse had been his disobedient wife, Maryam, driving the car against his express orders. Munir decided to discipline her tomorrow, first he would indulge himself and smoke cigarettes on the patio until he was ready for bed. Maryam hated the smell of cigarette smoke and hounded him constantly to quit. Tonight she would have to put up with it. And, if she had too much of a problem it might serve as a good segue into the beating she had coming for risking his life.

Munir had just sat down, when he heard a small noise over the back fence. Startled, he looked around for the origin which was quickly spotted when his mirror dressed in dull black stepped into the light. Putting his finger over his lips, he approached where Munir was sitting.

Munir was initially frightened, but then recognized the face as one of those who had also been at the hunt club during his training. He relaxed and motioned the mirror in closer, offering a cigarette as he did so. The mirror took the cigarette, accepted a light then leaned next to Munir's ear.

"The Hammer has disbanded the guild, due to a compromised network."

"Yes, I know that already. I started the destruction program earlier," Munir said impatiently.

"What you do not know, brother, is that you are the compromised link!" The mirror hissed as he drove a knife up deep into the throat and brain of Munir. Munir flopped once or twice then slumped back into his chair. The mirror wiped his knife on Munir's shirt, spit onto the ground next to the body, then faded back into the night.

Inside, the computer hard drive was still spinning as the best data destruction program available continued its tedious work; Maryam snored in the master bedroom, blissfully unaware that her husband was dead; and the FBI task force listened to the sounds of a household finished for the night.

The Hammer heard a beep from the phone in the burn bag. Pulling it out, he saw a short text, "Sullnpsych cleaned." He smiled, and put the phone back into the bag.

CLOSING DOORS

"..Sources say the FBI has been receiving thousands of calls from citizens after the President's special appeal. This reporter hopes the FBI has a real plan for stopping the Martyrs terrorists, as the global appeal suggests desperation.."

Farid Monsour al Haj for World News Corporation

All hell broke loose the next day. When Maryam Said got out of bed she noticed Munir had not joined her. Thinking he must have fallen asleep while playing his game, she tromped into his office anticipating a conversation where she would have the upper hand. He wasn't there, but his laptop was on with a small banner reading "Wipe Complete." Confused, she went into the kitchen and saw the back of his head through the patio window. Opening the sliding door, she started to admonish him before the pool of blood registered in her mind. What followed were screams and a panicked call to 911.

The FBI surveillance team was galvanized by the noise; they'd been half-asleep as they waited for the household to awake. Listening in on the 911 call, the lead agent Brian Ng recognized he didn't have to break cover to investigate directly. Tucking in his shirt and taking out his FBI credentials, he rang the doorbell.

Maryam opened the door very quickly, "That was very fast! Quick, come! My husband has been stabbed!"

"I'm not the main response team, but I heard the call and have a little training. I'm Brian Ng, FBI Special Agent. Please show me to your husband."

Maryam led the way onto the patio where the extent of Munir's injuries became apparent. Maryam was touching and pinching Munir in a manic attempt to deny what was already final.

"Ma'am, I apologize, but he was clearly attacked sometime during the night. This is a crime scene and I need you to stand back from his body. We don't want your fingerprints to cover any evidence that might lead us to the person who committed this crime. Please, sit at the kitchen table. Did you see a knife anywhere?" Brian asked.

Maryam went into the kitchen wailing about her lost husband, Munir, the love of her life. Brian knew she had not committed the crime, but he also knew procedure would treat her as a suspect. Taking out his phone, he told the rest of the team to get inside right away and to communicate the extent of the debacle to Dan Adams. This was going to be a very long day.

• • •

Justin had only been at the office for a few minutes the Thursday morning when Munir's body was discovered. Jameson was not in yet, but would have to be contacted. Justin went to the task force room where the conference call was still active.

"This is Justin Simons, is Dan Adams on the call?"

"Sir, this is Brian Ng. I've called him. He should be joining us shortly."

"Brian, are you at the homicide site?"

"Yes."

"We need to control the crime scene until forensics can get there. The wife has to be taken into custody for questioning and, because we don't know how much she is aware of Dr. Hammayil's activities, we do not want her loose in the house at all," Justin said urgently.

"I've got a team member watching Ms. Said, but we'll take her to a secure location as instructed. I took a quick look through the house and his office has a running laptop open with a disk-shredder program banner which says it is done. I hope the techs can get something useful off of it, but we might be too late. No one has touched it or the room, everyone is wearing evidence gloves," Brian advised.

"Good job, Brian. When are the techs expected to get there?"

"Any minute now. I called on Roseville PD to coordinate who gets into the house, they're fully aware of the situation and have been very helpful setting up the perimeter. The neighbors aren't too happy, but we'll deal with that. We had to head off the ambulance team with a national security need-to-know explanation, but they took it in good grace."

"Brian, do me a favor would you? Go out into the garage and see if you can open the trunk on the Honda."

"Sure, I'm headed out now. The driver side door is unlocked so I'll just pop the trunk. OK, the light in here isn't great." There was a long pause on the line. "Sir, looks like there's a rifle bag. We might have the weapon right here," Brian said.

"Don't touch it, for the love of God! Damn! Where are those techs? You don't see anything that looks like explosives, do you?"

"No, sir, I do not. We'll get the explosives dogs in once we get the body out."

"I'm going to step away for a few minutes," Justin said.

Leaving the war-room, Justin placed a call to Jameson to let him know things were moving. As it happened, Jameson was just pulling into the parking structure, and Justin briefed him on the overnight developments. Jameson wasn't happy about the loss of the suspect, but, after a few moments of ranting, recognized the surveillance team wouldn't have been able to hear the killing. What wasn't settled, was how easily the killer had skirted the surveillance team. Justin suspected there would be some fallout on that issue, as it appeared the team only set up a view on the front of Dr. Hammayil's house. That approach leaned too heavily on the wiretaps and sound-capture systems providing a full picture of what was happening inside. Justin knew also that putting teams on all sides of the house would have potentially compromised their cover, it had been a tough call to make and this time it would come back to bite them.

"I'm back, and Jameson will be here shortly," Justin announced to the call as he re-entered the war room.

The next two hours were filled with frenetic activity. The forensics teams were busy doing their respective work. The body had been removed to the local secure morgue for further examination. The laptop was in the hands of the data techs, after having been completely examined for fingerprints. The program used to wipe the hard drive was a good one, but the labs had a few tricks which might work to reconstruct it. The rifle was confirmed to be the same model used in the attacks, ballistics was testing to see if it matched the spent shell casing found at the scene of the first attack. No bullets were found for the gun inside the bag.

"Team, Kansas City field office here. We just served warrants on the owner of CryptProxy, and he doesn't seem to know much. The proxy server being used by Dr. Hammayil was a virtual server rental and the server instance was taken down last night. The owner claims he reimaged the server for some new clients overnight. We confiscated the physical server and it will have to be dissected by the tech agents. Supposedly, CryptProxy offers up a custom Linux proxy server image that does not log connections. So we may have some difficulty there. We reached out to the datacenter management team and they do have logs we can parse for traffic to and from the server. We'll need another set of warrants however."

"Justin, this Hammer seems to know what we're doing before we do it," Jameson complained as he stormed into the room.

"Sir, I think they simply executed a strategy incorporating multiple fail-safes. How we gather data on these types of systems is predictable, and they used it as a planning constraint in my opinion."

"Are you sure we don't have a leak internally, someone with Muslim friends who passes the information along without considering where it could wind up?" Jameson continued, staring at his second.

"I can't think of anyone who falls into that category," Justin said, knowing Jameson was thinking of himself and Farid again.

"I can, and I'm not going to let it pass if we keep getting stymied by these guys. That Muslim friend of yours better have a good story when it comes time to debrief him."

There was no point in responding to Jameson's rant. When things weren't going well, Jameson was known to lash out at whoever was in a subordinate role and standing in front of him. All you could do without being insubordinate was not to engage anymore than was necessary. Justin's size was generally enough to encourage respectful discourse from his superiors, but occasionally Jameson tested the limits. At the FBI, cold-cocking a superior was a good way to be shown the exit regardless of provocation. Justin was not hot tempered, but there was a limit to what verbal abuse he would take. Farid, on the other hand, wouldn't take any abuse from such a martinet. On a few occasions when faced with people like Jameson, Justin had seen Farid just walk away from working with them. In most cases, they came to regret having created the situation. *That's the best thing about being independently wealthy: it comes with a lot more options*, Justin mused.

"When is Ms. Said going to be interrogated, Dan?" Justin asked, snapping back to the conversation at hand.

"We have her in custody offsite, but haven't locked her up or treated her as a suspect. How do we need to handle this?"

"It's a dead certainty she knows something about her husband's activities. She may not have connected the dots previously, but we want to encourage her full cooperation and we don't have the luxury of time for extended negotiations. Mirandize then lock her up in a single; that should get her attention. Have someone drop the data her husband, and perhaps her as well, are the main suspects in the Roseville sniping attack. Mention she was observed driving the vehicle used in the shooting. If she wants an attorney, see that it happens, but under no circumstance is she to be allowed out of custody. Justin and I will fly out tonight for an initial interrogation tomorrow afternoon. By then we should have a lot more information to hand," Jameson said with the glee of a predator.

"Yes, sir. I'll check with Roseville PD to see if they have something suitable, otherwise we might need to move her to Sacramento," Dan said.

"Did we find any of the ammunition in the house?" Jameson asked.

"No, sir. No ammunition at all so far. Our guys are going through the place top-to-bottom. There are several different bank statements - maybe one of them has a safe deposit box. We'll probably need warrants there as well, but we should be able to learn if the doctor rented one."

"Good thinking. We're going to close down the bridge: we all have tasks to work. We'll send out a meeting invite for a status call later today. Let's get as much done as we can before then. The sooner we can crack this guy's story, the sooner we can roll-up the rest of the network. Let's not forget there are 30-40 more of these guys out there. Justin, you're with me," Jameson said as he exited the conference bridge.

"Let's go back to my office - we have to think about the merry widow's interrogation. I think we should run a good-cop/bad-cop on her. I'll take bad-cop just because you aren't convincing in the role," Jameson sneered as he made his way back to his office.

"I never thought the approach worked all that well, especially when dealing with fairly intelligent people. Plus it has been a plot feature of every television cop show since Dragnet, only the dumb suspects buy it. If she has a lawyer present, they will keep things on an even keel. In fact, the lawyer might help us, given the things we can charge her with at our discretion. If this goes to trial, it would be very emotional for the jury. Right or wrong, there isn't a lot of sympathy for the Muslim community right now."

"Maybe I should let you take the bad-cop role. That is a joke - I'll do it. It will be an emotional event to rattle her cage," Jameson said with anticipatory glee.

"Well, for starters we could charge her as an accessory just from driving the getaway car. We have video of that. Another thing we could do, and should do immediately, is seize all of their assets under the asset forfeiture provisions. We know money was spent on the operation and it isn't clear where it came from. This is the first terrorist who actually has a fairly profitable business in place, so the normal big data scans of bank spending habits wouldn't apply. I wonder if the rest of the shooters are similar or if he is an outlier. Maryam Said has a huge financial stake here, either she is a terrorist and loses everything or the widow of a terrorist who inherits most of his assets. If she doesn't have money to pay bills, or her lawyer, it gives her a powerful incentive to cooperate if she is innocent."

"I agree on the asset forfeiture seizure, if nothing else we can hold on to the money until things are sorted out. Make sure it happens before we interrogate her," Jameson said.

"Changing subjects a bit, what about all the other shooters? Right now, we think there are about 30-40 of them. If the Kansas City thing is a dry hole, and there are really no logs for the proxy server, I think the data center logs will be sufficient to point fingers in the right directions. The only fly in the ointment would be if the server instance was used by a lot of people not associated with the terrorists. The online game title should be knowable almost immediately once we get the logs from the datacenter. Then we can work back to the cities involved. It will be a tedious effort, but we should be able to zero in on the households in question. With Dr. Hammayil unable to fill in the blanks on means and methods, we really need a live shooter," Justin said.

"When is NSA getting the VPN traffic decryption back to us?"

"In the next few days, they're having to use brute force cracking since the data stream was handed to them. If they had been the ones capturing it, there were things they could do to speed it along, but it wasn't. So it depends on how lucky we get."

"How come our guys can't do it?" Jameson asked.

"We don't have the equipment budget they do and we don't pay techs as well as NSA. Our guys are good, they just aren't top drawer. We're a lot stronger on the physical science side of things. So we continue the big data scans of license plates, concentrating on the largest metro areas, until we get the IP address data back."

"We're going to have another problem when this is over, right now the spending is free-wheeling with the full agreement of Congress. But you know the software contractors who are providing the help now as a demo will want to get funded when it is all over. Congress is going see the bill for everything spent so far and cough blood. We had better have some warm bodies to throw in prison or it will be a hanging party for all hands," Jameson said grimly.

"I think we're probably due for another shooting too, which won't help the work we are doing now. What about the nuclear threat rumor we heard from Farid? We don't have anything on that so far," Justin asked.

"No, and while I would like to not have that worry it is just one more thing. We have notified all border security to watch for something, without being specific. We will ask Ms. Said about it. That should get the full attention of her lawyer. No lawyer wants to defend a client using weapons of mass destruction," Jameson said sensing a no-lose situation for the FBI. "Speaking of Farid, when was the last time you spoke to him?"

"Earlier this week, I did mention we had a lead after the President's address and to expect our call at a moment's notice. I think he and his network have handled this well, having other reporters take point on the domestic information we released. Due to his normal role of reporting overseas issues, he said he will be front and center if we identify any foreign involvement."

"Look, head back to your desk and break the travel plans to your wife. I'll do the same. I suspect we'll need about 20 more warrants to get to the bottom of Dr. Hammayil's activities. As you think of them, do a draft and have it ready. Brief the speechwriter over at the White House before we leave town. Look, Justin, this is a stressful time for all of us. Some of our careers are definitely on the line, I apologize if I get a bit animated as the bad news rolls in, but I want you to know you're still slated to replace me if we get through all of this," Jameson said.

"Thank you, sir. I'll keep that in mind. We'll probably have to head for the airport late afternoon, we should have a lot more in hand by then," Justin turned to go.

"We'll reconvene after lunch," Jameson said in parting.

• • •

At his desk, Justin placed a call to Farid. "Hi Farid, how are things in the Fourth Estate of broadcast journalism?"

"Not too much happening at the moment. You have something new for me?"

"Perhaps. I have to get on a plane to Sacramento tonight. We're running something down and may want to trickle some data to you folks."

"My boss is loving the access we've been getting, so I think we'll be eager to participate. Does this address the Roseville attack?" Farid asked.

"I can't say, sorry. I also wanted to ask if you had heard anything more on the rumor you mentioned?"

"Nothing material, councilor. The more I consider what I heard that day, the more I think "south". I don't think DC or New York were the targets. Obviously, you can't act on a hunch without some objective data, but that's all I have. I'm not going any further south than DC for the foreseeable future myself. Justin, would you be able to tell me if there were any indications the Board of The Martyrs al Sabra charity were part of The Hammer's campaign?"

"I don't see why not. We don't have any indication of ties. If anything, it is an imposition on the charity's good name. I imagine the contributions have dried up?"

"Yes they have - especially in the United States. I don't think it reflects an unwillingness on the part of donors, Muslims are easily capable of distinguishing between the two, but most of the donation jars have been put away so that other Americans wouldn't make an issue. We've had to trim back some of the work overseas until all of this is finished. Some of the other board members and I have made large stopgap contributions, but it doesn't replace what the donation jars used to provide."

"You never told me much about the summers you spent with your uncle in Lebanon. What was it like then for kids our age?" Justin asked.

"Pretty bad, by our standards. You and I, even then, were clearly destined for university followed by decent jobs. My extended family in Lebanon is rich. The teenagers in Lebanon have it pretty bad, and Lebanon is paradise next to Gaza Strip and the West Bank. No prospect of a good job or an education unless your family is wealthy. So the young boys wind up joining various militias, who are the de facto government in a lot of those places, to make a living. It is much worse for orphans. Orphans have it tough no matter where they are, but Palestinian orphans are really at risk of becoming cannon fodder for whoever offers them a square meal. The charity tries to help the ones with a shot at getting out. You know: kids with a gleam of intelligence in their eyes. So all of this turmoil here is hurting those efforts, which means fewer kids diverted from the destructive cycle. But, to answer the question you asked, my time there was privileged and I didn't experience the despair myself, only vicariously through those I met. Most of what I got there was immersion back into the language and customs. I left as a small child and hadn't had the chance to engage in learned discourse with adults of that culture. Even though I had tutors and went to mosque in Alexandria, it wasn't the same as being there."

"So it is unlikely The Hammer comes from the street?"

"I wasn't really saying that, but your observation is likely correct. The street boys wouldn't have the education or background to execute a long-term campaign like this one. Another thing to consider is that the money men in the Middle East are snobs, except perhaps for the Iranians. Most of them wouldn't be caught dead anywhere near the street fellahin. They make the kind of jokes like we, in America, have about rednecks or hillbillies. Not a lot of trailer parks in the Middle East, but the social class is definitely present. The snobs will barely talk to me, even though I am moderately rich and well-educated," Farid finished with a self-deprecating chuckle.

"These days we're talking mostly about Saudis?"

"Yes, although the Emirates have their share as well. The Iraqis are still pretty fragmented, so they are mostly out of that game. The Syrians would like to be a player, but they don't have cash laying around. The Iranians are the communists of the Middle East, always stirring up worker revolts and movements."

"What if these guys are connected more to the Far East, say Indonesia or Malaysia?"

"I'm not seeing that, for the simple reason that those two countries don't really care about the Palestinians. They have their own problems in spades. Although, maybe the whole Martyrs thing is a diversion? No, that doesn't strike me as matching the level of sophistication for Far East."

"Thanks, Farid! As always, I learn something new when we speak. Are you going to be available later tonight? I'll be spending some time with Great White Father Jameson on a plane, and we might have some information to release. If it gets too late, I'll text before calling," Justin said.

"No worries, my boss is out of town and I have a date with his wife tonight. She never lets me sleep," Farid joked.

"One of these days you're going to be caught at it, and I just hope you live through the consequences."

"It's a lot easier when you don't have to explain things to a spouse. She has to lie; I don't. The last time a husband asked if I was sleeping with his wife, I expressed surprise and said I didn't know she did that kind of thing, but would definitely be interested. That sent him on his way promptly. I think he forgot why he asked the question," Farid laughed.

Justin laughed, "I'll leave the hounding to Jan, when it comes to Nayla and her presumed-closing window of availability."

"Jan must have a direct line to Lindsey on that topic. I'd have to settle down or lie to Nayla if we were married, and I'm still not ready for that. She's a fine woman, and top of the list if I were thinking marriage."

"There's a list?" Justin laughed. "OK, I'll get back to you on the investigation later tonight. Have fun!" He hung up shaking his head. Justin knew Farid's viewpoint was almost certainly formed by having lost his family at such a young age, and it couldn't be forced. He only hoped that Farid would someday find what he and Jan had. He reactivated the phone and called Jan to give her the bad news.

She took it well, the wives of FBI agents had to live with uncertainty when it came to hours. She was pleased that progress was being made, nothing worse than living with an FBI agent getting nowhere in an investigation.

Justin finally texted the speechwriter Ashley, a query if she was available for a short call. Within a few minutes, she called.

"So, Justin. What do you have for us?" Ashley asked.

Justin briefed her on the developments of the last twenty-four hours, and explained he was headed for Sacramento that evening.

"So we have the suspect's wife in custody? Do you think she was directly involved?"

"We don't know at the moment. We should be able to confirm her husband's involvement through the deer rifle ballistics, which will be ready in the next two hours. The disconcerting thing here is that it appears his murder occurred due to our surveillance and was intended to silence him. I personally doubt his wife knows too much, otherwise she would been murdered as well. But, whatever she knows, we need to know," Justin said. "The terrorists acted quickly to eliminate the proxy server in Kansas City, so they are paying close attention or they have some insight into our investigation. Obviously, we hope the latter is not the case."

"There are no leaks on this end - only a small group is being briefed."

"We've had to cast such a wide net on this, it could be almost any of a thousand people on our extended task force. OPR will probably be looking into it at some point, but we need to press on with the effort. Oh, sorry, Office of Professional Responsibility. The President's address was important to move things along," Justin said.

"When are you getting back to town? We may want another briefing session," Ashley asked.

"I'm not sure at this point, I think we should be back in DC no later than Monday. I'll text you when it becomes clear."

"That will work. Be careful, we wouldn't want to lose you two on this."

"When you run a task force, you seldom get used as the sharp end of the spear; so it's pretty safe. We don't want to lose anyone, especially more sniper victims. I hope we can get a better handle on things from what we learn out there. Do you have everything you need to brief your bosses?"

"Yes, if they have more questions I can't answer I will text or call. Safe travels!" Ashley said as she hung up the phone.

Twenty minutes later, the ballistics report came back on Dr. Hammayil's rifle. It was definitely the weapon used to shoot Lorie Lampson. A local bank confirmed that Dr. Hammayil also kept a safe deposit box. The FBI were engaged in preparing warrants to gain access later that afternoon.

· · ·

Nayla had spent most of the day busily working a new project in support of target Congressional candidates in the upcoming midterm elections. The Democratic Party was determined to avoid an off-term election debacle and started planning almost as soon as the Presidential Election ended in a win for Lucinda Brown. There was a lot of fundraising to do in preparation and Nayla expected Friday would be a lost work day if Jonny Ray made good on his promise to spend the afternoon with her. She hadn't heard from him, but expected he would call when he returned.

As if the universe were completely in tune with her thinking, Nayla's mobile phone rang with Jonny Ray's ringtone. Nayla glanced around to confirm no one was within earshot as she closed the door to her office.

"Hello?"

"Hey, darlin', it's me, back from my tour of the hinterlands of this great nation!" Jonny Ray Brown boomed happily.

"Sounds like it must have been a success. I'm glad you're back! Does this mean we're still on for tomorrow afternoon?"

"I wouldn't miss it, doll! I'm in a car headed back to the big house right now, but wanted to call and check in beforehand."

"Excellent! I'll have everything ready for when you arrive. Just after noon, right?" Nayla asked.

"Absolutely! I really missed talking to you, we've got a lot of catching up to do."

"We certainly do, and then we can do some talking," Nayla teased.

Jonny Ray snorted laughter and rang off after a few more pleasantries.

Nayla walked over to the window and set the blinds requesting an evening meeting with The Hammer. Then she put her head down and worked on getting the fundraising project definitions completed for the party meetings the following week.

• • •

After work, Nayla went home and pulled on casual jeans with a t-shirt. She planned to spend the evening cleaning her extra Georgetown apartment and waiting for the appearance of The Hammer.

As usual, just as the evening transitioned into the full darkness of night, the door to the apartment opened quietly and The Hammer entered. He was dressed in dark jeans with a long-sleeved turtleneck shirt, nothing unusual except for the lack of any reflected color in his ensemble.

"As-salāmu ʿalaykum," Nayla said as she inclined her head in acknowledgement.

"Waʿalaykumu as-salām," The Hammer replied softly.

"Jonny Ray has confirmed his appointment for tomorrow afternoon; he arrived earlier today," Nayla said.

"Good. I see you were cleaning, did you see any evidence of the removed cameras and microphones?"

"No, it was well done. If I hadn't known they were there, I wouldn't have seen them. I know Jonny Ray hasn't a clue."

"Good. This is the last time for you, Nayla, but there is no need to tell Jonny Ray anything. After tomorrow, I would recommend changing your personal phone number. Not that he won't be able to get it from the Secret Service, but it will be clear the relationship is over by then," The Hammer said.

"Will I need to hide from the media at any point?"

"No, I don't think so. The plan doesn't involve a public exposure of that kind. Remember, most of the footage was taken with your face obscured. Were there any other questions?"

"I'm not going to have to do anything like this for the cause again, I have your promise?" Nayla asked.

The Hammer placed his hand over his heart, "As I said, this is the very last time. I promise."

"One final thing, after your time tomorrow, wait here to meet with me for the final debriefing. I will come after the Secret Service has left the area," The Hammer said.

"Very well," Nayla agreed. "I would ask you to stay a while longer, but I just cleaned the place for tomorrow and do not want to prematurely rumple the bed."

"No, I don't want to create more work for you, and there would be if I stayed. There is plenty of time for that after tomorrow," The Hammer kissed Nayla's forehead in benediction. "Be careful this one last time."

Nayla hugged him close and released him as he departed back into the night.

• • •

Jonny Ray walked into his bedroom suite in the White House and decided to wash some of the travel dust off of himself. *No matter what class of travel you choose, you still end up smelling like something musty that was left sitting in a closet for a few days*, he thought to himself. He hadn't seen Lucy yet, but was looking forward to delivering good news from the fund raising tour. Several of the Party's poor up-and-comers would now get enough funding to make it a real contest in their district. One of the candidates was an attractive young black woman who had served in the District Attorney office and Jonny Ray could not help but be stirred. The fact that she was married with several small children meant absolutely nothing to him, but so far she had resisted his charms. He was used to that response initially, and fully expected he would grow on her.

In the meantime he had his lovely Palestinian mistress, who was a done deal, waiting for him tomorrow afternoon in Georgetown. He might have to finagle the White House staff doctor for some more Viagra; there was no way he was going to fold his tents after just one bout with the lovely Nayla.

A small knocking at the door - captured his attention.

"Come on in while I'm still decent," Jonny Ray called.

A nervous looking staffer entered, immediately identifiable as one of Sidney Rosenbloom's young bloods by the overall fatigue visible on his face.

"What does Sid want now?" Jonny Ray said to help him out.

"Yes, sir. Sid, Mr. Rosenbloom, asked if you would stop by his office at your earliest convenience."

"Well sure, son! You tell him I plan to wash off some of the road, but I'll head over after. Does that work?" Jonny Ray asked.

"Yes, sir. Thank you, sir," the staffer said as he awkwardly exited the suite.

Did I ever seem that green?, Jonny Ray laughed to himself. *Probably, but I would be the last to know.*

After taking a long hot shower in the splendid spa-like bath, Jonny Ray got into a fresh suit, minus the tie since he wasn't working, and walked over to Sid's office in the West Wing. Jonny checked in with the administrative assistant, who Jonny swore never left her seat to take a break, and sat down to wait. After a few minutes, Sid's door opened and the man himself emerged to fetch Jonny Ray.

"Jonny, thanks for coming over so quickly. Come on in. What are you drinking?" the President's Chief of Staff asked.

"Thanks for asking, I wouldn't mind a stiff gin & tonic, with a slice of lime if you have it," Jonny directed the answer to another of Sid's minions who was manning the small bar set-up on the interior side of the room.

"Have a seat. How did the fundraising trip pan out?" Sid asked.

"Not bad, we ran into some of the usual donor fatigue after a big win, but were able to convey the message that it was no time to stop working after building some national momentum. The candidates looked pretty good, too, they all seemed to know their assigned roles and appreciated the administration's support."

"Any future leaders in the mix?"

"Most were just good foot soldiers and, let's face it, we need a gross of those. Davita Johnson seemed to have a gleam in her eye, but she is new to the national stage. If we were identifying potential, my money would be on her," Jonny Ray said.

"Black attorney, mother of two, running for the House?" Sid asked with his near-perfect political recall.

"That's the one. Her husband is a civil engineer, so he's probably not interesting enough to be a liability."

"Engineers make the most boring presidents, that's well established," Sid laughed as he referred to Jimmy Carter.

Jonny Ray laughed, "Somehow, I don't think James Johnson is quite that boring. So, Sid, do you want to stop beating around the bush and tell me what you've got to say?"

Sid motioned the staffer to leave the room. "Jonny, you know me too well. I have the sorry task of talking to you about the ongoing recreation with Nayla Kaldah. We're in a pretty sensitive place politically due to the Martyrs al Sabra terrorists. You know how the people are, they blame the president when it rains hard in a swamp. I've met Nayla, I think well of her and trust her. But my concern is related to her past. Did you know she was personally involved in the real Martyrs al Sabra incident in Gaza City?"

"No, Sid. Oddly enough, we haven't spoken much about her teenage years. You're saying she was involved. How?"

"Hamas and Fatah shot each other up in Gaza City in 2006 and incidentally killed 23 schoolchildren during the gun battle. Nayla herself was not there, having just moved to Paris for her education. Her indirect involvement was due to her brother, who instigated the battle while working with Fatah. Now, we aren't saying Nayla had anything to do with it, we're just concerned about what would happen if your affair leaked out to the tabloids and the connection was made. It would be bad for the President. Shoot, the media can't keep the current terrorists separate in their minds from the charity foundation," Sid said.

"Sid, any affair that was caught would hurt the President. We all know this. In the last nineteen years, there have been rumors, but not a whiff of proof. You and I have worked hard to keep it that way. How is this any different?"

"It's different because the level of risk is a lot higher when the woman is someone with Nayla's cultural connections. I was fine with her up until we started seeing a lot of anti-Muslim sentiment welling up in the polls. In a perfect world, I wouldn't ask you to stop seeing her. If you two enjoy each other and Lucy accepts the situation, I don't have a problem with it personally. You have to know that. The problem is that it isn't just another infidelity for the electorate, it is an infidelity with a Muslim possibly connected to the terrorists. Lucy could survive the former, the latter would pose more of a problem. Surely you can see that?"

Jonny tossed back the rest of his drink and set the glass down sharply. "I do, and I understand what you're asking. I'm willing to call a halt to things, but I want to do it my own way. We have a liaison set up for tomorrow afternoon. I'll break the news to her then. Does that work for the President?" Jonny Ray asked through a grimace.

Sid stared at him, "I haven't troubled her with this, Jonny. She has a lot on her plate already." He waited for Jonny's nod before continuing. "Tomorrow should be fine. Just be sure to work closely with your detail lead to keep things low-key. I really appreciate this, Jonny Ray. Maybe you should take a few more trips out to help this Davita Johnson step up, in order to take your mind off of it."

"Yes, that would probably be best. I really like Nayla, though, Sid. She is good people. We really ought to take care of her. I know she will be discrete. From what she has told me, Muslims aren't real happy when they find out about affairs with non-Muslims, so she would have a huge incentive to keep things quiet."

"We certainly would want to reward discretion. In this case, it is win-win as she is very accomplished and would add significantly to the administration's initiatives. The President wouldn't have to know about Nayla's past connection to you."

"That's good, then. Was there anything else, Sid?" Jonny Ray seemed tired as he thought through what he would be saying to Nayla the next day.

"No. Again, the President is very pleased with the results of your fundraising and mentoring. She has mentioned many times how helpful it is to our efforts."

"I'm sure she'll mention it when we meet for dinner tonight. You know I want to help, and that seems to be the only thing folks trust me with at this point. Thanks for letting me clean up the Nayla situation my own way," Jonny Ray headed out the door back to his private quarters.

• • •

The Roseville Police Department didn't have suitable accommodations for Ms. Said, so she was transported to the closest facility in Sacramento: the Sacramento County Main Jail on I Street. That facility was fairly close to full as well, but they did have a couple of solitary confinement cells. The FBI's prisoner was granted the use of one, along with an interrogation room located on a different floor. The facility itself was old, damp, and full of faulty equipment. The cell that Ms. Said drew was a standard six by ten foot concrete-walled room housing a stained mattress with a pillow and blanket, and a stainless steel commode without a seat. Even though she did not share the cell with other prisoners, they could see her within the cell as they passed including when she used the commode. Overnight, she wasn't able to sleep due to the unfamiliar setting and the noises of a working jail: the sounds of screams, loud talking, rapes in progress, and snoring combined to keep her alert.

Breakfast was to a very low standard compared to what Maryam was accustomed to. She hadn't eaten in more than a day, refusing the cold, greasy fare when the FBI had checked her into the facility. The one bright spot was that her cousin Fatima was busy finding a lawyer for her. Maryam expected to be released once the authorities realized she was not involved in anything. That fool husband of hers had made his last mistake, clearly getting mixed in with the wrong people. For whatever reason, Maryam had not considered Munir's murder to be random. He had been spending more time away from the home, in association with his friends at mosque. Maryam suspected he was really spending time with another woman, especially that two week "hunting" trip to Wisconsin. The fact that he had come back with both deer meat and a rifle didn't do much to change her assessment of the situation. If the other woman was married and her husband found out, that might explain who killed Munir so brutally. So Miriam had no inkling whatsoever of the real reasons she was locked up. If anything the police might suspect her of killing Munir herself. She looked forward to her lawyer coming in this morning and triumphantly setting her free.

After choking down the breakfast with its decaffeinated coffee, Maryam settled in to wait. Lawyers weren't allowed to speak to their clients until after 9 a.m. At 9:15 a deputy came to the door of Maryam's cell and told her to get ready to meet with her lawyer. Maryam quickly looked herself over and followed the instructions of the deputy who showed her into a large room with ten small tables. At most of them, a lawyer and a prisoner were talking over their specific cases. Maryam was ushered to one of the tables where only an attorney sat.

"As-salam alaykom, Ms. Said? My name is Mohammed Albiz, I was contacted by Fatima to speak with you."

"Wa aleikum ah salam, I am she. How soon can you get me out of here?" Maryam asked.

Reaching across the desk, Mohammed handed Maryam a cup full of Starbucks coffee. "I didn't know what you prefer but knew it was better than what they serve here. Dark brew coffee with cream and sugar. I'm not sure when you can leave yet, do you know why you are being held? Please tell me everything you know or can remember."

She gratefully accepted the coffee and took a small sip. Maryam walked Mohammed through the events of the last thirty hours. Mohammed was a good listener, interrupting her narrative when a clarification was needed, but otherwise letting her tell the story her own way. At the end of her story, he set down his pen as if in thought.

"Ms. Said, you said the FBI were the ones giving the orders?"

"Yes, the agents initially said they were passing by and heard the 911 response call on radio. But later they took over the entire operation. The Roseville police followed the FBI agents' instructions. They were going through the entire home, looking for Allah knows what."

"I ask, because it is very unusual for the FBI to get involved in a simple murder, normally that would be the local police jurisdiction. Were you questioned about anything else?"

"No. Initially they wanted to know where things were in our home, but after they said nothing to me other than the fact that I would be taken to the jail until I could be questioned. They seemed very upset, even more than I would expect in the face of a murder. Surely, I am not suspected of killing Munir? He was much larger than me and was killed cleanly with a knife. I am not strong enough to have done so."

"Again, I am not sure. No information has been shared with me yet, other than to advise me that your first interrogation will take place at 2 p.m. this afternoon. I'll try to get a private meeting with them beforehand, but it might not be possible. Is there anything else you can tell me which might explain what happened to your husband?" Mohammed asked.

"The only other thing is that I suspect Munir of having an affair for the last year or so. It's possible such a woman was married and her husband or family sought revenge by killing him. We had grown into our separate lives, but he was a good husband for the most part."

"Thank you, Ms. Said. One final question, how do you plan to pay for my services?"

"We have sufficient money to pay. We aren't rich, but he was a prosperous man with a good dental practice. We own our home without a mortgage. My family would help, if needed, as well," Maryam said.

"I would expect no less. I bill at $150 per hour and require an initial minimum retainer of $3,000 to start work. This discussion is not charged against the retainer, but further work would be. If the retainer is exhausted I'll bill every two weeks."

"If I had a credit card, I could pay. But I have nothing in the cell. Fatima will advance the retainer on my behalf," Maryam said.

"Very well. Please sign the following documents which engage my services and we'll get started. With luck, we may have you out of here no later than this evening. You won't be able to go home for a few days as it is still considered a crime scene, but it will be better than spending another night here."

"I would hate to be kept here another night. There is no sleep or peace."

"I'll take my leave and try to speak with the persons responsible before the meeting this afternoon," Mohammed signaled the guard and stood politely for Ms. Said to be escorted out before leaving himself.

Mohammed asked after the people managing his client's case, but received another reiteration there would be a chance for discussion at 2 p.m. He had a bad feeling about the whole situation. This had to be more than a murder, but what? The FBI never really provided warning when moving on a suspect. It was possible that Munir Hammayil was under investigation for something and had been killed by parties unknown. That scenario would explain the way Ms. Said was being treated, especially if she was suspected of being involved. Normally, with well-to-do Muslim clients, there were a number of financial transgressions which could get the attention of the FBI. Muslims tended to ignore currency movement restrictions when sending money to relatives overseas, using a hawala cash transfer system instead. While it was safe to do so for the most part, occasionally the FBI grew concerned with possible money laundering or support to terrorist organizations. A dentist with money might be arrogant enough to disregard the rules in favor of saving some money on exchange rates.

There is no way to know until this afternoon, Mohammed thought to himself. *At least the client has sufficient funds to pay my fees, praise to Allah for that blessing.*

Several hours later, Mohammed found himself back at the jail waiting in the lobby to be admitted for Maryam's questioning. A uniformed police officer approached him and showed him to a small interrogation room. Seated at the table were two men in suits, FBI from the look of them. Several large case folders were sitting in front of the bigger agent. Behind their chairs was a full video camera setup with microphones on the table, managed by a technician. The seat of honor was left vacant, waiting for Maryam Said.

"Mohammed Albiz, council for Maryam Said? I'm Special Agent Justin Simons and this is Section Chief Quinton Jameson. We are assigned to the Joint Terrorism Task Force out of the DC office," the largest agent spoke.

"Yes, I am Albiz. Where is my client?"

"She will be here shortly. Earlier, you attempted to meet with us but we were unavailable, so we decided to give you a few minutes prior, in the event a private discussion was in order," Justin explained.

"I was hoping to have a discussion with the prosecuting attorney to better understand the situation, before counseling my client."

"I am an attorney, admitted to the Bar in both Virginia and DC. Prosecution will be handled by others, however, but perhaps I can answer your questions," Justin said.

"What is it my client is suspected of doing?"

Justin glanced over to Jameson, who nodded once in affirmation. "Are you familiar with the Martyrs al-Sabra terrorist attacks?"

Mohammed's heart shrank within his chest; this case was not going to have a simple solution. "Surely, Ms. Said is not a suspect in those attacks."

"That is exactly what we are trying to determine. Her husband, Munir Hammayil, has been confirmed as the shooter in the Roseville attack. He became a target of our investigation and was clearly killed yesterday to hinder our efforts. Obviously, we will need to understand everything Ms. Said knows about Dr. Hammayil's activities very quickly. If she cooperates and was verifiably not involved, she may be released. If she does not cooperate, she could be detained indefinitely without trial as provided by law," Justin said.

"Correction, she <u>will</u> be detained indefinitely without trial if she does not cooperate," Jameson interjected forcefully.

"That would violate her constitutional right to due process," Mohammed stated.

"Perhaps the counselor is unfamiliar with recent federal law concerning detention of terrorism suspects?" Jameson said.

"I know that those provisions are being challenged as unconstitutional."

"Even if true, Counselor, we have her and will keep her until she provides the information required or until the Supreme Court rules on the challenge. We also seized all of her and her husband's assets under the asset forfeiture provisions of the RICO statute," Jameson said.

Justin looked genuinely apologetic, "We aren't taking these actions arbitrarily, and if we get the cooperation we need there is every chance she will be released and the assets repatriated."

They are running a good-cop/bad-cop routine on me, Mohammed thought sourly. "When may I see the evidence supporting the statements just made about Dr. Hammayil?"

"During the meeting with your client," Jameson said. "Do you have any other questions for us before we bring her in?"

"Yes, may I speak to her privately before the meeting?"

"As private as any other attorney-client consult in this facility; I'll have the guard set you up with that. You have fifteen minutes and then we start," Jameson said.

Mohammed was escorted back to the large room where he had met with Maryam earlier. It was considerably less crowded in the afternoon. He took a table removed from where others were in conference. A few minutes later, Maryam arrived clothed in prisoner coveralls and looking as though her makeup was on its last legs. Her face brightened when she saw him seated.

"Mr. Albiz! Am I being released?" Maryam said wishing that the whole experience would soon be a bad dream.

"Not immediately. Please sit down. I only have a few minutes to brief you before the meeting."

Maryam sat and waited for Mohammed to elaborate.

"Ms. Said, I was informed by the FBI that Dr. Hammayil was the confirmed shooter for the Roseville attack by the Martyrs al-Sabra terrorist organization. This investigation is a national security matter and it will be very difficult to obtain your release in any reasonable time."

Maryam's face blanched in complete shock, "Munir was not a terrorist - he was a dentist! Why am I being held? I did nothing for terrorists!"

"It is bad, Ms. Said, I will not lie. They have seized all of your family assets, which they can do with suspected terrorists or drug dealers. They can hold you without charges for a very long time. The agents stated that they wanted your cooperation and answers to their questions. If you were not involved, the best thing is to cooperate fully."

"I knew nothing about it, and can't provide the answers they seek. My husband and I had separate lives even though we were a family. I've never heard him say anything that would lead to the murder of innocents," Maryam said.

"I will be there to offer what protection I can, but you need to understand the FBI treats terrorism suspects under different rules than other crimes. They have the ability to keep you incarcerated indefinitely, if they so choose. Be very certain you tell them no lies, if you choose to cooperate. Lies will keep you in jail. I'm sorry this has happened to you, and I hope we can navigate this situation successfully. If you are unsure whether to speak on a topic, look to me for advice. Are you ready to go in?" Mohammed asked compassionately.

Maryam's legs felt as though they could not support her weight, "Yes, thank you for the warning. I might have had a heart attack if I learned this in the meeting." She stood and waited for the deputy to transport her to the interrogation room.

Mohammed followed as they walked down the noisy and smelly corridors of the Sacramento Main Jail. Maryam was ushered by the deputy into the meeting room, and Mohammed held her chair as she sat down. Maryam looked at the faces across the table. One had a neutral expression on his face which was reassuring on a man of his size. The other older man, however, had an almost menacing air about him.

The large man started, "Start the video recording, Samuel. This session represents the first formal questioning of one Maryam Said on the matter of the Martyrs al-Sabra terrorist attacks by myself, Special Agent Justin Simons, and Section Chief Quinton Jameson."

"If possible, I would like to make a statement before we begin," Mohammed interjected.

"Certainly, please fully identify yourself while doing so," Justin said.

"My name is Mohammed Albiz, attorney retained by Maryam Said. I have spoken to my client concerning the overall issues before us. Ms. Said maintains that she is fully innocent of any terrorist plots or activities of her late husband Munir Hammayil. Furthermore, she fully deplores and condemns the actions perpetrated by the Martyrs al-Sabra terrorists. She has pledged to offer her full support and cooperation to the investigating team. Thank you."

"Thank you Mr. Albiz," Justin turned to Ms. Said, "Your name is Maryam Said, wife of Munir Hammayil, DDS?"

Maryam nodded her head.

"Ms. Said, please answer the questions aloud for the record. Again, your name is Maryam Said, wife of Munir Hammayil, DDS?"

"Yes."

"How many years have you been married to him?"

"More than thirty. Thirty-three."

"Do you have children by him?" Justin asked.

"Yes, two boys and a girl. They have all graduated college and live separately out of state."

"Ms. Said, I am now going to show you some photographs. This is a photo of a deer rifle found in the trunk of your Honda Accord. What can you tell us about the rifle?"

"That was my husband's gun. He brought it back with him from a hunt camp he visited in February."

"Does your husband own any other guns to the best of your knowledge?"

"No, he never did. I was very surprised when he told me of his planned trip; he had never hunted in the past. When he came back, he had the gun and an ice chest full of deer meat. He told me it was hallal, so we have been eating it. There should be some left in our freezer at home." Justin made a quick note.

"Tell us more about this trip. When was the first time you discussed it?" Justin asked.

"I think it was sometime in December of last year. He told me of his plan to spend three weeks at a hunting camp in Wisconsin. He purchased the used Honda Accord at that time, saying it made more sense to drive a car like that across country than his normal BMW."

"Didn't you find it unusual that he would suddenly take up hunting? Had he ever shot a gun before?" Justin asked.

"Yes, it was very unusual. I was very surprised when he said he planned to hunt, because he always talked about how lack of good gun control laws was why there were so many murders in the United States, and he didn't approve of gun ownership. To my knowledge, he had never shot a gun before the camp. He also wouldn't drive a car like a Honda before, he said they were an indication of low class."

"Where do you think he got these new ideas?" Justin asked.

"I don't know. Most of his friends are from our mosque and, as far as I know, none of them hunt."

"Where else could he have learned of it?"

"He had no," she paused, "non-Muslim friends he spent any time with other than at the office. There he knew pharmaceutical representatives who would occasionally buy him dinner. Other than that, he kept to himself."

"I apologize for this question in advance," Justin said. "Is it possible your husband engaged in affairs with other women?"

"I believe so, but I never much looked for proof or confronted him about such things. In fairness, I was pleased I did not have to provide such service as I got older." Maryam seemed to grow self-conscious and quickly added, "Put yourself in my position, I was married to a successful man who provided well for his family. Even if I pursued divorce, winning half of the property, I could not live as well as I could staying. Plus, it would hurt my children to do that, even though they are grown."

"You say you never much looked, when did you become aware of the possibility and how?" Justin continued.

"Ever since the children left home. There were times he would become distracted, spending less time at home. At one time, I used to do the accounting for the dental practice. I noticed diversion of money that didn't arrive in our household accounts. When I raised the question, he told me not to worry about it, as it wasn't my business. Several months later, he hired our current accountant, so you would have to ask him. With him, it was always obvious. He would dress better, get haircuts more often, and stay late at work."

"So, in essence, you did know," Justin pressed.

"Yes, you could say that. But not the details, I could ignore it if the details were not known."

"Did one of these distracted times occur just before deciding to go hunting?"

"Yes and no. I knew he was spending more time at mosque than usual, but didn't suspect a woman."

"Let's leave that for now. What can you tell us about the hunt club?" Justin asked.

"It was somewhere in Wisconsin, and he had to drive there. The camp itself was for two weeks, the extra week was him driving there and back."

"Didn't you find it strange that he was planning to attend?"

"Yes, but it gave me a chance to have relatives visit and entertain during his absence. He is a family man, but doesn't like to spend as much time with relatives as I do. I also got to drive the BMW. He seldom allowed me to drive at all, once the children left we only had the one car until the Honda."

"So it was an opportunity for yourself when he left?"

"Yes. I could do the things I liked to do without having to ask permission first."

"Ms. Said, have you had an extramarital affair yourself?" Justin asked.

Mohammed interjected, "How is that relevant to the subject at hand?"

"I don't know that it is relevant, I am trying to fully understand the marriage relationship between Dr. Hammayil and Ms. Said," Justin said.

"Besides, Ms. Said pledged cooperation, did she not? Humor us and answer the question," Jameson said brusquely.

Mohammed and Maryam shared a glance, "I don't have a problem answering the question, although it is very personal. I have not had extramarital affairs. I am not interested in sex at this stage of my life. That is why I did not object to my husband's activities as long as my marriage was unthreatened."

"Thank you. Back to the rifle. Did you know it was in the trunk when you drove the Honda for shopping? This picture shows you driving the car, the date stamp is on the upper right," Justin said.

"I knew it was in the trunk, but I forgot about it as it was tucked in the back."

"This is another traffic picture of the car, can you identify the driver for us?"

Maryam looked closely at the picture, and then the date stamp, "Yes, this is Munir driving, but he is wearing strange clothes."

"This is a picture of the suspected Roseville sniper as he was leaving the scene of the crime," Justin said.

"Suspected. So you don't know?" Maryam grasped at the straw.

"At the time, suspected. Now it is proven. The gun which was kept in the trunk was proven to be the same one used in the Roseville attack. One more thing, have you seen this box of rifle cartridges?" Justin showed a close-up picture of a box with nine shells remaining.

"No, I have never seen that," Maryam said.

"We took this out of his bank safety deposit box this morning."

"We don't have a bank safety deposit box."

"He did, at your regular bank. He kept the bullets there, and took one out the same day of the attack. Here is another picture of one of these shells, notice anything unusual?" Justin asked.

"There is engraving, in Arabic. It says Martyrs al-Sabra," Maryam's face turned pale and she felt as though she would faint.

Mohammed sensed her distress, "Special Agent Simons, is it possible to get Maryam some water?"

Justin nodded, having seen her reaction as well, "Samuel, if you don't mind?"

Samuel went to a small cooler set in the corner of the room and pulled out a small bottle of water, handing it to Mohammed.

"Forensics has confirmed the shell casing left at the scene matches the rest in this box. In fact, it matches the shell cases of all of the Martyrs attacks." Justin said giving Maryam some time to compose herself.

"So your husband returned from Wisconsin with the murder weapon and presumably the ammunition as well. What else did your husband acquire on that trip?"

"All I noticed was the deer meat and the laptop computer. The deer meat from his trip is in our freezer."

"Laptop computer? What did he use it for?" Justin asked.

"He said he needed entertainment on the road. I think he used it to stream movies and play that stupid game," Maryam said.

"What game?"

"I don't know the game title, but it is played by a lot of people online. He used to lock himself up in his home office to play for hours at a time. I always knew, because there were sounds of sword fighting, shouting and spells along with the music sometimes. He played a lot, but always without fail on Monday, Wednesday and Friday nights. He said it was a regular group activity - a guild meeting? He was very angry with me when he found out I had told my friends about it."

"Did he play the game before his trip?" Justin asked.

"Not that I knew. I only saw it on his laptop. You should check that, it would have everything."

"We would do that, except that Dr. Hammayil erased everything on the laptop the evening before he was killed. Think back, were there ever any telephone calls from strangers in the last six months?" Justin asked.

"No, we only received calls from people we knew, or tied to businesses we knew. We have one wired phone number which we shared for the house, and of course we had our own personal mobile phones."

"Ms. Said, here is another picture of a mobile phone. Have you seen it before?"

"Yes that is my husband's spare phone, a pre-paid that he said he bought on the trip when his regular phone died. When he got back, he said the phone store was able to fix his old phone."

"Did you ever have occasion to use the new phone?"

"No, I had my own phone and, besides my husband told me not to use it."

"Did your husband approve of your use of the Honda?"

"No, he was very angry when he found out. He threatened my life and hit me."

"When did that happen?"

"The night he was killed. He never hit me in the past, the only time he was cruel was verbally when very angry. As I think about it, he might have been afraid."

"Where did he hit you?" Justin asked.

"My left cheek, here. It still hurts a little bit, but didn't bruise," Maryam said.

"Did your husband contact any of your children the night he was killed?" Justin asked.

"I don't think so, but after he hit me I went to my bed."

"Did you contact your children that evening?"

"No, I called them the next morning to tell them their father had died. They should be on their way to our home, if they are not there already."

"I'm sorry, but the home is still considered a crime scene until the investigation is concluded. They will have to stay elsewhere. Mr. Albiz will see to briefing them on the situation when we conclude. Ms. Said, do you remember where the hunting camp was located in Wisconsin?"

"No, I have never been to Wisconsin and am not familiar with it. But, I understand that mobile phones and the car GPS system have a record of where they have been? I never erased any records in the car and when I used it, I thought one of the entries was for Wisconsin."

"We will check into that, thank you. My question was really aimed at whether your husband told you anything about it," Justin said.

"Ah, no. My husband was not always open with me on his activities. He often acted as though everyone else was stupid and beneath him. The only people he didn't treat that way were his dental patients, to them he was friendly and kind. He wasn't a bad husband, as these thing go. Until this situation I would have said he was a good husband.

He provided for his family and was mostly home at night. If you marry a doctor, you have to accept some arrogance."

"He was just a dentist, not an MD, right?" Justin asked.

Maryam smiled ruefully and said, "Yes."

"We'll need a list of Dr. Hammayil's and your friends, as many listed as you can remember. Mr. Albiz will see to getting you pen and papers. We're close to finishing for this session, but will want the list as soon as possible. It does not have be perfect, if you remember others you can add them later. We have to speak with all of the friends as soon as possible to learn how this happened. We'll have another session this evening or tomorrow morning."

"I will do that immediately. Attorney Alviz said that all of our assets have been seized pending the investigation, when can they be returned?"

"Not for some time, I'm afraid. We have to review where the funds came from and how they were used. If they were used for terrorist activity, it will not be returned at all. Think months, if not years," Justin said.

"But I'm being cooperative, and had nothing to do with the terrorist activity, what about my own money?" Maryam asked in distress.

"Would it be possible to determine Ms. Said's money and separate it from the investigation early?" Mohammed asked.

"It might be possible. Section Chief?" Justin looked in inquiry.

"It may be possible, but Ms. Said needs to recognize a few unpleasant truths. First, at this moment we have a case against her as an accessory, with the photos of her driving the murder car. When news of this breaks, people will want someone to punish and her husband is no longer alive to answer for it. At bare minimum, she might be an accessory. Her reputation and social standing here is very likely ruined, no matter what. Depending on how money was being used, she might have also spent funds that came from a terrorist source, which taints all of the cash. Second, we have a lot of things to investigate, based on what she has said here today. If anything she provides turns out to be untruthful, even in omission, we will not be doing any favors for her. If we decide to release her pending the investigation, she will not be allowed to leave Roseville or Sacramento for quite a long while.

Personally, I have a hard time believing she knew nothing," Jameson said dismissively.

"If we validate a few of the items quickly, to confirm her good-faith, we might be able to release her with an ankle kit," Justin suggested.

"If we do that, we'll confiscate all passports first. And if that ankle unit goes offline for anything other than a battery failure, she gets the full load of charges in the worst place I can find. I hear the weather in Cuba is lovely this time of year," Jameson purred.

"There will be no need for such measures, Ms. Said will fully cooperate. Shall we conclude and start working on her list of contacts?" Mohammed interjected smoothly.

"Yes, we all have work to do. No press conferences for now, Mr. Albiz. We wouldn't view that as cooperation. I will contact you if we need another meeting tonight," Justin said as he called for a guard to escort them back to the attorney conference room. Justin fell in beside Mohammed quietly, leaving Jameson and Daniel in the interrogation room.

"I apologize for my colleague's way of phrasing things. He is under a tremendous amount of pressure on this case. If you follow the news, you know what he said is not that far off of the actual situation. If there is any reason to believe Ms. Said is involved, the entire government will seize on it and act accordingly. Let's work together to clear her name as soon as possible. Here is my card with mobile number, call me with anything material at any time," Justin said.

"Thank you, we will work on this immediately. Well, the good-cop/bad-cop thing has played out, and I guess you're the good-cop," Mohammed said.

Justin smiled slightly, "We play the roles we're accustomed to in this matter." Justin waved to the pair and returned to the interrogation room.

"What do you think, sir?" Justin asked.

"She pretty clearly didn't know much of what went on with her husband. I'd say she is pretty motivated to cooperate at this point. The lawyer will help in that regard, as his fees won't be paid if he can't get the funds released from forfeiture. We'll need to check all of the leads she provided, but she probably wasn't involved. How about the GPS data from phones and the car?"

"I'm pretty sure the team already has it, but we know what to focus on now," Justin said.

"Didn't we have a meat expert somewhere in the system? The meat-whisperer? You know - the guy who can identify where game was taken from a sample?" Jameson asked.

"I thought that was just a tech joke. Really? I'll look into it. We definitely have some deer meat samples. What does he do, eat it?" Justin asked.

"No, he does a chemical breakdown somehow and can predict where from the results. Maybe he does eat some of it," Jameson laughed.

Just then, Justin's mobile phone, seconds later Jameson's did as well.

"This can't be good," Justin said as he accessed his text messages.

"Another sniping attack, this one in Harrison, New Jersey," Jameson read aloud. "They missed hitting anyone, but the spent cartridge casing was found on site. It was down near the river in the old industrial section of town."

"The press is going to be crazed, even more so than usual. Which brings us to the question of when to release information about having found the shooter for Roseville? Your thoughts?" Justin asked.

"You're right, we need a success under our belts to stave off some of the furor. I am thinking we release information that Dr. Hammayil was the person responsible for the Roseville attack, and that others have been detained pending our investigation. Maybe show one of the pictures from the getaway car, ammunition from the safe deposit box, and the rifle used in the attack. It would make a good series of news stories and won't hurt our investigation as most of that data is static or not subject to change. What do you think?"

"I think that would help, I would leave the circumstances of Dr. Hammayil's death as unclear, as we need time to work that angle. On the release, how do you want to handle it? Do we play favorites or do this one with a press conference announcement?" Justin asked.

"I'll schedule a press conference for a couple of hours from now, with some show-and-tell pictures and no questions from the press. We'll promise a Q&A session for next week as we learn more. In the meantime, call your contact Farid and send him the pictures we'll use so that they can have a leg up on the competition. I'll call upstairs and get permission to hold the press conference."

"We should probably have the venue be the Roseville FBI office, right? Maybe get the Roseville PD Chief and Mayor to stand behind you?" Justin asked.

"Good idea, in fact we may want to open it up for some State politicians as well. I'll get calling and you do the same."

Justin sat down at the other end of the table so that the phone conversations wouldn't interfere with each other and dialed Farid's mobile number.

"Justin, how did you find things on the West Coast?"

"Some good, some bad. We have identified the shooter for the Roseville and will probably be holding a press conference in a few hours. We wanted to give you a heads-up and send you some of the photos we will use in the announcement. Of course, you folks are asked not to publish anything until after the presser."

"What was the bad?"

"Besides the shooting today in Harrison, NJ? The Roseville shooter was a local dentist, one Munir Hammayil and he did not survive to be questioned," Justin said.

"Ouch! Were you able to get some evidence that would help on finding the others before he died?"

"Not as much as we would have liked, but enough to be encouraging. Obviously, we are going to soft-pedal any details around that aspect of the investigation. The data implicating Dr. Hammayil is conclusive as you'll see from the photos."

"Send the photos to my email in the highest resolution you have available. My folks will process for publication. Thanks, Justin. What is the angle for the Harrison shooting?" Farid asked.

"We got lucky there - the sniper missed. One shell just like all the others, ballistics is still reviewing the rifle ID but it is probably a different rifle from the other shootings. Off the record, we may have as many as forty shooters nationwide. Don't report that obviously, we still have a lot of work to do."

"One further question, was Dr. Hammayil killed during the attempted arrest or in some other way?" Farid asked.

"I can't comment on that at this time."

"Got it. I'll get my folks ready to attend the conference. Where will it be held?"

"Right now, we're thinking the Roseville FBI office. It will be handled by Jameson in a few hours if approvals come through," Justin said.

"Good deal. When are they going to put your giant frame behind a podium? I want to be in the press gang when that happens."

"I'm still a spear carrier on these. Public or political announcements get handled by the boss."

"I have faith in you, although I will be taking bets you stutter on your first one," Farid jibed.

Justin laughed, "You're probably right. You should have the photos in the next fifteen minutes. Give me a call back if there are any hiccups. Cheers!"

Justin called Samuel over and selected the three photos that were needed. The picture of Dr. Hammayil in the Honda was grainy, but Maryam had easily identified him. The pictures of the rifle and ammunition were crystal clear. Justin wrote a short note to Farid, attached the photo files, and sent the email.

Jameson was just finishing his call as well. "Looks like we're a go with the press conference. We should head back to Roseville and start putting it together."

"We won't need to have another session with Ms. Said today, right?" Justin asked.

"No, we won't. We'll do one follow-up tomorrow morning and then head back to DC. The Roseville team can do any follow-ups that we need. Another thought occurred to me, the victim's family will probably sue the estate of Dr. Hammayil for wrongful death, this being California. No matter what happens on the forfeiture side, Ms. Said is in for a tough ride."

• • •

In a DC mosque, the terrorist known as The Hammer prostrated himself before Allah as he prayed for the strength to finish the task which was his alone. The Hammer always found prayer to refresh a sense of mental peace within whatever storms assailed his life. He drew strength from the memory and didn't always have the ability to observe the full cycle of prayer on a daily basis, but yearned for a time when it would be possible.

The network of snipers had been deactivated pending the FBI's investigative net tightening around the answers that lay as needles in their data haystack. The Martyrs communication via MMORPG would never be deciphered because the protocol took advantage of in-game activities that were unlogged by game servers. No, the best the FBI could do is to track the IP addresses back from the proxy datacenter in Kansas. In every case but one, the Martyrs snipers had already changed Internet service providers, wiped the laptops before disposing of them, consigned their rifles, deer meat, and ammunition to the deepest body of water that could be found locally. The one exception would be taking his shot tomorrow and then would finish his cover-up as well. The new Internet services were all installed with an insecure WIFI guest network, which would allow any of the snipers to assert that other persons used their network without their knowledge and therefore IP address tracking would not be definitive. Lawyers were standing by to ensure none of the snipers were charged without physical evidence of their involvement. This door was well and truly closed in the FBI's face.

The second and third doors to unravel the Martyrs network needed to be shut by The Hammer himself. Those were the tasks that filled his mind as he knelt in humble submission to Allah's will. An hour later, The Hammer rose refreshed and ready to finish what had been started in Allah's name.

LAST CALL

"..FBI identified Munir Hammayil, a Roseville dentist, as the person responsible for the death of Lorie Lampson in a Martyrs al-Sabra terrorist attack. Reports indicate Dr. Hammayil was killed prior to being taken into custody. No confirmation of the circumstances of his death has been released at this time..."

Farid Monsour al Haj for World News Corporation

Nayla left the office just before lunch, planning to make her last tryst with Jonny Ray that afternoon memorable. She had already stocked the apartment with an assortment of food and drink, even knowing that Jonny's appetite for the latter far exceeded the former. She also had a new black leather corset with matching red and black thong and knee-high black stiletto heel boots. The ensemble made a perfect contrast to her olive skin and raven hair; in short, it was an outfit to capture Jonny Ray's complete attention.

Nayla put the finishing touches on the apartment, donning an overcoat in anticipation of the usual Secret Service screening. Thirty minutes before Jonny Ray's scheduled arrival, they came through. By now, the routine was established. First two agents would come in with explosive-sniffing dogs and canvass the entire apartment. Next, came the RF screen - which would detect any listening devices transmitting in radio frequency bands. The cameras and recording devices The Hammer had recently removed were passive and did not transmit signals and therefore had never been detected. Finding passive gear required opening walls and air ducts, which the Secret Service had not done.

After the RF scan, drawers, closets, and cabinets were searched for firearms or other weapons. Nayla's kitchen knives were always examined, but left in place. Finally they searched Nayla herself with wands. Early on, she had learned to avoid wearing metal which only invited closer scrutiny. In one closet was an assortment of sadomasochism paraphernalia.

"What is all of this?" the agent asked.

Nayla smirked, "Do you really want to know?"

The agent's face turned red as he realized he did not, "No, no, that's fine." He bustled about some more but then gave an all-clear signal and the team left the apartment for the last time. Nayla took off the overcoat and got Jonny Ray's favorite drink ready for his arrival. Usually, you could hear him coming from a ways off as he joked around with the Secret Service detail while walking down the hall. Today was no exception, but he seemed to be in an even more jovial mood than usual.

Jonny Ray opened the door with a flourish as the Secret Service stepped back into their places within the hallway.

"Well, darlin', if you aren't a sight for sore eyes! My, you look like you need yourself a spanking, do a turn for me," Jonny gestured with his hand.

Nayla turned around slowly, smiling when she heard the catch in his breathing. *Most gratifying*, she thought, *I will miss this*. Nayla took out a hanger from the coat closet and helped Jonny Ray out of his suit jacket.

Jonny Ray found his feet, "Is that a drink I see over there? Set me up, come over, and let's talk about the lousy two weeks we just had," Jonny Ray planted himself at the end of the couch and waited for his cocktail. Nayla brought him his drink along with a plate of assorted small snacks. Jonny Ray took the drink in his left hand and rested it on the couch arm. The right hand patted the couch next to him and Nayla sat down, draping herself across him while resting her head against the same couch arm. In the past they had spent what seemed like hours in that position while resting between carnal engagements. Jonny Ray would take the opportunity to idly caress her olive-skinned breasts as they talked.

This was new for Jonny Ray. Normally, he was like a bull at the gate for the first consummation of a tryst, but today he almost seemed reflective, which suited Nayla as well. Jonny Ray rambled on about his recent political trip and Nayla listened in a perfunctory way.

"So that's the sorry story of my last few weeks. How about you?"

"Sadly, all I did was wait for your return. We're making progress with funding mid-term campaigns, but there is still a lot to do," Nayla said as she unconsciously removed the hair from her face.

"Nayla, I wish I could talk business all the time with you wearing this outfit and lying in my arms. My, how does this ensemble come off of this perfect body?"

"Maybe it doesn't all need to come off," she said with a smile as she stretched up to kiss his lips.

Jonny Ray placed his forgotten drink on the side table and stood taking Nayla with him once more into the bedroom.

• • •

At the coffee shop across the street, The Hammer had watched the shades of Nayla's apartment come down in the signal Jonny Ray was coming. The Hammer had no difficulty identifying Secret Service detail members as they maintained their positions of guard. One was actually sitting in the same coffee shop with a view of the street and had done a cursory visual examination of everyone there including The Hammer. But the Hammer was busily typing into a small laptop, without seeming to pay attention to anything in his surroundings other than his coffee. In short, he looked like a thousand other people affiliated with the law firms and universities in the area. He had no plan to stay for long, he just wanted to visually confirm the final act of Nayla's operation was in play.

Having confirmed the entrenched presence of the Secret Service, the Hammer made a show of looking at his mobile phone, cursing to himself, and closing his laptop in preparation for departure. The Secret Service agent glanced at him, then back at the street itself. The Hammer left the coffee shop behind as he set off for Nayla's home, there were a few tasks that still needed to be done and it would get him off of the street to do it.

Having several hours to kill, The Hammer sat down in Nayla's living room and logged into the new Martyrs proxy server. Communication with the snipers had been completely shut down. When the operation was complete, they could be reactivated when needed. One more sniping attack was scheduled for Riverside, California which would happen the next day.

The sniper part of the organization would now become sleepers, fitting in as normal Americans until the call for their services came once more. Amin would have to physically make contact again, but such was normal when an organization went dormant. The mirrors would remain active for several more months to ensure none of the deactivated snipers became a risk to the organization. There was a small risk the FBI would catch one or two of them, but now the mirrors were fully alert, the general lack of subtlety in FBI operations would guarantee a small window of time to eliminate a problem.

The Hammer checked his messages in a secure mail site, noticing immediately he was being summoned by Prince Zufar to come to Riyadh. The Hammer replied in the affirmative, smiling to himself as he now would not have to make an excuse to see the Prince. It would be difficult to make the schedule work, but the theatre potential of the Prince's bomb detonation would be worthwhile to coordinate. To that end, he sent a coded message to Amin, who was still waiting in the Caribbean. Amin's last report was all was on track, and the Qatari crew were behaving themselves while waiting.

A message was also sent to Reem instructing him to facilitate several network applications to spot scans that would indicate having been found by the FBI, as well as arrange for a small satellite-relay circuit for a Caribbean spot-beam. Reem would also have to prepare a relay-switch and ship it to Amin as spare parts for the Butler's Dosh.

After getting his message traffic completely up to date, The Hammer decided he would take a nap so he would be fresh for the night's activity to come. He set his mobile phone alarm for two hours later and set it upon the end table. Sitting down upon Nayla's long couch, he took off his shoes and then laid his head back against one of the end pillows. Within several deep breath cycles he was asleep, solving problems in vivid REM dreams, killing the waiting time in the most productive way he could.

•••

Mohammed Albiz had spent most of his afternoon helping Maryam put together a coherent list of known associates of the former Dr. Hammayil. Her own list of friends was more problematic, as she was reluctant to have her friends become aware of her husband's crimes.

"Ms. Said, you have to recognize that your life will never be the same after this becomes public. My guess is that you will have to move to a new city and make new friends. You will be tarred by your husband's crimes even if the FBI decides not to charge you with anything. I'll explain. Suppose the FBI releases you and reimburses all of the money they have seized. The victim he killed, Lorie Lampson, will have family who will undoubtedly sue Dr. Hammayil's estate for wrongful death. Jurors will have absolutely no sympathy for your problems. So it is possible you will spend much of the money in legal fees and then have to give the rest to the survivors. She had small children, which means the jury will award their upkeep costs through college and any additional funds they think appropriate. So at the very least, you will lose your home and have to move. Losing your friends is a small price to pay when you consider everything else that will be happening. So please make sure this list is complete. The FBI will get it anyway, make it easier for them. My job right now is to get you out of this jail. The rest will have to be dealt with later."

"It's not fair; I did nothing to deserve them taking all my money," Maryam complained.

"If we can establish your lack of involvement, we can also stake a claim for your share of the community property. That will limit the possible claims to fifty percent or less. Property you owned separately will add to your portion. If your husband didn't have a will, you might be in line to receive the whole thing, but you will have to defend against any wrongful death lawsuits and clear any other liabilities of your husband's. So it is bad, but not as bad financially as it sounds. Your bigger issue is living in this community afterwards."

"That man ruined me! Absolutely ruined me! And for what? Being part of a terrorist plot against the country which made him wealthy and successful?" Maryam lamented.

Mohammed thought about expressing that her husband was probably dreaming of doing something for the faith, which meant the things which normally would have been precious, like family or home, might be disregarded. But he knew it would not be well received at this time, so forbore. "Ms. Said, one thing you need to consider closely for subsequent questioning sessions of the FBI is the truthfulness of your answers. They will ask questions you have already answered again, phrased in different ways, in order to see whether your story changes in any way. You need to be consistent from session to session or it will not go well for you. Another thing, if there were any answers given today which were not 100% correct, we need to identify those before starting the next session. Maybe you omitted something important, maybe your memory was incorrect in retrospect. Regardless, we need to be the ones who find the inconsistencies. Do you understand?"

"Yes. I don't think there is anything major, but will have to think if there were any answers where I should have added more. When is the soonest you think I can be released?" Maryam asked.

"I doubt it will be any earlier than Monday, the week is essentially over and it is unlikely you'll be released over the weekend. The investigation needs a little time to validate your testimony. Also, I received a news update earlier on my phone saying another Martyrs attack in New Jersey took place today while we were in the meeting. I can't say whether that will help us get you released, but there won't be another session today."

"So I have to endure this confinement over the weekend? Can I have visitors?"

"I'll check into it. If the answer is yes, give me a list of who would you like me to contact. Normally a prisoner would get two visits of up to three people a week, but I hope to have you out prior to a full week," Mohammed said. "I'll come back tomorrow morning with the information on visitors for you, and, of course, attend the next questioning session. For now, though, we need to get you escorted back to your cell."

"Please do your best, this is very hard for me. Three more days of no sleep and being filthy all the time will be very close to my limit. If only three can visit, my children or cousin would be good choices. My cousin will make sure you are paid, too, so don't worry about that."

Mohammed had, in fact, been worrying about that, but now politely waved it off. Signaling a guard to escort Maryam back to her cell, Mohammed stood respectfully as she left the room. There was a lot to do before tomorrow, but he would start by contacting Justin Simons with the lists Maryam had prepared.

• • •

Farid sat watching the televised news conference taking place in Roseville, California. Quinton Jameson read a brief statement on the capture of the Roseville terrorist, Dr. Munir Hammayil, illustrated by the photos Farid's network had ready for their stories. Justin stood behind his boss, accompanied by many of the local Roseville worthies. Farid's management had already rounded up interviews with some of Munir's former patients and employees. They all said variants of the standard "he gave no sign of being that kind of person" statement you often see in these types of stories.

All of Dr. Hammayil's employees appeared severely shaken by the news and every one of them were now unemployed and looking for work. Farid decided to recommend a short news segment on how difficult it would be for them to find work, without any fault of their own. This story would feed the network for a few news cycles.

Not for the first time, Farid wondered how much longer he should spend working in the industry, which had turned to practices that would have scandalized even the most hardened yellow journalists of the past. Everything today was about viewers, website clicks, and audience trending.

Farid had never really needed to work as a news personality, it was something which paid reasonably well for the modest amount of work that went into it, enabled the meeting of many beautiful women, and kept one close to what was going on in the world. Knowing what was happening early had allowed Farid to greatly enhance his fortune with judicious movements of money from one type of investment to another, whenever it made sense to him. Journalists could be tried for insider trading of corporate stock if they knew details about the company that were not public knowledge, but that wasn't the edge he used. Farid knew what macroeconomic events were imminent, and translated it into an understanding of which firms could be impacted. That was not generally considered to be insider trading. Occasionally, he didn't pick a winner, but it was usually a mistake in the timing not in having chosen the event itself. As he watched, he wondered where his money should be shifted given the new terrorist approach in America.

Something in security, he mused, *or perhaps a larger play based on people being less willing to go out and spend money on impulse.* If people were hiding from snipers at home, general retail industries would suffer, impacting mall property firms. This one would take some thought.

While Farid had been thinking, Jameson had ended his televised press conference with a promise to take questions on the morrow. Farid was amazed someone as transparently slimy as Jameson could maintain a leadership position within the FBI. Farid's television network began releasing the avalanche of stories they had prepared. He doubted that Justin and Quinton would be too happy with the stories asking why shootings were still occurring. Farid knew such questions were inevitable, given the shooting that very day, and felt his network should be the one asking them. He also knew better than to invest in the stock of his employer, the added income from a good day like today was not nearly sufficient to make it a good investment. The impression he had gotten from Justin was that the FBI had identified one shooter and was hoping to find all the others from clues left behind. It would be interesting to understand how the shooter died, but, so far, Justin was cagey on that topic. *Time would tell*, Farid mused, *it always does.*

• • •

Jonny Ray and Nayla lay spent upon the bed which had seen a lot of use over the afternoon. Jonny Ray had even opted for the S&M hanging rig which choked a submissive Nayla if she did not provide the perfect response to his every move.

Jonny Ray lay nude with Nayla entwined next to him. This afternoon was something he would never forget - but now the time had come to deliver the bad news.

"Nayla, darling. I have some bad news for us that we should discuss," Jonny Ray said.

"Bad news?" Nayla asked as she sat up beside him. She was still wearing the leather outfit but for the red panties, which were missing in action.

"You've heard of this Martyrs al-Sabra situation?" he asked.

"Yes. Terrible people doing terrible things, and misusing the name of a great charity as well," Nayla said.

"That's right. Your friend, Farid, is on the board over there, isn't he? No matter. That isn't what I have to talk about, other than as an explanation. You know I love spending time with you. This last half year has been one of the best in my life. But I was called into Sidney Rosenbloom's office yesterday and he told me that you and I have to call it quits for a while in order to protect Lucy from potential scandal."

"Potential scandal? I thought all of that was handled by your arrangement with the Secret Service. How are you going to resist slipping out for very long?" Nayla asked.

"Sid wasn't saying I should stop slipping out, he meant I should stop doing so with you. Before you get angry, though, there are some good reasons which have very little to do with you and more with the possible perceptions of those who learn of it. In fact, Sid is very aware of what you have done for the Party and wants you to come work in the White House. The only caveat is we cannot continue whatever this was."

"Still lying there damp from lovemaking and already speaking in the past tense. I'm amazed," Nayla said calmly.

Emboldened by Nayla's calm, "The issue is that you and your brother were tied to the original Martyrs al-Sabra incident in Gaza Strip. If it were known I was having another affair, but this time with someone that half the country would assume to be guilty of something, it would not end well. I could be outed a number of times with women without that background story and it would be merely inconvenient for Lucy. But with you, it could cause a major scandal that might bring down her presidency, or damage it severely. That's why they asked me to stop and I agreed. I'm sorry, darling. You know how I feel about you."

Nayla stared past him to the curtained windows. "I wasn't even in Gaza when it happened, but I've suffered for it over the years. From losing my brother, who was the last of my family, to being alone in a strange country. I understand the political necessity, Jonny Ray. Sadly, I do understand. You're right. What we had was very special and I will always treasure the memory of it." She had been instructed not to inform Jonny Ray that today was their final assignation; therefore, she found it easy to portray the sadly jilted lover.

Jonny Ray had been expecting to see some of the fiery temper Palestinians were known to possess, so seeing her calmly accepting his news was somehow harder for him than weathering the screaming match for which he was prepared.

"Somehow I expected you would be disappointed, but you seem like it was expected," Jonny Ray said.

"Of course, it was expected, Jonny Ray! You're married to the President of the United States and I am the occasional mistress. There is nothing wrong with that, as I went into it with my eyes open. I've had fun, and I will remember it as a good time. I didn't know when it would end, but the outcome was never in doubt. We're both adults. I never expected you would restrict yourself to just one mistress either. Everyone knows you're a man with large appetites."

"I am at that. But sometimes it is fun to pretend it isn't my nature. I have to say I don't know what I'll do with three more years of Secret Service protection."

"Three more years? Seven more years if you or I have anything to say about it! Look, on the White House job, I think I would rather stay where I'm at - it pays a lot better. I would also get a twinge every time I saw you, which would be more often there than in my current role," Nayla said.

"There it is, I knew you cared, Nayla!" Jonny Ray chortled.

Nayla shook her head in mock surrender. Jonny Ray got up and started putting his widely scattered clothes back together, "I've got a reception this evening at the big house. So I need to get moving. Aren't you going to change as well?"

"No, I think I'll see you off dressed this way. At a minimum, it will give you something to think about in days to come," Nayla said as she arranged herself artfully upon the sofa.

"Strike a pose, darlin'!" Jonny Ray said with a booming laugh. He checked his ensemble over, patted pockets to confirm things were where they were meant to be, and kissed Nayla once more on the forehead. "I'll see myself out, doll. Listen, if you ever need help with something I can provide, don't hesitate to reach out. We may no longer be lovers, but that doesn't mean I don't care. Know that!"

Nayla nodded her head silently and blew a kiss as he waved back before closing the door. Through the door Nayla heard a low conversation with the members of the detail and the unmistakable sounds of footsteps leaving her floor. It wouldn't long before The Hammer came. Jonny Ray hadn't spent much of his afternoon eating, so there were snacks to freshen up as well as the array of drinks. Nayla went about her chores wearing the same outfit, although she did re-don the red panties which had been recovered from under one of Jonny Ray's socks. Normally, she would have jumped immediately into a shower and changed into something fresh, but The Hammer had ordered her to maintain the same clothes for an additional set of pictures. So feeling a bit less-than-fresh had to borne for a few more hours. It was still dusk outside and Nayla knew The Hammer would not come until it was fully dark.

• • •

Justin was sitting in the eye of a hurricane of task force activity in Roseville. Teams were running down IP address leads obtained from the Kansas data center logs in over forty different cities. Other teams were engaged in interviewing the friends and acquaintances of Dr. Hammayil in the Sacramento/Roseville area. Financial analysts were looking at the past five years of tax and business income paperwork for his dental practice. The MMORPG game the terrorists used for communications was identified as Fantasy Conquests, first by the data center logs and then by the decrypted wiretap take of Dr. Hammayil's Internet use. There was a team on the way to see what logs were available from the game servers, search warrants in hand. In fairness, the game company had offered full cooperation almost immediately when they understood the suspected misuse of their platform. The company had partnered in the past with the government for studies on crowd behavior in virtual environments, and kept extensive logs of chat sessions/game mail for that very reason. Added to that was the continued input from stolen license plates and traffic cam footage analysis from more than forty cities. In short, there was a lot on Justin's plate.

Now, it appeared his boss was suffering from some grievance which he had yet to share with Justin. Every so many minutes he would look over at Justin and scowl. Justin had suffered through Jameson's moods and passive aggressive lashing out before, but now was not really the time for any extra issues. There was no percentage in calling him on it, though. At the FBI that behavior tended to be labeled as insubordination in spite of the surrounding facts. Justin kept his head down and worked on all the other things clamoring for his attention.

Jameson was watching the television network coverage of the Roseville story. In many respects, the press conference had been a success, but almost all of the news sources had moved early to the questions that had not been addressed. How had Dr. Hammayil died? What about the attempted shooting that afternoon in Harrison, New Jersey? What had the FBI done to capture shooters in the other cities? When could results be expected on the entire terrorist ring? Who was The Hammer? Every news report which explored the follow-up topics seemed to darken Jameson's mood. Unknown to Justin, Jameson had been given an ultimatum by the executive team. To whit: FBI management was starting to have their own questions about the overall leadership of the task force, even going so far as to state that imminent success wrapping up the Martyrs matter was the only way Jameson could aspire to higher position. Jameson's attempt to deflect the blame onto Justin and the team for missing the murder of Dr. Hammayil was rebuffed with prejudice.

To paraphrase the leadership's viewpoint, Jameson had known of The Hammer for over six months but still had made no progress identifying him or his organization. Jameson recognized that the executive suite was looking to firmly fix the blame at his level before it rose to their own exalted heights. No matter your level, if you played the political game, you needed to have a Judas goat ready for the occasional balls-up. Justin was supposed to be that person for Jameson, but he wasn't cooperating.

"Simons, conference room," Jameson barked across the room where the task force was camped.

Here it comes, Justin thought to himself. "I'll be right there." Justin finalized his telephone call to the Kansas team and headed into the small conference room that was kept secure from wiretaps.

"Come in and close the door," Jameson said as Justin came into the room.

Justin sat down, with a pad of paper in hand for taking any notes that were necessary. Sometimes having something in the hand had prevented an overreaction to Jameson's provocations. Otherwise, the hands might form up into fists.

"What the hell is your friend, Farid, doing?" Jameson said.

"I'm sorry, what are we talking about?"

"We gave his network first access to the photos and story, and they end up stabbing us in the back with all of the speculation! I spent about an hour on the phone with the Director and his team, and they are calling this a complete cock-up," Jameson said.

"I'm still not seeing it. You mean the logical next-step questions that everyone, including Farid's network, are asking? What is the old Chinese saying? Expecting otherwise is like trying to wrap fire with paper. If we had their job, wouldn't we be saying exactly the same things?"

"Fuck old Chinese sayings! I've about had it with your boy, Farid. I still think he has some involvement in this, and I don't think your mind is right on that due to your childhood friendship. I think we're going to pull him in when we get back to DC and see what comes out in the sweat lodge."

"I've said it before, if you feel there is a conflict of interest take me off of the portion of the project assessing Farid - I'll recuse myself. What more do I need to do?" Justin said with some heat.

"You need to decide whether your loyalty is to childhood friends or the Bureau," Jameson said.

"I'm not seeing a conflict, sir," Justin said flatly.

"I do, and it is my opinion that matters on this."

"Permission to speak freely?" Justin said.

"Of course, here it comes," Jameson sneered.

"It is my loyalty to the Bureau that makes me urge caution when trying to bulldoze Farid Royce. I've known him from childhood, and I guarantee you he has a plan should the FBI decide to detain him without proof. I personally don't believe he is involved, but let's say he is for the sake of discussion. There is to date no material evidence he is involved. If he were detained without evidence he would hit the Bureau with the best lawyers in the country, and he can afford them. How long do you think it would be before the Director was receiving calls from Senators, Congressmen, and maybe even the White House? Without proof, nothing stands up to that kind of pressure. All the time I've known him, various people have tried to hurt him for whatever reason: he was Muslim, he was small, he was Palestinian - the list is endless. In every case, he bided his time and got even. Look, he is my best friend, but when he has been treated unjustly he is ruthless."

"Sounds to me like you are describing The Hammer," Jameson sniped.

Raising his hands in the universal *I-give-up* pose Justin said, "I'll recuse myself on handling Farid, and the entire investigation if you think it is appropriate."

"For now, you're off of anything to do with Farid. Handle the rest of the things you were doing while I think about next steps. I'm headed back to DC tomorrow morning. You can handle the follow-up discussions with Maryam Said then head back to DC in the afternoon. I think Maryam's contribution is already mined out, but it still needs to be validated for consistency."

"Is there anything else?" Justin asked through his clenched jaw.

"Consider yourself on probation with me. I'll be watching you closely and deciding whether you really do have a career in the FBI."

"You are my supervisor and that is one of the expected roles: assessing your employees."

"You don't have a very good attitude, Simons," Jameson said.

Justin didn't justify the comment with a response as he stood and left the conference room. He headed back to the task force room already dialing Jan with the news of his changed schedule.

• • •

The Hammer waited until all activity of the Secret Service had ended, and then waited another thirty minutes for full safety. The light was still on in the apartment, which he took to be a sign that Nayla had been successful.

Moving quietly as a cat stalking a mouse, he crossed the street and entered the stairwell leading to Nayla's floor. He was always amazed at how a city with millions of people could shut down so early in the evening. He had never run into anyone in the stairwell, but perhaps that simply reflected an aversion to exercise. The Hammer took the stairs two at a time. His breathing was slightly higher than normal as he hit the destination landing. He peered through the glass panel in the door. The hallway was clear, so he strolled up to Nayla's door, knocked once and opened it with his key.

The first thing he saw was Nayla sitting in full regalia on the couch. She smiled and stood up.

"As-salāmu ʿalaykum," she said bobbing her head.

"Waʿalaykumu as-salām," he said seriously.

"Will you take some wine?"

"Certainly, if it is ready. I can go without if it is not," he said.

"I have it right here," Nayla went into the kitchen area and came back to find him sitting on the couch. "Here you are," setting a glass close by his hand.

"So, how did it go with the estimable Jonny Ray?"

"You are not going to believe this, but he broke up with me tonight. So we don't have to do anything on that front," Nayla said.

"Tell me everything which was said," The Hammer ordered then sipped from the wine glass.

Nayla related the entire conversation to him. Nayla's ability to recall was most extraordinary, it was one of the things which had made her a star student. The Hammer listened to the entire story, only interrupting once or twice with soft-spoken requests for clarification. It didn't take long to take it all in.

"So they are concerned about the Martyrs al-Sabra campaign being generalized to others?"

"I think it was a case of a bridge-too-far: an affair they can deal with, an affair with someone the public might link to the campaign is too much."

"I'm impressed with their logic. You say it was Sid Rosenbloom who initiated the breakoff?

"Yes, from what Jonny Ray said. He might have said it anyway if he were trying to get out of a relationship, but I didn't catch a whiff of that. He seemed genuinely remorseful. The White House offer wouldn't have come from Jonny Ray, so that is another point in favor of it being Sid," Nayla confirmed.

"Do you think the President was aware of the relationship?"

"I would say she knew there was a relationship, or many, but not the details. That would be supported by the job offer as well. No way she would offer that up! I don't care how open minded she is about Jonny Ray's activities."

"I agree. My, that outfit has been through the wars a bit, hasn't it?" he asked.

"Yes, it has, but I kept it on per the instructions. Did you say there were more pictures needed?"

"Yes, in a few more minutes. I know you want out of those clothes, but I want to tell you about the scope of the final strike against the infidels, now that your part is nearly finished."

The Hammer told the story of a country paralyzed by random sniping attacks in the thirty largest metropolitan areas, a new president with a major sex scandal about to consume her attention, and the crowning glory of a light mimicking the sun about to be born in the Caribbean. So far, the FBI had nothing on the snipers, who were about to go deep cover once more. The FBI would also be caught completely flat-footed on the bomb, even though the knowledge it was in play was well-documented in the Martyrs case files.

Nayla gasped at the scope of The Hammer's plan, "Are you hoping for a change in the presidency? They might be able to survive this. What is the main objective?"

"Destabilization, fear, and erosion of American institutions for a start. As for the President, I hope she survives. She would make the next phase much easier for us. As a progressive, she will resist demonization of Muslims to the very end, but it has to happen eventually. You see the goal is change in Palestine's future, and that will never happen while the Muslim world remains fractious. To make steel, the ingredients must pass through fire. While Muslims talk about a religion of peace, nothing happens. If Islam regains its martial potential and acknowledges no peace will be granted to infidels, then something new happens. If all of the Palestinians went back to Palestine, how long do you think Israel would survive? It was our cowardice which lost us Palestine. Only bravery and sacrifice can regain it. Israel will be no more eventually regardless. An infidel once noted Palestinians inside Israel will outnumber Jews within the next fifty years. How long can a Jewish democracy exist while Palestinians are granted a vote?"

"The Americans will start killing innocent Muslims in the cities."

"I hope so. That might unite the Muslim groups in self-defense. It will be bloody and America will never be the same. No, I hope for a Muslim holocaust here in America, Either the American Muslims will stand up and fight, or they will be persecuted and killed. Americans will feel guilty about it after the dust clears, and Palestine will be ours once more. Americans don't care about Palestinians dying in Palestine; they will care about Palestinians killed in America by Americans."

"That is a change I cannot begin to contemplate, but I do support a return to the homeland. Even with the problems and stupidities," Nayla said.

"Now that you understand, let's finish here and get the last few pictures," The Hammer set his glass down and walked into the bedroom. The choke harness was still hanging from the ceiling, with other paraphernalia strewn about the room. "Perfect, we didn't get good profile shots of you in the harness. Let's have you on knees facing the head of the bed with your neck in the harness, and your hands bound behind your back with the handcuffs. Good, perfect. Let me flip your hair to this side, so the face can be obscured." The Hammer took several photographs with his expensive camera. No flash was needed with this model, it adjusted itself automatically to lighting conditions for perfect exposures.

"Alright, I think that is enough," The Hammer said as he walked over to her side. Grasping the choke harness, he pulled it tight enough to fully constrict Layla's neck.

Nayla started kicking and flinging herself around, despite knowing that it was futile against his strength. The Hammer took hold of both ankles and suspended her by her neck. The kicking and thrashing continued while he held her ankles tightly.

"You see, Nayla, for this part of the operation we need a sacrifice and Jonny Ray suspected of murder. I'm glad you didn't see it coming, as it should be as painless for you as possible. I love you, and you could have refused this task, but you did not. We could never go on with that behind us. No, we both do our part for a free Palestine. I love you."

Nayla's kicking had subsided to the point where it was probably post-mortem reflexive twitching. When it stopped, The Hammer placed her knees back in place and posed her once more. He stood back inspecting his handiwork and made one final change, pulling the red panties down to rest at her knees. It looked as though someone had stood at the end of the bed engaged in sex while she died. The Hammer took several more pictures then left the bedroom for the living room couch. The bedroom door was left half open.

The Hammer sat down on the couch and cried for his lost love, holding his head with both hands, given over entirely to his grief, hitting his forehead repeatedly upon his knees as he grieved. It might have been thirty minutes, it might have been an hour. To him time had stopped with Nayla's heart. His fixation was broken by the sound of a mobile phone, insistent.

Farid Amir Mansour Royce al-Haj looked down at his ringing phone, took a deep breath and answered, "Justin, what can I do for you?"

"I just wanted to give you a heads-up. Jameson has removed me from handling you due to a perceived conflict of interest. So don't be surprised when he reaches out directly."

"What happened?"

"I can't talk about it. In fact, I am taking a career risk just making this call, but I can present it as a confidential informant transition announcement should it come up," Justin said heavily.

"Alright, I'll act surprised. Thanks for letting me know. I appreciate it. When are you coming back to the right side of the country?"

"Tomorrow night. Jan was not happy, but she understood."

"Thanks again, Justin, I have to run. Good night."

"Good night."

Farid resumed his scan of Nayla's love apartment for anything that would tie him personally to the scene. Finally, he placed a single engraved 30-06 cartridge on the coffee table with gloved hands and left the apartment for the last time, never once looking back into the bedroom at the lifeless husk of his former love.

COMMAND PERFORMANCES

"..The Martyrs terrorist campaign has been hurting, not only the children of the United States, but also those who would normally have benefitted from the orphan's charity of the same name. The terrorist appropriation of the name should not taint the good work the charity performs around the world. I have with me tonight one of the orphans..."

Farid Monsour al Haj for World News Corporation

Quinton Jameson sat back in his exit row seat aboard the 9:30 a.m. direct flight from San Francisco to Washington-Dulles. He wouldn't arrive until late afternoon due to the three-hour time difference and five-hour flight. Enough time to decide how to best handle Farid Royce. He would have to be brought in as a terror suspect to give Quinton enough time to lean on him sufficiently. Otherwise, Farid would be out within hours and protected by a phalanx of lawyers. Quinton had a federal judge classmate who owed him a favor or two, so getting a warrant to search Farid's office and home should be easy to obtain in conjunction with an arrest warrant.

It would be best to take him by surprise, so a meeting request is out of the question, Jameson thought. The task force could show up at Farid's home unannounced. That might not work so well if he was inclined to resist arrest, though. Quinton had no compunction against using force with Farid, but wasn't as eager to involve his influential neighbors.

Maybe his office would be the right place to take Farid down. The problem with that approach was having to share too much information with the news network, which was publicity he didn't really want at this juncture.

Farid also had an office at the Martyrs charity, but he seldom spent time there in a predictable way. Jameson frowned. *Everything keeps coming back to a meeting request.*

Resigning himself to the inevitable on that front, he circled back to consider why he was so convinced Farid had something to do with the Martyrs attacks. In too many instances, Farid seemed to be close by another possible suspect. First was the election night party of last November, when they first heard of The Hammer. Then there was his ties to the Martyrs charity organization, and foreign sponsors of terrorism. Some of the case information had also come from Farid in his role as informant.

As a matter of personal policy, Quinton didn't trust confidential informants. They have too many reasons to be less than truthful. A person volunteering as a confidential informant doesn't make sense, unless they meant to feed the FBI misinformation. Each one of these facts, taken on their own, could be dismissed as coincidence. But all of them together, might actually be an indication of something more. The irrational part of Quinton's brain screamed that Farid was The Hammer, but his rational mind couldn't get the known facts to properly support that conclusion. The FBI wasn't a huge fan of unsupported assertions, unless they decided to use it as a strategy, so Quinton would need more evidence before saying anything on record.

Without question, the next few weeks would be critical for Quinton's career. He had enough years on the job to retire comfortably and perhaps work occasionally as a highly-paid consultant to pay for any extra toys he might want. His wife had fossilized into a society maven, banking on her Ivy League background to acquire standing in the glittery DC social scene. They weren't particularly well-heeled but were accepted at many of the right parties. As a couple, they were seen as having power and connections but not money. Quinton knew it was unlikely they would accrue any significant money by DC standards, so his only path was to remain on career track within the FBI.

Another possibility was to saddle Justin with the brunt of the blame for the lack of progress. Eventually, very soon now, the public will collectively lose its patience about Muslims and start lashing out. The President and FBI will come in for a lot of criticism. The President would blame the FBI, the FBI would blame a few sacrificial field agents or Section Chiefs, and everyone would hope the issue passed promptly into obscurity. Making sure it stopped with the field agents was Quinton's goal.

That Simons is a real boy scout in all of this, Quinton thought. *What if I could dirty him up a bit before the shit hits? The trick is deciding how to get that done.* Quinton hated men who were built like football players and had all their hair. *Simons even has a brain. Life just isn't fair sometimes.* Quinton scowled as he recalled his last conversation with Simons. *I'll give it some thought.*

Quinton reclined his seat and quickly passed into a fitful sleep for most of the flight.

• • •

Justin's morning session with Maryam Said went pretty much as they expected. She really didn't know anything useful, and was consistent in telling her story. If it were up to Justin, he would have released her that afternoon under ankle bracelet constraints, but Jameson had vetoed that before his departure. Maryam's interrogation had revealed where to look, even though she was apparently clueless about her husband's activities.

The quick analysis of the family's accounts showed an unaccounted $15,000 coming into Dr. Hammayil's personal checking account in early January. The Honda was purchased shortly thereafter. The road trip to Wisconsin was reconstructed by the trail of hotel, restaurant, and gasoline charges Dr. Hammayil had left behind. The rental agent at the Oversight Hunting Lodge confirmed a large group called the Sons of Italy had leased their facilities for two weeks, paying cash through several Caribbean wire transfers. The group even received their damage deposit back in full after the rental. From what special agents on scene could determine, the snipers had been taught to shoot at the club and probably trained on everything else. The Kansas data center log identified an extensive series of sessions between the hunting lodge IP address and the proxy server during those two weeks.

Justin couldn't help but feel that every time the FBI got close, the terrorists adjusted to remain just out of reach. The Kansas data center list of IP addresses included approximately one thousand regular users, about seven hundred of whom were within major metropolitan areas. There was no way to track all of them down for investigation in any reasonable amount of time. The terrorists had stopped using the game as a communication platform, and Justin wondered what had replaced it. More questions than answers, and no suspects who were alive.

Oddly, he found himself yearning for the old schema, where young zealots would brag on social media before actually performing an attack. Even a suicide bombing would be better. In those cases, you knew it was over afterwards. This current terrorist had tapped into the true meaning of terror: continued uncertainty and nothing deemed safe. America, as it was, could not survive in that kind of environment. The state would have to lock things down in order to stop campaigns like The Hammer's. Justin didn't know if the price of giving up personal freedom was worth paying for public security. It wasn't for him. It seemed to be the epitome of what the USA had fought against in the past: Nazis, Communists, and the like. *We would have to become more like them if our primary goal is safety*, he mused. *You haf' your identity papers?* A German accent from bad movies spoke the question. *If the FBI comes to that, I'll jump to a law practice. Jan would be a big fan. Maybe I'll ask Farid if he needs a lawyer on retainer.*

Justin had no worries for his friend. He knew Farid would read between the lines of last night's call and prepare himself. Jameson might bite off a piece that would break a tooth or two. Justin didn't have any problem reconciling his loyalties to Farid and the Bureau. The Bureau's interests were not synonymous with those of Jameson. If Jameson chose to bend the rules while pursuing a suspect then he deserved the blowback. He had been warned.

The Martyrs task force now had over one thousand people working nationwide on various aspects of the case, which did not even count the subcontractors who were carrying the HORUS data loads. No matter who was running the project, it was going to be difficult to justify the cost when the final reviews were being done. There would have to be more efficient ways to work cases like this one going forward. The public was a feather away from forming mobs and lynching Muslims. The recent good news was eclipsed by the shooting in Harrison, New Jersey. Justin hoped losing the terrorist communication channel of the game would slow or stop new sniping incidents. It seemed recently every time Justin got on a plane a shooting occurred, destabilizing the balance of the investigation until a new allocation of resources could be done. No point in worrying about it now, though, he had a plane to catch.

• • •

The call came into the DC e911 center early Saturday morning.

"Emergency Services, what is your emergency?"

"There has been a murder or something worse at her apartment. She didn't leave last night after meeting her very important lover, and there were sounds of breaking or a fight there. I watched for her later like usual, and she never came," an electronically modified male voice said.

"Sir, who are you and where is the apartment?"

Farid spoke into the voice modulation device, gave the address of Nayla's love apartment in Georgetown and her name, but didn't answer the question about his own identity.

"Sir, what is your name?"

"I think she is dead, and he might have killed her. I've told you on the record, so it will go hard if it is not investigated. I suggest you get to it, otherwise the Secret Service might get there first and cover it up. That would be bad for you, them and everyone," Farid hung up the burner phone and dropped it into the Potomac River. He slipped the voice modulation device into his pocket and walked the rest of the way off of the Theodore Roosevelt Island bridge into Virginia.

The e911 operator had been through many hoax calls before, but she'd also been through similar situations where the call was all too real. Regardless, it didn't pay to make the judgment in this case, so she escalated the call to her line supervisor.

He played it back several times, calling up the address on his monitor. Recognizing the high net worth of those living within the building, he said. "Thanks for bringing this to me, I think we need to get a crew over there. The caller was obviously disguising their voice and, from the tracking, I'll bet the phone is in the river by now." He tasked a patrol unit to investigate the apartment. All told, the decision took twenty minutes.

• • •

Sid's phone rang insistently, groaning he reached across the table to pick it up. "Yes?"

"Sir, Michael Costello, Secret Service. We have a problem that needs to be discussed immediately, concerning Jackalope."

"Certainly, where should we meet?"

"Your home, sir. I am outside in a service car, your detail knows I am here."

"Sure, a bit irregular but come on in," Sid said as he closed up his bathrobe.

Michael Costello, the Detail Lead for Jonny Ray Brown, was shown into Sid's kitchen by his own agent. Michael had a very serious expression on his face.

"OK, son. Out with it, what has the asshole done this time?" Sid asked.

"That's just it, we don't know. We monitor e911 calls in DC to assess threats to principals 24/7. There was one twenty minutes ago, anonymous caller, said that there may have been a murder at the apartment of Nayla Kaldah last night. Jonny Ray was there with her yesterday afternoon for what I understood to be the last time."

"Shit!" Sid was now fully awake.

"Did DC's finest investigate yet?"

"They are on their way as we speak. I took the liberty of scrambling a team over there to secure the area, they should be in control of it as we speak. They were not to enter the apartment, however. How do you and, of course, the President want to handle this?" Costello said.

"Secure it, but let DC Police open the apartment up first. Accompany them in without compromising anything if it is a crime scene. Does our team have their body-cams? I want a full record of what is found for our use. I don't want the media, or anyone, to say the Secret Service is covering up here. I have a really bad feeling."

"I agree, this is almost certainly something impactful to the President. Give me a second, I'll relay the instructions."

• • •

JeMeign Jones and Devon Marshall, Jem and Dev, uniformed minions of DC Metro Police, exited the apartment building elevator on the floor indicated by dispatch. They were alert but not excessively so; the building was quiet and seemed fairly secure. It was even more secure than they had imagined because when they rounded the corner there were four Secret Service agents standing athwart the entrance to the apartment.

"What's going on here?" Jem asked.

"Secret Service, Special Agent Higby, here are our credentials."

Jem and Dev presented theirs as well, "What are you folks doing here?"

"We're here to assess a possible threat to our principal, but we're not going to get in your way. We know a crime was called in, so DC has the lead unless it evolves into something within our domain. Jones and Harris, keep the hallway secure. Ng, you're with me behind Jones and Marshall." The Secret Service team split as instructed without making any comments.

Jem hated working with Feds; they usually wouldn't spit on the ground where local police had walked. Always tying the city in knots when one of their principals wanted a special hot-dog. JeMeign saw the Secret Service lead activate his body-cam. *Great! One of those special career opportunities*, he thought to himself as he activated his own.

Jem rang the doorbell and knocked. There was no sound from within the apartment. He escalated the knocking and ringing with the announcement, "DC Police, please open the door." There was still no answer or response. "Dev, we're going to need a key, see if the manager is in."

"No need for that," Higby said and handed a key to Jem.

Jem's eyebrows raised as a number of questions flashed through his mind. "We'll have to chat shortly on how it is you have a key, but we can table that for now."

Jem drew his gun, inserted the key into the door, nodded to Devon as he opened the door in a rush, swinging to cover the entrance of his partner. The two Secret Service agents entered behind the DC police.

There was nothing obviously out of place in the main living area. Two empty wine glasses sat on a table. The kitchen lights were on, but otherwise the apartment was orderly.

Jem motioned towards the half-open bedroom door and walked cautiously to where he could peer in. Caution gave way to interest, then a frown.

"We have a body. Dev, get on the horn while I check for a pulse," reaching into his jacket pocket, he extracted a pair of evidence gloves which he put onto his hands. "Gentlemen, you need to stand back and not enter the room. I don't want any more contamination than necessary."

Jem entered the room quickly, crossed to Nayla's side looking into her face for signs of life, of which there were none. Taking two of his fingers, Jem pressed against Nayla's neck in the vain hope of a finding a pulse.

"Don't touch or move anything, this is a murder crime scene. Dev, get the murder squad out here stat. OK, gentlemen, now is the time to tell me how you have a key. Do you know the victim?"

"I think you will find the victim is Nayla Kaldah. She is a K Street lobbyist and lawyer. We've had to secure these premises in the past for meetings," Higby said.

"What kind of meetings? She's not wearing a business suit at the moment," Jem asked remembering what Nayla was wearing.

"I can't say at the moment. If it becomes important to the investigation, the conversation can happen above our pay-grades," Higby said while shaking his head.

"Sir, you have to see this," Agent Ng called from the living room.

Jem pulled the bedroom door closed and walked over to where the others had gathered.

"Is that what I think it is?" Agent Ng asked.

Agent Higby took out a small flashlight and looked closely at the small object sitting on the coffee table, "God damn it! I think it is. Excuse me, I have to make a phone call."

Jem and Dev looked closely at what looked to be a deer rifle round with Arabic engraving upon it. "Holy shit, Dev. This is connected to all that Martyrs shit. Don't touch a damn thing, this whole apartment will have to be dissected."

Agent Higby dialed Detail Lead Costello who was waiting in Sid's kitchen for the call.

"Higby, I'm going to put this on the speaker," Costello said in response to Sid's gesture. "OK, go ahead it is just us and the Chief of Staff."

"Really bad, it looks like Nayla was killed sometime after Jonny Ray left the building. Not too long after, as she is still wearing the same outfit she had on yesterday."

"Higby, this is Sid. How do you know she was killed after?"

"Good point, I just assumed. I'll have to check whether anyone on the detail saw her as Jonny Ray was leaving. I know I didn't, now that I think about it. There is something else, though, there's a deer rifle shell on the coffee table with an Arabic inscription. Also, she was apparently strangled using one of those sex-strangulation devices that hang from the ceiling over the bed. DC has blocked off access to the room, but I did get body-cam footage which can be sent over later," Higby said.

Sid's face pulled into grim lines. "Two things: first, provide whatever assistance DC Police might require now; second, get the FBI over there as soon as possible. This is part of the Martyrs terrorist campaign. I'll get on the phone with the mayor and arrange for some DC participation in the FBI investigation. This belongs to the FBI, but we don't want the smell of a cover-up. You can tell the officers it is being arranged," Sid said.

Sid's mind was racing. When this hit the press, it would become known that Nayla was involved in the original Martyrs incident, even though tangentially. Today's press wouldn't make the distinction. Once the connection was made, the story would be Jonny Ray and every sordid thing he had ever done would be rehashed over and over again for weeks. Past administrations would have scrambled a black bag team to clean up the mess and hope for the best. President Lucinda Brown had made it clear that there would be no cover-ups of clearly illegal behavior on her team. It was one of the things that distinguished her from past Party colleagues that would do anything, even if illegal, to stay in power. People trusted Lucy Brown, they didn't trust her predecessors, and that was the difference. The question right now was whether to brace Jonny Ray before or after the President was briefed. Sid picked up his phone and dialed.

"Ashley? Sid. I'm sorry to bother you this morning, but I need the mobile phone of Justin Simons, the FBI Special Agent running the Martyrs case."

"Sure, I'll forward it in a text. What's up?"

"I'll fill you in later. Get your rest today, we're going to probably be on a war footing late today or early tomorrow. Jackalope got caught up in the Martyrs tarball."

"Jesus effing Christ! Should I head in this afternoon?" Ashley asked.

"Exactly. I'll call you in when I have more, I was serious about you getting some rest. Cheers," Sid hung up and immediately redialed Justin.

"Justin, this is Sid Rosenbloom. I need to speak to you, somewhere private preferably. Sure, I'll hang on." Sid had a large swallow of coffee.

"Sir, I am in the secure room," Justin said.

"I'm going to cut right to the chase. Nayla Kaldah was murdered sometime last night," Sid said.

There was a choking sound on Justin's end. "No - not Nayla!" he croaked.

"Yes. Sometime presumably after Jonny Ray Brown left her apartment yesterday. Whoever killed her left a rifle round with Arabic engraving sitting on a coffee table. The bedroom has been secured by DC Police and one of our Secret Service go-teams. I think the FBI probably has jurisdiction on this, although you will likely have help from DC Police. You'll need to get a team over there immediately," Sid said.

"Does the press know about this yet?"

"Not that I am aware, but I would assume the Martyrs themselves could release information if it suits them."

"Sir, I'll scramble a team, I'm currently in Roseville, California but am headed back tonight on a red-eye. Jameson should be getting back in a few hours, around 5 p.m.," Justin said.

"Thanks, I was going to call him next. I'll send you contact information for a couple of Secret Service agents who are on-scene at the apartment. Keep us informed, Justin. There will be no cover-up. If Jonny Ray was involved, I want to know about it immediately."

"In the spirit of full disclosure, I might have to recuse myself as I know Nayla personally. She is very close to my childhood friends, Farid and Lindsey Royce. That will be something to work through later, though. I can get things kicked off and we'll see what Jameson says about my connection," Justin said.

"Thanks, Justin. I knew calling you first was the right move. Keep this number handy and call anytime with updates. I'll let you get to it," Sid hung up the phone and leaned back in his chair. Pulling up Jameson's mobile number, he composed several short text messages summarizing the issues, deployment of Justin's team, and requesting an urgent call back upon landing.

Sometime over the last few minutes, Sid decided the President needed to be briefed earlier than later.

He turned to Agent Costello, "Thanks, Michael. I'm going to get cleaned up and head over to brief the President. Have our folks hold the crime scene intact until the FBI gets there and then turn it over to them. This is a national security issue and considered part of the Martyrs terror campaign unless proven otherwise. My guys can show you out."

A shower and shave would give him a fresh perspective on the problem. But before that, he rang the President's personal assistant to schedule a private conference in the next few hours.

• • •

Justin sat in shock from the news. He had called the Martyrs task force members still in DC and scrambled the team into action. He wondered whether he should tell his friend Farid before he learned of it some other way. If so, he would have to do it in person and that was almost a day away. Another possibility was to call Lindsey and tell her. No that didn't feel right either, Nayla was like a sister to Lindsey. He dialed a number and waited for the answer.

"Hi Baby! Don't you even tell me you are delayed coming home, I won't stand for it," Jan said playfully.

"Hi Honey, no I am coming home on time, assuming the airlines cooperate. I have some bad news, you might want to sit down, sorry. I just found out that Nayla was killed last night," Justin said heavily.

"Nayla, no! How?"

"I don't have all the details yet, but it appears to be connected with the Martyrs case I'm working on, which is why they called to tell me about it. I wanted to get in touch with Lindsey to let her know, but didn't feel right calling her on the phone with that. Same thing with Farid. I can't get back there until tomorrow, but they should be told in person, don't you think?"

"Justin, Farid will be devastated. He loved that woman, even though he acted like he wasn't attached."

"I'm thinking Lindsey will be pretty upset, too. Hell, Jan, I'm upset myself. I've got to hold things together looking into it, but definitely feel strange about putting her through the normal investigative process. Hopefully, Jameson will recuse me when he gets back to DC this afternoon."

"Justin, I will go talk to Lindsey, and Farid as well. It is probably best to do it as soon as possible, otherwise they might hear from other sources. I'll drop the kids at Mom's and head from there over to see Lindsey."

"I was hoping you would do that. You and I go back a long way with Farid, and all of Lindsey's life. They're family in all but name. Nayla was well on her way to that status as well. I always had her married to Farid in my mind."

"Me too, me too. Are you going to be alright, my Mr. Strong Silent type?"

"I will now. You've taken a huge load off of my mind. I couldn't see any way round calling them with the news, but I didn't want to do it with a phone call. It felt disrespectful to Nayla and what she meant to everyone. Thank you, honey! I'm sorry to lay this on you," Justin said.

"That's why you pay me the big bucks, love. Let me get them on the phone, maybe I can get Farid to come over to Lindsey's and tell them both at the same time. I'll check in with you later. Love you," Jan said.

"Love you too," Justin said as he rang off.

• • •

Sid sat outside the Oval Office waiting for the promised break in the President's schedule dreading the conversation he was about to have. It wasn't that he expected her to kill the messenger. No it was more that it would hurt her personally and possibly professionally. Sid loved Lucy Brown, not romantically, but as a person he respected and didn't want to see hurt. There was no way to avoid the pain that was to come - all he could hope for was to minimize it.

The assistant called, "She's ready for you now. Go right in, Sid."

"Thanks, Steph," Sid said courteously.

Entering the Oval Office, he could see Lucy still had her eyes fixed on a report on her desk. He walked over to stand in front of the desk, waiting to be acknowledged.

"Good morning, Sid. What is so urgent that it takes you away from your grandkids this weekend?" the President said as she looked up. Seeing Sid's serious expression she gave up all attempts at small talk.

"Madame President, we have a very serious situation that you need to be made aware of. It may involve Jonny Ray."

The President stood up from behind the Resolute Desk and walked over to the comfortable couch. "Do I need a drink to hear this, Sid?"

"Perhaps one for both of us, Ma'am."

Lucy walked over to the sidebar, "The usual, Sid?"

"Yes, please."

"Sit on the couch, Sid, I'll bring this over." She poured a generous portion of an aged Scotch Whiskey brought by the Ambassador of the

United Kingdom as a gift. She set one glass in front of Sid, and settled in next to him. "Cheers," she said with glass raised and took a swallow.

"Madame President, some background. Jonny Ray has been spending time with a local lobbyist for the Party, one Nayla Kaldah here in DC. Recently, we discovered Nayla had a personal connection to the Martyrs al-Sabra incident in Gaza City; her brother was one of the principals. As the current Martyrs incident has escalated, I became less comfortable with Jonny Ray spending time with her. In fact, when he came back from his last trip, I talked with him and we agreed he would put an end to the relationship. Supposedly, he did end it yesterday afternoon. This morning, I got the news from Secret Service that Nayla was murdered sometime last night. There is more, supposedly a rifle cartridge was left on a coffee table, just like the ones the Martyrs snipers use. I reached out to the FBI Martyrs task force and they are in the process of taking over the crime scene."

The President sat through the recitation of facts with various expressions ranging from hurt to shock. Sid's summary ticked all of the main points but one.

"Sid, you don't think Jonny Ray had anything to do with her murder, do you?"

Sid reached over and patted her hand, offering what small comfort he could. "I don't. But several problems are presenting themselves. First, she died in a very provocative outfit and was apparently strangled by a bondage sex device around her neck. Second, it is entirely possible Jonny Ray's DNA and fingerprints will be discovered at the scene. The connection with the Martyrs terrorists makes me wonder whether Jonny Ray was actually set up by her. If so, other pieces of evidence will make their way to the press: photos or videos. The Russians used to do it a lot, get someone important to commit transgressions in an apartment they controlled which was wired for sound and cameras, then use the take to blackmail, embarrass or discredit them," Sid explained.

Lucy's face turned hard as the implications for her presidency replaced her shock. "This just gets better and better. Has anyone talked to Jonny Ray yet?"

"No, Madame President."

"I thought the worst I could expect from Jonny Ray were the usual issues he has keeping his pants zipped. I discounted someone actually using him to hurt us politically. Damn! I should have cut him loose years ago, but I just couldn't bring myself to do it. What are the options, Sid?"

"It's too soon to call it. We should also be able to rule out any chance Jonny Ray was involved once we know how she died. Then we'll see if any additional data hits the streets from the terrorists. This is an attempt to further destabilize our administration, in my opinion. We're already reeling from the sniper attacks and then will be further embarrassed by this situation. Also, I keep thinking about that tip saying these terrorists have access to a small nuclear weapon. Maybe it is the knockout punch?" Sid shook his head and sipped his whiskey. "I still have no idea what their goal is. They know we're not going to free Palestine from Israeli rule, so what do they hope to achieve?"

"What is our current stance in regard to the murder investigation?" Lucy asked.

"I made sure the crime was discovered by DC Police rather than the Secret Service. I also got the FBI involved as soon as a link to the Martyrs was discovered. I told the FBI there would be no cover-up as far as we were concerned, in spite of Jonny Ray's apparent involvement," Sid explained.

"Thank you. Sid. That is exactly what I would have wanted."

"I have been working with you for quite some time, Madame President," Sid inclined his head.

"Should we take away the terrorist's advantage and announce the killing ourselves?"

Sid wobbled his hand back and forth as he considered the idea. "Normally, I would endorse that approach. In this case, where there might be photos or videos of Jonny Ray, I recommend waiting. You know the public will completely forget our coming clean if there are lurid photos to see. One exception would be if you planned to cut Jonny Ray off, then trouble such as that would all accrue to him. You would still get dinged as the first President to divorce their spouse while in office, but more than half the country would find it appropriate."

"Let's keep that as an option. Please do an assessment of what would need to be done to make a divorce happen quickly. I get the sense it is not as simple as it would be for most; the Secret Service issues alone would complicate the process. Let's get Jonny Ray in here right now, and tell him about Nayla." Lucy's voice was flat and hard.

"Madame President, I recommend a White House Counsel sit in that meeting as well."

"Set that up," she said draining her glass and walking back to her desk.

"Yes, Ma'am."

• • •

Jonny Ray helped himself to a drink and sat on the sofa next to Sid. Lucy took the chair next to Sid and the hastily-summoned White House Counsel sat in one next to Jonny Ray. Jonny Ray raised his eyebrows at the guest list, but waited to hear what was in the offing.

"Sid, will you tell Jonny Ray what you told me this morning?" Lucy asked calmly.

"Yes, Madame President," Sid said. He shifted to face Jonny Ray.

"Jonny Ray, this morning I was woken by a member of the Secret Service with distressing news. Something happened to Nayla Kaldah yesterday, and the DC Police were summoned to investigate. I instructed the Secret Service to secure the entrance to the apartment and wait for the police. Upon entry, they found Nayla had been strangled to death sometime last night. That's not all, on a coffee table was a rifle cartridge like those used in the Martyrs attacks."

Jonny Ray's face turned gray, and his hands shook as he set down his drink. His fingers fumbled at his shirt pocket for the cigarettes he had given up thirty years before. His eyes were wide and unseeing.

"Jonny, we have to ask you some questions now. I'm sure you understand," Sid said smoothly after giving the man a moment. "Jonny, when did you leave the apartment yesterday and was Nayla alive when you left?"

Jonny Ray snapped back into the here and now. "When I left can be verified by my Detail, it was sometime between 5 and 6 pm. Yes, she was alive when I left. Surely, you don't think I had anything to do with this?" He directed the last question to Lucy, the others falling away as he stared at his wife.

Lucy said nothing. It wasn't really Lucy at this point but the President who watched Jonny Ray's face closely for his reaction. The Counsel was taking notes nonstop.

"No, I don't think so," Sid pulled Jonny Ray back into the conversation, "but I want to hear your answers before I have to speak to others on this matter. As you know, the Martyrs terrorists are the province of the FBI so the entire thing has been handed off to them. How was Nayla dressed when you left?"

Jonny Ray glanced again at the President then turned his eyes back to Sid. "She was wearing some small leather outfit with boots."

"Do you think anyone on your Detail can corroborate your statement that Nayla was alive when you left her?"

"No, I don't think so unless they heard her speak. I let myself out and made sure she wasn't in line of sight to the door."

"Why?"

"Privacy. She wasn't wearing much and the agents aren't entitled to see that."

"Did you break the news that you were ending the … relationship?"

"Yes, she took it very well all things considered."

"Did anything strike you as unusual during this last visit?"

"Do you really want to hear this, Lucy?" No response in word or gesture was forthcoming from the President, so Jonny Ray plunged on. "No, other than the fact that she was more kinky than usual. I didn't break the news until just before I left."

"Jonny Ray, this is very important. Did you ever get the idea you were being recorded or photographed?" Sid asked.

"No, but now that you mention it, she was always setting up our tableaus. I just thought it was artistic preference or role-playing on her part."

"Did you ever choke Nayla during sex, using an overhead suspension device?"

Another furtive glance at the President, "She liked being choked while making love, I never took it as far as she seemed to want, and I never liked doing it."

"One last question. How likely do you think it is that medical examiners will find your DNA on the body?"

"What kind of question is that? Of course, they will easily find my DNA unless she had cleaned up afterwards. Even so, there is a good chance it will be there."

"I think we have everything we need for now. Thank you, Jonny Ray."

"What happens next?" Jonny Ray asked.

The President answered the question, "We see what develops in the case and media coverage. Until then, you are indisposed for public appearances and will stay here. Make no mistake, if my Administration is holed below the waterline by your indiscretions, you will be the ballast thrown off the ship. Work with Sid as he needs and we may yet make it."

"That's hardly fair, Lucy. Didn't the Secret Service look into her background? The first I heard of a problem was two days ago, and I did as Sid asked."

"That is a good question, and I will look into it, but you know fair has nothing to do with our problem here. Thank you, gentlemen, for coming," she said in dismissal.

Sid stood up, took Jonny Ray's elbow gently, steering him out the door. Once they got into the hall, Jonny Ray turned to Sid.

"How did she die, really?"

"I'm told she was wearing a black leather corset, panties, and thigh-high leather stiletto boots. They found her on all fours, hanging by her neck, with her panties at her knees. It looked like someone rode her hard and then left her as she was. The only other piece of information is the rifle cartridge, which puts a whole other spin to the murder. If it weren't for that, it would appear as though you were the murderer. You need to make yourself scarce, stay in your rooms and out of public sight."

"Won't that be noticed by the press?" Jonny Ray asked.

"It might, except that you don't do any of that First Lady shit. I expect we'll get a week for free, then you'll have to develop a bad flu."

"Shit," Jonny said as he walked towards his own suite.

• • •

Pulling up to Lindsey's home, which she'd inherited from her parents, Jan couldn't help but remember how she, Justin, and Farid used to play with young Lindsey when they wanted a break from school homework. Jan's parents lived in the same neighborhood so she had been a regular visitor to the house throughout her childhood.

Feeling oddly formal, Jan parked the car and walked to the front door. She hadn't heard from Farid yet, but she had to put that out of her mind for the time being. She knocked on the door and heard an excited gabble of sound within that served as early warning of two mobile toddlers.

Lindsey opened the door, "Hi Jan, come in. It has been too long. Margo! Come and take the children for a while," Lindsey called to their nanny.

Jan bent down and seriously greeted both children, gathering sloppy kisses as the price of admission. Margo appeared, expertly slung a child on each hip, and headed for the back of the home with the promise of cookies.

"I don't know what I would do if I didn't have help from Margo! It is damn hard raising kids. But you would know," Lindsey said with a conspiratorial smile.

"Absolutely! Although mine are finally getting to be less in a constant state of upheaval. You have it a lot tougher than I did, working full time and balancing your time. I wouldn't have had the energy for that. It makes me tired just thinking about it."

"So, Jan, why the sudden urgency? Is my brother trying to elope without the requisite parties?" Lindsey asked.

"Is there somewhere we can talk privately? It is serious and not for any other ears."

"Sure, why don't we use my office?" Lindsey suggested, looking at Jan strangely. Jan was a very direct, no-nonsense person and the reticence was unusual.

They walked together back into the office, which was furnished tastefully in a classic style. Lindsey motioned Jan over to a small couch, then sat down in a comfortable-looking leather chair.

"OK, Lindsey. I don't know where to begin. It is really bad news. Justin is currently in California working on the Martyrs case, and he asked me to speak to you since he wouldn't convey the news by telephone."

"It's Farid, isn't it? He's hurt?" Lindsey asked in a panic.

"No, no. It's not Farid. I tried to reach him so I could tell both of you at the same time, but he wasn't picking up. It's Nayla, Lindsey. She was killed last evening in Georgetown, and apparently there is a connection to the Martyrs case."

Lindsey couldn't move her body, it felt as though the world had dropped all of its weight onto her. Nayla had been her best friend since law school. Lindsey depended on Farid and Nayla as her immediate family. Nayla had been bridesmaid at Lindsey's wedding.

"How did she die? What happened?" Lindsey whispered.

"No one really knows much at this stage. Justin wanted to make sure you found out about it before seeing in a newspaper. He did say it was linked to the Martyrs attacks. Given all of the hysteria over the shootings, this will be getting a lot of publicity."

"Nayla must have had an inkling of trouble. She came over recently and asked me to do some things if anything happened to her. I didn't think anything of it, but enjoyed the afternoon catching up. Why wouldn't she tell me if she was scared of something?" Lindsey started to sob in between great gasps of air. Jan came over and held Lindsey as she cried.

"I know Justin will tell us more when he gets back. Do you know where Farid is today?"

"I don't know exactly," she said through tears. "He always checks in before leaving the country, so he should be here somewhere. Let me try him again now."

Lindsey disengaged and picked up her desk phone, dialing Farid with the speaker activated. It rang four times and as Lindsey moved to hang up Farid picked up.

"Hi Linds, just came in from a kayak run and barely made the phone. What's up?"

"Farid, I'm here with Jan. Can you come out to the house right now? We have to talk to you."

"Hi Jan, I just got your message and was meaning to call, sorry. Yeah, sure, I can grab a quick shower and head over. What's going on?"

"We'll save that for when you get here, alright?" Jan said.

"So mysterious. Is Justin lurking in the shadows to try my martial arts skills once more?" Farid joked.

"No, he is still in California until tomorrow. Just come as quick as you can, OK?" Jan asked her childhood friend and first lover.

"Milady's wish is this humble one's command. Give me thirty minutes," Farid said as he rang off.

"Jan, let's see what they have on the news about the murder," Lindsey said.

They scanned the news channels including one devoted to the District, and the story had yet to appear. Lindsey fired up her laptop and started searching with several search engines. The most that any site had was a woman had been killed in Georgetown inside an apartment. Either the FBI was keeping a close lid on this one or no one was interested in another death within the District. The minute it was linked to the Martyrs case, media coverage would explode. The shooting today in Riverside already had multiple stories published online as well as short editorials on the continued failure of the FBI and, by extension, the government to make progress against the terrorists. Some of the more right-wing sites had started to say the previously unsayable, namely that it was a mistake to admit any Muslims at all to the United States.

The fact Dr. Hammayil was a prosperous dentist had strangely opened up the debate to include all Muslims when considering potential solutions. Before, it was always a small disaffected group who participated in terrorist acts, so most Muslims could be given the benefit of any doubt. Now that the terrorists weren't necessarily disaffected, the old search criterion would not work, and a new one was needed. Some were advocating the same security approaches Israel did internally, checkpoints and mandatory identification, but without the recognition such steps would apply to everyone including themselves. All told, the nation hadn't quite decided which way to go, but the debate was well underway.

Lindsey knew Nayla suffered some discrimination due to her Palestinian heritage, but it was much easier for someone beautiful and rich than it would be for the average immigrant. Nayla's status had been a benefit during the Harvard application process, but Lindsey remembered how surprised Nayla had been upon arriving in DC and finding those unstated, but nonetheless real, obstacles ingrained in the city's culture.

Lindsey heard the sound of Farid's car as he parked it in the driveway, and met him at the door with a huge, teary hug.

"What's this all about, Linds?" he asked as he was pulled through the house to her office when Jan sat waiting.

Lindsey closed the door to the office, motioned Farid to the couch. As he sat, Jan placed her hand gently upon his shoulder.

"Farid, there is bad news about Nayla," Jan went on to tell him what she'd told Lindsey. Lindsey watched Farid's face as his expressions ran the range through shock, disbelief, and finally anger. She sat down on his other side and, together with Jan, held him as his body shook. Jan noticed that, like most men in the United States, Farid was not letting women see him cry, but his tearing eyes betrayed his internal state utterly.

"Where did this happen? I saw her several nights ago and there was no indication of anything, she was delightful as always. I joked as I often did about making an honest woman out of her, and she asked if I really was so confident she would say yes, with that maddening smile. This does not feel real."

"We don't know much yet. Justin found out about it due to the connection with the Martyrs case, and wanted you to hear it from us first," Jan said.

"Lindsey, did she have any gentlemen friends she was seeing in particular? Don't worry about my feelings, we both agreed to pursue our own interests, I am wondering if it was a lover who became angry for some reason."

"No, she never shared anything like that recently. The last one that I know made a move on her was Jonny Ray Brown on election eve," Lindsey said.

"Not the President's husband!" Jan said.

"The very same, but that was back in November," Lindsey said.

Farid shook off the women's arms as he pulled out his mobile phone and speed-dialed Justin.

Justin picked up the phone on the first ring, as if he had been waiting for the call. "Farid?"

"First, thank you for letting me know about this before I see it in the newsroom. I owe you once more. Second, I'd like to speak with you as soon as possible when you get back."

"I get in on the United red-eye tomorrow morning."

"Did you leave your car at the airport, or are you getting a taxi?"

"Taxi, I wasn't sure how long I was going to be out here. I need to get to the airport right about now actually."

"I'll drive you home tomorrow and we can talk on the way," Farid said.

"Fine, I'll be less than fully awake probably, but coffee will fix that," Justin said. "See you then."

Farid sat as though he were lost in thought. Then he seemed to come back into himself. He patted Jan's knee in thanks then put his arms around Lindsey, "You can stop being stoic for my sake, Linds, she was your best friend in the world," He held her as she gave in again to sobs of anguish.

Jan stood up, "I'll let myself out, you both know you can count on Justin and me. Don't hesitate to ask." They nodded and grasped her outstretched hands in farewell. Jan sighed deeply as she drove the short distance to her parent's home, working on her emotions so the children wouldn't learn about their Aunt Nayla before Justin came home.

• • •

The FBI had not been idle. The forensics team was in their glory, picking the apartment over with a fine-toothed comb. Detectives from the DC Police were working the murder aspect of the case as well. The team had established the time of death to be approximately 9 p.m., which let Jonny Ray off of the hook for murder. There were large amounts of biological evidence being sequenced for DNA as fast as the scanning devices could run. No blood evidence had been discovered, and there were no fingerprints on the matching wine glass to Nayla's. In the sink of the kitchen, glasses and utensils had been found with Jonny Ray's finger prints, which supported the theory of a second visitor or visitors after Jonny Ray. There was no sign of forced entry, therefore Nayla either knew or trusted the person. Nayla's clothing at the time of the murder argued for someone who was intimately acquainted with her.

One sharp-eyed technician noticed a series of holes in the dry wall ceilings of the bedroom. They removed a square of ceiling drywall and saw unmistakable signs of electronic equipment having been mounted against the ceiling joists. There was no equipment left in place, but the discovery led to the removal of other sample areas with unexplained holes. The uncomfortable conclusion was the apartment had been wired for sound and possibly video at some point.

The results of every screen were being uploaded into the Task Force drop box, which Justin was watching closely. His flight was boarding in about an hour, which barely left time for dinner, but even the airport had better food than the flight itself. He sat in the corner of a small Mexican restaurant and ordered a combination plate, indulging himself with a top-shelf margarita. After ordering, he opened his laptop angling it away so the other diners couldn't see his screen. He looked through the pictures of Nayla's extra apartment; the team had discovered her name on the rental agreement. She was clearly doing something she didn't want to come back to her home.

Justin flipped through the photos of Nayla as she was posed and later found. There were no marks of a struggle, but it would have been hard to struggle wearing the handcuffs. Nayla must have trusted the person who killed her, which meant Nayla was part of the Martyrs operation. Whether she was an active participant or someone simply being used was hard to determine. However, an active participant would probably not volunteer for their own death. It followed that there would be photos, videos, or audio recordings of her trysts with Jonny Ray Brown. The Hammer must be planning to either blackmail the Brown Administration or simply further destabilize it. Justin's mind turned to his friend Farid and his heart ached. If The Hammer made a point of putting the pictures on the Internet, it would hit Farid hard. Furthermore Justin knew Jameson had plans to lean on Farid when he got back. Jameson still thought Farid was related to or possibly the Hammer himself. The Farid that Justin knew from childhood wouldn't kill Nayla, he just wouldn't.

Justin turned his mind from Nayla and started to read up on the latest Martyrs sniping episode today in Riverside, California. It was no longer feasible to chase around the country, one step behind the terrorists the entire time. No, going forward he would stay close to the command center in DC until a break was made in the case. Being too far away from the center created problems for command authority. The field agents were capable men and women, and it was easy to conference when necessary.

• • •

Farid's mobile phone rang insistently in his darkened townhome. After returning from Lindsey's he had drawn up a chair beside the window with the best view of the Potomac and sat drinking a glass of wine. The cold calculating portion of his intellect which held The Hammer was content plans were proceeding down their proper course. The part which held family and friends was distraught and inconsolable. Which part was in ascendency changed from minute to minute. Love and hate were of equivalent emotional power and only the mind determined which to indulge.

The phone stopped ringing, but several seconds later his landline started ringing instead. Farid stood with a look of annoyance and read the Caller ID which said "Q. Jameson."

"Hello," Farid said shortly.

"Farid, this is Quinton Jameson. I assume Justin told you I am taking over his role when it comes to you," Jameson said baldly.

"Oh, does that mean you're my new best friend?" Farid needled.

"No, when it comes to your informant role in the Martyrs investigation."

"Alright," Farid said noncommittally.

"I want to see you in my office tomorrow morning at 9 a.m., I have some further questions."

"I'm sorry, that doesn't work for me. I have other engagements all day tomorrow. I'll be working from my downtown office on Monday, but then I head out to the Gulf for a week. How long will this take?" Farid asked.

"It will take as long as it takes. You're treating this request too lightly. I'm asking right now, but I can escalate the request if that is what will get your attention."

"I think you just set a new record for a handler getting off on the wrong foot. You do understand I am a volunteer, correct?"

"Maybe you are a suspect too. You need to come in for questioning, or we can come to get you. I can turn off your passport with one email, which will then give you plenty of time to answer my questions. Your call."

"Suit yourself. I'm no longer willing to be an informant and I quit. I'll be at my office on Monday if you want to show up with an arrest warrant. Good night," Farid hung up his phone.

Farid then took his mobile phone, "Prince Private Security? This is Farid Royce, I would like to arrange for bodyguard services starting Monday morning. Is that feasible on such short notice?"

"Yes, Mr. Royce. We can send your usual team. Does that work for you?"

"Excellent! Please have them report to my home at 7 am and we can go from there," Farid said.

The service confirmed Farid's address and other contact information before ringing off.

Farid made another call, "Ralph? Farid Royce here. I may need your assistance come Monday, if a certain FBI Section Chief gets too big for his britches. Let me tell you the situation -"

After another twenty minutes of discussion Ralph Stephens, feared attorney to the powerful and wealthy, was on the job.

Farid went back to the window, poured another glass of wine, and mourned for his Nayla.

• • •

Justin's plane landed fifteen minutes early, but the arrival gate was occupied and they had to wait on the tarmac for it to clear. By the time his flight arrived at the gate, it was ten minutes late. *Classic good-news/bad-news scenario*, Justin thought to himself. *Have to get some coffee on the way to Farid's car.* Justin texted Farid he was on the way, stopping at a coffee stand to pick up their favorites. It was a short ride home, but Justin expected he would be talking to Farid for a while.

Walking out the automatic doors to the arrivals level, Justin waved when he saw Farid's car moving slowly past. Farid nimbly moved the car to the curb, popped the trunk, and got out to take possession of his coffee.

"Welcome back, and thanks for the coffee. I knew you'd do that," Farid said.

"It would be rude to drink mine in front of you," Justin smiled.

"How are you feeling right now?"

"I got some sleep on the plane, believe it or not, so not too bad. How are you doing?" Justin asked awkwardly.

"I'm wondering why these terrorist shits would kill Nayla. I saw her about a week ago and she was perfectly fine. I can't believe she would be involved with something like that," Farid said.

"I can't share specifics, Farid, you know that. But it does look like she was involved in something sketchy. There wasn't any sign of forced entry or struggle, she knew or trusted her assailant," Justin said.

"Is the FBI going to release any statement about her murder being involved with the Martyrs attacks?"

"I don't know, I haven't spoken to Jameson since yesterday morning. I guess I'll find out on Monday." Justin said.

"I got a call from him last night. He ordered me to report to FBI HQ on Monday. When I declined, he threatened me with arrest," Farid laughed. "Don't worry, it's being taken care of at the highest levels."

"Be careful with him, even if he is prevented from taking you into custody he can still do a number of passive aggressive things to make life difficult," Justin said.

"Assuming, of course, he is still in a supervisory position at the FBI?"

"Not necessarily. As an example, he could put you on the do-not-fly list and even if he is long gone from his current role it would take months to clear that up. There are a host of little bureaucratic turds he can throw into your punchbowl without much work on his part."

"Actually, one of the Muslim organizations I belong to has been planning to test the constitutionality of some of the Patriot Act measures which disproportionately target Muslims in court. Perhaps this would be the time, especially since I work for a news organization that would love to be the ones breaking the story. These Martyrs terrorists are trouble, but so are government officials who abuse their power in search of the terrorists. Remember when poorly trained paramilitary police in Boston were turning homeowners out of their homes illegally at gunpoint when searching for the two remaining marathon bombing suspects? That is wrong and unconstitutional, Justin, you know it is. Not one of those police criminals lost their jobs or were prosecuted."

"No argument from me on that topic. One thing I am becoming more concerned about, is the increased pressure and 'do something' mindset I am beginning to see in the leadership. Situations like that, is when you see departure from procedures designed to protect constitutional rights. The Patriot Act is an embarrassment, from that perspective, but no one has had the stomach to do much about it so far. I have to be frank, in the atmosphere of fear which currently prevails, I doubt Congress will do much to change it as it could prevent their reelection in the next cycle," Justin observed.

"Monday will bring what it brings. I've done what I can to prepare, we'll just have to see how things go. Different topic, my work with the FBI was voluntary and unpaid. As such, I felt within my rights to withdraw the support. Is there any precedent within the Bureau for confidential informants? Most of the informants are criminals with deals, right?"

"I'm pretty sure most of them are, but a significant number are people like yourself who simply wanted to help. There should be plenty of cases where volunteer informants stopped for whatever reason. I wouldn't expect any problem being able to quit, it isn't a job," Justin said.

"I was thinking about those bureaucratic turds you mentioned earlier. I can see a scenario where something like asset forfeiture is threatened if I don't cooperate, in essence creating leverage he didn't have before."

"It's a possibility. It is a very difficult and time-consuming process to get seized funds released, even if you are completely innocent of what is suspected. We don't even have to charge or prosecute the people involved, but we keep the money."

"I guess it is a good thing that most of my wealth is beyond his reach."

"Yes, most of the people we hit with that tactic don't have those kinds of resources to fall back upon. But, it is definitely better to not have it happen in the first place," Justin said.

"I agree, that is why I hope to bring the whole thing to a head on Monday morning," Farid said. "I'm scheduled for another round of interviews in the Gulf later next week. We're trying to get the perspective of those in power of the effect that the Martyrs campaign is having on U.S. business within the region."

Farid turned right and made an immediate left onto Kentwell Place to park at Justin's home, "Here you are, safe and sound," Farid popped the trunk and helped get Justin loaded back up.

"Thanks for the ride home, Farid. For what it's worth, I'll keep an eye on your status and if you vanish suddenly into FBI custody I'll tell Lindsey so she can release the hounds of Congress," Justin said.

"Thanks. They'll certainly take her call, as much money as she raises for them," Farid said.

Justin entered his code into the garage opener, waved once to Farid and closed the door, entering a household that was still asleep.

Farid backed his car out of the driveway, turning right onto Algonkian Parkway and made his way back to Georgetown.

• • •

Quinton spent most of Sunday morning on the golf course with an old college friend who now served as a Federal Court judge in Maryland, trying to convince him there was enough evidence to issue a sneak-and-peek warrant for Farid's home. So far he hadn't had much luck, as normally the FBI had some tangible evidence prior to requesting one. Judges wanted some objective evidence before they actually put their names on a warrant. Part of the reason was political winds shift all of the time, and it wouldn't pay to be seen as having been less than fair when they did. In Farid's case, he was a Muslim, connected to a charity with the same name as the terrorists, and knew one of the victims very well. That wasn't enough for a judge to act upon. It probably hadn't helped that Quinton was having a great day on the course and their customary wager of $100 was on the line. After desultory consideration, the judge allowed that he would issue the warrant if and when Quinton brought back something definitely tied to Farid.

Quinton had other worries on his plate as well. The Nayla-Jonny Ray relationship was going to be very public very soon. Both he and Jonny Ray's Secret Service Detail head had known about the relationship. If the Martyrs started publishing videos of Jonny Ray's amorous adventures on the Internet, some uncomfortable questions were going to be asked. At the time, Quinton had decided a wiretap was not needed in the apartment because it was the President's husband and the Secret Service had the ball. There had been nothing of note captured from the wiretaps of Nayla's home or telephone. There were one or two calls with Jonny Ray, scheduling times to get together, but they didn't spend a lot of their time on the phone. There were no mysterious calls to anyone other than work and friends.

Quinton couldn't delegate the Nayla investigation to Justin without waiving a normal recusal situation. He could assign it to one of his other leads, but it would take a significant amount of time for them to get up to speed on the entire scope of the investigation. However, regardless of his concerns about Justin, he had never failed to protect Quinton's interests whether allocating credit or deflecting blame. In that respect, he was a very good foot soldier. Quinton might be able to short-circuit the whole issue by assigning another task force lead to work closely with Justin and step to the front when dealing with things where Justin should be recused. Quinton decided he had arrived on a winning plan as he went home for Sunday dinner.

• • •

In the Caribbean port of Andros Town, the Qatari crew of the Butler's Dosh spent their days in search of the best fishing spots within walking distance. They were experts and the sport available was some of the best seen. Amin had picked the port due to its quiet, out-of-the-way reputation as well as the fact that it matched the name of his Italian alter ego, Andro Simonetti. Andro stayed close to the boat for a number of reasons, the most important was the hundred-pound backpack stowed in the back cabin. Today he was on-hand when the special package arrived from Reem.

Andro opened the shipping box and found a sophisticated actuator controlled by satellite VPN link. The design allowed for communication of package status, GPS coordinates, and whether someone was tampering with the package. Not for the first time, Andro was grateful for Reem's participation in their enterprise.

The device would allow the entire crew to easily escape the area of any explosion, by not having to be within sight or radio range of the detonator. Amin's original plan called for the Qataris to meet their end after the successful operation, but this device would provide a few more options in that regard.

The Go Team, would be Andro and one or two Qataris in a small, black, inflatable boat with a quiet trolling motor. If they played their cards correctly, the Butler's Dosh could stand by off the coast of Pirates Cove while the boat silently approached the giant cruise ship scheduled to be docked there overnight. The plan was to plant the device on the ship's hull several hours after dark. The best option called for a moonless night or overcast skies, and they could wait for the right night as more than one ship docked each week.

Andro was only waiting for the final schedule from Farid before becoming operational. He logged into their international proxy host and sent a message to Reem the package had been received without incident.

• • •

Early Monday morning, Farid opened his front door to the security detail he had ordered. Sitting down the team in his living room, he briefed them on the situation with the FBI and specified what they were to do in the event of his arrest. Farid's intention was not to resist arrest, but to make it very difficult to snatch and hold him without charges. He expected Jameson to make his move today, or not at all.

The security detail would be doing all of the driving today, so Farid donned his suit jacket, picked up his briefcase and left his townhome. He had left a number of surveillance measures in place to capture footage of any sneak-and-peek efforts on the part of FBI technical teams.

The drive to his network offices was uneventful, and the security team deployed themselves around his office with their guest badges. No one would be able to just walk in on Farid during the work day. At 9 a.m., attorney Ralph Stevens walked in with a briefcase full of books, checked in with Farid and sat down to read. As he had told Farid on Saturday, the best part of today's job was being paid while catching up on his reading. Farid considered the expense worth every penny when it came to high-stakes games with the FBI.

Several hours later, a commotion was heard at the security desk, and the receptionist rang back to Farid the FBI was on its way to his office. Farid picked up the phone and dialed four digits, saying "They're on their way in," to the party on the other end before hanging up.

Quinton Jameson and two other FBI agents ran into the gauntlet of Farid's security, and produced their credentials which were photographed by the security team and politely returned.

Farid appeared at the door, "Jameson, please come in, you are expected."

Jameson's face is beginning to assume the angry, mottled red of a bureaucrat accustomed to generating a fear response on the part of their prey. Farid isn't showing any fear, however, and the natural caution of a bureaucrat started to whisper words of concern in Jameson's mind. Unfortunately, he had already built up a full head of steam and now it was difficult to back down.

"Jameson, have you met my attorney, Ralph Stevens?" Farid asked. "He'll be sitting in on our discussion today. Now, I understand you have some questions for me."

Jameson had heard of Ralph Stevens, after all, who hadn't? "We haven't met formally."

"Please consider this our formal introduction. As Mr. Royce's attorney, please outline the basis for today's discussion and under what status are they being held?"

"What do you mean? I asked Farid to come to the FBI building today, he refused so I came here instead."

Ralph rustled his notes until he found what he was looking for, "According to my client, you threatened him with arrest if he didn't comply with your request. You also threatened to place a hold on his passport, which he needs to conduct normal business. Did you make those threats, Section Chief Jameson?"

"I might have in the heat of the discussion."

"Do you have a warrant for his arrest today?" Ralph asked crisply.

"I don't need a warrant to hold him on terrorism issues."

"Actually, since Farid is an American citizen, you do, unless you witnessed him committing a crime. Did you witness him commit a crime?"

"I'm not going to respond to that. Farid, are you going to come with me peaceably, or should the agents put you in restraints?" Jameson asked.

Turning to Ralph, Farid said, "I'll let him dig his hole a bit deeper, since he isn't inclined to obey the law. Please work things on your end as we discussed."

Facing Jameson, he said, "I think the restraints will be needed just to make your point, Section Chief."

Jameson angrily motioned to one of his agents who duly produced a pair of handcuffs and placed them on Farid's wrists. Taking Farid's arm, the agents started taking him out of the office. As they emerged, Marc Crosse had his camera gear operating, catching excellent footage of the FBI agents, and Quinton Jameson in particular. A network reporter started asking questions.

"Section Chief Jameson, can you confirm Farid Royce is being arrested in connection with the Martyrs terrorists?" the reporter called out.

"It's too soon to say he is under arrest," Jameson said.

"He's wearing handcuffs and you have him doing a perp walk. What is he being detained for?"

"No comment," Jameson said as he shielded his face from the lights and cameras.

"Farid, do you have a comment?"

"Yes, this harassment is because I am Muslim and knew one of the victims who was killed here in DC last night, Nayla Kaldah. My constitutional rights are being violated as we speak, by Quinton Jameson of the FBI."

The agent holding Farid's arm said, "That's all." The FBI team made their way through what was now a small crowd of onlookers operating cameras.

Ralph Stevens watched the procession head out of the building and turned to Marc, "That went well. Do you have the video from the office?"

"Yes, here it is on this thumb drive. It is the one marked Farid_Office with today's date. Do you have everything you need?"

"I believe so, thank you for the fast response. How long do you think it will take the network to put this out to the public?"

Marc laughed, "This is the age of the Internet, I imagine some of the folks lining the halls have already posted their videos to blogs. The formal story might be a couple more hours. But I bet Drudge has it in 20 more minutes."

"Good enough. Can you show me out? I have some calls to make," Ralph said.

Justin saw the first news reports of Farid's arrest less than thirty minutes after it happened. It already had stirred up a firestorm of online debate, from Muslims outraged that a prominent fellow was being humiliated without evidence, to many others advocating the arrest as a good first step towards securing the country from malign Muslim influence. Given the level of online vitriol, it was a good thing the two factions were not within arms-reach otherwise a riot might have ensued.

Justin knew enough to stay away from Jameson until he was called. As for Farid, Justin wondered what he was up to. It was very unlike Farid to meekly submit when provoked. From the video footage released so far, Jameson looked like he had indigestion, especially when named in Farid's statement. Justin thought he saw Ralph Stevens lurking in the background, too. That alone would give any federal employee indigestion if he had to sit on the opposite side of the table. *Shit, I warned Jameson about Farid*, Justin thought, *He'd better have something solid or Ralph is going to give him a chainsaw enema.*

Justin's phone rang, and he saw that it was Sid Rosenbloom, "Simons."

"Sid Rosenbloom. Justin, can you come over here at 11 a.m. to brief us on the Martyrs case, including the Nayla Kaldah developments?"

"Sir, I need to speak with Section Lead Jameson to be fully up to date, and shouldn't he deliver the briefing?" Justin said.

"I suspect Quinton will be occupied in a different meeting. He kind of lost the bubble this morning. Check in with the Director's office for clearance and text me when you arrive. By the way, bring an evidence technician for a DNA screen. I'll explain when you get here."

"Yes, sir. I'll get right on it," Justin said as Sid hung up.

That was strange, Justin thought. He dialed the Director's office, "This is Special Agent Simons. I just spoke with Sid Rosenbloom who told me to clear a Martyrs briefing with the Director."

"Yes, Justin, we were expecting your call. The Director approves a full briefing of the case, with one caveat. Try not to be drawn into speculation if at all possible. There are too many unknowns in the case to support hard conclusions. The White House is being drawn into this as well, which you will understand better after the meeting. Any questions?" The Director's assistant said.

"Yes, should I check in with my line authority, Quinton Jameson, as well?"

"Certainly, if it can be done promptly. But if not, do not delay the meeting waiting to do so. The Director has approved the briefing."

"Understood, thank you," Justin hung up his phone. He then spent the next few minutes calling several numbers of Jameson's, leaving a message at one. Justin thought about it for a few more minutes and decided to take the extra step of sending an email to Jameson which explained the entire White House request and discussion with the Director's office. Later, it might be useful to counter accusations of working behind Jameson's back. Cover your ass, the first rule of government service.

• • •

Jameson wasn't available because he had Farid chained to an interrogation table like a violent offender and was attempting to interrogate him. Every question Jameson asked was answered by Farid's request for his attorney to be present. Farid, evidently to amuse himself, started making the same request in the various languages he spoke. Jameson, who spoke only English, would get a rush of optimism that Farid was finally cracking, only to be told by an interpreter what was actually being said.

"I don't think you're taking me seriously, Farid. You're sitting here in a reasonably comfortable room to answer my questions, but if you aren't answering questions, you need to join the rest of our detainees in the dirty, smelly, part of this facility. What's it going to be?"

"I will not answer any questions without my attorney present."

"All right, that's it. Transport Mr. Royce to the holding cell. Farid, we might have another session later today or we might wait a couple of days so you can fully enjoy our hospitality."

"I would like my attorney present at any questioning sessions," Farid repeated.

"I'm sure you would, and he will be at the time of our choosing," Quinton spat out. "Get him out of here."

Farid received a cavity search and a semi-clean pair of institution coveralls. His ankles were shackled, and the guard connected the handcuffs to the shackles, forcing Farid's arms to remain down. His gait was a shuffle to keep from falling over onto the floor. Jameson had kept Farid inside the interrogation room long enough time to miss what would have been a forgettable lunch. Farid knew the next trial would be the proper introduction of himself to the others in the holding cell. As he approached the lockup, the snide comments started.

"Look at the new pussy, must be dan-ger-ous to be chained. Who are you, New Pussy?"

"This one is an Arab motherfucker, probably one of those terrorists shooting people," the guard said.

Others just did "The Stare", the aggressive unblinking look that fighters aim at their opponent in an attempt to win a mental advantage. There were twelve other men in the cell, which had one official toilet and no beds. Three of the occupants were clearly in the throes of drug withdrawal, they would be no problem. Several burly gentlemen hanging in one group looked to be bikers from the gist of their tattoo sleeves. The balance was made up of gangbangers, two Black and four Hispanics who were split by the bikers. Farid took in the room with a glance, then turned his attention forward as the guard went through the exercise of removing his restraints. Making no sudden moves, Farid stretched muscles fatigued from being in a crouched position for several hours. The guard instructed the prisoners to stand back from the door, then opened it to admit Farid. The guard pushed him into the room and clanged the cell door closed.

Farid looked around the room, and saw security cameras were installed. That made things more difficult, but it could be managed.

The biggest biker had been elected to talk to Farid, "Who the fuck are you, new pussy?"

"Farid Royce. Are you the bellboy who will help me to my private suite?" Farid asked.

Not believing what he heard, "Did you just call me a bellboy? Do I look like a fucking bellboy?"

"Yes, I did, and actually, yes, you do," Farid said calmly.

The biker threw himself at Farid clearly intending to overwhelm the smaller man with his bulk and strength. Doubtless, the approach had worked well for him in the past. Today, however, was different. Farid spun in and twisted the biker's right arm out of his shoulder socket. Before the pain had even registered in the biker's brain, Farid kicked hard against the side of the big man's engaged knee breaking it as well. Farid glided out from under the biker's collapse and waited to see what the biker's crew would do. The entire takedown had taken less than five seconds. The gangbangers moved to the opposite wall, clearly wanting no part of this action.

"We're going to fuck you up, sand nigger," the biker's second said.

"Are you sure you want to try that?" Farid said calmly. "If you'll notice, I merely disabled your friend instead of killing him. If you four were to try to even the score I might have to kill one or two of you, just because I'd be in a hurry to defend myself."

The bikers were used to their numbers providing the overwhelming factor in fights, and four of them rushing one man wasn't going to end well for the one man. As one they charged Farid, true to his word, began doing his utmost to seriously hurt them. One went down with a strike to his Adam's apple, another with a broken leg, but the final two succeeded in getting Farid off of his feet. The bikers hit with fists like sledgehammers, and then stood to kick him. He may have been hit twenty or more times before the guards finally arrived to put a stop to the fight. He had earned a spot in solitary confinement for his own safety.

Upon arriving at his new cell, he took stock of himself physically in the reflective, stainless steel surface of the toilet. There were several ribs which might be broken, or at a minimum cracked, but he wasn't spitting up blood, a good sign. His face had a contusion on one cheek, but was otherwise intact. No teeth were loosened as well and nothing else presented itself. He owed the relatively light punishment both to the ineptitude of his attackers and his own knowledge of how to best turtle while being beaten. Inventory complete. He knelt down upon the floor and began the praying which would yield a calm mind.

• • •

Justin did not hear back from Jameson, so he called on the best evidence technician in the group, Evelyn (Evie) Wu, to accompany him to the White House. Together they walked the several blocks to the same entrance that Justin had gone to before, Justin with his briefcase and Evie with her evidence kit.

"Justin, how many times have you been to the White House? On business I mean," Evie asked.

"Just once, so I am an old pro. The administration was very open, comparatively, and nice to the rank and file. It hasn't always been the case, I understand. I don't know who will be in the meeting, other than the Chief of Staff and perhaps their political analyst/speechwriter."

"Why am I there?" Evie asked.

"They told me to bring an evidence technician, so I brought our best. I don't know why they asked exactly, but I expect the two of us can handle it," Justin said and smiled.

Evie smiled a bit at the flattery and was not about to correct his assessment.

Justin showed Evie how to check in at the guard station, Evie's evidence kit got a lot of examination, but shortly each had their White House visitor badge and could proceed on to Sid's office. Upon arrival, Sid's assistant told them the meeting had been moved to a conference room due to more attendees. Justin raised his eyebrow a bit at that news since he knew how big Sid's office was and wondered who else was on tap for the meeting. Soon enough they were shown to a medium sized conference room which could seat 10-12 comfortably around a large table; there were also chairs along the walls. Justin took advantage of being a few minutes early to hook up his laptop to the room's computer monitor system. He asked Evie to set up behind him, until they fully understood how many would be in attendance.

Within a few minutes, people started trickling in. Ashley came into the room, saw Justin setting up, and came over to say hello.

"Hello, big guy. Back in the White House so soon?" she teased and took the opportunity to set up next to him.

"Hi Ashley, on short notice, too," Justin said. Turning and indicating Evie, "This is my associate Evelyn Wu, who will handle any forensics or evidence collection issues."

"Hi Evelyn, I'm Ashley Cohen. You can take a seat at the table, it's more comfortable and we only have a few more coming in. Just don't sit in that chair," Ashley pointed to the chair opposite Justin's in the middle of the table's span.

"Thanks, I won't. Evie works in place of Evelyn if you're so inclined." Evie moved her kit up to the other side of Justin.

Sid Rosenbloom entered and sat on the right of the forbidden chair. Secret Service agents entered and went through the room, examining Evie's kit once more before leaving.

"I think we're about ready to start. Justin Simons is the FBI Special Agent running the Martyrs terrorist task force under Section Chief Jameson. He is here to brief us on the Martyrs investigation and progress made to date. Justin, the three scruffy folks to my left are Department of Justice, the two to the right are White House Counsel's office. To Ashley's left are representatives of the Party's Congressional leadership, and to your colleague's right are their counterparts from the

Senate. It's an odd assortment, but the reasons for it will become clear as we proceed," Sid said and, catching a signal from the Secret Service detail, continued "Ladies and Gentlemen, the President of the United States."

Surprised, Justin stood along with all of the others. Lucinda Brown entered briskly trailed by several handlers who set up shop behind the President's seat.

"Please be seated, everyone. I can't stay for the entire meeting, but I did want to hear this one first hand. Sid, please continue and make sure we've gotten into the Nayla Kaldah murder before I have to leave."

"Yes, Madame President. Justin, the floor is yours," Sid said.

Justin asked for the lights to be dimmed and started the presentation. His initial nervousness faded quickly and he soon found a good rhythm. He started by discussing the events of last year's Election Night, when The Hammer first captured the FBI's attention.

"Justin, was Nayla Kaldah present at the Gaylord that evening?" The President asked.

"Yes, Ma'am, she was present at the ballroom party along with many of the large campaign donors."

"Thank you, please continue."

Justin went on to discuss the subsequent investigation which didn't yield definitive results when it came to a potential threat, or indeed the identity of The Hammer. Using a time line graphic, Justin overlaid the current understanding of events against what was understood at each phase. The FBI had confirmed that 40-60 snipers were trained at the Wisconsin hunt camp in February and operational in March when the first shootings had begun. The methods of targeting appeared to be opportunity-based, with a premium on the sniper being able to escape. Communications and orders were handled somehow within a popular online game. Justin presented a slide representing the Kansas data center proxy server user locations which happened to be the top forty metropolitan areas of the Continental United States. He covered the way Munir Hammayil, the Roseville Dentist, had been uncovered and what had been learned about the means and methods used by the terrorists.

At this point the President interrupted, "So the takeaway is the Martyrs terrorists have changed the rules. They do not use disaffected youths to kill themselves and others, but rather well-established family men who aim to survive their acts?"

"Yes, that is correct. They are technologically sophisticated and familiar with the culture of the United States, most likely due to the fact they are long-time residents, if not citizens. There is no evidence Dr. Hammayil even knew how to fire a gun before the hunt camp training. If I had to guess, they learned tradecraft and shooting skills from one or more experts during those two weeks. Dr. Hammayil made a major mistake in that he did not change the plates on the getaway car after the shooting. If he had, we might not have found him at all."

"I'm hearing we have no other sniper suspects at the moment," the President said.

"Yes and no. We have too many suspects. We're systematically working our way through the list, each local FBI office running down the leads in their metro area. To illustrate the issue, we have IP addresses assigned from local Internet Service Providers to compare to those we pulled from the Kansas proxy server. The problem there is IP addresses are often reassigned by ISPs, so there isn't a one-to-one correspondence. In each case, we have to quickly review the millions of traffic log entries from the ISP for the prior several months, then identify users from the account lists. That's one activity.

We also have lists of all Honda Accords registered in each metro area and we're working our way through thousands of those. Our current profile is a mature Muslim male with a decent job. Multiply that effort by the number of cities involved and it is a daunting task. I don't mean to sound negative though; each of these efforts will contribute to finally catching the terrorists. The biggest challenge will be to capture one alive and interrogate them. The terrorists somehow found out we were on to Dr. Hammayil and promptly silenced him. They might have someone watching the shooters and noticed the surveillance we put in place. We don't know. In the future, we're going to operate as though we're on enemy soil to make sure the undercover work stays undercover."

"Thank you, Justin. Let's jump to the second part of this, the connection of Nayla Kaldah to the terrorists," Sid said.

"Yes sir. The evidence suggesting a connection is circumstantial so far, but it seems strong. There was no sign of forced entry into the apartment, so Nayla knew her killer. The killer left behind the same token left at the scene of all of the sniping incidents. Furthermore, the apartment showed signs of extensive surveillance equipment which had been uninstalled prior to the killing. Nayla leased the apartment, apparently solely for her amorous liaisons, so it appears to be a tool for blackmail or something similar. We don't have any leads on where the equipment and possible files could be, we're going through Nayla's things now."

"When was the apartment leased?" Sid asked.

"Mid-December."

"How many lovers did Nayla bring to the apartment?" Sid asked.

"We only know of one, but there was ample evidence left at the scene which is under analysis so there may be more," Justin said carefully.

Sid started to ask another question when the President motioned him silent and said, "I'm going to cut to the chase. We all know Nayla's lover was Jonny Ray Brown. We also know the relationship started in November of last year about two weeks after the election party. Assuming Nayla was involved with the terrorists, what would be the purpose of the surveillance gear?"

"We have several theories on that, Ma'am, one would be simple blackmail. Another would be using it as a means of destabilizing this Administration. We know from forensics that Mr. Brown was not there when Nayla died, but the public might not believe it under the wrong circumstances. I think the terrorists are hoping for a cover-up," Justin said.

"I agree, we need to manage to the worst case. There will be no cover-up," The President made eye-contact with the legal teams from the White House and Justice Department. "Justin, the FBI and the Justice Department have my full support to pursue this no matter where it goes. To that end, and to save work that the FBI could fruitfully use elsewhere..." She signaled her assistant who left the room. A few seconds later she came back with a strangely subdued Jonny Ray Brown.

"Jonny Ray is going to supply a portion of his DNA in the presence of these witnesses," the President said firmly.

Evie now understood her role and opened her case for the DNA mouth swab kits, taking one out. Jonny Ray meekly came over to the chairs behind the table without comment. Evie carefully took two samples from Jonny Ray's mouth, sealing each in separate bags for lab analysis.

"Thank you, Jonny Ray, that will be all. Justin, a copy of his fingerprints will be made available to the investigation as well," the President stated.

Justin didn't bother telling the President they already had them on file as part of his security screening. The DNA sample would definitely speed things up though and create less FBI internal angst over whether to ask a sitting president for her husband's DNA.

"Thank you, Madame President, that will be most helpful," Justin said respectfully.

"We will stay tuned on what the terrorists do with their media cache. We do not plan to deny the affair at all. I recommend the Bureau release news of the affair before then, so the terrorists will be robbed of the sensationalism impact," President Brown said. "Then when we are asked during the next news cycle, we will confirm it."

"I will communicate that guidance to our leadership. One thing we haven't talked about is the nuclear device threat, which was also linked to The Hammer. Our information is very thin on this topic, we've heard nothing on any of the normal communication channels terrorists have used in the past. The last piece of information we heard was the target is somewhere in the Southeast. We've made sure all entry points are being monitored closely, especially in the South, but it is a large area to cover when we're not sure what the target will be," Justin said.

"Justin, how are all of these separate efforts linked in the minds of the terrorists?" Sid asked.

"With the caveat that this is pure speculation, I think the terror efforts work together well and are meant to be complementary.

The snipers build a sense of ever-present fear with the random nature of their occurrence, exacerbated by the fact that few perpetrators have actually been caught or eliminated. The people start to be frustrated with law enforcement and the government's inability to remedy the situation. Then, the second attack, Nayla's death, is aimed at further erosion of the people's trust in the FBI, Presidency, and Congress. After that event, the people would perceive the terrorists are winning and the angriest would start taking matters into their own hands by attacking Muslims. I can see The Hammer, who is reputed to be a Palestinian, being able to consolidate support from other Muslims being thus repressed, who normally have zero interest in Palestinian causes. Then the final blow of a nuclear device, which eclipses the losses of 9/11, concludes a staggering terror campaign. If the terrorists wanted, they could have the snipers go silent for years, and then reactivate for another round of terror. Again, this is what I come up with when I try to incorporate all of the elements."

"I understand an arrest was made this morning of someone possibly connected to the Martyrs," Sid said.

"I'm aware of it from arms-length, as I've had to recuse myself due to my long-time friendship with the party involved. He was a close friend of Nayla's, who was present at the Gaylord election night celebration. Nayla was a good friend of mine as well. We'll have to see where the rest of the evidence takes us." Justin didn't put a name to Farid as he wasn't completely sure everyone was cleared for the information.

"My, we are an incestuous bunch here, and it seems everyone's chestnuts are in the fire," President Brown said. "Thank you, Justin, for the briefing. Keep Sid informed on any need for resources, especially if there are any leads on the nuke. If there is any way to shake that tree I want to be sure we do it. Who is the task force liaison with the Pentagon? We might want to schedule some full-strength training exercises in the seas off the South. Sid can handle pulling that together. Everyone, thank you for your time," President Brown stood and everyone stood as well until she had departed the conference room with an aide whispering in her ear.

"Sit down, everyone, we're not quite done," Sid announced. "I want to emphasize that what has been discussed today is highly confidential, until the investigation principals decide otherwise. This group needed to hear the whole situation in order to be best able to do their part in facilitating the capture or elimination of the terrorist threat. The President's personal problem has very little to do with that activity, however it may appear on the surface. Let's remember that as we proceed. Are there any questions for Justin prior to wrapping things up here?"

The Department of Justice participants wanted to know more about Farid's arrest, but Justin reiterated he wasn't privy to that detail and referred them to Jameson. No more requests were forthcoming and Sid closed the meeting.

"Good job," Ashley said squeezing Justin's forearm before leaving. As he packed up the laptop and supporting notes several other attendees complimented him on their way out the door. Finally, it was just Justin and Evie making their way back to the east gate guard station.

"Man, that was something to tell your grandkids about! I don't have children yet but taking Jonny Ray's DNA evidence will definitely be memorable," Evie said.

"I know you won't tell that story prematurely. And you thought this was just going to be another day," Justin said.

"Yeah, I just wish I could have been to the hairdresser first."

"Me, too," Justin said tossing his head to Evie's outright laughter.

"This is good though, right? We can easily eliminate the Jonny Ray contribution to the crime scene and look for anything else," Evie asked as they walked towards the FBI building.

"Yes, it is. Especially since the President took a cover-up off of the table. I don't know if you remember prior administrations always putting pressure on the political appointees in our building, who then put pressure on everyone else. President Brown has her act together. Enough different functional groups in the room witnessed Jonny Ray giving samples so it will be hard to dispute."

"This suspect who is a friend of yours, do you think the arrest was merited? Or was it another one of Jameson's moves for a win?" Evie asked.

"I don't know, to be honest. I'd hate to think I could be so wrong about someone I've known since junior high school, but it is possible. Farid's my best friend, he was the best man at my wedding. He has had the bad luck to be connected to several things in the investigation. If there is more evidence than that, Jameson hasn't shared it with me."

"Farid? You mean the broadcast journalist Farid Royce? Damn. That is one handsome man! If he's released, you should introduce us."

"Come on Evie, we're both old enough to be your father. In Appalachia, anyway."

"Why would I care about that? He is still better looking than half the pallid drones I meet in DC, smarter too."

"Alright, if I get a chance to talk to him, I'll let him know so he has something to look forward to," Justin teased.

"You do that. I'll take it from there," Evie appeared to be deadly serious.

The singles scene in DC has to be worse than I suspected. No wonder Farid is keeping his options open, Justin thought. Justin wondered how Farid's loss of Nayla would change things for his friend. For all of his joking around, Justin knew Farid had loved her.

Justin's desk had a series of notes placed upon it. Jameson had dropped by after Justin was in the White House meeting and asked him to check in when he got back. Justin picked up a notepad and headed that way.

As usual, Justin tapped the door frame several times before sticking his head into the room. Jameson gestured him in to take a seat while finishing up a heated telephone call.

"That was about your best friend, Farid. He just got himself beat up in the holding tank, so we had to move him into solitary. That was after he broke the arms and legs of several other prisoners," Jameson said.

"Self-defense?" Justin asked.

"Of course. There was a group of bikers in on a conspiracy-to-distribute beef and they took immediate exception to his presence."

"Where were the guards in all of this?"

"It happened fast, but their boss is who I was just yelling at on the phone. You never said he was skilled in martial arts," Jameson accused.

"Why would I? He mostly needed it when he was a small student. Now he has other strengths. Why is he in lockup?"

"Refusal to cooperate in our investigation, for a start. Being a suspect in a terrorism investigation."

"Yes, I've seen the news coverage. Was that Ralph Stephens I saw in the background? I hope there is more evidence than the last time I looked at it," Justin said.

"Not your problem. Tell me about the White House briefing."

Justin recounted the events of the briefing, as well as the taking of DNA evidence from Jonny Ray.

"Jonny Ray did that quietly in front of the entire room? Talk about humiliation - that had to be horrible! Did the President ask how long we knew about the affair?" Jameson asked.

"No, but she did fill in the detail about how the affair had been ongoing. The White House appears resigned to seeing whatever video or photos were captured by the Martyrs go public. They are very concerned on the nuke possibility, even to the point of positioning more naval assets in southern waters. One other thing, they asked about the Farid arrest, and I begged ignorance. Sid might call to speak with you directly."

"I still think Farid is the key to the whole thing. He is The Hammer, I know it in my gut. You should see the tape of him thumping those bikers."

"I thought you said he got beat up?"

"He did, there were four of them. He put two in the hospital before the last two got him down. He's not in the hospital; cracked bruises, facial abrasions, no broken bones, nothing else of note. I'll let him stew a bit more in the cell then interrogate him again."

Justin held his tongue tightly against the urge to respond, "Anything else?"

"Not right now," a knock at Jameson's door. "Come in."

The Director's assistant popped her head into the room, "Quinton, the Director wants to see you in his conference room immediately. Ah, Justin, you're to go as well."

Summons like this usually do not bode well for those summoned, Justin thought. He had no doubt his briefing at the White House had been reported back to the Director by Justice Department attendees and he mentally reviewed the things he had said in that meeting as he walked behind Jameson. Normally, he could identify things which might prove politically fraught, but there was nothing that came to mind.

The assistant plucked at Justin's arm and whispered, "Don't say a word in this meeting, no matter what is heard, unless the Director speaks to you."

Justin nodded his understanding of the instructions, but was now even more baffled than before.

They entered a conference room, similar to the one in the White House, but much more poorly furnished. Already seated were the Director, General Counsel, Internal Affairs, Human Resources and Justin's entire command chain. There was one seat opposite the Director available, and Jameson was told to take that spot. The Director himself apologized for the lack of spot and asked Justin to take one of the wall seats. The assistant joined him behind Jameson's seat.

"Quinton, what is the status on the Martyrs case?" The Director asked.

Jameson went on to display his excellent short-term memory skills and regurgitated the report he had just heard from Justin. The Director and the rest of the room listened without comment until it got to the Nayla Kaldah affair with Jonny Ray Brown.

"Quinton, how long have we known that Jonny Ray Brown was having an affair with a Martyrs suspect?" The Director asked softly.

"Since early January. We were tipped off by the Secret Service," Jameson replied.

"What measures were taken?"

"We decided not to bug the apartment, due to the political considerations of Jonny Ray's position. But we did a full cover of Nayla's home, all of her telephones, and Internet use. We had eyes on her the rest of the time."

Justin was surprised that he had known absolutely nothing about this portion of the investigation. But he, as instructed, held his tongue.

"Did we do that with any of the other suspects?"

"No, Nayla was resistant to our questions and engaged a lawyer early on. Furthermore, shortly after my last discussion with her, which was contentious, I was mugged. There seemed to be a possibility the two were connected," Jameson said.

"This would be the recent incident where your service weapon, badge, and identification were stolen?" Internal Affairs asked.

"Yes. The balance of those interviewed were cooperative and their stories fully vetted, so there was no need to pursue further corroboration."

"What were the questions Ms. Kaldah was resistant to?" the General Counsel asked.

"Questions about her brother, his current status, and whether it was possible he was The Hammer."

"What is Ms. Kaldah's background?"

"She's a lawyer for a prominent K Street lobbying firm, graduated Harvard Law."

"As a lawyer, is it reasonable to assume she would want a lawyer early in any discussion with law enforcement officials?"

"Put in such a way, yes. But there were other lawyers on the list of interview subjects who didn't go there."

"Were the other interview subjects asked about family members being potential terrorists?"

"No, they weren't. None of them had anything similarly suspicious in their background," Jameson explained.

"Quinton, what would have happened if we had run a black bag job on the apartment?" the Director asked.

Jameson thought for a moment until he saw the obvious answer to the question, one that promised extremely negative consequences. "We would have found the Martyrs equipment," he said.

"That seems like a very good possibility, doesn't it? Who decided not to do it?"

"That would be our team and the Secret Service," Jameson said.

"We'll get to the Secret Service in a bit. Didn't you say earlier that the Nayla portion of the investigation was performed by you?"

Jameson now saw the trap and hanging party sitting before him. "Yes, Justin here was a friend of Nayla's so he had to step aside."

"The same situation which applies to the handling of Farid Royce?"

"Yes, Farid was Justin's best man. The appearance of impropriety was too much of a risk," Jameson said.

"Just to confirm, Justin Simons hasn't been involved in the investigation once Farid was escalated to a suspect?"

"No. Farid was a confidential informant for years, with Justin as his handler. Once the direction of our search clarified, I removed Justin from the role and that line of the investigation," Jameson said.

With a sigh, the Director turned towards several of the persons in the room, "I'm sorry you had to hear this, it is classified information. Those of you without full clearance will be asked to sign a non-disclosure agreement with rather severe consequences for breach, no later than close of business today. Quinton, please remember the audience before sharing any additional classified information."

The Director's assistant was clearly perturbed, making extensive notes to herself. Justin listened in fascination to Jameson's explanations.

"Which brings us to today's events. Please tell us the circumstances leading up to the FBI jailing a confidential informant as a terrorist suspect," The Director asked.

Jameson started listing his reasons as if counting them off on his fingers. "Farid Royce was at the Gaylord election party, The Hammer was tracked to the same area that night. Farid Royce was very close to Nayla Kaldah and we've now seen that Ms. Kaldah was involved in the Martyrs terrorist efforts. Farid Royce is a board member of the Martyrs al-Sabra Muslim Children's Charity, the terrorist call themselves the Martyrs al-Sabra. Farid Royce knows a prominent Saudi terrorist sponsor who is connected to The Hammer. Farid is the one who received The Hammer's letter taking credit. Farid is the one who provided information on the possible weapons of mass destruction. I'm convinced Farid is involved at minimum and may even be The Hammer himself."

"Those appear to be your reasons for suspecting Royce, on what basis was he arrested this morning?" the Director asked.

"He stopped cooperating as an asset. I wanted to force some answers from him."

"Is it true that Saturday evening he declined to continue cooperating with you at the helm, and in response you threatened him with arrest?"

"He wasn't being cooperative, yes," Jameson said.

"Did you attempt to get an arrest warrant? What was the result?" the Director asked.

"The judge wanted more objective evidence before issuing a warrant for arrest or sneak-and-peek."

"You warned a suspect you planned to arrest them, then failed to get an arrest warrant. So what we saw today on the television was not an arrest?" the Director pressed.

"I arrested him as a material witness under the Material Witness Statute to begin interrogating him," Jameson said.

"Was the witness checked into the facility through the suspect intake process? Stripped, cavity searched, and placed within the general population of criminal suspects?"

"Yes, he needed to lose some of his arrogance before his interrogation."

"We're going to listen and view some media now. Dim the lights and proceed."

Jameson sat and listened to the audio of his telephone call to Farid, watched a full video of his foray to arrest Farid at his office, and finally saw an excruciating twenty minutes of his failed interrogation.

"Why was the witness wearing full shackles during his interrogation?"

"So he would have a full appreciation for the serious situation he is in."

"Will I be further surprised and embarrassed in the future by discovery of water-boarding footage?"

"No, sir," Jameson said.

"In summary, we have a Section Chief who lost objectivity early in this process. First, he interviews a potential suspect without a partner and consequently loses his badge, weapon, and ID. Second, the same potential suspect is given a pass due to the fact she is fucking the

President's husband, with severely negative consequences. Third, he doesn't like the attitude of a witness and decides to teach a lesson by illegally arresting him. Fourth, the same witness is a prominent news correspondent who made sure the arrest was captured in real-time Internet coverage. Give me one reason to think this Section Chief hasn't lost his mind."

"The telephone call was captured without informing me first, which is a felony. Also, he is no shrinking violet. You should see what he did to the bikers in lock-up."

"Have you forgotten the wiretap you authorized for his phones as part of the investigation? We didn't get that from his lawyer, but the rest was helpfully forwarded to my office, and the White House Chief of Staff by Ralph Stephens. I have also seen the surveillance video from the lockup, looks to me and others as though the man fought a losing battle in self-defense. Quinton, if I find out the guards were slow to respond by request, more than your career will be at stake."

"No, I gave them grief for the delay already," Jameson said.

The Director looked around the table and confirmed consensus with the various functional representatives. "Here's what we're going to do. Quinton, up until this case you've done a good job, one that justified your rank as a Section Chief. I think you lost the bubble after you were assaulted and may be too invested in the case emotionally to be effective. Therefore you will retain the nominal title of Section Chief for the near-term, however you will not be engaged in the line prosecution of the Martyrs case. We'll reconsider matters after the conclusion. Justin Simons will take over full responsibility for the case; however, on all matters concerning Farid Royce a peer will be involved in order to maintain impartiality. As soon as this meeting concludes, you will personally release Farid Royce and tender your most sincere apologies for his mistreatment."

"Sir, I understand the viewpoint, but there is more to Farid that bears upon the current investigation. He's guilty of something, I know it."

"Unfortunately, Quinton, you've tainted that well with heavy-handedness. Right now, the Bureau is facing a wrongful arrest lawsuit that could do more than just damage us monetarily. You yourself are facing an abuse of power lawsuit asking for millions of dollars, and the Bureau might not defend it on your behalf. I personally am not amused to be a defendant in a similar draft lawsuit as your ultimate supervisor. I think we can sort this out without it coming to that, but even a whiff of perceived mistreatment of Mr. Royce will unleash the hounds of hell. Your career with the FBI and federal government would also come to an immediate conclusion. So, Quinton, if you like working at the FBI you will go in there and humble yourself before Mr. Royce. If he asks for a blowjob, you should consider being a swallower. Do I make myself clear?" the Director asked.

"Yes, sir," Jameson's face had an unnatural pallor as he faced the ruin of years of scheming and positioning. Friends around the conference table wouldn't even meet his gaze.

"What are you waiting for, Quinton? You have a man to get out of jail," the Director said.

"Yes, sir," Jameson gathered up the remaining scraps of his dignity and walked stiffly out the door.

The room started to buzz back and forth with conversation. The Director called his assistant over and indicated which people would need the non-disclosure agreements. She bustled out of the room purposefully.

"Justin, I estimate Jameson will have Mr. Royce out in about thirty minutes. You might want to arrange for his transportation home. Please convey our apologies to him and explain that the entire episode should not have happened. It would be helpful if Mr. Royce's lawyer doesn't involve the Bureau or the leadership in the matter."

"Yes, sir. I will convey the message."

"And, Justin, continue to investigate Farid as needed within the scope of the Martyrs task force, but do so using proper methodology. We'll assign a peer lead to assist in all of the instances where you may have a conflict of interest, but you'll have the balance of the responsibility. Keep doing the good job you have been."

"Thank you, sir. I'll go now so that I can meet Farid as he is released," Justin left the room for the elevators.

"The White House likes that man; I just hope it doesn't come back to bite him," The Director said mostly to himself.

• • •

Farid was taken out of his cell to a private shower facility where he was given back his street clothes minus the contents of his pockets and encouraged to get cleaned up pending release. He smiled to himself, knowing Jameson's methods were the catalyst to his prompt release. Once again, Ralph Stephens had been worth every penny. After getting dressed and groomed as best could be, he was taken to a small waiting room. This time he had no handcuffs or shackles and didn't have long to wait. Jameson entered the room carrying a small tray which held the balance of Farid's possessions.

"You're being released immediately, and I want to personally apologize for the misunderstanding," Jameson said.

Farid picked up his belongings and placed them within his pockets, "Ralph must a struck a nerve somewhere in the building, upper floor if I'm correct? They needn't worry, I know exactly who was responsible for this ... misunderstanding. Someone who doesn't look like they have $20 million dollars to lose, judging from the Mens Wearhouse rack suit he's wearing."

Jameson looked as though he were swallowing his tongue. A slow flush of red crept up his neck above the buttoned shirt collar. He stood and opened the door leading to one of the building exits.

"Cat got your tongue? Mom always said if you didn't have something nice to say, it's best to not say anything. I think that advice serves you well, Quinton, although I would also find a way to vent your anger before you develop heart problems," Farid continued to needle Jameson as they walked the final fifty feet together.

Gritting his teeth, Quinton held out his hand at the door. "No hard feelings I hope?"

Farid looked at Jameson's hand and taking it leaned in close, "Don't worry Quinton, you did exactly what you were supposed to do, kill your own credibility. I'll recover from my bruises and doubt that you will ever trouble me again. I'd call that a win. I'm still debating whether I should litigate for my incurred costs." Releasing Jameson's hand, Farid stepped out the door into the late afternoon sun.

Justin called out, "Farid, over here." Justin looked over Farid's bruises and guessed his ribs hadn't escaped unscathed due to the careful way he was moving.

"I'd say you should see the other guy, but you've already heard that one," Farid said with a laugh that turned into an immediate wince.

"Yes, a few times actually. So, I heard it was a biker gang this time? I thought we agreed you weren't going to fight a gang again without my help."

"Hey, you get thrown alone into a group cell, you have to find a level you can live with. I was a bit disappointed the dark-skinned contingent didn't consider me qualified as a brother, but what can you do? You have a message for me?"

"I do, but let's get you home to recover in a more congenial setting, shall we? I'm double parked over here," Justin said.

Justin opened the passenger door of the unmarked service car, and Farid gingerly lowered himself into the seat. Justin went to the driver's side, snatched up the ticket DC's finest had placed under the wiper blade. "You'd think these idiots would recognize a government car and know they'll never see a dollar of payment, but this is DC after all." He reached over to the glove box and put the ticket inside with all of the others.

Farid laughed in spite of himself, "Why are you collecting all of these?"

"Because some day, I'll catch one of those twits writing one of these up and give them back the whole bundle. Farid, what happened to you since we last talked?"

Farid told the story, some of which Justin had guessed from the media coverage, but the details inside the FBI building were new.

"It shouldn't have happened, and wouldn't have if Jameson hadn't fixated on you for some reason. By the way, the Director wanted to convey his personal apologies and his assertion that it should not have happened. Left unsaid was that Jameson is facing some real internal affairs problems as we speak. I doubt he will bother you any further. What are your plans concerning Ralph's hard work?"

"I'll see how things go over the next few weeks and decide then. The Director is off the hook if that is what you're asking."

"I'm sure that will please him. I'm pretty sure they won't be circling the wagons around Jameson, but you already suspected it. I sat in a meeting reviewing your arrest and they were appalled."

"Does that mean I'm no longer a suspect?" Farid asked.

"It means that no one at the FBI will be using illegal means to investigate you going forward."

"I can live with that. I suppose everyone who was close to Nayla will be considered a suspect until the case is solved. Speaking of Nayla, has there been any progress on finding her killer?"

"I can't say much, but she did have a prominent lover she met in the apartment. We've ruled out the lover as a suspect based on time of death, but we're looking into details from that point. I told you this much because we think the information will be public soon. If you, as a reporter, were to ask about the involvement of the lover, I'll go on the record with that data."

"Any chance the lover covered his tracks with a false alibi?"

"None. I've seen the data myself and the chain of evidence is rock-solid. You'll understand when and if the identity becomes public."

"Now I'm intrigued, I'd like to talk to this lover and hear how Nayla got herself into this mess," Farid said.

"That, I cannot recommend. Again, you'll understand later."

"Alright. I'll table it for now, but I'm not letting go of finding out what happened to her. Justin you remember I was headed to the Gulf for work. Am I going to have any problems at the airport thanks to my good friend Mr. Jameson?"

"I hope for Mr. Jameson's sake you do not, but I will check into it when I get back to the office. Here we are. I'll let you out in front of the lobby if you don't mind. I can come back after work, to check in on you before heading home."

"No need. I'm sure Lindsey will have her maid bring me some chicken soup and make a fuss. No need to drag you into that," Farid said.

"Jan might elbow her aside on the same quest, and she will be greatly relieved when I tell her you're more or less intact. When were you planning on leaving town?"

"Originally it was tomorrow, but I'll have to postpone that a day or two as there are things that need to be cleared up at work and with Ralph," Farid said.

"I'll find out whether there are any restrictions on your passport and call. If it is too late, I'll just send a text because you really need some beauty rest. I'm happy you're safe; it was a nasty surprise when I learned about it along with everyone else on the Internet."

"Jameson didn't tell you his plans on Sunday?" Farid asked.

"No, he doesn't trust me for some reason. Actually, he seems to have trouble trusting anyone. It isn't the first time he has gone in on his own with negative results. I used to think it was just because he wants all of the credit, but he gets credit for anything his organization accomplishes anyway."

"Maybe he thought you might be a contender for his job," Farid said.

"I would have said so, too, up until recently when he began talking to me about taking over his job when his promotion came through. So he was probably conflicted. I hate that crap, as you know, but it is what you have to deal with in government service."

"You have it in the private sector too, believe me. Being able to say 'shove it' anytime you like makes a huge difference. Self-centered men with small minds are everywhere, my friend. In fact, I'm expecting to meet with a few of them on this trip," Farid said as he gingerly raised himself out of the seat.

"Get some rest - I'll be in touch," Justin promised as Farid shut the car door. Farid waved and turned towards the lobby of his building.

Justin returned to his office in time to see the Internet release of several graphic photos showing Jonny Ray in action. One matched how she was posed when found dead, except that Jonny Ray was in frame taking Nayla from behind as he pulled her hair. Another was of him laying back on the bed nude with a drink in his hand. Justin assumed the woman in the photos was Nayla, but in each shot the woman's face was angled away from the camera so it wasn't completely clear. Jonny Ray's face was definitely identifiable and in good focus. The third photo was one of Nayla after her death, but this time the face was in perfect focus.

Justin picked up the phone and dialed Sid Rosenbloom's number, which went immediately into voicemail.

"Sir, this is Justin Simons - FBI. I wanted to let you know the first Jonny Ray photos have been leaked by the Martyrs and are out on the Internet. I'm sending you a link via text message."

The caption on the photos had the tagline, "Killed While Making Love? WH Cover-up?" Justin reflected it would take seconds for the post to go viral. He emailed the technical leads that they needed to find the source of the post as soon as possible.

Justin then went on to check whether there were any holds or travel restrictions placed on Farid's passport and the search came up clean. Thinking his friend probably would appreciate not being disturbed that day, Justin sent a text relaying the good news.

Having seen to the welfare of his friend, Justin turned his mind back to the problem of finding the rest of the snipers as well as the persons releasing the Nayla photographs online. This was going to get bad.

• • •

Two days later, Farid reclined in his first-class Emirates Air flight to Riyadh nursing a gin and tonic. The aches and pains from the beating were on their way to healing although his ribs were still sensitive. He had sneezed once the day before and learned quickly he didn't want to do that again. His face still had a significant bruise on one side, but it could be covered with makeup if an interview opportunity presented itself.

The trip was being made under the auspices of Farid's news network, but the real reason was to do The Hammer's work. He would find some way to generate news content upon arrival, but the most immediate concern was the meeting with Prince Zufar.

It had taken an extra day to replace all of the electronic devices taken during his incarceration at FBI headquarters. It was simply too time consuming to check them over for newly installed spy applications, far easier to simply replace the devices. Make the FBI intercept his traffic the old-fashioned way, with Echelon.

Reem had sent a package of equipment to Riyadh which was waiting for Farid in a safe house Amin had set up during the previous visit to Saudi Arabia after the American election. Amin had also dispatched two mirrors as backup support for Farid should it be necessary. Farid would mostly be alone on this trip and a great deal hinged on his accurate assessment of Prince Zufar. Everything had been set in motion, it only required the right signal to bring it all together. One of the pieces set in motion was sitting in the back of the plane: a very poorly disguised Quinton Jameson, who Farid spotted almost immediately upon boarding. Quinton must have accessed the airline ticketing ID checks for Farid's flight information, and decided to follow him. It would be interesting to see whether Quinton leveraged his FBI credentials with the Saudi security services or if he was following on his own account. It might be worth a call to Justin upon landing.

After the excellent dinner, Farid decided to close his private compartment in order to get some decent sleep prior to landing in Riyadh. The residual body aches from the beating conspired to help him drift immediately into a deep sleep.

The next day, prior to landing, the flight attendant knocked softly upon the door to Farid's compartment. He gathered his kit, shaved and took a shower to ready himself for the day. He smiled when he considered Quinton would be ruffled and fatigued after riding in coach class. Farid looked himself over in the mirror and decided it would do.

Upon landing, Farid walked through the First Class entry lane, getting into a hotel silver Mercedes that sat waiting for him. The last he had seen of Jameson, was in a long line at immigration. Farid knew without local help, Jameson would have no means to follow his movements. And Prince Zufar would be aware if the FBI Section Chief leveraged local resources.

Taking out his new mobile phone, Farid dialed Justin's number.

"Hi Farid," Justin said.

"Good morning, Sunshine! Just wanted to let you know that Jameson was aboard my flight to Riyadh. Given the recent unpleasantness, it came as quite a surprise. Was it a sanctioned trip or is he off the reservation?"

"I don't know, but I doubt it's official. I'll check at the office. Stay away from him. If he is going rogue he might do something stupid."

"I will. He would have to be really stupid to do something here in the Kingdom; his credentials wouldn't help at all if he violates Saudi law. You guys might want to reel him in before something like that happens," Farid advised.

"I agree. Thanks for letting us know, it wouldn't do to be surprised on this," Justin said.

"Off to my favorite 5-star hotel, I'm pretty sure they can make my bruises feel better. Did you have anything you wanted me to ask Prince Zufar? He's on the list of worthies I'm talking to on this trip."

"Actually, yes. I would be very interested in how he responds to a question about the Martyrs," Justin said.

"Easily done, as it was already on the agenda. Glad to be of service. Go get yourself some coffee. Later!" Farid hung up and watched the street scene through his car window.

His appointment with Prince Zufar wasn't until later in the evening after prayers, more than enough time to retrieve his gift from the safe house. The best part about being back in the Gulf is time doesn't move on the same rhythm as it does in the United States. He might even be able to get a massage in the hotel spa before heading out. But first a nondescript disguise and short visit to the nearby safe house.

Several hours later, fully refreshed, Farid called for a hotel limousine, providing the address of a home near Prince Zufar's fortress-like residence. Upon arrival, Farid walked several blocks to verify he was not being tailed, then made his way to Prince Zufar's backdoor. Ringing the small buzzer, he waited in the building's shadow, holding a gift-wrapped box. Mussa opened the door and admitted Farid inside. After the usual security screens, Mussa took the gift box away for a thorough security screen. It had a removable lid to facilitate a security examination and protect the festive covering.

Once more, Farid sat waiting for the appearance of Prince Zufar in patience. Mussa showed up with the requisite platter of refreshments and coffee, which Farid sampled briefly.

Without fanfare, the Prince entered the room, motioning Farid to reseat himself.

"Thank you for coming so promptly, although I was beginning to have my doubts when the FBI picked you up two days ago. How is it that you were released when you are so clearly guilty of something?" Prince Zufar laughed.

"A little advance warning and no real evidence. I'd still be sitting there if it hadn't been for publicity and a lawyer who eats fools for breakfast. On the topic, the disgraced person responsible for my being detained happened to be on the same flight to Riyadh," Farid said.

"Really, how interesting. What is his name?"

"Quinton Jameson. I would be interested in whether he has support here or if he is touring this lovely city as a tourist. I'm thinking of ways Mr. Jameson can contribute to our current campaign, as I am not quite done with him."

"I should say not, given the state of your cheek. Did he do that?"

"Not directly. Jameson had me thrown in with a cell full of common criminals to soften me up. I had to fight several before the guards removed me to solitary confinement."

"Are the criminals still alive?"

"Sadly, yes. I merely broke a few bones. Anything more and they wouldn't have released me no matter how much pressure they were under."

"It's hard to restrain yourself in the heat of battle, I know how hard it can be. I commend your self-control. Mussa, please find out everything we can about the redoubtable Quinton Jameson. You know who to call," Prince Zufar said. Mussa nodded and left the room.

"We'll know something about him shortly. Tell me, how is the Martyrs campaign going?"

"Very well, in some ways better than expected. The United States is like an angry bear trying to fight a bee, they have only caught one of the shooters and it was solely due to him not following his training. I don't know if you saw the media reports, but the fool's wife drove the car he had used for his shooting without permission and the FBI found her. But the common people are afraid to leave home, and it is starting to affect the overall economy. The rest of our sniper network has been protected and we'll re-establish contact with the shooters over the next few months with a new communication method," Farid said.

"I noticed that Dr. Hammayil was killed before he could be questioned. I have to admire the professionalism which expects a failure and then leaves a system in place to deal with it."

"It makes things complicated, but much safer. We lost one man and our communication method was compromised, but we had already shut it down before the FBI found out. They will eventually decipher the entire puzzle, but by then we'll be doing something completely different. So, for the near term, the snipers will go dormant and wait for reactivation. Now, the implication of the American President's husband is just getting started," Farid said.

"I saw the first release of photos. Shocking what the infidels do when they think no one can see! Who was the woman in the photos?"

Farid knew some of Prince Zufar's favored sexual activities would not have been well-received in Riyadh, but he reserved comment. "The woman was one of our doomed spies, Nayla Kaldah."

"Why do I know the name?"

"She was the sister of the instigator of the Martyrs al-Sabra incident. She worked as a lobbyist in Washington, DC until she was killed," Farid said.

"Now I remember! How long was she one of yours?"

"Four to five years. This was to have been her last campaign," Farid said.

"*Doomed spy*, subtle Sun Tzu reference. She was killed by your team?"

"Yes. Her work would have been useful with her alive, but dead it became invaluable. A dead person involved with politicians gets attention in the United States. Much more than a simple affair."

"Did she know of her impending martyrdom?"

"No. I regret it was not possible for her to know in advance, in order to achieve the necessary staging. It had to be a surprise."

"An unpleasant one, I must say, if you're the one being surprised. The FBI does not fully appreciate how subtly they are being played, do they? Whatever else you are, Hammer, you remain a consummate artist. I commend you! Now, what are you doing with my small contribution to your symphony of mayhem?" Prince Zufar asked.

"I am very pleased you ask, as we've arranged something special indeed. I brought a small gift for you, which is in the process of being examined by security. Originally you instructed the weapon be used for an urban target, which would be difficult to accomplish with the excellent border-sensing of the Americans. But then I realized, the weapon's effect would be minimal when deployed against an urban area due to its low yield. In fact, the device itself is a tactical battlefield model, which means the destruction is limited to a fairly small area."

Prince Zufar bridled, "I want something which rivals the blow struck on 9/11. I sense that you are about to propose an alternative. You know what I instructed."

"I do, but please hear me out. This plan combines both approaches and lets you decide when to detonate the device. Some background, DuChard Corporation operates a fleet of large cruise ships which carry more than 6,000 people when at sea. They also have an island in the Bahamas that is theirs, where all of their cruises stop overnight. My plan is to attach the device to the hull of one of these large ships and detonate remotely by satellite VPN link. Were it me, I would detonate the device when the ship is well at sea, but the option also exists for a detonation as it approaches their home port in Florida. The target port would be Port Canaveral, which is right next to America's primary spacecraft launch facility. Think of it: over 5000 casualties, more than double the lives lost in 9/11," Farid said.

"Interesting, please go on," Prince Zufar said, his annoyance giving way to interest.

"The small gift I brought is a remote detonator. You would have the pleasure of activating the device from here personally, via multiple satellite VPN links. The device will upload GPS coordinates continuously until detonation, which can be shown in a tracking application. It also sends a signal if someone starts tampering with the detonator. What do you think?"

Prince Zufar resisted his urge to shout with joy, "I am speechless with admiration! How will the bomb be attached to the ship?"

"My team will approach a ship on a moonless or overcast night in a small Kodiak boat. They will attach the device to the hull below the waterline using magnetic grapples. Originally we thought to put it above the waterline, but realized it would far be too easy to spot. It proved to be less work to waterproof a small black container than to devise some camouflaged cover above the waterline. The only thing above the waterline will be a small antenna set. So no matter which way the ship turns, an Iridium spacecraft will be in line-of-sight view. The VPN circuit is active, even now, but the bomb is not activated."

"Show me how it works," Prince Zufar said. "Mussa, bring in my present, it should be cleared by now."

Mussa came back into the room with the gift box, which he handed to the prince and spoke softly into Zufar's ear.

"Your friend Jameson checked into the Novatel, his only calls thus far have been to the American Embassy. My cousin in the security service will keep me informed as to his movements. What do we have here?" Zufar asked as he opened the box.

"Do you have a laptop and a USB connector? We can program the VPN connection into the device and use your internal WIFI," Farid said.

"How is this protected from scrutiny, can't the FBI and CIA track this back to me?"

"That will be very difficult, but there are several cloaking steps that were taken to make it even more so. For instance, this connection will be routed to a private proxy server in Ukraine, then one in Romania, then one in the UK before finally tapping into the Iridium telecommunications network. Once the explosion occurs there will be nothing left to indicate how it was detonated, so the only way to even track it back to the UK would be to know Iridium was involved. Once they got to UK, there are too many possibilities to get to Romania, let alone Ukraine. I'd say it is pretty safe for you. Run the concept past an IT expert you trust and see what they think. If you do not want the honor, we can do it instead. I thought, though, it might give you a unique experience which would be hard to duplicate," Farid said.

"Show me how it works. Here is Mussa with the USB connector and laptop," the Prince said, all eagerness now.

Farid sat down with the operating laptop and connected the USB cable to access the device using a browser. When it came time to set up access to Zufar's WIFI network, he turned the laptop back to Mussa. Without comment, Mussa entered the code and handed it back to Farid, who then proceeded to activate the previously programmed device and rebooted. Disconnecting the USB connector, Farid handed the laptop and USB cable back to Mussa as it was no longer needed.

"Your Highness, the detonator circuit is active. If you look here, there is a small LCD window with the current GPS coordinates of the weapon. If you take these and use Google Maps it should show the device is located somewhere close to Andros Town in the Bahamas. The top left LED light indicates an active VPN connection when it is green, as it currently shows. The top right LED light indicates if the weapon is armed, when it is green and yellow if it is active but unarmed. Note that it shows yellow at the moment. The button, under the cage cover, is the one that detonates the weapon. The weapon will not detonate unless both LEDs show green, even if the button is pushed. The other time the weapon would detonate is if it was armed and someone tampers with the detonator."

Farid handed the activated device to the Saudi Prince who was struggling to hide his excitement.

"There is a small battery icon on the LCD screen which indicates the charge. It can be charged with any USB cable like a mobile phone. I recommend keeping it charged and active. So the decision of whether to detonate as the ship approaches port or on the high seas rests with you, if you so command," Farid said with an inclined head.

"I do command and I am grateful for your planning," Prince Zufar said.

"You had also asked about investment opportunities, I think it is safe to say all cruise ship line stocks will be vulnerable to short-selling gains post-explosion. DuChard corporate stock price will tumble. The question is whether the DuChard troubles would be a boost for Las Vegas and other entertainment venues. I think it would. We have scheduled the attack to occur sometime during the span from April 7th and April 15th, looking for a full dark evening with a ship in port. Can you make the financial moves necessary before then?" Farid asked.

"Yes, my buying proxies have already been supplied with the cash necessary. I just need to send the instructions to them."

"Good, unless there are further questions or issues to cover, I should depart for my hotel."

"No, but I will have Mussa get a car to take you back. Don't worry, it will be anonymous. Stand, my brother! You have made me very happy and added significantly to my wealth," Prince Zufar hugged Farid effusively in the traditional manner, with kisses on both cheeks. Farid had never been clasped as a brother by Zufar in the past, so it was clear Zufar was completely overcome by his excitement.

"I hope you are taking financial advantage as well," Zufar said in farewell.

"Yes, your Highness. I should make a fortune as well, but somewhat more modest than your own. It will help me maintain the struggle for years to come."

"Don't forget to come to me in the future, brothers should work together for the glory of Allah!"

Farid bowed his head in acquiescence and took his leave into the night.

Terminal Sacrifices

"..Muslim leaders in the gulf states are concerned by the continued Martyrs terrorist campaign, and its impact upon relations with the United States. So far, they support the efforts of President Brown to protect the safety of American Muslims and relations with the Muslim world, but are shocked by the recent scandalous behavior of Jonny Ray Brown..."

Farid Monsour al Haj for World News Corporation

Amin enabled the detonator satellite connection, as Farid had instructed, so Prince Zufar could be properly impressed. He fully expected Prince Zufar to be narcissistic enough to want to activate the weapon. Amin had to salute Farid's creativity; he had turned a liability into an asset. The biggest problem with this aspect of the plan was evading the enraged giant that was the United States when they threw everything into pursuit of those responsible. The Prince would be best served if he didn't press the button himself.

This was safer for Amin and his Qatari crew, though, as they would be able to put hundreds of miles between themselves and the explosion. The time of greatest risk would be when Amin connected the device, hoping the Prince wouldn't immediately press the actuator. By the time the United States accessed archival satellite imagery records to identify and track the Butler's Dosh, the entire crew would be long gone.

Tomorrow, they would fuel up the boat and run night sea trials to become completely familiar with the capabilities of the battery-driven Kodiak boat. It was important to understand the range of the boat when fully loaded.

Amin had created a harness to hold the waterproof container and ease in the attachment to the cruise ship's hull. The idea was to attach two magnetic grapples below the waterline, place the bundle between the grapples and cinch the straps to the grapples. Amin had tested the concept in the privacy of the forward cabin, but it would need a full test against a real ship. There was a medium-sized ship for delivering mail to the islands that docked a few miles from their base in Andros Town; they would use that as a dry run. Or a wet run, since the Butler's Dosh should sit offshore and deploy the Kodiak for the test. Amin would fill the backpack with rocks to simulate the weight of the actual device. If it worked, the only variable left unknown was when the operation was slated to take place.

Farid should be meeting with the Prince already, so word would come back soon. In the meantime, it was time to call a drill and get the crew back into the shipboard routine necessary to succeed when fully operational.

"Mohammed," Amin shouted in order to be heard throughout the boat.

Several minutes later, Mohammed came to the bridge station wearing cutoffs and sandals. "Yes, sir?"

"Gather the crew as quickly as possible and prepare to get underway," Amin said.

"Yes, sir. It will take me a few minutes to get Nassir, he went down to the rocks to do some fishing. Khalid will go get him while I start the preparations."

Amin nodded and pointed to his wrist chronograph whose stop-watch function was already engaged.

Mohammed nodded quickly and ran towards the cabins yelling, "Khalid!" in an urgent fashion.

Amin sat at the wheel of the ship and watched the crew scurrying to obey his orders. Mohammed had changed quickly into more sensible working clothes and shoes, Khalid hadn't bothered; running down the dock towards the rocks where the good fish were often caught. Local tourists used to a slower pace watched him run by in bemusement, but not really paying much attention. Shortly they were treated to the view of two men running back in sandals, one carrying a fishing pole.

Khalid and Nassir stowed the equipment quickly below deck while scrambling to change into their working clothes. Within five minutes, the Butler's Dosh engines had rumbled into a steady idle and lines were being retrieved.

"Not bad for an unexpected departure: nine and a half minutes," Amin announced. "Mohammed, set a course for Chub Cay. We will be doing sea drills today."

"Yes, sir. What kind of sea drills are we to perform, Captain?"

"I want to understand how well the Kodiak performs under various loads. In short we'll load it up with different weights, measure full speed, and see how long a battery charge gets us. It will drive how many people are in the Kodiak for the operation as well as how far offshore the ship can be during the operation," Amin said.

"If I may make a suggestion, Captain. Do we know what the sea will be like at the target location, in terms of winds and which side of the island we approach? It might be useful to do the tests somewhere similar to where the target is situated."

"Yes, a very good suggestion. We don't know the weather yet, but we do know the target location. Let me show you the chart, here at Buccaneer Cay on the western shore where the cruise ship dock is located. I was thinking we would lay off of Chub Cay's western shore for our exercises. What do you think?" Amin asked.

"Let's look at the depth charts, see Buccaneer Cay's west side drops deep very quickly, whereas Chub Cay's west side is much shallower. I recommend we use Bird Cay, which also has fewer people to notice the activity."

Amin looked over the charts and had to agree with Mohammed's recommendation, "Bird Cay it is, let's get there as soon as is reasonable. The conn is yours."

Amin went down to the forward cabin to check the gear once more. Upon their return to Andros Island, they would do a mock run on the mail ship and leave the package installed until the next evening. Hopefully the strapping system would prove durable enough to resist the rushing water while the boat was underway. A cruise ship would be much faster than the mail boat, so it would still be a risk but they could take whatever lessons were learned on the trial and apply them for the real thing. Amin had six magnetic grapples, and thought he only needed to use two given their strength rating. If being conservative he should probably use three. Attach the grapples in a pattern like two eyes and an open mouth, attaching the payload to the bottom grapple first, then the upper left and right. The cinches would then be tightened and the device should be fully secure, come what may. The uplink antennas could be taped to the hull above the waterline and still be very difficult to see. The cruise ships stay some of the night at Buccaneer Cay, leaving early enough to make Port Canaveral in the early morning, so the likelihood of detection would be even less.

Mohammed had the Butler's Dosh moving through the slight swells at about 3/4 speed, which is a wise captain's maximum sustained speed. Top speed ratings on most pleasure hulls are not meant to be sustained for any extended length of time, without creating maintenance problems, whereas 3/4 could motor on without incident until the bunkers ran out of fuel. Butler's Dosh had full fuel bunkers and her range was over 3500 nautical miles at 9 knots cruising speed.

Several hours later, Mohammed called down to inform Amin Bird Cay was coming up on the horizon. Amin took a pair of high-powered binoculars and looked the island over. It was very lightly developed on the west side, and the island was actually for-sale at the current moment. That would provide enough of a cover story in the event they were questioned by any passing U.S. Coast Guard ships. Theoretically, the Coast Guard were not permitted to board foreign-flagged vessels in International waters, but it had been known to happen when drug trafficking was suspected. The local islands were known for their fishing variety, so the team would use that cover as well. Amin smiled as he considered how the men would hate to do more fishing.

The island itself appeared to be completely deserted, but there were sport-fishing boats coming and going from Chub Cay. Mohammed's suggestion was definitely on the mark, and Amin's estimation of the Qatari boat captain rose.

Upon arrival within a mile offshore of Bird Cay, they loaded the Kodiak with three hundred pounds of ballast and Khalid. The men watched as Khalid steered the boat towards the beach. Amin was timing the total running time of the batteries. Khalid made six round trips before the batteries ran out of power. Amin was fairly certain there would be a decent operating margin, if the Butler's Dosh was standing off the coast about five miles. The crew recovered the Kodiak on board and commenced to charging the batteries for another run. In the meantime, Amin had Mohammed take the boat out the requisite five miles for the next test.

The crew sat down for a meal as the Kodiak batteries attained another full charge. The crew launched the Kodiak once again with the same load. Khalid duly set off on his ten mile round-trip. Nassir broke out the fishing poles, to the general ribbing of Mohammed.

"By the time we are finished, you will never want to see another fish, Nassir."

"The fish in these waters are so tasty, I don't think it will ever be a problem," Nassir replied.

"Besides it is a great cover. But you should wear one of those floppy straw hats we bought in Andros City, it shows that you are serious about recreation. We should have loaded up Khalid with fishing gear and clothes as well," Amin cracked a rare joke, but noted to himself it should be done for the real operation.

Amin kept his eyes on the horizon, and saw Khalid run the boat onto the beach. *What the hell is he doing?* Amin thought as he got the binoculars out for a better look. Then he started laughing, Khalid was peeing on the beach. Amin had to admit it made more sense than trying to go with the boat cresting swells all the way in. When finished with nature's call, Khalid got back into the boat and headed back towards the Butler's Dosh.

Amin hoped the operation schedule would be set within the next ten days, because he was getting tired of the islands, and the company, if truth be told.

Khalid was practically back to the boat, with his fist pumping the air in triumph. The crew waved him in and secured the Kodiak on deck once more.

"Captain, there is still 15-20% in the batteries so I think we have the right distance," Khalid said.

"The test may be invalid," Amin said with a straight face.

"Sir?"

"I saw you unloading the boat on the island, we might have to do it over."

Khalid panicked for a few seconds then realized he was being teased about his quick restroom break. He started laughing, "Well I had to go. Better out than in I've heard it said."

Amin smiled and nodded back. "Brothers, we wait now until nightfall, then we test loading the Kodiak with the weapon and trying to attach it to our boat."

"But Captain, our hull isn't metal," Mohammed pointed out.

"Yes, true. For that test, we will use the mail boat in Andros City. But this one will allow us, or rather me, to see how hard it is to maneuver the package from the Kodiak and in the water. I want to be familiar with the process before having to do it on the cruise ship."

"Captain, one suggestion," Mohammed said, "Why wait until dark, it might help to see what happens for the first test."

Amin thought it over for a few seconds, "Mohammed, you continue to provide wise counsel. Very well, let's get the battery charge up a bit and do it before sundown."

Amin went below deck to prepare the device for the test run. He didn't see any alternative to using the actual device, because the center of gravity would vary between it and an equivalent load of ballast. If handling the device in the water proved awkward, he needed to know it in advance. He planned to wear a black wetsuit with mask, fins and snorkel for the job. Amin was fairly comfortable in water, he had done well during the underwater demolition training he received as a young man, but he had not kept in practice over the years as it had never been necessary. In the last few weeks Amin had spent hours snorkeling while the rest fished, which should help get him through the exercise.

Amin slung the device pack over his shoulder and carried it out onto the deck. The hundred pounds felt as though it weighed more, by the time he placed it next to the Kodiak. A slight roll of the deck added to the instability. Amin hoped the buoying effect of water would make the package easier to handle. Amin pre-installed the magnetic grapples to the device pack before being placed in the water, as making the necessary connections while wet had proved to be very difficult. The task would not be any easier when bobbing around in the water. Amin planned to connect the bottom magnetic grapple, then the left and right, to hand tightness. Then he would tighten each of the straps with a ratchet winch until it was very tight. The ratchet winches needed a small wrench to operate, but that was the only tool necessary to attach the device.

Mohammed indicated the batteries had a 50% charge, which would be sufficient to run the test. Khalid helped deploy the Kodiak and climbed in once more to captain. As it bobbed in the sea, Amin handed down the heavy pack which was fairly ungainly with grapples appended to it. The task was difficult, because dropping it into the bottom of the boat was not a good idea. The Russian device was robust, but there was no point in stress-testing that aspect of its design.

Amin was starting to have some doubts about how easy this was going to be, based on how difficult it had been to gently load the Kodiak. He stepped into the Kodiak and pushed off the hull of the Butler's Dosh.

Khalid took them on a wide loop to then approach the Butler's Dosh from the bow, slowly warping the Kodiak until it was close by the hull of the larger boat. Amin got into the water and Khalid moved to hand the pack down into the water. It quickly became apparent that they would probably want an extra pair of hands, as someone would need to maneuver the boat while a handoff was being made.

For now, it was set aside as Khalid slowly lowered the pack into the water. Unfortunately a small swell caused Khalid to lose his, already tenuous, footing and he dropped the device into the water. Amin was caught by surprise as the device proved to not be buoyant at all, dragging him underwater and towards the bottom.

Amin struggled to reorient so he could engage his fins to surface, but quickly lost what little breath he had been able to take prior to being swiftly dragged down. Reluctantly, Amin released the strap he was holding as he descended. From there Amin watched the precious device continue downward until it disappeared into pitch darkness of the ocean depths.

• • •

While Amin and his team worked through their tense few days, Farid made the rounds in Riyadh interviewing those willing to go on the record with him concerning the Martyrs attacks. The public responses were pretty much as expected, they hoped Americans wouldn't generalize the behavior of the terrorists to all Muslims. Stopping well short of condemnation for the terrorists, the Saudis didn't understand average Americans would see it as approval. The powerful classes in Saudi Arabia were typically much better educated than the average American and understood the advanced concepts of nuance. Farid knew the seemingly innocuous interviews would be taken as negative in the United States and served The Hammer's purpose well.

The interesting undercurrent in all the discussions was a pride the terrorists were able to keep the most powerful country on earth off-balance. The only Saudi who knew of Farid's alter ego was Prince Zufar, so the feedback was genuine rather than an attempt at flattery. As for Prince Zufar, his new role in the operation had transformed him from an arrogant posture into an almost obsequious manner. Farid knew Zufar wouldn't stay in that frame of mind for very long, the habits of a lifetime do not vanish so easily, but it was only needed for the next two weeks.

Justin had sent a text to Farid confirming Jameson was operating off-script. So far the man hadn't done anything other than engage Farid in visual surveillance, and Farid wasn't much concerned on that account. He had been leading Jameson on a merry chase around the city, meeting every contact in the open and spending evenings at dinner with interviewees or in a mosque. Jameson hadn't leveraged any Kingdom resources, rather he depended on Americans from the U.S. Embassy. If Farid had to guess, they were probably CIA, as the known FBI representatives were pointedly uninvolved. Prince Zufar had appreciated the opportunity to identify CIA resources for himself and his coterie.

Farid was tempted to stay a few more days in order to further drain Jameson's resources and toy with the man, but his work was mostly complete.

The final evening of his visit was reserved for an interview with Prince Zufar in his role as an international investor. This time Farid would enter the palace through the front door, and Jameson would be left at the curb while he feasted inside. Farid's few clandestine movements had all occurred before Jameson got his feet underneath him and began watching. Farid booked a flight early the next morning which would put him in DC later in the evening. He knew an acceptable solution to the problem presented by Jameson would become apparent during the long flight. Some of his most creative past actions were conceived on such flights and he looked forward to the process. Now to get his formal wear pressed and perfect for the Prince's dinner.

• • •

Amin was pleased the miscues suffered off of Bird Cay appeared to have run their course. After a tense twelve hours of searching, the device was successfully recovered intact and total disaster averted. Throughout, the Qatari crew didn't panic which made quite an impression on Amin. Mohammed had suggested putting the device in a blackened life-vest to improve bouyancy and prevent another disaster. When tested, the idea worked perfectly.

Yesterday, the team had successfully installed a dummy payload onto a mail boat undetected and the next morning it duly motored off on its daily route to the other islands it served. Tonight, the team would recover the payload and see how it had fared with the extended exposure to seawater currents.

Amin was beginning to think that the Qataris might have a use which transcended the current operation. They had each shown a facile willingness to assume the cover identities and behavior, as well as remain in character during the times it was important. Each had contributed useful suggestions to the operation which were in the process of being implemented. Amin would give serious consideration to assigning them larger roles in upcoming operations. First, of course, they had to survive this one.

Once more, the team warped the Butler's Dosh off of its dock and headed out to sea. They planned to motor over the horizon then return to a point approximately 8 km offshore from the target, deploying the Kodiak and team to perform the objective. Picking up the dummy payload shouldn't be very difficult, but they weren't going to take any operational risks. Afterwards, the Kodiak would head out to sea flashing a directional signal light towards the larger boat, which would then move to intercept. That change allowed for simplification of the Kodiak steering, all they had to do was maintain an opposite compass bearing from their target approach and the Butler's Dosh would do the rest. Nassir was left ashore so he could assess how noticeable the Kodiak was coming in, both in sight and sound. Amin suspected the electric trolling motor was quiet enough not to be noticed over the normal dockside noises. The sight element was very important, though, as the DuChard island was almost certainly better lit than normal Caribbean islands at night.

Mohammed signaled when the horizon's edge had been attained and started the boat back towards the target. Amin and Khalid deployed the Kodiak then boarded once the 8 km offset distance had been reached. The mens' dull black clothes, Amin's was actually a wetsuit, and their naturally brown skin combined to make them very hard to see. They approached the mail boat from the shadow side until they were next to the hull. Khalid slowly maneuvered the Kodiak to the place they had installed the dummy load. Amin slid into the water and discovered the pack was still firmly in place. He fastened a darkened life jacket to the casing, then disconnected the magnetic grapples one by one. Floating the load next to the Kodiak he positioned it so Khalid could easily lift the payload into the boat. Khalid stowed the package amidships while Amin pulled himself into the boat quietly. Once they were both secure, Khalid turned the Kodiak and headed back out to sea. Khalid set course on the reverse heading using an old-school compass, while Amin took the signal light and held it pointed over the bow. All told, they were next to the mail boat less than five minutes, a quite satisfactory result and risk window.

Butler's Dosh intercepted them easily, the Kodiak was recovered and the crew headed back to their leased dock space in Andros City. Upon docking, they waited for Nassir's return. Within half an hour,

Nassir sauntered down the dock as if he fully expected the presence of the Butler's Dosh, boarding without any fanfare.

"Nassir, how did the operation appear from the dock?" Amin asked.

"If I did not know you were coming, it would have been very hard to notice. The sound was there, but it wasn't clearly coming from where you were. I could barely see you, and then it was mostly the wake wavelets, not the boat or you two. Once you were next to the ship, it was still very hard to see anything. I did think of something, though, if someone saw you and challenged. You could say you were getting barnacles to eat. Maybe we should carry a bucket of barnacles to show, that could explain the diver's presence," Nassir said.

"Excellent. I think your idea is a good one. We act as if we have permission, and when they go to check we leave. The payload will be below the waterline and hard to see. Do you know where we can get a bucket of barnacles?" Amin said.

"Yes, Khalid and I can get some in the next few days snorkeling. We'll keep them in fresh seawater until needed."

"Perfect! Alright, good work my brothers. All we have to do between now and the operation date is relax and keep our skills tuned. I'll take a look at the dummy payload and see if we need to make any further adjustments, but it looks like it weathered the seawater environment very well. Keep in mind, our actual payload will only have to survive for less than twelve hours, so I am very pleased. Over the next few days we need to determine the best way for everyone to disperse after the operation. I am open to requests on an end destination, assuming you have papers which will allow admission. Think about it and we'll talk," Amin then turned to the task of dissecting the dummy load.

• • •

Quinton Jameson was met at the airport post customs by a small delegation of people attached to the Bureau's Internal Affairs department.

"Section Chief Jameson?"

"Yes," Jameson said tiredly.

"You need to come with us. The Director has some questions about your vacation in the Kingdom of Saudi Arabia."

"What, I'm not allowed to take a vacation?" Jameson asked.

"Did you meet with internal security to register your trip in advance?"

"No, I forgot to do that."

In the United States, if one has security clearances which exceed a certain threshold, permission for foreign travel must be granted by their department's security office. Forms listing itineraries and planned foreign contacts had to submitted well in advance in order to maintain clearances. Upon return from the trip, the traveler had to sit in debriefing sessions to detail exactly where they went and who they met with during the trip. Jameson hadn't bothered to file a travel request and was in danger of losing his security clearance at a bare minimum.

Somewhere in the back of Jameson's mind he had felt that all would be forgiven if he brought back a smoking gun on Farid's activities. But Farid hadn't done anything at all out of the ordinary for a news correspondent during his trip the entire time that Jameson watched him. Unless Farid had done all of his illicit business when Jameson was sitting in the slow lane at Riyadh's Customs. There was a five hour period where Jameson hadn't known Farid's location, but it couldn't be helped given the nature of his arrival.

"Alright, I'm with you." Jameson knew there was no point in resisting or explaining anything to this team, they didn't have the option to let him off of the hook.

As he was driven down the Dulles corridor towards DC, he wondered how news of his transgression had made it back to the watchdogs so fast. Normally they wouldn't see data on something like this for several weeks after the fact. The implication was that he was being watched, which made sense given the last conversation he had endured with the Director. All it would take is a flag on his passport and they would be notified. Jameson wondered why he hadn't thought of it in advance, but had to acknowledge his state of mind had been blind rage when he booked the trip. A week sober in Saudi Arabia had given him a lot of time to think. While Jameson still thought there was more to Farid's story, he no longer felt the need to personally take the man down.

The black SUVs traveled significantly above the speed limit of the toll road in the car pool lane, pulling into the FBI building garage a mere forty minutes after leaving the airport. Jameson was hustled upstairs into a small meeting room, which held representatives from the Security Office and Human Resources.

The Security Office team took the lead, "Section Chief Jameson, I'll get right to the point. Please explain why you left the country without the proper authorizations."

"I simply forgot to do so, it was a spur of the moment thing and in the rush to make the flight it didn't get done," Jameson said.

"What was the purpose of the trip?"

"I wanted to get a better understanding of the culture which supports terrorists like the Martyrs. I knew I would have to do it on my own dime, given my current status."

"So this trip had nothing to do with Farid Royce, who was on the same flight as yourself?"

"I didn't approach or trouble him in any way," Jameson said.

"Did you use any embassy resources to follow and observe Farid Royce? Think very carefully before you answer the question."

"Yes, I used some company men to help me. I wanted to know all of the people Farid met with on his trip."

"Were you planning to write a report on it or was this another example of your operating alone?"

Jameson clenched his teeth. "I'm on suspension in all but name. No one is listening to my concerns. I'll be happy to write a report if someone wants to read it. I was hoping to find something material which would exonerate my standing in the Bureau."

"By breaking the rules under which the Bureau operates and orders specifically given to you by the Director concerning Mr. Royce?"

"That wasn't my intention, but I can see why you'd see it that way. Is the Director going to join us?"

The HR lead spoke. "No, he has other things which require his attention. Quinton, after your last discussion with the Director, did you not feel you were treated fairly by him? You maintained your staff position and pay grade without suspension. If one of your subordinates had performed in a similar fashion, would you have been so lenient?"

"Probably not," Jameson had to admit.

"And if they went on to do something like what you just did, how would you view it?"

"I'd probably have their badge or assign them to a North Dakota field office."

The HR rep nodded. "Glad to see we are on the same page. You are suspended immediately, with pay, pending a formal inquiry into all of your behavior over the last six months. Please surrender your badge, mobile phone, identification, and weapon now. We will be placing your passport on the restricted list until the inquiry is concluded. Do you have any restricted-access information in your home?"

Jameson threw his badge, mobile phone, and ID onto the table. He unbuckled his shoulder holster and laid it on the table as well. "Other than my laptop, no I do not."

"Where is the laptop?"

"Here," Jameson took it out of his briefcase and handed it over.

"These agents will take you back to your home or car. We will be in touch on your next steps in this process."

Jameson reflected on how quickly a promising career with the FBI had gone up in smoke. Even if he somehow survived the inquiry process, his service jacket would always be tainted by this episode. Maybe it was time to leverage his experience with national security in the private sector or politics. But that would have to wait. His anger at Farid had reignited and that called for a few things to be taken care of prior to any serious pursuit of those options. Right now, he had to walk out the doors a chastened man, keeping his opinions and plans to himself.

•••

Lindsey still hadn't come completely to terms with the death of her best friend Nayla. She had watched the slow leak of Nayla and Jonny Ray's lurid pictures on the Internet as well as the increasing shrill denunciations of the Administration over the last week and a half. Headlines like "Administration in Bed with Terrorists", "Terrorist Connection", "Killer Martyrs", the list went on. It didn't matter that Nayla wasn't actually proved to be a terrorist, nor that Jonny Ray was guilty of nothing more than lust. The news outlets did whatever it took to drive Internet traffic to their sites. Time for corrections later.

The Administration appeared to be completely forthcoming. Spokespersons explained the involvement of Jonny Ray with Nayla, and denied any connection to the Martyrs terrorists. Oddly enough, that stance spurred distrust, as the conspiracy theorists asked, "If they admit to this, what they're hiding must really be bad - what is it?" The instant pundits had no end of theories, some of the most outlandish involved extraterrestrials.

Nayla's will named Lindsey as executor of the estate, but the government had yet to release her body. Lindsey suddenly remembered the envelope Nayla had left her, and wondered what was inside it. It didn't matter, she had to see it delivered just as her friend had asked. The address and name on the letter meant nothing to Lindsey. So, she left the children with the nanny and drove to the nearest DHL location. Her father, Benton Royce, had always said that if something important needed to be sent internationally, it had to go DHL.

Lindsey asked the clerk which service would guarantee the letter arrive fastest and purchased it. Tucking the shipping receipt into her purse, she handed the sealed letter over to the clerk and thought nothing more of it. She needed to go look through Nayla's apartment and make sure there was nothing rotting in the kitchen or otherwise amiss. She had to arrange for disposition of Nayla's goods, but it could wait until after the funeral. Lindsey expected Farid to return from his latest trip yesterday, but hadn't heard from him yet. She hoped the trip had helped; he hadn't looked well the last time she'd seen him, on television being arrested by that idiot FBI agent. Hopefully, the jackass got what was coming to him, but, if not, Lindsey could make a few calls herself. Nayla had told Lindsey the same guy harassed her about the election night party. Lindsey hadn't been treated poorly during her interviews, so maybe the man had it in for Muslims specifically. Regardless, it wasn't going to stand. Lindsey pushed aside a swell of anger at how her friend died, and how her reputation was being treated afterwards.

She'd call Farid and ask him to meet her at Nayla's, if he was up to it. She wasn't sure she was up to it either, but she would do it alone if she had to.

• • •

The morning of April 14th dawned with beautifully clear skies for their departure from Andros City. They would not return and felt oddly sad as the memories of leisurely fishing expeditions along the mostly deserted shore presented themselves.

Amin ordered Mohammed to set course for Buccaneer Cay, the idea was to deploy fishing gear and cruise around the island to get a feel for the target site. They would arrive late in the day, with enough time for one night-time circuit of the island before heading over to Grand Abaco island to anchor off of Sandy Point for the evening. The next day would be spent fishing and observing the local traffic with several passes around Buccaneer Cay, making sure to be close in to Sandy Point at sundown. Then, in the full dark of night, the operation would proceed.

As the sun began to set April 15th, the crew of the Butler's Dosh spent time indoors praying, and gathered for their last leisurely meal in the galley. Everything they had seen so far indicated the plan would work. Khalid picked up a bucket of barnacles, as Nassir had recommended, setting it next to the Kodiak, ready to be loaded.

Amin wasn't one to make speeches to whip up the troops, so he simply gave the order to set course for the west side of Buccaneer Cay, just over the horizon, approximately 7 km west. At that distance the DuChard Duchess radars should barely detect the Butler's Dosh, and visual sighting would not occur. The crew was ready for the night's challenges and the ride would take a little over an hour and a half at the Butler's Dosh's cruising speed.

Amin sat in the cabin with the device as he checked the detonator packaging and the seals for any flaws. The life-jacket was attached to the middle of the device which looked almost like a man slumped over with the grapple assemblies loosely resembling arms and a single leg.

Amin sent the coded message to The Hammer indicating the operation was underway. Upon completion, Amin would send another message to indicate completion. Prince Zufar would see the right-hand LED turn green to indicate successful arming of the device within a minute of it occurring. Amin prayed the Prince wouldn't push the button immediately killing them all. Amin wouldn't arm the device until the very last minute to reduce the risk. Mohammed, staying on Butler's Dosh, had orders to leave the scene immediately heading for Nassau, if a detonation occurred while the team was still on the Kodiak.

The DuChard Duchess could carry up to 4,000 passengers and 1,400 crew. Amin was aware that Prince Zufar had wanted to hit an urban area with his weapon, but knew the size of the device wouldn't do much more damage in a city than on the single cruise ship full of passengers. By setting the device off on the bow, it was even possible the back end of the ship would survive the explosion intact. The fireball itself would be approximately 30 meters, and the deadly radiation exposure zone would only be about 500 meters from detonation site. The DuChard Duchess was 340 meters bow to stern. Most of the ship would be completely destroyed, but there would be wreckage. Of course, the ship will sink anyway and those aboard would be killed from radiation exposure, if not from the blast itself.

Amin packed four rounds of the engraved Martyrs sniper shells into his utility kit. He would drop those into the water next to the dock once the device was installed and operational. Four rounds for the four freedom fighters who set the device. U.S. Navy divers would be all over the site after the explosion and it was a good bet the shells would be found.

The sun was down and the sky fully dark as the Butler's Dosh reached the western turn towards the target. Mohammed was trolling back and forth as though the boat were engaged in sport fishing, waiting for the order to approach the target.

"Mohammed, it is time. Khalid and Nassir prepare to launch the Kodiak. Mohammed, don't forget, if the explosion occurs do not wait for the Kodiak unless you can actually see it coming back. Allah willing, we will be all together again in two hours," Amin said.

The Butler's Dosh stopped for a moment to drop the Kodiak, Khalid and Nassir boarded immediately and Amin carefully handed down the device to Nassir and joined them in the boat. As previously agreed, Nassir held onto a line from the Butler's Dosh so it could tow them slowly into the Kodiak's working range of 5 km. The sea had a slow roll, but nothing major, so it wasn't difficult to ride the Butler's Dosh's wake for the twenty minutes of free ride to their release point. Upon reaching the right distance, Mohammed turned the boat to the South as if trolling, and Nassir released the line. The Kodiak was now on its own.

Khalid had the compass heading to reference as he steered; the Kodiak hummed quietly towards its giant target. Shortly the light glow over the horizon resolved into the visual details of the dock and moored ship. The passengers except for Mohammed sat in the bottom of the boat in order to be less visible. The night behind the Kodiak was black as ink, but the team took no chances.

As the small boat approached the DuChard Duchess, Amin looked for security details that might be watching their approach. As expected, the starboard bow side of the ship was in full shadow as no lights other than those on the ship itself were deployed. Khalid nodded as Amin gestured towards the proper direction. The Kodiak slowed to make an absolute minimum of noise. The men were tense, and the only sounds were those of the small electric motor and the rasp of rubber wetsuits on plastic seats. Amin moved only as necessary and very deliberately; as every sound seemed as loud as a rifle shot. By now, the noises of the island were beginning to take over: music from several restaurant areas, children being children. There were even muffled noises from the ever-running generators of the DuChard Duchess.

After twenty minutes of tension, the boat warped to a position next to the ship's bow, fully in the shadow and underneath the ship's deck view. Amin slipped into the water, a dark shadow in the night. Nassir carefully set the device into the water next to Amin. The casing rose floating just below the surface, thanks to the life-vest. Amin was able to position it approximately 5 meters from the bow's edge. He dived down about a meter with the bottom grapple and activated it against the metal hull. The grapple gripped even better than it had on the Andros City mail boat. From there, it was simple to connect the left, then the right grapple. Taking the winch lever from his kit, he tightened the straps on all three grapples until he could rotate each winch no more. The bomb was on the hull tightly, one meter underwater. Taking the antenna sleeves, Amin taped the two foil antennas against the hull above the waterline. Using his underwater flashlight, he looked over the installation once more, then armed the detonator. Turning off his flashlight, he surfaced and gingerly got back into the Kodiak. Amin pulled out the four shells and dropped them into the water. Khalid turned the boat back towards the Butler's Dosh and got ready to depart.

"Hey, you there in the boat! What the hell are you doing?" An industrial grade security flashlight lit the boat from further out on the dock.

"I've got this, keep quiet and smile," Amin said low.

"Barnacles, got to get them at night. See? We have permission," Amin yelled as he held up the bucket, shining his flashlight into the bucket for the benefit of what must be security staff.

"I didn't hear anything about it. Come around the dock and show me some identification."

"Alright, we're screwed here anyway with all the light - barnacles locked up tight," Amin was making it up on the fly, he motioned to Khalid to head along the dock toward the ocean.

Behind them, the security guard noticed their direction and started running down the dock after them, his flashlight casting erratic stabs of light into the ocean as he tried to keep them in view. Khalid turned the course slightly off of the dock so the Kodiak was getting further and further away.

The guard stopped and yelled something inarticulate at the Kodiak. Amin gestured he couldn't hear what was being said, then waved goodbye and sat down. Khalid took that as his cue to bear back out to sea and did so. Amin kept an eye back on the dock and didn't see any signs of a water pursuit. Nassir went to the bow and started the signal lamp aimed back out to sea towards presumably the Butler's Dosh. Forty-five minutes later they could see the Butler's Dosh under way towards them. By now, the boarding drill was second nature and the Kodiak was stowed on deck quickly, the crew headed into the cabins for a change of clothing. Mohammed turned the Butler's Dosh due south at the cruising speed they would maintain for several hours before turning east towards the Dominican Republic. The bomb was in place successfully. Amin sent the coded message of complete success to The Hammer, receiving a rare "Well Done". Amir then tossed the satellite mobile phone overboard, along with all of the spare hardware related to the bomb: grapples, detonators, satellite VPN cards, leaving only the laptop. Over the course of this night, he and the crew would scrub all evidence of their business from the Butler's Dosh. The rush of adrenaline from narrowly escaping death had yet to diminish, and every kilometer they put between themselves and Buccaneer Cay would make them even safer.

• • •

Prince Zufar smiled as the amber LED on his detonator turned to a bright green. Mussa had arranged for the large multi-monitor display comprising the wall of the office to show a GPS map which updated when the detonator changed its reading. The location of the coordinate pin was centered on Buccaneer Cay in the Bahamas. Prince Zufar had become obsessed with the operation since The Hammer's visit. On another screen, a picture of the DuChard Duchess was displayed along with the stats concerning its size and capacity.

He picked up the telephone and made several calls, inviting a number of like-minded people to brunch at his home later in the morning. He wasn't taking no for an answer. Zufar's knew prudence dictated no one should know of his involvement, but the lure of notoriety among his contemporaries was too good to resist. In fact, he might be able to take credit for all of The Hammer's activities if he played this right. No one knew who The Hammer was, after all, and it might be interesting to have them think Zufar was the string puller. After all, he had acquired the device. The Hammer hadn't done anything remotely as useful, and he was only a Palestinian anyway. He would have to find a way to reach out to Amin, though and convince him to change his loyalties. Amin was the key to The Hammer's organization. Farid had some strategic vision but, without the arms and legs of his organization, he was a snake without fangs. He would have to be killed, of course, but that was an easily-managed trifle.

• • •

The security team at Buccaneer Cay reviewed video footage of the small Kodiak boat motoring into the west. The cameras had picked it up once it emerged from the ship's shadow, the silent gestures supported the guard's recollection of what was being said.

"Barnacles? Why would anyone want barnacles?" the security lead asked.

"Some people around here eat them, say they are pretty good. Most of the time they harvest them off of the dock pilings, crack them open and eat them cooked in butter or raw," the guard said.

"Why would they then motor out to sea after being caught?"

"I don't have any idea. Did we check if there were any boats waiting out there?"

"There are always boats out there. I have another theory, I'll bet these are just yachtsmen who came ashore for the free meals and decided to brazen it out." That had been a problem at Buccaneer Cay for a long time: freeloaders sneaking in to use the facilities with the ships' passengers. "Did we send a team to check out the perimeter of the ship for anything unusual?"

"Yes, sir. We didn't find anything. It was a small boat. I was mainly worried about graffiti, as it would be a pain to get paint crews out at this hour. I didn't find any."

"I'm going to recommend we go back to requiring a room key for using the facilities, but we both know that isn't going to happen. You know, for people with enough money to buy yachts they always seem to try to get free meals here. Asshats! I'll enter it into the incident log as closed."

The overlooked small device attached to the enormous ship signaled "All Systems Operational" over the satellite VPN channel and waited patiently for a command signal.

• • •

Justin and the Martyrs task force had endured a difficult week. The furor surrounding Nayla's murder had turned a titillating tale of politicians acting badly into something resembling a lynch mob baying for Administration heads. The Administration, of course, was pressuring the FBI to do something, anything, to show progress on the Martyrs case. The Director and his staff had started partipating in some of the task force meetings, which is never a good thing when you want to run an orderly investigation.

The forensic evidence from Nayla's extra apartment was mostly useless when it came to finding evidence which could lead them to the Martyrs. All the organic evidence had come from Jonny Ray. The contents of Nayla's purse hadn't yielded much of anything. There were recent magazines and a small packet of vacation tour brochures. Most were to adult venues in the Caribbean or Mediterranean, but one was for a DuChard Cruise Line. Somehow, Justin had never thought Nayla would want to be on a vacation with wall-to-wall children, but here it was. The edge of one of the pages even bent over as if marking a place.

That's strange, Justin thought, *it doesn't fit*. The page referred to a giant DuChard ship named the DuChard Duchess, based out of Port Canaveral, Florida. Suddenly Justin got a sinking sensation in his gut and the blood drained from his face. Picking up his phone he dialed Farid.

"Farid, Justin here. I have a question about Nayla. Did she ever mention wanting to go on a cruise vacation, a DuChard cruise vacation?"

"No way! That is the last place she would want to be on vacation. Those ships are huge, over 3,000 passengers but that just means there are even more poorly-behaved brat kids. I could see her on an adult cruise, like a Windjammer or something. But why do that when she could just leverage one of her yacht-owning buddies? Look, she loved her friend's children, but not all children." Farid trailed off sadly.

"Yeah, that's what I thought too. Thanks. How are you holding up?"

"Not too well, I still get really angry. I don't want to tell you how I feel about Jonny Ray. Every picture that hits the web just makes me want to ... nevermind. Why did you ask about cruises?"

"Nothing as of yet, just wanted follow up on something. Given Jonny Ray's exalted position, it probably isn't best to articulate rage, especially on a voice link," Justin said.

"Understood. Anything else?"

"No, thanks. Are you going to be around for the next week or so?"

"Maybe not. I was thinking of heading up to the cabin for a week or so. Might help me decompress from all that has happened."

Farid had a cabin deep in the Canadian Alberta forest, it took several hours of small road driving from the airport closest to it. Justin had been there once over the years. Due to the multiple airport connections necessary; you had to be serious about wanting to be there, plus stay a while to make the trip worthwhile. Farid went up every so often, mostly by himself.

"I can understand that, should be nice this time of year. Let's get together in a few weeks if things settle down."

"Sounds good. You're going to be busy for a while, though, especially since Jameson was put on suspension."

"What?"

"Yes, a reaction of management to his little trip to Riyadh. He did follow me around, but there wasn't much to see. I thought about inviting him and his CIA buddies in for dinner when I met with Prince Zufar, but that might have created an international incident."

"CIA?"

"Yes, I assume so anyways. It wasn't the local FBI guy at the embassy; I've met him in the past. So … congratulations, I think? No one ever inherits a kingdom when they expect it, it just kind of lands on them unannounced. Check that out internally, I'm sure the memo is working its way to you as we speak. Make sure they give you Section Chief and a salary bump, kemosabe. I've got to run, I'll let you know if I head north."

"See you," Justin said.

Farid nodded to himself in a satisfied way. Justin had taken the bait and put the pieces together himself. It was a calculated risk to place the brochures inside Nayla's extra apartment, but Farid had been pretty sure Justin would figure it out. He wanted Justin to rise within the FBI, and something like this would help make a place for him.

Justin had better get moving, though, the package was in place and only the whim of a megalomaniac Saudi prince decided when the DuChard Duchess would meet her end.

Justin, in the meantime, had walked upstairs and planted himself outside the Deputy Director's office, telling the executive assistant it was Martyrs-critical business. Twenty minutes later, Justin was permitted inside.

"This had better be important, Justin, there is a lot going on right now."

"Yes, sir. I'll get right to it. Remember the rumor with the Martyrs investigation that a small tactical nuclear device was in play, somewhere to the south?"

The Deputy Director nodded assent.

"I think I may have found a clue as to the target. In Nayla Kaldah's apartment, there were some travel brochures and not much else. One of the brochures involves a superb target for that size of weapon: a DuChard Cruise ship. A detail page was even folded down, on the ship DuChard Duchess which is based out of Port Canaveral. We've been looking for the terrorists to sneak a weapon past our border controls. What if they planted the device while a ship was in a Caribbean port, and blew it up as it approached Cape Canaveral? We know the security in the Bahamas is bad, really bad. Each of those ships can have as many as 4,000 passengers and up to 1,400 crew members. That would be quite a target. DuChard cruises are full of families and children, too, which these terrorists have not hesitated to attack."

"How did you come up with this line of reasoning again?"

"I was looking through the evidence gathered at Nayla Kaldah's extra apartment where she met with Jonny Ray Brown. I knew Nayla, she was a friend of my family. The Nayla I knew wouldn't have anything to do with a DuChard cruise. The other brochures were more indicative of her tastes, adult cruises and resorts. So I called a friend we had in common, Farid Royce, and asked him. He agreed that Nayla wouldn't be interested in a DuChard cruise. That is when I made the connection, sir."

"Farid Royce again? That man pops up like a bad penny on this investigation."

"Yes, it only seems that way because we all know each other. I knew Nayla through Farid. Farid's sister, Lindsey, was Nayla's roommate at Harvard Law. Farid and Nayla dated for a while but it never evolved towards marriage. They were all at the Election Night party which kicked off our pursuit of The Hammer. Farid actually helped us several times with insight on Muslim viewpoints and rumors. No question we have all been caught up in it from the very beginning," Justin said.

"We don't know that there is a bomb on the DuChard Duchess from this evidence - it is just a hunch at this point. Don't take it the wrong way, I'm very pleased that you made the connection from the data, but we don't want to be wrong on this. It wouldn't do to disrupt all those people's vacation if it turns out to be incorrect."

"Sir, how about I call DuChard Cruise Lines and speak to their security teams? I can outline the situation and see if there is anything to worry about before we stop everything to check," Justin suggested.

"I agree, go ahead and do that. Keep me in the loop, no matter the time if something material is discovered."

"I will, sir. One question, is this something to share with the White House Chief of Staff? I got a request for another briefing a few minutes ago."

"Normally I would say no, but we are talking a nuclear weapon. Brief them right away and their armed forces liaison, we're going to need their help if we have to move on the DuChard Duchess. Justin, you'd better get moving."

Justin nodded and walked briskly back to his desk. Stepping into an empty conference room, he placed a call to Sid Rosenbloom, expecting the assistant to pick up. To Justin's surprise, the Chief of Staff answered his own phone.

"Yes, Justin. What do you have for us?"

Justin outlined the same information he had just relayed to the Deputy Director for Sid. Sid asked some of the same questions, which Justin duly addressed.

"Justin, I am going to recommend a special forces liaison join your task force, immediately. I am sending over our own guy right now, Major Brad Spokes, until they can assign one for you. You might need to marshal armed forces assistance, having him there will shorten the time. In the meantime, contact the cruise line and keep me posted. I'll brief the President now."

Justin had to search for the DuChard Cruise Lines corporate offices, which turned out to be in Ocala, Florida. He worked through several administrative levels before he was put in contact with Gerald Kelton, Vice President of Operations.

"Hello Mr. Kelton, I'm FBI Special Agent Justin Simons. I wanted to speak to you about a possible terrorist threat against one of your cruise ships, the DuChard Duchess. Are you the right person?" Justin asked.

"Yes, security falls under my group. You said possible threat, what does that mean?"

"I lead the Joint Terrorism Task force that is investigating the Martyrs attacks, are you familiar with it?"

"Yes, we increased perimeter security at most of our facilities. But those were just snipers, right?" Kelton asked.

"Primarily, yes. But we've recently discovered some indirect evidence pointing to the DuChard Duchess. Combined with some previous information, we think it may be very serious."

"What kind of threat are we talking about?"

"A large explosive device set to destroy the ship. We don't have a timetable or method determined, but I did read up on the DuChard Duchess cruise routes and I'm thinking it would happen when docking in the Bahamas," Justin said. "Look, I know it isn't the best information, but I wanted to talk with you and understand if it is a possibility."

"We have pretty good security for what gets on the ship, even in the Bahamas. It would be very difficult to get a bomb on board through those controls. It works just like TSA at the airport; in fact it is TSA for domestic ports. The processes elsewhere mimic the controls. How big would the bomb be?"

"90 to 120 pounds, if it is what we think it may be. Tell me, Mr. Kelton, do your teams deploy neutron scanners at the dock perimeters in the Bahamas?"

"We use the large ones to scan luggage and any freight that is brought aboard. Is that what you meant?"

"No, I meant for the perimeter of the secured areas surrounding the ship when docked," Justin explained.

"No, we don't. That kind of thing is handled by the port authorities where we dock. In the United States, it would be handled by TSA and the like. In the Bahamas, it would be the local equivalent."

"How about Buccaneer Cay? That is a private island, isn't it?" Justin asked.

"Yes, we have a long term lease and manage it completely ourselves. But the only people allowed on the island are DuChard staff or cruise ship passengers. We don't have as much security there because the public isn't allowed in."

"So if a terrorist team infiltrated the island would there be a way for them to board the ship?"

"I'm not saying it is impossible, but it would be very hard to do. We still screen passengers trying to board the ship, and scan any luggage they bring back," Kelton explained.

"How about an approach from the sea? Are unauthorized people ever caught on the island?"

"You know, we have had a bit of trouble with people in yachts coming ashore and eating free dinners. The way the cruise works is that everything food or recreation related is free on the island for the cruise passengers. We got away from having the passengers provide a room key as identification, which is why some of the free-loader yacht people have been able to take advantage. Any time we find them, we boot them off, but we can't arrest anyone ourselves. By the time the Bahamas police get there they are usually gone."

"Is it possible a commando crew in a boat could approach the ship in the dark, attach a bomb to the hull and escape unnoticed?"

"I don't like to think about that, but maybe. One question, 100 pounds of TNT explosive attached to the outside hull of that ship would perhaps buckle the metal, but the large ship would barely notice that. How much explosive equivalent are we talking about?"

"Perhaps as much as 70 tons," Justin divulged.

"What the fuck! The only thing that could do that is something like an artillery nuke round. Are you saying there could be a nuclear bomb attached to one of my ships?"

"Mr. Kelton, we don't know anything for certain on that topic. We had a threat concerning one somewhere in the southern part of the country, and the ports have been on high alert for the last month. The Navy is patrolling more there as well. Getting a small nuclear device into the United States is very difficult, maybe so much so the terrorists decided to attack a United States vessel filled with innocent vacationers instead of trying to sneak past the barriers. There are a lot of passengers on these ships, right? More than 4,000? The 9/11 total death toll was barely over 2,000 people. How many would die if they attacked a cruise ship like the DuChard Duchess and it sank fast? Look, before we get carried away, can you verify the location of the DuChard Duchess now and increase security?"

"She just left Buccaneer Cay on her way back to Port Canaveral. She should dock there tomorrow morning. Agent Simons, you are giving me a heart attack thinking about a sea-based threat. I don't think we have a robust solution for it. We don't worry about it on the high seas because we are big and a lot faster than most ships, but at dock there might be ways to circumvent the security."

"Mr. Kelton, do you have security teams on Buccaneer Cay? Can you contact them and see if there were any unusual security-related events during this last stop? We can improve future security now that the threat is known, but if the terrorists have already made their move we need to think about the current passengers. I'll give you my direct contact information, can we reconvene after your discussion with the Buccaneer Cay team?"

"Yes, we'll do that. What should we do if there is a bomb in place?"

"We get the passengers off and the Armed Forces will try to disable it. Believe me, you will get all the support needed. Half of our Atlantic navy will be steaming at full-speed to get there. The satellite-based assets will be available as well, President Brown wants these people caught and stopped," Justin said.

"These ships cost close to a billion dollars to build, we're going to want to make sure the ship is saved too. I'll call the chairman after I'm done talking to the Buccaneer Cay folks. Let's chat again in about thirty minutes."

Justin hung up and went back to his desk. Sid Rosenbloom was true to his word - there was a note saying Major Spokes was waiting for him in the FBI lobby. Justin took the stairs two at a time.

"Major Spokes? I'm Justin Simons, thank you for coming so quickly. I'll sign you in and get a non-escort visitor's badge. There, let's head back up the task force bullpen."

Major Spokes was a young but hard-looking man. Being assigned to the White House meant a certain dress uniform standard had to be achieved, but Brad Stokes exceeded it looking like something out of a Marines recruiting brochure. At six foot and fit, he looked as though he could deal with a much larger Justin without even raising a sweat.

"Major Spokes, what level of security clearance do you have?"

"I'm cleared for Top Secret, and you call me Brad. Mr. Rosenbloom briefed me on some of what you're dealing with, and the DOD is forming a team as we speak to deal with the situation. It would help if we do a quick sit down to understand which bus might hit us first."

"Great, Justin is fine with me too. Let's go in this secure conference room, I spoke to the VP-Operations over at DuChard Cruise Lines, the DuChard Duchess just left Buccaneer Cay and will arrive in Port Canaveral tomorrow morning. He was pretty adamant that nothing could be brought onto the ship through the security checks, but was a lot less sure about whether a commando team could attach a device to the hull."

"You know, I am surprised as hell this hasn't happened already. There is a retired admiral who talked himself hoarse saying that American cruise ships are at risk from a terrorist attack, but not many paid attention to him. I guess this terrorist, The Hammer, did. Do we have any ideas where the device came from and what yield we're talking about?"

"We have no intel on source, other than the usual suspect of the defunct Soviet Union. As for yield, we're thinking it has to be man-portable so that limits it to around 70 tons."

"Let's see, that level of blast isn't very big. It would definitely sink the ship but not much else. Radiation kill zone would be something like half a kilometer. How big is that ship?"

"A little over a thousand feet."

"About the size of an aircraft carrier then. So you think the terrorists would move when the ship is in the Bahamas?"

"Yes specifically, and you should check me on this assumption, Buccaneer Cay the private island that DuChard has. I think that Nassau would be too busy to make it easy to slip in and out of. The one thing about these terrorists, they plan to survive their attacks, not be suicide troops. Here, let me project some pictures of Buccaneer Cay I pulled off of Wikipedia. What you think?"

Justin projected a few pictures of the dock and facilities. "According to the documentation, the ship always backs into port so they can just head straight out on departure, no tugs or anything."

"I can see some immediate concerns. If I were a wily terrorist with a small thermonuclear device, I would approach at night, in the shadow of the ship, attach it under the waterline, activate and leave. You could do it in a small commando craft with high-certainty at night. It would be almost impossible to stop someone using rebreather gear with an underwater propulsion sled. You could even do that in broad daylight and the security team might not see it happen. The only way to be sure is to have a dive team do a hull sweep before departure."

"The ship is at sea as we speak. I hope we caught this in time," Justin said. Just then Justin's phone rang, it was Gerald Kelton of DuChard Cruise Lines.

"Hello Mr. Kelton, I'm going to put you on speaker if that is alright. I have Major Spokes here with me."

"That's fine. Justin, I called you back so soon because there was an incident that was logged in Buccaneer Cay earlier tonight. A security guard saw three men wearing dark clothes, coming out from the front of the DuChard Duchess' bow. When hailed, they said they were after barnacles to eat, showed some, but when they were instructed to dock, they just headed out to sea. I've got divers in the water right now with lights, to see if there is anything suspicious down there. The security team thought it was probably personal yacht freeloaders like we discussed earlier, so they just logged the event. They did do an inspection circuit around the hull to see if there was any damage, but were mainly looking for graffiti, which happens sometimes."

"Mr. Kelton, Bradley Stokes here. The security guard didn't see anything other than the men and the barnacles?"

"No they didn't. The yachtsmen usually aren't dressed in black, though. I think the security team missed this one."

"At least they logged it, otherwise we wouldn't know about the situation. Mr. Kelton, what would it take to stop the ship at sea for a hull search by a dive team?" Stokes asked.

"We can be in touch anytime and make it happen. I don't think we have anyone aboard who can deal with a bomb, though."

"Yes, sir. We'll send the divers and the experts. I just don't want to set off a panic with all of your passengers. We don't know for sure there is an issue, but the last thing anyone needs here is a false alarm. Where is the ship right now?"

Gerald rattled off a pair of GPS coordinates which Brad wrote down. "Mr. Kelton, you need to stay available for the next few hours or someone does. I am going to scramble a team to meet the ship as fast as we can. Justin and I need to do some work right now, but we'll be back in touch shortly with the details."

"This is really happening, isn't it?" Kelton said in shock.

"Yes, sir. I think it is, but I hope to God I am wrong about that." Brad hung up the phone. "Justin, you need to head upstairs: this is the big one. I'll get on the phone with the Pentagon and White House. Let's move! We don't know how long we have."

Justin ran upstairs to the Director's office, "I need to see the Director immediately - Martyrs terrorists!" he said to the surprised executive assistant. He was admitted promptly into the Director's office. The Director had been meeting with the Deputy Director who stayed in place to hear what news Justin was bringing.

"Sirs, we think we know where the Martyrs put their nuclear weapon. We checked out the DuChard Duchess and it appears a team of commandos successfully did something earlier this evening then escaped out to sea. The ship left port on schedule, but we think the bomb is attached to the hull below the waterline. The White House sent over an armed forces liaison Major Stokes who is getting a dive team scrambled now, we're coordinating with DuChard management to set up a rendezvous," Justin said quickly.

"We're sure about this?" the Director asked.

"No sir. Evidence points to it, time is of the essence if true, and there's the possibility of a catastrophic result if we ignore it," Justin said.

The Director sat still for a moment, "I agree. Justin, you stick with the Major. We're going to head over to the White House and get the President's situation room spun up. Good work. We'll talk more after all of this is sorted out."

"Yes, sir." Justin bolted out of the office and headed for the stairs.

He burst into the conference room where Brad was talking in code bursts to someone on his phone. Brad raised a hand to indicate a need for silence, listening to the voices coming from the receiver. Justin's phone rang. He moved over into the far corner of the room and answered.

"Agent Simons? This is Gerald Kelton, I wanted to tell you the divers discovered something on the sea bed underneath the dock. Several rifle shells with Arabic script on the casings. Does that mean anything to you?"

Justin's stomach twisted, up until now, he could hope that somehow they were wrong about the DuChard Duchess. "Mr. Kelton, I am afraid it does. Have your team put those in a plastic bag and don't touch further, it is key evidence. What it means is the DuChard Duchess is confirmed as the target, and the bomb is almost certainly now attached to the ship. Hold onto the line, I need to confer with the Major."

Justin walked over to where the Major was pacing and sat down to wait. Major Stokes noticed and when there was a short break had his call wait for a moment.

Justin said quickly, "DuChard divers found Martyrs rifle shells on the sea bed underneath where the ship was docked: the Martyrs al-Sabra calling card."

Stokes nodded and turned back to his call with a vengeance. As an aside, "Justin get your things and meet me in front of the building, we're going on a trip."

Justin went back to Kelton, "Sir, we're headed for the DuChard Duchess right now. I'll need to call you back to coordinate. Navy divers will probably arrive first on scene." Justin hung up as he scrambled to collect his laptop and headed for the front door.

Washington, DC was quiet at that time of night, not knowing the horrible event in progress. Justin called Jan, "Jan, something big has come up and I won't be coming home tonight." She wasn't pleased but wished him luck and demanded he stay safe. After all this was over, he'd make it up to his family somehow.

Justin saw Major Stokes come running out just as a black SUV pulled around the corner with its lights flashing. "Here's our ride, Simons. Get in!" Stokes said.

They scrambled into the SUV which headed full speed with sirens engaged back towards the White House. The SUV slowed slightly as the barriers were lowered then sped again to the White House helicopter pad. Sitting there was a Marine Sikorsky SH-3 Sea King with the rotor already turning.

"That's our ride, let's go," Major Stokes said.

Justin and Brad climbed aboard, and the crewmen had the door closed immediately. The floor moved as the helicopter took off, headed for Andrews Air Force Base. Justin selected an empty seat and took in his surroundings. Sid Rosenbloom and a Navy admiral sat next to each other. Stokes saluted the admiral and started to brief him on the situation. It was clear the admiral would be taking command authority for the armed forces. There wasn't much opportunity to speak as the ride was quite noisy and short. The helicopter approached the end of the Andrews Air Force base runway, where it appeared Air Force 1 was waiting. Justin corrected himself, the President wasn't here, so the plane was just one of several used to transport her. The Sikorsky flared and landed gently on the tarmac. Crew members ran forward to open the doors for disembarking. The admiral and Sid walked briskly out of the helicopter and boarded the waiting Boeing 747 aircraft.

"Come on, Simons, let's go. They decided to use this aircraft at President Brown's insistence, as it was the fastest way to get us all down to Florida," Spokes said as he climbed the boarding stairs into the well-appointed plane. The plane was full of Secret Service and different flavors of military. Justin followed Spokes over to an empty seat and sat down.

"Why all the Secret Service? The Chief of Staff has a smaller detail doesn't he?" Justin asked idly.

"Forgot to mention, Vice President Rodriquez is on-board as the President's proxy. Don't worry, he won't get anywhere near the action. They are going to set up a command center at Patrick Air Force Base, just south of Port Canaveral." Spokes said. "Good news, AWACS is already in the air over the theater of operations. The Navy divers are in-route to the DuChard Duchess and should be in the water within 15 minutes. By the way, the Navy has assumed command of the Duchess for the duration of the emergency. The DuChard Corporation executives will be allowed to observe and recommend, but they are not running the show."

"Truth be told, they are probably relieved, because now the liability for what happens rests with the United States Government," Justin said.

"That's right, I'm talking to a lawyer! If there is a bomb on that ship, we don't want to spend time arguing about doing something. We can say sorry if we're wrong later."

Justin was pressed back into his comfortable seat as the plane took off. A 747 is a fairly fast plane when cruising, but in a hurry the Presidential fleet contains the fastest passenger planes in the world. It was about 800 miles to Patrick Air Force Base - their flight time would be approximately an hour and a half.

Justin and Brad were called into the conference room after takeoff to brief the high-octane team assembled. Vice President Rodriquez, Sid Rosenbloom, various high level military personnel, and the Washington-based participants on the conference bridge. The FBI Director made it clear in his comments that Justin was the person responsible for the conclusion there was a nuclear weapon in play. Sid and Brad looked at Justin with something like sympathy in their eyes. This one was so risky the Director didn't even want the credit if correct. *Politics*, Justin thought to himself.

Soon, the conference room began receiving night video feeds from the helicopters holding position over the DuChard Duchess, which had stopped its main drive using only its side-thrusters to stay under control. The Navy divers dropped out of the helicopter four to each side of the huge ship and began their survey of the ship's hull.

The diver closest to the bow on the starboard side found a device almost immediately. He began taking high-resolution video of the device which was fed to the tender helicopters, to the AWACS and onto Air Force 2. By that time the rest of the divers had been recalled except for several that came to assist. As one diver shot video, another held up a portable radiation detector next to the casing, with positive results. Several experts in the conference room began loudly debating which warhead was involved, but all agreed that it was Russian in origin.

"What is that taped to the hull?" Sid asked.

The question was relayed to the divers and back. "Sir, it looks like a telecommunications uplink, satellite probably. It seems to lead into the detonator bundle."

"Admiral, we need to get the passengers off of that ship immediately. How quickly can that be done?" Sid said.

"It depends. If we do it as an evacuation drill and try to maintain calm it might take as long as an hour and a half. If a panic ensues people will get hurt and it will take longer. We have ships in-bound to pick up passengers but they won't be there for a couple more hours. The life rafts will have to do until then."

"We don't know how long until the device will explode, do we?" Vice President Rodriquez asked.

"No sir, we don't. It might be on a timer, it might be satellite-activated, or it might blow if we tamper with it."

"Lucy, are you there?"

"Yes, Michael," President Lucy Brown said.

"I recommend we immediately evacuate passenger mothers with children first, getting them out of the potential blast zone. Then the rest of the passengers would follow. I think that is different from the way cruise line evacuation drills operate. What do you think?" the Vice President asked.

"I agree. Make it happen," President Brown ordered.

"Madame President, I recommend we deploy 50 Marines on board to maintain order during the evacuation. This can get ugly and we're separating families," the Admiral spoke up.

"Agreed. Sid and Michael, I'm going to monitor the situation from here, but I trust you to make the right decisions being on-site. Call me in on tie-breakers or escalations."

"Yes, Ma'am," the Vice President and Chief of Staff chorused.

"Admiral, please get the Marines aboard immediately. Have the Captain of the Duchess prepare for full evacuation, save for skeleton crew. Let's get the evacuees a minimum of a mile away from the ship. Don't touch the bomb until the evacuation is complete. Contact the AWACS and see if there is any way to see what telecommunications link is being used by the device. I want to know who it is talking to," Vice President Rodriquez said.

The night vision views of the ship and growing presence of military assets gave the scene a surreal touch as the 747 powered its way through the night skies towards Florida.

• • •

Prince Zufar went to his bed very pleased with plans for the next day. He had a number of guests arriving for a mid-morning brunch during which he planned to detonate the bomb in full sight of those attending. The Prince was an early riser, usually waking no later than 5 a.m., and this Friday morning was no different. Walking through his bedroom to the attached marble and gold bathroom, he noticed that he must have left the detonator in his office. For some reason, he had to see it before anything else. He walked into his office wearing only pajamas and saw that the detonator still showed two green lights. Glancing up at the television monitor, he noticed the GPS tracker was close by where it had been when he went to bed. Thinking there must be a mistake, he sat down to check the GPS coordinates being reported by the device.

A wave of panic gripped the prince, the GPS coordinates were current according to the detonator. The Hammer had provided a mobile telephone number for emergencies, to be used once, but Prince Zufar decided to wait a few minutes to see if the numbers updated. In the meantime, he didn't want the detonator out of his sight until it was ready to be used so he took it with him into the restroom.

The prince was a vain man. His morning ritual went far beyond a shave and quick shower. As he was in the midst, he rang for Mussa who appeared as though he were anticipating the call.

"Mussa, the ship's GPS coordinates look as though they didn't update overnight. Take a look at the laptop and make sure the GPS feed is working properly before I'm done here."

Mussa nodded silently and went to his task. There were several network technicians who had been brought in to automate the map update, and Mussa summoned them.

Prince Zufar later appeared in the doorway of his office resplendent in his thawb of flawless white cotton and red checked keffiyeh. "Well?"

"Your Highness, the GPS update appears to be working perfectly. The ship seems to have stopped. If you'll notice, we plotted the ship's course on the map and it has been in the same place for the last hour or so," Mussa explained.

"Why would they stop?"

"Mechanical trouble or they may have found the device and are trying to evacuate the ship."

"Clear the room, except for you Mussa. Get me a coffee service, my usual," Prince Zufar ordered.

Mussa gestured that the technicians should leave the room, then proceeded to prepare the Prince's coffee.

Prince Zufar took up his telephone and dialed the special number which had been provided.

A slightly mechanical voice answered, "Yes?"

"The GPS has stopped its progress, what has happened?" the Prince asked.

"I would expect mechanical difficulties, or they may have found the device. Is the GPS changing at all, like turning a circle, or is it stopped completely?"

"It has stopped completely; it hasn't changed for almost an hour."

"They found the device, and are trying to evacuate the ship."

"What should I do? I wanted this for my brunch entertainment!"

"You could do nothing. In such case, when they tamper with the device, it will detonate. Or you could choose to send the signal yourself, and might catch them before the evacuation is complete. A full evacuation will take over two hours at night for full safety. They will remove the women and children first, then the rest of the passengers."

"What if I choose to cancel the detonation?"

"Alas, my brother, it is not an option," The Hammer advised.

"Quite right, nor would I want it to be. Watch the news, Brother, and see what can be accomplished in Allah's name."

"Allahu Akbar!" The Hammer hung up.

"Mussa, get the studio ready for a recording immediately. After my coffee, I will make history."

Mussa placed the coffee service convenient to the Prince and hurried out to prepare the video studio.

After ten minutes, the prince picked up the detonator and made his way into the studio. The lights were warmed up and bright.

"We'll forego the makeup, Mussa. Just ready the cameras." Prince Zufar tucked the end of his keffiyeh across his nose and mouth, leaving only a view of his burning dark eyes.

"Start the cameras now," the Prince said.

"Today, the faithful strike another blow to the infidel, one larger than the blessed events of 9/11. From the other side of the world, Allah's faithful reach out and erase them as though they never existed. This device, is the key to Allah's fire, which cleanses the earth. The United States is shown as impotent to stop the will of Allah, running after the Maryrs like hungry dogs, but never catching their meal. Allahu Akbar!" Prince Zufar slowly removed the cage protecting the detonate button and then pressed the button with an exaggerated motion. With a signal to Mussa, the recording was stopped.

The signal worked its way through the multiple proxy servers dedicated to confusing its trail, electronic bits traveling thousands of kilometers in several seconds to their final destination and holy oblivion.

• • •

Farid knew that he must dispose of the burner phone as soon as possible, but given the news, he should provide some guidance to Amin before so doing. Activating his voice filter, he called Amin's satellite phone. It rang many times before being picked up.

"Hello?" Amin's voice over the sound of engines at full throttle on a swelling sea.

"Input. Device probably detected, suggest routing through #2, and a Viking funeral."

"Understood. Out." Amin hung up the satellite phone.

"Mohammed, set course for Nassau, Bahamas," Amin said.

Mohammed didn't ask any questions, and set the new course as ordered.

"We've had a change in plan, due to the device being discovered early. We need to disperse as soon as possible and it would take too long to get to the Dominican Republic on board Butler's Dosh. I'll drop you three off with cash for the airport, and ditch the boat somewhere safe," Amin said.

"I can help you ditch it, and the other two can go to the airport first. The task is something which should be done with two people," Mohammed countered.

"Yes I agree. I'm going to make a dead man's throttle on a seaward course, then come ashore in the Kodiak," Amin explained.

"Are you planning to scuttle after a few hours? I can rig something that opens valves below-deck."

"You've read my mind. We'll just leave the Kodiak wherever we land. All of our current flights are out of Dominican Republic, but we can get short hop flights there first thing tomorrow morning. Let's get Khalid and Nassir set up, we're only an hour out of Nassau."

Amin knew that the United States military had already re-tasked spy satellites to track all ocean traffic within 500 km of Buccaneer Cay and that the Butler's Dosh was not fast enough to evade being detected. It would be a few hours, though, before anything would be done. Hopefully it would be enough time to make their escape.

Mohammed piloted the boat into an area where private yachts docked for dinners along the Nassau waterfront, setting Khalid and Nassir ashore with their belongings in hand. Both were more than capable of catching a cab to the airport, and primed to state they were finishing a fishing trip prior to returning to work in the Dominican Republic. If Amin and Mohammed didn't make it back in time, they also knew how to buy the requisite short-haul flight tickets. They would say the boat developed trouble which is why they needed a one-way flight. Both slung their bags over the shoulders and waved as they headed out to find a ride to the airport.

Mohammed backed the Butler's Dosh expertly out of the docking area, heading back towards the open seas east of the island. The Kodiak was already prepared, with Mohammed and Amin's small bags as well as having a full battery charge. Since the small boat did not need to return to the Butler's Dosh, they could leave even further offshore which would make the whole exercise more safe. There was a risk of missing the port, but Amin's mobile phone had a full charge and the GPS would stand-in for bad navigating. The Butler's Dosh itself had an autopilot option where it would correct heading automatically. More problematic was the opening of the stop-cocks after several hours of heading out to sea. Mohammed had a solution for the problem by repurposing a valve actuator attached to a timer. When the time elapsed, the valve would open and the Butler's Dosh would sink.

Farid had specified a Viking's Funeral which meant a fiery end, but Amin had overruled that as calling too much attention to the boat. The watching satellites would definitely see a fire at sea. They would still see the Butler's Dosh anyway as one of many boats, but then it would simply vanish by sinking. All in all, a better result. The Hammer was always quite reasonable when field teams made good changes to plans, but Allah help them if the plan was damaged by the change.

The next hour was spent watching the ships grow fewer and fewer on the horizon. In a perfect world, there wouldn't be any witness to the abandoning of ship. But it was a dark night, and with the lights down it would be hard to see the change. Amin laughed to himself and thought the only fly in the ointment would be if the Butler's Dosh inadvertently set a collision course without responding to a hail. It was unlikely, but stranger things happened on occasion.

The time came for the parting of the ways. Amin set the autopilot to half-speed, helped Mohammed launch the Kodiak off of the back of the ship, secured by a line being towed. Mohammed went below deck to set the timer for the stop-cock then came up. Amin pulled the line close to the stern of the Butler's Dosh until Mohammed could jump directly into the boat. Then Mohammed put the Kodiak under his control and maneuvered close so Amin could clamber aboard with the tow rope. The Kodiak changed course back towards Nassau, as the Butler's Dosh headed deeper into the night's darkness.

• • •

The Marine platoon had boarded the DuChard Duchess almost immediately after being given the green light and stood ready to facilitate the orderly evacuation of passengers. The Captain of the ship called a normal lifeboat drill and all of the passengers were staged at their respective evacuation stations. Why the ship was being evacuated had not been shared with the full crew or the passengers, so belligerent half drunk passengers were a bit of a problem. The Marines were in no mood to trifle, they did know why they were there. If a few drunk passengers needed to be knocked unconscious to make it happen, the Marines knew how to do it. The first problem was separating the mothers and children from their fathers. Again, however, the Marines were not inclined to debate the issue.

The first lifeboats loaded with women and children launched within fifteen minutes of the order being announced. The crew member assigned to each lifeboat was told to head West for one to two miles and hold station with the other lifeboats. From the helicopter videos that Justin observed, it looked like a sea of corks bobbing up and down with the swells, but each cork represented more than 150 people safe. Approximately fifty-five percent of the passengers were minor children. Forty-five minutes after the announcement, all of the children were safely evacuated with a female parent. Now lifeboats with the remaining parents started to make their way towards the rally point. At seventy-five minutes, all of the remaining parents had been evacuated.

The 747 landed at Patrick Air Force Base to a fleet of waiting vehicles ready to transport everyone to the mobile command center which had been activated for the crisis. Vice President Rodriquez, Sid Rosenbloom, and their attendant military coterie took the first available car. Justin found himself fidgeting from being momentarily out-of-touch with what was happening 150 miles away.

Brad noticed Justin's unease, "Justin, don't waste time worrying, we'll be in the situation center shortly. I suspect you and I will be catching a helicopter to the scene afterwards. I checked progress of our military assets separately a few minutes ago. There is a Coast Guard Cutter which should be getting close. It isn't big enough to take in all of the passengers, but they can keep the lifeboats together and provisioned."

"How are we going to get all of those people out of there? The fast boats don't really have all that much extra room do they?"

"No they don't. Now if we had an empty cruise ship or even a half-empty one it would help a lot. We're checking now whether there are any cruise ships docked in Miami or Port Canaveral who could beat us up here, but if not there are several battle groups headed this way and should arrive within 8 hours. There will be at least one hospital ship which can hold quite a few people as well. It will be midnight shortly, so we will have a real problem staying on top of the evacuees the seven hours until first light. Here's our ride, get in."

Justin checked his mobile phone, "Shit, someone already has the story of an evacuation under Marine guard. One of the passengers must have uploaded it before comms were shut down," Justin said.

"Or the passenger had a satellite phone. Relax, nothing to be done about it yet. The technicians are still debating whether they should attempt to disarm the device or interrupt the satellite link. Any thoughts given what you know about the terrorists?"

"I think the terrorists would have anti-tamper provisions in place, given their sophistication. Who knows, breaking the link might set it off as well. Any luck on figuring out which satellite network is being used?" Justin asked.

"Yes, Iridium, the low-earth satellite constellation. Our guys have already contacted them and we'll find out where it terminates. It would be ideal to track it to the active user, but it will take some time."

"These guys are pros with proxy servers, they'll have several hops in places we can't easily access. We might want to get our guys off the ship as soon as possible. If the Martyrs hit the detonate command the whole contingent will get wiped out."

"The Marines will pull out once the passengers are fully evacuated. The crew can handle their own exit without traffic cops. Most of the passengers should be off by now." The van arrived outside a concrete-walled building with metal doors. Justin and the rest clambered out of the van into a large room with low lighting. Large television monitors carried the scenes from the DuChard Duchess and the small fleet of evacuation boats.

"What is the status of the passenger evacuation?" Vice President Rodriquez asked.

After a few seconds of relayed communications, the answer came back from the Marine Platoon Leader, "We're down to the last 600 passengers, I gave the crew a green light to launch theirs in parallel. It won't interfere with the last four passenger life boats."

"Thank you, good job to you and your team! Admiral, maybe the Marines should be redeployed to the lifeboats afterwards. The passengers are going to have to sit still for a while longer correct?"

"Yes, sir. We'll do just that as soon as the last passengers are off."

"Just ten more minutes and we'll be in much better shape to deal with next steps," the Admiral said to Vice President Rodriquez.

They didn't have ten minutes. The signal which had started in Riyadh several seconds earlier was sprinting through the last network on its way to the DuChard Duchess. Upon receipt the detonator closed the circuit and the night was lit by a small sun.

Pandemonium broke out in the Patrick Air Force Base situation room as all of the video feeds died as one. Technicians scrambled to radio the circling helicopters to restore contact. Almost immediately, radio voice traffic was reestablished, but there was no video feed.

"Task Force, what just happened? This is Vice President Rodriquez."

"Sir, the device has detonated. I repeat, the device has detonated. We lost all of the video cameras due to the EMP blast, but the radio and helicopter electronics are better shielded. No helicopters lost as of yet, but there was a wave generated by the exploding ship. We'll need to see how the life boats are holding up. I saw the explosion, it seemed to lift the front bow of the ship into the air but then it collapsed back down. The ship is sinking fast, only a little stern is left. We've lost contact with the Marines and the Bridge of the ship."

"The first priority are the passengers and civilians, please determine their situation as soon as possible."

The pilot sounded shaken, but acknowledged the commands.

The admiral walked over to a television monitor which had a map showing the progress of the various battle groups. "We need to break some speed records getting help out to the scene. Any suggestions?"

"Sir, the carrier group is about three hours out, but their aircraft can get here earlier. No luck on the cruise ship option. The Coast Guard will be here in a half-hour. There is a nuclear sub in-bound which should arrive in about an hour."

"Are there any merchant marine vessels nearby?"

"Send out a Mayday call and see if we can't get some help. We just presumably lost a Marine platoon, scramble more troops. I want one or two Marines on each lifeboat until it is picked up," the Admiral ordered.

"Michael? Do we have any eyes on the status of the lifeboats?" President Brown asked.

"No, Madame President other than the helicopters who are in the process of rounding them up," Vice President Rodriquez said.

"I'm going to address the nation within the next 30 minutes to break news of the attack. It would be helpful to know how many survivors were extracted successfully. You have Special Agent Simons on site, correct? Send him on a helicopter to see it with his own eyes. Sid, see if Brad Stokes can go as well. If it wasn't for the work of those two gentlemen, we would have lost everyone."

"Yes, Madame President," Sid and the Admiral chorused.

Justin felt the eyes of the entire command center staring at him, and didn't know how he felt about the notoriety. If he had made the connection an hour earlier, more would have been saved. Right now, there were too many questions about the blast to know what really occurred. Was the detonation due to inadvertent tampering? Was it due to a timer elapsing? Was a remote detonate command given? No one could say at this juncture.

Brad had been speaking in low tones with the Admiral, and gestured Justin to approach. "They are sending a fast helicopter for us right now, I would take this opportunity to use a restroom as there isn't any on the chopper. We'll be gone 4-6 hours."

Justin ran off to do so, pulling out his mobile phone and dialing. A sleepy Jan answered the telephone. "Jan, sorry to wake you, honey, but I will be out of touch for the next few hours. You're going to hear some really bad news on the television, but I wanted to tell you I am safe and should remain so."

"OK," Jan muttered, still half asleep.

"I love you, go back to bed."

"I love you too," she said as Justin closed the connection.

Justin finished up and headed back to find Major Spokes. An approaching deep rumble was heard as multiple helicopters approached the building to land in the empty parking lot.

"There's our ride, let's go!" Brad said.

Justin followed Brad out, ducking under the rotating blades of the seagoing helicopters and climbing aboard. As Justin and Brad found their seats, Brad motioned to the crew to take off. They closed the door promptly and the twin turbines began to whine as the helicopter rose into the night air. Before long the aircraft was positioned for maximum speed on a direct vector to the site of the explosion, 150 miles from Patrick AFB.

"Will we be able to hear the President's address during the flight?" Justin shouted over the noise to Brad.

"Yes, but no need to shout, hold on." Brad got up and talked to a crewman who provided two can-earphone headsets with patch cable. Brad showed Justin how to plug in and set the channel. The headsets canceled most of the ambient noise and allowed the two to semi-privately converse without affecting helicopter operations.

"This day is both a success and a complete debacle," Brad said. "How are we going to catch the assholes who just blew up the Duchess?"

"Our best lead will be the digital trail back to the terrorists, as well as some old fashioned surveillance analysis. If we can compare satellite imagery to track the terrorist's boat, we may be able to get the crew who planted the bomb. But it has to be done quickly, we're focused right now on saving the passengers' lives, but the terrorists are running. We have to get them before they can vanish into obscurity among the millions of other travelers. We have less than eight hours to do that. The good news is that we know they were on a boat, and it takes time to get to an operating airport. The closest ones would be Freeport, Marsh Harbor, and Nassau; all of those could be reached by now, but will not open for flights until morning. We need to get people on the ground in time to catch them," Justin said.

"Does Bahamas have a fast-track way to coordinate permissions? You're going to have to get people approving this right now. Should we set up a call to anyone while we're in route?"

"Yes, here is the mobile number for the Deputy Director, he can manage getting that aspect of things kicked off. Frankly, that kind of diplomatic activity is above my pay grade anyway," Justin said.

"I don't know, the President knows your name, that can't be all bad for the next review board." Brad handed the telephone number to a waiting communications specialist who started setting up the call. Within minutes, the specialist held up four fingers to indicate a channel 4 setting, and Justin began having the same conversation with the Deputy Director.

At the speed the aircraft was moving, there was little to see in the darkness of the night. Forty minutes in, there were lights on the sea just over the horizon. As they approached the scale of the devastation became clear. The DuChard Duchess was nowhere to be seen, but the sea was littered with debris which floated above the site of her demise. A small fleet of lifeboats bobbed a little over a mile from the site. Helicopters were engaged circling the site in a futile search for additional survivors.

"Brad, is it my imagination or do the lifeboats look to be bobbing around uncontrolled?" Justin asked.

"If I had to guess, I think their electronics got fried by the EMT blast and they might not have propulsion. Normally, there is little to no reason for lifeboats to have shielded electronics. The Coast Guard Cutter should be able to take them in hand. Look, they appear to be alright, but I'm not sure on the boat count."

Justin could see the Coast Guard cutter shepherding the large flotilla of lifeboats, keeping track with spotlights and crew. As long as the situation was kept under control on-board the lifeboats, the evacuees should come through their experience relatively safe. He could only imagine what the children were doing cooped up in the lifeboats. In a normal world they would be sleeping, but somehow he doubted their ability to do so with the ongoing noise of helicopters surrounding them.

Justin asked the communications technician to reconnect him with the Deputy Director. He briefed the FBI executive on what he was seeing as he circled the area.

"Brad, how deep is the bottom here?" Justin asked.

After conferring with the navigator, "About 500 feet, too deep for standard dive gear. When the sub gets here we'll ask them to determine if there is any indication of survivors in the wreckage of the Duchess. It's possible someone could survive in a closed-bulkhead section which has some air, but it is unlikely that they'll survive the radiation exposure. Regardless, the sub has a lot better gear to detect human activity rather than just sounds of mechanical wreckage or adjustment. But, Justin, the clock is definitely ticking. We'll need to get dive teams down pronto, if we're to have any chance of an extraction. Speaking of the sub, I think they've arrived."

Justin relayed the news to the Deputy Director, then released the channel. The sub had surfaced about a mile away from the flotilla and was proceeding there carefully on the surface. Soon the issue of trapped survivors would be determined, one way or the other.

• • •

The President looked into the cameras from the Oval Office.

"My fellow Americans, I come before you now with news of a horrible terrorist attack connected with the Martyrs al-Sabra faction. At approximately 12:10 AM Eastern Time, a small nuclear device was detonated against the DuChard Duchess cruise ship, offshore approximately 150 miles from its home port in Florida. The ship itself has been sunk and efforts are being made to determine whether survivors are still trapped aboard. A significant number of passengers were evacuated prior to the explosion and are safely being recovered."

"The terrorists appear to have attached a device to the ship at one of the foreign ports of call in the Bahamas. We are actively searching for the terrorists and hope to apprehend them alive. We have asked the Bahamian Government for their assistance, which was granted a few minutes ago."

"As horrendous as this event is, it would have been much worse but for the actions of a few brave people. The FBI investigation into the Martyrs campaign of terror provided a key clue as to the target. A combined team of military and FBI resources, led by the Vice President Michael Rodriquez himself, determined that there was an unexploded device upon the ship. Working quickly, almost all of the passengers, including a large number of children, were safely evacuated from the ship before the explosion. A full platoon of Marines, 50 soldiers, were lost as they stayed aboard the DuChard Duchess in order to ensure saving lives. The Navy divers who were monitoring the underwater device were also lost. The ship's crew were to be among the last evacuated, and most of them are presumed lost. We have taken a great blow this morning, but, as always, American heroes stepped up without regard for their own safety to protect their fellow citizens."

"We will know more in the coming hours. Hospital facilities in Florida are being prepared to receive survivors, and U.S. Navy and Coast Guard ships have arrived on the scene."

"Please take a moment to join me in silent prayer for those who lost their lives in this brazen attack against innocents." Lucy bowed her head in silent prayer for a few seconds before continuing.

"This Administration, and indeed our entire government, will not rest until the persons or states responsible are brought to justice. Time will not detract from our full resolve. To those responsible, there is no escape, there is no forgetting, there is no pardon. We will find you."

"Finally, my fellow Americans, do not assume all Muslims are responsible for this act of terror. I am certain there were Muslims among the lost heroes this day. I am certain there are Muslims who were saved. In this crisis, we were all Americans. Keep it in mind as we search for the real villains, the Martyrs al-Sabra terrorist faction."

"Stay strong, and may God bless America in our time of suffering."

Justin listened to a replay of the President's address as the helicopter continued to circle the site. The sub had submerged shortly after arrival to listen for any sign of trapped survivors within the wreckage on the sea floor. It had been a mere hour and half since the ship went down, debris was still popping up to the surface to sit sullenly with other odd pieces of buoyant trash. Justin could only imagine how the wreckage appeared on the sea floor. Strangely, he kept thinking of television documentaries about the Titanic, where the back half of the ship settled in a different location than the bow. The last video footage and eye witness accounts of the Duchess suggested the stern was relatively intact when it went underwater.

The eastern skyline had started to pale, when the helicopter crew reported they would be refueling off of a ship within the approaching carrier group. A small container ship was also standing by outside of the exclusion zone refereed by the Coast Guard cutter.

"Brad, any chance we can get the helicopter to head over to Buccaneer Cay for the evidence DuChard Security has on hand? I'm hoping there is some photographic evidence. The radar signature data probably went down with the Duchess," Justin asked.

"Not a bad idea. We might want to take some techs along also, see if there is any residual radiation. I'll put it to the Admiral," Major Spokes said.

A few minutes later he nodded affirmatively and sat back down next to Justin. "We might be in luck on the satellite imagery front. Evidently there was an ongoing wide area drug-trafficking-related satellite surveillance of Bahamian waters, trying to track suspected drug boats for DEA. I think we can use it to find where the terrorists went, but the timeline from the DuChard security logs will be critical to help identify the ships. As soon as we're fueled, we'll head over to Buccaneer Cay."

• • •

The morning brunch had been a mixed success. Servants had seen to all of the guests being well-fed. The conversations remained light and without much substance, certainly nothing to indicate why they had been importuned to attend. As they sipped dark coffee, a restive strain permeated the room.

"My brothers, you are doubtless wondering what made my invitation more important than usual. Wonder no more, follow me into the theatre room. We have something to view which all here should see first," Prince Zufar said.

The men stood up, adjusted their garments and filed into the small movie amphitheater located down the hallway. Prince Zufar himself directed traffic, seating persons according to his own desires. The servants followed up with another round of fresh coffee, served to each seat, and dimmed the lights. Prince Zufar stood at the front of the theatre where he could easily see the faces of his guests. Unknown to the guests, the entire room was being videotaped for the Prince's future viewing pleasure.

"First, we have a short announcement from the Martyrs al-Sabra," Prince Zufar said.

The short video that Prince Zufar had recorded earlier that morning played. Everyone there knew Zufar was the person hidden behind the scarf, as his features were familiar to all and his voice had not been modified in any way.

The guests conversed with each other in a low buzz, but without any overt excitement. Zufar smiled, "Now, we have a breaking announcement from the President of the United States."

Prince Zufar watched his contemporaries reactions as they listened to President Brown's speech, given less than an hour earlier, indeed while all were eating their meal. The persons who did not understand English were informed by those who could of the President's message.

Prince Zufar signaled for the room lights to be raised. Holding the detonator aloft in his right hand, "My friends, only you know the truth of these events, and I am holding the instrument of the infidels' loss. I imagine you will tell your descendants the story as a cherished memory, one you were a part of, when the struggle against the infidel is won."

Now the room erupted with shock, elation, fear; the full panoply of emotions within a few seconds. The guests crowded around the Prince, congratulating him and wanting to hold the detonator themselves. Prince Zufar hadn't noticed before, but it had the same inscription that was emblazoned on every rifle shell casing. The Prince chortled to himself. If it hadn't been there already, he would have had to get Mussa to do it. Prince Zufar was already getting very comfortable with people thinking he was The Hammer.

"Please continue to partake of my hospitality, while I speak a bit on ways to take advantage of the situation when the United States markets open today. As I had some prior knowledge of these events, I had my financial proxies sell many Put options on DuChard's and other cruise companies' stocks during the last two weeks. I also had them borrow thousands of shares which I immediately sold short. For a limited time, I will sell the investment positions to those in this room for a quite reasonable finder's fee. Come with me into my office suite."

As the crowd approached the office, it became clear that Prince Zufar's entire finance team was waiting patiently behind multiple desks ready to make sales. Above, a wall covered with computer monitors detailed the positions in play and available to guests. Some of the attendees who were quick studies, immediately sat down and started to haggle with the finance men over the right fees to assume the positions. As deals were made, the overhead monitors showed a reducing inventory. Greed gripped the rest of the group as they scrambled to get their own portion of what was sure to be a killing.

Prince Zufar stood back and watched as the deals were closed. He stood to make tens of millions from these sales alone, but would make hundreds of millions in the next round with much less risk. He knew sharing the proceeds today would commit everyone in the room to his side. Saudis, no matter how wealthy, never forget someone who has made them money. As Zufar had expected, the demand exceeded availability, but everyone attending had been able to capture something. The guests were given printouts of their positions, and the financial men were given personal notes signed by the guests for the purchases.

"My friends, this is the beginning of what I hope will be an ongoing concern. As usual, I expect your notes to be paid within four hours; the market positions will be released to each of you once your payment has cleared. My team will be working into the evening. If the

Americans close trading on these stocks today, they will still trade on international exchanges for much reduced prices, or you can wait until you think the time is right. This concludes our time this morning, thank you for coming," Prince Zufar said.

The long process of farewells took place, with more than one of his guests offering to purchase any positions on which other guests might default. Prince Zufar nodded solemnly and had Mussa take note. The farewells were long and flowery, full of praise for the genius of Prince Zufar, and sincere gratitude for being allowed to participate. Finally, the last guest had departed and Zufar was alone with his staff. The finance lead tallied the net proceeds as exceeding 40 million dollars, which was an excellent return for the time spent. The finance team had no idea why the prices of cruise ship company stocks would be impacted, but would soon enough as the news worked its way around the world.

Prince Zufar chuckled as he considered his next move where he, as a supporter of free and open markets, would step in to purchase large quantities of depressed shares in order to stabilize the markets. It always worked for Warren Buffett, in essence getting a medal for buying sound companies on the cheap and making billions. Why would anyone be a mere terrorist? The concept of a waiting paradise in the afterlife for devout Muslims was designed to keep lower-caste Muslims in their place within the earthly sphere. Zufar preferred to attain paradise in both realms, why should he settle for less?

Friday The 16ᵗʰ

"..America has never been struck a blow such as this, and to consider how much worse it could have been had all the passengers been aboard. There is a sense on the street, Americans must pull together, first to comfort the survivors and then to punish the responsible parties. There will be a reckoning..."

Farid Monsour al Haj for World News Corporation

Most of the United States woke clueless of the President's early morning broadcast but, President Brown also issued a Presidential Alert to all mobile phones in the United States. The morning news shows started broadcasting footage of evacuees being retrieved by the Navy and several civilian vessels. Mobile camera videos of Marines boarding the ship went viral, with servers crashing under the strain of demand. All of the news outlets were screaming for footage and access to the survivors. Survivors were being transported to Port Canaveral where they would be screened for radiation exposure and other injuries before being released.

Initial information indicated that all passenger children had survived, but a few parents and adult passengers had not. The crew of the DuChard Duchess were not so fortunate, almost all of them had been killed by the terrible blast. The few surviving crew members had been manning the controls of the passenger lifeboats. The Navy's search for survivors in the sunken wreckage proved fruitless, as there were no responses to the submarine's sonic signaling. Normally ship's crews were trained to bang metal against the bulkheads in a steady rhythm, but there was only silence.

Farid woke to the news from a surprisingly good sleep after being woken in the night by Prince Zufar. He hoped his friend Justin had survived. It would have been almost too much to bear if he lost both Nayla and Justin. But, if there was one thing he'd learned during the teenage summers spent in Lebanon, it was that the needs of the struggle have to be divorced from those of the heart. Anything less was a recipe for failure or ignominious death. The Hammer was not created to be a failure - years of work had gone into the effort.

Farid turned on the cable news network to see what stories were in the current cycle. The initial reaction of the American people was blinding rage, much more so than the attack on the Twin Towers. 9/11 engendered a shock reaction, with people glued to the television to see what would happen next. The attack on the DuChard Duchess didn't seem to have the same uncertainty associated with it; the worst had already happened. People wanted to know how many had survived and what their stories were, but were more ready to fight this time. There were already demands to understand how a terrorist was able to get close enough to a U.S. flagged vessel to place a nuclear weapon in the first place. Followed almost immediately by a demand to know where the nuclear weapon was manufactured. President Brown's administration was noncommittal as to the origin of the device, saying that it was being investigated, but clearly placed the responsibility upon the shoulders of the Martyrs al-Sabra.

The conspiracy theorists were out in force, attacking the Brown presidency directly for being less than effective rounding up the snipers, the President's husband being suborned by the terrorist Nayla Kaldah, and failing to prevent a nuclear attack on Americans. Questions were being asked about what information Jonny Ray Brown provided to the terrorist, and those asking questions were not impressed with the logic that Jonny Ray didn't know any information needing a security clearance. Naysayers pointed out that he knew the President's schedule and location, which while not exactly classified, had national security implications.

All cruise ships with American ports of call immediately instituted a process involving divers checking a ship's hull completely before leaving a dock, no matter where it was docked. Other provisions to secure the sea approaches were also announced by the cruise ship lines in order to prevent a repeat performance. DuChard's cruise line executives were taking heat from an enraged public with perfect hindsight. Wall Street wouldn't open for several more hours but all of the cruise line stocks and, DuChard's in particular, futures pricing had dropped more than 45%. The entire market would participate in the drop, futures indicating a minimum 10% hit. Farid expected markets would suspend trading before noon, given past history of much smaller upsets.

Farid had made most of his financial moves a month prior and, like Prince Zufar, planned to take advantage of the decline to purchase value stocks temporarily impacted by the early morning events. The impact to DuChard's prospects could be longer lived, as the loss of a billion-dollar asset would not be completely covered by insurance. Replacing the DuChard Duchess would be covered by insurance, but even if the corporation placed an immediate order with the shipyards, it would take years to complete and place into service. The revenue capacity of DuChard Cruise Lines would be impacted for years, and that assumed the demand for cruises remained high. Many Americans would simply forego taking a cruise in the future, Farid expected. None of Farid's financial positions involved DuChard.

Farid polished off his morning coffee and then picked up his mobile phone.

"Farid?"

"Yes. Boss, I've been following the attack on the news. I think I should line up some reaction interviews with local DC Muslim leaders today, first thing, do you agree?"

"Hell yes! But make sure they don't waffle on condemnation of the Martyrs, it won't be taken well by folks on the street. We want to head off people coming for their Muslim neighbors, but it is going to be hard. When the rednecks get up this morning, there will be hell to pay."

"I think so as well. At a minimum we'll get expressions of regret and support for the survivors from the leaders. We don't have a passenger manifest yet, do we? I think President Brown is probably correct some Muslim families were on that ship. It would be a better story if we had those names," Farid said.

"I'll try to see what I can get for you. Mark should be in the studios today, so grab a mobile camera unit and get going."

"Thanks, I don't want to just sit here and watch the bad news come in," Farid said. "I'm planning to take some time off in the next few weeks, but I'll loop back with you after this story runs its legs."

Farid hung up the phone, laid suitable interview attire on the bed, and headed for the shower.

• • •

Andro Simonetti sat in the Lynden Pindling International Airport in Nassau Bahamas waiting for his flight to be called. Mohammed, Khalid, and Nassir had already left on an earlier flight. The local police had increased their presence within the terminals, due to the news of the DuChard Duchess. But, Amin thought there was a good chance the Qataris would get away without incident. The Bahamians were not the best police force in the world, more suited to dealing with tourist-related crime and local slums filled with illegal Haitians than with international terrorism.

The local police were spending a lot of time taking videos of the passengers in the departure lounges, though. In Amin's mind, that meant United States antiterrorist task force assets were going to analyze the take of the locals. He had spent some time in the restroom working on changing key features on his face: adding putty to cheekbones and darkening eyebrows. He wore a holiday hat which covered his ears and sunglasses to obscure the distance between his eyes. The new biometric techniques identified people by the relationship between key elements of their face and were very difficult to fool. Amin hoped the Royal Bahamas Police Force were not that advanced and their video feeds were without the necessary calibrations to support later analysis by those who were sophisticated.

He sat with his back to the glass windows overlooking the tarmac, reading a worn paperback novel written in Italian. In such a position, cameras would have a very difficult time resolving his image for lighting automatically as they would default to the brighter light source. The hour of waiting went by quickly, and the gate attendants called the flight for boarding without any sign of a security stoppage.

Amin boarded well within the press of passengers and didn't have any trouble when his pass was scanned. His route included stops in Dominican Republic, Cuba, Canada, and finally his home city of Columbus, Ohio.

It had been several months since he had been home and he was looking forward to getting some rest. Depending on The Hammer's next plan, he might have to reactivate the sniper network which was now dormant, thanks to the apprehension of Dr. Hammayil. Plus there was some unfinished business in Riyadh. Amin shelved his concerns for the future, knowing it would be moot if he didn't successfully navigate the trip home. He rested his head on the hard coach airline seat and closed his eyes. By the time the plane was in the air, he was asleep.

• • •

Justin and Brad Spokes arrived back at Patrick AFB a little after 9 am. It had been a night without much sleep for both of them. They had seen the last of the lifeboats empty their cargo onto U.S. Navy ships. At the last minute, it was decided to not utilize the commercial boats offering assistance to keep the survivors within their custody. United State destroyers and guided missile cruisers set up a perimeter to the area to allow unfettered access for the teams of forensic specialists who would get to the bottom of how the DuChard Duchess was destroyed. Russia had long-since denied culpability for the loss of portable nuclear devices in the transition from the USSR to Russian governments. Some of the small former Soviet states had Muslim majorities and many things were lost as those countries broke away from the Soviet regime. This had long been known in defense circles, but after so many years the urgency to track or find the missing weapons had abated. Regardless, those in charge wanted to know everything there was to know about the device.

The initial tallies of survivors were heartening only if you accepted that it was better than losing everyone. No children or parents were lost to the terrorist's weapon. None. There were several cases of broken bones, which happened during the evacuation and during the stressful few moments when the life boats rode out the sea turbulence engendered by the blast. In total, 2,527 parents with children survived. A further 742 adult passengers without children survived. That left 253 passengers unaccounted for. Of the crew, only 16 people remained out of the 1,423 working the ship. The Marine platoon died to a man, 50 soldiers. A demolition diving team of 8 also perished. A total of 1,718 people missing and presumed dead. If the bomb had not been found, it was entirely conceivable over 5,000 people would have died in the attack.

Justin tried to find some consolation from those facts, but the weight of those who died remained a bone in his throat. What if he had made the connection 30 minutes earlier? Would it have saved most of the rest? The passengers were being brought back to Port Canaveral after being examined and cleared by Navy physicians on the hospital ship which arrived after Justin returned to Patrick AFB.

Vice President Rodriquez planned to stay in the area until the survivors were fully released. Justin and Major Stokes gathered in the command center to listen to the satellite imagery analysis from the last forty-eight hours.

"We think we have identified the terrorist vessel used in the approach to Buccaneer Cay. In this photograph, with a timestamp shortly after the DuChard security log entries, there is one craft approximately 3 miles to the west of the dock. From orbit, it looks to be a small ocean-going yacht or sport fishing vessel. Apparently, the boat passed by the entire island several times during the twenty-four hours prior to the operation. The night of the 14th, it anchored off the coast of Bird Cay to the east of Buccaneer Cay. On April 15th, it circled Buccaneer Cay several times before returning to Bird Cay. From there, it is clear they approached Buccaneer Cay under cover of darkness. Approximately an hour after departing the dock in the small craft, the boat heads south and then turns east mid-channel. It lands in Nassau for a short time, then heads back out to sea on a northeast course. At some point afterwards, we completely lost track of the boat. We are examining footage for any occlusions or discrepancies, but for now we don't know where it is."

"Question," Major Stokes said, "When the boat left Nassau, was the smaller boat visible on the deck?"

"Just a second, sir. Scrolling back to those slides. There, it does appear the small boat is secured to the deck."

"How about comparing that one to the final one we have of the boat? I'm wondering if they sent the boat off to be scuttled and made their escape on the Kodiak?"

The technician put both photos up on the screen. It was clear the Kodiak was no longer there on the final shot.

The Admiral nodded approvingly, "Good thinking, Brad. Captain, see if we can't get a Navy ship over to the last known location to search the bottom for the boat. You'll have to coordinate with the Royal Bahamas Defense Force, but the liaison should be available."

"Yes, Admiral. We're on it," the Captain said.

"So the terrorists must have fled from the Nassau airport this morning. The DuChard security team identified three men in the Kodiak, with the boat offshore there must have been at least four. Do we have any data on where the boat was prior to closing on Buccaneer Cay?" the Admiral asked.

"Yes sir. We tracked it as far south as Andros City, but we lose track beyond several days ago due to the weekly recycling of storage capacity due to the data arrays."

"Captain, are you hearing this? We'll also need to get a team on the ground at Andros City to see if anyone there knows anything more about the terrorists."

"Yes, sir!"

"The stock market is about to open, can we get a stream of what's going on there put up as well?" Sid Rosenbloom asked.

The technicians quickly cleared one of the larger monitors, turned on the closed captioning to prevent the current operations live audio from competing with the cable feed. The cable pundits were predicting a halt to trading early, once the session started.

The market opened with a crash in stocks across the board, but cruise line firms were the hardest hit. DuChard, predictably, was dramatically down. One of the network talking heads mentioned that there had been a marked increase in short sales of DuChard stock in the prior 45 days.

Justin made a call to the Deputy Director who, like Justin, was running on fumes and caffeine by then. "Sir, I just saw a comment from a television financial analyst which mentions DuChard stock has been sold short in higher volumes than normal within the last 45 days. I wonder if those investors knew about the terrorist target in advance and were trying to cash in. I recommend we get our securities team trying to identify all of those investors, it might lead us back to those responsible. In fact, I would look across that market segment for similar patterns, as the drop in cruise lines would be predictable if the investors knew."

The Deputy Director agreed and told Justin to expect a call from that group shortly. He also instructed Justin to catch the next flight back to DC, as there were too many threads to the investigation to manage remotely.

Justin acknowledged and rang off. Heading over to Major Spokes, he relayed the need to get back. Major Spokes told him there were a couple of small flights headed back with some of the Pentagon staff which had accompanied the Vice President on Air Force 2. The Vice President was planning to meet with the survivors as they offloaded in Port Canaveral but it would happen later in the day. Several small executive jets were being made available to shuttle the Pentagon staff back to Washington, DC and Justin was able to claim a seat without too much difficulty.

The ride back had a stilted and strained atmosphere. The military didn't always see the value in working with other branches of government service, and junior generals or admirals could be prickly in that regard. Justin wasn't going to apologize for being an FBI Special Agent and was too tired to make an effort to be sociable with the status-conscious functionaries on the flight. Instead, he slept as best he could for the two hours they were in the air.

Upon landing, an Air Force Lieutenant came up to Justin and informed him a ride was waiting to provide transport back to FBI Headquarters. Justin slept an extra half-hour in the car before being deposited outside the door. Thanking the Staff Sergeant who drove the car, he turned and entered the building. The entire building thrummed like a beehive hit repeatedly with a stick. This morning's attack was the first time that the United States had suffered the attack of a nuclear weapon. The fact that it was small as those things go, the weapon which hit Hiroshima was roughly 200 times larger, mattered for very little. It was a matter of pride and the loss of a perfect record. Already, the services responsible for security were finding ways to subtly blame other organizations.

As predicted, Wall Street had suspended sales of DuChard stock within the first thirty minutes of trading. It looked as though the overall market might close early as well so information about the terrorist attack could be better assessed and the first wave of hysteria could pass. Justin sat down and started reading the task force work which had continued while he worked out of Florida.

Before noon, the Director's executive assistant appeared with a summons. Picking up his notes, Justin made his way to the top floor of the building. After a short wait, he was shown into the Director's office.

"Justin, good work today, it looks like many of those families owe you a great deal," the Director said. The Deputy Director nodded warmly at Justin as well.

"Thank you, sir. But I can't stop thinking about how thirty minutes earlier might have made all the difference for the ship's crew and the Marines. The Marines were just getting set to evacuate when it went off."

"Conversely, thirty minutes later would have seen most of the children killed, correct? We can't win them all, or be perfect, even if the people of the United States expect us to be. Brief me on where we are currently, across the board."

Justin, mindful of earlier briefings, provided an edited version of the entire task force investigation which focused on developments the pair may not have heard. Both men asked questions to clarify the thinking and strategy being utilized, but overall were very supportive of the current approach. Justin found himself flagging as he explained the investigations being undertaken in real-time by the armed forces.

"Justin, I don't mean this in a negative way, but you look like hell. I know you worked a full day yesterday and didn't sleep most of the night, correct?" The Director asked.

"Yes sir. I was able to get naps during transport, but nothing remotely normal."

"Tomorrow is going to be very busy, the District will be very surprised to see all of us here on the weekend, but we're going to be working pretty much nonstop until we catch these bastards. You need to go home, get some overdue sleep and family time. Kiss the wife, pet the dog. We're going to be asking a lot of you for the near future. The White House is making noises about awarding a medal, but can't seem to make up their mind which one it should be. You're being credited as the hero whose actions saved all of those children and their families. We can't have you doing interviews or the like with a day's stubble and a wrinkled suit," the Director said and smiled to take the sting out of his words.

"I don't feel like a hero, sir. I just happened to be in the right place at the right time."

"Real heroes never feel heroic, son. If they do, further questions should be asked by their superiors. Doors are going to open for you here, Justin, but keep your mind on how we close the Martyrs down for good. It is the most important thing we can do. Enough, get your stuff and clear out! Believe me, it will be waiting for you tomorrow morning."

"I will, and thank you, sir." Justin stood and headed back down to the task force room to gather the rest of his things. One thing surprising about DC Metro traffic is a mid-day lull when commuting time is often less than half of rush hour. Justin was pulling into his driveway just before 2 p.m. Jan's car was in the garage, which lifted his spirits considerably. The last week had been very hard on everyone, and even after many years of marriage Justin missed spending time with her the most.

"Justin!" Jan said as he walked into the kitchen from the garage, hurrying over and embracing him. Over her head he could see the news reel she'd been watching. Beth danced about in canine ecstasy as she greeted him. *Nothing warms the heart quite like your dog being happy to see you,* Justin thought, as he leaned down to rub Beth.

"The Director threw me out of the building for time spent, but expects me there tomorrow morning. I'll grab a quick shower then come back down. Are you up for an afternoon nap before the kids get home?"

"Since it is you asking, sure. I'll make you a sandwich while you shower. When was the last time you ate?"

"The sandwich will be great! I'm running on coffee and donuts."

"Get upstairs and wash off, Bucko. See you in a few minutes." Jan set to work making a loaded sandwich she knew Justin would like. He looked pretty ragged, the Director made the right move sending him home; although why it wasn't Justin's boss making the call didn't make sense to Jan. Within a minute of sandwich completion, Jan heard the pounding of large feet coming down the stairs, with Beth's smaller paws as counterpoint.

Wearing clean loose shorts and a tee-shirt, Justin sat down at the kitchen counter and set to with a will. The sandwich was gone within a short minute. He drank the glass of water Jan had set next to the plate with several large swallows, paused as if he had forgotten what was next, then brightened. "Alright, woman! Time for an afternoon nap with your husband. That's all you'd want from me until after I get some quality sleep."

Jan followed him upstairs, kicked off her shoes, and joined him in the queen-sized bed. When they were first married, an afternoon nap was a treat. Sometimes sex was involved, but most times, it was simply the pleasure of being alone with each other without other pending commitments. Justin fell asleep almost immediately, followed by Jan, lulled by his slow breathing. Beth, ever the opportunist, hopped onto the bed into an empty space and joined them in slumber.

After the children came home, the Simons enjoyed an almost normal evening, Justin told Jan what had happened to the DuChard Duchess. Jan was brought to tears as he described the frustration of being too late to save everyone, and looking at her own children resolved, like many Americans this day, to support those working to stop the Martyrs terrorists.

• • •

"This has been a very profitable day, Mussa," Prince Zufar said as he looked over the financial analysis of his current holdings. Before the market was closed early by the exchange, the Prince's nominees had been able to acquire significant positions in solid companies affected by the market rout. The entire market had crashed, enabling his strategy of buying in market segments unrelated to cruise lines, Eventually the FBI would get around to investigating all of the cruise line short selling of the previous few weeks, but Zufar's tracks were well-covered. If anything, the FBI would find the worthies who had attended Prince Zufar's brunch gathering. The Prince was not concerned they might point a finger at him, as there were severe consequences for such behavior in Saudi society. None of those persons would be tied to the attacks regardless, so the FBI could do nothing really to affect the outcome unless the principals traveled somewhere U.S. law prevailed.

Prince Zufar had already called in his personal gold artisan to build a special display case for the detonator. Within a few weeks it would be ready to occupy a place of honor in the Prince's trophy room. Even though keeping it might place him in some danger of being identified, the personal sentimental value of having it far exceeded the potential risk of discovery. The Hammer would not approve, but, upon reflection, Zufar felt the Hammer might have outlived his usefulness. He would have to find a way to get The Hammer and Amin to Riyadh, to eliminate one and to co-opt the other.

• • •

"I'm here today with Mr. Mahdi Aziz, a prominent Muslim businessman from Alexandria, Virginia. Mr. Aziz, can you share the thoughts of the local Muslim community concerning the attack on the DuChard Duchess?" Farid asked.

"Certainly. Our hearts are filled with compassion for the families affected by this terrible and immoral attack on innocents. As President Brown stated earlier this morning, Muslims were among the many victims and Muslims were also among those evacuated safely. They attacked children without concern, against the basic precepts of our faith. The actions of the Martyrs al-Sabra terrorists are not supported by the vast majority of Muslims."

"Are you concerned about Americans categorizing all Muslims as terrorists in the wake of these attacks?"

"Of course I'm concerned! We live and work with mostly non-Muslim Americans, but in our society it is recommended that religion is kept private, mostly so that no one is offended. I would say to the people who encounter me, if they wonder how I feel about terrorism, how I feel about being an American, and what I would do if I knew something about the terrorists - simply ask me. I think we have to start talking about these things. Too much is made of our differences and not enough made of the things we all share. I think we should strive for more of the latter," Mr. Aziz said.

"Do you have any concerns of a backlash from the Martyrs for sharing your views?"

"It is an issue, although I know my views on the topic are held more widely than those of the Martyrs. While it is possible I will be targeted for speaking out, it is more likely I will be involved in a fatal auto accident on the Beltway. Most American Muslims feel the way I do. I have to believe."

"Thank you for agreeing to speak with us," Farid said. "This is Farid Monsour al Haj for World News Network."

• • •

In his Arlington home, an unshaven Quinton Jameson watched Farid's broadcast with bitter interest. His fashionable wife had gone on an extended vacation until Quinton pulled himself together. He barely noticed her absence.

He knew Farid was involved in this up to his armpits, but no one would listen to his thoughts on the topic. Quinton consoled himself with the knowledge that the nuclear detonation would reopen all previous threads of the investigation, including Farid's. Sources within the FBI, who still returned Quinton's calls, had confirmed that evidence within Nayla Kaldah's extra apartment led to the weapon's discovery. Everything and everyone would be reexamined. Farid Monsour would not be so fortunate this time.

RENDEZVOUS IN RIYADH

"..In spite of the full resources of the United States and other concerned countries, none of the terrorists responsible for the sinking of the DuChard Duchess have been publicly identified or apprehended. The Brown administration also has yet to fully explain the circumstances connecting Jonny Ray Brown to the killing of alleged Martyrs terrorist Nayla Kaldah. Sources indicate secret discussions of the unthinkable, impeachment, have begun on Capital Hill.."

Farid Monsour al Haj for World News Corporation

Two weeks after the sinking of the DuChard Duchess, Justin was discouraged with the lack of progress. The FBI had little to show for the hundreds of thousands of hours spent chasing the elusive evidence threads for signs of the Martyrs terrorists.

The trail of the commandos, who had placed the lethal weapon, was lost in the Bahamas. Investigators now knew there were four men, who had spent a long period of time fishing while docked in Andros City. The Andros City docking slot had been paid for in cash, but the ship's name was Butler's Dosh. Ownership records for the Dominican-registered vessel led to multiple dead-end corporate shells. Neighbors described the men as friendly, always waving as they passed by carrying their fishing gear. How the nuclear weapon got aboard the boat was still undetermined. The men themselves were a mystery as well. FBI investigators narrowed the search to three Qataris assumed to be involved. Passport photos were shown to the Andros City neighbors, who confirmed them as the fishermen. The fourth man was initially overlooked as he was traveling under an Italian passport, but the neighbors confirmed him as the fourth member of the crew.

The FBI had names and photos, but were stopped in their tracks by the flight itineraries chosen by the fugitive men. Their first stop was Havana. While the failed communist country to the south of Miami was on much better terms with the United States, they were not going to roll over when asked by the FBI or U.S. Armed Forces. All four men had made connections to other International flights and were long gone before discussions with Havana started to bear fruit. The Qataris had debarked to Venezuela, another country with a prickly relationship with the United States, before heading on to the Persian Gulf. The fourth man, one Andro Simonetti, flew into Toronto and promptly vanished. The FBI held this man up as the leader, possibly The Hammer himself, and expected he was already back inside the United States.

The satellite imagery of the Butler's Dosh provided an indication of where it was last seen. The U.S. Navy found many boats on the floor of that section of ocean, though. Unless they were very lucky, searchers wouldn't find the Butler's Dosh any time soon.

The weapon itself was identified by the trace elements remaining at the blast site. As expected, it was a former Soviet weapon lost during the breakup of the Soviet Union. Russia's military had lost track of the weapon more than twenty years prior. It could have been anywhere during that time.

The Iridium telecommunications channel being used by the device was traced back to an IP media gateway in the United Kingdom. From there, the trail was muddied considerably by numerous proxy servers in less-than-friendly-jurisdictions. The FBI and NSA could not do a traffic meta-analysis to find candidates for the next leg of the path because data centers in Ukraine and Romania would not immediately provide a data log dump. Presumably, diplomacy might be deployed to gain access to the global logs, but it could take weeks. In the meantime, the user was long gone.

There was a telephone call made by Prince Zufar the morning of the explosion which suggested culpability, but the State Department insisted on legally obtained corroborating evidence, before engaging Saudi authorities about one of their own. There were some financial indications Prince Zufar had made substantial purchases in the stock market the day of the attack, but then every investor in the world with cash had done so as well.

The investors who had sold cruise line stocks short in the weeks prior to the attack were varied, but most of the open interest came from Saudi investors, many of whom had immediately cashed out the day of the attack.

On other fronts, the extensive log data from the proxy server in Kansas had been fully analyzed. Many of the IP addresses targeted turned out to be dynamically assigned. Furthermore, most involved Internet service providers public WiFi networks, where users could be connected as long as they had an account. The worst problem was the ISPs' now routine use of the WiFi routers installed in customer's homes to add additional public WiFi network coverage to residential areas. Knowing an IP address was no longer definitive proof of identity in such networks. The IP address could belong to anyone within range of the router.

The hunt club in Wisconsin had been tracked down and investigated. The engagement contract had been signed by the omnipresent Andro Simonetti, on behalf of the Sons of Italy. When contacted, the Sons of Italy had no idea who Andro Simonetti was, but confirmed they didn't have a hunting club. The rental payments came from offshore banks in jurisdictions which didn't automatically share information with United States law enforcement. Nonetheless, there were multiple persons of interest identified in the proxy server data investigation, so warrants were issued for a number of searches. In each case, no suspicious laptop, mobile phone, gun, ammunition, or deer meat were found. When questioned, the persons who had received the search warrants were no longer in a mood to cooperate with law enforcement. None of the questioned parties would admit to attending a hunt camp in Wisconsin. After a number of heavy-handed failures which were publicized, the Bureau pulled back, trying less direct methods to make the cases, such as surreptitiously analyzing credit card statements and mobile phone call records during the time span of the camp. In time, the effort would bear fruit, but it would require much more work.

The murder of Nayla Kaldah remained unsolved. Lewd pictures of Jonny Ray in action continued to leak onto the Internet. There were even some videos with sound tracks. Comedians had started making jokes Jonny Ray was taking his public relations cues from the Kardashians, with the slow serial publishing of his own sex tape. Rocksolid Entertainment, a well-known porn publisher had publicly offered one million dollars if Jonny Ray gave permission to release a full compilation DVD. By the last tally, there was more than forty-five minutes of video released. The White House was completely humiliated, but if the terrorists had intended for them to be politically discredited by the scandal, it had simply failed to deliver. The White House was embarrassed, and the butt of every second-tier comedian's jokes, but the government was able to make the distinction between private and public affairs. No one had suggested that Jonny Ray gave up any national secrets in the process, on the contrary the tapes suggested he was interrogating her.

Congress had convened hearings, in camera, to understand the progress of the entire investigation. Justin, the Deputy Director, and Director all had their time in front of the Committee of Homeland Security. Congressmen were hearing calls from constituents asking why the terrorists had not been brought to justice. The meetings were very uncomfortable, as the Congressmen were posturing toughly for the record, rather than engaging in a serious working meeting. The White House sent representatives as well, who stressed the need for budget support if there was to be any progress made.

During a short intermission, Justin was walking through the halls to counteract the hours spent sitting, he felt a tap on his shoulder.

"Well, if it isn't my favorite FBI hero!" Ashley said with a smile. She was wearing a smart suit similar to what the lobbyists wore.

Justin turned and smiled as well, "I wish you wouldn't say things like that, I don't know how to take them."

"Just my luck: an innocent hero, not the veteran campaigner for which I was hoping." She smiled mischievously.

Justin smiled in response, but didn't leap into the implied gambit.

"Have they contacted you about the medal?" Ashley changing the subject.

"It was mentioned the day of the attack, but haven't heard anything since. Honestly, I am fine with it not ever coming up again. The real heroes are the ones who died trying to get those passengers off the ship. Plus, if we don't get traction with the investigation soon, they'll be looking for someone to hang instead."

"That is true pretty much across departments, but so far no one has had a bad thing to say. The sense I get is that you aren't really identified with a Bureau faction, so you aren't a natural first choice for the knife. After all, your removal wouldn't change the balance of power one iota," Ashley said.

"And to think I thought I couldn't be more depressed about my career," Justin joked.

"Seriously now, just keep grinding away the way you have been doing and things will work out fine. If you get stuck, give me a call and we'll decide whether Sid should take a hand. I won't let you waste that chip! On the investigation, is it really stalled or are there obstacles which need to be overcome?"

"Obstacles - mostly in foreign climes. Things we could look into quickly for clues in the United States aren't as easy when the State Department gets involved. That isn't a criticism. It is exactly how these terrorists planned things. They knew enough about our methods to plan accordingly. While we're stuck or slowed down, they move like quicksilver through the cracks. Take the commandos: we knew who they were, we knew where they went, but we were always one step behind until they vanished," Justin groused.

"Keep the faith, something will break. Oh look, there goes the chairman back into the room, time to reconvene. It was good seeing you, Justin. Keep working it," Ashley said as she walked back into the committee room.

• • •

In a small secure conference room, Quinton Jameson sat waiting for whoever had called the meeting to arrive. He'd received a call from one of his remaining friends at the Bureau asking how eager he was to earn reinstatement. Quinton jumped at the opportunity, and the meeting was set up. He was told to maintain absolute secrecy otherwise the entire opportunity would be reconsidered. That was easy - he didn't have anyone to tell. Besides, he didn't know what the deal was to begin with. He sat alone for a half-hour before he heard footsteps approaching the room.

The Deputy Director entered the room by himself and sat down opposite Quinton. In better days, the two of them had been on a first name basis. Quinton didn't expect it to be the current case.

"Quinton, I'm told you are interested in resurrecting your career here at the Bureau," the Deputy Director said.

"Yes, sir, I am."

"What I am about to say to you cannot be repeated. Ever. To anyone. Are we clear?"

"Yes, sir," Quinton now had a feeling of faint unease, but then again there weren't any palatable options left.

"Good. During your time in Riyadh, how much time did you spend learning about Prince Zufar's habits and compound?"

"A fair amount. I was tracking Farid Monsour primarily, but he did spend several hours there for dinner with the Prince."

"How were you able to operate in-country? From our records, it looks like you didn't engage the local FBI liaison."

"That's right, I had several local representatives of no such agency help me out. I knew them personally from previous campaigns and they owed me."

"Do they still owe you? Enough to help you one more time?" the Deputy Director said.

"I believe so, but it really depends on what needs to be done," Quinton said.

"Some background. In the wake of the DuChard Duchess attack, we investigated worldwide short selling of DuChard and other cruise line stock. I am sure it won't surprise you to learn that most of it came from Saudi Arabia. All of the holders made fortunes the day of the attack. While there were many investors involved, there have been rumors the initial positions were taken by Prince Zufar alone, then sold in private transactions to the others. No proof of course. It doesn't take a penchant for rocket science to connect those dots, though, does it?"

"No, sir, it doesn't. Our investigation got started in the first place because we intercepted a call from Prince Zufar to this Hammer character. But him knowing in advance is a bad sign."

"Listen to this telephone call we captured, but cannot use in court." The Deputy Director played back a call from the panicked Prince Zufar about a GPS signal that wasn't moving.

"That certainly sounds as though the Prince has a detonator, doesn't it?" Quinton was beginning to flush with anger, both at the Prince and the Bureau who hadn't listened to him sooner.

"Yes, it does. In retrospect."

"Where was the other caller?"

"Somewhere in Georgetown, talking on a burner phone."

"Goddamn it! Has anyone ruled out Farid Monsour as the other caller?" Quinton asked. "I fucking had him in a cell, but you made me release him."

"We did. Then, as now, there was little direct evidence of his involvement. Believe me, a number of people are starting to wonder whether you had the right approach all along. But no one is going to bite that apple without better evidence. Which brings me to your situation. I want you to go back to Riyadh and work with your contacts to do a black bag job on Prince Zufar. When we have the evidence, then we'll lower the boom on everyone involved. If you succeed, you will be fully reinstated, and the previous personnel actions will be rescinded retroactively. Conversely, if you fail, we'll deny we ever said anything of the sort."

"It is pretty expensive to get there, how am I going to swing it?"

"Quinton, at your age surely you have sufficient funds for this? If successful, your expenses will be more than covered by the special success bonus that will be paid out once you're reinstated. Obviously, we cannot expense the trip. It is off the books. You will also receive a public commendation, which should help repair your public reputation somewhat."

"As long as it isn't the Memorial Star," Quinton said, alluding to an award given to family members of agents killed in action.

"If you're careful, it shouldn't come to that end. To be very clear, we're looking for sufficient evidence which can be used to take Prince

Zufar into custody. We'll have a lot of questions for him, about the entire Martyrs organization. Don't let your cowboy friends decide to just assassinate him if things heat up."

"I won't. When did you want me there?"

"As soon as you can get there, naturally. I've removed the flag on your passport. Here is a card with a special email address and mobile phone number along with your computer as well. Use this to communicate or send photo evidence. Do not call the office lines under any circumstances. We don't need this coming back to haunt any of us in ten years. Are you clear?"

"Yes, sir. Thanks for giving me another chance, I won't let you down or forget who helped me back into the fold," Quinton said.

"See that you don't. Leave in five minutes please, and send updates when you're able to do so," The Deputy Director left the room briskly, as Quinton read the card several times over.

A sense of relief permeated him. He knew the work would be risky, but it was better than dying a slow, friendless death in Arlington, Virginia. Farid thought he was finished, did he? Time to get moving.

• • •

When Amin arrived home, there were no indications of illicit interest. The security systems reported all was well, and the young neighbor boy had faithfully done his duty keeping the walkways clear of trash. Things were exactly as he had left them.

Amin renewed his acquaintance with his home and his mistress in exactly that order. He knew he would be hearing from The Hammer soon, but tried to enjoy springtime in Columbus. The attack had gone quite well, even though the Americans were able to evacuate all of the children. *Not truly a payment for the Martyrs,* Amin thought to himself, but he had to admit the Hammer was right about a partial success being worse for the Americans than a total loss. Dozens of television shows had sprung up to discuss the psychological damage to America's youth due to the attack on a childhood icon. Pundits were holding forth on the best ways to appease the Martyrs terrorist demands which drew frenzied lobbying efforts by Israeli interests. In short, it was a delightful increase in chaotic activity without any resolution or end in sight. By contrast, if the DuChard Duchess had gone down with all hands, there would have been less continuing drama. But to almost succeed in fully stopping the plot, that had to be a chafing bone in the craw of the FBI. Being unable to arrest even the low-level commandos had to rankle as well.

The next steps would be the most difficult. In a special Internet chat room that Amin used to contact assets overseas, a note was left for him. It contained a message from Reem saying, in coded language, that Prince Zufar wanted to speak with him directly. It was an odd request for several reasons. First, Reem had no contact with Prince Zufar as far as Amin knew. Second, Amin's contact with the prince had been minimal and always as a second. Before contacting the prince, Amin sent a coded message to Farid asking for a conversation on the encrypted VOIP channel. Within fifteen minutes, the sound of an incoming VOIP request chimed.

"Andro?" A mechanical voice asked.

"Yes. Contacted by Zufar Saud, asking for direct call. No topic of discussion. Channel was Nico, who I didn't think knew Zufar."

"Yes, that is odd and will have to be examined further. As for Zufar's request, I think he is determined to help with the next stage as well. Listen to his words and report back. Our next move will be next week, unless events require an earlier resolution."

"Understood. Same channel or a set time for the report?" Amin asked.

"Same channel, out." The circuit hum ceased to be active.

Interesting, Amin thought, *The Hammer was expecting Zufar's contact.* Turning to his message from Nico-Reem, he gathered the information needed to make his call. Following the same process as The Hammer, he raised a small masking device between his mouth and the handset after dialing.

"Salaam," a non-committal voice said.

"I was asked to call his highness, the prince," Amin's mechanical voice intoned.

"One moment, please," the assistant's voice escalated to brisk.

Several minutes later, the Prince came onto the line. "Hello, to whom am I speaking?"

Amin shook his head at both the Prince's unmodified voice and utter lack of tradecraft. It was a dead certainty the NSA was monitoring all of the Prince's telecommunications lines, but you didn't have to make things easy for them. "This is he whom you requested to call from the United States by way of Iraq."

"Very good, the voice doesn't sound a bit like you," the Prince laughed at his own joke. "I wanted to congratulate your recent efforts and see whether there might be interest in a promotion?"

Amin wondered where the Prince would have heard his voice, but set that aside for the time being. "I am very content with my current circumstance. After all, a man can only eat one chicken a day."

"Yes, that is true, but is it the very best chicken one could buy? Also, you never get the credit for your work, which I think is something to change. Only people within the business know of your expertise."

The Hammer was right again, Amin marveled. "There is always a better class of chicken, I find. However, personal credit in this business is very overrated, in my opinion. I find it tends to be positively correlated with the wrong end of a cruise missile."

"Perhaps so, perhaps so. Why don't you come to visit, and we can talk more over a feast of the finest chicken. I would be offended if you didn't at least agree to hear me out."

"I would not want to offend such a person as yourself. It may take a week to break free. Would that be acceptable?"

"Certainly. Contact my man, Mussa, upon arrival and we will continue our discussion. By the way, I felt the signal in my very bones when I used your device. A most singular experience! I look forward to meeting with you very soon." The prince broke the connection.

So the Prince is testing the waters for a change in employment, Amin mused to himself. *The Hammer is right again.* Amin took a few minutes to check the availability of flights into Riyadh. His Andro Simonetti alias had been destroyed prior to entry in Canada, according to plan. Perhaps, he would use his Rafael Perez alias on this trip. It might be amusing to travel to Riyadh as a Mexican-American sales representative. In the United States, there were many Mexican-Americans who didn't speak Spanish, so it would be fairly easy to pass.

Amin signaled again for The Hammer. Shortly, a connection was made.

"As expected, our friend is trying to recruit me," Amin said.

"Excellent! When do you plan to travel?" the mechanized voice asked.

"I'm thinking May 6th or 7th."

"Perfect! In the meantime, please look into Reem's sudden connection with Saudi royalty. I may have a task for him in Canada. Depending on what you learn, Qazi may need to be pulled in as well."

"I understand and fully concur."

"Right now, three people know who I am. If the number is actually four or more, it needs to be reduced back to one or two. Those two would be you and possibly our Riyadh contact," the Hammer said.

"Perfectly correct."

"Thanks, and out."

Amin organized his thoughts while purchasing a roundtrip airline ticket to Riyadh as Raphael Perez from an online broker. After completing his purchase, Amin sent Reem a secure message requesting a conference. Reem had been extremely useful helping with the technology side of operations. It would be a shame if he knew too much about The Hammer, as it would likely warrant a death sentence.

Several hours later, Amin placed the call to Reem over the secure network.

"Salaam. I want to understand how you came to be the conduit for the Prince's recent communication," Amin said in his metallic voice.

"It was pretty clever of them, actually," Reem's admiration for technical expertise was audible even with voice modification. "They used the detonator code to send a message. You see, when I was programming the device, I had to test the connectivity before it was finished so I embedded a test routine which would communicate with my application development environment. When it came time to finish up, I simply left the inactive test code within the device rather than removing it. They found the address of my environment space and sent a datagram message asking for you."

"Are you saying they sent a blind message without even knowing your identity?"

"Yes, exactly. I thought originally that the remote detonator would be immediately destroyed after use, but it appears to not be the case. I had to move my entire environment after receiving the message, otherwise it would be blown from a security standpoint. I've also cycled the old IP address through several new owners, so that it will never come back to us. I got the message to you immediately, but then got busy fixing the hole. What are they thinking keeping the detonator intact?"

"I think the device has assumed the status of a precious memento and won't be willingly discarded or destroyed."

Reem paused, processing this information. "That is unfortunate. I just thought of something else I need to do. I'll have to fudge the proxies we used for the routing of the VPN connection, otherwise there might be something there to connect to us. They have already been torn down, but I haven't put up any smokescreen yet," Reem explained.

"By smokescreen you mean…?"

"Connections that are wild-goose chases. The idea is to generate thousands of data points to obscure the one that could be used against you."

"Makes sense, and I think you've done very well. One thing I do want to mention, for future consideration. This business we are in is very dangerous, and people are betrayed occasionally by those they trust. You receiving a message from someone you aren't supposed to know, can raise difficult questions and extreme precautionary measures. In this case, there was a very good explanation. Just be careful."

Reem was shocked and silent for a few seconds as the magnitude of the situation suddenly became clear. "I certainly did not mean to do anything of that kind," he sputtered.

"Be at ease, brother. As I said, there was a good explanation," Amin reassured. "Please make sure the tracks from the device are fully-covered. We will be doing something next week, which requires two men in Canada. I will brief you within the next few days."

"Very well. Using the hunt club aliases?"

"Yes, exactly. Thank you for being proactive on the technical front, it is one reason why your work is so valuable."

"I certainly don't want my fingerprints on that remote device, which is why I am moving so fast. Next time, I will do something which erases itself, if there is any possibility of something similar occurring," Reem said.

"Hopefully, future work will stick to the agreed-upon script, but this last one was a special case. Let me know if there are any difficulties cleaning it up."

"Will do."

Amin terminated the connection, relieved that Reem had a good reason for receiving the Prince's message. It would have to be verified, but if the Prince didn't know who received the message that would work in Reem's favor. Amin wrote a coded message to The Hammer, relating what he had just learned and his opinion of its veracity.

If he had to leave home again for several weeks, it might be a better solution to bring the late Dr. Hammayil's mirror to Columbus for additional training and to watch over Amin's home. The automated security systems were top-notch, but any system can be beaten with sufficient skill and the FBI certainly was capable. There was enough loose data and gear in the home to raise the eyebrows of any law enforcement personnel who happened to see it. Having a man, a cousin from abroad perhaps, living in the home would greatly improve the situation while Amin was out of the country. There was a lot to accomplish over the next two days.

• • •

Quinton Jameson's phone rang, the caller ID flashed the special number provided by the Deputy Director. He picked it up quickly, "Jameson."

Without preliminaries, the Deputy Director got right to the point. "Quinton, there have been further developments in the matter of Prince Zufar. He recently contacted someone appearing to be from The Hammer's organization, perhaps even The Hammer himself, inviting him to Riyadh. The contact committed to be there within one week.

Obviously, if we catch Zufar and The Hammer it would be a major coup. Keep your eyes open and see what you're able to learn."

"What if The Hammer is Farid Monsour, as I've suspected all along?"

"Then you will have our abject apologies along with your new position. We're monitoring Farid's movements and should be able to give you warning if he leaves the country."

"No, if Farid is our man, I'll want a promotion as well. It's a small price to pay for keeping the whole matter confidential, wouldn't you agree?" Jameson said with a hint of his old imperiousness.

The Deputy Director paused for a moment, then smoothly continued, "Yes, I believe it would be."

"Very well. I leave for Riyadh tomorrow night and will check in once I arrive."

"Good, be careful over there, this can easily go wrong if you aren't."

"I will be, thanks for the update." Jameson hung up the telephone, excited there might be more reward from this trip than just rehabilitating his personal reputation. It was a gamble, though. If he went over and nothing was accomplished, he would be out the travel expenses. If the trip led to an arrest, not only would he be reinstated, he would also be famous as the man who brought the DuChard Duchess terrorists to justice. Much more fame than what Justin Simons had accrued for simply saving lives. If he were to return the FBI, he would have to consider what to do about Justin. The man was much too popular and competent. Jameson preferred subordinates who needed his continued guidance.

Two days later, Jameson's plane landed in Riyadh. Once more, he endured the hours of immigration processing and baggage retrieval. Checking into his hotel, he took a quick shower before visiting his CIA contact at the United States Embassy on Abdullah Alsahmi Street, across the street from the Turkish Embassy. Jameson was dressed in a nondescript business suit, looking like nothing so much as a harried businessman. The CIA man was a part of the embassy trade mission staff, but his duties lay elsewhere.

"Colin, how are you?" Quinton asked, standing to shake hands. "Is there a secure location where we can chat? I don't want any of my competitors hearing what we're doing in the Kingdom."

Colin Jones, whose name everyone assumed was an alias, looked the part of a career government bureaucrat. He wore a white dress shirt, with a loosely hanging tie which didn't manage to cover his belt buckle. He hadn't quite given up on his thinning hair but the comb-over was beginning to be a challenge. At first glance, he gave the impression that his heart might decide to stop beating at any moment. Such an impression would be a serious mistake, but it did make for a believable cover story.

"Welcome back to the Kingdom. Certainly we can use my office. I think most of the conference rooms are taken." Turning about, he led the way back to his office with a brisk walk. After the door was securely shut, he asked, "OK, Quinton, what's up?"

"What's up is that I have a bead on who called the shots for the DuChard Duchess attack. I'm here to gather some evidence which will allow us to arrest or detain the person responsible. How would you like to be a hero, Colin?"

"I always like being a hero, it does wonders for my reputation with the ladies. What kind of intelligence led to the identification of a suspect?"

"NSA intercept of voice communications. The suspect didn't bother to disguise his voice or identity and asked for a status on the detonator GPS coordinates. The terrorist answered the question with some scenarios and recommended the suspect initiate detonation. The detonation occurred shortly thereafter."

"I must confess you have my full attention. Who is the suspect?"

"Our old friend, Prince Zufar Azziz," Jameson said.

"Interesting, didn't we sit outside his residence for an extended amount of time during your last trip?"

"We did. At the time, I was focused on Farid Monsour as the potential leader of the Martyrs terrorists, Zufar happened to be one of his stops in the region. In the past, we have liked Zufar for funding terrorist activities but evidence has been difficult to acquire."

"I can well understand why it would be! I've heard some interesting rumors concerning these matters recently. One of my local contacts, well-connected but not courageous at all, mentioned a brunch hosted by Zufar where a video was shown of terrorists claiming to have detonated the DuChard Duchess. There wasn't enough detail or corroboration to justify looking into it or even reporting back to the mothership," Jones said.

"But the data seems to be something important, you know every agency is mobilized to find these terrorists."

"Yes, and we're no different at the Agency. The problem is, I myself heard more than thirty similar rumors being bandied about with different players. Every pretender with money here wants others to think they're close to the action, wherever it is. Most of these stories are dead wrong or wishful-thinking fabrications. The way power works here is difficult. The Saudis are very conscious of being perceived as lackeys to the United States. It would be hard to arrange for the arrest of a prominent Saudi without extensive negotiations state-to-state. We have to be very careful here, to not upset the diplomatic status quo."

"But now, it seems as though the Prince Zufar link is independently corroborated, right?"

"I would say so, yes. I was only explaining why we aren't passing every data point upstream. So, what do you need from me?" Jones asked.

"Ideally, a black bag job into the Prince's compound, looking for evidence and planting some surveillance devices if possible. Also, I need an unregistered weapon - handgun - as a carry."

"Wow, you aren't asking for much! There are several difficulties with that, but let's first deal with the gun request. You are aware that unregistered handguns are forbidden, correct?"

"Yes. I assume your team carries them despite the risk?" Jameson asked.

"Yes, they do. However, they do not live in a hotel with metal detectors in the front lobby."

"Then why not set me up in a safe house? I don't have to stay in a hotel," Jameson said.

"Are you planning to be hands-on for this exercise? Otherwise, it is very unlikely you would need a gun here." Colin clearly didn't want Jameson caught with a gun.

"Yes, I'm planning to enter the compound with the team, because I understand what kind of things we're looking for. My field operations skills aren't terrible, haven't used them in a while, but I was part of a black bag squad coming up."

"Alright, alright. We have a small apartment you can use with one other person. There isn't anything hugely secret about it, foreigners cannot be hidden in this city without disguises. It is an apartment for executives temporarily assigned to Riyadh. Of course, the executives are all company men of one stripe or another. But having settled the issue of lodging and a firearm, we still come back to the first issue. Normally, with a black bag job we go in to an empty space, when the target isn't there. I don't think you understand how many servants and family live within these compounds. If he is out for some reason, there is no guarantee the offices will be empty. In fact, I would wager the exact opposite, sight unseen."

"How do you go about looking in on these folks?"

"Mostly with remote electronics, wired informants, and informants within the household."

"Do you have anyone there?" Jameson asked.

"No, we do not. You have to understand, most of the servants are lower-class members of their own tribal units, they aren't hired off the street. Usually there will be a few foreign workers, especially for menial jobs, but they are never fully trusted or have access to secrets. It takes a long and arduous campaign to either subvert or place an asset inside a compound such as this."

"I'm not prepared to give up on it just yet, maybe an opportunity will present itself."

Colin shrugged. "Perhaps it will. How long are you planning to be with us?" Jones asked.

"As long as two weeks, which I could extend if I'm using the apartment rather than a hotel. Once successful, I'll head back to DC."

"One last question, I heard your status with the Bureau is, how should I put this, somewhat tarnished. How does that square with you being on this mission?"

"I'm here by myself, but fully expect to be reimbursed by the Bureau. Does that clarify matters?"

"It does. God, I hate bureaucrats! You have to make good, but they have perfect deniability if it went the other direction. Quinton, we'll take care of you, both for old times and the mission itself. I think I know just the two men I want on this project. Look, stay in the hotel tonight, you're already on the hook to pay for it anyway, check out tomorrow morning and I'll send them over to fetch you. OK?"

"Yes, thank you," Jameson said.

"We'll have an embassy driver take you back to the hotel, wait in the lobby until they fetch you. Hopefully you know never to get into a street-hail car, right? Not much crime here, but enthusiastic locals thumping or humping lost infidels is not uncommon." Jones led the way back to the lobby.

Jameson sat as he imagined different ways to gain access to the Prince's residence. Every scenario seemed to be doomed without the intervention of movie-like capers to empty the building. You couldn't just wear gas company overalls and order an evacuation in Saudi Arabia. Jameson wasn't used to being somewhere he couldn't blend when needed. Americans are easily identified by the way they move, upright and purposeful, culturally quite different than the street traffic in Riyadh. No, this situation called for a different approach. Jameson was still deep in thought as he entered the hotel lobby comfortable in his role as a businessman and confident of being perceived as just another foreigner. His confidence was misplaced.

After the American had entered the hotel lobby elevator, a man reading a local paper set it down. Taking out a mobile phone, he dialed a number. "Mussa, this is Fazil over at the Hilton. Remember the American whom I watched a few weeks ago? He's back. I just saw him go upstairs."

Fazil listened to the voice give lengthy instructions on the other side, then hung up as he walked to the front desk to consult with a manager.

• • •

Justin was at his desk when the flagged list of international travelers leaving the United States came in for review. Persons of interest and those who had earned a notation from the scanning algorithms made the list. Justin and every other case leader with international interest routinely scanned the list for familiar names which may have come up in their investigations. As Justin perused the list, one entry caught his attention. Quinton Jameson had boarded a flight bound for Saudi Arabia the previous day. Taking the report in hand, Justin headed upstairs to speak with the Deputy Director.

"Sir, I apologize for interrupting, but I thought you should be made aware of this report. Quinton Jameson left the country yesterday for Saudi Arabia. I didn't flag him but he came up on the list. Is this something to be concerned about?"

"Thanks for bringing this to me. He shouldn't be on the flagged list, but I think I know how it happened. When he was first suspended, he was probably flagged as a matter of standard practice. But I have to admit, I'm not sure why he would be returning to Saudi Arabia. Wait, is Farid Monsour on the list as well?"

"No, sir, he's flagged as part of our Martyrs investigation so it would have made the list. I'll go back over the last few days reports in order to be sure I didn't just overlook it," Justin said.

"Do it. And would you find out where Farid is right now? He might be planning a trip or something that Jameson knows about, in which case I would be very concerned. He is completed fixated on Farid, almost irrationally so."

"The Bureau isn't worried about Jameson in a foreign jurisdiction, while under suspension?"

"What kind of trouble can he get into? He doesn't have any of his credentials or access to Bureau support. If a foreign inquiry came in as to his status, he would be disavowed."

"I don't know, sir. It just seems odd that he would pick up and return. I understand following Farid, but absent Farid's presence it doesn't make sense to me. Quinton is a competent agent, it seems strange he would go out on his own."

"Exactly! Which is what got him in trouble with the Farid situation. Let's stay informed on the topic. Send me an email as to Farid's location when you find out, will you?"

"Yes, sir!" Justin turned and went back to his desk. He had been sure the Deputy Director would take exception to news of Quinton's return to Riyadh, but he was seemingly unconcerned. Justin didn't understand it, but shelved the issue in favor of his assigned task.

Justin reached out to Farid and, without mentioning Jameson's trip, confirmed he was home in Georgetown. Farid reminded Justin of his planned two-week vacation to his cabin in Canada once he broke free from the office. Justin sent an email to the Deputy Director with details of Farid's location and plans, then went back to the forensic accounting of securities-trading irregularities following the sinking of the DuChard Duchess. The State Department was still working on the proper approach to gain access to Prince Zufar at its own glacial pace.

• • •

The next morning, Jameson stood with his suitcase outside the Hilton lobby waiting for his ride. A small BMW sedan which had seen better days pulled up and the driver hopped out. "Mr. Jameson, I expect?" He had about the most obnoxious Australian Outback accent that Quinton had ever heard. The voice came from a seemingly wizened man with scruffy sun-blonde hair and dark skin like leather.

"Yes, I am."

"Gary Beard here, let's get your stuff situated in the boot for our comfort," Gary said as he opened the car's trunk and flung Jameson's bags inside. Slamming the door shut, he walked around to the driver's side door. "Get in, mate. No one's going to hold your door."

A bit disgruntled, Jameson got in the back as the shotgun seat was filled by a wiry Arab.

"Don't mind Sadaq, he doesn't speak English worth spit. He has other skills which are useful. Right! We're to take you to your temporary home in the Kingdom. Have you given any thought to your cover story? You came in on your own paper, didn't you?"

"Did I need a cover story? I wasn't necessarily trying to hide my FBI background."

"You mean to carry a handgun and live in a safe apartment while here in the Kingdom. Yes, you need a story. FBI doesn't mean shit here. If anything, it makes you a target," Gary explained as he pulled out from the hotel.

"I came in on my own personal credentials, without reference to the FBI connection."

"Not all bad then. When showing your documentation, say something vague like you're investigating or improving business ties with the Kingdom. All the coppers like hearing it, even if they don't believe you. Saudi Intelligence services definitely know you're in-country, but there is a chance it isn't a concern. Hold on now," he swore. "It looks as though someone is following you, mate. What the hell have you stumbled into?"

"I briefed Colin, didn't he give you a summary?"

"No, he didn't. Colin will be getting an earful from me! We weren't expecting to be followed. Who are the baddies?"

"Potentially a terrorist group or local thugs associated with someone we suspect is connected," Jameson said.

"Have to admire the size of your balls, coming alone into the lion's den! Or were you just clueless? We'll save that for later. First, let's lose these lads and continue our drive. Excuse me while I converse with Sadaq for a bit," turning to Sadaq he unleashed a torrent of Arabic gutturals with a will. Sadaq sat up, checked the side mirror for a view of the car which was hanging back and had two heads showing. His dirty suit coat gapped enough to reveal a shoulder holster.

"Don't tell me we're about to do some evasive driving here, wouldn't that call even more attention on us?" Jameson asked.

"Oh, hell no, I flunked that course! Not really, of course, but no way am I about to bring the weight of Riyadh's finest down on my head. We'll just go park our car in the building over there."

Gary expertly pulled the car into the entrance, pressed a remote which opened the gate, then slowly drove forward so the gate closed behind him. The following car drove slowly past the building. Gary drove the car around the parking circuit until coming up to an exit on a different street. "We'll just wait here for a bit," he said. Keeping the car in idle, Gary watched the street outside the building until he saw the tailing car drive by in a hurry. "Now we go. Guy had to go 'round the block to get back to the entrance we used. We'll take a left and bid them adieu, shall we?"

"Damn, I am going to have to remember that one. Smoothly done."

"All part of the extra-special service. Gratuities not required, but definitely appreciated," Gary said with a guffaw. Quinton couldn't help but laugh as well.

"How are you tied up with Colin's team? Your accent has you coming from down under," Quinton asked as Gary resumed his deceptively relaxed driving.

"I'll tell you sometime when we're tying on a bender. Bad form to ask it on a first date, though," Gary said as he turned right into a parking structure next to a modern apartment block. "We're home, the flat is upstairs, follow me."

Gary led the way, Quinton followed carrying his suitcase and laptop. Sadaq hung behind keeping an eye on the parking spaces for any interest by third parties. The few people there appeared to be going about their own errands.

Gary opened the apartment door and ushered them inside. "Deep breath. Here is a key for you during your stay. Take the bedroom on the left, it should be set up for you with a private bath. This apartment has only two bedrooms, but three baths, go figure."

"Who stays here?" Jameson asked.

"We all do. I have the bedroom on the right and Sadaq gets the sleeper couch when staying over. We'll be here for the duration to provide for your security as well as convenience. Go unpack and get sorted, I'll start some coffee for when you're done. Join us when ready."

Jameson went into the surprisingly well-appointed room and unpacked his bags. There was a small desk for his laptop, which he plugged in to the familiar wall sconce in order to keep a full battery charge. Then he walked back into the common area next to the kitchen. As he took in the scene, he saw about ten small handguns arrayed.

"I had Sadaq lay out an assortment for you. Pick one you like, and we'll fix you up with a holster. I cannot emphasize enough that you do not want to be caught by the security services with one of these weapons, think Turkish-prison ugly. I have to ask, have you ever fired one of these in the line of duty?" Gary asked.

"No, I haven't had to as of yet. I served on the line for about ten years, had it drawn several times but never used it."

"Good! Glad you won't be impulsive about it. So, tell us what we are trying to accomplish. You can trust Sadaq with our lives, I do."

Jameson explained the entire situation just as he had for Jones at the embassy. "We are sure that Prince Zufar is involved somehow in the sinking of the DuChard Duchess, and The Hammer will be visiting the prince soon. We have to get proof, before we drop a ton of bricks on him. The powers that be want a live defendant rather than a dead one. Otherwise, we might have done something different."

"Makes sense, I guess that is why you are on your own rather than coming over in a conspicuous pack. Tell you what, let's get your weapon set up and we'll do a drive-by of the Prince's compound. I'd like to see if there are alternate ways to get this accomplished before we start thinking Mission Impossible bullshit."

While Quinton tried various handguns for feel, Sadaq started putting together electronic gear that looked like a black bag kit. Raising his eyebrows, he caught Gary's eye.

"Fucking Americans, you think because someone doesn't speak good English they won't be skilled in technology. Tell it to 4 billion Chinese and Indians, wanker!"

A bit abashed, Quinton turned his attention back to firearm selection. He selected small 9mm pistol with a 12-shot clip, plus two spares. For someone who didn't expect to be shooting, it still felt more comforting to have extra on hand, something about the solid weight of it. Gary came around, looked over Quinton's arrangement of his holster, and nodded his approval. Quinton couldn't see that Gary had any weapons, but knew he probably did.

"Gary, what do you and Sadaq normally do for Colin? Mostly surveillance? Black-bag?" Quinton asked.

Gary looked at him as though the question was beneath an answer, but finally said, "Whatever is required, Mate, whatever is required. Enough chit-chat, we're ready to roll. Jameson, I'll want you to sit in the back seat. Do you have a pair of sunglasses?"

"Yes, I do."

"Good, given our episode this morning, I do not want you to be spotted on this ride. Sit back in your glasses and try not to attract attention. I think we'll be fine as long as you're not walking about or have your head out the window."

They exited the apartment and were shortly in Gary's car once more. Sadaq had a large cache of equipment on the front passenger floor, while he sat in the seat. The trip to the Prince's residence was driven in a leisurely way, Gary pointed out various landmarks along the way. If anyone were to look into the car, it would simply appear as though a local was showing a visitor the sights of the city. Upon arrival, Gary cruised slowly by the front entry gate with a circular drive for dropping visitors at the front door. It was unclear where the parking area was located, but the security guards manning the gates were armed with rifles. Gary whistled tunelessly and drove around the block. The Prince's compound took up an entire city block, with a service alley which looked to dead end into a loading dock. Gary parked the car in an open spot just past the alley entrance.

"Let's have a look at the alley, shall we?" Gary spoke some rapid Arabic to Sadaq who pulled out a small drone about two times as wide as his hand. Turning on the drone, Sadaq took Gary's mobile phone and paired the devices. When he confirmed the video feed was operating properly, he opened the car window and after a quick look for passersby, released the drone into the air.

Quickly it rose to thirty feet, high enough to not be immediately obvious to any bystander and above the presumed viewing angle of the security cameras. Sadaq navigated the device slowly down the alley, panning the camera back and forth. Gary watched as device made an orbit of the alley. He spotted additional security cameras mounted high on the walls of the compound. After a short reconnaissance, the drone returned to the car. Flaunting his expertise, Sadaq flew the drone into the car and caught it before powering it down. Sadaq and Gary had a long conversation in Arabic, with Gary shaking his head ruefully.

"OK, a physical approach will be difficult without some help. Sadaq is going to monitor WiFi and see what joy there is on that front."

Jameson couldn't help but be impressed with what he had seen so far. Sadaq took out a small laptop and started scanning for WiFi routers. Gary translated Sadaq's comments as he worked. The WiFi system was an enterprise system installed within the Prince's entire compound which utilized the same name across multiple access points. It was secured using WPA2-PSK, which normally would require a brute-force computing attack to guess the network key, guessing the password over and over until it found the right one. Sadaq's aspect brightened somewhat at something he found, which he explained to Gary as he shut the laptop casing.

"Our lad just found something we may be able to use. Evidently the network was set up to be very secure, however it maintains a segment using older, less-secure protocols, probably so they can support older devices. We might have something back at the shop we can use for it. Alright, we're done here for now," Gary explained.

He drove back to the apartment, watching alertly for any signs they were being followed. If anyone was there, they were skilled enough to remain undetected so Gary continued without taking an indirect route. The three men walked up the stairs silently and entered the apartment. Gary made the rounds checking his security, making sure no one had taken the opportunity to visit while they were gone. No one said anything of note until Gary gave a thumbs-up gesture to both men.

"Sadaq is going to update his laptop with the routines needed. In the meantime, let's look closely at the captured video on bigger screens, shall we?"

Sadaq handed Gary a USB-drive which he promptly plugged into a flat screen television. Sadaq opened his laptop and began working on something feverishly. Gary cursed creatively as he navigated the clunky television interface to play the videos.

"OK, I think that's got it. Here we are working our way down the alley. There are two doors into the complex, one is set onto the loading dock, and another is right here halfway down the alley. Both appear to be made of heavy metal. There are six security cameras. Let's get a good look at those and see if we can identify the make and model. Well, well, what do you know! It amazes me when people as rich as the Prince skimp on their security planning. These are not hard-wired cameras, they run off of the same WiFi as the rest of the compound. Undoubtedly on their own network segment and dedicated bandwidth, but if the network goes down, these do as well. Better double check and make sure all are the same type. What do you think?"

"That makes perfect sense. Are we talking about somehow cutting off their WiFi network before going in?"

"Not so much that, as being able to insert ourselves into their network. If Sadaq is successful in his quest for a hole, we can, perhaps, get what we need without going into the facility itself. Going inside isn't the difficult problem, but getting out afterwards is quite another matter. Therefore, I am not fond of the notion. They have backup power generators, I saw the exhaust manifolds as we circled the block. From the size, I would guess they are full backups running on natural gas, so cutting the power to the block won't get us anywhere. There is another possibility of doing a man-in-the-middle with their Internet feed, but it doesn't get us past the firewalls," Gary said. "Go ahead and hang loose for a while, I think we'll be going back over there tonight if Sadaq comes through for us. Could be a late night, you might want to take a nap. When hungry, help yourself to what's in the fridge and make a list of requests if nothing suits. We have an assistant that stocks the food and beverages every few days. Alcoholic beverages are not on the menu, however."

"I'll catch up with things online, then probably will take the nap since I am still a bit lagged from yesterday's travel," Jameson headed for his bedroom and the desk. He hoped they had not been noticed or followed by the Prince's security crew.

• • •

"How could you lose an American in Riyadh? Their block-heads are visible a kilometer away," Prince Zufar was not happy with the news Mussa was relaying.

Mussa was endlessly patient with Prince Zufar. "Highness, evidently Jameson was picked up by a private car, and they became aware of our car following. They went into a private garage and didn't come out. When our men went inside, the car was nowhere to be found. They discovered a second exit to the parking structure, which presumably is how they lost him."

"Do you think we're dealing with professionals? That doesn't sound like an amateur," Prince Zufar asked.

"Perhaps, but, if so, they are not connected to the FBI in Riyadh. I'm told Jameson met with the Trade Mission, a fellow named Colin Jones."

"Probably CIA then. Do you think the driver was CIA?"

"It's possible. The hotel manager told us Jameson checked out this morning. I've queries out to all of the major hotels, plus a few of the smaller ones. If he checks in, we'll hear about it. If this is CIA, he might be staying at one of their apartments."

"Assuming it is CIA, why is Jameson here?"

"I expect it is because they learned something and he is here to follow up. CIA would be the natural party to engage for illegal activities. Perhaps he couldn't get the job done through the normal processes," Mussa replied in his soothing deep voice.

"This Jameson broke his tooth trying to chew on Farid, maybe he is here on personal business. But I cannot imagine Farid would share any plans where Jameson would find them."

"Perhaps Jameson was the recipient of an informant's tip," Mussa smiled.

"I haven't spoken to Amin yet, so it would not have been me. Besides, it would have gone through you regardless. When does Amin arrive for our discussion?"

"This evening, he will come after it is dark. I have taken the liberty of having dinner prepared in the event you want to so honor him."

"Yes, I think it fully appropriate. We may want to provide a short video entertainment for his amusement as well," Prince Zufar enthused.

"Highness, you know I think we should dispose of everything connected to the DuChard Duchess, the video, the detonator, and the bullets. I have already eliminated the men associated with the transfer of the weapon in order to protect your house. If someone should tell of what they have seen, even in passing, enough pressure could be brought by the United States for the King to remove your protections."

"No, absolutely not. These items are now the proud relics of my family, to be passed down to future generations!" Prince Zufar strode to the new display case to once more admire its contents. "They will not leave my office unless something happens within the Ministry. If the United States brings diplomatic pressure, it will not happen all at once. We will have warning enough to spirit the heirlooms to safety," Prince Zufar stated.

"What if they raid the compound to take the evidence and you captive?"

"If it is their intent, they have to go through you first, dear Mussa. I have confidence you will be careful and make sure it doesn't happen. Besides, when Amin joins us, we'll have our own offensive capability. You are my defense, Amin will be my sword."

"What if Amin declines to join with us? I wonder what motivates a man like Amin, he never wants to lead, but has the capabilities to do whatever he should desire," Mussa said.

The Prince waved away the question, annoyed. "Enough, we'll deal with Amin tonight. Once he understands Farid is no more, but The Hammer is to remain, he will make the obvious choice. If not, then perhaps Amin will be no more as well. Try to find out which alias he is using, we may want immigration to place a flag on it."

"As you command," Mussa said with his head inclined.

• • •

Amin sat in the living area of a small apartment the Martyrs owned in Riyadh. He allowed a young government employee to use the space for a nominal fee. In return, he accepted packages when they were not there and visited his family in a remote village whenever

Amin or Farid needed the apartment. Amin smiled as he thought of the fastidious young man, who would be shocked to discover his landlords were wanted terrorists. Farid had arrived several minutes earlier and immediately headed for the shower to wash the road dust from his body.

Both men had used new identities to enter the country from Brazil. It was getting harder to create false identities in the old way: finding a forger and paying large sums for their services. Now, you simply suborned a government employee in a passport office to create false records. Paradoxically, it was less expensive than the old way, because the bureaucrats didn't understand yet how valuable their service could be.

Farid came out of the bathroom a new man. "How was your trip over? Mine was not as nice as usual, had to travel business class. Have you heard from Reem yet?"

"Yes, he crossed the border successfully and was on his way to the cabin. He has your mobile phone and he knows what to do," Amin said.

"Great. I am relieved he proved to be innocent of dealing with Prince Zufar. His work is top-notch and there is a lot more for us to do. Speaking of which, did you confirm whether we were able to open the backdoor to Zufar's home network?"

"Yes, the routines propagated when the detonator was attached to their WiFi network. Reem used something from a past life, so I doubt that our friends will have found it."

"How about your Qatari friends, did they make it back home?"

"They did indeed, and frankly are a good choice for us if we need to expand our activities in the Gulf. They traveled under false papers, so their trail stopped once they arrived home," Amin explained.

"Good. I'm fairly certain that Zufar has become a problem, but we don't have many options in dealing with him. If the FBI or CIA take him alive, he will identify us in a heartbeat. The question is how to best accomplish safety on that front with a minimum of risk. I would prefer something more elegant than mere assassination, something that effectively closes the book without further investigation.

Let's both think on those goals. Do you think anyone has noticed the flaw in his network security besides ourselves?"

"Hard to say, but I would guess not. It wouldn't be obvious to a general attacker, unless they were trained by some of the same people. NSA or CIA would spot it pretty quickly, as it comes from their toolkit, but I have doubts about others," Amin explained.

"How are you going to present things to Zufar?"

"I'm going to listen and try to escape noncommittal. Why? Do you think this is a good time to ask for a raise?"

Both men laughed freely at something only the two of them could fully appreciate.

• • •

Under cover of darkness, Jameson and his borrowed CIA team drove back to the Prince's compound. They set up next to a dumpster which served a small coffee shop. The foot traffic was sparse, but there was enough for the men to blend into the area. Sadaq kept his head down, focused on his laptop full of tricks, as his fingers tried one approach after another. Gary sallied forth and purchased three coffees from the establishment next to their parking space. Jameson kept his face under cover and watched Sadaq work. Suddenly, Sadaq said something which sounded triumphant, but then he remembered Jameson's language handicap and gestured a thumbs-up with a wide smile. Gary came back into the car with his precious cargo and got the news in Arabic. He slapped Sadaq on the shoulder in congratulations, then handed him a well-earned cup.

"My young genius has just found something important, and we're into the Prince's network. Someone before us must have left a small gift in place, because it was vulnerable to an Agency-approved approach. We'll figure out later how it got there, but for now we use it," Gary said.

"You mean our colleagues might have already arranged an access method to be available? Doesn't the coincidence make you a bit nervous?" Jameson asked.

"Not particularly. I'll explain. We have no idea how long it has been in place, could be weeks, months, or years. The Agency does this sometimes. When an opportunity comes up they'll package a payload in something else the target uses, just on the off-chance we'll need it someday. So, we don't really know how old this hole is, but we really don't care anyway. One time here in Saudi, we packaged it into a USB drive packed with porn which was passed around here like it was Star Wars. We're still seeing systems and networks infected with that one."

"What will Sadaq go after first?"

"I've got him trying to gain access to the video surveillance cameras, so we can look over the inside. Then I'll have him start looking at any storage networks or live PCs for other opportunities. No way will we have digested everything tonight, but he'll be downloading a lot once we find something. If you have any ideas on that front, let me know."

"I would be especially interested in the Prince's office and the surrounding areas," Jameson said.

"I'll tell him, but in the meantime, do your part and keep an eye out for anyone taking an unnatural interest in us," Gary instructed.

Gary was positioned to where he could see the beginnings of video camera feeds, Quinton watched over the seat in between his scans of the surrounding area.

"Here, lad. It appears that a banquet will be served tonight and soon now, look at this setup. Makes my mouth water and I can't even smell it. Look, someone's coming down the alley towards the back door. Who is this?"

Jameson struggled to see a face, but the small format of the screen worked against detail. "Are we able to capture this feed? We may want to look into this person a bit more."

"Already ahead of you - Sadaq is pulling it in."

"Let's follow this guy with the cameras. If he is a guest, something useful might come of it," Jameson said. Gary rattled off a string of Arabic instructions to Sadaq.

Sadaq sectioned the screen into two halves, one with the ongoing video feed and another with file systems being searched. Jameson tried to maintain his guard duties, but found his eyes drawn back to the small screen mesmerized. So much so, he failed to notice the slight but powerful man who had spotted and recognized Quinton Jameson. The Hammer pulled back into the shadows and vanished.

• • •

Amin walked down the dark alley towards the back door of the Prince's compound. The ornate front entry hall was too noticeable for a man who lived for being ignored. The Hammer had briefed Amin on the exact placement of the surveillance cameras and Amin kept his face at an angle which made it difficult to capture biometric data. The Prince's cameras weren't placed to enhance that technology, but Amin saw no point in giving anything away. Reaching the door, he pressed the call button and waited. Within a few seconds, he heard the unmistakable sounds of someone approaching.

The door opened a crack against the shoe of a very large man.

"Your name and purpose?"

"Amin Zafir al Tikriti. His Highness is expecting me," Amin said clearly but quietly.

The door opened wide, "Pleased to make your acquaintance. I am Mussa, we have spoken in the past. In addition, your reputation is well-known to me."

"I'm flattered, but I'm sure it is exaggerated. I've heard your name in the past as well," Amin said politely.

"Please step over here for a security screen, please hand over weapons at this time. I'll return them before you depart." Amin submitted to the various changes in position necessary to complete the screen with fatalistic good humor. The small arsenal he carried was collected in a plastic bin and set to one side.

"Come with me, the Prince asks you to join him in his theatre room." Mussa turned and led the way deeper into the palace. Amin continued to present sidelong views to the security cameras he passed. Soon, he entered a small theater to meet the Prince, who waved up at a large screen showing a stylized logo of several rifle bullets engraved with "Martyrs al-Sabra".

"Welcome to my home, Amin Zafir al Tikriti! It is a pleasure to finally meet you in person. How do you like the logo?" Prince Zufar asked. "I had it made in honor of the great success achieved!"

"I confess it makes me nervous, as marketing is the last thing we would want to do. Too dangerous and risky to the principals, but I like how it appears certainly."

"Understandable, please take a seat, I have a short video to show you," Prince Zufar eagerly said.

Amin walked to the area indicated and sat down. Zufar pressed a remote control which dimmed the lights. Amin watched as the Prince made his speech and pressed the detonator button. In the days following the sinking of the DuChard Duchess, the Prince had gathered news coverage video of the rescue attempt and victims gathered in Port Canaveral. Interspersed throughout the stolen footage was the stylized logo for the Martyrs al-Sabra. Privately, Amin was appalled that the Prince kept such incriminating evidence within his home. Once more, the Hammer was correct in his analysis of personality tendencies. As the house lights came up, Amin politely clapped his hands in congratulations.

"Amin, tell me. What do you think of my special movie?"

"I think it is one-of-a-kind and special. It has been kept very close, yes? No chance the infidels have seen it I hope," Amin said.

"None. The day of the blessed event I hosted a small meal for a few special friends who saw the portion from our own studio, I had planned to do the detonation in their presence, but we had move early. If I had risen earlier, I would have gotten them all instead of mostly just the crew. What was it like to plant the device onto the ship itself?"

"I do not hesitate to say it was a very uncomfortable thirty minutes, especially because of the anti-tamper provisions we built into it. We were very lucky and were able to do the work without any losses. In fairness, the secrecy and lack of publicity is primarily aimed at our survival. We want to run many more operations over the next few years."

"Speaking to your last point, I am of the opinion the organization needs new thinking. Thinking only a man with more resources can provide. How would you feel about a change at the top?" Prince Zufar said.

"What exactly do you mean?"

"The Hammer's organization has been primarily a Palestine-focused group, even when engaged in other activities. I think it should broaden its worldview to include Islamic struggles worldwide. The goals currently stated are all of the old tropes about a return of

Palestine to its rightful owners, which few Muslims really care about, at least not to the point of risking life and limb. We all care about the rise of Islam in the world, and it might be a unifying principal which delivers much more power. The world's Muslims need the leadership we can provide. I think the persona of The Hammer is important, but it can be anyone, couldn't it?"

"What of the current Hammer?"

"If he agrees to take his rightful place within the organization instead of the leadership role, he can be a part of it. But he is a proud man, and may not accept the demotion gracefully. In that case, he would have to become a real martyr for the cause. I know you are a loyal man, otherwise I wouldn't be talking of this plan. I value your contribution much more and want you by my side."

"How would this work, in operation?" Amin asked.

"We'd establish a chain of command and communication protocols to support leading the effort from here. We'd maintain the United States team in place, including you. Come with me to my office suite, we can dine together as we discuss the future of the Martyrs al-Sabra." The Prince turned aside and led the way.

Amin followed the Prince. Mussa's looming presence followed Amin.

"Come over here and see the possession of which I am most proud. Please, come," Prince Zufar urged Amin over to a standing gold-trimmed case built around the small detonator, which rested upon black velvet. Gold-plated rifle shells with the Martyrs name indelibly inscribed on the casings nestled on the cushion beside the detonator. Amin, again, was surprised that all of these things were not destroyed after completion of the operation. It was akin to someone wanting to keep documentation proving they had taken flight lessons in Florida with the Twin Towers terrorists from 9/11.

Just then, Mussa heard a bell ring for the alley door. "Your Highness, we weren't expecting anyone else, were we?"

"No, we were not. Let's check the cameras, shall we? A man by himself, obscured to the cameras. Wait! The Hammer? What is he doing here?" Prince Zufar wheeled on Amin.

Amin's look of shock was all too real, The Hammer wasn't supposed to reveal his presence until they had a chance to talk after the meeting. Something must have happened. "He isn't supposed to be here," Amin managed with conviction.

It must have been enough for Zufar, as he then turned to Mussa, "Go let him in, but search him very thoroughly. We'll see him here." Mussa bustled off to admit him.

"Amin, let's have some refreshments while we wait. Maybe this is fortuitous, as we can settle all of our discussions this evening."

Amin wasn't hungry, but one of things he had drilled into all of his students is to be underestimated when it came to being dangerous. No one worried about a man holding a small plate of food as an imminent threat. Especially with a large person like Mussa by their side.

In a few minutes, Mussa reappeared with a rumpled Hammer still rearranging his clothes from the thorough search.

"Hammer, to what do we owe this honor? Even though you were not invited, as my brother you are ever-welcome."

"In our organization, one invitation counts for all. But before we get caught up in what I mean, did you know there is a group of three men sitting outside the east side of the compound next to the coffee shop? Americans, CIA probably, at least several of them. I thought it important this was known immediately rather than my original plan of remaining unseen."

"Three men? Mussa, the monitors," Prince Zufar shouted. The men watched as one of the large television monitors lit with the security camera feeds, Mussa selected the camera for that part of the compound wall.

"There, that one, Mussa," Farid pointed out the car.

"Did you recognize any of them, Hammer?" asked Zufar.

"No, it was dark and the windows are tinted. However, it did appear they were watching a laptop closely. Can you check your network to see if there is an unauthorized visitor?" Farid said calmly, but expected he already knew the answer.

"Mussa, get the guards out and capture those men. I want to find out who they are and why they are here," the Prince commanded.

Mussa hurried out of the room talking into a small radio. The remaining three watched the camera feed as the security team closed on the car. The occupants were clearly ready for trouble as the car leapt away from the curb and away from the running guards.

"Hammer, did you know your favorite FBI man is in Riyadh? We lost track of him this morning after checking out of his hotel. Does his presence here have anything to do with you?"

"Not possible he knew I was coming. If I had to guess, I would say he is probably here for you," Farid said calmly.

"Why would you think such a thing?" Prince Zufar asked.

"Who used a standard voice line to contact me the night of the DuChard Duchess to ask questions in the clear? You know NSA records and investigates all of your telephone calls, correct? The only reason they learned of my existence is when I used that channel to tell them after the American election. I distorted my voice and used a burner phone, they suspected but couldn't prove anything. You, though, did nothing to protect yourself. Therefore, I think he's here for you. But don't despair, I expect he was very pleased to see me on the surveillance cameras just now: a bonus. I didn't recognize Jameson in the car, but it makes the most sense," Farid lied without compunction.

"Don't be impertinent, remember where you are standing. If it is Jameson, he will find out what it means to challenge a Saud at his home. Where is Mussa?"

"I apologize. I meant no disrespect, but we do not have much time. We have to find those three men immediately and learn what they know," Farid said.

Mussa ran back into the room, and hastily conferred with Zufar.

"Highness, is it possible you have a friend or contact with access to the public security camera network? We can track the car from here if we hurry, then make plans to deal with them once we know where they hide," Farid said.

"Yes, yes. Mussa, do we have the access link and password for it? If not, you know who to call."

"In the meantime, did we ever determine whether they successfully penetrated your network? Amin can help search the router logs if you grant access to the network management platform," Farid asked. "I think they came in over your WiFi network, which was why they had to be close by. An Internet attack could have been launched from anywhere. That side of the building is no good for visual surveillance, they wouldn't see anything. It had to be electronic."

"After we get the traffic cameras up, Mussa will set up a terminal for you, Amin," Prince Zufar said.

Farid walked over to the gold display case and admired the craftsmanship. "This is a beautiful relic and displayed so well. I would be too fearful of the Americans to keep something like this in my home."

Prince Zufar warmed at the oblique compliment to his bravery, "This is the Kingdom, not the United States. They wouldn't be able to take me without giving plenty of warning. Soon they will have forgotten and stop looking, after such time they won't even recognize the significance if they did see it."

"I respectfully disagree with the assessment. The Americans will never stop searching until they find the persons responsible for the attack. Never. They will examine every thread of evidence until they find something," Farid said with conviction.

"Why are you not worried, then?"

"My Prince, of course I am worried! What intelligent person wouldn't be worried? Our whole operation was planned to be a slowly evolving reveal of evidence. When the FBI finds something, we are long gone and their time is wasted. The difference between us and your situation here, is we present a moving target to the pursuers. As long as we, the Martyrs, continue to move they will have difficulty finding us. If we stop moving, they will find us as surely as tomorrow's sun rises in the East. If those three men found anything useful, you might unfortunately have to start moving as well."

Mussa was able to successfully access the city surveillance network, which was run by Prince Zufar's cousin, and was busy reviewing the camera feeds for the car in question. Switching from camera to camera, each labeled by small lettering in frame detailing the camera's mounted street location. Soon he had the car as it sped away from the Prince's compound. As Mussa grew more adept in the tracking, Amin sat down next to him on another computer and pulled up a copy of a street map on a separate overhead monitor so turns could be discerned more readily. What most foreign visitors to Riyadh don't realize is the prevalence of surveillance cameras in the Kingdom's capital city. There were very few places one could go which would not have an active camera watching. Prince Zufar and Farid offered options of route choices as Mussa worked to keep the car in view, switching from camera to camera using the timestamps. It took time, but after about thirty minutes, they saw the car pull into the parking garage of an apartment block.

"There it is, we need to go fetch our shy friends for a long debrief here. Do we know anyone at this apartment block, Mussa? Get on the phone and find which apartment they are in while we come up with a strategy to capture them," Prince Zufar ordered.

Amin looked up from the computer terminal which Mussa had set up for him, "Highness, from what I can tell, they did breach the perimeter of the network and downloaded a large amount of data from the storage arrays. There is also an indication they were into the surveillance camera feeds, I'm not sure what they actually saw but it is really bad if they captured all of us on tape."

"Then I guess this is your problem as well, isn't it? Can we count on your help bring them in?"

Farid looked at Amin, who nodded. "Your Highness, I see no other alternative. I believe we can do it with just Mussa and us two. No disrespect against any of the rest of your men, but this should be kept to as small a group as possible. If Jameson is there, he is the only target of value. The other two regrettably should die immediately, it is the only way to work with a high-success probability. We need our weapons obviously, but I just had a notion. Do you have any Beretta Model 70s at hand? If we have to kill a couple of CIA assets it might be nice to muddy the water with Mossad fingerprints."

"We do have two or three of those. No one will believe Mossad would be so stupid, but it does buy some time. Especially, if the information somehow gets into circulation that Mossad killed two CIA men in Riyadh, the fellahin will be in the streets rioting. Mussa will go, but I also want him to take one more of my men. He can choose the right fighter. Who knows how many people are in the apartment?" Prince Zufar said rhetorically.

Farid raised his hands in acquiescence.

Mussa came back in, "Highness, I spoke to the apartment manager. There is an apartment on the third floor leased to a commercial firm. Normally, there is an Australian who speaks Arabic and a Pakistani staying there. Not much is known about the company, other than they pay their bills on time. He will be waiting for us in the office."

"Mussa, choose one good man from your team to accompany you. You two are to support our friends here while capturing Jameson. Please get them properly equipped and be on your way as soon as possible. We will ready ourselves to meet Mr. Jameson in the studio. I think his end should be properly advertised. Use the black panel van, the security forces won't stop that license plate."

"Hammer, I wanted to work with you more directly, it seems as though the time has come. Let's plug this leak and then decide what is next for the Martyrs al-Sabra," Prince Zufar said.

"As you say, your Highness," Farid stood up and followed Mussa in order to gear up. Regardless of what the Prince wanted, Jameson would have to be removed from consideration in a final way.

• • •

"It looks as though they are in a movie theater, see the seating and the big screen? Clearly the Prince wants to show something to the visitor," Jameson said. "Is there any chance we can download the video file as they play it?"

Gary rattled off some Arabic to which Sadaq nodded in affirmation. In the meantime, the video feed darkened as the Prince and his guest sat down to watch. Quinton had a hard time making out what was on the screen, but saw what looked like a terrorist ranting and holding a device in his hand. There was large Arabic banner behind the man.

"Gary, can you make out what the banner says on the film?" Quinton asked.

"Let me see," Gary had to close in on the laptop while Sadaq was typing furiously pulling in files, the video window took up a quarter of the screen. "Hard to say mate, looked like a hundred banners I've seen. The video Sadaq is pulling will be a better view, may just want to wait for that to come in."

The two men watched as the video completed and the camera feeds followed Amin to the Prince's office.

"What is that trophy case the Prince is showing the visitor? Can we get a better view of that?" Jameson asked.

Gary spoke to Sadaq who uttered a short reply to Gary. "Damn prince is a narcissist, or extremely paranoid, he has six cameras in that large room. Sadaq is looking for the best view."

"Are we capturing this feed?" Jameson asked.

Another quick conference, "We're trying to, but he's prioritized the video files over the live streaming. Our bandwidth on the WiFi network has been fluctuating, but that is perfectly normal. We'll have to see what we got when we get back to the ranch."

The men continued watching for a few minutes, as the Prince and his guest began to serve themselves some food. Jameson was reminded by his growling stomach that coffee isn't a permanent substitute for a meal. Sadaq was humming something to himself in the strange musical keys found in the Gulf region, or maybe he just wasn't a good singer. Jameson was encouraged, thinking the files must be coming in properly. He took a few moments to scan the area for potential danger, then turned his eyes back to the small screen. A fourth man had joined the group, someone who looked familiar to Jameson.

"When did that new man arrive?"

"Just now, you should have seen it, looked like security roughed him up pretty good as his clothes were a mess," Gary said dispassionately.

The man turned in profile to the camera Quinton was watching. A cold feeling of dread gripped him and he felt as though he needed to vomit. "Gary, we have to wrap up and get out of here, right now! That man is Farid Monsour, the same man I was convinced is The Hammer. He is extremely dangerous, and I have a really bad feeling he already knows we're here."

"Why do you think so? It doesn't look as though he is all welcome there, although there is a lot of talking going on. OK, I'll get Sadaq to wrap up as much as he can." Gary hurriedly spoke to Sadaq, who nodded and, if possible, his fingers moved faster. Gary started the car and it sat idling. "Jameson, keep a watch, if you see anything: we fly."

On the screen, Jameson saw the large man who appeared to be the Prince's bodyguard run from the room. Quinton rotated his head back and forth between the two directions a security detail would appear. His neck craning was rewarded less than a minute later, as a group of guards with rifles ran around the corner of the compound.

"Go, go, go!" Jameson shouted.

Gary put the car in gear and stomped the gas aggressively. The car sprang from its resting place and flew past the security detail. Looking back through the rear-view window, Jameson saw the guards aim their weapons at the car, but the large man waved them down.

"Gary, you might have just saved all of our lives, thank you."

"My pleasure, Mate. Sadaq just lost the WiFi signal, so he will work on making sense of our take while we head back to the roost."

Sadaq spoke at length to Gary. Jameson sat back in his seat relieved and stunned by the danger escaped.

"Sadaq said the room was wired for sound within the camera feed, we didn't hear it because he was using the earphone, but you were right about the 4th man. The Prince addressed him as Hammer. The first guy was called Amin. Finally, the writing on the banner said Martyrs al-Sabra," Gary said.

"Shit, Gary! We're in great personal danger now, our priority has to be to get somewhere we can upload the video to FBI HQ. Then we have to find somewhere safe to hide until reinforcements get deployed. Believe me, we could wind up in a shallow grave in the desert before morning. This is the man who ordered a cruise ship destroyed by a nuclear weapon, not to mention shooting children by sniper. I had him in jail and he personally put three bikers in the hospital with his bare hands," Jameson said urgently. Quinton's normal arrogance and personal attitude of being safely in charge was shaken at last.

"The safe house is the best place for us, for a number of reasons. First, the Internet connection is excellent and should make short work of sending the data to HQ. Most important, it should be fairly secure and non-obvious," Gary said.

"What if they are tracking the car?"

"Extremely unlikely, but we'll check the undercarriage before we make the final turn home. Did anyone get close enough to the car to do something along those lines?" Gary asked as he wove through the half-empty nighttime streets.

"I don't think so, but I was looking for people watching us and weapons of course. If someone walking by dropped to tie a shoe while placing a transponder, I might have missed it."

"Alright, we'll do our garage trick again and then get a quick look underneath. Don't worry, I have the bomb detection mirror in the boot, this is something we have to do normally anyway," Gary said.

"I'm going to call my contact now, to tell him what's coming," Jameson said.

He fumbled with the screen of his mobile phone to dial the Deputy Director. The first dial didn't go through as he hadn't entered the country code for the USA, the second went to voice mail.

"Sir, it is important that you contact me immediately. We have electronic proof of the Prince's involvement, and will be sending the video file to you shortly. More, man I had arrested was here with the Prince and the Prince addressed him as 'Hammer'. I should have video proof of it as well. We were spotted by the Prince's security and are trying to evade capture now. I recommend spinning up Lucy, it will be hard to arrest these guys without a lot of cover and men with pointy sticks. Please call me as soon as possible, sir!" Jameson terminated the call and checked his battery charge. It should be sufficient to get him through the evening. Quinton had been burned in the past, by engaging in loose chat of classified materials, and had learned his lesson well. He assumed the message was monitored. Thus, his indirect identification of Farid and the President. The Deputy Director would understand Quinton's references easily, however, which was the true goal.

"Hold on, here comes the garage," Gary called out cheerfully. He pulled close to the side exit and got out of the car. Holding the bomb detection mirror and a flashlight, he carefully walked around the entire perimeter of the car. After a couple of orbits, he placed the mirror and flashlight back into the trunk closing the lid with a slam. Gary jumped back into the driver's seat, restarted the car, and drove back out onto the streets.

"Nothing down there but a lot of caked mud and offal. Seriously be hard to place a magnet with all the slop down there, makes it easy when searching since you have to find a clean spot to attach. Now for home, lads."

Jameson sat in his seat, checking his phone every few seconds for a missed call. Every minute seemed an eternity as the lights of the city sped by. Finally, the car pulled into the apartment block parking structure. The men exited the car within the empty garage, and briskly climbed the stairs, walking fast but not in a run until they finally entered the privacy of the apartment. Sadaq rattled off a long address to Gary who asked a few questions before turning to Jameson.

"Sadaq has some good and bad news about the downloaded imagery, Mate. He has the theater video in its entirety and much of the discussion with Amin in the Prince's office, but we don't have any of the Hammer footage. Evidently it was backed into the download queue: first in, first out. I'm sorry, but I think you have what the men in shiny suits wanted most. Sadaq said there were a lot of what look to be financial documents and spreadsheets as well."

"Can we see the theater video on the television or a larger screen?" Quinton asked.

"Certainly, you don't think we watch our porn videos off the laptop, do you?"

"Nothing gets you down does it?" Quinton asked. "I'm barely holding it together here and I thought I was experienced."

"No point in whinging, is there? Plus, the rest of the world sees nothing wrong with bottling it up. Americans always have to share. That's what put me off my first American wife, all the sharing. Then she has the effrontery to object to sharing me!" Gary declaimed before snorting a short burst of laughter. A few words to Sadaq and they gathered around the large, flat-panel television in the living area.

All three men listened to what appeared to be the Prince wearing a scarf over the bottom half of his face. Gary provided an English translation for Jameson's benefit as things progressed. It was the smoking gun of smoking guns. In the event a viewer didn't know what had happened after the Prince pressed his button, the newsreel highlights which followed removed all doubt. Jameson sat stunned for a few minutes, then went and gathered up his laptop case.

"Gary, I need to get the video file at minimum uploaded to DC. I'm guessing the file is too large for email? I have a secure dropbox through VPN back to the Bureau. Please ask Sadaq to transfer the files to this empty USB thumb drive. It is 64 GB, is that large enough?" Jameson asked.

"Sure, it will be a few minutes to copy all of it over, but that should be plenty of space for what we have."

"No worries, it will take Windows 7 awhile to boot and connect to VPN anyway," Jameson said with a smile.

"There you go: a joke! Might make an International Man of Mystery out of you yet! How about a good, stiff drink? I'm planning on one for myself and the lad here."

"How about a Lost Empire Special? You know, a gin and tonic," Quinton said.

"I'd laugh, were it not so tragic," Gary said.

Just then, Jameson's phone rang. Hurriedly, he picked it up and answered.

"Jameson here, sir. Thank you for calling back so promptly. I am about to upload the proof of the Prince's involvement to the secure dropbox. We also got some additional surveillance video and financial files from the system."

"How good is the proof?"

"Sir, he made a video of pressing the detonator button, then added footage from the news reports of the Duchess, with Martyrs al-Sabra banners in the background. By itself, a pretty damning piece of evidence. But in the surveillance videos of his office, the detonator is apparently displayed in a gold and glass exhibit case."

"Good work, get the video to me immediately. How was the evidence obtained?"

"We broke into the WiFi network for his compound. We were spotted, though, and had to escape. One thing, the person I mentioned? There is no surveillance video for him, there wasn't time to pull it in.

I'll swear to him being present and being called 'The Hammer' though."

"Don't worry about it, we'll try to get him when we sweep up the Prince. How soon can you take the Prince into custody?"

"I can't, remember? I'm unofficial. Furthermore, we're going to need all the local help we can get, a team of SEALs comes to mind. No way to get it done quietly, I'm afraid. It will have to be official and facilitated by Kingdom security forces. The compound is in the city, guarded by staff with automatic rifles. Lucy will have to demand it, or the Prince might just vanish with the evidence."

"Look, Quinton, you've done very well and believe me when I say we'll reinstate you. Hell, we'll probably give you a medal, too. I'll call Lucy's folks now and ask them to be available as soon as possible. Get that file to me immediately!"

"I will, sir. I will text you when the send is complete."

The VPN connection with FBI HQ finished its slow setup just as Sadaq come over with Quinton's thumb drive. Plugging it into the laptop, he opened the Explorer interface to examine the files. The video file had been named "Prince" and was 438 megabytes in size all by itself. The other files were smaller, but the entire package was more than 2 gigabytes in total.

"Gary, how big an Internet pipe do we have here?" Quinton asked.

"We have 12 mbps, which is very good for Riyadh," Gary said.

Doing the math quickly in his head, Quinton shook his head. He logged into the secure drop-box and started the upload of the most critical file, the one named "Prince". The upload started and he watched the progress bar slowly fill.

"This is going to take a while, I'm doing the video file first and will follow with the others. Are you going to brief Colin, or shall I? Saudi Arabia will be having to make some very difficult choices shortly and he will need to be prepared. I'd tell the ambassador, too, but I don't give two shits for him. Where's my drink, Aussie?"

Gary laughed and handed Quinton his rich cocktail, "That's how to play it: spit in the eye of the storm. I'll read Colin in right now, you keep an eye on the transfer. I'll tell Sadaq off of the Internet while you upload, but, knowing him he is probably way ahead of the game."

Quinton's face was illuminated by the laptop screen as he willed it to finish, while he sipped the cold drink. The alcohol loosened a tension he hadn't fully recognized until it departed. A few more minutes and he would be back from disgrace, stronger than ever.

• • •

Justin was finishing another working day filled with dead ends and bureaucratic delay. His desk phone rang from the Deputy Director's office, "Justin, can you come up here right away?"

"Yes, sir, on my way."

He was shown directly into the Deputy's office, the Director was also sitting at the conference table.

"I've asked you both in because we've had a break in the DuChard Duchess attack. In minutes, we should be provided with a video obtained from Prince Zufar's compound in Riyadh. It is explosive and establishes Zufar as the person who detonated the device," putting up a hand to forestall questions he continued. "There's more. An eye witness claims to have seen Farid Monsour in Riyadh tonight and heard Zufar address him as Hammer. Justin, do you have any knowledge of his whereabouts?"

"Not today, the last time we spoke he mentioned taking a vacation in Canada. He has a cabin in the deep woods somewhere up there. His phone is still monitored, so we should be able to do a GPS query, if he has coverage. I'll look into it later, but I won't believe he is The Hammer on mere hearsay. Who is the witness?" Justin asked.

"Quinton Jameson. I know, I know! His record on Farid is far from objective, but let's see what data he has on-topic and not blind ourselves to the possibility."

"How did Quinton Jameson get involved in all of this, and how the hell didn't I know about it?" the Director said calmly in a voice that promised consequence.

"Plausible deniability, sir. Quinton came to me asking if there was any way to redeem himself with the Bureau. I shared with him the issues we have been experiencing surrounding the necessary investigative work in Saudi Arabia, and he volunteered to go in as a private citizen. He has personal contacts with the CIA types stationed there, and it seemed he might be able to help." The Deputy Director shaded the truth a bit in his explanation.

"Why would I need plausible deniability?"

"If he failed, then surfaced telling the world I had sent him over in an unofficial way, the consequences would land on me. If successful, no one would ask too many questions. Justin, can you access the task force secure dropbox and play the video to my television monitor?"

"Certainly, sir." Justin came around the desk to see an open folder labeled Riyadh up on the Deputy's screen. A video file named "Prince" was being uploaded, the grey ghosting effect testifying to it still being underway.

"You and I are going to have a chat about risk management after this settles down. What was the quid pro quo for Jameson?" the Director said.

"What he wants most in the world: reinstatement and a clean folder."

"I don't know if that's possible, too many agreements are in place which would be affected. We might take him back in, but he couldn't be anywhere near his old job. One note, we don't move on Farid Monsour unless we have dead-on proof. Hearsay won't cut it, especially coming from Jameson who has a large axe to grind. Our agreements with Farid's legal team would fall apart, and I would not be pleased with the results. Am I understood?"

"Yes, sir." The Deputy Director affected a chastened demeanor, but knew his plan had worked.

"OK, it just finished being uploaded. I'll start the player now," Justin said.

The three men watched the incendiary video, blood draining out of their faces, replaced quickly by anger and the need for revenge. Even in Arabic the intent was clear, and all three men recognized the banner script from the current case. The Director took out his phone and speed-dialed an office less than a mile away.

"Sid, Director Spencer here. We need an immediate conference with you and the President. There's been a break on the DuChard Duchess." He listened for a few seconds then rang off.

"Gentlemen, be downstairs in five minutes, this has to be briefed at the big house. Justin, get a thumb drive with this and meet us out front." The Director headed off to the restroom.

"Sir, Jameson has a bunch more files coming in," Justin said.

"They'll be there when we get back, this one the President needs immediately as she will need to get our forces mobilized. Jameson isn't safe right now, he was spotted. We need to move fast all around." The Deputy Director urged.

Justin ran back to his desk, grabbed a clean thumb drive and started the transfer as he pulled together his things. He wished he had a few minutes for the restroom as well, but it wouldn't work in the five minutes allotted.

Upon completion of the download, Justin snatched the USB drive and ran for the front lobby. Sitting by the curb was the Director's SUV and protective detail. The men waved Justin into the back and they were off, sirens blaring.

The entry into the White House was by the usual route, in terms of entry security, but the attentiveness of the security staff was significantly heightened. The Director led the way towards one of the larger conference rooms, where he was met by Sid Rosenbloom. Sid nodded his head at Justin and the Deputy Director as he waved the group into the room.

"Gentlemen, I took the liberty of adding Pentagon liaisons to the guest list. The President will join us shortly. Justin, you running the show and tell? Here, plug in and get set up," Sid said.

Justin sat down but nodded to Major Spokes before focusing on connecting to the projection system. He looked up and caught Sid's eyes when it was ready to start. Sid signaled his Secret Service lead and the President entered the room with her detail. Everyone rose and remained standing until she had taken her seat at the middle of the table.

"Madame President, FBI Director Spencer has had a break in the DuChard Duchess case," Sid explained.

"Finally, some good news! Director, please proceed," President Brown said.

"Madame President. As you know, we have been experiencing delays in following up on our Saudi evidence. A group within the FBI arranged for an unofficial investigation by a former FBI agent. Working with his CIA contacts, he was able to obtain the data I am prepared to show, along with much more which has yet to be analyzed. The reason for urgency will become plain as we go. Do we have a cleared Arabic interpreter?" Director Spencer asked.

"I can manage, but I am far from fluent," Major Spokes offered.

"Thank you Major. Agent Simons, please start the video. It is fairly short."

Sid dimmed the overhead lights and Justin pressed play.

As they all watched the video, the initial impressions were non-committal. Videos from terrorists taking credit for attacks was nothing new. Major Spokes did well translating, even going so far as to identify the banner text behind the masked speaker. The mood in the room changed dramatically when the man pressed the detonator button and celebrated. The media footage of the DuChard Duchess had been seen many times by those in the room. Sid had the lights raised once more.

"Director, I'm not seeing why this is any different from the videos we see from terrorists or pretend terrorists on Facebook. What am I missing?" the President asked.

"Madame President, this video was never intended for release or publicity. This is a home movie, made by Prince Zufar Azzizi al Saud for his own use. The voice in the video was not doctored and will match his voice. Remember we intercepted a telephone call from him to the United States the night of the attack which seemed to question why the ship wasn't moving. He was advised it was due to our knowledge of the target and probable passenger evacuation. Shortly thereafter, the movie was made and the device triggered. Our operative and the CIA, obtained this data directly from the Prince's palace network."

"I can play the telephone call as well, if it is helpful." Justin said. The President waved her hand to proceed. The call, too, was in Arabic, but a translator had already performed a voiceover in English.

"I'm convinced, Director. What is the current situation in Saudi Arabia?"

"Madame President, I can answer that," the Deputy Director said, "Our man was spotted in their surveillance post, but escaped and got to a safe house run by the CIA. They are in significant danger if the Prince finds where they are staying. We don't know how far the Prince's power runs, but he is a member of the royal family and it is possible the state would support him if it did not have all the facts. Another consideration is that our operative saw internal security camera footage of the Prince's office, which appears to have the detonator enshrined within a gold trophy case. We need the physical evidence and the Prince alive in order to roll-up the entire network."

"Sid, have the Secretary of State bring the Saudi ambassador over here immediately. I will not take no for an answer. Also, get the joint chiefs in here as well, they need to see this and start contingency planning." President Brown was electrifying in her decisive manner.

"Madame President, the Joint Chiefs are already on their way," Brad said.

"Thank you, Major. I'm going back to the Oval to write down what I want to say to the ambassador. Sid, keep the group together, bring the Chiefs up to speed on the evidence. Good job everyone. We have more to do tonight." The President and her detail departed the room.

"Sir, I think we have additional security camera videos uploaded, do you want me to preview them first or just put them up?" Justin asked.

"We have some time before the Chiefs get here, just play them," the Deputy Director said.

Justin started playing the security camera footage Sadaq had gathered several hours earlier. They watched as the unknown man was shown to the theatre, the movie was shown, and the move to the Prince's office. The viewers could tell the movie was the same as the one they had viewed earlier, and there was no mistake that Prince Zufar was proud of it. Major Spokes grunted when the gold display case clearly held the outlines of the detonator shown in the video. Justin was marking down which files had the corroborating evidence so the Chiefs wouldn't have to watch everything.

"Justin, is it my imagination, or were there some rifle rounds in that case as well?" Major Spokes asked.

"I'm not sure, let's slow it down and see if a clear frame will show it." Justin fiddled with the controls until it did appear gold-plated shells were indeed in the case.

"The contents of the case will be the crux of our evidence against the Prince. The President indicated earlier we were to arrest and prosecute whoever was responsible. We need to remember that some of our evidence is inadmissible, due to how it was gathered," Justin said aloud.

"The only way it will happen is if the Saudi government cooperates. It would represent a huge departure for them, to break ranks with a member of the royal family. Bin Laden they could explain away as a mere wayward son of a successful family from the Kingdom. Prince Zufar is actually in the line of succession, low down on the list, but still on it," Sid commented. "It's up to the President now and how the Saudis react."

The Joint Chiefs started filing in with their small staffs. Once settled, Justin played the videos pertinent to the situation. Sid and Director Spencer took the lead on context commentary. The men watching had various visceral reactions to the antics of Prince Zufar. These were men dedicated to the military protection of the United States. They were deeply offended by the nuclear attack, in particular the Chief of Naval Operations and Marine Corps Commandant. Both men looked as though they would prefer to soften up the Saudis with a device or two of their own.

"The President has asked this group for options. We're attempting to gain the cooperation of the Saudi government in apprehending Prince Zufar but it is far from certain we will get their assistance in time," Sid stated.

"Did I hear that we have operatives at risk in Riyadh? What if we sent a detachment of marines over to get them safely to the embassy grounds?" Marine General O'Malley asked.

"It would represent a great start, but before we have the Saudis on board it would have to be done discretely. None of us want Marines in a shooting incident with Saudi security forces."

"I'll get on it now. Four Marines in an embassy vehicle shouldn't be too much of a provocation. I'll reach out to the local base for support or extraction in the event things escalate on the ground." The United States had maintained a small, multiservice base in Riyadh since the Gulf wars.

"We can put surveillance drones up now over Riyadh, to watch the Prince's residence as well as the apartment block where the operatives are holed up. We can do that as a training exercise, and no one will think anything of it. How are we fixed for a mobile command center?" Air Force General Schmidt asked.

Justin sat still with his bosses as the military leaders worked through various scenarios in a collegial manner. Having little else to contribute, he started reviewing the files uploaded by Jameson, making notes on each for further investigation. In particular, he was looking for a familiar face, but dreading its appearance. After a cursory examination of the entire upload, he was unable to find Farid in any of it. Excusing himself for a moment, he slipped into the hallway and made a call to his best friend. The call went right to voicemail.

"Farid, this is Justin. Please give me a call as soon as you can, I wanted to run something by you. Also, did you head off to your cabin? If so, I hope the weather is great and you're having a good time relaxing."

Justin went quietly back into the conference room. Logging in to the Homeland Security passport database, he made a quick search for Farid. Sure enough, he came up on a flight to Vancouver, British Columbia three days earlier. There was no indication of a passage to Saudi Arabia other than the one from several weeks prior. *Not definitive proof,* Justin thought, *but combined with mobile phone use we should know.* Justin hoped Jameson may have seen someone who looked similar to Farid on a security video and made the cognitive leap.

• • •

In the Oval Office, President Brown put the final touches on the bullet points she wanted to cover with the Ambassador. Ambassador Suaved was a well-known fixture of the Washington DC cultural scene. A sophisticated patron of the arts, he had spent most of his life living abroad, first educated in the United Kingdom and finally assigned to the Saudi embassy in Washington. Over the years he had worked his way to the top position and was well-liked by most American Presidents. Of course, the previous years were turbulent times for diplomats in Washington, but President Brown felt the relationship had improved significantly during her administration.

Lucy had her personal assistant summon Sid for a quick chat.

"Madame President?"

"Yes, Sid. I am going to need a way to play the videos for Ambassador Suaved when he arrives. Can you take care of it? Also, what is the status on his arrival?"

"State says we pulled him out of a fundraising party, but he should arrive within a half-hour. State has been briefed verbally on the situation, but has yet to see the footage."

"Good. Hopefully, she will keep her mouth shut on this one. We have to play this hard and fast, and she has had weeks to do it the normal way."

"I'll make the suggestion to her when she arrives."

"The meeting is only you, State, the Ambassador, and I. What I have to say shouldn't leave the room."

"Are you citing WMD?" Sid asked.

"Can you think of a bigger stick?"

"No, ma'am, I cannot. I think you have no choice but to do so, especially if we want to debrief the Prince ourselves."

"Thanks, Sid. I have to go put on my Margaret Thatcher duds. Suaved is smart enough to know what it means. I'll be back in the Oval within twenty minutes."

Sid bustled out and called Ashley over to set up a laptop with the videos. She went into the main conference room, handed a small thumb drive to Justin and explained what was needed. He quickly put together the three most damning videos and gave it back to her.

Fifteen minutes later, the Saudi Ambassador arrived at the White House. He was shown to a well-appointed waiting room and offered coffee which he declined. The Secretary of State came in a rush, still wearing her evening clothes for a night at Lincoln Center. Ambassador Suaved rose and greeted his friend.

Sid looked into the room, "The President is ready to see you, Ambassador."

When the trio approached the Oval Office, Secret Service agents opened the door. Inside, standing behind the Resolute Desk was President Brown.

"Ambassador, I apologize for interrupting your evening, but there is a very serious matter between our countries which cannot wait for the next working day," President Brown said.

"Madame President, as always I am at your call. How may we in the Kingdom be of service?"

"Please sit, this conversation will doubtless be too long for standing." President Brown indicated a chair next to hers for the Ambassador; State and Sid sat down upon the expensive couch.

"Ambassador, I want to work together with the Kingdom to forestall a serious incident between our nations. Some background: you are aware of the DuChard Duchess terrorist attack which occurred last month. Some very damning information has come into our possession. Rather than explain, I would ask you to watch." The President signaled for Sid to play the videos.

The Ambassador watched the videos without comment, even when the recorded telephone call referred to detonation. Diplomats had to have a poker face if they were ever to be good at the job. After the final seconds of play, he turned to the President.

"Madame President, these are very disturbing but I question their provenance. I'm also unclear as to what you want from the Kingdom," Suaved sat back in his chair with a relaxed manner, in marked contrast to the others in the room.

"I'll be frank in the interest of time," President Brown said. He nodded agreement and she continued. "We want to capture Prince Zufar alive, with the evidence intact, in order to try him in the United States for his crimes. Clearly, we cannot do so unilaterally without impacting our relationship with the Kingdom. I value the strong friendship between our nations and would like to see it continue undamaged."

"Why not file an extradition request through the normal channels?"

"For several very good reasons. First, given warning the Prince could flee the Kingdom ahead of the extradition; he is a billionaire after all. Second, the crucial evidence would be destroyed or remain unexamined, making the scope of his activities unknown. Finally, and most important, because his actions were a causus belli."

"Surely you do not consider the actions of a private Saudi businessman to be those of the Saudi government?"

"The government of the Kingdom of Saudi Arabia is one of monarchy, is it not? Prince Zufar partakes of such status within the royal family, and is in line for the succession, even though far down the list. A case could be made that he is a member of the ruling Saudi government. But there is something else which perhaps hasn't occurred to you yet. What is the stated policy of the United States of America when it comes to a response after being attacked by a weapon of mass destruction?" President Brown sat back and waited for an answer. State started to speak up, but Sid placed his hand on her arm and she subsided.

"Surely you are not threatening an ally with nuclear attack?" the Ambassador sputtered.

"An ally would see the issue from our perspective and decide friendship is more important than one prince. Prince Zufar used an old tactical nuke of Soviet origin, we could use the same sized device on the Prince's compound within an hour. But then, we would endanger innocent lives and not achieve our goals for a full debrief."

"What if the government were to arrest and hand him over afterwards?"

"We passed that bridge several weeks ago when the Saudi government didn't respond to our diplomatic request for joint investigation. Now, we want to be there and ensure all the evidence makes its way back to us in one piece," President Brown said firmly.

"Obviously this is not something I can resolve without consultation, I should go back to my embassy to see what can be done," Ambassador Suaved said.

"Certainly. One additional comment, I am open to face-saving ways to make this public. I want Zufar alive, and I want all the evidence in his possession, both witnessed by our representatives. How it is reported is open for discussion. I am not like my predecessor and will not engage in a Twitter debate online."

"I'll take my leave then, Madame President."

"Ambassador Suaved, I apologize for the urgency of our requests. But we'll need an answer within three hours. It is difficult, I know, but events here are moving swiftly. After you leave, I have to walk down this hall and explain why the armed forces should wait three more hours. Americans have been attacked with a nuclear weapon, feelings are running high and the urge to do something is very strong. It is up to you and I to ensure that sanity prevails, for all of us." President Brown rose, extended her hand to the Ambassador in a friendly fashion and walked him out to where his assistant was waiting.

After the ambassador was out of the White House, Sid turned to the President. "Three hours? Why three?"

"Mainly to give them time for some additional sleep, given the time difference. Plus, we still have some work to do here. Did you mention the operatives who provided the information might still be in danger?"

"Madame President," State interjected, "Did we just threaten a sovereign nation with nuclear attack over a law enforcement issue?"

"No, we threatened a sovereign nation with nuclear attack over a WMD issue. There is a fairly sizable difference. Diplomacy isn't just about going to parties and socializing, sometimes a blunter approach prevails."

"We're not seriously thinking of nuking Saudi Arabia?"

The President sighed. "Katherine, we are considering every option. Do I hope we don't have to? Of course! It would be easy for me to order a SEAL team in to kill or capture Prince Zufar. We are taking a harder route because I want to preserve a working relationship with the Saudis. But if, at the end of their three hours, they refuse a joint approach, we'll decide how to handle it unilaterally. When negotiating life and death, you don't take killing off the table. Enough sermon from me, are you on board here or not?"

"I would like to think about it overnight," State said.

"Fair enough. If you decide to resign, I'll permit it without prejudice assuming there are no media leaks attributable to you on these matters. If you decide to stay on, you need to be fully on-board with where the administration is going. Otherwise, it would be a career-limiting decision for you, unless you decide to switch parties. Understood?"

"Yes, Madame President." State scuttled out of the Oval Office as quickly as her feet could carry her.

"You might have been a mite hard on Katherine, Madame President. She was having to shift paradigms on the fly. I think she will be onboard when she thinks it over."

"Unfortunately, these times are not kind to gentle souls. I can't have a Secretary of State who thinks she sets administration policy. You know, Sid, the American people would applaud if we nuked the Saudis, without any consideration for consequences. Hopefully, Ambassador Suaved is aware of that, and is concerned I might want a distraction from my personal humiliations."

"He is a very smart individual. I am sure he understood all of the points being made. What are we going to tell the military folks down the hall?"

"I'm going to order them to get the operatives to safety and plan for what we do if the answer from the Saudis is no. I suspect they will close their airspace to us during this time to prevent our bringing in more resources, so we're going to have to make do with what's already on the ground. Well, I've put it off long enough, let's go chat with the Generals, shall we?"

• • •

Farid and Amin looked through the Prince's weapons cache, picking and choosing the previously requested Berettas. Interestingly enough, there were also suppressors available which both men also took. After recovering their own gear from Mussa and securing it on their persons, they were ready to go.

Mussa and Bashir rounded out the quartet.

"We're ready whenever your team is, Highness." If you hadn't seen Farid picking up all of his weapons, you wouldn't know he carried any. The same could be said for Amin. Mussa had a tell-tale bulge on his shoulder, but Bashir got the prize for most obvious gunman.

"They are ready now. Bring back Jameson. I think he should be a star in my new video, this one to show to the world. Go, Mussa, follow

Hammer's lead and come back with my property. The studio will be ready for your return." Prince Zufar raised his hands in benediction.

The four men got into a small, unmarked black utility van, much like the ones used by the Kingdom Security Forces. Mussa drove, while Amin and Farid rode in the back. For such a large man, Mussa was a nimble and efficient driver.

"Any ideas on how to do the takedown?" Farid asked in English.

"I think it has to be in the garage, we don't know who is in the apartment or the layout, so the risk goes up dramatically," Amin said.

"I agree. How do we get them out to the garage? I think we should use the landlord to deliver some message which makes them want to leave. Maybe Saudi Religious Police called the landlord to ask about their use of alcohol, and he had to answer in the affirmative. But since they were good tenants, he felt he should warn of the impending arrival," Farid said.

"I think it would get them out, but alert to danger as they expect it is really the Prince's men. We'll need a distraction."

"I think Mr. Obvious gets the nod. Maybe have him looking over their car for contraband when they come out."

"A winner! You and I will shoot the CIA men at the same time, then Mussa can subdue Jameson with the handheld taser. We pile him into the van and depart the scene," Amin said.

"We need to grab any laptops or phones they have on them as well. I expect Jameson already uploaded the Prince's unfortunate video, so Washington is about to come unglued. If this works properly, it might be time to wrap up our work in Saudi Arabia, don't you agree?"

"Most certainly, yes. Road trip to Jordan, or the other direction?" Amin asked.

"I'm thinking Jordan, a long drive under a starry sky."

Amin laughed, "We'd need a convertible for the ride, boss. You're giving me visions of the highway from Vegas to Los Angeles." After a few more seconds, "This apartment building might have security cameras in the garage, we'll have to deal with it."

"I think it is something we bring up with the apartment manager," Farid said. "Mussa, do we know this apartment manager at all?"

"No, we know of him through contacts, but nothing personally."

"What do you think of our plan?" Mussa spoke a passable English, which Farid knew from previous visits.

"I expect it will work with the Mr. Obvious decoy. I'll tell him to show his wallet open as though he is a policeman. No, he doesn't understand English."

"I think we're ready, how far away are we?"

"About ten minutes."

"Drop Amin and I off in front of the manager's office, then go to the garage gate. We will get him to let you in to get set up. I'll disable the video equipment. We won't initiate contact with the targets until everything is in place."

Amin and Farid readied themselves to look completely innocuous when getting out of the van, as though friends had given them a ride home. Mussa pulled up next to the manager's office and stopped. Amin and Farid got out, thanked them and went to the office door.

"Farid, look what is circling overhead," Amin said in a very calm manner.

Farid glanced up at the sky for several seconds, "We have less time than we thought."

Farid started knocking on the door loudly, from within a voice called out asking who it was. The manager's office was part of the manager's living quarters, which was a very common pattern in the Gulf. Being woken in the early hours was never good, but normally it was due to some transgression of a tenant, so the manager opened the door. Amin and Farid pushed through, pulling the surprised manager with them at gunpoint.

"Two questions, your life depends on your answers. One: can you control entrance to garage from here? Two: where is the security camera control center?"

"They are in the same room. Come with me." The manager led the way gingerly to a second small closet off of the office, there a security camera had the van in view. The manager pressed a button on the console and the garage door opened.

"Where are the security videos stored?" Amin asked.

"In the server, under this shelf. It is self contained."

Amin opened the cabinet and pulled out the server appliance. Behind it was a honeycomb of incoming connections from cameras which were multiplexed into a single connection to the appliance. Spotting a pair of wire snips, probably used the last time they added a camera, Amin picked it up and started cutting the bundle of smaller cables. Within fifteen seconds enough damage had been done to render the cameras useless.

"Don't worry, old man, the damage is easy to repair, it just takes time and skilled hands. We'll wait here for our friends to arrive," Amin said.

Within a minute there was a quiet knock on the door, Farid admitted Mussa and Bashir into the room.

"How does it look?" Amin asked Mussa.

"The car is close to the stairwell, probably intentionally. There are several good spots for us."

"The cameras are down, I think it is time to disturb the tenants."

• • •

Upstairs, the excitement had begun to wear off for Jameson and the alcohol helped. The last of his files had been transmitted into the secure dropbox, now he just needed to get safely back to DC.

"The last files just went up, Gary, I think we are good."

"Excellent. I need to do a similar exercise for our lad Colin now. I told him to expect contact from the high and mighty, which made him forgive my waking him. Colin can be quite mean when he hasn't slept."

Jameson took out his phone and once more dialed the Deputy Director. The call went to voicemail, so Quinton hung up. No need for a message when he could just text the word "Complete". After the fact, the entire episode seemed somewhat unreal to him, almost as if it had been too easy. No one thing leapt out to support the notion, but it nagged at him nonetheless. The concern was crazy, they had been in real danger, hadn't they?

The only nit in Jameson's craw was lack of supporting evidence for his identification of Farid. No matter, he would use the statements of Gary and Sadaq to identify the man they both saw against a photo of Farid. Yes, Farid Monsour would pay for the slights Jameson had suffered.

Jameson had almost fallen asleep sitting on the sofa when Gary's mobile phone rang insistently. Gary picked it up, looked at the ID and muttered to himself.

"Yes?"

"Mr. Gary, I am sorry to be calling you so early in the morning, but it is urgent. I received a call from the religious police just now, asking about you and your fellow persons. I told them only what was on the lease documents, which I have to do legally when asked by police. They said you had been reported drinking alcohol tonight and they are coming to investigate. I just got off the phone with them."

"Mr. Mifsud, I appreciate the notice. Why would you take the risk of telling us?"

"Sir, you have been very good tenants and I don't want the police to damage the property, which sometimes happens," Mr. Mifsud explained.

"Fair enough. We'll pull out right now, and the place should be clean for them to inspect. Thanks again!" Gary said while hanging up.

"That was the landlord. Evidently the religious police are on their way over based on a tip. It could be the Prince's goons have found us and it is just a blind, too. Regardless, let's head over to the embassy grounds, it is safer there anyway and we can just break cover since the mission is largely accomplished. In the event it is the Religious Police, we'll take the booze with us. Let's go, now!" Gary ordered.

Jameson ran into the bedroom and threw his clothes into the suitcase without regard for the niceties of packing. A quick scan of drawers and the bathroom, and he was ready to go. The laptop closed and slid into his bag. He walked out into the living area, pulling his luggage with his computer bag on one shoulder.

"One hand free Jameson? Here's a bottle of gin. Good thing there wasn't much here - it is always depressing to lose a bottle. Sadaq, here is one for you, too. Let's go, gentlemen."

Gary and Sadaq hadn't bothered with their clothes. They had computer bags and the small arsenal case between them. The safe house wasn't completely clean, but nothing really important had been left.

Jameson followed the two down, lifting his luggage to deal with the stairs and cautiously stepping without the normal holding of a handrail. The three entered the basement only to see two armed men looking over their car. The nearest had an automatic rifle held down-safe as he peered through the windshield. The other, a very large man who seemed familiar was on the other side of the car.

"Here, what are you lot doing?" Gary asked assertively in Arabic.

"Religious Police. This is your car?"

Sadaq set down his load and tried to get to his weapon as Gary did the same. Jameson froze in the moment, still holding the unopened bottle of gin. He recognized the large man as one seen in the Prince's security videos, and was just going to warn Gary when the first shot clanked. The first shot was followed by three more shots. Both Sadaq and Gary were hit by someone behind him, Quinton dropped the bottle and reached for his weapon as he turned.

"Hello, Quinton. How lovely to find you here tonight," The Hammer said as he fired a taser. Quinton went down and lay twitching on the ground while Amin and Farid stood carefully away until the charge fully dissipated. Then Farid rolled Quinton over and secured his wrists behind with plastic zip-ties.

"Mussa, how are his CIA friends?"

"One dead, another soon to be," Mussa shot another, louder, round into Gary's head.

"Excellent, our work here is almost done. Bashir, move the bodies behind one of those cars. Mussa, we will use their car to return to the Prince due to drone eyes in the sky. Have Bashir drive the van to the airport, then wherever he wants for several hours as a diversion. Amin, the keys for our ride?" Farid said.

Amin walked over to where Bashir had stashed the bodies and went through pockets until the keys were found, and he held them up.

"Mussa, help get him into the car," Farid said. "Sit still, Quinton, otherwise we'll light you up with another round. It is just about back up to full charge." Mussa came over, the two men carried Jameson to the sedan and folded him into the back seat. Farid slammed the door shut just as Bashir took the opportunity to drive out the gate and turned for the airport.

"We'll wait for three minutes and go. Mussa, please drive."

The three minutes went by without further incident, Jameson sat cowed next to Farid who sat with the taser in hand. "Let's go, we should get back to the Prince's home before full light. No speeding, we do not want to get stopped for any reason."

Mussa set a steady pace back towards his home turf. The twenty-minute drive seemed much longer, but soon, they pulled into the alley of the Prince's compound. "Amin, can you see if we have flying visitors?"

Amin stepped out of the car as if he had business with the residence, surreptitiously looking skyward for the sign of U.S. drone aircraft. He bent down to the window, "Looks as though the Bashir gambit worked, let's get him in quickly."

Mussa parked the car next to the door, and entered the codes to open the locks. Grabbing Jameson by the armpits, Mussa dragged him into the building.

"Amin, please turn the car around so we can make a quick exit. This is going to be very hot in no more than two hours. Right now, the Americans are trying to find a way for the Saudis to allow a raid. We do not have much time."

Farid went to follow Mussa as he chivvied Jameson down the hall towards the studio. Soon Amin joined them. Farid opened the door for Mussa as he forced Jameson into the room. Sitting at ease wearing a robe and keffiyeh, marked with Martyrs al Sabra in Arabic script, the Prince stood.

"Mr. Jameson, we have never met, but I have followed your activities recently and decided we should remedy the situation. I even asked most of my staff to leave so we would not be disturbed. I understand you've stolen and watched my previous video. May have even sent it to others. I am about to make another video, but this time you will be the star." Prince Zufar indicated the small stage which had been set up. A scene played many times in the world of Islamic fighters. A single camera facing a lone chair, with a back drop of the

Prince's Martyrs banner. A large curved knife was also prominently displayed.

Knowing what needed to be done, Mussa set Jameson down in the chair, leaving his wrists tied behind the back of the chair. Then Mussa tied Jameson's ankles to their respective chair legs with zip ties and secured a scarf as a gag. It was when the black hood covered Jameson's head that he began to curse inarticulately through the gag.

"I'm a reasonable man, Quinton. May I call you Quinton? I'll take that as a yes. A lot depends on how you answer a few of my questions. Let's start, shall we? Did you see my movie?"

Quinton nodded his head.

"Yes? It's a shame when someone's home movies get stolen and sent elsewhere. Did you send it to someone?

Quinton's covered head was still for a few seconds then nodded sharply.

Yes? Where did you send it?" Prince Zufar asked. No answer was forthcoming other than an inarticulate jumble of sound from behind the gag.

"Mussa, please remove his gag and hood for a few moments. Answer the question, Quinton, in full detail please."

Jameson coughed several times then began, "I sent it to an FBI secure dropbox, from the apartment. They know about you now and will be coming."

"How long ago did you speak with them?"

"Maybe an hour or so. You're a dead man walking, Prince," Jameson taunted defiantly.

"Perhaps, but then it will take some time for their arrival. I probably should hurry things along. It is so tedious to have to pack bags, Quinton. But here is a scenario you probably have not considered, when they arrive, they find an empty home. No search reveals any evidence to support the accusations being made. The United States is humiliated by being wrong. Then it is discovered the Israelis ran a false flag evidence trail to incriminate me. Suddenly, I am living back in my home, protected by my cousin the King. But what about Quinton, what happened to him?" Prince Zufar toyed with his captive.

"You let him go so he can say it was a setup?"

"I wish I could trust you to do it, Quinton, I really do. But in actuality, you have a role to play that is far larger than your person. You get to represent the entire United States and die on camera."

"Your Highness, may I ask a couple questions of my own?" Farid asked.

"Please feel free to do so."

"Quinton, what is the password on your laptop?" Farid asked calmly while Amin waited with the laptop open.

"You're going to kill me anyway. Why should I tell you anything?"

"There are many ways to die, Quinton. One way is to do so with all of your limbs intact, so family has a chance to identify the body, and is relatively quick. Another is a slow, painful death. The thing is, Quinton, I know you'll give up the answer anyway with application of the right amount of pain. Why not cut to the chase and save us all of the unpleasantness?" Farid asked reasonably.

"They're going to catch you, you arrogant prick!"

"Mussa, is there a bolt-cutter I can use? I think we'll start with the middle finger of Mr. Jameson's right hand. Appropriate, don't you think?" Farid asked. Mussa muttered and left the room in search of the tool.

"Don't! The password is *StatelyHome68*." Quinton said through clenched teeth.

"A Batman fan. Movies, television, or comics?" Farid asked.

Quinton ignored the question, his eyes hating Farid with an inhuman intensity.

Farid shrugged. "Ah, Mussa, thank you but we won't be needing it after all." Farid looked over at Amin who nodded that he had access to the laptop. "Highness, I have no further questions."

"Good thinking, Farid. We won't have to guess what was shared. Excellent. Quinton, we are going to start with the filming. If you keep silent, I will not use the gag. Your role is not a speaking one. Mussa, tie his chest and back securely to the chair."

Prince Zufar wrapped his keffiyeh over his nose and lower face, leaving dark eyes shining with anticipation.

"Mussa, on second thought, gag him and cover the head with the black bag. It is too much to expect silence," Prince Zufar looked in the mirror at the image he presented. Persons who viewed the video would have no idea of the embedded irony: a freedom fighter wearing only the very best clothes.

"We're ready to begin, start the camera." Prince Zufar stood with the captive on his left, facing the camera.

Amin and Farid remained off-camera perusing the files Quinton had stolen earlier.

"Children of Allah! The Martyrs of al-Sabra have captured an infidel hoping to put an end to our struggle. He came into our stronghold as weakly as a lamb enters the den of lions, but arrogant nonetheless. He came with help of the American CIA, he himself is a leader of the American FBI. Who is he?" Zufar paused for dramatic effect as he walked to the chair, and pulled the hood off of Quinton Jameson.

"Quinton Jameson, minion of the FBI, behold his disgrace for the entire world to see. But the Martyrs were not fooled by his works, The Hammer is much harder to capture than Jameson had supposed. Now he is the captive. What is the justice of Islam for enemy spies? Death by the sword. I have such a sword here, engraved with the name of the Martyrs, with an edge keen as death."

Quinton didn't understand the Arabic of Prince Zufar but, hearing his name repeated and seeing the sword waved about, knew his end was near. He struggled against the ties to no avail. Finally, Zufar held Quinton's head up by grasping his hair and harangued the camera, waving the sword at his head. Quinton knew everything rode on what he did next. Zufar was working towards a climactic ending in rhetoric.

"Watch the justice of the Martyrs performed and tremble, infidel, for the same end comes for all of you."

Zufar held Quinton's head upright with his left hand and swung the sword hard with his right hand towards Quinton's exposed neck. Quinton threw his head forcefully to one side upsetting the chair to which he was tied. Zufar's blade scored Quinton's head but did not damage his neck. Zufar screamed down at his victim who would not accept the inevitable and struck Quinton on the jaw with the pommel of the sword stunning him. Bending down, Zufar grasped Quinton's hair once more and swung the blade against the exposed neck, but did not have the force to completely sever it. Zufar hacked several more times in a frenzy with similar results. Jameson's wounds were fatal but his head remained upon his shoulders. Zufar, frustrated, placed the blade and sawed until a final separation was made. Zufar then stood triumphantly and held the severed head aloft facing the camera.

"Thus, shall all the enemies of Islam perish!"

"Stop the video. What a mess, I knew it would be, but not this much." Zufar said as Mussa came forward to right Jameson's chair. "Mussa, start the video compilation using the footage I worked on earlier. I'll come help when I get my hands clean," Zufar placed Quinton's head in the lap of his body facing forward.

"So, Farid, what was on his computer?"

"Highness, the original video made for the detonation event as well as the security camera videos made during your meeting with Amin. We interrupted their download before they were able to get video of my entry. Fortunate, since it means my United States cover is damaged but not fatally so if managed the correct way."

"I wasn't joking earlier with Jameson, I'll be long-gone inside of three hours and all evidence will be eliminated."

"What were you planning to do with the video?" Farid asked.

"I'm going to upload it to the Internet."

"If I may suggest, why not modify the voice track to disguise yourself? Without the detonator, they have no proof the earlier video is real. The Americans have almost certainly matched your voiceprint against your telephone calls for that video. This one shows you killing an American agent, if they match your voiceprint, they will chase you for murder. I can show you how to do it easily."

"I believe you are right. As much as I would prefer to be known, it would remove much flexibility. Please, let's go to the production booth."

Farid followed him into the room where Mussa was putting the video inside a template already constructed with titles and banners of the Martyrs. Looking at the multiple tracks, he distorted the waveform using a utility and replaced it. Now the Prince sounded like a demon from a death metal band.

"I like it, let's watch the entire thing," Zufar exclaimed.

The four sat and stood within the booth watching the monitor as it played the entire video.

"Let's have some fun, shall we? We'll upload a copy to the FBI secure drop box where he put the stolen files," Farid suggested.

Prince Zufar laughed uproariously, waving his hand in permission as he couldn't speak for the laughter.

Mussa handed Farid a USB thumb drive and he plugged it into Jameson's computer. Within a few minutes, the 450MB compressed video file had been uploaded.

The four men walked back out into the studio. Zufar walked over to Jameson's body and laughed once. Turning around he found Farid was pointing the business end of the Beretta at him.

"What is the meaning of this? Why are you pointing a gun at me? Mussa, kill them!" The Prince screamed. Mussa held the Prince's eye and shook his head in negation.

"You've become a liability to our work, Zufar. The Americans will not be fooled, they will find and capture you. Then you will give them the Martyrs in hope of leniency. We cannot accept that possibility. Don't look to Mussa, today he is free of you. He has been ours for quite some time, because this day was inevitable. Commit your soul to Allah, and I will grant you peace," Farid said.

Zufar leapt for the still-bloody sword and swung about to rush Farid with a shout. Two quick shots rang out, Zufar's chest blushed red as he fell. Farid walked up to him, and shot once more through the temple. The Prince's body lay at the foot of Jameson's.

"Mussa, gather the security videos to eliminate the record of our presence and meet us at the car. Amin, we'll stop by our safe house to pick up a few things and then drive. I also need to make a telephone call before too long."

"We should probably ditch the car as well, it is only a matter of time before the Americans get serious about finding it," Amin pointed out.

They gathered up the few items needed and climbed into the car.

• • •

The conference room of the White House was still storming with debate over whether to send a small team of Marines to extract the operatives in Riyadh. The military was ready to move, but the State Department urged caution in movements which could be interpreted as provocative to the Saudi Government. Justin stayed out of the discussion as he had no standing to make operational suggestions. He listened to the arguments while continuing to process the files in Jameson's folder.

Suddenly, the system chimed and a new document appeared in the dropbox. Justin clicked on the largish video file and sucked in his breath. He wasn't projecting to the screens, those had been taken for the tactical discussions. Closing his laptop, he stood and walked over to Director Spencer, quietly letting him know there was something he needed to see. Director Spencer watched as Justin opened the laptop and played the video once more.

Visibly shocked, Director Spencer called for the attention of the room, "Everyone, there has been a development from Riyadh. Justin, play the video please. If anyone has a weak stomach, please excuse yourself now."

Justin played the video, with sound, for the assembled persons. As before, Major Spokes provided a running translation. When Prince Zufar inexpertly chopped Jameson's neck, there were groans of dismay, and several people left the room in distress.

Sid Rosenbloom stood, his face pale and grim. "People, the issue of rescuing our operatives is moot. Please concentrate on how we can find out what happened and where our oversight was when it did. I need to brief the President." Sid left the room in a hurry.

"Why would the Martyrs have uploaded the video into the drop box?" Director Spencer asked the room.

"Sir, I think it was their way of telling us they tortured Jameson and have his access into our systems. I just opened an emergency ticket to revoke Jameson's network privileges, but we won't know what they got until our forensic team can investigate. He had access to the entirety of the Martyrs investigation so the breach could be major."

"So, the Martyrs could leak out details of our investigation, wiretaps and surveillance reports?"

"Nuke the PC with the self-destruct application, immediately." There was an application installed on all field and senior agent computers to completely erase sensitive information, operating in the background, when a specific code was received over the Internet. It was a bit like locking a barn after the horses had fully escaped, but if the Martyrs hadn't backed up the computer yet, it might help minimize the damage.

"I'll get IT to issue the destruct code for his machine. When his laptop checks into the server, it will pick it up. I'll go check messages to see if I have heard from Farid or where he is.

Justin stepped out into the hall and sent an emergency text to the head of operational IT security which was immediately acknowledged. He then checked messages and found one which verified that Farid's phone had been seen in a remote area of British Columbia this morning. *Call me, Goddamnit!* He said to Farid.

Feeling impatient, he dialed Lindsey to see if she knew any more than he did.

"Hi, Linds! This is Justin. I've been trying to get Farid on the phone and am having a hard time. He mentioned he might spend a couple weeks in the woods of British Columbia, but didn't say when or where. Do you have a way to reach him?"

"Hi Justin, no I really don't. Whenever he goes up there, he is pretty much off the grid for a couple of weeks, no mobile phone signal. The only time he comes up for breath is when he goes into town for a meal or for provisions. I would leave a message and wait, it is usually less than a day before he gets back to you."

"I left a message yesterday afternoon, so if I get lucky…," Justin's voice trailed off while thinking of alternatives.

"How important was it?"

"Very, it had to do with the investigation."

"Are you any closer to finding the people who murdered Nayla?"

"I believe so, yes."

"Good! We don't have a punishment suitable for them, maybe they should just perish while being apprehended," Lindsey said fiercely.

"I need to talk to them in order to solve all the other murders the snipers committed, Lindsey. We only caught one and he was dead before we could reach him." Justin said gently.

He heard her huff out her breath. "I didn't think about that, I suppose you are right, but Farid and I are still trying to deal with her death. It is so hard! I get angry but there isn't a target for the hate I feel. I can't take it out on my husband or children, … it just festers. Farid is probably trying to exorcise his demons in his own way. He planned to marry her, you know, he just wasn't ready. It has to be eating at his soul," Lindsey said.

Justin felt remorse for some of the suspicions Jameson had sown in his mind against Farid. He had to be objective, but it was difficult when he heard her raw emotion.

"Thanks, Linds. I'll ring back to let you know if I hear from him."

"That would be appreciated," Lindsey hung up the phone.

When he got back into the conference room, a team of Marines had been unofficially dispatched in mufti to the CIA safe apartment. They were armed with handguns, carried concealed, and were wearing bodycams which uplinked to circling American aircraft. Justin learned the drone oversight had followed the Prince's black van from his compound to the apartment. Thinking it more important to watch the Prince's men, they chose to follow the van when it left the apartment.

Major Spokes was on record that the van was a diversion, given its aimless course since the beeline to the airport. Others weren't sure, but they could not know what happened until the men investigated.

The video from four bodycams were displayed on the large screen, as the men exited their car for the office. There was no answer to their knock other than a dull thud from inside. Trying the door, a marine was surprised to find it unlocked and they entered, calling out greetings. They found the apartment manager tied to a chair and gagged. He had thrown himself over in the hope that someone would hear. The marines untied him and asked about Gary.

The manager's English was poor, and the marine's Arabic was worse, but he indicated they should look in the garage. He opened the gate for them. As the men walked through the parking structure, viewers in Washington held their breath. The blood was rather obvious and one marine tracked it until the bodies were found. The marine finding the bodies made sure the bodycam had a good view and notified the rest of the team.

"Sir, we've found Gary Beard and his man Sadaq. Both dead, shot from behind. No sign of Jameson."

"Is there any way to get the bodies back to the embassy?" a calm voice from Riyadh asked.

"We should be able to get them in the trunk, sir. We're in a sedan, assume you don't want them to be noticed in passing?"

"Yes, bring them back now as quickly as you can. Leave two men to go through the apartment for anything sensitive," Colin Jones said.

"There was a laptop kicked under a car, probably Sadaq's, we'll bring that back now."

"Be careful, I think the bad guys are long gone, but you never know."

Director Spencer whispered over to Justin, "Who was just speaking?"

Justin whispered back, "Embassy agency lead, I believe. Those two men worked for him."

Justin's pocket began to vibrate, indicating an incoming telephone call. Seeing the number, he ducked out into the hallway.

"Farid, where the hell are you?" Justin strained to make out his friend's voice against the static and wavering signal.

"Bumfuck Egypt, where do you think? I'm up at my cabin, fishing, thinking deep thoughts about my lifestyle. Not right now, of course. I'm in town for a meal I didn't cook, and to answer the mail. I have to say the mobile phone service here is somewhat primitive, but at the cabin it is nonexistent. What's up?" Farid asked.

"The Martyrs case is breaking real hard right now, you're missing out on the story of the century."

"There will always be another story, 'Time. Besides I got too close to this story, probably should keep my distance, given everything."

"Fair enough, when will you be back in DC?"

"Probably about a week. I've got a battle with this large brook trout who keeps breaking my lines. I'm going to catch him if it kills me. If I catch him tomorrow I might be back sooner, I'll let you know. I have to head back to the cabin now, if you need anything leave a message. Hey, if you wrap up the case, maybe you could take a few days and join me up here."

"If I do, I might take you up on the offer. Stay safe, I hear drinking and driving is legal in the Canadian wilds."

"I wouldn't have it any other way. Talk to you soon," Farid terminated the call.

Justin called the technical team who were monitoring Farid's line, and asked where the call originated. The technician confirmed it came from a remote part of Canada. *Good*, Justin thought, *at least I won't have to arrest Farid in all of this mess.* His mind relieved, he rejoined the rest of the task force. The State Department representative came in with the news the Saudi government had agreed to a joint raid upon the Prince's compound. The quid pro quo was that the Saudi's were to lead the raid nominally in order to save face within the Muslim world. The conference buzzed with discussion concerning the personnel composition of the team. Justin caught up with the discussion fairly quickly and wished he were in Riyadh to participate. Most of the persons around the table wished for it as well. The DuChard Duchess was a stain on American law enforcement and defense, one difficult to expunge.

• • •

Farid hung up the mobile telephone, then motioned Amin to drive on. "It went very well, Reem did a very good job relaying the call, it will show up as having originated in Canada, the GPS will agree, and when they come to pick me up next week there will be nothing to indicate being anywhere else." The trio had abandoned the CIA car in a slum area with unlocked doors, with luck it would be stolen before the CIA caught up to it.

"Mussa, first lesson: no one in the Martyrs takes unnecessary risks. We plan, we execute, and we live to do it again. Unfortunately, cousin, that is something the Prince was too arrogant to learn. Our enemies are powerful enough to eliminate anyone, even a billionaire prince. He made himself a target, and he died the way the enemies of Israel die," Amin said.

"The bullets aren't enough to pin this on Mossad, many have tried that ploy in the past to divert attention, right?" Mussa asked.

"Absolutely true. However, we have left them a small gift which will muddy the waters further. Mossad will play along, because they never comment on such things. Leading question: how many Jews were killed on the DuChard Duchess?"

"Probably not many, the passenger families got off," Mussa answered.

"True, but out of more than 1,000 people in the crew, would you agree it is likely there were some?"

"Yes."

"The Hammer knows the names of most of the Jewish victims, it was one of the first things he investigated. The next thing was to look for those with links to Israel, then keep the information in his pocket in the event it could be used," Amin said.

"Complicated."

"Yes, but complexity can mean the difference between being alive or dead, living in the open or in mountain caves," Amin lectured while driving.

"Amin, please! Don't scare our newest member! Mussa, most of what I know I learned at the foot of your cousin here when I was a teenager. The key difference between our efforts and the useless beards of Hamas or ISIS, is that we love living life and plan to continue doing so. I would also argue we are accomplishing more than the others."

"Make no mistake, Mussa, The Hammer is being modest. Yes, he learned from me, but he has taken it much further than I could. I work for him and will until I die. Someday you may come to feel the same way."

"If we're done patting ourselves on the back, there are some practical matter to be dealt with. I assume from the direction, we are headed for our friends in Qatar?" Farid asked.

"Yes, we can get Qatari passports easily, with a Canadian Visa. Then I'll go back to Columbus with Mussa, while you keep your date with the FBI," Amin said.

"I do not understand. Why are you two so unconcerned about a meeting with the FBI? I would be worried very much," Mussa said.

Amin shook his head. "We're concerned, but we've prepared for the situation. In the United States, most of the time the law enforcement agencies require firm proof of your participation before they do anything. Especially when the person is an ethnic minority with money. If the police are wrong in their arrest, the person can submit a case to the courts and win a large financial settlement. You've heard of juries? Good. Juries have a skeptical mind when it comes to police misconduct, but locking up a Muslim without proof is something they avoid. Farid is suspected of being The Hammer, and has been for months. But each time the FBI moved, it was without proof and it ended badly for them," Amin explained.

"I'm confused, what difference should there be in being Muslim or infidel? If a crime is committed it is the same, no matter who did it," Mussa struggled with the concept.

"Yes, it is true but not the way the United States is operating these days. When a Muslim terrorist attacks, the news networks will not even identify the crime as a terrorist attack for some time. The attackers could be screaming 'Allahu Ackbar' as they shoot children, but the news will resist saying the attacker was a Muslim. That creates much opportunity for our effort," Amin said.

"But it is crazy! Who would do such a thing? How can they manage maintain order?" Mussa asked.

"They cannot - it is their primary weakness and we take full advantage."

Farid looked forward to seeing Mussa's reaction to other things Americana. For someone who had lived within the strictures of the Kingdom most of his life, it would seem chaos. Amin's job would be to educate Mussa on the dangers residing within the chaos. Their American enemies were not incompetent, merely hampered by a set of rules which reduced their myriad advantages.

Farid sat back in the seat and dozed off, listening to Amin talking himself hoarse in order to bring his lost cousin up to speed.

• • •

President Brown reentered the conference room with her phalanx of Secret Service agents. As before, the room stood until she took her seat back from Sid. Sid moved into the spot Ashley vacated as she moved to the periphery of the room behind him.

"Thank you for spending this evening working this issue. We're going to run this the same way we did the rescue of the DuChard

Duchess passengers. Our team in Riyadh will consist of six people, who will uplink bodycam video footage to an AWACs team circling the metro area. I'm told the six includes the FBI and CIA local leads, two forensic technicians, plus two fully armed Marines. There will be a go-team assembled at the Air Force Base, in the event reinforcement is needed. The Saudis will deploy a full squad of armed security forces. They should be hitting the compound within the next fifteen minutes. Sid, do we have the drone feed, too?" President Brown took charge.

"Yes, we'll get it up. Did you want the six bodycam feeds shown as insets over the drone feed?" Sid asked as he anticipated the questions of the technicians.

"Yes, if we need to change we can do it in real-time. How is the assault going to proceed?"

"The Saudis are sending a couple of men to ring the front door bell, while the balance of the men hit the back door."

President Brown sat back and watched the video monitors.

The video showed an overhead view of the compound as the drone circled. The smaller windows of camera feeds from the six Americans, showed a different angle of the same view, as the men ran down the alley towards the door. The two Saudi security men had run into the Prince's guards, and so far nothing but shouting seemed to be the outcome. Eventually the Prince's men escorted them into the lobby area, and seemed to stop there.

"DC, we're hearing the Prince sent most of the help out for the day and left orders not to be disturbed. Good news in one respect: low risk of collateral damage," Colin Jones dry voice commented.

The lead Saudi team on the back door tried to open it, but it was securely locked. They took out what looked like small, explosive charges, set them on the door lock, and motioned the team back. The Saudi's readied assault rifles, the charges went off with a cloud of smoke, and they ran into the building. The Americans followed closely on their heels.

The video feed for the men was chaotic as they ran down the hallways.

"Check the office," Sid suggested.

There was a flurry of excited Arabic as the men ran to the studio and found the set piece.

"Are you seeing this, DC? We found Jameson's body and another that appears to be the Prince. There are shell casings on the floor and lots of blood. The Prince appears to be wearing the clothes worn during the making of Jameson's kill video."

The Saudis started to move the Prince's body, looking in vain for a pulse. Colin stepped in, and asked permission for the technical team to start documenting the evidence before things were moved. After some heated discussion in Arabic, the techs were permitted to get started.

"Colin, this is President Brown. You need to get to the Prince's office and take possession of the detonator and other contents of the trophy case, if it is still there."

"Understood."

Colin's feed walked over to one of the Marines and then both feeds were walking down the halls looking for the office. The security station was missing the video storage arrays, which looked to have been ripped out. The theatre was next, the people watching in DC matched what they had seen previously on Jameson's uploads. Finally, Jones found the Prince's office. There they found the remains of a small feast and one gold trophy case. The case itself was lit from overhead by small spotlights. Inside sat the detonator surrounded by several small, gold-plated rifle shells.

"Are you seeing this, DC?"

"Yes, we see and are capturing it."

"Marine! Secure the door, while I get this out." The Marine took up a position outside the door. So far the Saudis had been preoccupied by the bodies, but that would not last.

"The case is locked. I'll try to find a key in the desk, but will break it if I must." Colin kept up a running dialog of what he was doing, which did more to certify his professionalism than the slightly unkempt look he favored as a cover. Going through the drawers quickly and professionally, Colin moved swiftly as the DC team watched.

"I think we have a winner!" Colin held up a gold-colored key in front of his camera, then ran over to the case. The lock clicked and the case was open. Colin snatched the detonator and bullets from the display, stowing them in a small bag he carried, then relocked the casing. Just then, they heard Arabic voices at the door and the Marine answering in the negative. "Let them in, Marine! They can help me search," Colin commanded.

The security men came into the office and goggled at the furnishings. A painting which appeared to be a French master's work hung on the wall. Colin helped himself to some of the food and spoke to the Saudis in between bites. Gesturing towards the desk, Colin indicated he had already searched it for evidence. Walking confidently back to the door, carrying a small kabob in his hand, he rejoined the Marine and went back to the studio abattoir.

In DC, the various groups were already claiming right of first inspection of the detonator. Tiring of the hubbub, President Brown ruled, "The FBI is lead on investigation. However, the Joint Terrorism task force will be involved as well. We've lost the chance to interrogate Prince Zufar, but hopefully we can use what's left to get to the rest of the terrorists."

"DC, do we have any idea who killed Prince Zufar? We know the prince killed Jameson, we have that on video, but who killed him? I suspect he was killed very soon after killing Jameson. There are a number of small-caliber shell casings, look to be .22s," Colin said.

"Not sure who would do it," Sid Rosenbloom said. "There were security cameras installed throughout the residence, we saw it from the files Jameson was successful in uploading. Maybe there are suspects shown there."

"The video storage arrays are missing the hard drives. I guess we can check if there was a backup in a separate cabinet. First glance says not, though."

One of the technicians stood up from the Prince's body and came over to Colin. "Sir, I found this tucked inside the Prince's keffiya. It looks to be Hebrew text, anyone know what it says?"

"One of the many languages I'm not fluent in, unfortunately," Colin said.

"Hold it up to your bodycam, Colin," Sid said.

Colin complied with the request, holding as still as possible so that the autofocus could successfully do its job.

"Colin, it's a list of names, ten of them. Keep holding it still, I'm writing them down now," Sid said. "Director Spencer, please check these eleven names and find out their significance as soon as possible."

Director Spencer handed the list to Justin, who got cracking by logging into one of the HORUS tools still on loan to the Bureau. The results came back almost immediately, and Justin was a little ashamed he hadn't been able to identify them himself: all had lost their lives in the DuChard Duchess attack. Justin whispered the result to the Director, as the conversations had moved on.

"Sid, the names are people who died on the DuChard Duchess. Must be a list of Jewish victims, right? Israelis?"

The room erupted in noise as the various organizations spoke up all at once. Sid called for quiet.

"Colin, you hear any of this?" Sid asked.

"Yes, on the list, not so much through the resulting clamor, though."

"Do you think the Israelis could have run an operation to assassinate Zufar?"

"I think they could have done, but I don't think they would have. In recent years, they have become a major trading partner with the Saudis, even though it is done through intermediaries. There was even recent talk of normalizing trading relations. This could be a false flag operation, sir. I think someone went to the trouble of making us think it was the Israelis. Even so, I could be wrong about it."

"Thank you, Colin." Sid muted the microphone. "Madame President, I think we've done what we can do here tonight. The team in Riyadh can handle the next steps, and we don't need the combat-ready teams anymore."

"I agree, but I absolutely insist on getting the evidence back for the FBI investigation immediately. Make sure it is here in record time. Also, bring Jameson home, he died serving his country and we will want to make sure it is recognized. Everyone, thank you for your contributions. We'll reconvene in the next 24 hours to see where we go from here. Sid, join me in the Oval after you wrap up here."

"Yes, Madame President."

President Brown swept out of the room followed by her detail. The room immediately felt larger, as the President's presence always seemed to overfill the available space in a room. Justin thought it was probably the metric ton of Secret Service protection and remora-like assistants following in the President's wake. It was easier to breathe until he remembered his entire chain of command was also in the room.

Justin wondered what Jameson had been thinking when he knew his death was imminent. The execution was inept and if Jameson was beaten beforehand, it didn't show on the video. Jan would come over the counter if she thought for a minute something similar could happen to him. Justin found it odd to consider the possibility of dying from a regular criminal's bullet as a normal risk, but not feeling the same way about being beheaded by a terrorist on video.

Sid was shown into the Oval Office, where the President was working through her upcoming schedule which had been modified to deal with the real-time situation.

"That will be all, Marcy. I need a half hour now with Sid, move things around to make it work. Thanks!"

After Marcy had left the room, Lucy turned to Sid, "So what do we have here, Sid? Did we just hit another dead-end with these terrorists?"

"Madame President, I think we caught a break here, I really do. If the Prince had lived, we would have had a real problem interrogating him with the Saudis' sensitivity, plus we could expect a fair amount of interference during the process. It is the nature of bilateral cooperation. In this case, we pretty clearly found the man responsible for the DuChard Duchess attack. I expect the evidence the team has gathered will only reinforce the verdict. I am also remembering what Zufar said in the video, the bit about infidels chasing The Hammer unsuccessfully. I'm wondering whether Zufar was the brains of the outfit and The Hammer merely an invention to throw off pursuit."

"But what should be done about the men who set the bomb on the ship?"

"We go after them in the normal fashion: through good investigative work. This Justin Simons is good at his job, and well below the political fray at FBI. He'll do the work to eventually find those men. But when it comes to Zufar, I think we declare victory tomorrow similar to what happened to Bin Laden during the Obama administration. Release the evidence we have which implicates him: the videos, the death scene, pictures of the detonator and rifle shells to a favored news outlet. Convict him in the court of public opinion, do a press conference where you state a preference for having brought him back to the United States for trial, but you feel the victims received justice. Have a plant ask whether the Israelis were the ones administering justice, then fudge the answer saying the Israelis never confirm or deny operations. Go on to eulogize Quinton Jameson, who provided the proof we needed and paid for it with his life: a true American Hero. It should boost your favorability numbers significantly."

"It sounds so calculating and politically opportunistic," Lucy said in distaste.

"It is, but you didn't ask for the situation in the first place. It landed in your lap in the early days of your Presidency, and has stalled your agenda in a myriad of ways. This is us making lemonade out of a box of lemons. We chalk up the success, get off the dime with the immigration bill, and make hay while the sun is shining. We don't want to spend four years doing nothing but chase these terrorists."

"I'll think it over tonight, let's talk about it tomorrow."

"Thank you, Madame President. I'll have Ashley start putting together press conference drafts in the meantime. I'm optimistic."

"Yes, it is one of your strengths," President Brown sat back for a few seconds, took a deep breath and dove into the stack of paper her assistant had left for review.

• • •

The next day found Farid, Amin, and Mussa on a flight to Canada, sitting in business class. It had not been difficult to arrange for the new travel documents; Qatar is very efficient in that regard. It had mainly required a new picture being placed within the electronic record and simply issuing the new passport. The Canadian tourist visa stamp had been requested under the name and record previously. Payment was easy to arrange as The Hammer had multiple bank accounts there as well.

The six hour drive enabled Farid to do a full review of the files Jameson had uploaded to the FBI drop box. Luckily, it appeared as though he had not been shown in any of the uploaded video. Farid had no doubt Jameson knew he was there, as he had not been truly surprised when captured. But Jameson saying Farid was in Riyadh was quite different from having proof of the assertion. Farid had turned off the laptop's WiFi interface immediately after uploading Prince Zufar's incriminating video. The laptop itself had been discarded during the trip somewhere in the desert.

Mussa was starting to realize the major life change he had chosen. Prince Zufar had not been the kindest of masters, but he was relatively generous. Many servants of Saudi royalty were treated little better than slaves. But, the call of family trumps everything in the Gulf. Prince Zufar's security staff had neglected to do a full exploration of Mussa's family connections. It was true all of his immediate family was dead, but he had many cousins. As Mussa had risen within Zufar's service, it became easier and easier to forego clearance updates, and by the time he was Zufar's right hand no one would dare to ask.

Noting Mussa's quiet, Farid engaged. "Mussa, what languages can you speak already?"

"Primarily I speak Arabic, Kurdish, and Turkic. I can manage some English and Russian, but it is rough."

"All Russian is rough! English as well. Some skill is better than none. One of the first tasks for you will be learning better English, as it will help us immeasurably. No matter, there will be time. Tell me, are you a strict Muslim or one of the more tolerant sects?"

"It would have been difficult to maintain a strict religious lifestyle working for Prince Zufar. I drink alcohol, and have been known to provide discrete solace to young widows on occasion. Why?"

"Perfect, I am planning to have wine with dinner and didn't want to offend your sensibilities. I think you will find your new circumstances to be an improvement. In the meantime, relax and enjoy the flight. I think they have the latest Star Wars movie available," Farid nodded at Amin, and opened a book acquired at the airport. It was a very long flight.

• • •

Justin had shared most of the story with Jan the next morning. The execution video was already posted in numerous places on the Internet. Each time the Bureau had one video removed; five more sites would post it. Once out, it was impossible to contain.

"Justin, does it mean the sniping attacks are over?" Jan asked.

"I'm not sure. The men who did the attacks before are mostly still out there, but the head of their organization being killed might keep them from new attacks. It isn't 100% sure the Prince was their leader. There is no question he killed Jameson and probably detonated the DuChard Duchess device, but originally there was a phone call between him and someone he called Hammer. Jameson had some thoughts on it, which I will have to investigate. I repacked my go-bag with fresh clothes, as a trip might happen at any time."

"Whatever you do, don't get in a situation like Jameson, alone in a foreign land without backup," Jan said and shuddered, thinking about her Justin being killed instead.

At the White House, Lucy Brown sat back at the kitchen dining table, savoring her coffee after a good breakfast. The White House staff was among the best in the world when it came to day-to-day quality of meal preparation. It had not taken long to become used to it. Lucy tended to eat within the private residence kitchen as it felt more like her own space. Jonny Ray was still nominally living within the White House, but she had not had a conversation with him in weeks. When he tapped on the door frame before entering, it came as a surprise.

"Lucy, may I come in and share a cup of coffee?" he asked.

She waved assent and motioned him towards the coffee station.

"Luce, I saw the news coverage about this Prince Zufar being behind the Martyrs attacks. Does it mean the end of the attacks?" Jonny Ray said.

"I hope so, Jonny Ray, I really hope so. I have a question for you. How do you feel about his death as opposed to a big trial and conviction here in the United States?"

Jonny Ray swirled his coffee cup. "I think justice was done. We're lawyers first and always want a trial to be the sole arbiter of justice; it's engrained in us at law school. The rest of America, though, doesn't give two shits about a trial. Too often, Americans have been shortchanged with courtroom justice. No, I think you will have a grateful nation waking up today, just happy it is over and the bad guy was killed."

"Exactly what Sid said last night. The two of you are generally right when it comes to the pulse of things in the electorate. I should listen. He wants me to declare victory today and move on with my agenda."

"Good advice. It isn't often you are dealt a gift in this business, even more so being president. People will blame you if it rains and they forgot their umbrella. Taking credit this time won't be a crime."

"Thank you," Lucy said as she carried her cup towards the Oval Office.

• • •

Justin's day at the office started with a bang. There was a note left on his desk telling him to report to Director Spencer's office when he arrived. Justin groaned. He had arrived later than usual due to the late night. There was nothing wrong with it, but generally government employees like to be in the office when the boss gets there.

Justin set down his things, took a notepad, and set off for the Director's office on the top floor. He didn't have long to wait before he was being shown inside. As usual, the Deputy Director was present as well.

"Justin, come in. Let's talk about the Martyrs investigation. The physical evidence from Riyadh should be coming later this morning. Quinton's wife Betty will meet us later in the morgue to formally identify his body. I got her on the telephone last night to let her know before she saw it on the news. Unfortunately she had already heard the news, but hadn't seen any of the video coverage. We're planning for a Bureau burial with honors." He paused for a second in thought, then came back. "Now, where do we stand on the other threads of the investigation?" Director Spencer asked.

"On the Nayla Kaldah front, we have nothing new on her killer or killers. We're still running down IP addresses for the snipers themselves, we have a list of people we want to watch but it will take more time. The physical evidence coming in may provide a new set of

IP addresses to investigate. The detonator device, unless wiped, will have the programming necessary to connect to the bomb via satellite. In short, it should tell us exactly how or where the signal was routed. One more thing, I wanted to run down something Jameson said when he spoke to the Deputy Director, specifically his statement of having seen Farid Monsour Royce in Riyadh yesterday. I was able to speak with Farid yesterday, and he told me he was on vacation at his cabin in Canada. We double-checked where the mobile phone signal originated, and it was in the region stated. However, I think we should send someone to drop in on him, in order to confirm he is actually there. Mr. Jameson had a problem with Farid, but we shouldn't necessarily ignore what he said," Justin summarized.

"I concur. Coordinate with RCMP, they can pinpoint where the cabin is from property records. Take your peer reviewer along unless RCMP details one of their own to accompany you," Director Spencer said. "I wanted to brief you on the Press Conference announcement the White House is planning for later this morning. President Brown, doubtless at the urging of her Chief of Staff, is about to declare victory on the DuChard Duchess attack. She is going to imply it is only a matter of time before the rest of the network is rolled up, now that the leader has been killed. On that topic, before you head off to Canada, check in with your Israeli contact and see if he'll give any indication off-the-record of their involvement. I doubt they will, but we have to ask."

"If there is nothing else, I'll go speak to them now," Justin said.

"Justin, one more thing. The President wants you in Jameson's old job, in appreciation for the work done to date. Normally, I would be cautious when asked to do something along those lines, but you know Jameson had put your name in as a possible replacement before all of this occurred. Think about how you would like to run things in the department and let's talk about it."

"Thank you, sir. I will."

Justin went back to his desk and pulled out the contact information for Davi ben Judah, a local Israeli embassy resident who had been a back channel for communication between the United States and Israel on more than one occasion.

"Davi, this is Justin Simons over at the FBI, we've spoken previously during the course of our Martyrs investigation."

"Shalom, Justin. I was wondering who would be the first to call me."

"Yes, I imagine you are probably very well informed on what happened in Riyadh yesterday?"

"No more so than anyone else who peruses the Internet. Is there something in particular?"

"Davi, stop me when I repeat something you already know. The questions I have involve the early demise of good Prince Zufar, and whether our friends in Tel Aviv really had anything to do with it."

"It would be impolite to stop you, and besides a story told a different way can still be quite entertaining. What would indicate our involvement?" He sounded amused.

"There was a scrap of paper with the names of Jewish victims of the DuChard Duchess attack tucked inside the Prince's keffiyeh, and a few shell casings from what appears to be a Beretta Model 70 firearm. Shot twice in the chest, tight grouping and once more in the temple at close range."

"Interesting. Justin you know Mossad never confirms or denies any operation. It makes for uncertainty in the minds of our enemies and keeps them off-balance: our version of asymmetric warfare. Unfortunately, however, it also means Mossad is easy to false-flag or at least to attempt it. My off-the-record recommendation would be to not assume we took care of the problem for you. It may be a politically palatable solution to do so, but you might be ignoring the true agents of his death by closing the book early. I will say Prince Zufar deserved to die for his crimes, from what I've seen this morning."

"Thank you, Davi. It felt too easy to me as well, exactly what someone would do to confuse a trail."

"The next question you should ask, in my opinion, is where did the killer, or killers, go from there? It might open up some leads for the rest of the investigation."

"Thank you. Shalom Davi. We didn't speak," Justin hung up and smiled. Davi as much as told Justin the Mossad wasn't involved, which was more than the usual "no-comment". It complicated the investigation once more, but none of it had been easy.

Justin readied himself for a short jaunt to Canada, where hopefully he would find Farid chasing his big fish. Justin couldn't really picture his friend as the master terrorist, but he also had to admit Farid would be formidable as an opponent. But it was preposterous to think Farid was a terrorist when they first met, or later in college. He was a Muslim, but he was also as American as anyone Justin knew. Nothing in Farid's past with Justin gave any indication of the least bit of anger towards Western Civilization. Indeed, if anything, Farid reveled in it, knowing all the best museums and art galleries. Just one trip, Justin thought, and an end to the doubts.

• • •

The White House press conference went off without a hitch. President Brown was firmly and warmly in charge addressing the nation rather than the press corps. When the time came for the heavily edited videos and audio capture to be shown, gasps could be heard from around the room even though most had seen the unedited footage. Perhaps it was due to the English translation which had been added. The President offered her regret to have failed bringing the Prince home for trial, but allowed justice had been done nonetheless.

A question raised about a possible Israeli assassination team, was seemingly sidestepped by the statement that to the best of her knowledge it was not the case. She mentioned that even though the Israelis never confirm or deny such accusations, she had asked the question anyway, without result.

A question about the pursuit of remaining Martyrs foot soldiers, the snipers and bombers, was answered with an observation there had been no new sniping incidents since the murder of Ms. Kaldah. Whether it reflected an organization on the run, or lack of direction from the top, it would be hard to say. President Brown would only say the terrorists had been dealt a terrible blow, and the FBI would be dogging their heels until the last were finally apprehended.

President Brown then went on to tell a much-sanitized version of Jameson's story who, alone but for two CIA operatives, infiltrated the Prince's security apparatus, making the entire event possible. The fact all of them paid the ultimate price, made them instant national heroes.

The CIA declined to provide the names of their own, citing national security issues, which left the balance of the kudos for Quinton Jameson. The President announced there would be a memorial service held in coming weeks where all the heroes of the Martyrs campaign would be feted.

• • •

Justin decided to check in with the Joint Task Force team assigned to the Prince's forensic evidence before departing to see if any progress had been made on the detonator. He walked over to Michael Kang, his forensics lead.

"Hi, Mike, we have anything back yet on the detonator?"

"Justin. Nothing final or definitive, but I would testify this is the actual detonator. We were able to lift the Prince's fingerprints on the case and most damningly on the trigger button. The device itself is a marvel; a Linux server with custom applications to set up VPNs with multiple hops, terminating in the Iridium network IP space. This is the missing link, I'm sure of it. The thing that bothers me the most, Justin, is all the custom code. Whoever did this could run with our big dogs. Shoot, it even looks like some of our Maryland brothers' work. It could have come from inside, Justin. Another problem we discussed with the CIA at length was the vulnerability in the Prince's WiFi network. It was a toolkit exploit the agency has used over the years. You infiltrate a target network once and leave it vulnerable to anyone with the right codes. Jameson's crew had the codes, it is the only reason they were able to get in so easily. The problem is the CIA swears they had no such operations against the Prince ever. This again points to the idea that this might come from someone within the USA intelligence community."

"Just when I thought this investigation couldn't grow any more hair, it does. Good work on such short notice. Keep at it, I'll be in touch later this evening on the team call."

"We're backtracking through the proxies now, but I don't think it makes much difference at this point, we have the link at both ends, the middle doesn't really lead anywhere else. We'll double-check anyway."

Justin nodded his agreement and left for the airport.

Seven hours later, he landed in Kamloops on a small commuter flight from Vancouver. One clerk sat at the rental desk serving all rental car agencies. Luckily for Justin, four-wheel drive was standard in all available vehicles. He duly set off for the Holiday Inn Suites and his rest. He would attend the task force status call before getting dinner and much needed rest.

The mountain of data being reviewed by the task force was a daunting task and Justin wanted to make sure the team didn't get complacent. The Prince had been caught, but there were twenty to thirty snipers still at large, Nayla's killer, as well as the men who placed the bomb upon the DuChard Duchess. No news on the conference call was earthshaking, it was simply the normal progress of investigation teams. The evidence was a mass of differing data and somewhere within the haystack a needle of the snipers' identities lay. Time and effort would eventually provide the answers. Justin wondered how long the Bureau would continue funding the extensive search, given the President's public position of closure. The investigation was a long way from being closed, but the funding could dry up in an instant. *No point in brooding about it now*, Justin thought, *not when we have funding.*

After closing out the call, Justin went out in search of dinner before an early bed. James McManus, his RCMP contact, wanted a departure of 7 a.m. and Justin was still on East Coast time regardless.

James turned out to resemble the underfed hipster minions of Seattle, but for the official cut of his clothing and no-nonsense pistol strapped to his waist.

"Good morning, Justin, is it?" James asked. It wasn't hard to spot an American FBI agent, even when they were trying to fit in with the local surroundings. It was after ski season when the region was packed with out-of-town visitors bound for the seven major ski resorts within 100 km.

Justin didn't necessarily feel stuffy, but knew his haircut, clothing, and bearing tended to tell the story in such a way.

"That's right! Are we ready to head out?"

"Sure, we can go about this one of two ways. Ride along with me in the company truck, and I'll have you back sometime today.

The problem would be if I get called into something in the course of going about your business. Or you can follow me up to the cabin in your own ride and we part company afterwards."

"Makes sense to me. How often do you get interrupted this time of year?" Justin asked.

"Not often, since all the skiers are gone. But you still have remote crimes of passion, the long winters alone with the same person, the sudden urge to kill them. You know, the stuff of life," James joked.

"Don't I know it, and our winters aren't all that bad. I guess I'll follow you up in the rental. This whole exercise could prove to be nothing. If Farid is actually at his cabin, then our informant was mistaken. I'll want to speak with people in the closest towns for independent confirmation if possible, but I could do that on my own and cut you loose."

"Right! Let's top off our coffees and be off. It is a bit less than two hours up the highway to Bridge Lake and maybe another thirty minutes of private roads."

Justin grabbed his coat, laptop bag, and requisite coffee refill. James was driving a RCMP Ford Explorer, which made him an easy follow. Justin followed along in his wake, making their fellow punters wonder at the suicidal man clearly following a marked police car. As promised, the highway portion terminated at Bridge Lake, and the road became a bit more challenging. Nominally paved with loose gravel, after a winter's worth of snow plowing the way was pot-holed and rutted in places. The rental SUV had no problem with the footing, but it proved a bouncy ride for Justin. The GPS said they were close when an overgrown turnoff appeared on the right. Justin made the turn and drove slow behind James until the path opened into a small clearing. Parked next to the house was another rental car with what looked to be a season's worth of mud already caked to it.

Justin parked next to the rental, and James sensibly backed his Explorer in next to him. Justin approached the door and saw a note taped there, which said "Gone fishing, Loon's Shallows, be back around noon."

Taking out his mobile phone, Justin noted zero bars of signal coverage. Walking around the perimeter of the cabin, there wasn't a telephone junction box, just an electric meter and a satellite television dish. Coming back around, he met up with James who had set himself down upon a bench seat next to the door.

"Did you find anything useful?"

"Yes and no. Confirmed he is pretty much isolated out here, no phone service. How many people do you think use a satellite for Internet service out here?" Justin asked.

"It's either that or DSL, not a lot of good options. Something like this place it wouldn't make sense to run twisted pair copper for DSL, too far from town. The satellite has problems due to the low sky angle, hard to not have interference and the signal isn't great."

"How do you stay in touch with your dispatch?"

"Low-frequency police band radios and my trusty satellite phone here," James held it aloft.

"It doesn't have the same problem on the sky angle issue?"

"No, this is an Iridium network phone, their satellites are in low earth orbits rather than at the equator in geosynchronous ones. There is a satellite directly overhead most of the time. It's expensive, but it almost always works."

"Yes, we've seen our terrorists using them in recent days," Justin said. He looked down the road and saw someone walking with what appeared to be fishing gear. "I think this is him."

James opened up his coat to where his gun was both visible and available, sitting back in a relaxed posture. Justin stood on the edge of the wide, covered porch and waved when he saw Farid looking their way. Farid held up his right arm in a wave which was weighted down with the bag he carried. His left hand carried a fishing rod and tackle box.

"Justin! You took up my invitation. What's this? You need me to post bail with Canada's finest? I caught my white whale this morning: a beauty of a trout, easily more than 10 lbs. Come on in, you two, and I'll put on a pot of coffee."

"No bail required, this is RCMP Officer James McManus who helped me find your cabin." Justin said as he followed Farid inside.

"Farid Royce, officer McManus, pleased to make your acquaintance." Farid set the fish down in the sink and washed his hands thoroughly before starting the coffee pot. Behind him, McManus arched an eyebrow at Justin in question. Justin nodded in acquiescence.

"Pleased to be of service. If all's good, I'll take my leave after a coffee refill and the use of your facilities."

"Of course, down the hall on the left. I've milk and sugar for the coffee but nothing else I'm afraid. How do you take yours?"

"Milk and sugar is fine. I'll be right back." McManus stomped down the hall towards the restroom.

"You didn't come to fish, did you Justin?" Farid asked.

"No, I'm sorry to say. An informant said you were somewhere else, and it had to be confirmed. I'm really happy you are here."

"Ah, a parting gift from the lamentable Quinton Jameson I expect. I had dinner in town last night and saw the coverage. Horrible thing! I had my issues with the man, but no one should die like that. His wife has to be distraught. He had kids, too, didn't he?"

"Yes, two. Married with children of their own. His wife was already living with her parents, so there was someone to support her."

"I was actually writing an editorial which I planned to air when the President attends the memorial service. As much as I hated the guy, he died a hero. A true American hero. Who can ask more?"

James came back in with his oversized coffee mug, which Farid duly filled and returned.

"Mr. Simons, I'll be on my way. I trust you can find your way out without too much trouble?"

"Thank you, Officer McManus. I'll be fine," Justin assured. The RCMP Explorer spread the thinly-layered gravel even more as it left for the highway.

"Justin, why don't we go into town for lunch and get caught up? There is a place there with a waitress who hasn't quite decided to sleep with me yet. I tell her I'm a famous American television news personality, but she doesn't quite believe it. I'll buy."

"Sure, I know how lousy your cooking is, so this is the safest option."

"I'll get a quick shower to wash the fish off of me. Grab a beer and relax."

Justin went to the well stocked refrigerator, grabbed a Molson Lager bottle, and headed for the porch. Sitting on the bench, he reflected on his relief to find his friend but still couldn't stop his brain from asking how it would be possible for Farid to have both been in Riyadh and here today.

A few minutes later, Farid came out in fresh jeans and a fitted casual shirt with his dark hair damp from the shower. "Come on, I'll drive. You can bring the rest of the beer, as long as you don't drink it in front of a police officer."

When they got to town, they pulled into a busy parking lot for a small diner or café. Mom's, it was called.

"The jokes write themselves around here," Farid commented, "but the food is solid."

As they approached the cashier for seating, she lit up.

"Mr. Farid! It's good to see you again. I'm sad to say Bethany is off-shift, spending time at home trying to repair her marriage," she said with a wink. Farid shook his finger at her in mock dismay as she escorted them to an open table.

Justin looked over the reasonably priced menu and ordered the local catch fish fillet which looked promising. Farid pointed out the flat screen television which was tuned to news. "Things got pretty quiet in here during the President's press conference, so I heard pretty much the whole thing. Do they really think the Israelis were involved?"

"There was some evidence of it, but a lot of us have doubts."

"It isn't their style, and I am still unclear on the timing of all this. The Israelis came in after Jameson was killed? That theory seems strange to me. Is there any chance of an on-the-record interview with someone working the investigation?"

"I'd say probably not, due to your recent experiences at the hands of the Bureau. I'd wait awhile before trying. Trust needs to be rebuilt. Trust meaning you weren't just looking to revenge yourself on the Bureau."

"Shoot, if I were looking for that, my lawyers already had it. No, I'm a working journalist and I can't afford to burn bridges. Jameson had a bug up his ass when it came to me. I know the rest of the Bureau wasn't responsible for his personal vendetta. Journalists have no problem separating the personal from the professional, good journalists anyway."

Justin nodded his head, as his mouth was otherwise engaged. The fare was plain food, but very well executed. He watched as the various employees all seemed to know "Mr. Farid", stopping by to say hello or deliver some local gossip. Justin sighed in relief, Farid was not The Hammer.

• • •

"Those of us gathered here today at the memorial service for FBI Special Agent in Charge, Quinton Jameson can only acknowledge the sacrifice and dedication of the man. In the past, I had my disagreements with him, but today he has my utmost respect as a true American hero. Acting selflessly, he alone made possible bringing the terrorist responsible for the DuChard Duchess to justice. He paid the ultimate price without question or fear. The United States of America is diminished by his loss. For World News, this is Farid Monsour Royce al Haj at Arlington National Cemetery."

EPILOGUE

On the remote Greek island, Skyros, a man rose from bed to walk onto a large tiled patio overlooking the Aegean Sea. His home was a white plaster beacon high above the light blue waters. He sat at a small table laden with hot coffee and the hard-crust bread he loved for breakfast. Next to his plate sat a tray holding mail for his review.

On top, was an envelope with a Washington, DC return address. He picked up a knife and opened it quickly in anticipation. As he read the letter within, a cry of anguish escaped him, but was extinguished quickly. He read and reread the letter before sitting back in his chair.

Signaling the houseman over to attend, he asked, "When did this come and who delivered it?"

"Yesterday, sir. DHL delivery."

"Thank you. Please bring my tablet and enable our Internet for a time."

The houseman bustled away to do these things, and the man returned to his breakfast, ignoring the rest of the documents.

With quick motions on the tablet, he entered one name into a search field paired with Washington, DC. Hundreds of returns, many with lurid details of a murder on the other side of the world. With precision, which great anger produces in the man with steel-grey eyes, he set the tablet down and asked for a phone.

It was early at the location he dials, but no earlier than where he sat.

A voice answered in Palestinian Arabic patois, "Hello?"

"I want to speak with the big man, it is important," the man said in an aristocratic form of the same language.

"Who is calling?"

"A brother."

"One moment."

"Yes?" a rumbling voice said after a minute or two.

"Brother, I need your help once more. Nayla has been murdered in America."

A silence on the line, broken only by the intermittent background static, "How?"

"Martyrs al-Sabra in Washington."

"Such arrogance must be answered, Adeeb."

"I agree, I will come for you in a week. I'm sorry, my friend."

"No more than I. Until your return," the phone connection was cut.

Snapping his fingers to summon the houseman, Adeeb readied himself to return to Gaza and from there to America.

Book Two of the Martyrs Series, "Martyr's Revenge",
will be available late 2019.